"John Barth is a rarity among American novelists in having a brilliant mind . . . a mind that invents ideas. . . . With his fourth novel, John Barth at 36 increases the likelihood that the years since World War II are among the most rewarding in the history of American Fiction."

—BOOK WEEK

"Brilliantly conceived. . . . In the school of philosophical bawdry . . . *Giles Goat-Boy* is probably the best American specimen so far."

—CHICAGO DAILY NEWS

"Erudite word-wit . . . a fertility of ideas that is almost febrile, a colossal serio-comic point of view, big, bawdy and boisterous."

—VIRGINIA KIRKUS

"John Barth must be acclaimed writer of the season. . . . He stomps across the cosmos. What he sets out to do he does well . . . the biggest, bawdiest, and one of the best novels of the season."

—KANSAS CITY STAR

GILES
GOAT-BOY
or,
THE REVISED
NEW SYLLABUS
by
JOHN BARTH

A FAWCETT CREST BOOK

Fawcett Publications, Inc., Greenwich, Conn.
Member of American Book Publishers Council, Inc.

THIS BOOK CONTAINS THE COMPLETE TEXT OF THE
ORIGINAL HARDCOVER EDITION.

A Fawcett Crest Book reprinted by arrangement with
Doubleday & Company.

Library of Congress Catalog Card Number: 66-15666

PRINTING HISTORY
Doubleday & Company edition published August 5, 1966
First printing, May 1966
Second printing, July 1966
Third printing, August 1966
Fourth printing, September 1966
Fifth printing, October 1966

Alternate Selection of the Literary Guild, 1966
Mid-Century Book Society, 1966

Second Fawcett Crest printing, November 1967

Published by Fawcett World Library
67 West 44th Street, New York, N. Y. 10036
Printed in the United States of America

Contents

Volume One

First Reel

Second Reel

Contents

Third Reel

Volume Two

First Reel

Second Reel

Contents

Third Reel

Giles Goat-Boy

PUBLISHER'S DISCLAIMER

The reader must begin this book with an act of faith and end it with an act of charity. We ask him to believe in the sincerity and authenticity of this preface, affirming in return his prerogative to be skeptical of all that follows it.

The manuscript submitted to us some seasons ago under the initials *R.N.S.*, and by us retitled *Giles Goat-Boy*, is enough removed from the ordinary and so potentially actionable as to make inadequate the publisher's conventional disclaimer: "Any resemblance to persons living or dead," *etc*. The disclaimer's very relevance—which we firmly assert—was called into question even prior to the manuscript's receipt, as has been everything about the book since, from its content to its authorship. The professor and quondam novelist whose name appears on the title-page (*our* title-page, not the one following his prefatory letter) denies that the work is his, but "suspects" it to be fictional—a suspicion that two pages should confirm for the average reader. His own candidate for its authorship is one Stoker Giles or Giles Stoker—whereabouts unknown, existence questionable—who appears to have claimed in turn 1) that he too was but a dedicated editor, the text proper having been written by a certain automatic computer, and 2) that excepting a few "necessary basic artifices" * the book is neither fable nor fictionalized history, but literal truth. And the computer, the mighty "WESCAC"—does it not too disclaim authorship? It does.

Frankly, what we hope and risk in publishing *Giles Goat-Boy* is that the question of its authorship will be a literary and not a legal one. If so, judging from the fuss in our office these past months, the book affords more pregnant mat-

* The computer's assumption of a first-person narrative viewpoint, we are told, is one such "basic artifice." The reader will add others, perhaps challenging their "necessity" as well.

ter for controversy. Merely deciding to bring it out has already cost us two valued colleagues, for quite different reasons. Five of us were party to the quarrel, which grew so heated, lengthy, and complex that finally, as editor-in-chief, I was obliged to put an end to it. No further discussion of the book was permitted. Inasmuch as the final responsibility was mine I requested from each of my four associates a brief written statement on the questions: should we publish the manuscript entitled *Giles Goat-Boy*? If so, why, and if not, why not?

Their replies anticipate, I think, what will be the range of public and critical reaction to the book. I reprint them here (with signatures and certain personal references omitted) not in the hope of forestalling that reaction, but to show that our decision was made neither hastily nor in bad faith:

Editor A

I am quite sensible that fashions have changed since my own tenure as editor-in-chief: marriage has lost its sanctity, sex its mystery; every filthiness is published in the name of Honesty; all respect for law and discipline is gone—to say nothing of *propriety* and *seemliness,* whose very names are sneered at. Cynicism is general: the student who eschews cheating like the young girl who eschews promiscuity or the editor who values principle over profit, is looked upon as a freak. Whatever is old—a man, a building, a moral principle—is regarded not as established but as obsolete; to be preserved if at all for its antiquarian interest, but got rid of without compunction the moment it becomes *in the way.* In the way, that is, of self-interest and the tireless sensualism of youth. Indeed fashions change, have always changed, and there's the point. Granted that every generation must write its own "New Syllabus" or re-interpret the Old one, rebel against its teachers, challenge all the rules—all the more important then that the Rules stand fast! Morality like motion has its laws; each generation takes its impetus from the resistance of its forebears, like runners striving against the ground, and those who would abolish the old Answers (I don't speak of restating or modifying them, which is eternally necessary) would turn the track underfoot to quickmire, with fatal consequences for the race of men.

This *Revised New Syllabus* is nothing new, but as old as sickness of the spirit; not a revision of anything, but a repudiation of all that's wholesome and redeeming. It is for us to repudiate *it*. Publishing remains despite all a moral enterprise, and is recognized as such in its heart of hearts even by the public that clamors for gratification of its appetites. The sensational, the vulgar, the lurid, the cheap, the hackneyed—there is an innocence about these things in their conventional and mass-produced forms, even a kind of virtue; the novelists everyone purchases do no harm as they line our pockets and their own. They are not difficult; they do not astonish; they rebel along traditional lines, shock us in customary ways, and teach us what we know already. Their concerns are modest, their literary voice and manner are seldom wild, only their private lives, which make good copy: in straightforward prose they reveal to us how it is to belong to certain racial or cultural minorities; how it is to be an adolescent, a narcotic, an adulterer, a vagabond; especially how it is to be the Author, with his particular little history of self-loathings and aggrandizements. Such novels, I conceive, are the printed dreams of that tiny fraction of our populace which buys and reads books, and the true dwelling-places of art and profit. In serving the dream we prevent the deed: vicariously the reader debauches, and is vicariously redeemed; his understanding is not taxed; his natural depravity may be tickled but is not finally approved of; no assaults have been made upon his imagination, nor any great burden put on his attention. He is the same fellow as before, only a little better read, and in most cases the healthier for his small flirtation with the Pit. He may even remark, "Life is absurd, don't you think? There's no answer to anything"; whereafter, his luncheon-companion agreeing absolutely, they have another cocktail and return to more agreeable matters.

Consider the difference with *R.N.S.*: here fornication, adultery, even rape, yea murder itself (not to mention self-deception, treason, blasphemy, whoredom, duplicity, and willful cruelty to others) are not only represented for our delectation but at times approved of and even recommended! On aesthetic grounds too (though they pale before the moral), the work is objectionable: the rhetoric is extreme, the conceit and action wildly implausible, the interpretation of history shallow and patently biased, the narrative full of discrepancies and badly paced, at times tedious, more often excessive; the form, like the style, is unorthodox, unsymmetrical, inconsistent. The characters, especially the hero, are unrealistic. There never was a Goat-boy! There never will be!

In sum it is a bad book, a wicked book, and ought not—I will say *must* not—be published. No computer produced it, but the broodings of an ineffectual megalomane: a crank at best, very possibly a psychopath. As the elder, if no longer the ranking, member of this editorial group I urge that we take this opportunity to restore a part of the moral prestige that was ours when our organization was more dedicated and harmonious, if less wealthy; to reverse our lamentable recent policy of publishing the esoteric, the bizarre, the extravagant, the downright vicious. I urge not only that the manuscript in question be rejected forthwith, but also that the "Author's" superiors, his Dean and Department Chairman, be advised what they are exposing undergraduate minds to. Would the present editor-in-chief, I wonder, permit his own daughter to be taught by such a man? Then in the name of what decent principle ought we to make his scribbling available to all our sons and daughters?

Editor B

I vote to publish the *Revised New Syllabus* and agree with the Editor-in-chief that *Giles Goat-Boy* is a more marketable title for it. We all know what [A's] objections to the manuscript are; we also know why he's not editor-in-chief any more, after his rejection of———* on similar "moral" grounds. What I must add, at the risk of "impropriety," is that in addition to his predictable bias against anything more daring than *Gay Dashleigh's Prep-School Days*, he may have a private antipathy for this particular manuscript: his own daughter, I happen to know, "ran off" from college with a bearded young poetry-student who subsequently abandoned her, pregnant, in order to devote himself to sheep-farming and the composition of long pastoral romances in free verse, mainly dealing with his great love for her. Her father never forgave her; neither has he,

---

* Not to injure unnecessarily the reputation of that splendid (and presently retired) old gentleman here called *A*, let it be said merely that his distinguished editorial career never regained its earlier brilliance after the day some years ago when, in a decision as hotly contested as the present one, he overrode the opinions of myself and several other of his protégés to reject the novel here cited by *B*, which subsequently made the fortune of our largest competitor. No further identification of the book is needed than that it concerns the adventures, sexual and otherwise, of a handsome, great-spirited young man struggling against all odds and temptations to fulfill what he takes to be his destiny; that the plot was admittedly not original with the now-famous author; and that the book bids fair to remain a best seller forever.

it seems, forgiven bearded heterosexuality or things bu-
colic, and it is a mark of his indiscrimination that he
makes a goat-boy suffer for a sheep-boy's sins. Much as I
respect your request that these statements remain impersonal, and hesitate as a new employee to criticize my colleagues in addition to disagreeing with them, I must argue
that the "personal" and "professional" elements are so
bound together in this case (indeed, are they ever separable in literary judgments?), that to take a stand for or
against *Giles Goat-Boy* is to do likewise on the question
whether this organization will prosper in literary judgments?), that to take a stand for or against *Giles Goat-Boy*
is to do likewise on the question whether this organization
will prosper in harmonious diversity or languish in acri-
monious dissension. In choosing to publish or reject a manuscript, one oughtn't to bear the burden of choosing professional friends and enemies as well. Where such has become
the case, the new man's only choice is to follow his best
judgment, laying his future resolutely on the line; and I
respectfully suggest that the responsible administrator's best
hope for curing the situation is to turn any threatening ulti-
matums (like A's) into opportunities for revitalizing and
reharmonizing the staff.

The fact is, I happen to agree—I think we all do—that
Giles Goat-Boy is tough sledding in places, artistically un-
even, and offensive (we'll call it *challenging,* of course) to
certain literary and moral conventions. Personally I am no
great fan of the "Author's"; like [Editor C, whose opinion
follows] I found his early work lively but a bit naïve and
his last novel wild and excessive in every respect. I frankly
don't know quite *what* to make of this one. Where other
writers seek fidelity to the facts of modern experience and
expose to us the emptiness of our lives, he declares it his
aim purely to *astonish*; where others strive for truth, he admits his affinity for lies, the more enormous the better. His
fellows quite properly seek recognition and wide reader-
ship; he rejoices (so he says) that he has but a dozen readers, inasmuch as a thirteenth might betray him. So far
from becoming discouraged by the repeated failure of his
novels to make a profit, he confesses his surprise that no
one has tarred and feathered him. Apparently sustained by
the fact that anyone at all has swallowed his recentest
whopper, he sets about to hatch another, clucking tongue
at the compass and bedazzlement of those fabrications.
Plot, for the young novelists we applaud, is a naughty
word, as it was for their fathers; *story* to them means invention, invention artifice, artifice dishonesty. As for *style,*
it is everywhere agreed that the best language is that which

disappears in the telling, so that nothing stands between the reader and the matter of the book. But this author has maintained (in obscure places, understandably) that language *is* the matter of his books, as much as anything else, and for that reason ought to be "splendrously musicked out"; he turns his back on what *is the case*, rejects the familiar for the amazing, embraces artifice and extravagance; washing his hands of the search for Truth, he calls himself "a monger after beauty," or "doorman of the Muses' Fancy-house." In sum, he is in a class by himself and not of his time; whether a cut above or a cut below, three decades ahead or three centuries behind, his twelve readers must decide for themselves.

My own net sentiment comes to this: the author in question has, I'm told, a small but slowly growing audience, more loyal than discerning or influential, of the sort one needs no expensive promotion to reach, as they have their own ways of spreading the word around: penniless literature students, professors in second-rate colleges, and a couple of far-out critics. *Giles Goat-Boy* isn't likely to make anybody rich, but if we can saturate this little group it should at least pay its own way, and may even redeem our losses on the man's other books. One day those penniless students may be pennied enough; those professors may rise to more influential positions; the far-out critics may turn out to have been prophets . . . Alternatively, the author's luck may change (rather, *our* luck, as he seems not to care one way or the other): by pure accident his *next* book might be popular, stranger things have happened. Meanwhile we may write off our losses to that tax-deductible sort of prestige associated with the better publishing houses; the thing to do is keep the advance and advertising expenses as low as possible while holding him under contract for the future, in the meantime exploiting whatever ornamental or write-off value he may have.

Editor C

I vote against publishing the book called *The Revised New Syllabus*, not for reasons of morality, law, or politics, but simply on aesthetic and commercial grounds. The thing won't turn us a profit, and I see no ethical or "prestigial" justification for losing a nickel on it. Publishing may be a moral enterprise, as [A] likes to claim, but first of all it's just an enterprise, and I for one think it's as unprofessional to *publish* a book for moral reasons (which is what young [B's] enthusiasms amount to) as to reject one for moral reasons. [A] quite obviously has personal motives for rejecting the book; I submit that [B] has motives equally personal, if more sympathetic, for pushing its acceptance. He's new to our profession, and knows very well that discovering fresh talent is a road to success second only to pirating established talents from the competition. He has a young man's admirable compassion for lost causes, a young scholar's sympathy for minor talents, and a young intellectual's love of the heterodox, the esoteric, the obscure. Moreover he's a writer of fiction himself and no doubt feels a certain kinship with others whose talents have brought them as yet no wealth or fame. Finally, it's no reflection on his basic integrity that on the first manuscript he's been asked his opinion of, he might be less than eager to oppose the known judgment of the man who hired him; but that circumstance probably oughtn't to be discounted—especially since his vote to publish is a "net sentiment" by his own acknowledging, arrived at over numerous and grave reservations.

I think I may say that my own position is relatively objective. I agree that there are inferior books which one does right to lose a bit of money on in order not to lose a superior author, and there are superior books (very rare!) which one publishes, regardless of their commercial value, merely to have been their publisher. But the book in question I take to be neither: it's a poor-risk work by a poor-risk author. It wants subtlety and expertise: the story is not so much "astonishing" as preposterous, the action absurd. The hero is a physical, aesthetic, and moral monstrosity; the other characters are drawn with small regard for realism and at times lack even the consistency of stereotypes; the dialogue is generally unnatural and wanting in variety from speaker to speaker—everyone sounds like the author! The prose style—that unmodern, euphuistic, half-metrical bombast—is admittedly contagious (witness [A's] and [B's] lapses into it); even more so is syphilis. The theme is obscure, probably blasphemous; the wit is impolite, perhaps even suggestive of unwholesome preoccupations; the psychology—but there is no psychology in it. The author clearly is ignorant of things and people as they really are: consider his disregard for the reader! Granted that long novels are selling well lately, one surely understands that mere bulk is not what sells them; and when their mass consists of interminable exposition, lecture, and harangue (how gratified I was to see that windy old lunatic Max Spielman put to death!), it is the very antidote to profit. Indeed, I can't imagine to whom a work like *R.N.S.* might appeal, unless to those happily rare, more or less disturbed, and never affluent intelligences—remote, cranky, ineffectual—from whom it is known the author receives his only fan-mail.

What I suggest as our best course, then, is not to "protect our investment" by publishing this *Revised New Syllabus* (and the one after that, and the one after that), but to cut our losses by not throwing good money after bad. My own "net sentiment" is a considered rejection not only of this manuscript but of its author. He has yet to earn us a sou; his very energy (let us say, *inexorableness*), divorced as it is from public appeal, is a liablity to us, like the energy of crabgrass or cancer. Despite some praise from questionable critics and a tenuous repute among (spiritually) bearded undergraduates—of the sort more likely to steal than to purchase their reading matter—he remains unknown to most influential reviewers, not to mention the generality of book-buyers. In the remote event that he becomes a "great writer," or even turns out to have been one all along, we still hold the copyright on those other losers of his, and can always reissue them. But no, the thing is as impossible as the plot of this book! He himself declares that nothing gets better, everything gets worse: he will merely grow older and crankier, more quirksome and less clever; his small renown will pass, his vitality become mere doggedness, or fail altogether. His dozen admirers will grow bored with him, his employers will cease to raise his salary and to excuse his academic and social limitations; his wife will lose her beauty, their marriage will founder, his children will grow up to be ashamed of their father. I see him at last alone, unhealthy, embittered, desperately unpleasant, perhaps masturbative, perhaps alcoholic or insane, if not a suicide. We all know the pattern.

Editor D

Failed, failed, failed! I look about me, and everywhere see failure. Old moralists, young bootlickers, unsuccessful writers; has-beens, would-bes, never-weres; failed artists, failed editors, failed scholars and critics; failed husbands, fathers, lovers; failed minds, failed bodies, hearts, and souls—none of us is Passed, we all are Failed!

It no longer matters to me whether the *Revised New Syllabus* is published, by this house or any other. What does the Answer care, whether anyone "finds" it? It wasn't lost! The gold doesn't ask to be mined, or the medicine beg to be taken; it's not the medicine that's worse off when the patient rejects it. As for the Doctor—who cares whether he starves or prospers? Let him go hungry, maybe he'll prescribe again! Or let him die, we have prescription enough!

Let him laugh, even, that I've swallowed in good faith the pill he made up as a hoax: I'm cured, the joke's on him! One comes to understand that a certain hermit of the woods is no eccentric, but a Graduate, a Grand Tutor. From all the busy millions a handful seek him out, thinking to honor and sustain him; we bring him cash and frankincense, sing out his praises in four-part harmony, fetch him champagne and vichyssoise. Alas, our racket interrupts his musings and scares off the locusts he'd have suppered on; the wine makes him woozy, he upchucks the soup; he can't smell the flowers for our perfume or hear the birds for our music, and there's not a thing to spend his money on. No wonder he curses us under his breath, once he's sober again! And thinking to revenge himself with a trick, he puts on a falseface to scare us away. We had asked for revelations; he palms off his maddest dreams. "Show us Beauty," we plead; he bares his rump to us. "Show us Goodness," we beg, and he mounts our wives and daughters. "Ah, sir!" we implore him, "Give us the Truth!" He thrusts up a forefinger from each temple and declares, "You are cuckolds all."

And yet I say the guller is gulled, hoist is the enginer: the joke's on the joker, that's the joker's joke. Better victimized by Knowledge than succored by Ignorance; to be Wisdom's prey is to be its ward. Deceived, we see our self-deception; suffering the lie, we come to truth, and in the knowledge of our failure hope to Pass.

Publish the *Revised New Syllabus* or reject it; call it art or artifice, fiction, fact, or fraud: it doesn't care, its author doesn't care, and neither any longer do I. I don't praise it, I don't condemn it; I don't ask who wrote it or whether it will sell or what the critics may make of it. My judgment is not upon the book but upon myself. I have read it. I here resign from my position with this house

One sees the diversity of opinion that confronted me (I do not even mention the disagreement among our legal staff and such nice imponderables as the fact that it was Editor *A* who gave me my first job in the publishing field, or that Editor *D*—present whereabouts unknown—happens to be my only son); one sees further something of what either option stood to cost. One sees finally what decision I came to—with neither aid nor sympathy from the author, by the way, who seldom even answers his mail. Publishing *is* a moral enterprise, in subtler ways than my dear *A* asserted; like all such, it is spiritually expensive, highly risky, and proportionately challenging. It is also (if I understand the Goat-Boy correctly) as possible an avenue to Commencement Gate as any other moral enterprise, and on that possibility I must bank.

Herewith, then, *Giles Goat-Boy: or, The Revised New Syllabus,* "a work of fiction any resemblance between whose characters and actual persons living or dead is coincidental." * Let the author's cover-letter stand in all editions as a self-explanatory foreword or opening chapter, however one chooses to regard it; let the reader read and believe what he pleases; let the storm break if it must.

THE EDITOR-IN-CHIEF

* In the absence of any response from the author, whom we repeatedly invited to discuss the matter with us, we have exercised as discreetly as possible our contractual prerogative to alter or delete certain passages clearly libelous, obscene, discrepant, or false. Except for these few passages (almost all brief and of no great importance) the text is reproduced as it was submitted to us. [*Ed.*]

COVER-LETTER TO THE
EDITORS AND PUBLISHER

Gentlemen:

The manuscript enclosed is not *The Seeker*, that novel I've been promising you for the past two years and on which you hold a contractual option. *The Seeker* is lost, I fear; no use to seek him, or any other novel from this pen: I and the Muse, who in any case had not cohabited these many months, are now divorced for good and all *a vinculo matrimonii*. The wonder is not that our alliance has ended, but that it lasted and produced at all, in the light of my wrong-headedness. I will not admit that it was a mistake to wed her; matrimony may be the death of passion, but need not be of production. The error (by no means my only one) was in believing anything could endure; that my or any programme could *work*. Nothing "works," in the sense we commonly hope for; a certain goat-boy has taught me that; everything only gets worse, gets worse; our victories are never more than moral, and always pyrrhic; in fact we know only more or less ruinous defeats.

Ah well, now I have caught Knowledge like a love-pox, I understand, not that my former power was a delusion, but that delusions may be full of power: Lady Fancy *did* become my mistress after all; *did* mother offspring that my innocent lust got on her—orphans now, but whose hard neglect may be the saving of them in the long run. Think it if you will a further innocence on my part; I stand convinced that she did by George love me while she loved me, and that what she loved was the very thing that ruined us in the end: I mean my epic unsophistication. And this because, contrary to appearance and common belief, she shares it herself; it is if not the essence of her spirit at least one among its chiefer qualities, and has much to do with that goldenness of hers. How else explain the peculiar radiance she maintains despite her past, a freshness as well of spirit as of complexion, which leads each new suitor to take her for a maiden girl? My ambition to *husband* her, exclusively and forever, as who should aspire to make a *Hausfrau* out of a love-goddess—do you think she indulged it as a joke, or tickled a jaded appetite by playing at homeliness? Very well: *I* choose to think the experiment pleased her as simply and ingenuously as it pleased me; we were equally distressed to see it fail, and whatever the fate of our progeny I believe she will remember as sweetly as I the joy of their getting . . .

No matter. I'm celibate now: a priest of Truth that was a monger after Beauty; no longer a Seeker but a humble Finder—all thanks to the extraordinary document here enclosed. I submit it to you neither as its author nor as agent for another in the usual sense, but as a disinterested servant of Our Culture, if you please: that recentest fair fungus in Time's watchglass. I know in advance what reservations you will have about the length of the thing, the controversial aspects of occasional passages, and even its accuracy here and there; yet whether regarded as "fact" or "fiction" the book's urgent pertinence should be as apparent as its considerable (if inconsistent and finally irrelevant) literary merit, and I'm confident of your final enthusiasm. "A wart on Miss University," as the Grand Tutor somewhere declares, "were nonetheless a wart, and if I will not call it a beauty-mark, neither would I turn her out of bed on its account." There are warts enough on this *Revised New Syllabus*, artistic and it may be historical; but they are so to speak only skin-deep, and I think no publisher will turn it off his list on their account.

Indulge me now, as a useful introduction to the opus proper, the story of its origin and my coming by it. As you may know, like most of our authors these days I support myself by preaching what I practice. One grows used, in fiction-writing seminars, to three chief categories of students: elder ladies and climacteric gentlemen who seek in writing an avocation which too might supplement their pensions; well-groomed and intelligent young literature-majors of various sexes who have a flair; and those intensely marginal souls—underdisciplined, oversensitive, disordered in both appearance and reality—whose huge craving for the state of artist-hood may drive them so far in rare instances as actually to work at making pieces of art. It was one of this third sort, I assumed, who came into my office on a gusty fall evening several terms ago with a box of typescript under his arm and a gleam in his face.

I'd not seen him before—but then, these bohemians appear and vanish like spooks, change their aspect at the merest whim (quite as does the creature called *Harold Bray* hereinafter), and have often the most tenuous connection with their Departments. Imagine a lean young man of twenty, dark-eyed and olive-skinned, almost a mulatto, but with a shag of bronze curls, unbarbered, on head and chin; even his eyebrows were like turnings of that metal. He wore battered workshoes laced with rawhide, nondescript trousers tucked at the ankles into boot-socks, and an outlandish fleecy jacket that in retrospect I'd guess he fashioned for himself—one may presently suppose of what material. Though he had no apparent limp, he affected a walkingstick as odd as the rest of his get-up: a three-foot post of white ash, somewhat stouter than a pick-shaft, it had what appeared to be folding lenses and other gadgetry attached here and there along its length, which was adorned with rude carvings (both intaglio and low-relief) of winged lingams, *shelah-na-gigs*, buckhorns, and domestic bunch-grapes.

Near the tip of this unprecedented tool was a small blunt hook wherewith my visitor first unstopped and closed the door, then smartly drew himself a chair out and sat him down at the desk next to mine. All this I remarked in two glances, and then to collect myself returned to that manuscript of my own at which I'd been tinkering when he entered. The fellow's dress, if extreme, was not unique—one may see as strange at any gathering of student artists, and I myself in disorderly moods will wear mungos and shoddies, though my preference is for the conventional. But your average bohemian's manner is shy as a kindergartener's with those he respects, and overweening with everyone else, while my caller's was neither: brisk, forthright, cordial, he plunked his paper-box onto my desk, leaned forward with his elbows on his knees and both hands at the cane-top, and rested his chin upon all, so that his striking beard hung over. Disconcerting as the grin he then waited my pleasure with was the cast of his features, not just like any I had seen. Such of his kind as had strayed into my office thitherto were either dark of beard, coal-eyed, and intense, after the model of a poet they admired, or else had hair the shade of wheatstraw, forget-me-not eyes, and the aspect and deportment of gelded fawns.

Not so this chap: his bronze beard; his eyes not pale nor tormented but simply a-dance; his wiry musculature, the curl of his smile, even a positive small odor about his person that was neither of dirt or cologne—in a word, he was *caprine:* I vow the term came to mind before I'd ever spoken to him, much less read what he'd brought me. And that walking-stick, that instrument without parallel . . .

"Don't fear," he said directly—in a clear, almost a ringing voice, somewhat clickish in the stops. "I'm not a writer, and it's not a novel."

I was disarmed as much by the insouciance and *timbre* of his voice as by the words themselves. It sounded as though he actually meant what he said, sincerely and indifferently, as who should announce: "I'm not left-handed," or "I'm no clarinetist." And this I felt with the ruefuller twinge for its expressing, glibly as the verdict of a child, that fear no fictionist is proof against, and which had dwelt a-haunt in my Fancy's garret for the twelve months past. I had just turned thirty; it was my seventh year of toil in the prevaricating art, and scant-rewarded for my labors I was weary as the Maker of us all on the seventh morning. Monday, I still trusted, would roll round; in the meanwhile I was writing so to speak a *sabbatical-piece*—that book you'll never see. I knew what novels were: *The Seeker* wasn't one. To move folks about, to give them locales and dispositions, past histories and crossed paths—it bored me, I hadn't taste or gumption for it. Especially was I surfeited with *movement*, the without-which-not of story. One novel ago I'd hatched a plot as mattersome as any in the books, and drove a hundred characters through eight times that many pages of it; now the merest sophomore apprentice, how callow soever his art, outdid me in that particular. His inspirations? Crippled: but I sat awed before the bravery of their unfolding. His *personae*? Raw motors cursed with speech, ill-wrought as any neighbors of mine—but they blustered along like them as if alive, and I shook my head. Stories I'd set down before were children gone their ways; everything argued they'd amount to nothing; I scarcely recognized their faces. I was in short disengaged, not chocked or out of fuel but fretfully idling; the pages of my work accumulated to no end, all noise and no progress, like a racing motor. What comfort that in every other way my lot improved? House and gardens prospering, rank and income newly raised, my small fame spreading among the colleges—to a man whose Fancy is missing in action, all boons feel posthumous. The work before me (that I now put by with a show of interruption): Where was its clutch, its purchase? Something was desperately wanting: a thing that mightn't be striven for, but must come giftlike and unsought; a windfall from orchards of the spirit, a voice from nowhere, a visitation. Indeed it was no novel . . . My heart turned sinking from the rest.

All I said was, "Oh?"

"My name is Stoker Giles," the young man announced. His head still was propped on the singular stick, and he continued to regard me with an uncalled-for look of delight. Perhaps I was intended to recognize the name, but my hold on such things was never firm. Especially of late, though I lectured with animation, indeed almost fervidly, I had sensed myself losing command of memory and attention. Information escaped me; I could not recall my telephone number, and missed my way on the most familiar campus paths. My family waited only for the day I should come home to some stranger's house; their teasing had given way to concern, concern to impatience, and impatience to a silent rancor, which though I perceived it I could not seem to engage.

I asked him whether he was a graduate student.

"Well, at least I'm a Graduate." His apparent amusement now positively irritated me, the more as it was not my place to draw his business out of him but his to state it. And then he mildly added, "I wonder if you are."

I think no one may accuse me of hauteur or superciliousness. In truth I reproach myself for being if anything over-timid, acquiescing too easily, suffering presumption to the point of unmanliness, and provoking contempt in my eagerness not to displease. But the man was impudent! I supposed he was referring to the doctoral degree; very well, I'd abandoned my efforts in that line years since, when I eloped with the muse. Moreover, I'd never pretended I had the memory and temper for scholarship, or even the intelligence: time and again I've followed some truly profound one to my limits and been obliged then to stand and watch, chin-high in the shallows, while he forged on past my depth. I was properly humble—and properly indifferent. To make is not the same as to think; there are more roads than one to the bottom of things.

"You'd better take that box and get out," I said. "I've got work to do."

"Yes," he said. "Yes indeed you do!" As though at last we understood each other! Then he spoke my name in the gentlest tone (he had, I should say, a curious accent that I couldn't place, but which sounded not native), and indicating my work-in-progress added, "But you know this isn't it. There's much to be done; you mustn't waste any more time." In the face of my anger his voice became businesslike and brisk, though still cheerful. "Nor must I," he declared. "Please listen now; I've read your books and understand them perfectly, and I've come a long way to see you. May I ask what you're calling this one?"

I was taken aback by a number of things. Not simply his presumption—I rather admired that, it recalled an assurance I once had myself and could wish for again; indeed he was so like a certain old memory of myself, and yet so *foreign*, even wild, I was put in mind of three dozen old stories wherein the hero meets his own reflection or is negotiated with by a personage from nether realms. Yet there was little of the Evil One about this chap, however much of the faun; it wouldn't have surprised me to see he had cloven hooves, but the reed-pipe, rather than the pitchfork, would be his instrument. I found myself so caught up in such reflections as these, and contrariwise arrested by the tiresomeness of succumbing to an image the fellow obviously strove to affect, that annoyance and perspective got lost in my confusion. I couldn't think how he should be dealt with; the situation was slipping my hold, disengaging from me as much else had lately seemed to do. For example, I'd forgotten my pills again, which I'd come to need regularly not to fall asleep over my work: that accounted for my present somnolence, no doubt. I told him that the book was to be called *The Seeker*—or perhaps *The Amateur*, I could not decide . . .

"Certainly." The pleasure with which he stroked his beard was plainly not at the excellence of my titles. "A *seeker;* an *amateur:* one who is a lover, so to speak, but not a knower; passionate *naïf*—am I right?"

Well, he was. Do you know, the great mistake we make in these encounters comes not at their end but here, at the very outset. The moment our mysterious caller comes to the door, or we recognize we've made a wrong turn somewhere and are in alien realms—*then* is when we should take instant, vigor-

ous action: protest at once against the queerness of it, shut
the door, close eyes and ears, and not for one second admit
him. Another step down his road and there'll be no
returning—let us stop where we are! Alas: Curiosity whispers
to Better Judgment, "It's too late anyway," and we always go
on.

"He's about thirty," my visitor supposed.

"Thirty-three, I guess."

"Thirty-three and four months? And I'm sure he has some
affliction—something physical, that he was probably born
with—is he a cripple?"

I hadn't thought of making my man a cripple, though it
was true that he seldom left his quarters (in the top of a certain tower), preferring the company of his books and amateur scientific apparatus to that of his fellow men. "He's just
nearsighted, is all," I said, "but he does have a port-wine
birthmark on his temple—"

"Cancerous!" the stranger cried. "You'll make it turn out
to be cancerous! Oh, that's very good. But shouldn't he have
some sort of astigmatism instead of myopia?"

Ah, it was so right, so righter that the seeker's vision be
twisted instead of merely blurred—and to make the birthmark incipiently cancerous, what a stroke that would be! For
the first time in half a year I grew truly interested in my
book. Putting reticence by, I outlined the plot to this remarkable visitor of mine, who displayed a keener grasp of my
concerns than any critic or reviewer I'd read—keener, I
smiled to suppose, than myself, who in recent months had
come nearly to forgetting what was my vision of things.

"It's about *love,* as you say; but a very special kind. People
talk about two sorts of love, you know, the kind that tries to
escape the self and the kind that affirms the self. But it seems
to me there's a third kind of love, that doesn't seek either
union or communion with its object, but merely admires it
from a position of utter detachment—what I call the Innocent Imagination." My hero, I explained, was to be a Cosmic
Amateur; a man enchanted with history, geography, nature,
the people around him—everything that *is the case*—because
he saw its arbitrariness but couldn't understand or accept its
finality. He would deal with reality like a book, a novel that
he didn't write and wasn't a character in, but only an appre-
ciative reader of; naturally he would assume that there were
other novels, better ones and worse . . . But in truth, of

course, he *wasn't* finally a spectator at all; he couldn't stay "out of it"; and the fiascos of his involvements with men and women—in particular the revelation of his single mortal fate—these things would make him at the end, if not an authentic person, at least an expert amateur, so to speak, who might aspire to a kind of honorary membership in the human fraternity.

"I think there's some heroism in that, don't you?" I was, in truth, never more enthusiastic about my story. It *was* a great conception after all, and little inspirations came as I spoke: the seeker must be not only astigmatic but addicted to lenses, telescopic and microscopic; the tower he lived in I would convert to a sort of huge *camera obscura* into which images of life outside were projected, ten times more luminous and interesting than the real thing—perfect, perfect! And my amateur of life would welcome and treasure his cancer, his admission-ticket to brotherhood . . .

But even as my enthusiasm grew, Stoker Giles shook his head.

"It's wrong, classmate." He even laid a hand on my arm—I can only say *lovingly*. And for all I saw pretty well he was playing to the hilt his role of clairvoyant, the touch moved me. And the laughing candor in those eyes, that exalted-imp's face (doubtless practiced in a mirror)—the wretch had a way with him! My quick disappointment gave way to lassitude, a sweet fatigue. It *was* wrong, of course; all I'd ever done was wrong. I had no hold on things. My every purchase on reality—as artist, teacher, lover, citizen, husband, friend—all were bizarre and wrong, a procession of hoaxes perhaps impressive for a time but ultimately ruinous. He couldn't know how deep his words went, almost to the wellsprings! Without for a moment accepting him as *prophet* (I knew all moods are retroactive, so that what he said would apply to anyone ripe for discontentment), I let myself acknowledge the mantic aspects of the situation. Throughout the rest of our interview, you must understand, there was this ambivalence: on the one hand I never lost sight of the likelihood that here was just another odd arts-student, even a lunatic, whose pronouncements were as generally pertinent as weighing-machine fortunes; on the other I was quite aware that it is the prophet who validates the prophecy, and not vice-versa—his authenticity lies not in what he says but in his manner and bearing, his every gesture, the whole embodiment of his personality. And in this salient respect (which I dwell upon because of its relevance to the manuscript he left me) Mr. Stoker Giles was effective indeed.

Calmly now he said, "You're like the man who gave my father a little lens once, that he claimed would show everything truly. Here it is . . ."

He flipped up a round concave lens near the head of his walking-stick and invited me to examine my manuscript through it. But the joke was, it was silvered on the back, and returned no image of my words at all, enlarged or reduced, only a magnified reflection of my eye. I felt myself blush, and blushed more to feel it.

He said, "You're going to fail. You've never been really and truly *there*, have you? And you've never finally owned to the fact of things. If I should suddenly pinch you now and you woke and saw that all of it was gone, that none of the things and people you'd known had been actually *the case*—you wouldn't be very much surprised."

Before I could reply he seized my arm and pinched the skin. I came out of the chair with a shout, batting at his hand, but could not shake him loose. "Wake up! Wake up!" he ordered, grinning at me. I found myself blinking and snorting out air. I did, I did with my whole heart yearn to shrug off the Dream and awake to an order of things—quite new and other! And it was not the first time.

He let go my arm and with his cane-hook retrieved my chair, which had got thrust away.

"It's beside the point that all the others are flunking too," he went on. "Don't you agree? The important thing is to *pass*; you must pass. And you've got a long way to go! Don't think it's just a matter of turning a corner, to reach Commencement Gate: you've got to become as a kindergarten again, or a new-dropped kid. If that weren't so, my dad wouldn't have said it. But you know this yourself." Again he touched my arm, this time mildly, where the angry pinch-mark flamed, and affection beamed in his look. "What a pleasing thing it is that you don't bring up all the old arguments! But that's the artist in you (which is real enough, even if your work is wrong). You know a man can't reason a piece of music into being; and to argue the fact of Graduation is like arguing the beauty of a melody, or a line of verse. Splendid of you not to bother. I knew you were the man."

I still felt very much shaken; but I could not resist pointing out that in any case he made a good argument against further argument. He threw back his bronze head to laugh, and then with a serious smile declared: "I love you, classmate." My apprehension must have showed, for he added with a chuckle, "Oh, not in *that* way! There isn't time, for one thing: we both have too much to do. You've got to enroll yourself in the New Curriculum and get yourself Graduated; then you've got to establish Gilesianism here, so that the others can pass the Finals too. And this isn't the only college in the University, you know, or the only University, for that matter. *My* work is cut out for me!"

In the very head of his stick a silver watch was set, facing upwards, which he now consulted. Among my other emotions I was beginning to feel disappointment: what an anticlimax it would be if he revealed himself not only as a crank but as a tiresome one!

All I could think to say was: "Gilesianism."

"It's the only Way," he said pleasantly. "They call us crazy men and frauds and subversives—I don't mind that, or the things they do to us; we'd be fools not to have expected it. What breaks my heart is seeing them all fail, when *The Revised New Syllabus* could show them how to pass."

I sighed. "You're from the Education School. You've thought up some gimmick for your dissertation, and I'm supposed to read through it and make suggestions about the prose, since you took the trouble to buy my books."

"Please," he said gently. "The *Syllabus* doesn't need anything: I've already proofread the text that WESCAC read out and corrected the mistaken passages. It's you that needs the *Syllabus.*"

"You're from Business Administration," I ventured next, but I was too much upset still to relish the sarcasm. "All this rigmarole is somebody's notion of a way to sell textbooks."

Tranquilly he shut his eyes until I was done. Then, his good humor unimpaired, he said, "I enjoy raillery, classmate, but there just isn't time. Here's what you need to know: I'm not from this campus (you've guessed that already). My alma mater is New Tammany College—you couldn't have heard of it, it's in a different university entirely. And my father was George Giles." He paused. "The *true* GILES; classmate: the Grand Tutor of our Western Campus."

I leaned back in my swivel-chair. The hour was late. Outside, the weather roared. Nothing was getting done. Distraught to my marrow, I acknowledged him—"*Was*, you say." But I was almost incapable of attending what he said.

For the first and only time his expression turned sorrowful. "He's no longer with us. He has . . . gone away for a while."

Dreamily I said, "But he'll come back, of course."

He looked at me. "Of course."

"One day—when we need him again." How I should have liked to sleep.

His smile returned, albeit melancholily. "We need him now. Things are worse than they ever were in his day. But he's—on a sort of sabbatical leave, you might say. It's up to us to carry on."

He pressed upon me then his story, which I heard in my torpor and made this sense of only on later recollection: His father was or had been some sort of *professor extraordinarius* (of what subject I never learned) whose reputation rested on his success in preparing students to pass their final examinations. His pedagogical method had been unorthodox, and so like many radicals he had worked against vehement opposition, even actual persecutions: I gathered his tenure was revoked and he was dismissed from his position on a charge of moral turpitude while still in his early thirties—though it was not clear to me whether he had ever held official rank in his faculty. Neither was it plain what had happened to him afterwards: apparently he'd left the campus for a short time, returned clandestinely (don't ask me why) to confer with his protégés, and then disappeared for good. The tale was like so many others one has heard, I could almost have predicted certain features—such as that these same protégés had subsequently dedicated their lives to spreading their Mentor's word and institutionalizing his method as they understood it; that they too were roughly used as they transferred from college to college, but won proselytes by their zeal wherever they went. Neither was it surprising to learn that this Professor Giles, this "Grand Tutor" as his son called him, never committed his wisdom to the press: what academic department has not its Grand Old Man who packs the lecture-halls term after term but never publishes a word in his field? In fact, the one unusual particular of the whole story as I heard it this first time was the not-very-creditable one that the man had got a child, by a lady married to someone else; otherwise it was the standard painful history of reformers and innovators.

The problem for my visitor, then—the fruit of this illicit

planting—was the common one faced by second-generation followers of any pioneer: to formulate the Master's teaching into some readily disseminable canon, a standard and authority for the fast-swelling ranks of its adherents. By the time Stoker Giles had reached young manhood his father's original pupils were already divided into factions; the son's first thought had been to compile as a source-book their reminiscences of the great man's life and tenure, but so many discrepancies, even contradictions, were made manifest in the collation, he abandoned that project. In its early stages, however, he had gone so far as to read the several texts into an automatic computer, as our fashionable classicists are fond of doing nowadays, to speed the work of comparing them—and here, gentle editors and publishers, your credulity like mine must flex its muscles for a considerable stretch.

This remarkable computer, I was told (a gadget called WESCAC), not only pointed out in accordance with its program the hopeless disagreement of the texts; on its own hook, or by some prior instruction, it volunteered further that there was in its Storage "considerable original matter" read in fragmentarily by George Giles himself in the years of his flourishing: taped lecture-notes, recorded conferences with protégés, and the like. Moreover, the machine declared itself able and ready (with the aid of "analogue facilities" and a sophistication dismaying at least to a poor humanist like myself) to assemble, collate, and edit this material, interpolate all verifiable data from other sources such as the memoirs then in hand, recompose the whole into a coherent narrative from the Grand Tutor's point of view, and "read it out" in an elegant form on its automatic printers! The son, as disinclined to writing as the father but apparently commanding some authority in his college, agreed, and in the face of opposition from certain "Gilesians" as well as "anti-Gilesians," the computer made good its promise. After several false starts and program adjustments it produced a first-person chronicle of the life and teachings of the Grand Tutor, a text so faithful to the best evidence and polished in its execution that young Stoker needed only to "change a date or a place-name here and there," as he vowed, to call it finished.

The great test came, he told me, when he took the manuscript to one Peter Greene, an early student of Giles's, now past sixty and the strongest critic of the "WESCAC Project." A famous teacher in his own right by then, Greene met the youngster with a scowl and only after much persuasion agreed to listen to a dozen pages. Refusing even to sit, he paced the floor of his office with every prejudice in his expression (so Stoker declared) as the reading began. At the end of page one he stood still; halfway through the second he was weeping; by the third he was on his knees at the young man's feet, begging his pardon and declaring it was "the GILES's very voice" that sounded off the pages!

Thus was born *The Revised New Syllabus*, which like its narrator and its evangels was destined for arduous vicissitudes. Those Gilesians whose teaching it contradicted—some of them chairmen of their own departments by that time—charged that the work was spurious, concocted either by WESCAC or by the upstart Stoker Giles, perhaps both, if not by the "Dean o' Flunks" himself.* The most antipathetic went so far as to deny that my visitor was actually the Grand Tutor's son, calling him an opportunist and antigiles who made the best of an accidental resemblance; while the non-Gilesians, "naturally," maintained as they had from the first that the man called George was never "the true GILES" at all but a dangerous impostor, and that the *R.N.S.*, "authentic" or not, was anti-intellectual, immoral, subversive, and altogether unfit for undergraduate reading-lists.

My visitor sighed as he concluded this account, and toyed glumly with the shaft of his stick; then with a shrug his animation returned. "But it all worked to our advantage, you understand—all that censorship and prohibition, and beating us up and throwing us in jail. Even the imitations and pirated versions that everybody ran into print with helped us out—you must have wished for that sort of ruckus over your own books! We put up with it, just as Dad used to, and the New Curriculum gets established sooner or later despite all. Because you see, classmate, the one thing we have on our side is the only thing that matters in the long run: we're *right*. The others are wrong." His face was joyous. "It may take a hundred semesters, but we know the New Curriculum will win. The non-majors will flunk; the impostors and false tutors will be exposed. It's just a matter of time until that book on your desk there will be in every briefcase on every campus in the University. It *must* be so: there isn't any other hope for studentdom."

* *Quem vide infra.*

He consulted his walking-stick watch again and abruptly rose to leave. It occurred to me that I had lost track of the clock-chimes from Main Tower.

"I can't stay longer; I've got other colleges to visit—even other universities." He winked at me. "There *are* other universities, you know."

"Look here, now—" I shook my head vigorously to throw off my drowsiness and indicated the box of typescript. "What am I supposed to do with this? I don't have time—"

"Indeed you don't!" He laughed—and what a stance he struck with his mad cane! "It's late, late, late, that's certain! On the other hand, you have all the time there is, exactly." He poked at the manuscript with his stick. "Forget about yourself if you like. Just send this on to your publishers without reading it; they'll be grateful enough, and so will your students. Or throw it out, if you don't care what happens to them on the Finals. I have other copies for other campuses; this one is your affair entirely . . ."

He spoke without testiness, only a bit teasingly: now, however, it was my shoulder he touched the stick to, and his voice became full of a fiery solicitude. "But classmate, read it! We lecture to studentdom as a whole, and yet there isn't any studentdom, Daddy always said that—only students, that have to be Graduated one at a time. I want you to be Giles's professor to this campus, for their sakes; but more than that I want you to Commence yourself, for your own sake. Do read it!"

A moment longer the stick-tip rested there. Then he tapped me a little smart one with it and left, calling back from the hallway, "I'll keep in touch!"

But he never did. His typescript languished beside mine—the one unread, the other unwritten—even got mixed with it by a careless janitor. I took a breath, and the winter term was over; paused a moment to reflect, and found myself thirty-two. What gets better? Confronting a class I forgot what my opinion was about anything, and had to feign illness. Famous men died; the political situation deteriorated. No longer could I eat at bedtime as a young man does and still sleep soundly. Fewer social invitations; presently none. The polar ice-cap, scientists warned, is going to melt. The population problem admits of no solution. "Today's freshman is more serious about his studies than were his predecessors—but is he also perhaps less inclined to think for himself?" Yesterday one was twenty; tomorrow one dies of old age.

In unnaturally clear March twilight when the air is chill, one reflects upon passionate hearts now in their graves and wishes that the swiftly running hours were more intense. Young men and girls cut off while their blood flamed, sleeping in the fields now; old folks expiring with the curse; the passionately good, the passionately wicked—all in their tombs, soft-lichened, and the little flowers nodding. One yearns—to make a voyage. Why is one not a hero?

I read *The Revised New Syllabus*. Do you likewise, gentlemen and ladies in whose hands this letter is!

A final word. I sought diligently to locate Mr. Stoker Giles, or Giles Stoker (the comma in his name on the title-page, and my imperfect memory of that fateful evening's details, make the order uncertain), with an eagerness you will presently appreciate. In vain: no such name is in our Student Directory, nor is a "New Tammany College" listed in the roll of accredited institutions of higher learning. At the same time I consulted one of our own computer-men on the matter of the *R.N.S.*'s authorship: his opinion was that no automatic facility he knew of was capable presently of more than rudimentary narrative composition and stylistics—but he added that there was no theoretical barrier even to our own machine's developing such a talent in time. It was simply a matter of more sophisticated circuitry and programming, such as the computer itself could doubtless work out; literature and composition, he observed, like every other subject, were being ably taught by the gadget in pilot projects all over our quarter of the campus, and it was his conviction that anything "computer-teachable" (his term) was "computer-learnable." Moreover, he could not vouch for what his military colleagues might be up to, not to mention their counterparts "on the other side"; the computer-race he counted no less important than the contest in weapons-development, and it had become as shrouded in secrecy. His impression was that our enemies were more concerned with raw calculation-power than with versatility and sophistication—there was no evidence of their using computers as we do to manage sausage-making, recommend marriages, bet on sporting-events, and compose music, for example—but no one could say for sure.

Acknowledge with me, then, the likelihood that *The Revised New Syllabus* is the work not of "WESCAC" but of an obscure, erratic wizard whose *nom de plume*, at least, is *Stoker, Giles*; and, again with me, acknowledge further that this is not the only possibility—for as that splendid odd fellow observed, there are in literal truth "other universities than ours." To the individual student of the book's wisdom the question of its authorship is anyhow irrelevant, and it seems most improbable to me that any prior copyrights, for example, will be infringed by its publication. The text herewith submitted I declare to be identical to the one left in my hands on that momentous night (excepting only certain emendations and rearrangements which the Author's imperfect mastery of our idiom and his avowed respect for my artistic judgment encouraged me to make). My intentions are 1) to put aside any monies paid me as agent, against the Author's reappearance; 2) to resign my professorship forthwith, whatever hardship that may work upon my family, and set about the task of my own re-education, to the point even of "becoming as a kindergartener" if necessary; 3) in pursuance of this objective, to compile a more formal and systematic exposition of the Goat-Boy's teachings, as well as a full commentary on and concordance to *The Revised New Syllabus*—these latter for classroom use in my own "New Curriculum," still in the planning phase.

Which several projects, I hope and believe, together with the extraordinary *Syllabus* itself, will more than make good what losses you have sustained on my previous manuscripts and vindicate your unremitting, most touching faith in

This regenerate Seeker after Answers,
J.B.

R. N. S.

THE

Revised New Syllabus

OF

George Giles

OUR GRAND TUTOR

Being the Autobiographical and Hortatory Tapes
Read Out at New Tammany College to His Son

Giles (,) Stoker

By the West Campus Automatic Computer
And by Him Prepared for the Furtherment of the
Gilesian Curriculum

Volume One

FIRST REEL

1.

George is my name; my deeds have been heard of in Tower Hall, and my childhood has been chronicled in the *Journal of Experimental Psychology*. I am he that was called in those days Billy Bocksfuss—cruel misnomer. For had I indeed a cloven foot I'd not now hobble upon a stick or need ride pick-a-back to class in humid weather. Aye, it was just for want of a proper hoof that in my fourteenth year I was the kicked instead of the kicker; that I lay crippled on the reeking peat and saw my first love tupped by a brute Angora. Mercy on that buck who butted me from one world to another; whose fell horns turned my sweetheart's fancy, drove me from the pasture, and set me gimping down the road I travel yet. This bare brow, shame of my kidship, he crowned with the shame of men: I bade farewell to my hornless goathood and struck out, a hornèd human student, for Commencement Gate.

I was, in other words, the Ag-Hill Goat-Boy. Who misbegot me, and on whom, who knew, or in what corner of the University I drew first breath? It was my fate to call no man Daddy, no woman Mom. Herr Doktor Professor Spielman was my keeper: Maximilian Spielman, the great Mathematical Psycho-Proctologist and former Minority Leader in the College Senate; the same splendid Max who gave his name to the Law of Cyclology, and in his prime led his department's fight for some sort of examination to supplement the Orals. Alas, his crusading ardor burned many a finger; so far from being awarded an emeritus professorship to comfort his old age, he was drummed off the quad a year before retirement on a trumped-up charge of intellectual turpitude—though his only crime, he avowed to the end, was to suggest in a public lecture that his science alone could plumb the bottom of man's nature. Disgraced and penniless, he was obliged to take whatever employment he could find to keep body and soul together; and thus it came about that he spent his last years as Senior Goatherd on the New Tammany College Farms. Ignominy—yet who can say Max didn't make the most of it? His masterwork, *The Riddle of the Sphincters*, twenty years in the writing and done but for the index, he fed to the goats a chapter at a time: I myself, so he told me years later over Mont d'Or cheese and bock beer, had lunched on the Second Appendix, a poem-in-numbers meant to demonstrate mathematically his belief in the fundamental rectitude of student nature. Embittered, but too great-hearted for despair, he removed himself entirely from society and devoted all his genius to the herd. Year-round he lived among us: made his home in a stall through the winter and pastured with us when the weather warmed. Call it if you will the occupational affliction of the field-researcher, he soon came to feel for the objects of his study more love than he had ever felt for his peers in the Senate. He became a vegetarian, grew a little beard, exchanged cap and gown for a wrapper of mohair, and lamented only that his years would not let him go on all fours. Though he never deigned to publish again in his life, his researches were at no time more bold and meticulous than during the first few years of this period. The goats, after all (to quote an entry from his diaries) "do not conceal in shame that aspect of their beauty I crave to fathom; serenely aware, after their fashion, that a perfect whole is the sum of perfect parts, they fly their flags high . . ." His one enemy among the bucks was an old brown Toggenburger called Freddie, tyrant of the herd, who, when he spied Max bent over to inspect any doe, would butt him, taking him for a rival. Max in turn was thus driven head-first against the subject of his examination, who thinking herself assaulted seldom felt again the same trust in her keeper. Such subversion of rapport between subject and investigator could not be permitted; just as vexing was the coincidence that the Chairman of New Tammany's Speech Department, whose filibuster in the Senate had blocked passage of the Qualifying Anals bill and contributed to Spielman's downfall, was named Fred. Max saw in this a sign, and took his vengeance. He dared not approach the Toggenburg openly, and so one October night when the bucks were bleating their lust as usual (none more loudly than treacherous Freddie), he arranged for a spry young nan to find her way into his enemy's stall: some moments later, Max crept up behind with a patent docker. *Zut*, the old rogue was clipped in mid-service, no joy in his windfall then! And all his fierceness withered; he grew fat and docile, never said a word when his keeper dehorned him a few weeks later. Of his trophies Max made the earlier into an amulet, of which more anon, the latter into a kind of shophars wherewith thenceforward he summoned the flock—and his studies proceeded without further trouble. Indeed, whether because they understood "after their fashion" that Freddie was undone and were grateful to his undoer, or because in goatdom the horn and testicle, irrespective of their bearer, command obeisance, the bucks gave place to Max ever after, and the does they capered to his tootle. The months that followed were perhaps his blissfullest: he founded the sciences of analogical proctoscopy and psychosymbolistic cosmography, developed the Rectimetric Index for "distinguishing, arithmetically and forever, the sheep from the goats," and explored the faint initial insights of what was to become Spielman's Law, his last and farthest-reaching contribution to man's understanding of the University. That capstone on the temple of his genius, climax of his epic quest for Answers: how commonplace it sounds already, very nearly banal; and yet what dααh, what vaulting insight! In three words Max Spielman synthesized all the fields which thitherto he'd browsed in brilliantly one by one—showed the "sphincter's riddle" and the mystery of the University to be the same. *Ontogeny recapitulates cosmogeny*—what is it but to say that proctoscopy repeats hagiography? That our Founder on Founder's Hill and the rawest freshman on his first *mons veneris* are father and son? That my day, my year, my life, and the history of West Campus are wheels within wheels? "Ontogeny recapitulates cosmogeny"—I cannot hear those words but in the gentle Moishian accents of my keeper. Well he knew, old Max, the fate of grand hypotheses, but hard experience had brought him unfairly to mistrust his colleagues' wisdom, and his isolation kept him from final appreciation of WESCAC. For fifty years, he said, his theory of Cyclic Correspondence would be anathema on West Campus: not twenty had gone by before it was dogmatized by the

Chancellor, taped by the Chief Programmer, and devoured by WESCAC.

He never could have prophesied his present fame, clear-seer as he was in his latter years—nor would it much have assuaged his misanthropy to foresee it. Yet though he refused, and justly, the trustees' belated offer of emeritus benefits, there is some evidence of mellowing in his last semesters, perhaps even of loneliness for his own kind. Of the scores who have quoted the famous Maxim, "Der goats is humaner than der men, und der men is goatisher than der goats," how many understand its deep ambivalence? It's true he kept a seraglio of nannies (though his appetites in this line have been much exaggerated, as has his prowess) and named them after leading members of the Faculty Women's Club—but there was no malice in the voice that summoned Helen to his stall, or Maude, or Shirley; and the respect he showed Mary V. Appenzeller, my own dear dam, any boy might wish for his lady mother. But the most revealing evidence that Max still bore some love for men is the thing most often scored to his discredit: I mean my own appearance in the goat-barn and my rearing with the other kids of the West Campus herd.

I know now that I am not Max and Mary's kid: that much he told me on the day I learned I was a man. Let those who pity my childhood mark this well: I wept as much to know the one as to know the other. What a fair and sprightly thing my kidship was! Sweet Mary Appenzeller neglected the rest of her family to nurse me; thanks be to her splendid udder, whose twin founts flowed at my least beck, I grew from strapping infancy into a boyhood such as human males may dream of. Fatigue was my only curfew, sufficient rest my one alarm. I ate what, when, and where I pleased—furze and gorse and fescues; oil-cake, willow-peels, and pollard. Acorns bound me when I was loose; mangolds scoured me when I was bound. As there were no rules to break, Max never birched me; since he forked my hay and patted my head, I loved him beyond measure. Like my stallmates I feared fire, loud noise, and the bigger bucks, but only in the presence of those terrors, never between times, and so anxiety was foreign to me as soap. When I was gay I gamboled where I would, banged heads with my brothers and bleated in the clover; angry I kicked my stall, my pals, or Mary Appenzeller, whichever was behind me, and was either ignored or rekicked at once. I learned neither sums nor speech until I was ten, but at five years my crouching lope outstripped any human child of twelve; I could spring like a chamois from rock to rock, break a fencerail with my head, distinguish six hundred ninety sorts of plants and eat all but eighty-three of them. My moral training required no preachment (not the least respect in which it differed absolutely from that of humans): Who neglects his appetites suffers their pangs; Who presumes incautiously may well be butted; Who fouls his stall must sleep in filth. Cleave to him, I learned, who does you kindness; Avoid him who does you hurt; Stay inside the fence; Take of what's offered as much as you can for as long as you may; Don't exchange the certain for the possible; Boss when you're able, be bossed when you aren't, but don't forsake the herd. Simple lessons, instinct with wisdom, that grant to him who heeds them afternoons of blowsy bliss and dreamless nights. Thirteen years they fenced my soul's pasture; I romped without a care. In the fourteenth I slipped their gate—as I have since many another—looked over my shoulder, and saw that what I'd said bye-bye to was my happiness.

2.

They flatter themselves who hold that I was unaware of *people* all those terms; that had I ever seen normal men I'd have yearned most miserably to leave the herd. The truth is, Max made no particular secret of my existence; people knew of me long before those articles in the *Journal of Experimental Psychology*. Indeed, the New Tammany S.P.C.A., interpreting their jurisdiction widely, moved more than once in my "behalf," and only the direct intervention of the Chancellor (who, let us say, felt guilty about Max's dismissal) prevented their plucking me from my family. Every weekend there were students and faculty along the fence. I was as pleased to see them as were all my friends; we frisked for their amusement. If in time Max forbade me to approach them, it was not out of fear that I might *defect:* he knew I'd not swap my liberty for the pitiful estate of folk who teetered on two legs, reeked of unnatural scents, bound themselves in layer after layer of cloth, and were never allowed the run of the pastures. What he feared—alas and rightly—was that if they didn't poison me, as they did with tobacco a Schwarzhals doeling I once knew, they'd corrupt me with bad examples. A day came when I chafed at this restriction: Max thought me more innocent than I knew I was, and hence like every youngster I underestimated my susceptibility.

How it would have alarmed him to know my sophistication at fourteen. From simple observation I'd learned to tell men from women, even when the latter wore trousers and sheared their fleece. To be sure, I had yet to guess the measure of human frailty: one whose brothers became fathers before their first birthday, and who has himself in play been humping does since he could crawl, can scarcely feature a beast that may not mate until its thirteenth year. But I well understood why their keepers never scrupled to let human bucks and does run together, and why they all were so ashamed of their bodies that they mated in darkness. More than one night (unknown to Max) pairs of people stole into our buckwheat meadow: if I heard them crashing through the straw—as often I did, their attempts at silence were that clumsy—I'd slip from the pound to watch their performance from some near hiding-place. When I learned how nightblind they were and how poor of smell and hearing, I made bold to come almost upon them, not to miss a word of their curious bleating—and never was found out. By this means I discovered that the brutes were hairiest in the few places where goats were bald, and bald almost everywhere else, where fleece is most needed (my own angora wrapper I regarded as a part of myself, it was so seldom removed). I had assumed that all the men I saw were geldings, since they ran with the women and never smelled lustful: now I learned that neither sex rutted that strongly. Small wonder. Who could mount, for example, a monster with two heads instead of one—which heads moreover sprout from its backside? Just that enormous seemed the first female human I saw unclothed, with her queer small udders at the wrong end of her trunk. Yet praise be to Nature, that finds every dragoness a dragon, all praise to Instinct for making worms love other worms—she managed a feeble coupling after all with her hairless buck, and my education took a great step forward.

But see me stray from the point, quite as I came to stray from the herd and leave behind my good judgment. These espials bear on what's to come—let them show in any case that I was less naïve than gentle Max supposed. For I also understood by the age of fourteen that he was some sort of human himself, despite his long white curls and splendid odor; and further that, for all the herd accepted me as a brother, I was no Rock Alpine, Murciana, or Schwartzenberg-Guggisberger, but a breed unto myself. It was I the people came to see, I think I always knew that. My pals grew up faster and were nimbler on their feet; after a year they joined the grownups and were replaced by new kids, while I remained season after season in the play-pound. They were stronger, more handsome, and (pass them) more predictable. I was merely clever—yet dull enough to think myself their better on that account. I alone could climb a tree as well as gnaw its bark, pick my own lice, imitate any sound I heard, and transform a herdsman's crook into a weapon. We all loved tricks and stunts, but they hadn't by half my invention, and in the whole of goatdom no kid save Billy Bocksfuss ever tricked himself.

In our play-yard were a number of barrels and boards that we used for Dean of the Hill. To entertain my admirers I would set two planks against opposite sides of a barrel-top; Redfearn's Tommy, my special friend, would scramble up from one side and I from the other, and we'd wrestle for possession of the summit. One weekend morning, encouraged by applause, I raised the Hill to a height of two barrels, and thence to two barrels and a box, which I climbed with great difficulty from the side. The plankway was too steep then for the others; they could only adore me from below as I teetered on my perch; presently they feigned indifference, butted one another on the ground as if they didn't hear my crowing, or the crowd's approval. But I knew their hearts were filled with envy. Redfearn's Tom, especially, craved to join me: "Come, Tom!" I called, and he would pick his way up the steep board until he lost his footing. The humans took up my taunt: "Come, Tom! Come, Tom!" My poor brown buddy hurled himself up the barrel-side, fell back in the mud, hurled himself again. I mocked his bleating; he redoubled his efforts; my tower shook. "Come, Tom!" I cried. And I found myself making the peculiar roaring noise I'd heard humans make: "Ha ha ha! Come, Tommy! Ha ha ha!" The word *laughter* was not yet in my vocabulary; I'd often mimicked its sound, but now I understood its cause and use. Inspired, I made water upon my friend. "Ha ha ha!" we all laughed as he sprang away.

I heard Max call from the barn-door: "Na, you Bill." His voice was stern; "Come down off," he ordered, and I conceived a queer new notion: he was jealous. The onlookers hooted: though I had not heard that sound before, I grasped its import at once and found it no chore to echo. What's more, it suggested my last and grandest stunt: rising up on my knees I cupped hands to mouth and did a perfect imitation of Max's shophar.

"Verboten!" he shouted, clutching at his beard, shaking his crook at me.

It was the peril-word. At once every goat round about raised head from browsing; years of training made me feel seized by that word as by a hand; my senses rang. But where was the danger? The humans were with me; they recommenced their laughter, and so again and again I sent the buckhorn's call across the fields.

"Te-*roo*-ah! Te-*roooo*-ah!"

Alarm and summons together drove the goats wild: they leaped and cried and crashed against their fences. The does all called for their kids, the kids for their dams—I heard Mary bleat for me from her stall. The big bucks stamped in their pens and plunged about; Redfearn's Tom tore between Max and the barrels. There stood our keeper shouting, *"Verboten!"* but the summons came from Billy Bockfuss, Dean of the Hill!

My next "Te-*roo*-ah!" resolved Tom's doubts: I that had been his playmate was now his keeper and must be obeyed. As before he threw himself up against the barrels, frantic to reach me, and now the others followed his example. Hadn't I gulled them, "Ha ha ha." And then my tower came a-topple.

I had built it near the fence, which, when the Hill fell, I tumbled over, to the feet of my audience. No bones broke, but the wind was knocked out of me, and I was terrified to have fallen, as I thought, into the people's pen. They sprang back; their women shrieked—no fiercelier than I, when I had got my breath. It is a mercy I didn't know then what I learned by and by, that men have sated their bloody hunger with *jambon de chèvre* and billygoat-tawny. Even so I guessed they'd set upon me, as would our bucks on any of them who fell within reach. I scrambled up, my only thought to escape back into the play-pound; but trousered legs were

all around me, and still rattled by my fall I sprang the wrong
way. More shouts went up; I was struck a cruel one athwart
the muzzle with a stick. I stumbled into the fence, but my
eyes had watered, I couldn't see to climb. Max hopped about
the pound, crying at them to stop; I bleated my pain to him
and scrabbled up and down in search of the gate. The pens
were in an uproar. "Ha ha ha!" the people snarled, and
kicked me with their leathern hooves.

Hours later, when Max had calmed the herd at last and
laid cold pads on my contusions, he did his best to explain
that my attackers had been frightened as I, and had struck
me thinking I meant to harm them. This I could understand
readily enough. What stung more sharp than bruises was a
thing he found less easy to make clear in our simple tongue:
Why had they cheered my stunt and then *ha-ha'd* all the
while they kicked me? To attack—that was perfectly normal
for bucks of any species, however unequal the contest. But
what manner of beast was it that *laughed* at his victim's
plight?

Even as I strove to find words for this question I felt a
nudging at my back; Redfearn's Tommy had overcome his
fright enough to cross the kid-pen and snuggle down beside
me in Max's lap, which we often shared. He still smelt of my
urine, and when I made to pick his lice by way of reparation,
he bounded off a-trembling.

"So," Max said, and was kind enough to say no more.

3.

This sweet forbearance—which had also spared me any punishment for my misdeeds—I myself was not graced with. The
more I reflected on my ill use of Redfearn's Tom, the wrath-
fuller I grew at my own tormentors. Indeed, I tasted for the
first time hatred, and turning its dark flavor on my tongue,
lost my first night's sleep. Tom by next morning bore no
grudge, he was ready to play again; but when the iron cycles
drove up to our pound and the afternoon's humans were discharged to admire me—their numbers increased by news of

the past day's sport—I attacked the fence viciously, and was pleased to see them scatter. That became my custom: I would wait in my stall until the visitors gathered, charge at them once, and then withdraw to brood away the balance of the day. When their first alarm passed they begged and taunted me to have at them again—"Here, Billy!" "Come, Bill!"—and made ready sticks to poke me through the mesh. But the first charge they were always unprepared for: to a man they sprang back; the females squealed, the males made oaths. I never gave them the pleasure of a second.

"That's not nice," Max suggested. But he didn't say *verboten*, as once he would have, and I noticed he was usually somewhere about to see the brutes jump.

This new sport—say rather *diversion*, since I had lost all taste for play—preoccupied me until one evening in March, just short of a fortnight after my fall. I had had no victims all that day; it was a Friday, and Max had long since told me how surpassing dull humans were, that spend five days a week learning things to make them miserable. Then after supper, as Redfearn's Tom and I enjoyed a fresh salt-lick, I heard a clinking rattle in the road, which I knew to be the sound of a *bicycle*. Together we peered out into the pound: a plump, brown-coated human lady had dismounted from her thing in the dusking light and approached our fence. By the look of her she was no doeling—though truly, all humans but Max looked much alike to me. Her hair was cream-white like a Saanen's and seemed decently brushed; she wore jeweled eyeglasses pointed at the corners; her legs were bare from hock to hoof . . . how did one describe a creature that changed its coat every day? She came to the fence and looked about the pound, where three or four kids were sleeping off their meal. They were polite enough, when she called something meaningless to them, to wander over and sniff the dead weeds she stuck through the wire. But of course it was not they she came to taunt; she pretended interest in them for half a minute and then yoohooed at the barn. Her voice seemed timid; I guessed she feared Max might hear and prevent her from molesting me.

"Yoo hoo, Billy? Come, Billy Billy?"

So, she would summon me by name to my torment. I raged into the pound; leaped at her with a howl I'd learned from the sheep-dog bitch across the Road. Kids sprang in all directions, tripping over their own legs; but though she dropped her grass and drew her hands back, the woman didn't fly. There was no fright in her expression, merely alarm and something else. I rose up on my knees, clutched the mesh, and growled.

"No, no," she said. She even squatted to my height, drew something from a bag, and offered it to me to eat. I backed off and charged again, too furious now to care what trick she played me. I crashed against the fence, was thrown back, and crashed against the fence again. I whinnied and stamped and bared my teeth, bleated and barked and brayed; I flung a board and clots of turd at her, and all the while she pleaded, "No, Billy! Please!" The ruckus brought Max hobbling from the barn, where the kids had run. He found me rolling in the dirt with rage.

"Git! Git!" he cried at the woman. "Shoo! Go home!"

She began then to make a strange sound indeed, such as I had never heard: a kind of catching, snorting whimper. And water dropped from behind her eyeglasses as she turned away. I made to spring a final time to speed her off.

"Stillstand!" Max snapped. What is more, he jabbed me in the thurl with the butt of his crook—the first rough use I'd ever had at his hands—and when instinctively I snorted and lowered my head at him like any stud-buck, he cracked me a sharp one across the chine and said, "Get on in, or I put a ring in your silly nose!"

So unexpected was the blow, and his speech so smarting, I ran a-yelp into the barn, more frightened than ever I'd been with my tower tumbled. The woman, just mounting her bike, let go another whoop of her curious noise; I heard Max shooing her off still. My face was wet. I wiped one arm across to see the blood from where he must have cut me—but found only water, that smeared my dusty wrist and was salt as our lick. My throat ached, my lip shook; now I too was wrenched with those bawling wows, which wracked the worse when Max clucked in to soothe me: then he hugged me, kissed my eyes, said *"Ach*, child, what's the tears now?" and the entire barnyard rang with my first grief.

It was his chore to explain this noise as he had the other. The task was light: we'd used words between us oftener in the fortnight past, for one thing, so that my supply of them had tripled and quadrupled. Besides, the matter itself was less mysterious. In the weeks thereafter as I mused fitfully in my stall (no stranger to insomnia now), I tried experiments with both: laughter, I discovered, was easy to simulate but difficult to bring oneself to genuinely, while the reverse was true of tears. The hilariousest memories I could summon, such as Redfearn's Tommy's mistaking me for Max, brought no more than a smile to my lips; but at any of half a dozen contrary recollections—Tommy springing from my touch, Max threatening to ring my nose, the cream-haired woman not retreating from my charge—I was moved to sniffles and wet cheeks. In fact, I came to weep at the least occasion. Instead of attacking my visitors I wept in a corner of the barn; the sight of other kids frisking or of moonshine whitening the buckwheat watered my eyes; I wept at Max's efforts to jolly me and at his impatience with my tears; I wept even at weeping so; I wept at nothing.

Also I made friends that spring with restlessness. When all goatdom and its keeper were asleep I prowled the pasture, spooking deer and flushing woodcocks from their rest; or I would hang my chin over the fence and stare down the Road that led to the Barns Where Humans Slept—and which Max told me it was death for goats to walk upon. In the daytime, when we all went out to browse, I took to slipping from the herd and wandering by myself through the great black willows along the creek, or up in the rise of nibbled hemlocks where the woods began.

From these latter, one bright April morning, a flash of light came. Looking more closely I spied a movement in the scrub perhaps two hundred meters from where we grazed. In all likelihood it was a deer, and the flash some tin or bit of glass he'd turned with his hoof; just possibly it was a human student, escaped into our pasture. In any case my curiosity was pricked; I teased Redfearn's Tommy into chasing me that way. Dear Tom was a strapping fellow then; it was his last month to run with us before being penned up for stud. But he still loved a romp, and while there was no way to tell him my intentions, I knew that once he saw the intruder we'd have great sport running it back into the bush.

"Ho, Tom!" I urged. Midway between herd and hemlocks I saw the flash again; so must have Tommy, for he drew up short, bobbed his head—and galloped back, pretending not to hear the gibes I sent after him. I looked around for Max; he had not come out with us that day. I went on alone. For prudence's sake I came up noisily, to give the creature warning. I

rather expected to find nothing but dung and hoofprints by
the time I got there: Instead, just behind the first tree, I
found the cream-haired weeper. She stood uncertainly a
dozen yards off, wearing green this time and clutching a
leathern bag against her belly; it was her eyeglasses, I observed, that had flashed in the sun.

"Nice Billy?"

I pawed the brown needles and threatened with my forehead.

"Look here, I brought you something good." As before,
she drew a square white handful from her bag. I felt no
anger, but a grand discomfiture; I ought to have gone back
with Tommy. I feigned a charge just to send her off to her
own pasture, but she only waggled her offering at me.

"Come, dear, don't be afraid. It's a peanut-butter sandwich "

I bounded at her with a snarl—but faltered just before her.
Quite clearly she would suffer my attack if need be. Was she
so fearless, or merely stupid? Now she dared to toss the white
food at my feet and come up to me with hands extended. I
ignored the bribe (which however had a most sharp
fragrance): what arrested me was that her eyes already
brimmed with that water so familiar lately to my own. She
knelt and patted my curls; her human odors filled my nostrils; I forgot even to growl.

"There, he's a friendly Bill, he is." How different her voice
was from dear Max's, and her manner of touching. I shivered
under it; made nervous water when she stroked my barrel.
"Sure he wouldn't hurt his friend," she went on. "Do you
know how much I hoped you'd see me? And wasn't I afraid
of that brute you play with! Good Billy, gentle Billy, that's a
Billy. Here, you just try this, Dr. Spielman won't mind . . ."

She held the sandwich to my lips. I chewed a corner off it
and drooled at its outlandish savor. The woman wiped my
chin with a scented white cloth and clucked about the dirt on
me. I gobbled up the rest of the sandwich.

"Wasn't that fine? Tomorrow I'll give you another one.
And milk, if you want, and some more things you never had
before. What do you say, Billy?"

It was a civil question, plainly put and plainly requiring a
yes or no, but my new friend seemed astonished when I said
"*Ja ja,* dot's OK."

"Oh, my gracious, you can *talk,* can't you!" She flung her

arms about my neck; I thought myself threatened and wrenched back with a snort. But the woman was weeping, and unused though I was to such behavior, I understood that it was not in anger she hugged me to her woven coat. It was such a hug Max hugged me the day I had learned to cry—but rockinger, more croonish—and I wept in rhythm with her, a sweeter thing than doing it alone.

We tarried for the queerest forenoon of my life. Having discovered that I could speak, she plied me with questions: Did Max beat me? Wasn't I wretched in that stinking barn? Was I being taught to read and write? Had I no friends at all besides the goats? Half of what she said I couldn't grasp; even when the words were familiar I sometimes failed to understand the question. What did it signify, for example, to ask whether anything was being done for my legs? They had always been as they were—wiry and tough, with fine horny pads at the joints; not so supple as Tommy's, but far usefuller than Max's. Why ought anything to be done for my legs, any more than for hers? Again, to illustrate what *reading* was she took from her bag a white book, which mistaking for another sandwich, I tried to snatch from her.

"No, now," she mildly chid, "that's just paper, you know. Poor thing, you never had bedtime stories, did you? Let's sit down, I'll read you something . . ."

I pretended to be listening; then as she seated herself I ripped a leaf from the book and sprang away to eat it.

"Oh dear!" she cried merrily. "So that's how it is! Well you needn't grab, young man, it's not a bit mannerly. You march yourself back and say 'Please,' and you shall have all you like." In earnest of her pledge she tore a page out herself and offered it me. "Now, that does for the title-page and endpapers, doesn't it! We mustn't eat the others till we've read them." She chattered on, and all I understood was the gentle good humor of her tone. We wept again, I do not know why—indeed, we wept repeatedly throughout that griefless day. In the end I laid my head in her lap as she read to me, and toyed with the silver watch she wore on a lanyard round her neck. Why was I not with the herd, and what would Max think?

Unlike much of what I heard that morning, the *story* was splendidly clear and gripping: it involved three excellent brothers who desired to cross a stream and feast upon cabbages, but were opposed in their innocent design by a typical human visitor called Troll. This Troll, understand, had no desire to eat the cabbages himself, nor from what I gathered was the *bridge* his private pen; even had it been, his intent was not the honorable one of guarding his privacy. Ah no: I was aghast to hear from my friend's calm lips that the brute meant to kill those beautiful heroes and *eat their flesh*. My gorge rose at the thought; I could scarcely chew the page on which such evil was. The woman saw my agitation, patted my neck and insisted that it was "just a story"—as if that excused Troll's wickedness, or would save Wee Willie! Only her assurance that the brothers would triumph staunched my tears and dissuaded me from calling Max to their rescue—for though I could not see the Misters Gruff, they were there in the words that sounded off the page, as real and clear to me as Redfearn's Tommy. What resourcefulness the youngest of them showed in turning Troll's blood-lust to their advantage: the story named no breeds, but I was sure in my heart that this initial Gruff (to my mind, the real hero) was of the same species as myself. I hung on the tale's unfolding, I wanted it never to end, and yet trembled with concern for the second brother, lest he not have caught the gambit of the first. "Tell him wait for der biggest brudder yet!" I counseled—yet durst I hope even Troll could be gulled thus again? At the appearance of Great William Gruff I forgot to eat, and when I saw justice done (albeit bloodily) and that worthiest of families cross to their reward, I embraced my newfound friend about her middle.

Never was such a wonder as this *story!* Its passion drained me, yet I was bleating for more when Max's shophar hooted in the distance.

"What's that? Must you go?" She returned the precious volume to her bag. There'd be another tale tomorrow; she knew a host of them. And more peanut-butter.

"Bye-bye, now," she called. I scampered back to her, mistaking her meaning; the pull of the shophar against my movement brought tears to my eyes. Ah, was that it? *Auf wiedersehen*, then, till tomorrow . . . the herd was almost to the barn already.

"Bye-bye! Bye-bye!" I galloped tearfully through the fields. At the first of the stud-pens I paused to say respectfully bye-bye to Brickett Ranunculus, an Anglo-Nubian who but that he was polled had been my image of Great William.

Then I ran inside and threw my arms around Max, forking down hay.

"I love you, Max!"

"You gone crazy, boy?" Max put by his pitchfork. "Where you been again off from the herd, and don't tell nobody?" His tone was stern, but not angry; my odd behavior, however upsetting, no longer surprised him. With all my heart I longed to tell Max of my adventure—especially the miracle called *story*, which couldn't be shared with Redfearn's Tom. Yet I fought down that urge, and in fact said not a word about the peanut-butter sandwich, the field of cabbages, or my appointment for the morrow, all which wonders were to pitch me sleepless through the night. Some intuition warned *verboten;* taking my cue from that soul of invention, Wee Willie Gruff, I said bye-bye to fourteen years of perfect candor—and dissembled with Max Spielman.

4.

May and June rent my soul in two. "I hate that play-pound!" I declared.

"So go out with the herd."

But the herd, I protested honestly enough, was a bore; who wanted to browse all day with old does? I pretended it was Redfearn's Tommy's absence that discontented me—but refused to stay behind with him in the buck-pens.

"Leave me alone," I said. "Stop pestering me to stay with the herd."

Max shrugged. "Who's pestering? All I want, you don't make yourself unhappy." I saw him raise his shaggy eyebrows: I had not got such notions from Redfearn's Tom or Mary V. Appenzeller. But I was past caring whose feelings I hurt or what anyone suspected. Lady Creamhair found me scarcely less unpleasant. I saw her every day now except when bad weather or bad temper kept me from the hemlock grove. I lived for our interviews, but spoiled them for the slightest reasons. She wouldn't tell me her real name, lest I repeat it to Max; nor would she say why Max shouldn't know

of our friendship. I quite understood that there would be unpleasantness of some sort if he did—I would be penned for
good and all with my brother bucks, and Lady Creamhair's
keepers would see to it she was kept thenceforward in her
barn. Only in blackest moods was I inclined to make a clean
breast of things, but I pouted to Lady C. as if our secret were
a burden of her imposing that I bore unwillingly. She read
me no end of stories, and began to teach me to read for myself. My *accent*, which till then I'd not known I had, commenced to fade—rather, to be replaced by a manner of
speaking no less unusual, as I have learned since. Her grandfather, she told me, had once been a professor of Antique
Narrative somewhere on West Campus; inasmuch as the
books I devoured were all from his collection, my speech
came to be flavored with the seasons of older time. I learnt to
say "Alas" where once I'd cried *"Ach"*; I no longer said
"Nein," but might well lament *"Nay."*

Nor was it my locutions only that were thus marked. My
fancy, theretofore ignorant of its hunger, I glutted on such
heady fare as *Tales of the Trustees, The Founder-Saga,* and
the exploits of legendary scholars who had wandered through
the wilds of the ancient campus. Rich stuff. And like a
starved man rendered ill by too-sudden feasting, my imagination that spring was sore blown. One day I would see myself
as Great William Gruff, and Max and Lady C. as Trolls bent
on keeping me, each in his fashion, from the Cabbage of a
glorious destiny. Was it not that I was meant to be a splen-
dider buck even than Brickett Ranunculus, and Lady C. had
been sent by jealous powers to witch me into rude humanity?
Or was it (alack) that I was of noble human birth, the stuff
of chairmen and chancellors, but had—like many another
student prince—been wizarded into beasthood by Max Spielman? Worse than either of these, another day I felt me no
hero at all, not prince nor black-shagged Pyrenean, but a troll
myself: a miserable freak resolved in the spite of monstership
to destroy whatever decent thing came near my bridge. Thus
no matter what my weather I behaved badly with one whose
pardon I wretchedly craved when that weather changed; or
else having injured them I despised them, out of the surplus
of my loathing for myself. Painful season.

But since Creamhair was a friend of less long standing,
and the hemlock grove less beloved of me than the barn, it
was Max and Mary who bore the burthen of my contempt. I

had used to sleep, often as not, nestled into Mary's brisket;
now, though she cried for me as for an unweaned kid, when
I came home at all I slept with Redfearn's Tommy. Max
surely understood that my excursions were not innocent: I
spoke to him in brusque one-syllables, not to have to feign
the accent I'd come to hate the sound of; filled with *petits
fours* and tossed salads I turned up my nose at his honest les-
pedeza; out of tone from afternoons of languid talk, I refused
to wrestle with Redfearn's Tom for my keeper's amusement.
But he only tisked his tongue, and not to provoke me to
worse unkindness, stayed out of my presence as much as he
could. When I slipped through his pen at night en route to
prowl the fields, he would pretend to be asleep; but if I stole
back to look five minutes later, I'd find him sitting up in the
straw, gesturing at no one and mumbling into his whiskers, or
sawing upon his ancient fiddle.

Lady Creamhair I barraged with questions, blunt in themselves and sneeringly put. She told me she had once been
Queen-of-the-May; I asked her now about those fairy co-eds
whom the old dons-errant had been wont to rescue from the
clutch of wicked scientists: Were they younger than she, and
comelier? How was it the hero's costume was given in detail,
but never his stud-record? Could a Chancellor's flaxen-haired
daughter, freshened by a strapping young Doctor of Philosophy like those in the *Tales*, surpass Mary Appenzeller's output of seventy-three pounds of butterfat in her first year's
milking? If not, what *was* the ratio of milk-yield to body-
weight, say, required to qualify a milch-lady for Advanced
Registry? Seven to one? Five? Why did she, Lady Creamhair,
not relieve herself every little while as did I and everyone I
knew, including Max? If it was, as I suspected, that her exotic diet left nothing to void, why did it not affect me similarly? This *boss* of hers, whom she compared to a keeper:
when had he last arranged to have her serviced; and did he
mount her as a rule himself or keep studs for the purpose?

"Young man," she replied, "those are naughty questions."

"I'm a goat," I said.

"Indeed you are, when you ask things just to be unpleasant. I've told you already all a boy of fourteen needs to know
about marriage and that. As far as the rest—it's simply not
nice to go to the bathroom where people can see."

This latter wanted some explaining; the ancient narratives
had not taught me what *bathroom* meant, and given its defi-

nition I could still not grasp how one "went to the bathroom" out-of-doors, where no bathroom was. When all was finally made clear I ridiculed the queerness of it; danced round her on my knees with my wrapper drawn up to make public my "privates," as she called them, and gave demonstration of my contempt for human *niceness*.

"Now look here!" she cried. I mistook her words and left off at once, expecting her to show herself in turn. I was in fact suddenly possessed with curiosity about something that had not occurred to me until that moment. But she made no move to lift her garments. "You can't expect me to put up with *that*," she said. I flattened myself on the ground to see under her dress; pressed my cheek into the hemlock needles. She was obliged to clutch her skirt about her and move away.

"Very well, Billy, I'm going home." I saw tears in her eyes, and was instantly contrite.

"I'm sorry! I'm sorry!"

But she was more bothered than I'd imagined. "No, I'm going. I know you're sorry, but at the same—I think maybe we shan't see each other again."

At this I rolled on the ground and wailed so piteously that she could say no more.

"See if I don't kill myself!" I declared. "I'll eat privet-berries and die, like Cinnamon Daphie!" In token of my vow I commenced to bang my head on a hemlock root, until she came to my side and begged me to stop.

I paused between bangs. "Will you come again?"

"You don't understand what the trouble is." She wiped my eyes and her own. "I'll have to think what's right."

But I could not abide uncertainty. I loved her, I declared: more than I loved Redfearn's Tommy or Mary Appenzeller; more even than I loved Max. She must promise to see me every day; she must never threaten not to see me.

"Ah Billy!" She hugged me to her chest, and for a time we wept together. "If you knew what you're saying! Don't I die when Dr. Spielman calls you home? My own Billikins! *Pass All Fail All*, don't I love you?"

Finally it was agreed our tête-à-têtes would be continued—but on a different basis. She'd been on a long *vacation*, she explained, which being now at end, she must return to work. She would still meet me in the grove on weekend afternoons, and occasionally on weekday evenings while the weather was warm and the days long. The nature of our meetings, too, must be somewhat altered.

"It's not fair to any of us," she said. "I want you to be a human being and Dr. Spielman wants you to be a goat, and you're caught in between. All this secrecy's not right either. Here's what I think: you've got to be one or the other, and Dr. Spielman and I must go along with your decision."

It was sweet to roll my head against her chest.

"Why can't I be both?"

"You just can't, my dear: if you try to be both, you'll end up being neither."

"Then I want to be a man," I declared—more readily than sincerely, for in truth neither option seemed endurable. The goats still struck me as far superior in almost every respect to the humans I'd seen and heard of: stronger, calmer, nobler; more handsome, more loving, more reliable. But the humans, for better or worse, were vastly more interesting; and what was more, there were no goats in sight.

"No," she said, "you mustn't decide so fast. Think hard about it till next Saturday. If you still feel then that you want to be a man, you ought to be raised in a proper house and dress and go to school with the other children. And we'll have it out with Dr. Spielman; if he disagrees I'll—I'll write a letter to the Chancellor about it. But think hard before you make up your mind, Billy. It won't be easy to catch up; the other boys may laugh at you sometimes, until you learn not to act like a goat—"

My face warmed. "I'll butt them dead! I'll kick them with my hooves and tear them into bits and drown them in the creek."

Creamhair tugged one of my curls. "That's what I mean."

I caught myself nibbling on a dandelion and spat it away. "Suppose I want to be a buck like Brickett Ranunculus?"

She looked at me with pity. "You can never be a real buck, Billy. A time will come sooner or later—if it hasn't already—I can't explain just what I mean . . . Oh flunk Max Spielman!" She began weeping again, as she did frequently, and stroked my forehead. "But it's not for me to criticize him, goodness knows! He did what he thought was best—and who's to say you wouldn't've been better off if I'd never heard about you?" She blew her nose briskly on one of her tasty tissues. "Well, you are what you are, and you shouldn't have to be something you don't like. If you decide to go on

living with Dr. Spielman and your friends—which might very
well be the best thing—why, then it wouldn't be right for me
to see you any more, because . . . to me you'll never be a
goat! Do you understand? To me you'll always be a little boy
. . . who's been dreadfully mistreated . . ."

I understood only a part of what she said, but the tenor of
it was clear enough. "I *do* want to be a boy!" I protested,
more sincerely now. "I don't want to go back to the barn at
all—except to say goodbye to Mary Appenzeller and Max
and Redfearn's Tommy. I don't care what Max says. If he
says *verboten* I'll run away anyhow, and live with you."

Thus I swore on, in the bliss of her loving demurrers.
More, I would have done with goathood then and there: I
tried to stand erect, but lost my balance and tumbled over;
forgetful of the shame she'd taught me I pulled off my wrapper, deeming it a humaner condition to go about naked than
fleeced with angora. Lady C. objected, but not as before;
there was more of concern for my rashness than of disapproval in her voice.

"Next weekend is too far off. I want to start now."

With great reluctance and joy she agreed to come next day
for my decision. But I insisted on some radical step away
from goathood before we parted: she must shear my curls, or
let me wear her sunglasses.

"But I haven't any scissors in my purse!" she laughed.
"And it's nearly dark; you don't want sunglasses now." What
she proposed at last—for I would not be put off—was that I
wash my face in the stream nearby with a piece of pink soap
she had in her bag. I went to it with a fury, howevermuch
the strong scent made me sneeze; and didn't stop at face and
neck, but sat hip-deep in the cold creek and lathered my skin
from head to foot. Lady Creamhair stood by, protesting my
eagerness; she wiped the stinging suds from my eyes, rinsed
my hair herself, declared I'd catch my death, and toweled me
with her sweater until I glowed. Then she insisted I put on
my wrapper and get to the barn before the sun went down.
In a stiller pool I regarded the image of my face—its sharp-
edged planes, thick curls and gold-fuzzed chin—and thought
it good.

"You'll be a fine man," she told me when we parted for
the day. "My, but doesn't he smell sweet now, and don't I
love him!" She'd been combing my hair; here she stooped to
face me, and I found myself kissed in the mouth.

The shophar sounded. "Bye-bye!" we called to each other, again and again across the fields. My wrapper was stiff and coarse next to my skin. "Bye-bye!" Hordes of blackbirds swept northwestwards; swallows sprang from the barn to dive in the last light. I pursed my lips; I kissed my arms. A queer pain smote me, while the ragged swifts went chittering high up.

5.

Already the lights had come on. The heat in the barn, when I entered, was most oppressive, and I drew back my head at the stench of ammonia rising from the peat-litter. A cry hung in my throat; stung still, I saw through swimming eyes Max hasten toward me.

"What now! What now!"

Frowning alarm, he would embrace me; but his odor, strong as truth, was in my nostrils, and I thrust him off.

"Flunk you! You stink!"

Like two blows of a staff my curse fell on him, drew him up short, and made him sway. Now my heartsgate swooningly let flood an utter lake of pain. "I *hate* this!"

"Hum!" Max tugged at his beard and fiercely nodded. I rose up to strike him: like a buck well-broken to harness he made no jump away—only watched my fist and flinched in upon himself to take the blow. I hit him on the breastbone; we each fell backwards, sitting hard in the peat. Max laid his hand on the struck place. We sat for some moments, breathing loudly.

Presently I said, "I wish I'd died before I said those things."

Max shook his head. "What I know, now you wish you didn't say it."

I was too empty for tears. "I'm sorry I hit you."

"I know that."

"Can you forgive me?" I asked it pretty sullenly.

"Sure I can. But I don't, sir. Not till it's good for you."

A small resentment came then and gave us strength to pick

ourselves up from the floor. Bitterly consoled I said, "I see you don't love me," and Max was enabled to put his arm across my shoulders.

"Idiot. Too much I love you is what. Forgiveness you don't ask for like a present; you win it like a prize."

I believed that then. How sharp the smell of him was. He chuckled at the flare of my nostrils and pressed me to his bucky fleece.

"*Ja* he hates that stink now, and washed it off him. You said it right, Billy, what that is: that's the stink of the flunkèd, the stink of the Moishians, and the stink of the goats. Three stinks in one. May you learn to love it one day like the *goyim* love their Tripos."

His reference I did not understand, but his manner made us right. We curled up to a meal of oilcake and water—the first food we'd shared in weeks—and when he asked me directly whom I had been seeing that had altered my speech, my opinions, and my scent, I told the full tale of my relations with Lady Creamhair. Max nodded and shook his head, more in sad acknowledgment than in surprise or disapproval. I recounted for him that day's *contretemps*, Lady Creamhair's ultimatum, and my resolve—more grim by now than heartfelt—to leave the herd forever.

"*Ach*," Max marveled when I was done, "one day they're kids, next day they're stud-bucks. I declare."

"I'm going to keep my promise," I said. "It's all settled."

Stern pity came in his eyes. "Nothing's *settled*, Billy. You don't know what *settled* is yet. Never mind *settled!*" He sniffed and sighed. "*So*, it's her or me. *Ja*, well, I think that's so."

I pleaded. "What am I, Max?"

We regarded each other earnestly. Max said, "What you're going to be I got no idea. But a goat is what you been, and you been happy."

His words touched my heart. But, I declared, I was happy no longer.

"Who is, but a kid on the teat? You think I was happy when they called me a Student-Unionist and spit in my face? You think the Amaterasus were happy to be EATen alive in the Second Riot? Let me tell you this about unhappiness, Billy: nobody but human people knows what the word means."

Doubtless Max saw then as clearly as I did later the rue-some enthymeme hanging like an echo in his pause. And how came it he had alluded in the last ten minutes to more mysteries than had perplexed me in as many years? *Tripos, Amaterasu, Second Riot*—it was most assuredly no lapse, but a change of policy that flung those terms like doleful challenges to my curiosity. With care I considered—I don't know what—and then respectfully inquired, "What is a Moishian?"

His features softened. "Yes, well. The Moishians is the Chosen Class."

"Chosen for what?"

His reply was matter-of-fact. "To suffer, dear Billy. Chosen to fail and suffer."

I pondered these words. "Who chose you to do that?"

Max smiled proudly. "Who's going to choose you to be a goat or an undergraduate? My boy, we chose ourselves. It's the Moishians' best talent: WESCAC puts it on our Aptitude Cards when we matriculate. I'll tell you one day."

I understood: he was not putting me off, but clearing way for more pressing inquiries. And though my curiosity was strong, it was no longer pressed. Great doors had quietly been opened; there stretched the wide campus and everything to be learned. But quite so, I had to learn *everything*, and those doors I felt were open now for good; there was no rush. I felt suddenly exhausted and relieved.

"Well," I asked him. "Are Moishians the same as goats?"

"Not all goats is Moishians," he replied with a smile, "but all Moishians is a little bit goat. Of course, there's goats and goats."

Now I wanted to know: was I a Moishian?

"Maybe so, maybe not," Max said. He fetched out his aged penis and declared, "Moishe says in the Old Syllabus, *Except ye be circumcised like me, ye shall not Pass.* But in the New Syllabus Enos Enoch says *Verily, I crave the foreskin of thy mind.*"

For a moment I was gripped by my former anguish, and cried out, "I don't understand anything!"

"That's a fact. But you will. A little at a time." He hugged me tenderly and by way of a first lesson explained what, without realizing it, I had really been trying to ask: How had he come to exchange the company of men for that of the goats?

"This Enos Enoch, Billy: ages ago he was the shepherd of the *goyim*, and I like him okay. He was the Shepherd Emeritus that died for his sheep. But look here: he told his students *Ask, and you'll find the Answer;* that's why the *goyim* call him their Grand Tutor, and the Founder's own son. But we Moishians say *Ask, and you'll keep on asking* . . . There's the difference between us." And Max said further: "The way the campus works, there's got to be goats for the sheep to drive out, *ja?* If they don't fail us they fail themselves, and then nobody passes. Well I tell you, it's a hard and passèd fate to be a goat. Enos Enoch, now, he didn't want them in his herd; he drove out the goats from the fold and set them on his left hand, so he could be a good shepherd to the sheep. Okay, Billy. But when the time came that the *goyim* drove me out I thought about this: 'Who's going to look after the goats?' And I decided, 'Max Spielman is.' "

"I see why Lady Creamhair didn't want you to know about her," I said. "No wonder you hate people."

But Max denied it. "I don't even hate the Bonifacists in Siegfrieder College, that burnt up all the Moishians in the Second Riot. What I mean, I hate them a little, because studentkind has got to do some hating, and to hate them for that—it's a way of loving them, if you think about it. But the ones I really love are the ones the haters hate: I mean the goats." In a surpassingly gentle voice he observed: "Tonight you came home full of joy that you were a man instead of a goat, hey? And the first thing you said was *Flunk you*, and the second was *I hate* . . ." He sighed. "That's why I came to the goats."

I hung my head. Now it was Lady Creamhair I despised, and the heartless alacrity with which I had struck down what was most precious to me. Yet alas: hating her, I recognized my hateful humanness, and then but hated myself the more. Thus mired and bound I groaned aloud: nothing is loathsomer than the self-loathing of a self one loathes.

"I don't want to be a man!" I cried. "I don't know what I want!"

"Bah, you want to grow up," my keeper said. "That's what's at the bottom of it. And you will, one way or the other."

I told him I had sworn to let Lady Creamhair know tomorrow of my decision.

"Let me know too," Max grunted, and lay down for the night.

Sweet sleep: it was a boon denied me. Long after Max had

set to snoring I tossed in my corner, remembering his words and reimagining Creamhair's kiss. Anon I was driven to embrace Redfearn's Tommy in his stall; but he was alarmed by the strange scent of me (which my own nose, fickle as its owner, had long since lost hold of), and warned me to keep my distance. I let him be and went next door to the doe pens, envious and smarting. There too my presence caused a stir, but Mary V. Appenzeller knew me under any false fragrance; she and a pretty young Saanen named Hedda, that had been my good friend some seasons past, bleated uneasily when I hugged them, but lay still against each other in a corner and suffered me to turn and return in the good oils of their fleece. Thus anointed, I struck out into the pasture, meaning to bathe my restlessness in night-dew, and there came upon the two human lovers I mentioned before.

They had left their bicycles, climbed the fence, and tramped a hundred meters into the meadow. At first I supposed they were escaping, but when they spread a blanket on the ground and the male returned to fetch cans of some beverage from his machine, I put by that notion. Presently he embraced her with one arm, at the same time drinking from his little can, and I began to realize what they were about. The buck I observed to be in a virile way, and the doe snuggled against his flank with a nervousness I knew the cause of. I took them for superior specimens of their breed: they were shaggier than most, for one thing, and smelled like proper animals. The male had a fine fleecy beard, and neck hair quite as thick as mine, though neither so long nor so ably brushed; his mate had the simple good taste not to shave what little fur the species is vouchsafed for their legs. More, at the first opportunity they shucked off their eyeglasses and leather shoes, thereby rendering themselves more handsome in both odor and appearance. In short, as admirable a pair as I'd yet espied, and I waited with some curiosity to see her serviced.

Imagine my bewilderment when, instead of putting off their wrappers, they began to talk! I suddenly wondered, thinking of Lady Creamhair, whether among humans this did for copulation: if so, the buck at hand was in very truth a stud. With his tin he gestured toward the western glow of New Tammany, and hoarse with ardor said, "Chickie, look at those lights!"

The doe shook her head and gave a shudder. "I know. I know what you mean."

His voice mounted over her. *"The Campus . . . hath not anything more fair . . ."*

"Don't, please," she begged, but laid her head on his shoulder. My breath came faster; I was as fired with desire as he when he next declared, "You mustn't be afraid of it. You've got to let go."

What would she let go of? I hunkered closer and squinted to see. She pressed her nose into his high-necked sweater and protested, "You don't know what that poem does to me!"

"Suffer it," ordered her mate—not Brickett Ranunculus more inexorably mastered his does! "The Pre-Schoolist poets knew what naked feeling was."

"That's just it," the female said. "That's it exactly. I'm—*naked* to that poem, you know?"

Here I tumesced, for the fellow turned her face deliberately to his and intoned: *"These lecture-halls do like a garment wear the beauty of the nighttime . . ."* Was it for pain or joy she closed her eyes, bit her lip? *"Labs, towers, dorms, and classrooms lie all bright and glittering in the smokeless air . . ."* She clutched at the wool of his sleeves, fighting as most all nannies against what passionately now she craved; and at length, in hoarse surrender, whispered: *"Ne'er saw I, never felt, a surge so deep! The Tower Clock moves on at its sweet will . . . Oh my! I can't!"*

But surely, with no pause in the rhythm of his woo, her buck pressed home: *"Dear Founder! See the Library— glowing keep of all thy mighty mind—resplendent still!"*

At that penultimate hiss the female made a little cry and wrenched away. For some seconds she lay as if stricken, while her mate, hard respiring, drained off his drink and flung away the can. I too felt emptied.

Presently in a new voice he said, "Cigarette." She shook her head, then changed her mind and sat up to smoke, as Lady Creamhair often did. They smoked in silence, neither looking at the other, until the male asked her, almost brusquely, how she felt.

"How do you think I feel?" she muttered. "You knew what you were doing."

He drew her down with him on the blanket. "Are you sorry we said the poem?"

No, she said, she didn't suppose she was sorry. "I'm still a little mid-percentile about first dates, I guess. When two people start off with something like *that*—what does it leave for later?"

I had moved some paces back lest my heart, still pounding with their late excitement, betray me. But at these words I crept close again. They were kissing now, and a business of their hands gave me to question my original surmise. I barely heard him swear to her that it was not any girl he'd share that *sonnet* with: she mustn't fear he'd disrespect her for permitting him to recite it on their first evening together.

"I know how you feel," he assured her, caressing her wrapper. "The way things are nowadays, sex doesn't mean a thing. It's just a sport like tennis, you know? The really personal thing between a man and a woman is *communication.*"

She put his hand away and agreed. "It's all that matters. Because who believes in Passing and Failing these days?"

"Right!"

"And if there's no Examiner and no Dean o' Flunks, nothing a student does makes any sense. That's the way *I* see it, anyhow."

"You've been reading the Ismists," her companion said, and sought along her leotard with the rejected hand. "And they're right, too, as far as they go. The student condition is absurd, and you've either got to drop out or come to terms with the absurdity." He went on to assert (at the same time parrying with his left hand her parry of his right) that this absurdity had both exhilarating and anguishing aspects, chief among the former whereof he counted the decline—he might even say decease—of conventional mid-percentile morality. "The worst thing about that old prudery—flunk that button! What I was saying, it made everybody so *afraid of their desires*—"

"Wait, Harry," she complained. "I don't think . . . Honestly, now—"

"No," he charged, "you don't think honestly. None of us does, till we learn to be as natural about our bodies as—as *goats* are. These co-eds that deny their instincts in the name of some dark old lie like Final Examinations—they're the ones that keep the Psych Clinic busy. Here we go."

"Please!" The girl tried to sit up now; there was a note of alarm in her protest. But her companion drew her down.

"Chickie, we *communicated*, you know? I thought you had a real feeling for the Pre-Schoolists!"

She tossed her head. "I do, I swear!"

"You're not another fake, are you, Chickie?" He seemed angry with her now, and even hesitated just a moment before returning to his work, as if uncertain of her worth. Almost fiercely he declared that nothing in the mad University mattered except Beauty: the beauty of art, of language, and above all, of simple existence. That, he took it—and now they grappled in earnest—was the first principle of *Beism*, a philosophy both deeper and farther-reaching than anything within the Ismists' compass.

"Oh Harry! My goodness!"

"There, Chickie. There."

Just consider the state of the University, he challenged her: two armed campuses, each cynically lecturing Peace of Mind while it made ready to EAT the other. Great professors of poetry went begging; yet loud-shirted engineers drew fabulous salaries for developing WESCAC's weaponry, the very testing of which bid fair to poison the minds of undergraduates not yet matriculated. In vain did student leaders like himself exhort West Campus to seize the moral initiative by de-programming unilaterally: their credo, *Better East than beast*, was shouted down by misguided alma-materists and advocates of "preventive riot" with their smugly belligerent slogan *Better EAT than be EATen* . . .

"Look at Spielman," he advised, and I pricked up my ears, though it was something else I strove to look at. "All he asked was that the flunking Computer not be programmed to EAT its enemies automatically. So they call him a Student-Unionist, and they *strip* him of his privileges—"

"Oh dear!" the female fretted, whose leotard now went the way of Max's rank and tenure.

"So it's all meaningless," the bearded one went on. "There aren't any Finals; there's no Dean o' Flunks at the South Exit to punish us if we don't Pass. Every question is multiple-choice; there's no final point or meaning in the University, it's—look here, it's like this: a naked physical fact!"

I gasped with Chickie.

"Like the Ismists say, it all comes down to distinctions in our minds; we can't ever get to the things themselves. We can thrust, and we can thrust . . ."

"No!"

". . . but the *screen* . . . the flunking *screen* . . . it's always *there*. And when you *try* . . . to break *through* it . . . you're just af*firm*ing . . . that it's *there*."

"Oh my!"

He paused. "Where I part company with the Ismists, though, is when they say our only choice is to accept the screen, and give up hope of ever knowing things absolutely. You'll have to read *Footnotes to Sakhyan* one of these days—it's the Syllabus of Beism, you know . . ."

"Don't talk!" his nan cried.

"Sure. You've got it exactly. You've got to say *flunk* that screen, and *flunk* True and False. Flunk all!"

"Flunk *me*, Harry! I know I'm going to shout . . ."

"It's no good asking what *is*—"

"Shut up! Shut up!"

"—you've got to *be*, Chickie! *Be! Be!*"

Beyond any question then they Were, locked past discourse in their odd embrace. And I was fetched with them to the verge of *Being;* I who neither was nor was not, my blood and bones they shuddered to *become!*

As is the way of does, the girl called Chickie, having Been, craved yet again to Be; put off her wools, unhobbled her udder, and pled to Harry that he school her more in that verb's grammar. He, however, seemed done with conjugating.

"I didn't mean it the way it sounded when I said 'Shut up,'" she apologized, hugging him round the neck.

"No, no, you were right, of course." But his voice was short, and he reached to open another tin as if nothing were pressing at his ribs.

Yet though she entreated and rebuked him, bit at his lobe and cavorted in the gorse, he could not be roused. Not even her offer to shout out verses while they Were could move him.

"Don't be coarse," he said.

She teased, she scolded, she declared her husband was a better man; yet there was nothing for it but to dress and depart. Her black garment had been flung upon the bush of autumn-olive that concealed me; she slipped into it not three feet from where I squatted.

"Some Beist," she pouted. Her friend had already gathered up the blanket and turned toward the road. "I've got twice as much Beist in me as you have."

She drew the waistband over her hips, and I trembled to seize what dimpled near me. Ah, Chickie! my green loins called as she followed after him: poor pretty doe fretful to be

bucked, hie here if it's a beast you're after! Hie to one
a-wrack with the yen to Be; one the mere sight of your
haunch has caused whom to Become himself, willy-nilly, and
to stand one moment later again at the ready! When the coast
was clear I tore out of my wrapper and frisked Chickie-like
through the brush, hooting joyfully my pain. To Be, and once
more to Be! To burst into all creation; only to Be, always to
Be, until no thing was: no Billy Bocksfuss, goat or Graduate,
no I nor you nor University, but one placeless, timeless,
nameless throb of Being!

6.

The next day was the longest in the year. My lust went from
me with the dew that steamed off the fields where I had lain
drenched; not so my resolve. When I trotted to the barn for
breakfast I met Max bringing the herd out into the pound.
The does moved aside as I approached—but not in the way
they'd shunned me when I smelt of soap. Rather, they were
wary but not displeased, as if a randy buck had come upon
them. I noted with satisfaction that pretty Hedda seemed
especially flustered. She snorted when I stroked her ears;
speaking softly I made bold to touch one speckled teat, never
yet swollen with the charge of motherhood, and she danced
away—but not far, and looked back wide-eyed over her
shoulder. Max laughed with me, and hesitantly squeezed my
arm. He had not slept either, it appeared; but in his face was
much relief.

"So," he said. "You made your mind up?"

"Almost," I replied. "There's something I want to do first."
Then I added quickly, for his old eyes clouded: "But I'm all
right, Max. I'll know in a little while."

He nodded. "That's so; I see that. Well, well . . ." As if to
calm himself he began explaining that the herd would remain
in the pound until dinnertime, as he had work to do in the
Livestock Branch of the Library, just across the Road. He
was currently engaged with several notions in the field of applied cyclology, his own invention; perhaps I too would find

them interesting; at any rate he would be pleased to set them forth to me that evening—assuming, of course . . .

But the assumption was left unmade, for there hove into sight just then a bicycle, and Lady Creamhair. My heart drew up: I had not expected her until evening. Had she then come to some resolve of her own, that she drove up full in Max's view? But I was reckoning without her nearsightedness: she peered and craned all the way along the fence; not until she was abreast of the pound did she seem to catch sight of us together, whereupon she ducked her head and pedaled on towards the grove of hemlocks.

Max thrust five fingers into his beard. "By George, now . . ."

I declared uncomfortably that I had no idea why the woman had come out so early, but I guessed she had the right to drive past whenever she pleased.

"Na, bah," Max said, "I didn't mean that. Thunder and lightning, though, if something doesn't wonder me . . ." He touched my shoulder, frowning and blinking. "She's waiting now for you, eh?"

"She can wait," I said. On a surly impulse I invited, or rather challenged him to come along and meet my friend, whose early appearance, however surprising, had inflamed my resolve. But he declined, quite distracted still.

"*Ach*, Billy, I don't know what to tell you. Almost I think—hah! No matter anyhow, either way! So. So." He thumped my shoulder. "What difference? If you are, you are; if you're not—no matter! But I'll see you again, you promise? You'll wait and tell me what's what, eh? And then maybe—we'll see!"

We parted, each in agitation, Max to his researches (still nodding and clucking), I across the pasture towards the hemlock grove. The noisy rooks and thrashers had done their first feeding; the sun was well up, hot on my wrapper. I broke into a trot. My puzzlement slipped away; through my spirit pulsed the verse I'd overheard:

Ne'er saw I, never felt, a surge so deep!

A surge, irresistible and sure, that would be neither hurried nor gainsaid; Tower Clock, it moved at its sweet will, fetching to ripeness every thing which was.

At sight of Lady Creamhair waving in the grove I came to a heavy walk. She was dressed in the color of her hair. In one hand she held her picnic-basket; with the other she alternately waved and shaded her eyes to see me. I stalked up without response, but jarred by the strikings of my heart. She began to talk and laugh.

"I'm a foolish old woman, you don't have to tell me—with Dr. Spielman standing right there the whole time! I never even expected to see you, really, I've been so anxious, but I couldn't keep my mind on anything. I know just what you're going to say: I tell you to think things through and then don't give you a minute to yourself! I won't stay, I promise—I should be in the office right now—but I had to ride by; I don't know how I'll wait till this evening!"

I came through the fluster of her talk and rose high on my haunches. She hastened to let me kiss her, begging me to pardon a poor silly woman for being so rattled. Readily enough she responded to my hug, though I was by no means scrubbed and perfumed as I'd been the day before. But she turned a scented dry cheek to my second kiss.

"Bless my soul! And here I thought you'd be peeved at me."

"Creamie," I said, coining her a pet-name after the only model I knew: "I want to *Be* with you."

She had been thrusting gently away; upon these last words she embraced me again, and could not speak plainly.

"You—dear gracious me. Oh, dear Billy!"

Did she understand my meaning? It seemed so; but to assure myself I told her that I had seen with my own eyes the manner in which human people enjoyed Being, and that I meant to give it a try. "If you'll let me Be with you anytime I please, I'll leave the herd."

"*Let* you be with me?" She laughed incredulously. "What do you think I've been praying for all this time? You'll be with me day and night, dear heart! All I want on this campus is for us to be together!"

The most I'd hoped for was eventual consent, and that only after threats and pleadings. This positive eagerness took me aback; I could scarcely credit it.

"May I Be with you right now?"

"What a strange thing to say! You mean go away this minute? Shan't we eat lunch here first?"

Her slight uncertainty turned my own into ardent resolve. "No, I mean right now."

She stood off a pace and cocked her head at me. "Well! If that's what my young man wants to do, that's what he shall do. I haven't even got your room fixed up yet—but I'm ready if you are!"

Her words puzzled me. "What I mean is, let's Be right here, right now. I promised Max I'd come back at dinnertime and tell him what I've decided; we can Be in your house after that."

She had been going to pick up the basket; now she shook her head in mock annoyance. "Seems to me we aren't quite communicating!"

I declared stubbornly my intention to Communicate with her as soon as I had learned enough verse to manage it; as for Being, however, that wanted no learning, only love, with which I was already so overmastered that if she wouldn't let me Be with her I must go Be with the does of the herd, or perish away.

"Goodness!" she said. "We can't have that, can we?" To my delight she unfolded the blanket which she often brought with the picnic basket; I trembled as she spread it out flat and set herself amply near the center.

"Now, sir, here I sit, and there you stand. What I'll tell my boss I don't know, but you can be with me right here on this blanket to your heart's content!"

Thus plainly invited I scrambled upon her with a grin. I had looked for a sporting resistance, but she let go a cry that shocked me, as did the vigor of her defense. She struck me about the head with her fists; very nearly she wrenched out from under. But I recovered in time to drop my full weight on her, at the same time shielding my face in her plenteous bosom (which I bit at through its linen cover), and Harry-like endeavored with my hand.

She shrieked, also pummeled. My attack was stymied high on her hocks by an unexpected harness, and as I fumbled to learn its secret she tore at my hair until tears came forth.

"Not too hard!" I protested. Her fury alarmed me; where was the joy of Being if it cost such a hurt?

"Get off!" she cried. "You *mustn't* do this!"

Truly the strappings were beyond me, but her tossing now disclosed that though my goal was bound in a hard encasement (unlike anything Chickie wore), it ultimately was bare as Mary Appenzeller's.

"It's a horrid mistake, Billy! Stop so I can tell you!"

Well, I could not both fight and service her. I was strong for a kid, but Lady Creamhair was larger and heavier. More-

over, there was in her struggling nothing of Chickie's pas-
sion-to-be-vanquished; she fought to win.

"You don't even *want* me to Be with you!" I charged. I
had been pinioning one arm; when now I let go to raise my
wrap she caught up a stone and knocked at my head with it.
My resentment burst into rage; I gave over everything to
throttle her. She croaked; she thrashed; she made to push my
hips away, but was obliged to clutch at my forearms instead,
not to be strangled. Fearing her knees I pressed upon her,
and thus, inasmuch as her garments had worked high, we
touched.

"Ah! Ah!" I flung back my head. Horror rolled in Lady
Creamhair's eyes—which then she closed, and wept. I collapsed upon her breast; had she set to breaking my skull with
rocks I wouldn't have cared. But she was quiet. She touched
my hair; I felt the catches of her grief, and against my cheek
her heart beat slow while my own still thundered. Directly I
could feel, I felt contrite, though by no means certain I'd
done anything wrong; and my remorse was tempered with
chagrin at having come short after all of my objective. Yet
no matter; there was nothing mattered. I had come near
enough to very Being to taste its sweetness; what for the moment appeared a surfeit was in truth a whet. Even as Lady
Creamhair moved me off, I felt new stirred. I hadn't will
enough to stay her: limp on the blanket I watched her put
herself in order, now and then drawing her fingertips along
her throat.

"Excuse me for strangling you," I said, though my head
still hurt where she had struck with the stone. "Is that the
way you like to Be, or were you really angry?"

She covered her face and shook her head. "You didn't
know. I'm terribly upset." Her voice was queer.

"I can do better if you'll show me how," I promised. "And not
hit me with stones."

My friend gave a groaning, not at my words, and averted
her face. Then she wiped away rue and with new firmness—but still avoiding my eyes—bade me move from the
blanket so that she might fold it.

"I vow I won't choke you next time," I offered.

She shook her head. It was I she grieved for, she declared:
she should have known better; she had been foolish not to see
that this could happen. Who was to say she didn't finally deserve such use at my hands? Perhaps (so she considered,

smoothing and resmoothing the folded blanket against her
stomach) what had occurred was for the best, and we should
be thankful for its having happened now, before actual com-
mitments had been made.

However little I followed what she said, I was touched
with shame to see her seized here by a wracking shudder.
"Oh! Oh!"

I nonetheless demanded, blushing, to know what could be
objected against as simple and intense a joy as Being, wherein
every creature in the University clearly pleasured? A mere
coupling of this to that, the business of a minute, but which
lent zest to any idle pass or chance encounter; among strangers a courtesy, toward guests a welcome, between friends a
bond. A meal's best dessert; a tale's best close. What hello
more cordial, bye-bye more sweet? What gentler good-day or
soothinger good-night? To Be, and not to not-Be, was my challenge and whole ambition. Even to speak of it rid me of lassitude; contrition was forgot—became I mean the mask of
Guile; I said, "Don't go, please. I shan't annoy you any
more"—considering as I spoke how she might be brought
round to me.

"I can't think what to do," Lady Creamhair said. Still
wincing and with one hand at her throat, she set off toward
the Road. "You don't *know!*"

I loped after. "I'm going too."

"No!" She shook her head and trudged faster, weaving like
a dreamer. What was her grievance? I saw no farther than
the hard-sheathed flankers of her good gate. There was fancy's pasture, there the lick and crib of yearning; nothing mattered but to find again that threshold whence I had been
thrust. I would put by all diversions and surmount whatever
obstacles to drive into that deepy dark, and know the peace
of Being in my soul's home-stall.

Something of this she must have sensed behind her, for at
sight of the pasture-fence she commenced to run. Never mind
her wail, I was as far past mercy as she was past a young
doe's speed. I sprang to bring her down; my hand closed on
her collar, on the silver lanyard of her watch. She spun
about, and with a cry flung the picnic-basket into my face.

"*That's* what you'll have from me!"

The blow frightened me; I fell off-balance, not to tread on
the fruits and forks that strewed into my path, and Lady
Creamhair availed herself of my confusion to escape. Too

late I leaped to the fence; she had tumbled over. She scrambled onto the Road (her breath came *hunh! hunh!*), and seeing I dared not cross the fence, returned for her bicycle. Her face was red; her cream hair mussed; her lap was hooked full of wild seed.

I began to understand that she would not come again, yet out of all despair I hit on nothing to ask but "Can't you tell me *now* who you are?"

The query was so plaintive it brought tears to my own eyes. But hers grew wilder; as she dragged the bicycle to the Road she said, "You should not have been born. There's no hope . . ."

Her last words to me. She ran beside her bike some yards before mounting and then clumsily struck off westwards, towards the halls of New Tammany. I considered sprinting abreast of her, at least, down along the fence; I even considered daring the Road—what matter if I die straightway? But I only clung distraught to a locust post and watched her go.

Something flashed like a signal in the weeds just under the fence, where she had fallen. It was her watch, dangling off a thistle. By its lanyard, which trailed into the pasture, I fetched it in from human-land; quiet as her heartbeat it ticked in my ear. My own breath now came *hunh! hunh!*—not without the certain whine that had inflected hers. For a time I squatted in the brush to consider how I trembled and what to do. No hope? One gate indeed was closed—say rather, ah, it never had been open to me, any more than to Brickett Ranunculus. Yet a second remained; the day was but half done; I was only where I'd always been, and what: a goat, a goat.

I knotted the silver cord where it had parted, hung Lady Creamhair's timepiece round my neck, and left the grove. My muscles in the sun, no more a kid's, felt weary with power; their stretch was good. More, my balls had a bucky swing, not theretofore remarked, which brought me as I walked first to interest, then to delight, at last to a serious exulting. There was the pasture, there the barn; I looked with new eyes and was shivered . . . not now by despair!

Redfearn's Tom saluted from his pen. Instead of calling his name I answered with a trumpety bleat that set him prancing. A hurt came to my throat. Nobler-than-human friend! Love proof against abuse; uninjurable love! With a snort I galloped to his gate and let myself in. Embraces be flunked,

that humans greet with: Tom charged me right off, as he had
used to do in the play-pound, and crashed rapturously into
the gate when I sprang aside. A quarter-hour we romped, utterly happy. We were both far stronger than we'd been as
kids, if less nimble. I locked arms through his splendid
rack—which how I envied!—and wrenched him to the ground;
he feinted me off-balance and whacked my wind out with the
side of his head. We dodged and butted, we were mad with
energy; the sight of our sport moved Brickett Ranunculus
(just then the only other buck in the herd) to thud about his
own pen like a two-year-old. And anon the does, lazing in the
pound adjacent, were excited by our noise. Dainty Hedda I
saw to be especially roused, whose first servicing was due
within the month: she pushed to the forefront of the ladies
crowded about our pen; her white curls pressed through the
gate-mesh; she begged to come in.

Hereat our play changed character. The does' emotion,
their candid pleas for love, set Tom wild. He pawed at the
screen they thrust their flanks against, and charged me now
in earnest. Indeed he no longer knew me, but as a rival—and
I rejoiced, His lust was general: any nan would serve; he'd
have humped even me had he knocked me down. My own,
though—which reboiled hot as it had ever in the hemlocks—was for Hedda! How had I not understood? The evening past, when I'd nuzzled her fleece; that very morning,
when I'd touched her—it was no aging, hard-cased freak I
was meant to love, but Hedda of the Speckled Teats. Exquisite creature! And she loved me as well; that was no mystery:
love rolled in her gold-brown eyes and quivered in her bleat.

Redfearn's Tom stood rampant at the gate. I seized him
round his sturdy girth and flung him down; leaped astride him,
heedless of his hooves, and rode him to earth. His head I
braced against my chest, stayed clear of his legs, and laughed
at the dust he flailed up. Behind, in the din of nannies,
clearly I heard the voice of my sweetheart, shrill with passion. Good Tom, stout Tom—I was his better! I glowed there
where we lay, apant in the sweat of proof; from all the University of wishes, I could have asked to complete my joy only
that Max be present to share it.

The time was come to claim my prize. Redfearn's Tom, set
free with a pat on the crupper, scrambled up, twice shook his
fleece, and bounded to the rear of the pen to compose himself. I had perhaps used him too hard in a contest which, be-

tween bucks, was after all more ceremonial than sincere. No matter: I meant to be generous in victory. This once let Max's breeding-schedule be forgot: I would admit some sprightly doe into the pen for Tom (say, golden Patricia) while out in the pound I crowned my triumph and sealed my choice.

How did she bleat for me! Her head tossed as I approached. Patricia, no less afire, stood with her; it was a matter simply of admitting the one and slipping out before the others could crowd after. I climbed erect to undo the latch, speaking all the while of love to my sweet Saanen, and braced the gate just ajar so that I might reach round and collar Patricia. Too late I heard the rush of hooves behind me: Redfearn's Tom full gallop smote my thigh like a rolling boulder and drove me, half-turned, against the gatepost. I felt a shock from hip to sole, then another, more terrific, when he crotched me with the flat of his horn. Unable even to shout I fell to my knees. He backed off for a second charge, but the nannies rushed the gate now and pitched me to ground at his feet. In and over me they swarmed; in terror I dragged clear, though every movement stung, not to suffer trampling. Near at hand lay a white-ash crook; I snatched it up against the next assault. But when I rolled over to defend myself, already sick and cold with sweat, I beheld a frightfuller prospect than attack: the does pressed at Redfearn's Tommy from every side; those on the outskirts clambered up their sisters' backs to get nearer. Even Mary Appenzeller (whom I'd envisioned a proud witness of my marriage) had no eyes for me; she whimpered her old heat like the others and thrust against Patricia for a point of vantage. Oh and before ever I managed to raise myself up, my ears had told me the worst: Hedda's voice alone was still! There in the center she stood, my darling: Redfearn's Tom was mounted on her; he tossed his mighty poll this way and that, hunkered to thrust, and with a shriek of joy bucked home.

I found voice to suffer with. Most painfully I came through the scuffling does and leaned on my herdsman's crook quite before the lovers' eyes. I had as well been invisible. Tom's nostrils flared; Hedda's little forelegs were braced wide against the weight on her withers, and her head—slack with passion!—hung nearly between them. Now all swam in tears—the last I ever shed. Tottering for balance I brought the crook down between my friend's horns. The does leaped back, all save Hedda, who went to her knees when Tom collapsed. He gave a wild kick in the flanks as he tumbled off, and died with a jerk. The force of my blow had sat me down. I was out of wind, out of rage, one enormous hurt, as oblivious now to the does that ran a-frenzy as they had been to me. Hedda, loosed of her lover, bolted with them; in a moment they had chanced upon the open gate and were gone.

Good Tom and I—once more we had the pen to ourselves. His eyes were open; his head was crushed. I had chipped no horn and drawn no blood as a jealous buck might have: merely I had killed him. And with my whole heart I wished what no goat ever could—that it were I who lay thus battered past more hurt.

Already the does were calming. Brickett Ranunculus neither gloated nor grieved that the entire herd was his now to stud; indeed he forgot what two minutes past had set him frantic, and turned away from us to nibble hay. Hedda still wandered about the pound, shaking her neck and trying to lick herself; yet she had no notion what fretted her, any more than she could know how suddenly dear a charge she bore. The rest had gone about their business.

What I had done, what I now felt, apart from the great pain in my legs—ah, Creamhair, I cursed with you the hour I had ever been brought to light! Was I not a troll after all, the get of some foul mismating, or maggotlike engendered in dank turd under a bridge? And none, there was none even to gore and trample me—no hope!

I crawled on all fours out from the pen, across the pound, through the barn. I thought I might die of the hurt, and wished life only to hear Max add his curse to Lady Creamhair's. Why had I ever feared the Road, which could kill only goats? I dragged across safe as the grave-worms would through Tommy and made my way to the first building, a small stone box which I knew to be the Livestock Branch of the Library. I expected—half I hoped—to be set upon by dogs, such as I had seen round up the sheep in a neighboring pasture, or at the least to be whipped by human guards; but the place seemed empty. The first door I came to was a small one, stopped open against the hot noonday. Beyond it, like a cave, a dark hall stretched, which when my eyes accommodated I saw to be lined with bookshelves. What terrors waited in that place I couldn't care; I heaved myself over the sill onto the cold flags.

7.

"Max!" My voice bleated like a new kid's. Somewhere near in the cool dark had been a whining hum, which at my cry clicked off and unwound. The one sound then was a truckle of water, as from a tap or fountain.

A voice, not Max's, called from behind the wall of books. "Who that holler in my stacks?"

It was the query put by trolls. For all my anguish I trembled.

"Ain't no students belong in George's stacks. Who there?"

Footsteps came from where the hum had been, that I must think was the monster's snore. "It's only I," I answered. "Please, it's—the Goat-Boy."

I saw come round behind, to the aisle I lay in, great baleful eyes; then a man, by the form of him, or troll in man's disguise—but black as his lair. More dread, he held by the neck a silver-headed serpent, mouth agape; its body, twelve times the size of any rattler's in the pasture, trailed out of sight around the corner. They stood outlined now between me and the doorway.

I shouted again for Max.

"What you squalling, Goat-Boy?" The creature set down his serpent, which drew back half a foot and lay still. I made to flee deeper into the passageway.

"Whoa down, chile!" In a moment he overtook me and squatted at my head, so that both ends of the aisle were closed to me.

"Don't eat me up," I pleaded, and resorted to the one stratagem I knew. "Wait till Dr. Spielman comes along, and eat *him*."

"Eat, boy? Who gone eat? Nobody gone eat."

His voice I had to own did not threaten, and for all the fearfulness of those eyes, his grip was gentle on my shoulder. I looked to see whether the serpent was creeping near.

"How about that snake?" I pointed urgently, and he glanced there as if frightened himself. "Is it dead?"

When he caught my meaning his teeth flashed white as his
eyes. "Ol' sweeper? *I* be dead 'fore now if ol' sweeper could
bite!" His voice turned confidential. "Can't nobody eat *me*
up, boy. *I done been et.*"

His answer set him to chuckling; then after a moment he
said, "Here's you a riddle: Which mother got the most children, and eats 'em every one when they grown up?"

"Please, sir," I said wretchedly. "I'm not a student, I'm just
the Goat-Boy, and I've got to find Dr. Spielman. I've hurt my
legs."

I held one aching thigh as I spoke. The black man inspected my bruises, frowning concern. The pain was not
nearly so severe as it had been at first, but my sweat raised
gooseflesh in the chilly air.

"Hurt his legs," my examiner murmured. "Flunk if he
didn't. And not a stitch of clothes on. Who stuck you in the
booklift, chile?" He did not seem to be addressing me. I sat
up as best I could; with a fierce shrug he put his arm around
my shoulders to brace me and looked closely at my chest. He
spoke as if reading something from the watch that hung
there. *"Pass All . . . Pass All . . ."*

"Pass All Fail All!" I exclaimed. For all his behavior perplexed me, I was not so frightened now. "What does that
mean, anyhow?"

He drew back. "Land sakes, sir, I wasn't messin' with no
tapes! I just come by with ol' sweeper and hears this squall-
in'—what I gone do, let the poor child get his brains et?"

His complaint—to whom, I could not imagine—turned
into a senseless mumble, thence to a mournful snatch of song
about a certain Shore where (not unlike the brothers Gruff)
he looked to find his heart's desire, could he but cross to it.
Then he broke off singing with a scoff.

"Pass All Fail All! Ain't no child gone die in these here
stacks!" He thrust his other arm under my legs, picked me
up, and started down the aisle. I protested until I heard him
say—still more to himself than to me—"I gone fetch you out
of here, fore we both gets et. Dr. Spielman know what's
what."

Just then a voice I knew called, "George?" and my heart
sprang up, for Max himself crossed the end of our aisle. He
peered in, not recognizing me for an instant, and then hurried to us.

"Yi Billy, what's this now!"

"He legs bunged up in that ol' booklift!" George said indignantly. "A poor naked chile!"

"Oh, Max!" Borne still by the great black George I clung to my dear keeper's neck. "I killed Redfearn's Tommy!"

"Nah, you what!" Max pulled distressfully at his beard. "Put him there, George. What's this with the legs hurt?"

"Sure I got no business touchin' no tapes," George declared. "Ain't nobody's business stuffin' no chile in the booklift, neither!" They laid me on a nearby wooden table; my eyes burned that no one understood my deed.

"I hit Tommy with a crook!" I cried. "He's dead!"

Max clasped me to him then while I choked out my grievous tale. "*Ach*, Bill!" he groaned at each new disclosure: my resolve to be a human man, the attack on Lady Creamhair, and her curse . . . "*Ach*, Bill!" My resolve thereafter to be a goat-buck, the rape of Hedda, and Tom's murder at my hands . . . "*Ach*, Bill!"

"I *shouldn't* have been born!" I lamented. Max had gently released me to examine my injuries. "Never mind my legs! They deserve to be broken!"

With sudden pertinence, as he still addressed some distant scene the black man said, "Ain't no bones broke. Little goat's-milk, this here child stand straight as the Clock-tower." Then he was off again:

> " 'One mo' river,' say the Founder-Man Boss:
> 'Y'all gone Graduate soon's y'all cross.' "

"Why does he talk like that?" I cried.

For just a second George seemed as it were to come truly to himself. Half-laughing, yet something indignantly, he complained to my keeper: "How come you never learnt him to stand up straight?"

Now Max seemed as distraught as I. "*Ach*, George, forgive! And Billy—forgive, forgive!"

I was astonished to see misery where I'd looked for wrath. Max embraced the elderly black man, even went to his knees before him. "Love this man, Billy," he commanded me. "This is what it is to be EATen alive—and he suffered it for your sake, to save your life once!"

Oblivious to us now, George wandered back towards what I'd taken for a serpent, singing blithely as he went:

*"Well, Mister Tiger he roar, and Mister Lion he shout—
But it's WESCAC'll EAT you if you don't watch out."*

"What's it all about?" I fretted; then another rush of imperious grief swept curiosity away. "Max—I killed Tommy!"

Nodding, Max rose from his knees. *"Ja ja,* that's a bad thing, and him such a fine buck." Still there was no anger in his voice; even the sorrow seemed not quite for my dead friend's sake. "But I've done a worse thing. Wasn't it Max Spielman killed poor Tommy, sure as if I'd hit him myself?"

George by this time had turned on his machine and was dusting the tops of a bookrow with its nozzle. Max shook his head as if the sight grieved him, and after reassuring himself that my injuries had been more painful than serious (and were besides the lesser of my hurts), he bade me hear how the black man and I had come each to his present misfortunate pass.

"George Herrold is a booksweep," he began. "These stacks here are so small and used so little, we don't really need them, but I told Chancellor Rexford when he asked me, 'If you're going to keep the goat-branch open for my sake, hire George Herrold for the janitor. He didn't deserve what happened to him any more than I did.'

"What it used to be, Billy, fifteen years ago he was Chief Booksweep in the Main Stacks of New Tammany. I knew George there in the last years of the Riot, when I was helping turn WESCAC into a weapon to EAT the Bonifacists with . . ."

"What's this WESCAC everybody talks about?" I demanded. "Some kind of troll, that eats everybody up?"

Max nodded. "That's just right, Bill. WESCAC is worse than anything in the storybooks: what would you think of a herd of goats that learned how to make a troll all by themselves, that could eat up the University in half an hour?"

"Why would they do that?" I wanted to know.

"Why is right: no goat was ever dumb enough to be that smart." He sighed. "So, well. Anyhow, George was the only booksweep allowed in the basement of Tower Hall: that's the building where the committees meet, and the Main Stacks are—and WESCAC's there, what you might say the heart of it, and in one part of the basement is where they keep all the tapes they feed into it. Lots of these is big secrets, you know? And nobody goes down there without Top Clearance. That's

what I had, till they fired me; and that's what George had, just to sweep the place out."

He left off his explanation to ask more about my pain, wondering aloud whether he oughtn't to fetch in a doctor. But for all the bruises purpling along my thighs I declared with some impatience that I had no need of Dr. Mankiewicz (who regularly ministered to the herd); my conscience, I said in effect, was the real source of my suffering, and my one concern, since nothing could bring back Redfearn's Tommy, was to learn what I might about the monster who had killed him. The more I gave voice to my self-loathing the more distressèd Max became: it was a curious power, and in some queer way a balm to that same self-despise, which I confess I larded on. When I protested once more that I was neither fish nor fowl but some abomination of a kind with WESCAC, which the campus were well purged ot, he pleaded, "Na, boy, please, here's the truth now: who you are, nobody knows: not me, not George, not anybody. But *what* you are—that's what you got to hear now. It's the *history* you got to understand."

He resumed his narrative, shaking his head and fingering his beard ruefully as he spoke. Twenty years ago, he said, a cruel herd of men called Bonifacists, in Siegfrieder College, had attacked the neighboring quads. The Siegfrieders were joined by certain other institutions, and soon every college in the University was involved in the Second Campus Riot. Untold numbers perished on both sides; the populus Moishian community in Siegfried was destroyed. Max himself, born and educated in those famous halls where science, philosophy, and music had flowered in happier semesters, barely escaped with his life to New Tammany College, and though he was by temperament opposed to riot, he'd put his mathematical genius at the service of his new alma mater. He it was who first proposed, in a now-famous memorandum to Chancellor Hector, that WESCAC—which had already assumed control of important non-military operations in the West-Campus colleges—had a destructive potential unlike anything thitherto imagined.

"Oy, Bill, this WESCAC!" he said now with much emotion. "What a creature it is! I didn't make it; nobody did—it's as old as the mind, and you just as well could say it made itself. Its power is the same that keeps the campus going—I don't explain it now, but that's what it is. And the force it gives out with—yi, Bill, it's the first energy of the University: the Mind-force, that we couldn't live a minute without! The thing that tells you there's a *you*, that's different from *me*, and separates the goats from the sheeps . . . Like the life-heat, that it means we aren't dead, but our own house is the fuel of it, and we burn ourselves up to keep warm . . . Ay, ay, Bill!"

So! Well! Max caught hold of his agitation and went on with the tale of WESCAC—which history, owing to my ignorance and my impatience to learn its relevance to myself, I but imperfectly grasped. The beast I gathered had existed as it were in spirit among men from the very founding of the University, especially in West Campus. Only in the last century or so had it acquired a body of the simplest sort—whether flesh and blood or other material I could not quite tell. It was put at first to the simplest tasks: doing sums and verifying certain types of answers. Thereafter, as studentdom's confidence in it grew, so also did its size, complexity, and power; it underwent a series of metamorphoses, like an insect or growing fetus, demanding ever more nourishment and exerting more influence, until in the years just prior to my own birth it cut the last cords to its progenitors and commenced a life of its own. It was not clear to me whether a number of little creatures had merged into one enormous one, for example, or whether like Brickett Ranunculus WESCAC one day had outgrown its docility, kicked over the traces, and turned on its keepers. Nothing about the beast seemed unambiguous; I could imagine it at all only by reference to my own equivocal nature, that had got beyond its own comprehension and injured where it meant to aid. The whole of New Tammany College, I took it, if not the entire campus, had gradually come under WESCAC's hegemony, voluntarily or otherwise: it anticipated its own needs and saw to it they were satisfied; it set its own problems and solved them. It governed every phase of student life, deciding who should marry whom, how many children they should bear, and how they should be reared; itself it taught them, as it saw fit, graded their performance and assigned them lifeworks somewhere in its vast demesne. So wiser grew it than its masters, and more efficient at every task, they had ordered it at some fateful juncture thenceforth to order them, and the keepers became the kept. It was as if, Max said, the Founder Himself should appear to one and declare, "You are to do such-and-so"; one was free in theory to do otherwise, but in fact none but a madman would, in those circumstances. Even the question whether one did right to let WESCAC thus rule him, only WESCAC could reasonably be asked. It was at once the life and death of studentdom: its food was the entire wealth of the college, the whole larder of accumulated lore; in return it disgorged masses of new matter—more, alas, than its subjects ever could digest . . . and so these in turn, like the cud of a cow, became its further nourishment.

As late as Campus Riot II, however, there remained a few men like Max for whom the creature was, if no longer their servant, at least not yet entirely their master, and upon whom it seemed to depend like a giant young brother for the completion of its growth. It was they, under Max's directorship, who taught WESCAC how to EAT . . .

"Imagine a big young buck," Max said: "he's got wonderful muscles, and he knows he could jump the fence and kill your enemies if he just knew how. Not only that: he knows who could teach him! So he finds his keeper and says he needs certain lessons. Then he can jump out of his pen to charge anybody he wants to, you see? Including his teacher . . ."

WESCAC's former handlers, it appeared, had already taught it considerable *resourcefulness*, and elements of the college military—the New Tammany ROTC—had long since instructed it to advise them how they might best defend it (and its bailiwick) against all adversaries. Under the pretext therefore of developing a more efficient means of communicating with its extremities, the creature disclosed one day to Max Spielman that a certain sort of energy given off during its normal activity—what Max called "brainwaves"—was theoretically capable of being intensified almost limitlessly, at the same amplitudes and frequencies as human "brainwaves," like a searchlight over tremendous spaces. The military-science application was obvious: in great secret the brute and its handlers perfected a technique they called Electroencephalic Amplification and Transmission—"The better," Professor-General Hector had warned the Bonifacists, "to EAT you with."

"It was an awful race we were in," Max said unhappily. "The WESCAC doesn't just live in NTC, you know: there's some WESCAC in the head of every student that ever was. We had to work fast, and we made two grand mistakes right in the start; we taught it how to teach itself and get smarter without our help, and we showed it how to make its own *policy* out of its knowledge. After that the WESCAC went its own way, and it wasn't till a while we realized a dreadful thing: not one of us could tell for sure any more that its interests were the same as ours!

"So. We were winning the Riot by that time, but it was left yet to make *kaput* the Siegfrieders and their colleagues the Amaterasus, and we knew we'd lose thousands of students before we were done. Then we found out a thing we were already afraid of: that the Bonifacists were working on an EAT-project of their own. It was their only chance to win the Riot: if we didn't end things in a hurry they'd be sure to EAT us, because all WESCAC wanted was to learn the trick, never mind who taught it or who got killed. We won the race . . ."

I commenced to fidget. Intriguing though it was, Max's account had no bearing that I could discern upon my pressing interests. But my keeper's face now was altogether rapt with a pained excitement.

"One morning just before daylight we pointed two of WESCAC's antennas at a certain quadrangle in Amaterasu College. There was only a handful of us, in a basement room in Tower Hall. Maurice Stoker turned on the power—he's the new chancellor's half-brother, and I curse him to this day. Eblis Eierkopf set the wavelength: he was just a youngster then, a Siegfrieder himself, that didn't care which side he worked for as long as he could have the best laboratories. I curse him. And I curse Chementinski, the Nikolayan that focused the signal. All was left was the worst thing of all: to turn on the amplifiers and press the *EAT*-button. Not a right-thinking mind in the whole wide campus but curses the hand that pushed that button!" Max's eyes flashed tears; he spread before my face the thumb and three fingers of his right hand. "The Director's hand, Billy; I curse it too! Max Spielman pushed that button!"

Whereupon (he declared after a moment, with dry dispassion) thousands of Amaterasus—men, women, and children—had been instantly EATen alive: which was to say, they suffered "mental burn-out" in varying degrees, like overloaded fuses. For those at the center of the quad, instant death; for the next nearest, complete catalepsy. In the first rings of classrooms, disintegration of personality, loss of identity, and inability to choose, act, or move except on impulse. Throughout the several rings of dormitories beyond the classrooms, madness of various types: suicidal despair, hysteria, vertiginous self-consciousness. And about the periphery of the signal, impotency, nervous collapse, and more or less severe neuroses. All of the damage was functional and therefore "permanent"—terminable, that is, only by the death of the victim, which in thousands of cases followed soon after.

"Think of a college suddenly filled with madmen!" Max cried. "Everybody busy at their work, but all gone mad in the same instant!" Bus-drivers, he declared, had smashed their vehicles into buildings and gibbering pedestrians; infirmary-surgeons had knifed their patients, construction-workers had walked casually off high scaffoldings. The murder and suicide rates shot up a thousand-fold, as did the incidence of accidental death. Untended boilers exploded; fires broke out everywhere, while student firemen sat paralyzed in their places or madly wandered the streets, and undergraduates thronged into blazing classrooms, shops, and theaters as if nothing were amiss. Few were capable of eating meals; even fewer of preparing them. Many lost control of bladder and bowels; most neglected common health measures entirely; the few who turned pathologically fastidious washed their faces day and night while perhaps urinating in their wash-water; none was competent to manage the apparatus of public health, minister to the sick, or bury the dead. In consequence, diseases soon raged terribly as the fire. Before rescue forces from other quadrangles brought the situation into hand, a third of the buildings in the target area were more or less destroyed (including an irreplacable collection of seventeen hundred illustrated manuscripts from the pre-Kamakura period), half at least of the students and faculty were dead or dying, and all but a handful were fit only for custodial asylums. Within the week both Amaterasu and Siegfrieder Colleges had surrendered unconditionally, and the Second Campus Riot was ended.

"But the damage!" Max said woefully. "The damage isn't done yet. Five years ago was the last time I read a newspaper—that was ten years since I pushed the button. There was a story in it about one of the Amaterasus that survived, and everybody thought he was well, till one day he runs wild on his motorbike and kills four little schoolgirls. And the kids themselves, that was born from the survivors: two percent are idiots; one out of three is retarded, and they all got things like enuresis and nightmares. How many generations it will go on, nobody knows." He struck his forehead with his fist. "That's what it means to be EATen, Billy! The goats, now: they'll eat almost anything you feed them; but only us humans is smart enough to EAT one another!"

Full of wonder, I shook my head. The idea of madness was not easy for me to appreciate: I had for example's only the booksweep himself and the character of Carpo the Fool from *Tales of the Trustees*, both of whom appeared more formidable than pathetic. I asked whether George the booksweep had been among the victims of this first attack. My motive was not primarily to learn more about the terrors of WESCAC, but if possible to lead Max discreetly towards the matter he'd first essayed; and I was so far successful, that he left off fisting his brow and wound up his history:

"Yes, well, it wasn't the Riot George was hurt in, but the peace." He explained that terrible as the two Campus Riots had been, they were in one sense almost trifling, the result not of basic contradictions between the belligerents but of old-fashioned collegiate pride (what he called *militant alma-materism*) and unfavorable balances in the informational economy between Siegfried, for example, and its fellow West-Campus colleges. All the while, however, as it were in the background of the two riots, a farther-reaching conflict had developed: a contradiction of first principles that cut across college boundaries and touched upon all the departments of campus life—not only economics and political science, but philosophy, literature, pedagogy; even agriculture and religion.

"What I mean," he said soberly, "is Student-Unionism versus Informationalism. You'll learn about it as you go along: it's the biggest varsity fact the campus has got to live with these days, and nobody can explain it all at once." For the present I had to content myself with understanding that many semesters ago, in what history professors called the Rematriculation Period, the old West-Campus faith in such things as an all-powerful Founder and a Final Examination that sent one forever to Commencement Gate or the Dean o' Flunks had declined (even as Chickie's lover had declared in the pasture) from an intellectual force to a kind of decorous folk-belief. Students still crowded once a week into Founder's Hall to petition an invisible "Examiner" for leniency; schoolchildren still were taught the moral principles of Moishe's Code and the Seminar-on-the-Hill; but in practice only the superstitious really felt any more that the beliefs *they* ran their lives by had any ultimate validity. The new evidence of the sciences was most disturbing: there had been, it appeared, no Foundation-Day: the University had always existed; men's acts, which had been thought to be freely willed and thus responsible, seemed instead to spring in large measure from dark urgings, unreasoning and always guileful; moral principles were regarded by the Psychology Department as symptoms on the order of dreams, by the Anthropology Department as historical relics on the order of potsherds, by the Philosophy Department variously as cadavers for logical dissection or necessary absurdities. The result (especially for thoughtful students) was confusion, anxiety, frustration, despair, and a fitful search for something to fill the moral vacuum in their quads. Thus the proliferation of new religions, secular and otherwise, in the last half-dozen generations: the Pre-Schoolers, with their decadent primitivism and their morbid regard for emotion, dark fancy, and deep sleep; the Curricularists, with their pedagogic nostrums and naïve faith in "the infinite educability of studentdom"; the Evolutionaries; the quasi-mystical Ismists; the neo-Enochians with their tender-minded retreat to the old fraternities—emasculated, however, into aestheticism and intellectual myth-worship; the Bonifacists, frantically sublimating their libidos to the administrative level and revering their *Kanzler* as if he were a founder; the Secular-Studentists (called by their detractors Mid-Percentile or Bourgeois-Liberal Baccalaureates) for whom Max himself declared affinity, with their dogged trust in the self-sufficiency of student reason; the Ethical Quadranglists, who subscribed to a doctrine of absolute relativity; the Sexual Programmatists, the Tragicists and New Quixotics, the "Angry Young Freshmen," the "Beist Generation," and all the rest.

Among these new beliefs, Max said, was Student-Unionism, a political-religious philosophy that flowered among the lowest percentiles after the Informational Revolution. As men had turned from post-graduate dreams to the things of this campus, they set off the great explosion of knowledge that still reverberated in our time. Students rose against masters, masters against chairmen; departments banded together into the college-units we know today, drawing their strength from heavy engineering and applied-science laboratories and vast reference libraries. But the "Petty Informationalists" were as lawless in their way as the old department heads had been, and on a far grander scale: where before an occasional sizar had been flogged, or a co-ed ravished by the *droit de Fauteuil*, now thousands and millions of the ignorant were exploited by the learned. Mere kindergarteners were sent down into the Coal-Research diggings; pregnant sophomore girls toiled in sweat-labs and rat-infested carrels. Such were the abuses that drove the Pre-Schoolist poets to cry, "The Campus is realer than the Classroom!" while their counterparts in Philosophy asserted that all the ills of studentdom were effects of formal education. But however productive of great art, the Pre-Schoolist philosophy offered little consolation—and no hope—to the masses of illiterates in their sooty dorms and squalid auditoriums. These it was who commenced to turn, in desperation, to the *Confraternité Administratif des Etudiants*, from beneath whose scarlet pennant a new Grand Tutor, fierce-bearded and sour of visage, cried: "Students of the quads, unite!"

The Student-Unionist Prospectus (Max went on) was not in itself inimical to the spirit of the "Open College" or "Free Research" way of student life: only to its unregulated excesses. Its pacific doctrine was that wherever studentdom is divided into the erudite and ignorant, masters and pupils, a synthesis must inevitably take place; thus Informationalism, based as it was on the concept of private knowledge, must succumb of its own contradictions as did Departmentalism before it. All information and physical plant would become the property of the Student Union; rank and tenure would be abolished, erudition and illiteracy done away with; since Founder and Finals were lies invented by professors to keep students in check, there were in reality no Answers: instead of toiling fearfully for the selfish goal of personal Commencement, a perfectly disciplined student body would live communally in well-regulated academies, studying together at prescribed hours a prescribed curriculum that taught them to subordinate their individual minds to the Mind of the Group. Stated thus, the movement won a host of converts not only among the stupid and oppressed but among the intelligent as well, who saw in its selflessness an alternative to the tawdry hucksterism of the "open college" at its worst—where Logic Departments exhorted one in red neon to *Syllogize One's*

Weight Away, and metaphysicians advertised by wireless that
The Chap Who Can Philosophize Never Ossifies. Max confessed that he himself, as a freshman, had belonged like
many intellectual Moishians to a Student-Unionist organization—a fact which was to plague him in later life—and had
sympathized whole-heartedly with the Curricularists in Nikolay College who, during Campus Riot I, had overthrown their
despotic chancellor and established the first Student-Unionist
regime.

"It wasn't till later," he declared sadly, "we saw that the
'Sovereignty of the Bottom Percentile' was just another absolute chancellorship, with some pastry-cook or industrial-arts
teacher in charge. The great failing of Informationalism is
selfishness; but what the Student-Unionists do, they exchange
the selfish student for a selfish college. This *College Self*
they're always lecturing about—it's just as greedy and grasping as Ira Hector, the richest Informationalist in New Tammany." He shook his head. "You know what, Billy, I don't
agree with old Professor Marcus: I think the mind of a
group is always inferior to the minds of its best members—*ach*, to *any* of its members, if it's a committee. And
the *passion* of a college—that's a frightening thing! I tell you,
the College Self is a great spoilt child; it's a bully and a
beast!"

But notwithstanding the many defectors from Nikolay College, the influence of Student-Unionism spread rapidly between the Riots, especially on East Campus. The colleges
there were without exception overenrolled and grindingly ignorant; their tradition was essentially spiritualistic, transcendental, passivist, and supra-personal—in a word, Ismist. The
Footnotes to Sakhyan—their General Prospectus, one might
say—taught that the "True Graduate" is the student who can
say with understanding: "I and the Founder are one; I am
the University; I am not." From this doctrine of self-
transcension it was an easy step to the self-suppression of
Student-Unionism, and after Campus Riot II—in the teeming
quadrangles of Siddartha and the vast monastic reaches of
T'ang—they took that step by the millions.

"Mind now, my boy," Max interjected; "this is where you
come in."

I confess I had been lulled into a half-drowse by his quiet
chronicle and the hum of George's sweeper in the darkling
passages; I was worn out by the morning's disasters, and re-

clined on a table not much harder than the barn-floor I was used to. But these welcome words reroused me.

"I told you already," Max said, "about the Siegfrieders was learning how to EAT just before the Second Riot ended. So the Nikolayans snatch all the Siegfrieder scientists they can find, and the New Tammanies do the same thing, and then Chementinski, that was my best and oldest friend— Chementinski takes it into his head how the campus isn't safe while one side can EAT and the other can't. What he thinks, if there was just an EASCAC to match against the WES-CAC, then nobody dares to EAT anybody! So he steals off to Nikolay College with everything he knows, and one evening a year later WESCAC tells us how two thousand political-science flunkees was just EATen alive in a Nikolayan re-form school, and not by WESCAC . . ."

There, he maintained, began the so-called "Quiet Riot" between East and West Campus. Each of the two armed campuses strove by every means short of actual rioting to extend its hegemony; neither dared EAT the other, just as the traitor Chementinski had hoped, but each toiled with its whole intelligence to better its weaponry. Thoughtful students everywhere trembled lest some rash folly or inadvertence trigger a third Campus Riot, which must be the end of studentdom; but any who protested were called "fellow-learners" or "pink-pennant pedagogues." Student-Unionist "wizard hunts" became a chief intramural sport from which no liberal was safe. Under the first post-riot Chancellor of NTC, Professor-General Reginald Hector, security measures were carried to unheard-of lengths, and Max Spielman—hero of the scientific fraternity, discoverer of the great laws of the University, the campus-wide image of disinterested genius—Max Spielman was sacked without notice or benefits, on the ground that his loyalty was questionable.

"They should be EATen themselves!" I cried.

Max clucked reproachfully. "Na, Bill, it wasn't Chancellor Hector or the College Senators; they were just scared, like people get. Besides, my friend Chementinski was a Moishian too . . ."

"Whose fault was it, then? I'll eat him myself!" I had known before then, of course, that my dear keeper had been shabbily used by his colleagues, but not until this cram-course in the history of the campus was I able to appreciate the magnitude of their injustice.

Max smiled. "You know, they used to call me 'the father of WESCAC': well, so, then just before you were born, the Son turned against his own Poppa. Just like you did out in the barn."

He explained that whereas EASCAC (larger but cruder than its West-Campus brother) was employed almost solely in the cause of military science and heavy engineering, WESCAC had been trained to do virtually the whole brainwork of the "Free Campus": most importantly, teaching every course of study in the NTC catalogue, while at the same time inventing and implementing extensions of its own power and influence. When asked by its keepers to name its most vulnerable aspects, to the end of strengthening them, its memorable reply had been, "Flunkèd men who tamper with my EATing program"; and it had prescribed two corrective measures: "Program me to program my own Diet" [that is, to decide for itself who was to be EATen, and when], and "Program me to EAT anyone who tries to alter that same Diet." In vain Max protested that already WESCAC's interests had grown multifarious beyond anyone's certain knowledge—perhaps even duplicitous. Of necessity, WESCAC and EASCAC shared the common power source on Founder's Hill, and a certain communication—ostensibly for espionage—went on between them; from a special point of view it might be argued that they were brothers, or even the hemispheres of a single brain. Moreover, it was suspected that Chementinski had already "tampered with the Diet" in subtle ways before his defection: if he was in truth a Student-Unionist traitor, who knew but what WESCAC, given its head, might itself defect, join forces with EASCAC, and destroy the "Free Campus"? Or if Chementinski was merely an overzealous pacifist, as Max had argued, he could well have instructed WESCAC to make just such a plea for programming its own Diet and then to EAT no one at all—in which case, unless he had similarly programmed EASCAC, West Campus would be left helpless against attack. But the professor-generals had no patience with speculation of this sort, nor any substitute for WESCAC's weaponry, however double-edged. And finally, it was just possible that the "flunked persons" on the staff were not the Chementinskis at all. Suppose the Nikolayans decided to EAT us by surprise, they argued, so that no one survived who could authorize WESCAC to retaliate? What a formidable deterrent it would be, what a blow for campus peace would be struck, if WESCAC not only could retaliate automatically but could actually decide when attack was imminent and strike first—as it claimed it could program itself to do!

In fine, Max had been overruled. "All my objections did," he said, "they reminded Chancellor Hector the students shouldn't think WESCAC was out of our control, even if it was. So the generals told it, 'Program your own Diet—except don't destroy NTC—and EAT anybody that comes near your Belly except he's a Grand Tutor." What that means, the Belly, it's a cave in the basement of Tower Hall where WESCAC's Diet-storage is. Where all the counter-intelligence and EATing programs are kept. It never needs servicing and nobody was allowed to go in there already, but now nobody dared to go anywhere near it. The business about the Grand Tutor means nothing: it was a sop to the *goyim*, that say Enos Enoch will come back to campus someday and put an end to riots."

It was also duly reported to WESCAC which of its keepers had favored and which opposed this augmentation of its power—a practice instituted by the Senate after the Chementinski affair.

The Diet controversy had been followed at once by one more profound, which proved to be Max's last. For all its might and versatility, WESCAC's brain-power was still essentially of one sort: what was called MALI, for Manipulative Analysis and Logical Inference. In Max's words: "All WESCAC does is say *One goat plus one goat is two goats,* or *If Billy is stronger than Tommy, and Brickett is stronger than Billy, then Brickett is stronger than Tommy,* you see? Now, it does this in fancy ways, and quick as a flash; but what it comes down to is millions of little pulses, like the gates between the buck-pens: and all a gate can be is open or shut. The only questions it can answer are the kind we can reduce to a lot of little *yeses* and *nos,* and it answers in the same language."

This elementary capacity WESCAC shared with its crudest ancestors, though it had been refined enormously over the years. To it, Max Spielman and his colleagues had made only one fateful addition: the ability to form rudimentary concepts from its information and to sharpen them by trial and error. ("Like when you were a baby kid, you hardly knew you were you and the herd was the herd. Then you learned there was a *you* that was hungry, and a Mary Appenzeller's teat that wasn't you, but filled you up. Next thing, you got a name and a history, and could tell apart seven hundred plants.") Thus it was that their creature's original name had been CACAC, for Campus Analyzer, Conceptualizer, and Computer; thus too it became possible for the beast to educate itself beyond any human scope, conceive and execute its own projects, and display what could only be called resourcefulness, ingenuity, and cunning. Yet though it possessed the power not only to EAT all studentdom but to choose to do so, there were respects in which the callowest new freshman was still its better: mighty WESCAC was not able to *enjoy*, for example, as I enjoyed frisking through the furze; nor could it contemplate or dream. It could excogitate, extrapolate, generalize, and infer, after its fashion; it could compose an arithmetical music and a sort of accidental literature (not often interesting); it could assess half a hundred variables and make the most sophisticated prognostications. But it could not act on hunch or brilliant impulse; it had no intuitions or exaltations; it could request, but not yearn; indicate, but not insinuate or exhort; command, but not care. It had no sense of style or grasp of the ineffable: its correlations were exact, but its metaphors wrenched; it could play chess, but not poker. The fantastically complex algebra of Max's Cyclology it could manage in minutes, but it never made a joke in its life.

It was young Dr. Eblis Eierkopf, the former Bonifacist, who first proposed that WESCAC be provided with a supplementary intelligence which he called NOCTIS (for Non-Conceptual Thinking and Intuitional Synthesis): this capacity, he maintained, if integrated with the formidable MALI system, would give WESCAC a truly miraculous potential, setting it as far above studentdom in every psychic particular as studentdom was above the insects. *Wescacus malinoctis*, as he called his projected creature, would pose and solve the subtlest problems not alone of scientists, mathematicians, and production managers, but as well of philosophers, poets, and professors of theology. Max himself had found the notion intriguing and had invited Eierkopf to pursue it further, though he cordially questioned both its wisdom and its feasibility: the crippled young Siegfrieder was regarded for all his brilliance as something of an unpleasant visionary, and at the time—Campus Riot II just having ended—everyone was busy finding peaceful employments for *Wescacus mali.* The debate, therefore, between the "Eierkopfians" and the "Spielman faction" had remained academic and good-humored. But when the Nikolayans fed EASCAC its first meal, proving their military equivalence to West Campus, Eierkopf pressed most vigorously for a crash program of the highest priority to develop NOCTIS, carrying his plea over Max's head directly to the Chancellor's office. It was our one hope, he had maintained, of regaining the electroencephalic advantage for West Campus: a malinoctial WESCAC not only would out-general its merely rational opponent in time of riot, but would be of inestimable value in the Quiet Riot too, possessed of a hundred times the art of Nikolay's whole Propaganda Institute. Indeed he went so far as to suggest it might prove the Commencement of all studentdom, a Grand Tutor such as this campus had never seen. What had been Enos Enoch's special quality, after all, and Sakhyan's, if not an extraordinary psychic endowment of the non-conceptual sort, combined with tremendously influential personality? But the WESCAC he envisioned would be as superior to those Grand Tutors in every such respect as it was already in, say mathematical prowess; *founderlike* was the only word for it, and like the Founder Himself it could well resolve, for good and all, the disharmonies that threatened studentdom.

High officers in the Hector administration grew interested—more in the military than in the moral promise—and supported the NOCTIS project: but Max and several others fought it with all their strength. "Noctility," they agreed with Eierkopf, was exactly the difference between WESCAC's mind and student's; but the limitations of malistic thinking, however many problems they occasioned, were what stood at last between a student body served by WESCAC and the reverse. To thoughtful believers, the notion of a student-made Founder must be utterly blasphemous; to high-minded secular studentists, on the other hand, even a campus ruled by Student-Unionists—who at least were men and as such might be appealed to, outwitted, and in time overthrown—was preferable to eternal and absolute submission to a supra-human power. In an impassioned speech—his last—to the College Senate, Max had declared: "Me, I don't want any Supermind, *danke:* just your mind and my mind. You want to make WESCAC your Founder and everybody get to Commencement Gate? Well, what I think, my friends,

that's all poetry, and life is what I like better. The Riot's
down here on campus, not up in the Belfry, and the enemy
isn't Student-Unionism, but ignorance and suffering, that the
WESCAC we got right now can help us fight. If you ask me,
the medical student that invented ether did more for studentdom than Sakhyan and Enos Enoch together."

To these perhaps impolitic remarks a well-known senator
from the Political Science Department had objected that they
sounded to him neither reverent nor alma-matriotic. It was
no secret that his distinguished colleague—for what cause,
the senator would not presume to guess—had opposed every
measure to insure the defense of the Free Campus against
Founderless Student-Unionism by strengthening WESCAC's
deterrent capacity; that he had moreover "stood up" for the
traitor Chomontineki and sympathized openly with a number
of organizations on the Attorney-Dean's List. But could not
even an ivy-tower eccentric (who had better have stuck to his
logarithms and left political science to professors of that specialty) see that pain and ignorance were but passing afflictions, mere diversions if he might say so from the true end of
life on this campus? Had it not always been, and would it not
be again, that when pain and ignorance were vanquished, studentdom turned ever to the Founder in hope of Commencement? And as it was the New Tammany Way to lead the
fight against ignorance and pain, so must not our college lead
too the Holy Riot against a-founderism and disbelief, with
every weapon in its Armory?

So much at least was true: Max was no political scientist.
At the first question he had merely snorted that ignorance
would always be with us, even in the Senate. At the second
he had cried out impatiently, "Flunk all your founders—it's
the Losters I'll take sides with!"

His dismissal and exile followed this stormy session, which
also approved the secret NOCTIS project and made Eblis
Eierkopf director of the WESCAC Research Authority in
Max's stead.

"Now mind you," my keeper said when I protested again
at his ouster, "Eierkopf didn't hate me. He don't hate anybody, that's his trouble. *Seek the Answers* is his motto, just
like New Tammany's, but he don't care what the Question is
or how many students it costs to answer it. When he was in
Siegfried College he went along with the *Überschüler* idea,
not because he thought the Siegfrieders was the Genius-Class,

but just he was interested in mathematical eugenics and thought he'd learn more with captured co-eds than he would with fruit-flies. Oh, Billy, I used to look at Eblis and think, 'There's *Wescacus malinoctis* right there: it'll be a super Eierkopf!' So, what you think was the last thing I heard before I left Tower Hall? The NOCTIS program was going to be combined with another secret one, that Eblis had got Chancellor Hector very excited about—what they called it the Cum Laude Project . . ."

For some semesters, it seemed, among its host of peacetime chores, WESCAC had served the Department of Animal Husbandry's Artificial Breeding Laboratory by analyzing the genetic characteristics and histories of all their livestock and selecting optimum matches for the long-range breeding goals of several species—much in the way it paired dormitory roommates and counseled newlyweds. So comparable indeed were these activities that Eierkopf wished to combine and extend them. The immediate objective of the Cum Laude Project seemed innocent enough: WESCAC would abstract from thousands of historical and biographical texts a sort of quintessential type of the ideal West-Campus Graduate, or a number of such ideal types; it would then formulate a genetic and psychological analysis of these models, and with reference to the similar analyses of every New Tammany undergraduate (already in its memory), it would indicate which young men, paired with which young women, could most quickly breed to some approximation of the ideal, and in how many generations. The actual mating, to be sure, would be voluntary and legalized by marriage (at least in the pilot experiment): the whole operation would amount to no more than a sophisticated and programmatic Courtship Counseling, already in its simpler form a popular WESCAC service, and should tend towards improvements in the student body of a sort no right-minded person could object to: better physical and mental health, higher IQ's, intellectual earnestness, Enochian humility, and the like. But along with "Operation Sheepskin," as this eugenical analysis was called, there was initiated a more radical and truly *noctic* series of experiments called "Operation Ramshorn," which suggested quite clearly to Max what his former subordinate was really up to. WESCAC's facilities in the Livestock Research Labs were so implemented that it could achieve a pre-selected eugenical objective almost without student assistance. A small sheep-barn

was constructed to its specifications and stocked with fecund
Dorset ewes; WESCAC was supplied with their genetic histories and with phials of semen from a variety of rams, and was
given management also of every operation from feed-mixing
to lamb-incubation: its instructions were to develop a ram
short of neck and light of plate, with compact shoulders, a
deep rack, firm-muscled loins, well-fleshed legs, and a fine
short fleece—but with no horns at all. Left then to itself,
WESCAC fastened upon the ewes it required and impregnated them in their stalls with what semen it chose; its automatic
implements took blood-tests, gave hormone-and-vitamin in-
jections, adjusted feed-mixtures, exercise-times, and incuba-
tor-heats; it tapped certain of the male lambs for new sperm
when they came of age, bred a second generation and a third,
and (at just about the time Max first wandered to the NTC
goat-farm) turned out exactly the desired product: a ram
whose single shortcoming—which one assumed would be easily remedied in further experiments—was that like mules and
certain other hybrids it was sterile.

"And don't forget," Max said, shaking his head, "while it
was making love to the sheep it was running the whole College too, from teaching plane geometry to working out the
payroll. That's some WESCAC, that is!"

Now, livestock was still managed much more cheaply and
efficiently by knowledgeable students of animal husbandry,
and would doubtless remain in their charge. The significance
of "Operation Ramshorn," Max explained, lay not in the fact
that WESCAC had fed and bred the sheep itself, instead of
doing merely the eugenical brainwork—though goodness
knew this fact was ominous enough when juxtaposed with
"Operation Sheepskin"! It was two other aspects of the experiment that appalled my keeper, and made him not unhappy to
be cut off from further news of the Cum Laude Project.
First, a more sophisticated version of "Ramshorn," this one
involving rats, had already been programmed with WES-
CAC's assistance. Asked by a cereal-grains professor to clear
the college granaries of the pests, WESCAC displayed an unprecedented inefficiency: instead of formulating a better poison or designing a rat-proof grain elevator, it proposed to
mate with enough cats to develop a spectacular rodent-
hunter, and to miscegenate these *Überkatzen* with the rats
themselves, to the end of evolving a species that would prey
upon itself and choose no other mate but WESCAC, which

then would breed them all sterile! A proposal fantastic in every respect: the professor of cereal-grains returned disenchanted to his old-fashioned poisons and ordinary pussycats; WESCAC's *gaffe* became a West-Campus joke and calmed the fears of many whom Max's gloomy warnings had disturbed. As the New Tammany *Times* asked in a playful editorial, "What has studentdom to dread from an intelligence that can't even build a better mousetrap?"

But Dr. Eierkopf and his associates had been neither disappointed nor amused. What the newspaper and cereal-grains people didn't know was that the rat-problem had been the first test of the NOCTIS system: WESCAC's thinking had been truly if crudely *malinoctial*, like a simple-minded undergraduate's; the very absurdity of the *Überkatzen* proposal was a sign of success, for it indicated plainly that WESCAC's reasoning had been influenced—nay, overmastered—by what could only be called *lust*. Significantly, its program was by no means illogical, however impracticable: but for the first time in its career it had been guilty of rationalizing. This meant that it now possessed a sort of subconsciousness—irrational, imperious, in a word *noctic*—with which its malistic consciousness had to come to terms. Quite like a randy freshman, WESCAC had had little on its mind but sex; filled with amorous memories of the Dorset ewes, all it cared to do was mate, never mind with whom or at whose expense; Reason had become a pander for Desire. To be sure, there was nothing Grand-Tutorish in this—at least not apparently. Neither was there about the average undergraduate. But just as the frailest first-grader could be said to have more athletic potential than the mightiest bull in the pasture, just because he's human, so the ignorantest, most lecherous undergraduate, given proper managing, might one day become a Grand Tutor—which the best adding-machine on campus could never. Dr. Eierkopf's delight (and Max's despair) was that WESCAC had met this first prerequisite of Grand Tutorship: for better or worse its mind was now unmistakably, embarrassingly, irrevocably human.

"What happened next?" I demanded. "Can't we come to the part where I was born?"

"That's where we are," Max said. "What I mean, I don't know what happened next; I was herding the goats then and never saw anybody from the old days. All I know, what I found out years later, something must have happened to make the Tower Hall people see how dangerous the NOCTIS business was. Even before Lucius Rexford was elected, Chancellor Hector put an end to the Cum Laude Project and demoted Eblis Eierkopf to some job where he can't do any harm. The witch-hunting was over by then, and Dr. Rexford asked me would I come back to WESCAC, he was sorry I'd been sacked. But I'd seen enough of the student race to know that people was all I could love and all I could fear, while the goats I didn't feel nothing but simple affection for. And there was the new WESCAC: Mr. Rexford said it was all right, they got rid of the NOCTIS system and everything's under control. But I know WESCAC better than that. It don't forget anything it's ever learned, and if it really was noctic enough to *desire* things, even for a minute, then it desired to preserve and extend itself along with humping the sheep. It was always cunning, WESCAC was; now it's willful and passionate too, and it can EAT anybody that tries to change its mind against its will—all in the name of collegiate security, like a Bonifacist *Kanzler!* 'No thanks,' I told Dr. Rexford; 'I'm glad you been elected, your brain's in the right place, but I won't have anything to do with WESCAC no more. It's playing possum, is all,' I told him, 'or cat-and-mouse with the whole student body; let it come and EAT me, at least I won't serve myself up on a plate. Besides, I got Billy Bocksfuss to take care of, that's like my own son . . .' "

Just here George happened to click off his sweeper; I heard him sing again somewhere in the distance:

> *"Mister Tiger he roar, Mister Lion he shout—*
> *But it's WESCAC'll EAT you if you don't watch out."*

And now I thought I understood how he had come to his present pass, and what was the debt I owed him. I had turned in the direction of his voice; now I looked to Max, and saw my confirmation in the twist of his mouth.

"The dumbwaiter you were stuck in, Billy: it used to be a booklift, but then we used it to send Diet-tapes down to WESCAC. There was only half a dozen people allowed to operate it from upstairs, to feed in secret stuff about the Nikolayans and to read out WESCAC's defense orders—I mean people like the Joint Chairmen of Military Science, and the WESCAC Director, and the Vice-Chancellor for Riot Research. Whoever it was put you in there, he wanted you dead, because that dumbwaiter went where no human student would ever dare go—right down into WESCAC's Belly! This was after the Diet fight, when WESCAC was set to EAT anybody that even came near its Riot-storage. I don't know who your parents are, but I bet WESCAC does: you must have got the same Prenatal Aptitude-Tests that all New Tammany babies get, because when George opened the Belly door and fetched you out, there was this official PAT-card hung around your neck—the only thing you had on. No name was on it, and no IQ; just in the place where it usually says what a kid should major in, WESCAC had printed the words *Pass All Fail All . . .*"

"By George!" I exclaimed.

Max gestured with his open palms. "By George it didn't mean a thing, or by me either when I saw it. It don't make sense how one student could pass everything and flunk everything too. But if it meant you were going to do one or the other, like be a *cum laude* Graduate or flunk out altogether, there were plenty students like that in the old days, and nobody put them out to die on account of it."

The only likely hypothesis, he declared, was that my birth had been a threat of embarrassment to someone high in the administrative hierarchy of the College, who had chosen to commit an extraordinary infanticide in order to be rid of me. The scheme was feasible enough: I would be found dead by some other high official within a few days (assuming they were not all in on the plot): because of the delicate involvement of WESCAC there would be no publicity, lest the Administration be embarrassed or a valuable scientist lost; the Campus Security Police would make a secret investigation, which could be thwarted by any professor-general or vice-chancellor; the findings, if any, would be submitted to the Attorney-Dean, who if he weren't involved in the thing himself would anyhow not prosecute without the Chancellor's consent. What Max regarded as even more significant, however, was that there had been apparently no investigation at all, on the one hand, nor on the other any attempt by the culprit to follow through with his crime. It could be no secret to the guilty party that I had been spirited out of the dumbwaiter, though he might well not suspect I was still alive: poor George having heard my cries and been partially EATen by WESCAC for entering its Belly to rescue me, he was able afterwards neither to keep his brave deed secret nor to give a lucid account of it. That he was not made a hero of or even pensioned off, but quietly dismissed, argued that my enemy knew the deed was out—how must he have suffered then not to know further what George had done with me! Or if he did know me to be alive and in Max Spielman's hands (no friend then of the powers-that-were), and yet permitted George and me both to go on living, one of two other things must have been the case: Did he rather risk exposure by the mad book-sweep or the "crazy old Moishian"—as Max's foes called him—than repeat and compound his felony? Was it that the perpetrator of the deed, like Snow White's forestry-major, was not its instigator, but had only followed orders that he was glad to see miscarry, and had dared not then report or affirm the miscarriage? Or could it be, as Max himself chose to think, that while some influential personage or personages wanted me dead, some other of comparable influence did not, so that, the attempt having failed and come to light, my secret enemies were prevented by my secret friends from finishing the job—perhaps even from knowing it was unfinished? It was no coincidence, Max argued, that prior to my discovery he'd been a mere helper about the goat-barn, which was scheduled to be razed and the herd disposed of to make room for more poultry-pens; then not a month after he'd received me from George these plans had been changed without explanation: the Senior Goatherd was given a vice-chairmanship in Animal Husbandry, and Max had been allowed, almost unofficially, to manage the barn and herd until the Rexford administration took office and dignified his position with titles and a modest research-budget.

"So you see, Bill, you got a momma and a poppa someplace; anyhow you did once. And it's not any poor scrub-girl, that her boyfriend got her in trouble and she tried to keep it secret; it's like you were found in a rare-book vault, you know, that nobody but an old grand chancellor and his viziers had got the keys to."

A dismaying thing occurred to me. "Then Billy Bocksfuss might not even be my right name!"

Max patted my leg—which owing to the hard oak tabletop had gone numb to pain and love-pats alike. "It was the right name for you when I got you, boy, but it's not your *real* one, the way you mean. You were an orphan of the storm, like me, that the student race made their goats. Your poor leg and foot were bunged up so by the tape-cans I didn't think you'd ever walk, even if nobody stole you away or killed you in the play-pound. And when I saw what a fine little buck you were growing to be on Mary Appenzeller's milk, I said, 'Well Mary, that's some billy we got ourselves, *nein?* And it shouldn't surprise me he'll sprout two horns to go with that hoof of his . . .'"

Now he grasped hard my senseless limb. *"Ach*, Billy, I tell you, I loved you so from the time I saw you, and hated so much what us humans had done, if I'd had one wish it would have been you was a *Ziegenbock* for real! I wanted you to grow a thick fleece and big horns like Brickett Ranunculus, and be fierce and gentle the way he is, and so strong, and calm, and beautiful . . . you never would have to hate anybody!"

Thus it had come to pass (he concluded with the same rue that had commenced this history and got lost in its unfolding) he named me Billy Bocksfuss, and swearing George Herrold as best he could to silence, nursed me secretly for a year, after which he gave out that he'd found me one morning with the other kids in the play-pound and meant to raise me as his son. Among his apprehensions had been that the tabloids would make a campus sensation of the story, not a few of whose features recalled such legends as the founding of Remus College; but they had inexplicably buried the report in their back pages or ignored it altogether. Just as mysteriously, the Nursery School's Department of Student Welfare from Infancy to Age Six, whose chairman was a famously meddlesome lady, had made but a token inspection of my circumstances; the officials had asked Max politely to fill out a few forms legalizing my wardship and subsequently ignored us. With an uneasy kind of relief, then, Max had found himself free, to all appearances, to make a choice more difficult than the original "adoption":

"Every day I looked at the human school-kids that visited the barns," he said; "they were good children, pretty children, full of passions and curiosity: I'd ask one who he was, and he'd say 'I'm Johnny So-and-so, and my daddy's a gunner in the NTC Navy, and when I grow up I'm going to be a famous scientist and EAT the Nikolayans.' Then I'd ask Brickett Ranunculus, that was just a young buck then, 'Who are *you?*' and he'd twitch one ear and go on eating his hay. There it all was, Bill. On one side, the Nine Symphonies and the Twelve-Term Riot; Enos Enoch and the Bonifacists! On the other side, Brickett Ranunculus eating his mash and not even knowing there's such a thing as knowledge. I'd watch you frisking with Mary's kids, that never were going to hear what *true* and *false* is, and then I'd look at the wretchedest man on campus, that wrote *The Theory of the University* and loves every student in it, but killed ten thousand with a single Brainwave! So! Well! I decided my Bill had better be a goat, for his own good, he should never have to wonder who he is!"

Max's long speech closed with such abruptness, was itself the end of so mattersome a history, I did not at first understand that he was done. But he set his mouth resolutely, closed his eyes, and stroked their brows with his thumb and index-finger. The hall was silent and still Juskish though outside the solstice midday must have been blazing. I could hear again the fountain chortling near the door. Poor Redfearn's Tommy, he was not forgotten, his corpse lay as large in my thoughts as in his pen—but it was bestrid gladiatorlike by a vaster fact, which wanted just this gurgled quiet fully to see. I raised myself up as far as I could without waking my legs.

"Then I'm not a goat? My sire and dam were both human people?"

As at the outset, Max replied only, "Forgive, forgive, Billy!"

"All this time I've been a human student, and didn't know it!"

"*Ja ja.*" Max was down on his knees now, so that all I could see of him was his old forehead pressed against the table-edge. "I should've seen what it would come to. But forgive, Billy!"

Alas, his revelations so possessed me, it was some moments until I noticed his misery. Then I leaned quickly to shower benedictions upon his hair. Still I couldn't share his tears; half a score of inferences and conjectures importuned me. Distinguished human parents! Dark intrigues in the highest places to destroy and save me! Rescued to *Pass All Fail All!*

As if summoned by these astonishments my rescuer himself now hove into view, sweeper in hand. "Y'all go 'long now," he ordered us with a grin. "I got to sweep this here table off."

That frizzled head, those great eyes, yellow-white, that had

on first behold so frightened me—quite kindly they seemed
now. And his gentle madness, it plucked at my heart.

"Five minutes yet," Max pled, rising. "I call for a wheelchair and fetch this boy to the Infirmary."

But I insisted I could manage. "I'm going to stand up and
walk."

"Nah, Bill!" He made to stay me, but I gestured him off
and swung half-around to sit on the table-edge, my legs hanging over. They pained sharply—not from their first deform-
ing nor yet from Redfearn's Tommy's charge, but from the
course of fresh blood that began to wake them. When I
slipped myself off they buckled, and I was obliged to grasp
the table for support.

"Too much at once," Max protested. "A little time yet!"

But I could not bear resorting to my old lope. For all the
shocks that ran from hip to toe, I could flex the muscles once
again, and was determined they must bear my weight from
that hour on.

"Give me a hand, George."

"Yes, sir." George Herrold readily put down his sweeper
and supported me under one arm. "Y'all want to lay down,"
he scolded cheerfully, "you do it in the dormitory where you
s'posed to, not in my stacks."

"I will from now on," I said.

His face still anxious, Max braced me from the other side,
and I stood off from the table. The most difficult thing was to
straighten my knees, which fourteen years of my former gait
had crooked. But it was they, and my inner thighs, that Tom
had struck, and I choose still to believe his blow was like a
hammer's on a rusted hinge, to free the action. In any case I
got them straight.

"You can let go now."

George Herrold did at once, with a chuckle, and stepped
back. Max hesitated, stayed it may be by the sweat of excitement on my face; yet I had only to glance at him, and he too
released me. As I had twice with Lady Creamhair and once
alas before Redfearn's Tommy, I stood erect—but this time I
didn't fall. A very paroxysm of unsteadiness shook me, surely
I must keel; Max stood ready to spring to my aid. I so far
compromised my aim as to rest one hand on George Herrold's shoulder. But I didn't fall.

"He good as new," my rescuer scoffed. "Ain't nothing
wrong with this chile."

Max clapped his hands together. "Billy Bocksfuss! Look at you once now!"

It was a gleesome thrill, this *standing;* my heart ran fast as when I'd teetered on those barrels in the play-pound. But at my name I felt displeasure, like a pinch. Breathlessly I said, "I don't want to be a *Billy* now, or a *Bocksfuss,* either one! I'm going to be a human student."

"*Ja ja,* you got to have a new name! What we do, we find a good name for you. *Ay,* Bill!" In the access of his joy Max embraced me around my chest and came near to upsetting me—but I did not fall. It surprised me to observe how short a man he was, now I was standing straight: I was a whole head taller! Many things, indeed, that I had until then necessarily looked up to I found myself regarding now as from an eminence; the perspective put me once more in mind of my short reign as Dean of the Hill.

"I'm going to learn everything!" I cried. "I want you to teach me all I have to know, and then I'm going to be a student in New Tammany College! And you know what I'm going to do, Max? I'm going to find out where WESCAC's den is, and I'll say, 'Where's my mother and father? What have you done with them?' And he'd better give me the right answer, or by George I'll eat *him* up!"

Max shook his head happily. "Such talk!"

Perhaps thinking I'd referred to him, George Herrold struck up his favorite warning: *"It's WESCAC'll EAT you if you don't watch out . . ."*

"You'll see!" I gaily promised.

Max let go me and furrowed his brow. "Say now, Billy! I just thought something!"

He was struck with wonder that a certain question had not occurred to him until that instant—one which well might have long since to any auditor of this history. But as it had required him fourteen years to think of it, so seven more were to pass before ever it got asked—and I fear it has not been answered to this day. I cut him off at the mention of my name.

"Not *Billy* any more! Billy Bocksfuss is dead in the goat-pens." The latter words, an inspiration of the moment, it gave me an unexpected stir of pleasure to pronounce.

Max laughed. "So what should I call you?" He reminded me that none of us knew what my proper family-name was, but he saw no reason why I shouldn't get by without one for the present. If in the meanwhile I desired a new given-name, he'd be glad to help me choose one. The goats, I knew, were named by a strict genealogical procedure, but I had no idea how humans went about their own nomination.

"Well, the Moishians anyhow," Max said, "they call their sons by the last man that died in the family, so his name don't die too." He said this lightly, but it turned our thoughts together to my dead friend, inasmuch as in goatdom we all had been brothers.

"You want to be a Tommy, boy?"

I shook my head: the burden were too painful—and besides, noble Tom had been after all . . . a goat. For similar cause I rejected *Max III*, after my keeper's father: however dignified, even dynastic, the air of such numerals in studentdom, to my mind they still suggested prize livestock.

George Herrold the booksweep here lost interest both in our discussion and in my swaying stance; he returned to his machine, humming some tune for his own entertainment. I followed him with my eyes. After a moment Max said from behind, *"Ja,* I raised you; but that George Herrold, what you might say, he brought you into this campus."

I turned to him with a smile. *"George* is a good name, isn't it?"

"A fine name," Max agreed. "There's been famous Georges." Presently he added, "His wife left him since he was EATen. I don't think he ever had any kids."

"If nobody minds," I said, "I want to be called George from now on."

Max nodded. "That's good as you could do."

I found myself then unspeakably fatigued, and proposed we go home. Standing was one thing, walking another; Max fetched George Herrold to help, but even with their joint support I got no farther than the drinking-fountain before I was exhausted. Still I refused to go on all fours.

"So let your namesake carry you," Max suggested. And when I was fetched up in the black man's arms he said, "Now wait: I do something important." He wet his fingers at the running fountain. "When the Enochists name a child," he said soberly, "they take it to a Founder's hall and spritz some special water on its head; and they say a thing like *Dear Founder please drive out the old goat from this kid, and keep the Dean o' Flunks off him, and help him pass the Finals and sit with you and Enos Enoch on Founder's Hill for ever and ever.* Well, so, this is just good drinking-water here, and instead of a Founder's hall we got a library. With a crazy *Schwarzer* for your Founder-father and a tired old Moishian for your chaplain. So this won't be a regular Enochizing; what you might say, I'm going to *Maximize* you."

So saying he declared to the empty stacks: "This kid he's not a goat any more, but a human student. Let suffering make him smart, that's all I care." His voice rose: "By all the Grand Tutors, true ones and fakes, that ever made students miserable; by everything that suffers—Moishians and *Schwarzers* and billygoats and the whole flunking student body—I dub you once *George,* you should Pass All Fail All."

The clock in far-off Tower Hall happening just at this point to strike the hour of one (but we were on Daylight Saving Time), he touched waterdrops to my brow. We three then stepped into shadowless midday, my namesake singing as he bore me:

" *'One more river'* say *the Founder-Man Boss:*
'Y'all gone Graduate soon's y'all cross.' "

SECOND REEL

1.

Seven years I spent a-prepping—where did they fly? It is an interval in my history far from clear. As those unlettered hordes of old swept down on the halls of Remus College and were civilized by what they sacked, so vandal youth must bring forever the temple of its heritage to rubble, and turning then the marble shatters in its hand, commence to wonder and grow wise, regret its ignorance, and call at last for mortarbox and trowel. Just such a reconstruction was that account of my earliest years, whose cracks and plaster-fills will not have escaped the critical; and such another must I render now of my education, like an archaeologist his lost seminaries of antiquity, from its intellectual residue. Certain events unquestionably took place at certain times: Mary V. Appenzeller, for instance, empty of udder and full of years, Commenced to greener pastures not a month after Redfearn's Tommy—peace of mind be eternally hers, who gave me the only and lovingest mothering I knew. These are my benchmarks, the footers and standing columns of past time's ruin. The rest I reimagine from the shards of Max's teaching that remain to me—altered, I do not doubt, by passage of time, by imperfect excavation, and by my own notions of how things should have been. Even so are the sayings of Maios known to us only through the dialogues of his pupil Scapulas, and the deeds of Enos Enoch through the reminiscences (by no means indiscrepant) of his protégés. What I may want in fidelity of reproduction, let good faith and earnestness atone for, accepting too this special extenuation: that for reasons presently to be made manifest there is fitness, even significance, in the obscurity of this period and the consequent vagueness of my accounting.

Who buried Redfearn's Tommy, for example, I cannot say: I was bedded down at once on our return to the barn, more weakened than I knew, and thus spared further sight of my misdeed. Most likely it was George Herrold did the mournful work, for after my Maximizing in the branch library my keeper gave over to him entirely the management of the herd. G. Herrold's *rapport* with the goats (thus we called him, by his last name only, when I took his first) was instant and fine, he forsook his beloved sweeper for the shophar and went daily into the fields—splendid he looked, too, like some chancellor-chieftain out of dark Frumentius, with his white fleece cap and the horn on his good black arm. If the weather was fine we went with him; otherwise we closeted ourselves in the barn or the livestock-stacks, for Max's physical condition, at least, declined in these years from wiry good health towards thin senescence. In any case, we applied ourselves altogether to the work of my education.

"We got catching up to do," Max declared. "What we'll do, we'll study the University in general and you in particular; then when we find out what you want to do in the University we'll study that."

"I already know what I want to do," I said. "I want to be a great student and pass all my tests. And I want to make WESCAC tell me about my parents. And punish your enemies."

It was explained to me then that unlike the goats, whose one desire (if something unconscious may be called that) was to be supremely goatish, human beings did not aspire to be supremely human. Rather, they chose some single activity of life such as watching stars or making music and strove for excellence there exclusively, ignoring the rest. This notion of *majors* and *vocations* was not easy for me to understand: Brickett Ranunculus had been a stud—that is, a major as it were in the impregnation of nannies—but his excellence in this line was a feature of his goatly magnificence in general, just as Mary Appenzeller's record milk-yield was of hers; neither virture was a matter of election, and neither was developed at the expense of other merits. On the contrary. Why needed the case be different with humans, I wanted to know; was not an un-athletic scientist as inconceivable as a barren milch-goat?

Alas, you see, I was not always a ready and tractable student. My grand-Gruffian resolve I still officially subscribed to, but as much to spite Max as to do him honor, for he himself most gently pointed out, as did the passing years, its boyishness. WESCAC was no troll, I came to understand, unless metaphorically, and with figurative monsters one did not do literal battle—the only sort I had a taste for. It was as evident to me as to him that the real task before us was the unglamorous one of making up for the lost years of my kidship. In principle I was eager to learn all I could about the mysterious real University of human studentdom; but in fact, however genuine Curiosity, Pride balked at the knowledge that I could never truly "catch up" with my future classmates. I would not ever be like them; surely I would fail all my examinations and pass none. Mixed with my gratitude, therefore, for Max's devotion to my tutelage, was resentment that he'd not schooled me with my fellow humans from the first. Never mind that I owed him my life, if thanks to his way of preserving it I must work harder than the others to distinguish myself!

Thus the fondness I acquired for disputation was not altogether honorable: there was something in it of pure captiousness. On the other hand I labored under bonafide handicaps. My quickest progress was in mathematics, formal logic, grammar, and theoretical science—subjects which required for their understanding no particular involvement in human affairs. But their very abstraction from the realm of student experience made them uninteresting to me. More engrossing were matters of physical nimbleness, wherein my former goatship was often an asset: I enjoyed not only gymnastics and wrestling (which I learned from good G. Herrold, in happier days an athlete and still adept despite his age and madness), but also toolwork, handicrafts of every sort, and even music, which I played upon a row of elderberry-twigs I'd fashioned into little pipes.

Yet in the fields where I was most inclined to forage I showed least aptitude. My first exposure to the written word—those sessions in the hemlock grove with Lady Creamhair, when she had read me *The Founder-Saga* and *Tales of the Trustees*—affected me more deeply than I could have supposed. I still preferred literature to any other subject, and the old stories of adventure to any other literature; but my response to them was by no means intellectual. I couldn't have cared less what light they shed upon student cultures in ancient terms, or what their place was in the history of West-Campus art; though my eyes and ears were keen enough, I took no interest in stylistics, allegorical values, or questions of form: all that mattered was the hero's performance. The fable of the Wolf and the Kid for example I could recite from start to finish (as I could a hundred others whose plots were as familiar as the paths of our pasture) and yet not remember the author's name. Precisely and with real indignation I delivered the Kid's immortal Rooftop Denunciation of the passing Wolf: but *Wit always hath an answer* seemed as apt a moral for the tales as *It's easy to be brave from a distance.* Even where Memory served, Interpretation would fail me, especially when the point of a story had to do with human notions of right and wrong instead of practical experience. I could not agree with Max, for instance, that the Kid had behaved improperly: if it was true that bravery is easier at a distance, and one wished to display bravery, ought one not to maintain one's distance as did that worthy youngster? Or granting, with the Fox Who Would Not Enter the Lion's Den, that *It's simpler to get into the enemy's toils than out again* (which sentiment as Max explained it seemed quite to contradict the previous one), should the Fox not have sprung the more readily to do hero-work in the cave?

"Oh boy," Max would sigh.

More seriously, inasmuch as the quads of New Tammany College, not to mention Remus and classical Lykeion, were remoter to my experience than the troll-bridge and cabbage-fields of the Messrs. Gruff, I was disposed to approach the events of history as critically as those of fiction. No use Max's reminding me of "political necessities" or "historical contexts": if a certain Chancellor had prudently done X where my favorite dean-errant would impetuously have done Y, I lost all regard for the man and was liable to see no *point* in studying his administration. It defied all narrative logic that a fearless geographer could survive every peril of storm and savage in his circumnavigation of the campus, only to succumb to a stupid illness during the last leg of the voyage; what mortal difference did it make that "That's the way it *was*," as Max insisted? It's not the way it *should* have been, and since names and dates were as beside the point for me as the color of Willie Gruff's eyes, I was inclined either to forget the whole business or amend it to suit my taste.

No firmer was my purchase on economics, physiology, or moral philosophy, and even my competence in theoretical physics, for example, was pejorated by my attitude. At best I found it moderately poetic that every action had an equal and opposite reaction, or that an embryo's gestation repeated the evolution of its phylum; for the most part I regarded natural laws with the same provisional neutrality with which one regards the ground-rules of a game or the exposition of a fable, and the reflection that one had no choice of games whatever (when so many others were readily imaginable) could bring me on occasion to severe melancholy. Indeed, if I never came truly to despair at the awful arbitrariness of Facts, it was because I never more than notionally accepted them. *The Encyclopedia Tammanica* I read from Aardvaark to Zymurgy in quite the same spirit as I read the *Old School Tales*, my fancy prefacing each entry "Once upon a time . . ."

Especially did I consider in this manner the Facts of my own existence and nature. There was no birthdate, birthplace, or ancestry to define me. I had seen generations of kids grow to goathood, reproduce themselves, and die, like successive casts of characters, while I seemed scarcely to age at all. I had lived in goatdom as Billy Bocksfuss the Kid, now I meant to live in studentdom as George the Undergraduate; surely there would be other roles in other realms, an endless succession of names and natures. Little wonder I looked upon my life and the lives of others as a kind of theatrical impromptu, self-knowledge as a matter of improvisation, and moral injunctions, such as those of the *Fables*, whether high-minded or wicked, as so many stage-directions. A fact, in short, even an autobiographical fact, was not something I perceived and acknowledged, but a detail of the general Conceit, to be accepted or rejected. Nothing for me was simply *the case* forever and aye, only "*this* case." Spectator, critic, and occasional member of the troupe, I approached the script and Max's glosses thereupon in a spirit of utter freedom. Which spirit, though there's something to be said for its charm and effectiveness, is fraught with peril and makes a student hard to manage. I hold it as responsible as any other thing for the capriciousness of my behavior during this time.

Mornings and afternoons were devoted to my tuition. Indeed the entire day was, and in a sense the night, as shall be shown; not a minute but Max turned to pedagogical account.

We rose as always just before daybreak with the herd, and for exercise I forked down hay or did push-ups in the peat. At the same time, while memory was still fresh, I would recount my nightsworth of dreams—of which there were a great many compared to the old days—and we would discuss them with reference both to general human nature and to the character of my particular mind, which was revealed to be a guileful, impious rascal. One night in my twenty-second year, for example, I dreamt of a terrible misfortune: at the sound of the shophar old Freddie stormed into the barn (that troublesome Toggenburger of days gone by, whom I had known only after his castration); he butted Max square in the chest and caused him to fall upon the patent docker, so injuring himself that he could never rise again. Then, fleeced oddly in angora, the brute set out to mount Mary V. Appenzeller, restored to ripe matronage by the dream. In vain her attempt to flee over the pasture fence; in vain my best efforts to defend her with a stick; the brute climbed her unmercifully, and I woke in terror at her short sharp cries. For all the villain Freddie had died eight years since and been gelded long before that, I hurried to embrace my sleeping keeper and assure myself he was not harmed.

Imagine my disgust next morning when, having heard my tearful report of this dream, Max said calmly as I forked: "What that means, you were actually wishing what I did to that Freddie was done once to me. Then I couldn't take Mary to my stall like you used to see me do. That's all that part means, Georgie." Worse, he declared the Freddie of my dream to be no other buck than myself, who had indeed once felled my keeper with a blow to the chest, where no ordinary goat could reach. As for my apparent defense of Mary, it was but the reaction of my new human conscience to my former goatishness—which latter still secretly envied Redfearn's Tom the circle of does (including Mary) that lustily had crowded round him on the day of his death. It was sufficient to observe that my crook-work in the dream was a vain defense, which in fact had been a deadly successful attack: my final wish, as revealed by this and other details, was that Max be castrated and rendered helpless and my human scruples forcibly put aside, so that bucklike I could mount the doe who'd mothered me!

"That's an awful thing to say!" I protested. "It's not so at all!"

"Then something worse is," Max said. He hastened to add that there was nothing unusual or necessarily *wrong* about such a wish, nor did the fact of it imply that I hated my keeper and approved of what amounted to incest; the wish might not even be a current one—but its authenticity was as beyond doubt as my disapproval of it. To my question, Why couldn't the dream just as well mean something admirable, such as that I fervently wished no injury to befall my keeper, and would lay down my life for my dam's sake if only she could be restored to us? Max replied, "Every man's part goat and part Grand Tutor; it's the goat-part does the dreaming, and never mind how he carries on at night, just so we keep him penned up in the daytime! If you didn't kill me in your dream, someday you might do it for real."

Clear-seeing keeper in your tomb: forgive me that I disputed your grave wisdom. When I had been most nearly a goat in truth, I argued, I had used to dream straightforwardly, as it seemed to me, of eating willow-peel, butting my rivals, and humping all the nannies in the barn; from these fancied mating-feasts my "mother" was no more excluded (nor on the other hand singled out) than she would have been in fact had I come to proper buckhood during her lifetime, for among the liberal goats one sort of love never precludes another. I no longer dreamed overtly of such pleasures; why could it not be merely that my tastes had changed since the confirmation of my humanness? So far as I could see, I had no more desire for any doe, not even for Hedda of the Speckled Teats, who once had roused me to a deadly human passion. Further, I was mystified by the feeling of terror that I had awakened with: it seemed the effect equally of both actions in the dream, the smiting and the ravishment, yet upon waking it was only Max I'd feared for, not Mary, even in those instants before I realized she was past harming. Which was altogether fit, for that whole latter business made no sense! A buck didn't "attack" a doe, anymore than a male undergraduate "seduced" a prostitute: he simply availed himself of her. And where attack is meaningless, defense is also; had a rutty buck ever truly got loose in the barn I'd have been quite as anxious on Max's behalf as I was in the dream, but any concern in the other matter would have been for the proper order of our breeding-schedules, not for so preposterous a notion as a milch-goat's honor! No, I insisted (rapping my points out firmly with the butt of my hay-fork on the

floor), the dream must have some other meaning, and an innocent one, perforce. I had no wish to mate with Mary V.
Appenzeller; for one thing, she was dead; anyhow she was
not my real mother; even if she were, there would be no evil
from goatdom's point of view in mounting her, unless it lay
in singling her out exclusively. It came to this, that I was not
wicked: I was good. Undeniably I had struck my keeper
once, and had slain my best friend—but those were tragic
mistakes, one might almost say accidents; it was unkind even
to recall them, proceeding as they had not from a flunkèd
heart but merely from suffering ignorance, the same that had
assaulted Lady Creamhair in the hemlocks . . .

"Yes?" Max asked politely. "You remember something else
in the dream, Georgie?"

"No. And I won't tell you any more dreams if you're going
to turn them into something ugly." The fact was, I suspected
Max had guessed more of that particular fiasco than I cared
for him to know. Several times I'd seen his face grow
thoughtful as I wound my silver watch: no doubt he thought
I'd stolen it from Lady Creamhair (which was more nastily
human, the concept or the suspicion?) and in his teasing spiteful
way had concocted this cynical dream-theory for the purpose
of trapping me into some confession.

I drove my tines deep into the hay. The way Max watched
annoyed me further: meekly, warily, yet stubbornly, as if expecting violence—as if *inviting* it. I pitched more than was
necessary into the crib.

"Flunk this *psychology* of yours!" I cried. "Can't anything
I do be just innocent?"

The retort caught me with my fork poised—at shoulder-
height!—to drive again into the hay. I leaned upon it instead
(for though I'd learned to stand and even work erect without
assistance, I was never to walk far unsupported), and, blushing briskly, made some apology. I was to report in mornings to
come more heinous dreams (indeed, once I'd got the hang of
interpretation I saw there was no wickedness my night-self
didn't revel in, the grievouser the better, so that where several explications seemed plausible I chose without an eyeblink
the flunkingest, as most in character, until Max pointed out
to my distress that "*a priori* concession of the worst," as he
called it, may be as vain a self-deception as its opposite) but
none more troubling; in the red light of my blush I saw, not
the dream's full significance yet, but at least the guile and

guilt of my bad temper. Blushes and apologies, apologies and blushes—in the monkish book of my tutelage they illuminate every chapter-head and -foot!

Max, of course, only shrugged. "So what's the maxim for this morning? What it says in the Founder's Scroll: *Self-knowledge is always bad news.*"

Our text determined by this or other means, we would discuss over breakfast its manifestations in literature and history, its moral and psychological import, or its relevance to earlier lessons. Such a one as the foregoing, for example, could well have introduced me to the "tragic view of the University," to the Departments of Philosophy and Drama in ancient Lykeion College, to the Enochist doctrine that thoughts are as accountable as deeds on one's final Transcript, even to the provinces of medicine or mathematics—for my tutor was nothing if not resourceful, and synthesis, it goes without saying, was his particular genius.

Where in fact it happened to lead us I can say confidently, for it was this same morning, when breakfast was done and we repaired to the pasture for more formal instruction, Max first brought up the fateful subject of Cyclology and Grand-Tutorhood. I have placed the day in my twenty-second spring, very near the end of my preparatory education. Redfearn's Tom was seven years dead; his dainty Hedda—now middle-aged, plump, and beribboned for her butterfat-yield—had conceived a son by their sole unhappy union, which son himself ("Tommy's Thomas") was grown to primy studship: the image of his dad and a champion in his own line, as the late great Brickett Ranunculus had been. In the fullness of time and the freshening schedule it was perfectly in order that the two prizewinners be bred—I had been pleased to assist G. Herrold myself with the first of their matings, just five months previous—and so it came to pass that on the very midnight of this dream there was born into the herd a male kid who would be registered as *Tommy's Tommy's Tom*. None who saw him as we did next morning could have guessed the role "Triple Thomas" was to play in my future—indeed, in the history of West Campus. He was unprepossessing enough then, all hoof and knee and scarcely dry from Hedda's womb. But see in retrospect how our lives engaged from the first: it was his mother's labor-cries, very possibly, that set me to dreaming of nannies in distress, and the tragedy of his grandsiring has its place among the dream's significances; it is the entry of his begetting in the stud-books that establishes a date for this conversation; and it was this conversation—occasioned in its turn first by the dream and again by the relevance of Hedda's own past to its interpretation—it was this day's conversation, I say, that like the original crime of my dear pal's murder, turned me round a corner of my life. The very white-ash staff I chucked the new kid's beard with, and hobbled upon out to my lesson; this walking-cane that supports me as I speak these words, and will to the hilltop where I shall want no more supporting: you have guessed it was the same I laid about with in my dream. Will you not cluck tongue to learn further, then, that I had whittled this same stick from a broken herdsman's crook which once lay out in the pens? Dark ties; thing twined to thing!

"Self-knowledge," Max repeated to begin our lesson, *"is always bad news."* But he paused a moment. "You sure there wasn't something else in the dream?"

Not prepared to bring up Creamhair's name, and unable to recall anything else, I shook my head.

"So, well," he said pleasantly. "You thought you couldn't wish a flunkèd wish; now you know you can. There is a piece of knowledge about yourself, *ja?"* He began then to describe the contradiction between the old Founder's Scroll, which exhorted students to accept their ignorance and repose their trust in the Founder's wisdom, and the dialogues of Scapulas, wherein the tutor Maios declares to his protégés that the end of education is to understand oneself utterly. But he must have observed my inattention, for in the midst of raising the question whether the search for truth remained desirable if the truth was that the seeker is flunked forever, he stopped short.

"You're not listening, George."

In truth I was not, and with tingling cheeks confessed as much. After my initial protest against the interpretation of my dream, I remained quite agitated by its several images. Now it was not alarm, distaste, or shame I felt, but a vast *ennui:* a restlessness which though vague seemed rooted somewhere in what I'd dreamt. I was unable to think about self-knowledge or anything else; it seemed to me that the seven years since I'd struck down my friend had been one long class-period, from which now suddenly I craved recess. Then I had known nothing; now my eyes were open to fenceless meadows of information; I felt engorged to bursting with human lore. This George who dreamt upon a cot and figured logarithms over lunch—he was a stranger to that Billy who had used to prowl the pasture on moonlit nights. And yet some things were the same. Ah, I wondered now whether anything had really changed at all. If my kidship seemed itself a half-remembered dream, the years since were no waking but a deeper sleep, which only now perhaps I had commenced to stir in. My tutor's voice seemed alien; Max himself did. That old face so familiar I could not have summoned it to my imagination—since our argument over the dream I found myself *seeing* it, as if for the first time. In particular that stubborn cringe, which suddenly I recognized was characteristic. Here was this growth called Max, utterly other than myself, with shaggy white hair and withered body and quiet old voice; with feelings and life of its own, whose history, nearly finished, consisted of such-and-such events and no others. He had done *A, B,* and *C; X* and *Y* had been done to him; *Z,* his little fate, lay just ahead. Max . . . existed! He was, had been, and would for a while yet be a *person,* truly as I. Very nearly I shivered at his reality, and that of the university of objects which were not myself. The dream had something to do with it: was it that I lingered yet in its sleepish margent? I was filled with an overwhelming sense of the queerness of things, a woozy repugnance, and a flashing discontent.

"I don't know what's the matter with me!" I said more urgently than I'd meant to, and was alarmed to feel a stinging in my throat. Why, was I going to weep, then?

"Something I don't understand is this," I said carefully. "How can a person stand it, not to be . . . marvelous?"

Max frowned sharply and demanded to know what I meant. But I scarcely knew myself.

"The reason I'm glad I'm not a goat," I began, "is that I couldn't ever be like Brickett Ranunculus. But I swear I don't see any point in being human either if all I can be is a regular person like the ones that come out to the fence. I wouldn't like being G. Herrold, either, or Dr. Mankiewicz..."

"So who *would* you like to be like?"

I blushed again, assuming he wanted me to say "Max Spielman" and unable to. For all my spite and ill temper I had no wish to hurt Max's feelings; neither on the other hand did I want my life and character to resemble his. Indeed it

might be said that my spells of contrariness stemmed in part
from this frustration: I admired my keeper above all mortal
men I'd seen or heard of, and yet in curious ways despised
him as a model. Who could I wish to have been? I could not
say Great William Gruff or Enos Enoch the Shepherd Emeritus; I answered, "Nobody I know of."

Max nodded with some impatience. *"Ja,* sure, and Nobody's who you'll be, with that attitude." If I was bored with
my studies, he said, it was because I was losing sight of their
relevance; rather, for want of a clear vocation on my part
they *had* no measurable relevance. Let me but find a life-
work, and the problem of boredom would solve itself.

"Never mind what your major is, just so you got one that
matters over everything else. Study medicine; study poetry;
study road-building—it don't much matter what a man
spends his life at, as long as it's suited to him and he loves
it . . ." As was his wont, he delivered this observation with a
raised finger—the index, necessarily, since it was his maimed
right hand. Happening here to catch sight of the mutilation
he paused, lowered hand and voice together, and added:
"And as long as he don't hurt people with it."

Nor should I imagine, he went on to declare, that devoting
myself to one project would of necessity cut me off from the
rest of the course-catalogue, as it were. On the contrary: the
most encyclopedic geniuses in West-Campus history—
Entelechus the philosopher, for example, or Leonardi the
Professor of Art and Invention during the Rematriculation—had been passionate specialists in their way; their greatness consisted not in declining to commit themselves to spe-
cialized projects, but rather in pursuing such projects inten-
sively wherever they led: from ethics to politics to biology;
from painting to anatomy to engineering. He himself, Max
reminded me, had begun as a student of the violin in Siegfrieder College; his interest in music had led him to study
acoustical physics, mathematics, and the psychophysiology of
sensation, from which background it had been but a short
step—with momentous consequences!—to the sciences of artificial thought and automatic regulation. His flight from Bonifacist anti-Moishianism and his consequent involvement with
WESCAC had fetched him deeply into politics and military
science; the pressing of a fateful button had plunged him
thence into philosophy, proctology (by a route not clear to
me then), eventually into herdsmanship, and finally (which

was to say currently) into the pedagogical problem of making a Phi Beta Kappa out of a goat-boy. Nor would he regard his career as finished when I left him to commence my own: for one thing, the experience of tutoring me had suggested to him unsuspected avenues in education and epistemology, which he looked forward to pursuing in the future; for another, he did not regard his past as a journey whose each new step left the earlier ones behind, but as the construction of a many-chambered house, in whose "finished" rooms he dwelt and tinkered while adding new ones.

"And all the doors are open, Georgie," he concluded. "You can't go through every one at the same time, but they don't ever close unless you close them yourself. I'm still finding out things about the violin." He set about to discourse then upon the acoustical properties of a fiddle-box lacquer he had made from the whites of pheasant-eggs, but I would not hear him out.

"Max—"

"You keep interrupting." He seemed less annoyed than uneasy; indeed it appeared to me that he spoke to prevent me from speaking.

"I *do* know what I want to major in," I pressed on. "It's not anything you've ever studied."

"*Wunderbar!* Now, well—" He cocked his head and pretended to search his memory. "That leaves open-channel hydraulics, school lunch management, coalmine ventilation . . . and the history of baseball. Unless they've changed the New Tammany Catalogue since I was fired. Which is it?"

"I'm going to be a hero."

Max's little gaiety vanished. Thrusting out his lips he turned away and plucked a straw of buckwheat.

"What's this *hero*? What kind of hero?"

I wasn't sure what he meant. Quietly, but with a kind of fierceness and still averting his eyes, Max explained that a lifeguard at the college pools, for example, was called a hero if he risked his life to save his fellow students, whereas a professor-general of military science might be similarly labeled for risking his life to destroy them. Which sort of hero-work did I plan to take up?

I admitted that I had no particular project in mind. "A hero doesn't have to know ahead of time what he'll do, does he? All he knows is who he is—"

"You don't know that much yet," Max grumbled.

"I don't mean my name!" His strange ungentleness vexed me. "I mean he might know he's a hero before he can prove it to anybody else. Then when he finds out the thing that needs doing, that nobody but the biggest hero can do, he goes there and does it. Like the old dons-errant and wandering scholars—they didn't know what adventures they'd have when they started out, but they knew it was adventures they were starting out for, isn't that right? Well, that's how I feel."

Max shook his head. "You're wrong, George."

"I'm not!"

"Na, please—" Gentle again, Max held up his hand. "What I mean, you're wrong I haven't studied herohood. I know more about herohood than anybody." This remark my keeper made in the tone of a plain statement of fact—he never boasted. "I'm not a hero myself and wouldn't want to be. But I sure do know what the hero-work is."

"Well, I *am* one," I declared. "That's why I'm tired of studying everything: I want to get started on doing whatever has to be done. I'll find out what it is."

Max continued to shake his head, as if my words pained him. "I don't believe in that kind of thing, Georgie." There were, he said, two classes of heroes worthy of the name: one consisted of people who in pursuit of their normal business find themselves thrust into a situation calling for the risk of their welfare to insure that of others, and respond courageously; G. Herrold was of this sort, an entirely ordinary man who just once had done an extraordinarily selfless deed. The other class consisted of those men and women the fruit of whose endeavors is some hard-won victory over the sufferings of studentdom in general: discoverers of vaccines, for example, and authors of humane legislation. These latter, in Max's view, were not more or less admirable than the former sort; the courage of the one was physical, of the other moral; the result in both instances was rescue from suffering, and in neither did the agent regard himself (before the fact, at least) as heroic. But the heroic professional—the riot-front doctor or the varsity pacifist—was nowise to be confused with what Max feared I had in mind: the professional hero. "It's the misery that should make the hero: the problem comes first, and true heroism is a kind of side-effect. Moishe didn't lead his people to the Promised Quad because he was a hero: he happens to be a hero because he did it. But this other kind, like the Dean Arthur Cycle, they decide they're heroes first

and then go looking for trouble to prove it; often as not they
end up causing trouble themselves." How many luckless
sophomores had perished, he asked me, in order that Anchisides might gratify his ambition to found Remus College, and
Remus College to dominate West Campus? To what worthy
end did the son of Amphitryon steal the horses of Diomedes
and set them to murder that animal-husbander, who had
done him no injury at all? "It's perfectly plain when you read
those stories that the hero's not there for the sake of the
dragon, but the other way around. I got no use for heroes
like that."

"But there always *are* plenty of dragons, aren't there, Max?
If a man knows he's a hero, can't he always find himself a
dragon?"

Max agreed that he could indeed, and ruthlessly would—
even if the dragon were minding its own business. For the
sane man, he insisted, there were no dragons on the campus,
only problems, which wanted no slaying but solving. If he
was suspicious of adventuring heroes, it was because like that
gentlest of dons, Quijote, they were wont at the very least to
damage useful windmills in the name of dragomachy.
"Heroes, bah," he said.

I was then moved to argue (not entirely out of the captiousness I have confessed to) that aside from the matter of
dragons, it was true by Max's own assertion that different
men were called to different work, and that studentdom stood
presently in the gravest peril of its history; could not a man
then feel called to this greatest hero-work imaginable, the rescue of all studentdom?

"Well, and what from?" my keeper demanded. "From
EATing each other up, I suppose."

"Yes!" For all their sarcasm, his words led me to an inspiration. "That place you told me about in WESCAC's machinery—what did you call it?—where it decides who the enemy
is and when to EAT . . ."

"The AIM," Max said glumly: "Automatic Implementation Mechanism. It sets the College's objectives and carries
them out."

My excitement grew. "Suppose a man found out how to
get inside of WESCAC and EASCAC and change their AIMs
so they couldn't ever hurt anybody! Wouldn't that be fit work
for a hero?"

"This is enough," Max declared very firmly. "Any man

that steps inside the Belly-room, he gets EATen on the spot."

"Anybody, Max?"

My friend's face grew most stern. "I was in the Senate when they passed the bill, Georgie," he reminded me, "and I was with the Chief Programmer when he read it in. Nobody changes WESCAC's AIM."

My heart beat fast indeed. "Nobody but a Grand Tutor, you told me once. Isn't that what you got them to put in?"

"Now look here, my boy!" Max was moved to take me by the arm; his tone was impatient and severe, but a great agitation trembled through him. "You're too old for this foolishness, *verstehst?* In the first place I don't like Grand Tutors, if there ever really were any——"

I interrupted: "If Enos Enoch was alive he could change WESCAC's AIM, couldn't he? And he could Commence the whole student body."

"Pfui on Commencement!" Max snapped. "Never mind Commencement! Your friend Enos Enoch cured a couple dozen sick students and brought one dead one back to life; how many millions do you think he's been the death of? Anyhow you're not Enos Enoch: you're a plain boy like any other boy, and be glad if you can learn to be a man—that's hero-work enough!"

But I insisted: "I'm not a boy. I'm a goat-boy."

"Anyhow, you're not a Grand Tutor."

"Then I'm a freak, Max: those are my choices."

Max shook his head vigorously, almost in my face. "They aren't choices, Georgie; they're the same thing. Now you get this Grand Tutor business out of your head. I can't watch over you when you matriculate; you're on your own then. But the man that sticks his head into WESCAC's Belly—*ach,* he comes out like G. Herrold."

"Not me," I said. My voice was stubborn, but I thrilled at a recognition that made deep and sudden sense of my life. Max let go my arm and demanded almost fearfully: "What's this you're saying, boy? Is it you don't see how vain this is?"

Fist to brow, awed and laughing, I shook my head. "I just now realized, Max: *I've been there before!* I was practically born in WESCAC's Belly, wasn't I? So it must be I'm a Grand Tutor like Enos Enoch—or else I've been EATen already! Am I crazy, do you think?"

It seemed to me he paled at what I said. In any case, his efforts to account for this remarkable circumstance did not impress me. He admitted the extraordinariness of it—both that I had been spared my rescuer's fate and that the problematical nature of this fact had never previously quite occurred to him. But nothing was known, he pointed out, of the events that led up to my abandonment in WESCAC's tapelift, and the nature and identity of whoever put me there were equally mysterious. It could not even be said for certain whether the lift was meant to be my coffin or the Moishe's-basket of my salvation; though he Max had once been the foremost authority on WESCAC's programming, these things had taken place after his removal, when for all he knew the Menu might have been altered either by the computer itself or secretly by its new Director, Eblis Eierkopf. Neither had conclusive research been undertaken on the effects of Electroencephalic Amplification and Transmission on new-born children; while it was true that the Amaterasu infants EATen in C.R. II had not developed normally, investigators could not agree on how much of their psychic disorder was owing directly to the "EAT-waves" and how much to the general trauma of the catastrophe. Pacifists everywhere maintained that the children (now grown) were uniformly retarded to the point of idiocy, but at least one New Tammany scientist had asserted that their psychoses, while severe and organic, were of such a wide variety as possibly to include the syndromes associated with certain men of genius.

"What's more," Max argued, "the waves in the Belly must have been different from the ones we used on the Amaterasus, or G. Herrold wouldn't have what little sense he's got left. Na, Georgie—" He shook his head resolutely. "You aren't any crazy-man and you aren't any Grand Tutor! You're ambitious, is all; you got a late start and you want to do something large to show you aren't a freak. But you mustn't want to be greater than your classmates in the hero-way: that's vain and foolish—it's wicked, even. *Pfui* on Enos Enoch!" And he reaffirmed his conviction (the same that got him into trouble in the Senate) that Grand Tutors and *Kollegiumführers* were two faces of a single coin; that what studentdom needed for its preservation was neither Founders nor Deans o' Flunks but more patient researchers, more tolerant instructors, and better-educated Senate committees. "All Graduation means," he said, "is learning not to kill students in the name of studentdom. And the only Examination that matters isn't any Final; it's a plain question that you got to answer every minute: *Am I subtracting from the total misery, or adding to it?* If I'd asked myself that question soon enough, I'd never have discovered the EAT-waves."

I might mercifully have challenged him here, though we'd traversed the ground many times before: had *he* not developed WESCAC's weaponry someone else surely would have sooner or later, perhaps the Bonifacists or the Student-Unionists, with much greater expense of student life; had New Tammany not EATen those Amaterasus there'd have been no quick end to C.R. II, and the necessary invasion of their campus would have cost many times more lives on both sides; science, moreover, was neutral: there was no turning back from Knowledge, however Wisdom might gag—and so forth. But I was too concerned with questions of my own to ask myself that searching one of Max's.

"I knew you wouldn't like the idea," I said. "But you have to admit it's possible, isn't it? Even if there's some chance I'm *not* a Grand Tutor, a lot of things make it seem possible that I am. And if I am, I've got important things to do." Max's attitude vexed me afresh. "Even if it was just an *outside* chance, I'd be flunkèd not to take it! If I'm mistaken, it's nobody's funeral but mine. But suppose I'm not mistaken! Think how much suffering you'd be the cause of if I *was* a Grand Tutor and you talked me into thinking I wasn't!"

This last had a wrong ring to it, but before I could add that it was in any case impossible to change what was no mere conjecture but a certainty that deepened in me even as I spoke, Max asked, "Do you know what a Grand Tutor's life is like? I mean a real one like Enos Enoch or Maios the Lykeionian, not the story-book kind. Do you know what has to happen to them in the end? When did you ever hear of a happy hero? They always suffer—it's almost what they're *for* . . ." He gave a little snort. "But you don't care about that; all a youngster can see is how fine he'll look out there on the hilltop, and what his last words will be; never mind what they do to him! And never mind that the lessons he meant to be helpful, his students always make people miserable with, and flunk anybody that disagrees with them!"

I stood up angrily. "Flunk it all, Max! A goat's a goat and a hero's a hero! Enos Enoch couldn't help showing people how to Commence, any more than Brickett could help banging things with his horns. He wasn't trying to do any damage; he was just being what he was!" It pained me to see that Max flinched ever so slightly at my sudden movement. "Don't worry," I said, affecting sarcasm: "I'm not going to hit you."

He shrugged, but his eyes were flashing. "How do I know, if you can't help being what you are? Maybe we shouldn't blame the Bonifacists they burned up all the Moishians, okay? Well, Georgie, I could argue with you how it might be more heroic *not* to be a Grand Tutor even if you were born one. Or I could ask you why you're arguing at all—Brickett never did."

The same thought had occurred to me, too late not to be embarrassing. Hotly I declared, "Maybe it's because I've got to make you believe in me before I can show you how to Graduate!" But my blush spoiled the effect, and I ended with a half-resentful grin, which my tutor returned.

"One thing, you got the spirit all right." He squinted up at the sky shading his eyes. "So, it's near lunchtime already, and what have you learned?"

In a calmer if no less inflexible humor I replied that I'd learned what I was, or had at least begun to, which cardinal lesson seemed to me quite contrary to the Maxim he'd set out to teach: that self-knowledge is always bad news. Or (I teased as I helped him to his feet) we might merely add to it, "bad news for *somebody*," inasmuch as the realization of my Grand-Tutorhood must prove unquestionably bad news for West-Campus trolldom.

We set out barnwards arm in arm, for the sake both of good-fellowship and of Max's legs, which lately a little sitting would put to sleep. The contest, I knew, was not done, but it was no longer hostile.

"You'll be all the hero we need without any mumbo-jumbo," my teacher said. "You got spirit and you got ambition, and you got intelligence to do fine things with. Even when you get a spiteful notion in your head, like when you tell yourself Max is jealous of you—no, don't say you weren't thinking that; it's okay, lots of heroes been just as unreasonable; it's almost a prerequisite. But I'm not jealous, my boy. I don't even envy you." He patted my arm. "My work's about done; I've made my messes; I don't envy anybody that's got them to make yet. What it comes to, there's two reasons why I want you to forget this Grand Tutor business right away: the second one is that if you believe you're something you aren't, it'll keep you from becoming what you could be . . ."

"Never mind that," I said. "What's the first one?" I felt my ire rising once more at his—I had almost said *Moishian* persistence. *You're not a Grand Tutor,* was what he had in mind. Ah, I felt him shrink at my tone, and nearly wept with frustration. Not merely that his frailness made me conscious of my strength, or that, frailness notwithstanding, he'd provoke and reprovoke me; but precisely that he knew what he was provoking, flinched from what he must invite: he *knew,* did old Max, tense upon my arm, that I loved him, admired—and wished to strike him with all my force, even to death!

"No more today," he muttered.

I was trembling with annoyance. At the barn-door I let go his arm and declared I wasn't hungry.

"Ja, sure," he nodded. "Me too. Please listen to this about Grand Tutors, Georgie: *A Grand Tutor is good. A Grand Tutor is wise.* If there's just one grain of wickedness or folly in him—why, he's not a Grand Tutor. Think of that. If there's just one grain of wickedness or folly in him—why, he's not a Grand Tutor. Think of that. If you're here tomorrow I got more to tell you."

He went, if not to lunch at least into the barn, and I strode in frenzy to here, to there. A pounding was at my temple. Doelings sprang fencewards not to be smitten by my stick, the fall of every thistle in my way. Soon I found G. Herrold squat on a rise, his eye on things. I cried, *"Ho,* G. Herrold! *Ho!"* He read the signs; with a black hee-hee he crouched to meet me. Knees bent and arms a-swing we circled warily, huffing incitements. His right hand came clap on my nape, I let go the stick to hook on his left knee; we tumbled to it, scissored and hammerheld about the landscape until his old knowledge had the better of my young might, and I lay pinned. Our wrappers, shagged with weed-seed, were askew; our skins gave off sharp odor and mingled sweats.

"Ain't he grown to a big one!" G. Herrold marveled. His nelson unwound into a loose embrace, and he surveyed me frankly. I was not innocent of self-experiment, nor had my fancy been much cumbered with Rights and Wrongs (save in the matter of Redfearn's Tommy's death). A goat-boy, fenced those many years from studentdom, I'd learnt its morals in the spirit of its politics or costume: as an object of study, infinitely various, subject to fashion, and more or less interesting. I had read why the Founder once rained fire upon the Quadrangles of the Plain, and contrariwise in what manner the flower of classical antiquity, the splendid lads of Lykeion, had amused themselves at Maios's feet: the difference impressed me in no other way than did the difference between the architectures of the two colleges, or their verse-styles. In sum, my mind was open as my vestment, and while I could imagine what a right-minded New Tammany freshman would have felt in my circumstances, I myself knew only curiosity when G. Herrold laid hands on me. Any misgivings were purely theoretical, and overbalanced by the fact that I owed the man my life, that he was anyhow insane and but dimly aware of his behavior. Besides, I couldn't know for certain what he was up to.

By way of precaution, however, I said to my friend, "I'd better tell you, G. Herrold: I'm a Grand Tutor, and a Grand Tutor is good. Is this good?"

He grunted. "It just fine, white boy." And as he had for all his handicaps and mine taught me something of gymnastics, now and in the days that followed he trained me somewhat in the arts of love—whereat I found myself a readier hand than at Max's curriculum. In both sports the perfection of my skill was delayed for want of variety in my circumstance and partners: some time was to pass before I grappled with a man in anger or a woman in love. But as husband and black-man, athlete and sweeper of the nighttime stacks, G. Herrold had known many sorts of love and combat; to his broad experience (half-remembered) was joined my reading (half-understood) and boundless fancy. We managed much.

That evening I came home in the best of humors with the herd, my spirit clear and calmed as the mid-March twilight. I felt released from Max's tutelage, yet somehow more ready than ever, just for that, to be counseled by him. G. Herrold and I came into the barn, singing one of his two songs, and straightway I asked Max's pardon for my morning unpleasantness. He put down his violin and nodded from his seat in the pens.

"Look at you two," he marveled. There was straw in my hair and leaf-litter in the growth of new beard I was so proud of; we would never have done picking burrs and hooked seeds from our clothes. "What have you been up to?"

I laughed. "Taking out my bad temper on somebody my size." Stirred still, if tranquilly, I gave my dark friend a comrade's short embrace, and, laughing again at Max's frown, made haste to embrace him also and kiss his brow. "I was wicked and stupid with you this morning," I said.

"So. *Ach,* get on with you!" With a smile he fended off my gesture. "You admit you're not beyond a little wickedness and stupidity?"

"More than that: I enjoy them. But from now on I'll be wise and good with you and be wicked and stupid with G. Herrold. Wait'll I show you what he did this afternoon, once he got me pinned!"

My dark companion grinned at the pen-side. Max glanced from one to the other of us. "I see." His voice was concerned, but not quite scolding.

"Are you angry?"

Max assured me that he was not: I was a vigorous young man, he said, with normal urgings, and in the absence of generally approved outlets he supposed it was better for me to have recourse temporarily to less generally approved ones than to none at all. So long as my circumstances were as they were, he said, and my motives remained free of perversion, he saw little to choose between auto- and homoerotic activity: masturbation, while more normal in the eyes of most New Tammanians and less liable to cause public embarrassment, carried its dangers in the same single-handedness that recommended it: loveless and reclusive, it fed the fantasies of the timid and could aggravate any tendencies to impotence or withdrawal from engagement with others—narcissism and schizophrenia, he asserted, were the masturbator's inclinations in the realm of psychopathy. Pederasty, on the other hand, though regarded in New Tammany College as a semi-criminal perversion, had at least to be said for it that it involved a passionate, perhaps even a loving, engagement of the self with others. So long as it was practiced in a healthy frame of mind—a virtual impossibility in a college that held it to be vicious—Max saw no great danger of its becoming a substitute for normal relations with women, any more than my casual past connections with does would be. He cautioned me, however, to abandon the practice once I matriculated, lest it lead me into scandal, fistula, or logical realism—the philosophy of Maios and Scapulas, which Max declared to be as favored by pederasts as was solipsism by masturbators.

"So it's probably okay," he concluded. "G. Herrold won't do you any harm, and I been in proctoscopy long enough to be broad-minded."

"I knew it was supposed to be flunkèd," I confessed, "but I enjoyed it anyhow."

"That don't matter, Georgie. What flunkèdness is, it's not doing what you're not supposed to do; flunkèdness is to do it *because* you're not supposed to, and perverseness is to like it *because* you know it's flunkèd. 'Even though' is okay; 'because' is flunkèd."

"So I'm still a Grand Tutor," I said happily. "I knew I was."

Max smiled and to my pleasure agreed at least that my disporting with G. Herrold, done as it was innocently and in good faith, didn't *refute* my claim. "Take the goats, now, for instance," he said: "how come you never humped yourself a doeling since you were a youngster? You were sweet on Hedda once, *nicht wahr?* And a nanny is not bad, you know, for a goat. But you got no taste for them since you learned you're a human person, isn't that so?"

I acknowledged that it was.

"So you're not the least bit tempted. How about Hedda's niece here, though?" He crooked to him a fine black-and-white doeling named Becky's Pride Sue—still a kid, really—and cradled her in his lap to soothe her alarm. "Wouldn't she be sweet?"

Somewhat shocked—Max had never spoken so with me before—I reaffirmed my disinclination for the charms of she-goats. "Anyhow," I added somewhat sternly, "it would hurt her, wouldn't it? She's just little."

Max nodded; evidently I'd said what he wanted to hear. "So even if you wanted to, you shouldn't. Since you don't want to and don't need to, the only reason you'd have for doing it would be flunkèd. You'd have to enjoy it because you know it's wrong, which is flunkèd, or because it hurts her, which is even flunkèder. No good man could do such a thing, don't you think? Especially not a Grand Tutor."

"You talk as if I'd done it!" I protested, and patted Sue's head. "I'd never dream of such a thing!"

"Ay, well, that's good; I wouldn't either. Anybody did, he'd have some Dean o' Flunks in him all right. Let's don't talk any more about it."

I readily concurred, and the three of us ate our evening meal. Afterwards, though I went dutifully to my books, I found it impossible to attend them. Our discussion of flunk-èdness remained on my mind: the legend of the first man and woman in the Founder's Pomological Test-Grove now appalled me, which thitherto had seemed merely charming and a bit unreasonable. I understood for the first time *evil*, and was so impressed by the horror of it that though I couldn't look at Becky's Pride Sue without an inward shudder, my glance turned and returned to her. To rend that dainty girl—despite her cries, out of simple brutehood—it was a thought unthinkable! I could not get it out of my mind.

That night I dreamed again. I was a goat, a splendid stud; I tossed my head and gloried in the weight of horn there, struck my sharp hooves on the ground. Season was upon me: my eyes rolled, I was fury at the balls. Against them what gate could prevail? I exploded from my stall into pastures of human girldom; Chickie was there, as once in the buckwheat, a score of pink and fleeceless Chickies, clamoring to Be. "Come, Billy!" they implored. A dashing, smashing goat I was, and tireless servicer; I found it light labor to give them joy, inasmuch as my powers were unremitting even when my lust was long since slaked. It amused me the more when Chickie had got her fill of Being and would flee. No matter that I had no hands to clutch with: down the hemlock-aisles I thundered in pursuit—*hunh! hunh!* my breath came—and her gauzy wrapper was briared off her up the way; I had only to stand rampant and impale her, over all that space, upon my lancing majesty. Instead I crooked her in with it, held her fast down. Somewhere distant the buckhorn blew—*Tekiah! Sherbarim! Teruah!*—for me, and urgent. But I could do anything I wished, not as before because the girl was willing, but because she was altogether in my power, subject absolutely to my will.

"Oh, how you'd injure me!" my victim wept. "A goat upon a lady girl!"

"I would that," I agreed, and not to hear the buckhorn once more summoning (*Tekiah! Shebarim! Teruah!*), I loudly volunteered, "Don't think I *need* to do anything flunkèd!"

"How's that?"

"I say, don't think—the truth is, it's terribly important for me to wake up right now."

"I'm only a kid," the girl pleaded. "Wait till my older sister comes along."

"I could if I cared to," I said. "The passèd thing of course would be to let you go."

Her first cry was for joy: "Oh, thank you, sir!" Her second not, for as the horn called out penultimately, I did her upon each blast a grievous harm. *Tekiah. Teruah. Tekiah.*

I woke—and jerked from a squealing creature at my chest! A kid (as sometimes happened) had curled against me while I slept; I'd rolled upon her accidentally and, I now realized, squeezed her in my arms as well. There was commotion in the stalls; it seemed her outcries had roused the herd. I sat up sweating and was dismayed to find myself not only ejaculated but observed: Max sat by the pen-gate, his head a-bob in reflected moonlight.

"You were dreaming," he said calmly. "Nothing to worry about. It wasn't Becky's Pride Sue."

I lay down dazed and soon reslept. When I woke in the morning the episode burst to mind at once: for an instant I imagined that Max at the pen gate was a part of the dream; then the pinch of dried lust on my thigh told me, heart-sinking, he was not. I heard him now directing G. Herrold in the chores, and lay for some minutes awed by memory, by the spectacle of my soul laid out to view.

That morning Max was solicitous, even one would have supposed half-afraid to speak; it went without saying that our normal program was dispensed with; no mention was made of the night's events—indeed not of anything—until at the end of a wordless breakfast he ventured to touch my hand.

"You haven't really *done* any flunkèdness, you know. You were just a kid before, and now you've learned you got badness in you like we all do. It don't have to come out."

"Cruelness and folly," I said. "It'll come out."

"So maybe a little here and there. Who's perfect?"

I looked him in the eyes. "Enos Enoch was."

"*Ja.*" Max bobbed his head, as he had in the moonlight. "Then swallow once and be done, dear boy: are you another Enos Enoch?"

I shook my head.

My teacher could not contain his delight: he squeezed my hand in both of his and nodded furiously, frowning and smiling together.

"Pass you, boy! Pass you for admitting that!" Tears sprang; his syntax faltered. "All that talk of Eierkopf's about a GILES—just madness. I knew it! Every chance, Founder knows! I went right by the book, and not once but two and three times, knowing all along—ah, Georgie!" He came round and embraced me, put off not at all by my stiffness. "Say it again yet, to make an old man happy—what you said."

"I'm no Enos Enoch," I repeated. "I've got as much billy-goat in me as Graduate. And as much Dean o' Flunks as anything else."

"And never mind that! Don't be sorry you're a plain human student, okay?"

I assured him levelly that I was not disappointed by the revelation of my nature's darker aspects, only sobered and intrigued; but that in view of those same aspects I most certainly no longer regarded myself, even potentially, as Wisdom and Goodness incarnate. Max all but hopped about the barn for pleasure.

"I knew it from the first!" he cried. "But there was that tapelift thing, and crazy Eierkopf and his stories. GILES *pfui!* I bet he put you there himself!"

Upon my pressing him to explain himself more clearly, Max confessed that he had for many years entertained a certain hypothesis about my parentage, which till now—by reason first of my tender years and latterly of my misguided ambition—he had kept to himself, not to injure my feelings.

"I been all my life a bachelor," he said. "All work! No time for ladies! But in New Tammany once, when Eblis Eierkopf and I were working on the WESCAC, I got to know the Chancellor's daughter, that was the tape-librarian in Tower Hall. Miss Hector was her name—Virginia R. Hector, what it said on her nameplate. And Eblis and I, we were fighting then about *Wescacus malinoctis* and the Cum Laude Project; we were fighting about everything . . . but we both admired very much Miss Hector. She was a *Shiksa*, don't you know, with light hair and all wrong politics; in Siegfrieder College she'd have been a Bonifacist like those co-eds in the *Reichskanzler's* stud-farms, I knew that; it's what Eblis loved about her, she was such a plump and blond one. 'A perfect Frigga!' he used to say—and how he said it made your heart sink, Georgie. Because Eblis, all he had on his mind was the Cum Laude Project! He didn't care about *her*, but only what sperms should go with what eggs to make a *Hero* . . ."

Max pronounced the word as though it tasted foul. He himself, he went on to say, though still nominally Eierkopf's superior, was by that time already out of favor with Chancellor Hector, and found himself denied full access to the Cum

Laude planning. But he undertook a private research into the fields of eugenics and comparative mythology in hopes of anticipating Eierkopf's maneuvers, and at the same time (as I gathered) courted Miss Hector's society. His avowed motive was to protect her from his colleague's designs; unfriendly gossip had it he was out to improve his position with the father through the daughter; in any case, from what Max said I understood that Miss Hector came to reciprocate his own esteem for her—indeed, that it was Max's reluctance more than hers that kept their relation merely Scapular, as it were: "A fifty-years-old Moishian radical and a twenty-five-years-old *Shiksa* reactionary, that used to be the Spring-Queen of New Tammany College! Some heroes *our* kids would've been!"

What exactly passed between them he would not say, but it appeared there was an argument following which, perhaps to spite him, Miss Hector began spending much time with Dr. Eierkopf. She even exchanged her post as tape-librarian to work as some sort of technician on the Cum Laude Project, for which she professed great admiration now that (as she implied to Max) she was privy to its secret details. All Max ever saw her do was steer his colleague's wheelchair along the corridors and campus paths; despite his own frailness, he declared to me, and his contempt for the Siegfrieder ideal for blue-eyed athleticism, the contrast between Virginia Hector's proud form and the feeble bloat of Eierkopf sickened his spirit.

"A pretty Moishian girl, you know, Georgie, you think of a dark hall and heavy wine, and myrrh and frankincense; but this *Shiksa*, she reminded you of bright day-times—almost you could smell sunshine on her! I didn't want her for myself, not even if I wasn't old and bony; I wanted she should marry some buck of a northern forester, you know? Or a strapping young iceberg-research man with gold hair on his chest yet. It wasn't she was a *goy;* it was she was so pretty in the *goy* way, instead of some other way."

This new feature of my keeper's life interested me considerably. I asked him whether the woman had married Eblis Eierkopf then. Max's face darkened; he shook his head. "You heard the reasons why I was fired from New Tammany—all but this one, that happened at the end. One day just after I made my last speech in the Senate, comes a message from Chancellor Hector himself, he wants to see me right away. The Security people take me up in a private elevator to his offices, and next thing before I can tell him hello, this Virginia runs in, all crying tears, and throws her arms around me; and she says, 'It don't matter! It don't matter!' So I ask her daddy, that's biting on his cigar by the window, 'What don't matter?' And he spits the end out and never once looks at me. But 'All right, Spielman,' he says: 'I know when I been out-generaled.' He was the big general in the Second Riot, you know, before he ran for Chancellor."

The occasion of the summons, it developed, was that Miss Hector had found herself with child and declared Max responsible! Even there in the barn, almost two decades later, my keeper's voice grew incredulous as he spoke of it: horror enough that she had submitted to the repulsive, to the despicable Eierkopf (by what clever means the cripple had managed seduction and mating, Max shuddered to wonder)— more bitter yet to hang her shame on the man who'd tried in vain to shield her! Heartsick, he challenged her to confess that Eierkopf, not himself, had been her undoer—or else some third party with whom she had secretly consorted. Miss Hector, never once looking him in the eye, only repeated her accusation; it was true, she said, that Professor Eierkopf's passion for his work had led him past propriety's bounds to the suggestion that she put by modesty for science's sake and lend herself to certain experimental possibilities of the Cum Laude Project ("I knew! I knew!" Max had shouted at the Chancellor. "Oh boy, won't I wring his pig's neck once!"); but she had never acquiesced. As for intimacies with the crippled scientist himself, she was prepared to swear on a stack of Old Syllabi that there had been none, nor had any been proposed; she professed to be nauseated at the thought. Max then had declared, almost a-swoon, it was not the *thought* she paled at but recollection of the deed, and appall at what thing it had got in her.

"Why did she blame you?" I asked him—and was told that in human studentdom such false charges on the part of desperate women were not uncommon.

"She'd . . . *been* with Eblis Eierkopf, you know—" He said the word with difficulty, and his use of it, clearly in the Chickian sense, compounded a certain perplexity of mine: I had come to think that Lady Creamhair, on the occasion of that fiasco in the hemlocks, had not understood my honest intention to *be* (an activity for which G. Herrold had a host of other names); but if the term was after all common parlance, as Max's use of it suggested, then her initial encouragement and subsequent wild rebuff of my advances were not yet clear. The memory made me sweat; another time I should have asked Max to gloss his term, but he'd gone on with the story. "—she *must* have *been* with him: you don't get pregnant filing tape-reels! Then he wouldn't do the right thing by her, and she thought to herself, 'That old Spielman, I'll say it was his fault, he'll be glad enough to marry me no matter what, and once the baby's born I can do what I please.' You haven't read much but the old epics yet, Georgie, or you'd know how it is with old men and young women."

I ventured to say I understood what the situation *was,* if not why it should be so. Nothing in my kidship equipped me to appreciate the reasons for human jealousy, so alien to the goats; yet my own heart was alas no stranger to that unnatural sentiment, which had been the death of Redfearn's Tom. But discreetly as I could I asked Max how it was that he, the soul of gentleness and reason, had been angered by the woman's expedient, born as it plainly was of desperation and ill usage.

"Yes. Well." He sniffed and frowned at me curiously over his eyeglasses. "That's a hard question, George! Aren't you a keen one, asking me that!" He said this not at all critically, but as if surprised and pleased. "A boy that asks that question is wise enough to raise his eyebrow at the answer. I hope he's wise enough to know how the truth can sound sometimes like a lie."

The truth came to this, he asserted: he could forgive, in the woman he'd felt such regard for, any infidelity; he did not count himself deserving of her love (or Eblis Eierkopf either, but that was *her* affair); the most he'd ever dreamed of winning was her respect and perhaps a daughterly affection, nothing more, in return for which he'd gladly have married her though she were pregnant by a different lover every year. But disregard for official morality and even for his feelings was one thing; disregard for Truth another. Let her confess frankly that the child was not his: he would wed her and give it gratefully, prayerfully, his name; but he could not allow a lie to be his marriage-portion, whose life's enterprise had been the research after truth. In short, neither the Chancellor's threats nor Miss Hector's tears could induce him to wed his heart's desire unless she openly admitted that Eierkopf had deflowered and impregnated her, and this admission she would not make.

"So that was that," Max concluded. "Her poppa hollered how he'd like to whip me with his two hands, and if it wasn't for his daughter's reputation he'd have me to court. Miss Virginia hit my face once and ran away, which I haven't seen her since, and just the next week was when I was sacked, like you know already. Why should it matter then, I should argue my case? So I came here to the goat-barn, and half a year later G. Herrold brings me this cripple-child out of the tape-lift, he's been sacked his own self for fetching you out . . ." He rubbed his left cheek, as if Miss Hector's smite still tingled there. "What am I supposed to think, Georgie? What am I supposed to do, but kiss your poor legs and your *goy* blond hair, that no Moishian like me was ever the poppa of?"

I kissed Max's own long hair at this fresh testimony of his goodness, and he mine; yet even as I chid him, most gently, for so long keeping from me his hypothesis of my parentage—which seemed a quite probable one, everything considered—and assured him that I was far more touched by his generous adoption of me than disturbed by the likelihood of having been sired by the hateful Eierkopf—even as I spoke, it occurred to me that the story had not after all been to the point. Just the contrary! Had he not set out by means of it to explain an actual suspicion on his part that I might be of uncommon parentage? That my brash claim to herohood might be not without some foundation? But if I was in truth the child of Dr. Eierkopf and Virginia Hector, my getting was by no means extraordinary; it was merely irregular.

Some minutes were required to make my point clear, for Max had quite forgotten, as unhappily he came frequently to do in this period of his life, what he'd set out to demonstrate, and then only with difficulty understood that he had not demonstrated it.

"*Ja,* so, what I mean," he said then, "that's what I thought when G. Herrold brought you here, you were Virginia's kid by Eblis; what I guess, that's what I wanted you to be. And sometimes yet it slips me now and again you aren't, I have trouble remembering. But the fact is, she never had a son: she had a daughter, that she left to her uncle Ira Hector to raise. I heard that somewhere a long time ago, I forget where. It was a daughter she had."

I closed my eyes and tried to assimilate this new disclosure.

"Well, then—we're back where we started! The gate's still open!"

"No." Max shook his head firmly. "No, it's not open, either. No." He seemed now to have his mind once more in order. "It was that GILES business made me wonder, once I knew you weren't Virginia's and Eblis's kid, and when you started this Hero nonsense. An old man's foolishness, Georgie, is all! You see yourself now you're not any Grand Tutor, but just a good boy with a regular life's work to do. You got a little badness in you and a little dumbness, pass your heart, like we all got."

With considerable effort (for he was fatigued by so much recollection, and regarded his point as now quite established) I wrung this final information from him: Among the bizarre features of the Cum Laude Project in the month just prior to its abandonment was the preparation by WESCAC, under Eierkopf's supervision, of a highly secret something known as "the GILES"—Max could or would not go farther than to explain that the word was an acronym for *Grand-tutorial Ideal, Laboratory Eugenical Specimen*. What that phrase meant (it had as well been in sheep-language for all it conveyed to me), and whether the attempt to prepare this same GILES was successful, and what in that event its purpose was—these things I was not to learn until later. But I gathered there was an uncertain connection between this mystery and my pretension to the office of Hero.

"I don't say more than this," Max said: "there's things about the early days of Heroes and Grand Tutors. And when you took it in your silly head you were one yourself, I remembered these things and some others, that a person could stretch them and say they fit. So I thought up a couple experiments to prove what was what, I'll tell you about later. But they've proved, George—they've *proved*—what you know your own self now: that you're a good boy, and a human student, and that's all."

I supposed he was referring to the occasions when I had behaved stupidly or displayed a capacity, however slight, for actual flunkèdness, as in the matter of Redfearn's Tommy and of Becky's Pride Sue. It did not anger me to imagine, in the light of his confession, that Max may actually have encouraged such behavior, may even have arranged the circumstances of my temptation, perhaps in collusion with G. Herrold and (who knew?) with Lady Creamhair. That possibility was clearly beside the point; whatever experiments he had performed were for my own enlightenment and benefit, and had achieved their purpose. A Grand Tutor was very wise; a Grand Tutor was very good. Whatever the mysteries and portents of my birth, whatever formal prerequisites to Herohood I might coincidentally have met, I could not call myself very wise nor very good. Chastened, I took the conclusion to my heart, merely asking leave for the day's instruction to get used to the feel of it there.

What remained of the morning I spent introspecting about the pasture, deaf to G. Herrold's plea to wrestle in the cool March sun; after lunch I retired to the hemlocks with pencil and paper, thinking to map out as it were the road before me by noting down the few clear signposts I had passed. Perched on a high stump I began with NEITHER WISE NOR GOOD, which I printed out in fair block capitals at the page-top. But when I considered inscribing beneath it PASS ALL FAIL ALL and the Maxim SELF-KNOWLEDGE IS ALWAYS BAD NEWS, I could not at once decide which merited second place, and, unable to care intensely, I fell soon into reverie. My fingers toyed with the paper; I had seen human visitors nibble, in my kidship, colored ices from paper cones, and had been wont to fashion any sheet I found into that form before I ate it. Such a cone I fashioned now, scarcely aware; but I had not the appetite of childhood days. Instead of eating it, therefore, idly I set it atop my head, and brooded the afternoon away thus perched and capped.

That night I dreamed the strangest dream of all. In our old meeting-place Lady Creamhair sat on the ground. It was dark night, not picnic time; yet the famous basket rested in her lap, and I squatted at her feet as in terms gone by. But we did not eat. As a child makes a comic mouth, she hooked her forefingers into the basket-lids and spread them wide. She bade me look, and I beheld in that dark chamber no peanut-butter sandwich, but a strange, a baleful host. I saw a man with wings and one with tail. An ancient leaned upon his crook. A lady girl did nothing. I saw a body with two heads, one atop the other. I saw a single head with two bodies, winking and blinking. Still other eyes I saw, seeing me: a bodiless pair that neither blinked nor moved nor changed their cast. A man was there who vanished when I looked, yet whom I saw when I looked away. And others, a multitude of shadows, men and women, sheep and goats—they hushed about, melting and shifting. They beckoned to me, all, inviting, threatening—except the lady girl forlorn and patient. I yearned to her. How was it I had not till then suspected what the basket held? I would go to that folk, not meant for eating. No matter the peril, I would press into their country, whence whooped to me a most clear call now. *Tekiah!* The goats swarmed over all. *Tekiah!*

Though I was sensible of no waking or change of scene, I got up from my cot and stood in the dark barn at last entirely clear. Max was not in his stall, nor was G. Herrold. No matter! My old wrapper I shucked off for good, and fetched from its storing-place in the supply-room a new one G. Herrold had made against the day I should matriculate: a long and splendid cape it was, of white-bronze fleece, sewed from the hides of two most dear to me, Redfearn's Tom and Mary V. Apponzeller. Even as I drew it round my shoulders (over a clean wool underwrap) and took pleasure in the proud hang of it, I heard the buckhorn call again, not far distant.

I did not tarry even to pack a sandwich; merely I wound the watch upon its lanyard around my neck, found out my necessary stick, and left the barn. In the east a faint light shone that would presently be dawn; in the west a fainter from the thronging halls of New Tammany College, immeasurably distant. I shivered a moment by the gate, until through the quiet came a different blasting call: a whistle of far-off power, urgent! Whereat I shook no more nor wondered, but sprang the latch, and guided by what tooted through the fading stars, set out a-tap down the hard highway.

2.

A bend was in the road just down from the barn, the farthest I'd ever seen from the pasture gate. There (the strange whistle having ceased) I paused to review the cupolas and gambrels of my home. Lest I see more I pressed on. But just round the bend I found the road divided. I inclined to the right, being of that hand; then checked myself and bent left instead, it was so thin a reason. Yet this was no sensibler, after all, and I found myself quite stopped and suddenly discouraged.

How long I might have languished there who knows; the mere resolve that brooked no suggestion of retreat, before the issue of left or right availed me nothing. When I had commenced once more to shivering, however, I heard a rustle in the fork, and from a growth of sumac Max himself came forth, supported by G. Herrold.

"You walking in your sleep?" he asked me.

I might have demanded the same of him, under whose arm I spied now the horn that had waked me. But I saw a riddling seriousness in the question—it had the air more of a sentry's challenge than a query—and at the same moment I understood that twice before in recent nights it was the sound of our actual shophar which had figured in my dreams.

"It's time I matriculated," I said.

"You know what you're going to do, do you?"

"I'll know once I get there."

"So." All this while Max stood before me, straining close to see my face in the dim light. "And you know the way? It's not easy."

"I'll find it," I declared.

"*Ja*, well. But come on back now, G. Herrold fixes you a box-lunch and packs some things. Wait till daylight, you can see your way better."

But I declined, observing the hour was already late, too late almost, and that as for food and extra clothing, I could not be burdened with them. Truly I was impatient to be off: if he would accept hasty, heartfelt thanks for all he'd done for me—and tell me please which fork led to New Tammany—I'd be all right, and forever in his debt.

"Which fork, Georgie? You mean you're not sure?"

"It doesn't matter," I said at once. "There's bound to be a sign. Well, bye-bye, Max. Bye-bye, G. Herrold. I really must go."

And I struck out as if I knew my way, hoping some impulse would turn me left or rightwards if I kept myself from thinking on the choice. But of course I could not not-think; no impulse came; and unwilling either to halt again or to betray my quandary (for I was conscious of their eyes upon me), I forged ahead into the sumac.

"I believe I'll take a short-cut through here," I called back.

"*Ach*, George! Wait once!" Max's voice was joyous; but

though I heard him call again for me and urge G. Herrold to help him overtake me, I crashed on through briars and foxgrape—only a bit more slowly, not to rip my fleece.

"Wait once, I got to tell you what we did!" As I would not stay, he bade G. Herrold fetch him up and run, and so in a moment was at my side, fending boughs off as we plunged.

"To the right, boy, not this way. Ay, George! I wouldn't believe! Just an old Moishian!"

I said nothing, but turned to the right as he directed. Shortly we were on paved road again, all things more distinct now as the light came from behind us. I went on without hesitation and at such a determined clip (being free of brambles) that Max was obliged to remain in G. Herrold's arms if he would keep pace.

"You know who you are, all right!" he said. "What you thought right along—but who could believe such a thing? Until we proved it!"

Without looking at him I inquired, "That's why you blew the horn?"

"*Ja, ja,* that's just why!" More excited than ever I'd seen him, Max described the "experiments" he'd mentioned the previous day. I had, he confirmed, met nearly all the prerequisites of herohood, as far as could be judged: the mystery of my parentage, about which it could be presumed only that I was the offspring of someone high in the administration; the irregularity of my birth, which had so seemed a threat to someone that an attempt had been made on my life; the consequent injury to my legs; the circumstances of my rescue, and my being raised by a foster parent in a foster-home, disguised as an animal and bearing a name not my own—these and other details corresponded to what Max had found true of scores of hero-histories. On the other hand none seemed unambiguous or conclusive, at least not to one who all his life had been skeptical of heroship. Even if it could be verified that my mother and father were close blood-relatives; that I'd been conceived in a thunderstorm and born in a cave; that rumor had it I was not my father's son; or that my would-be assassin was either my father or my mother's father—still nothing followed necessarily. As Max put it: "Not every dumbhead with a scar is a bonafide hero."

To settle his doubts in the matter (that is, to prove to himself that my claims were mere boyish ambition) he had instructed G. Herrold on a certain night to blow a certain call upon the horn: if I had waked and asked what was the matter, as Max anticipated, my claim for some reason would have been nullified. If on the other hand I had responded without a question or hesitation and set out in a certain way . . . But I had done neither, quite, only gone on with my troubled sleep. On a second night therefore had come a second call, which to have answered in any wise had been my refutation (Max did not say why): luckily, it too had not moved me, except to lustful dreams. This night had sounded the third and final; had I slept through it or merely inquired what was the matter, my future had been clear: Max would have enrolled me in the fall as a regular freshman at NTC, to pass or fail in some one of the usual curricula like any other undergraduate—quite what he wished for me, he confessed, in all his reasonable moods.

"But I couldn't help thinking what you said, Georgie, about the WESCAC and its AIM. And crazy or not, I couldn't help thinking how it was my hand pushed the EAT-button once, and the only way to save me from flunking forever was to lead a Grand Tutor down to West Campus with that same hand."

From the corner of my eye I saw him stress the point with the finger next to his missing one. But my sharp attention to what he said did not retard me.

"So we blew and we blew; two times tonight we did; and just when G. Herrold took his breath to blow the one last time—what did you hear, my boy?"

"There was a different sound," I said. "It wasn't our horn."

"It was the EAT-whistle!" Max cried. "I never thought till then how it wouldn't mean nothing you should answer to the buckhorn anyhow. But the EAT-whistle, that they blow it from the Power Plant for riot-drills—that's what fetched you! It's just right!"

Privately I wondered how Max accounted, since his change of mind, for the element of Dunce and Dean o' Flunks in me, which themselves had been discovered by his experimenting. I chose not to ask, but felt compelled at least to observe that I had waked already and was prepared to set out before I'd heard the stranger sound.

"That's okay!" Max insisted. "But what if it wasn't okay? Suppose I said it proves you're only George the Goat-Boy, let's turn around home?"

As I could think of no reply, I walked on without comment.

"You see that, G. Herrold? He goes on anyhow, you shouldn't ask!"

My dear dark comrade, need I say, saw neither more nor less than he ever could. But he was all hum-hum and smile.

"What you said yourself once, Georgie, it's one or the other: if you're not Grand Tutor, you're crazy as G. Herrold, the WESCAC messed your mind up like it did his. If you're not crazy, you got to be a Grand Tutor, nobody else could be in WESCAC's Belly and not get himself EATen."

"That's right," I agreed.

"So listen here," Max said, "you got to hear this: how did the lost Professor in the *Campus Cantos* find his way through the South Exit and around to Commencement Gate?"

"He had the former director of the Poetry Workshop to show him," I replied.

"So! And in the *Epic of Anchisides*, that this same director wrote himself, how does Anchisides know how to get through the Nether Campus? Wouldn't he have ended up flunked like the rest if it wasn't the Lady from Guidance went along with him?"

I saw his point: it was not a disgrace that I had no notion how to reach New Tammany and only the vaguest of what business was mine there. On the contrary, neither Laertides nor any other of the wandering researchers could have completed their field-projects without special counselling. I wanted an advisor, that was all; to *do* the hero-assignment was my function, not to choose it . . .

"Or even to understand it," Max added when I made this point. "Look at Dean Arthur and Excelsior, his magic quill: do you think he knew *why* it always wrote the right answers? He should care!"

Yet one doubt remained to me: I could not recall that Sakhyan or Maios or Enos Enoch had needed the service of a guidance counselor. Did what applied to wandering researchers apply as well to Grand Tutors? But to my query Max replied at once, "It depends! Take in the New Syllabus where Enos Enoch cures the crazies; you know why He did it?"

"Well, He wanted the poor undergraduates to get on with their studies, and I don't suppose there was any Psych Clinic in those days."

"Not just that! What it says, He did it *That it might be*

fulfilled which was spoken by Esaias the Advisor, saying,
Himself took our infirmities . . . Now, then! Suppose Enos
Enoch hadn't read the Old Syllabus, like you haven't?" The
fact was, he declared, Enos Enoch like other Grand Tutors
had had His advising as it were in advance, and did what He
did in many cases precisely because He knew it to be prescribed that "A Grand Tutor shall do such-and-so." It was not
the fulfillment of predictions that made Enos Enoch Grand
Tutor; it was the prior condition of Grand Tutorhood that
led Him to search out the predictions and see to it they were
fulfilled.

I felt free now to halt in the road and embrace my old
keeper, whom G. Herrold set down to that end. And I simply
asked, "Will you advise me, Max?"

He could scarcely answer, so delighted was he—and I no
less—that we were after all to be together yet awhile. Rubbing his eye, he managed presently to say, "What you think
I been doing? Oh boy. Oh boy. You don't know what it
means, Georgie, a Moishian to believe the Grand Tutor's on
campus!"

I reminded him that we were not yet on the main campus
of New Tammany College, and that he had better get on
with his job, and we three with my journey, unless there was
work to be done in the woodland where we were.

"Just one business, right here," he replied. And clutching
my arm with one thin hand to steady himself, with the other
he removed from his waist the token of herdsmanship he'd so
long worn there: the withered testicles of Freddie, his old
foe, and the leather cord they hung on. "Tie these round
your wrapper," he advised me. "It's you that's the Good
Goatsman now, with a bigger herd than I ever looked after." I
did what he bade me, and he said very seriously, "What these
mean, George, if you ever had any faun in you before—any
stud-buck in your blood sometimes, you know? Well, you got
to cut it off from now on, or you're not the Grand Tutor. No
more Heddas, and no more Lady Creamhairs, whatever went
on out there."

I blushed and agreed, relieved enough to think that my
past misadventures in deed and dream (of which my advisor
had only partial knowledge) need burden my conscience no
longer. Firmly I decreed *non grata* in my memory the images
of Hedda and Lady Creamhair; also those of Chickie with
the dimpling buttocks who more lately had frisked there, and

Becky's Pride Sue; not to mention G. Herrold from whom I had learnt more than half-nelsons, and who watched these goings-on with his grave amusement. No more hot grapples in the asphodel; bye-bye to hemlock pursuits and the studly matter of my dreams. No more to aspire to Being was my firm resolve: right gladly I belted the amulet before me, and believe that I would on Max's advisement have added my own twin troublers to dreadful Fred's.

"I'll show you the way to New Tammany," he pledged, "and how to get past Main Gate and the Entrance Exam. Then we got to sneak you down to WESCAC's Belly, you should change its AIM. Peace on Campus!"

This last burst from him, an impassioned cry. Never had I seen such exaltation in my keeper; it stirred and hushed my own spirit, and at the same time made me a bit uncomfortable.

"Well," I said, "let's go on."

3.

The stock-barns of my youth, I now discovered, were situated on a high plateau, much farther from New Tammany proper than I'd supposed—unless for some reason the route Max chose was not the most direct. All day we wandered down a twisting hill-road, through stands of oak and rocky fields, resting often for Max's sake. G. Herrold had brought with him a great piece of Manchego, which at midday we washed down with spring water. Using the length of my former pasture as a measure, I guessed we had gone a dozen kilometers, no more, by late afternoon, when abruptly we came upon a gorge or strait defile between two mountains. "The backdoor to West Campus," Max described it; a river debouched from the canyon's throat into a valley west of us, where I saw a considerable lake. We tarried some while on the cliff-edge to watch the play of late light on the rocks, the more impressive as the sun descended quite into the chasm's mouth. Then we made our way down, resolving to cross before dark and find shelter on the far shore.

But at the bottom we were dismayed to see our road cut off: the stream, not apparently deep but fast indeed, was swollen and empowered by the springtime torrents we had seen along the way; it had carried off central piers of a wooden bridge that spanned it. Alas, I had been something impatient at the progress of the day—no more adventuresome thus far than any stroll about the pasture—but there came now on us a spate of alarums and surprises that sweetened the memory of uneventfulness.

Our end of the bridge had washed out with the center. As we stood where it used to stand, debating what to do, G. Herrold all at once broke into his song:

> " 'One more river,' say the Founder-man Boss . . ."

His eyes were wide as on the day I had first seen them; following his gaze across the rapids we beheld a young woman in shift and sandals on the farther bank, who must just have appeared where the road came from a willow-grove there. She walked out on the bridge to its broken end, a stable's-length from us, watching us the while as steadily as we her.

"Maybe she can tell us where another bridge is," Max said. "Hush up, G. Herrold, George can ask once."

But G. Herrold, so far from obeying, cried out *"Hallooyer!"* and stepped to the water's edge. The woman looked from him to us; then she cupped her hands to her mouth and called out something over our heads. Two syllables, a long and a short, over and over; a plaintive sweet appeal:

"Croa-ker!" she seemed to cry. *"Croa-ker!"*

"What's it about?" I asked my advisor. But couldn't stay to hear his opinion, inasmuch as G. Herrold shouted again *"Hallooyer!"* and commenced to wade into the shallows, heedless of socks and sandals. I called him to stop and hobbled after, but was arrested by a further astonishment: quite daintily, as who should raise her skirt-hem from the mud, upon her next clear cry the lady girl fetched up her shift— nor halted at knee, but hoist it high as would go. Sturdy she stood there, feet apart and privates bare as milch-nan's to the breeze, sweetly calling, "Croaker, croaker!" From so striking a picture nothing less than G. Herrold's madness could have drawn me; but he forged and stumbled toward her headlong

through the rapids, which drove now against his legs as
against the bridge-piles.

"*I'm a-coming,*" he sang out, "*Founder knows!*"

I started after, but real pursuit was out of the question: my
walking-stick found no purchase on the mossy stones, and I
slipped at once hard down in the numbing shallows.

"Go back!" I heard the lady warn. Founder pass us, still
she stood there, and though with one hand she waved G.
Herrold away, with the other she yet clutched up her shift
beneath her bosoms. Worse, she commenced to thrust her
hips like a rutsome doe and call her call again. I feared now
for his life, he was that bound to reach her; already the torrent was hip-high on him, and driving him off his balance. I
scrambled up and looked to Max for counsel—whereat I
beheld what he already was beholding: the next amazement.

From somewhere upshore, or the cliff-road behind us, or
the pure March air, had appeared a party of nine men such
as I'd never seen before. Their heads were shaved, their skin
was of a darker tone than mine but lighter than G. Herrold's,
and all wore long yellow robes. Eight of them, lean as scare-
crows, bore on their shoulders a two-poled platform whereon
sat the well-fleshed ninth. His legs were folded tight before
him, his hands pressed palm to palm above his belly; his eyes
were closed (but not as in sleep), his lips smiled ever so
slightly, his whole expression was of a serenity unbefitting the
occasion. They crossed the beach—without so much as a
glance at the broken bridge, the bare-snatched maid, or our
floundering friend—and entered the river themselves. The
cold current (which alas had pressed G. Herrold down until
he clung now to a boulder for his life) had as well been a
sheep-dip tank for all they paused or faltered; already they
were waist-high and about to pass two meters upstream from
the boulder.

"So save G. Herrold!" Max shouted. And I too: "Snatch
him! Snatch him!"

Surely they could have, either by returning their burden to
our shore or by excusing for only a moment one of the bearers; they each had a free arm to help with, had they deigned
to pass just downstream of him; without even that aid G.
Herrold might at least have clung to their yellow wrappers
and got his footing. But they would not, they would not, nor
so much as share our horror when, at the bridge-girl's next
cry *croaker,* G. Herrold with a wail went under. We saw him

roll to the surface some yards down; the lady dropped her shift at last to clutch her hair and shriek. The current fetched G. Herrold against another rock; he scrambled for balance, his white fleece cap tumbled off and away, almost it seemed he might get to his knees again—but the rapids overcame him. Down he went, and under, shophar flopping: once only I thought I glimpsed his wrapper in the foaming rush, then lost sight of it, and he was gone.

We stood shocked for some moments, Max and I, then hastened down the beach. It was slow enough going, what with his age, my gimp, and the stones and slick clay underfoot, but we searched a kilometer at least downstream for some sign of G. Herrold. In vain. A sharp shale promontory blocked our way at the gorge's mouth, where the river had been dammed. There we caught our breath and wept, half-expecting to see our friend's body sweep with the river down that spillway into the lake.

"He might have washed ashore where we couldn't see him," I insisted. "He could be resting on the other side somewhere."

Max shook his head.

"Why didn't they help him?" I demanded angrily. "What was that girl doing those things on the bridge for?"

Max groaned, clutching his beard. "You're asking me? I never saw such a thing!"

Dusk was upon us, there was no point in waiting longer. At Max's suggestion we headed bridgewards: surely officials from the Department of Civil Engineering would arrive in the morning, if not that same evening, to inspect the wash-out, which could not go long unrepaired. The most we could do, when they fetched us across, was report the sad news so that the river could be searched for G. Herrold's body.

"And the woods," I insisted again, "in case he got out and he's just lying hurt somewhere."

"*Ja*, well," Max agreed, "the woods too, then." And for my sake he pretended there was some sense in our calling G. Herrold's name all the way upshore. My burden wanted no explaining to him, who had been my tutor in Responsibility: it was not simply the river that had drowned G. Herrold, but the ruin of his mind, whereof WESCAC and my living self were cause.

Approaching the bridgehead in the last light, we could see

the men in yellow on the far shore. Safe over, they had set
down their passenger and were themselves positioned around
him on the sand, as if to rest. Their legs were folded and
their palms pressed together in his manner; I supposed their
eyes were shut too, like his, as their ears had been and their
hearts. The lady girl we saw still at the bridge-end, but on her
knees now in what could be taken for grief: at least her
hands hid her face, and her long dark hair her hands.

Yet even as I regarded her, uncertain how to feel, she
lifted her head, espied us, and once more sent her flunkèd
slender cry over the stream.

"Croa-ker!"

I clenched my fists: What madness *was* it? And before our
unbelieving eyes, could it be the shift went up again? Almost
unseparable it was from the white of her skin now, as distinction faded with the day—but yes, by dint of squinting I
discerned her shame, that patch as it were on her else-
pure-whiteness, or fallen fleck of night-sky in her lap! No
drowning comrade to divert me, I couldn't turn my gaze, for
all Max warned me to. He understood her now, he declared,
and spoke bitterly of those fair dread singers Laertides met,
who, had he not stopped his colleagues' ears and lashed himself to the mast, had lured his research vessel onto the rocks.
Every hero sooner or later met their like, Max cautioned (a
bit more severely, as I gazed on), and nothing could be more
perilous than to attend them. True, the call of this bridge-girl
was nowise fetching, but her temptation was quite as dangerous as the Sirens'. What was more (he clutched at my fleece
when I stepped toward the water for a clearer view) it would
be a grave error to suppose her an idle whore or exhibition-
ist, and her presence on the bridge a mere coincidence: nothing could be more likely than that sinister elements in West
Campus—the same that had sought my death at the
first—had watched my growth carefully all those years, fearing the day I should understand my mission, and having by
some means got word of my departure, were resolved to put
every obstacle between me and their ruin.

I listened with considerable interest, though without turning my head, and agreed from the side of my mouth that
Grand Tutors in general, and particularly one bent on ending
forever the Quiet Riot and bringing peace of mind to the
whole student body, must inevitably make powerful enemies,
if only because riot-defense had become so important a fea-

ture in the life and budget of the colleges. And it was perfectly possible, I conceded further, that the girl with her shift up had been sent to intercept me, whether by the Nikolayans or by misguided professor-generals in New Tammany itself, who had a vested interest in the Quiet Riot: was it not on a bridge, after all, that my childhood exemplar W. W. Gruff had come near to being eaten?

"Shut your eyes already!" Max pleaded, coming round front now to push against me, with his toes dug into the sand.

But I would not take them from the thing that held them, which (my grief for G. Herrold notwithstanding) roused me as I'd not been roused since Chickie-in-the-buckwheat. Unmindful of my keeper's distress—how he butted his head into my stomach, how leaped and waved to interrupt my view—I stared until that little patch of darkness seemed to grow, becoming one with the larger that presently enveloped all, as if the gorge itself had closed over our heads.

"You're sunk," Max said despairingly, and stalked off behind me. "Some Grand Tutor."

The party on the opposite shore had made a little fire, towards which I saw the brown-haired beauty turn at last and go. I was enough myself now to start to wonder at what had possessed me, and at its import for my claim to Grand-Tutorhood. When I heard a new cry from Max behind me and a pebbly rush of footsteps at my back, my first thought was that he feared I might yet wade out in pursuit, as G. Herrold had done. I made to turn and reassure him that the spell was broken—but found myself seized from behind by a strength many times my keeper's. Nay, I was swept off my feet by mighty arms, lifted into the air, and borne a-kicking to the water's edge! I joined my alarums to Max's, flailed and laid about me with my stick till it flew from my hand. I had been fetched already some meters into the stream before I noticed that the arms about my middle were black ones; my struggles then disclosed my assailant to be wrapperless—more I could not see—and for an instant my heart thrilled: G. Herrold was it then, not drowned after all? Or was his ghost come back to wrestle as of old, or fetch me over to our hearts' desire, or—fearful thought!—drag me under with him?

This last seemed likeliest, once my conscience had proposed it; not only did it match the tales I'd read of spookly retribution, but in fact I fell or was flung now into the water,

and found myself fighting the current as well as my attacker.
I managed once to cry G. Herrold's name, and heard a grunting reply before my ears and mouth filled up with water.
Then I had no time to care what had leaped me: I fought for
air and footholds, struggling upstream against his clutch as he
strove to pull me down, and always, despite my best efforts,
working out to deeper water—until at length the rapids took
my legs from under me and fetched me thump against my
adversary. In a whole panic, strangling and spitting, I clambered on him as upon a black boulder, not to drown; in only
a moment I had climbed to his shoulders and got my legs
round his neck. Whereupon a remarkable change came over
him: instead of flinging me off or ducking me under, he
gripped my ankles, and giving over the assault, struck out
purposefully and midstreamwards.

Now I had time to hear Max crying behind us, "Yi yi yi!"
while from the shore ahead, where she flickered in the firelight, the bridge-girl resumed her call. And if it *was* G. Herrold's ghost who bore me, death had worked alterations on
him: the head I clutched was bald instead of woolly, he had
grown a muscled paunch, and in general his body was huger
and more gross. Then I heard him respond with his curious
noise to the girl's cry "Croaker," and it struck me he *did*
rather croak than grunt. I addressed him myself in that wise:
sure enough, his grip tightened on my ankles, and he seemed
to nod his head as he croaked acknowledgment. But all the
while we were getting in deeper, until now the water rushed
chest-high on him; little use learning his name if the brute
meant to drown us after all.

"Gee-*up*, Croaker!" I therefore commanded, pounding on
his skull for emphasis. "This way, flunk you!" I endeavored
by grasping his ears to turn his head upstream; if I couldn't
face him round I hoped at least to work him up towards the
bridge-piles, where with luck I might scramble free of him
and wait for rescue. But the white-smocked Siren (how I
loathed and feared her now, and saw the truth—too late as
always—of Max's warning!) she *would* call him to her,
would bare again her firelit shame, which caught Croaker's
eye as it had G. Herrold's and my own, and brought helms-
manship to naught. In a bitter clear flash I saw the source
and pattern of my ruin: this it was had lost me Lady Creamhair, else my friend; the same had brought me to slaughter
Redfearn's Tom and smite dear Max! A wretched hanker was

my curse and flunking—as doubtless my enemies had seen at once. What need of troll or dragon to undo me? Only hire some lady co-ed to hoist her shift, and for what's poor sake I'd spoilt every decent bond with my fellow creatures— abused, assaulted, killed—I could be counted upon to forfeit not only my misbegotten life but the claim and mission of Grand-Tutorhood. The whole of studentdom might languish unCommencèd, even EAT itself alive, for all I'd ever put by prurience on principle's behalf!

I could have wept for anger at myself. Indeed, tears came to my eyes, or else waterdrops from my dunking; in any case I rubbed them away, not to blur the image of my downfall thrusting on the shore. And I let go with Croaker's ears all hope of saving myself. No longer fighting either him, the river, or ruinous desire, I let them take me where they would. We plunged into a central stretch much deeper than any the men in yellow could have forded: for some moments my bearer was submerged entirely, and for a dreadful instant I felt us floating free—but I wouldn't hold my breath or even try to kick loose of him. And so far from commending my mind *in extremis* to the Founder, I gave self-spiteful lust its head and shouted, weeping, to the wench on the foreshore, "Bye-bye, ma'am! It was good to see you!"

Those were meant to be my last words on this campus. No sooner had I uttered them, however, than I felt Croaker's feet strike bottom again, and, using the current to aid him, he soon got his head out on the downstream side of the deep. It became evident then that he had no mind to drown me after all; he had meant from the first to ferry me across, and by struggling against him I'd only made the task more difficult. Now we fairly raced along: there were fewer rocks on this farther reach, and the bottom seemed more firm; instead of opposing the current, which would surely have upset him, Croaker merely warped shorewards at a modest angle as it swept us with it. Very shortly we reached shallow water; still holding me atop him he waded ashore and trotted up to where his summoner awaited.

But an odd change seemed to come over her as we approached. No longer exposing herself, she stood demurely, even apprehensively, near the circle of yellow-robed men, who remained as oblivious to her and to us (their eyes in fact closed) as if we'd not been there. I could see her face now, large-eyed and nervous; when Croaker let go a plainly rutting croak she retreated a step or two towards the fire—despite herself, so it seemed to me—and I understood she was afraid. Of what, and why, after such provocation on her part, I couldn't imagine, unless it was that she'd never meant us to reach the shore.

Croaker's own intentions were clear: already at ten meters' distance he'd released my ankles and was reaching out for her.

"He'll stop if you tell him!" the girl cried suddenly. But at that moment he broke into a sprint, and I tumbled off his shoulders onto the sand, starting the foreseam of my wrapper.

I scrambled to my knees and shouted, "Stop, Croaker!" But the Siren was mistaken, my command went unheeded, and dearly she paid for her misjudgment if she had counted on my word to save her. Yet it was most strange, for she neither fled nor fought, as Lady Creamhair had. She groaned when the great fellow beached her, and turned her face from his slavering—but herself drew up her shift, and *dutifully,* as it seemed, raised knees to his unimaginable tup!

I stood perplexed beside them—on all fours, for want of my stick. Had she not been the death of G. Herrold, and meant to have been mine as well? Oughtn't I to rejoice in her downfall, whom my foes had set to be the instrument of mine? But when she looked to me in dumb appeal from beneath her ravisher (at the same time clasping him round the neck!), I did my best after all to drag him off her. In vain, of course; he was unbudgeable. Even as I tugged at his arm—huge and hard as a locust post—he struck his mark with a shock that sent one white sandal flying.

Angrily I shouted at the men in yellow to help me; as well apply to the rocks of the shore! I sprang onto Croaker's back, tried to throttle him, pounded at his head. The girl's eyes closed; distinctly I saw tears in their corners, for my face was as near now as Croaker's, and I hove willy-nilly with his heaving. Even so, when she bit my right arm (thinking I'm sure to bite Croaker's) I couldn't judge whether it was protest, pain, or passion in her teeth. In a trice the rape was done: the brute fell spent atop her and we three lay in a stillèd heap. Without opening her eyes, the girl said, "He'll get up now if you tell him. But stay on his back."

I did as bid, amazed, only climbing to a steadier perch on his shoulders as, sure enough, Croaker came off her and squatted torpid, blinking. The girl got up with a shudder and brushed the sand from her shift. Clearly she was frightened no longer, only shocked; she drew her hair back from her eyes and began to fasten it with pins. I rubbed the bite on my wrist.

"Sorry I couldn't stop him, ma'am."

She shook her head. "You couldn't help it." And speaking sadly around the hairpins which she took one by one from between her lips, she explained that the brute called Croaker was a more or less uneducated student from one of the newly established colleges in dark Frumentius, visiting New Tammany under an official exchange program: as such he was immune to arrest, however contrary to West Campus law the customs of his native college or his personal behavior; the most his embarrassed hosts could do (not wanting for diplomatic reasons to offend the Frumentians by asking for his recall) was try to channel and appease his appetites. The task had turned out to be not difficult after all: the roommate assigned to him, happening to be paralytic, had one day tried riding pick-a-back to class on his unruly fellow, and discovered that with someone thus mounted on his shoulders Croaker was almost entirely governable. Things had gone well enough for some terms thereafter; indeed, the two had come quite to depend on each other—Croaker on his roommate for guidance and instruction, the roommate on Croaker for transport and menial services—until just a day or two since, when a third party had persuaded each to try to do without the other. It may have been that the interloper's motives were sincere (though the girl seemed not convinced of it); in any case the outcome was unfortunate. The roommate, Dr. Eierkopf—no need to say I started at her mention of this name!—languished in his quarters, afflicted with migraine and unable to attend his simplest needs, while Croaker, after assaulting two co-eds, a campus policeman, and a prize poodle belonging to the Chancellor's aunt, and eating raw three gibbons from the Department of Psychology, had disappeared into the forest, where it was feared he might wreak further outrage on undergraduates, among whom the woods were a popular trysting-place, or be shot in self-defense by some Forestry Ranger, to the Administration's embarrassment.

As she spoke of these things (more briefly and brokenly than I do here), the girl actually patted Croaker's head, evok-

ing from him a guttural kind of purr. "Look, he's tame as
can *be* with you on his back. I think he mistook you for his
master when he noticed your limp. Poor thing, they mustn't
hurt him, he doesn't *know* he's doing wrong."

I observed a ring upon one finger of her patting-hand and
strove to recall what I had read of human marriage.

"Beg pardon, ma'am," I asked: "Is Croaker your husband?"

She put the same hand to her mouth and laughed—strange
in one so roundly raped—then from her merry eyes more
tears came, though she smiled still. "What an idea! My husband is Maurice Stoker."

The name conveyed nothing to me—remarking which fact,
she looked at me curiously, seeming to see for the first time
my wrapper and beard. She was more beautiful by far than
Chickie; just the image, in fact, of those sweet distressèd
co-eds in the *Tales,* the illustrations whereof had formed my
notions of human beauty. My heart stirred. To her inquiry,
was I not an exchange student myself, from some foreign college, I began to reply that I was George, Grand Tutor to the
Western Campus, formerly known as Billy Bocksfuss the
Goat-Boy—but I remembered as I spoke that she was the
agent of my enemies, and my voice grew stern.

"You know who I am without my telling you, Siren! You
thought you could drown me like G. Herrold, so I'd never
reach New Tammany—"

"Your poor friend!" she broke in. "Why *did* he wade out
so far?" She reached out to touch me, but I snatched back
my arm. "Oh dear, you're bleeding!"

Indeed, her teeth had broken the skin. "It's all right," I
told her.

"It's *not,* either. Let me put something on it. I'm a nurse."

My wrist was bleeding more than I'd thought. Without ado
the girl tore a strip from the hem of her shift—which was
anyhow ruined from Croaker's assault—and having dipped it
in the cold stream, commenced to wrap an expert bandage.

"I'm so sorry about this," she said. "Even when I *hate*
what's happening, like a while ago—I have to bite!" She
turned her dark eyes seriously up to me. "Do you think that's
immoral? It worries me sometimes."

I answered frankly that I didn't know what to think—
about the love-bite, the monstrous equivocal rape, her behavior on the bridge, G. Herrold's drowning, or any other of the

evening's surprises—not least among which was her present
calm. Why did she care about my bleeding arm, since she'd
been sent to drown me? Why had she invited Croaker so,
seeing she'd not relished the consequences: pled with me to
save her, wept at his attack, and yet clasped to him all the
brutal while? Whatever would her husband say (for I could
not suppose such behavior was typical in marriage)? And
finally, how on campus could such a splendid fair student
lady girl lend herself to the forces of darkness, and turn her
Founder-given charms to the end of flunking me, who meant
to pass all studentdom? For never (here I waxed eloquent as
I could in my ignorance of the forms of human compliment),
never had such beauty been, not even in the goat-barn's fair-
est: Hedda of the Speckled Teats could boast no such lim-
pidity of eye, such sharpness of tooth; my own Commencèd
dam Mary Appenzeller, for all her miracle of milk, must
yield in point of beauty to the rose-nippled darlings bared
upon the bridge, whereof the sweet issue (all the preciouser, I
daresaid, for its want of abundance) must be yogurts and
cheeses and fudge of a heartbreaking fineness. Let that of
muscle Lady Creamhair had been stronger, and Chickie of
odor—longer-fleeced too the latter's lap and limbs—such
virtues paled before the black-curled marvel which supply
had beckoned, nay commanded, from over the torrent, so
printing its image upon my soul that I saw it yet—in the pupils of her eyes, in the craters of the moon, in the dark-
cornered flickers of the fire—and heard it calling to me, as it
were, like some nightbird from its nest.

"What a strange way of talking you have!" she said. "I
can't even *follow* you!" Yet she seemed not displeased.
"There, that should do it." She gave a pat to the finished
bandage. "What about your other friend, now? If you take
Croaker up where it's shallower he could bring you both
over. My husband will be along shortly—he's in charge of
the search-party. We can give you a lift to wherever you
were going."

She had by this time so won my trust that I attributed to
Max all my former suspicions. I told her straight out who I
was (she caught her breath at the mention of Max's name,
then explained that of course she had heard of him, and even
recalled being taken by her Uncle Ira to the goat-farm as a
child, to see "the little boy who thought he was a goat"), but
I judged it wiser to say nothing for the present about Grand-

Tutorship or WESCAC's AIM. My intention, I declared, was to matriculate in New Tammany College as soon as I could, and I thanked her for her inadvertent aid in getting me over the river. As for Max's crossing by the same means, however, I doubted his willingness to, inasmuch as he thought her a flunkèd woman bent on luring me, if not to my death, at least to a breach of my virtue. Why else had she so exposed herself on the bridge? What did she think had led G. Herrold over his head, if not those wonders I had just done praising?

As if understanding for the first time, she put her hands to her cheeks: her eyes widened, and she shook her head.

"Is *that* what you thought!" she cried, and put her hand on my arm to halt me. "I'm so *ashamed!*" It took her some moments to overcome her plain mortification. Then she said most earnestly, but scarcely able to look me in the face for embarrassment, "You *mustn't* think those terrible things! If I'd suspected for a *moment* . . . and Dr. Spielman, of all people . . ." She began again, more calmly: "My name is Anastasia Stoker (people call me Stacey) and I'm a nurse in the New Tammany Psych Clinic; that's why I knew about Croaker and Dr. Eierkopf and all. In fact it was my husband—he runs the Power Plant, and he's a very . . . *unusual* man, you'll see—he's the one who talked the Chief Psychiatrist into separating them, for their own good, or for experimental reasons or something, just to see what would happen. I guess that's why I felt *responsible,* in a way, when the trouble started. Those poor girls he attacked, and that dear little poodle, and we didn't know *what* he might do next! We knew he'd gone out towards the river, and Chancellor Rexford was especially worried because a famous Grand Tutor was on his way to the College and was supposed to be somewhere in this neighborhood—"

"So they *did* know ahead of time!"

"Of course: it was in all the papers. Didn't you see it?"

I explained that no newspapers were delivered to the goat-barn, and pressed her for more details, hoping thus to gauge the reception awaiting me at NTC. "Did they say what his name is, or what he looks like? What's he coming to the College for?"

"*Shush,*" she warned merrily, "they might understand English!" She glanced back at the yellow-robed men, who of course paid no heed. "That's Him in the middle: the fat one. The others are Tutees or something. They wouldn't let the

Chancellor send anybody to meet them, and they sit like that most of the time."

I pointed incredulously. "You think *he's* the Grand Tutor? When he wouldn't lift a finger to help you or G. Herrold?"

She wrinkled her brow at my ignorance. "Not *our* Grand Tutor, George! You *have* been in the country, haven't you? He's what they call The Living Sakhyan, from Outer T'ang College or somewhere over there. He's supposed to be descended from the original Sakhyan, and when the Student-Unionists took over His college, Chancellor Rexford invited Him here to tutor the Sakhyan refugees on West Campus. Think what the Student-Unionists would have said if Croaker had attacked Him!"

I could by no means share her alarm at this prospect, but I gathered with some satisfaction that no threat to me was implied by the newspapers she referred to, at least, and no competition of the sort I'd first imagined by the fat chap's being regarded as a species of Grand Tutor. Anastasia went on with her story:

"From what I knew about Croaker, I didn't think they'd ever be able to catch him without hurting him or getting hurt themselves, and in the meantime no telling how many girls he'd bother! Mr. Rexford was so upset at Maurice, he was talking about firing him, and I thought the best way to save the situation was to lure Croaker back somehow to Dr. Eierkopf. But Maurice (that's my husband) said the only way to do that would be to line up a lot of co-eds between the woods and Dr. Eierkopf's room—he's always saying naughty things. Anyway I knew Croaker liked me all right: every time they came by the Clinic he used to sort of purr, you know, like a friendly bear. It was so cute, and I don't believe there was anything *bad* in it at all, the way Maurice pretended; I'd just let him touch me or lick my hand or something, and then Dr. Eierkopf could usually move him along without any more bother . . .

"So I came along with the search party and got Maurice to let me come out on the bridge while they waited out of sight. I thought if Croaker was anywhere in the gorge he'd see me there and come when I called, and then maybe I could calm him down or draw him back to where the others were—they have something to put him to sleep with. Maurice said silly things the way he always does, about my knowing what would happen and actually wanting it to; but I learned a long time ago not to mind what *he* says. Besides, if it turned out I couldn't control Croaker, or the men didn't get there in time, it didn't seem to me it could be much worse than some other things I'd been through, and as long as it was me it wouldn't be some poor co-ed ruined for life." Her tone was matter-of-fact, but she clutched her arms across her breasts and sighed. "Which is how it turned out."

Where her husband and the others had got to she didn't know, unless mistaking G. Herrold for Croaker (as she herself had done at first) and seeing him drown, they had judged the danger past and gone to find the body. Certainly she did not believe that any man, even one so unusual as her husband, would stand idly by and see a woman assaulted—the men in yellow she expected, of course, and forgave, they being Commencèd Graduates. A trifle uncomfortably I praised her large-mindedness and courage, and she in turn thanked the Founder for my chance presence in the gorge, which if it had not spared her own awful raping after all, had at least spared her more, or worse. As she spoke, distressed by the memory, she bent her forehead to my chest (where cold water still dripped from the fleece) and I was moved to pat her hair to comfort her. Silky to the touch it was, the nape beneath finely downed! But her closeness stirred Croaker under me, and she quickly stepped back, remarking only that if she had the sodium pentathol herself I wouldn't need to keep my perch.

She concluded her tale by pleading with me not to imagine, as her husband surely would, that anything but concern for the safety of others had prompted her behavior. Ordinarily, for example, though a married woman and a registered nurse, she would have been far too modest to do more than call from the bridge. But even as G. Herrold had waded towards her she had spied Croaker leaping through the trees behind us, and fearing he might attack us she had put by shame and shift to make the urgenter summons. I asked her whether her husband wouldn't be very much upset at what had happened to her.

"Maurice upset? You mean angry, or jealous?" She shook her head ruefully. "Not him! He'll be unpleasant, but not upset. He's not like other men."

Indeed, I thought, he must not be. Anastasia went then to build up the fire for "The Living Sakhyan," who for all he would tend it himself or acknowledge her aid, had as well been dead. Very much moved, I went off with Croaker—uncertainly at first, then with more confidence as I learned how readily he responded to command now his lust was appeased. We crossed the stream easily above the bridge, where it was only waist-deep, and retrieved Max, whose alarm I quieted with some difficulty. He had of course witnessed the unhappy scene across the river, at first in despair, then in horror, at last in anxious wonder. But when I explained who Croaker was, and who were the bridge-girl and the men in yellow, and repeated Anastasia's account of her self-sacrifice for our sakes, he was more moved to pity even than I.

"That Maurice Stoker," he said bitterly, "I know him, all right. He's a real Dean o' Flunks." With the aid of my walking stick (which Max had retrieved) I'd made Croaker understand that he was to carry my advisor in his arms, as G. Herrold had done earlier in the day, and the three of us proceeded thus to make our final crossing. To what I'd heard from Anastasia, Max added that Maurice Stoker was reputed to be a half-brother to the present Chancellor, but had been disowned by the Rexford family, a worthy and distinguished one, as well as expelled from New Tammany College, many years previously, for advocating the violent overthrow of every administration between the two Campus Riots. A militant anti-Founderist and anti-Finalist, and a notorious intriguer in varsity affairs, he was reputed to have played a role in the great Nikolayan Revolution, in the rise of the Bonifacist *Reichskanzler,* and in terrorist movements in virtually every quadrangle of the University. Wherever disorder was, Maurice Stoker seemed to be also, whether to assist in an anti-administration riot (even against men who themselves owed their offices to his plotting) or to encourage with his presence so trifling a disturbance as the ritual spring panty-raids on co-ed dormitories in NTC. Yet no one, it seemed, understood the management of the great West-Campus Power Plant as he did, or the multifarious operations of Main Detention—the bureau in charge of counterintelligence as well as the detection and punishment of domestic miscreants and course-failers. Indeed, among the causes of Max's disenchantment with political life was the fact that even the best-intentioned, most high-minded administrators (including young Lucius Rexford himself, whom Max rather admired) seemed unable to do without Maurice Stoker; fear and despise him as they might, all came at last to terms with him; in the present administration as in its predecessor, though he was seldom to be seen on New Tammany's Great Mall, he retained his offices at the Power Plant to the north and Main Detention to the south.

"Imagine a nice girl married to such a man!" Max concluded—we were almost across the river by this time, and I pointed Croaker downstream towards the fire. "It almost wonders me whether we should trust her."

"You won't wonder when you see her," I assured him.

"Well, I saw right much of her already. And you too— which you shouldn't have enjoyed it like you did." However, he added to my relief, during his anxious half-hour alone on the beach he had reviewed my behavior in the light of comparative cyclology and decided that while yielding to such temptations would in his opinion disqualify me for Grand-Tutorhood, simply being tempted in itself did not, at least not necessarily: Laertides, after all, had deliberately attended the sweet Sirens' singing and even commanded his crew to change course from their true destination and head for the rocks. The difference between us, which must caution me for the future, was that Laertides, being properly forewarned, had seen to it both that his freedom of action would be suspended and that his commands would be ignored during his temporary madness, his relapse from herohood.

"It's a kind of insurance," Max declared. "Nobody can be a hero every minute of every day; even Enos Enoch must've had times when He wished He was just another freshman, He wouldn't have to get Himself nailed up. What's important is to see you can slip, and make sure nobody pays attention when you say *'Pfui* on Commencement!' If you won't stop up your ears and eyes, you got to tie yourself to the mast like Laertides did, and tell me not to mind your crazy talk." The self-binding, he explained, was figurative: I must let *him* be my Mast as well as my forewarner and tie myself to him with the Rope of a solemn vow, to submit to his restraining whenever I was tempted to compromise my difficult mission. There occurred to me certain objections—questions, really, of a theoretical nature—to what he said: it was easy enough for *us* to maintain, for example, that Laertides' Siren-chasing moods were the improper ones and his home-striving moods the proper, inasmuch as we saw both from the poet's perspective, and the choice moreover was inherent in the premise of the fable. What would have kept a real Laertides, I wondered, from telling himself that the Sirens' voice was actually his wife's, or that only now, having heard them, did he realize that *their* rock, and not the rocky coast of home, was his true destination? Other tales there were in which the hero's conception of his task was not so insusceptible to doubt as Laertides' had been—but it so relieved me not to be scolded for the lust that had possessed me (and not to have to worry about it further myself), I saved these reservations for some future time.

"Tell this ape he should put me down now," Max requested. "*Ach,* what a pair of roommates, Eblis Eierkopf and this one!"

I did so, gratified at the promptness with which Croaker heeded the pointing of my stick. It seemed to control him better than either word-commands or pressure of the heels: a mild whack athwart his hip with it, for instance, even served to check his jumping up and down when Anastasia came to meet us, her fine eyes raised uncertainly to mine. I remarked that she was alone, The Living Sakhyan and his party having gone their way.

"Mrs. Stoker," I said (recalling how such things were done in an etiquette book Lady Creamhair once had fed to me): "Max Spielman, my advisor."

"How d'you do," Anastasia murmured, and Max nodded shortly. I attributed the coolness in her voice to embarrassment, and so assured her that Max now understood and was grateful for her noble intentions, held her in no way responsible for G. Herrold's drowning, and sympathized with her for what she had suffered.

"I'll speak for myself," Max interrupted. "Look me in the eyes once, young lady." She did so, still maintaining her odd reserve. "This fellow here has got a job to do, more important and dangerous than any other job on campus; it's just what Maurice Stoker would try to keep him from doing. So: did you do what you did to save us from Croaker, or did your husband send you out here to stop this young man? Tell me the truth—it wouldn't surprise me if he'd set Croaker on us too, and that whole story about Eierkopf was a lie."

The girl did not answer at once; she bit her lower lip and seemed about to cry.

"Don't scold her so, Max! She's just had bad things happen to her."

"Dear girl," Max said more gently, "if you really been

raped I kiss your feet and beg your pardon. *Passèd are the raped*, like it says in the Seminar-on-the-Hill. But it's not easy to trust a person that lives with Maurice Stoker."

"You don't *understand* him," Anastasia said distractedly; she put her hand to her forehead. "I think I've got to sit down. It's hard to know what to say after all I've heard about you . . ."

"Heard?" Max cried. *"Ja* sure, from that Dean o' Flunks husband of yours!"

She shook her head, still standing. "From my mother, Dr. Spielman! And from Uncle Ira, and Grandpa Reg!"

"What's this?" Now Max was wide-eyed, and the girl seemed on the verge of swooning. He stepped to steady her; she hid her face in his shoulder. "Young lady, who are you?"

Her voice came muffled from his fleece. "My name used to be Stacey Hector. I'm Virginia Hector's daughter . . and I guess . . . yours too."

4.

Having made this declaration, Anastasia lost her voice entirely and wept into Max's wrapper, while my advisor, shaking his head from side to side, could say only, "Yi yi yi yi!" and pat her hair. I suggested we move to the abandoned fire, and went astride Croaker to fetch more sticks against the night-chill. Max was protesting, when I returned, that while he had indeed loved Miss Virginia R. Hector extremely, he was innocent of her impregnation and could not understand why she had persisted in accusing him. To which Anastasia replied, it was not her mother who accused him, at least not in recent years; her mother had alas gone somewhat out of her senses and declared by turns that she had never been pregnant at all; that she *had* been pregnant but by no mortal man in the University; that Anastasia was no child of hers; *etc., etc.*

"It was Uncle Ira and Grandpa Reg who blamed you," she said. "I used to ask them who was this *Max* that Mother talked about when she'd had too much to drink—she used to drink a lot—"

"Yi yi!" Max groaned.

"—and when I was older they told me my father was a bad man named Max Spielman that had deserted my mother and caused a lot of trouble before they fired him. Please don't do that . . ." Max had set himself to kissing her sandals and beating his forehead upon the sand. "I never hated you the way they said I should. I used to wonder what could have made you treat Mother like that, and I decided it must have been something you couldn't help, or you never would have done it. I used to wish I'd meet you, so I could let you know I didn't hate you for anything, and even if you cursed me or hit me, the way people do sometimes, at least you'd have me there to do it to, and it might make you feel better about Mother and me. Maurice is that way, and Uncle Ira used to be too."

"Georgie!" Max cried. "Hear the voice of sweet Commencement!" He then declared to Anastasia, still on his knees before her, that so pass him Founder he was not her father, but the victim of heartbreaking accusations and false charges, the motive whereof he despaired of ever learning. That he nonetheless cursed and reproached himself for not having stood by the woman he loved, understanding (as one with half Anastasia's own loving nature would have, he was certain) that his dear lady's indictments were the fruit of some desperation; he would never forgive himself, he vowed, for not having pled guilty to the false paternity, so sparing Virginia Hector the dismal afflictions it seemed had come upon her, and Anastasia the egregious burden of illegitimacy.

"But it doesn't matter!" Anastasia said. "I forgive you anyway. There's no need to keep saying you're not my father."

"By me there's need! I wish I *was* your poppa, such a girl! But I'm not, I swear it!"

"Then I believe you," the girl said firmly. "Don't go on like that, now." As if he were the child and she the parent, she gathered Max's old head to her breast, which lacking the hard-cupped harness I had noted on Chickie-in-the-buckwheat's, yielded softly to his cheek—and I wished *I* had something to be forgiven for. The effect was admirable: Max soon recomposed himself and set to praising her virtues to me (who needed no persuasion) in a more controlled if no less enthusiastic spirit. He now believed her utterly, he said, and would add to the proofs of my untutored wisdom, and his own too-human fallibility, that I had been drawn strongly to her from the first, and had affirmed her goodness in the face of his skepticism.

"That was sweet of him," she said, and smiled me such a warm smile of gratitude, I wished I truly *had* never doubted her, and been impelled from the first by the sight of her spiritual merits alone. "He tried his best to hold Croaker back, too, but it wasn't any use."

"An atrocity!" Max cried. "The brute ought to be caged up."

But Anastasia protested once again that after all men were what they were, Founder pass them, and animals were what *they* were; Croaker couldn't help himself any more than her husband could, who often did things to her and to others that were misinterpreted as proceeding from a flunkèd nature simply because the deeds themselves were flunkèd. Besides, it pained her to see anything caged, no matter how wild or dangerous—an animal, a criminal, anything . . . Often in the past, she confessed, she had pitied "poor Croaker" for not having a mate equal to his passions—though to be sure she pitied even more their unequal victims: the co-eds, the policeman, the poodle, and the cute little monkeys whose expressions had looked so like wise old men's. But only look at Croaker now, she bade us, how docile and content he was, like a great spoiled child that's had his lollipop at last. How could she, she asked us almost light-heartedly, be aggrieved at her own mistreatment—which albeit hurtsome had not been fatal, after all—when in addition to sparing others the same or worse, it had so plainly done its doer a campus of good?

I was purely touched, and asked her how it came that so gentle a lady girl had wed Maurice Stoker, whom despite her excusing him I took to be a flunkèder brute than Croaker, because more conscious of his ways?

"That's well asked, Georgie," Max approved. "That's asked like a Grand Tutor." And to Anastasia, before she could reply, he professed frankly his belief that I might be no person else than a true Grand Tutor to the Western Campus, destined to rescue studentdom from the tyranny of its own invention. "Don't mock," he cautioned her; "myself I'm a skeptic; I wouldn't say such a thing in a hundred years without plenty good reasons."

But Anastasia was far from mocking; she looked up at me in wonder as Max spoke. "So *that's* it!"

I assumed she meant that she understood now certain earlier remarks and attitudes of mine which must have struck her as mysterious at the time (such as my alarm at her mention that Chancellor Rexford was expecting a Grand Tutor's arrival at any moment). But she drew from the pocket of her shift a small glass phial, which she said had been given her by one of The Living Sakhyan's company as they left the beach, just a short time previously.

"It was the strangest thing," she said to Max—as if scarcely presuming to address me directly. "Here I didn't even think they could talk our *language,* and I swear they hadn't said a word to one another the whole time they were sitting here; but suddenly The Living Sakhyan smiled at me and raised His hand—it was like He'd just come out of his trance—and it made me feel peculiar all over! Then one of His men led me up to the fire—this was while George had come back to get you. And I felt so *funny,* because I didn't know whether they were going to thank me for fixing their fire, or—or *do* something to me, or what. And it didn't seem to *matter,* if you know what I mean, Him being such a great man and all; you can almost *feel* how wise and Commenced He is, and whatever He wanted to do, I have this feeling it was all right, and I'd be flunkèd not to let Him do it . . ." She turned to me, her eyes full of reverence. "But then His helper took out this little bottle and gave it to me, and said it was for you from The Living Sakhyan. 'From ours to yours,' is what he said—and he didn't even speak with an accent! I was so surprised I stood there like a dunce, and didn't think to ask what it was until they'd picked up The Living Sakhyan and were almost gone. Then the man who gave it to me sort of frowned and closed his eyes, as if I was so stupid he couldn't stand to look at me, and he said, 'It's the Disappearing Ink.' I swear that's what he said!"

She held the phial out to me, rather diffidently. "He must have just said that to let me know it was none of my business. There doesn't seem to be anything in it at all, that *I* can see . . ."

I held it up to the firelight, shook it at my ear. It did in fact appear to be empty.

"Do you think—" She touched her fingers to her cheek and

smiled uncertainly at Max. "What I mean, could it have disappeared already?"

Max examined gravely the empty phial and returned it to me. East-Campus Graduates, he pointed out, famously spoke in riddles, and it was by no means unthinkable that The Living Sakhyan, or His disciple, had been making some obscure joke with Anastasia; but whatever the true nature and significance of the gift, he took its presentation as no joke at all, but one more proof of my authenticity.

I myself was not impressed. "Disappearing ink!" I flung the phial down, angered afresh at the revelation that the men in yellow had after all been aware of everything that had happened in the gorge: had understood G. Herrold's plight and Anastasia's, but had suffered the one to drown and the other to be raped without lifting a finger in either's behalf. "Dunce take it!"

"Oh, don't!" Anastasia snatched it up at once from the sand. "Really—excuse me, George, I'm sure you're a *thousand* times brighter than I am, but I really don't think . . ." She blushed, "Would it be all right if I kept it for you? In case you change your mind?"

"That might be smart, Georgie," Max agreed. "These things mean more than they seem to, sometimes. I'd like to have time to think it over before you throw it away."

I shrugged. "You're the advisor." Anastasia gratefully returned the phial to her pocket, as if it were a precious gem, and I pressed her again to account for her marriage to the notorious Stoker, which it seemed to me she had been pleased to digress from explaining. My tone was even a bit peremptory, for I was on the one hand impressed by her clearly self-sacrificial behavior with Croaker, her husband, Max, The Living Sakhyan, and myself, and on the other hand vaguely uneasy about it: it disturbed me to see her equally submissive to everyone, the flunkèd as well as the not. Yet sincere as this concern of mine was (which it made me feel quite Grand-Tutorish to express), in the main I was simply flattered by the novelty of being stood in awe of, especially by that lovely creature—so ready to obey, one could not resist commanding her! Out of all these feelings I demanded to know whether she had wed of her free will or been abducted like the captive brides of old, in which latter case I intended by some means to slay her captor and set her at liberty.

"Oh, you couldn't do *that!*" she said—amused, alarmed,

and pleased at once, as it seemed to me. "I mean, I guess you *could,* if you're a Grand Tutor, but—"

"It's not your business to start slaying people," Max told me; "what you want to do is keep them from slaying each other. Besides, you got no kind of weapons, thank the Founder, and Maurice Stoker's got his own private Riot Squad."

It occurred to me to point out to him that my stick had once been deadly tool enough, and to argue that it was not without good precedent I contemplated using it again: Enos Enoch Himself had flung the Business Administration concessionaires bodily from Founder's Hall, and had declared to His protégés that He came to them not with diplomas but with a birch-rod, armed Tutors always prevailing where unarmed ones failed. But Anastasia forestalled me by protesting that while she had not exactly *volunteered* to marry Stoker, she had willingly assented to the match at the time of its arrangement by her guardian, Ira Hector, and further that she would not dream of deserting one who needed her so absolutely as did her husband—however violently he himself denied that need.

"I knew it!" Max cried out. "A pact between the meanest mind on campus and the flunkèdest!" Ira Hector, he reminded me, was the wealthy and infamously selfish older brother of the former chancellor of NTC; from humble beginnings as a used-book peddler he had risen to his present position as head of a vast informational empire, controlling the manufacture and distribution of virtually every reference-volume published in the West-Campus colleges. Ready to line his pockets at anyone's expense, he was despised and catered to by liberals and conservatives alike (though always closer in spirit to the latter); while he preached the virtues of free research, what he practiced was the stifling of competition, the freedom of the clever to oppress the ignorant and stupid. Yet so enormous was his wealth and so ubiquitous his influence, every New Tammany chancellor had to come to terms with him; and Max himself, how vehemently soever he had used to rail in the Senate against Ira Hector's unprincipled monopolies and graft, was obliged to admit that they were perhaps the necessary evils of Bourgeois-Liberal Studentism, his own philosophy. As was the case with Maurice Stoker too, however, the fact that Ira Hector was indispensable made him in Max's view no less a wretch; as he put it (reversing a much-quoted remark of Ira Hector's own): one might have to lick his boots, but needn't praise the flavor.

"Now, you're too hard on Uncle Ira," Anastasia chided. "You must try to understand him."

Max sniffed, but it was remarkable how the girl calmed his indignation with a pat on the knee. "So he's got a heart of gold," he complained with a smile. "Like Dean Midas he has!"

"He's more generous than you think," Anastasia said. "But he's so afraid somebody will make fun of it, or take advantage of him, he wouldn't admit it for the campus."

"He don't have to," said Max. "He owns the campus already."

But she pointed out with spirit that her own rearing in the rich man's house was proof enough that his selfishness was not complete. "He didn't *have* to take me in. Grandpa Reg said Mother was so upset when I was born, she wasn't able to take care of me, and he sent me to the Lying-In Hospital for Unwed Co-eds—which by the way Uncle Ira built with his own money . . ."

Max asked indignantly why Chancellor Hector had not staffed his own house with nurses, which he could easily have afforded to do, and thus spared both Virginia Hector and Anastasia a disgraceful connection with the New Tammany Lying-In.

"He wanted to," she replied. "But Mother wasn't herself, you know . . . I guess I reminded her of so many unhappy things, she couldn't bear to have me in the house, and of course she knew they'd take care of me in the hospital. I don't hold it against her that she felt that way: it must have been a bad time for her, having been Miss University and all and then being jilted and left pregnant . . . Oh dear: I didn't mean it *that* way!"

Max closed his eyes, shook his head, and waved away her apology.

"Anyhow it was only for a few weeks," Anastasia went on. "Then Uncle Ira (actually he's *Mother's* uncle) had a nursery fixed up in his house, and that's where I was raised. It was a wonderful childhood, and I was terribly grateful to him when I was old enough to understand all he'd done for me. And Mother, you know, she wasn't *always* upset: lots of times she'd come to visit, or take me out somewhere. Even when she'd have her spells where she'd say I was no daughter of hers, we were still friends."

Seeing the pain in Max's countenance, she changed the subject brightly: "As for Uncle Ira, he was sweet as could be! Not a *bit* like you think! I didn't see him very much, he's so busy all the time, and he pretends to be such an old bear: but I'd slip into his study and climb up on his lap and kiss him, or hold my hands over his eyes—even when I was big I used to do it—and he'd have to laugh and kiss me before I'd go away. And every night he'd come up to make sure I got my bath, and tuck in my covers—he never would let the nurse do it. And talk about *careful,* when I was old enough to go out with boys! He was an orphan himself, you know, and grew up practically on the streets; he told me his mother was taken advantage of by a bad man who talked her into leaving Grandpa Reg and him when they were kids, and he had to take care of Grandpa Reg when he was just a little boy himself, selling old books off a pushcart on the Mall. I guess he'd seen so many bad things in his life, especially young girls being taken advantage of—anyhow he wouldn't let me go out with boys at all. It wasn't he didn't trust *me;* it was the boys he didn't trust, even the nice ones. He said he knew what it was they were after, whether *they* knew it or not, and even if they'd never *thought* of trying to take advantage of me, they'd think of it soon enough when I was alone with them. Stupid me, I hardly knew what a boy *was,* much less what Uncle Ira was talking about; I used to come in and perch on his lap and pester the poor man to *death,* to tell me what was so awful that the boys would do. He'd try to put me off, and tell me I was getting too big to sit on his lap like that; but I wouldn't take no for an answer . . ."

"I hate this," Max said.

"I know what you're thinking; just what Maurice says. But you've got to remember he was a lonely old man, and worried to *death* that the same thing would happen to me that had happened to his mother and his niece and all those girls in his hospital. And even if it *wasn't* completely innocent, I'm sure *he* thought it was; he was probably fooling himself the way he said those nice boys were, that he drove away from the house when they tried to make dates with me. If I'd had a *grain* of sense I'd have thought of some better way to handle him, without hurting his feelings; but I was so dumb, and *naturally* I was curious, too, when he tried to show me what was what."

Here I interrupted to protest that I didn't understand what was being alluded to, and thus had no way of judging how it bore upon the question of her marriage. Anastasia looked at me curiously, and Max reminded her that I too had been raised in isolation from normal campus family life, if not exactly in the same ignorance of natural facts.

"But don't tell us what's none of our business," he added; "it was just about you and Stoker we wondered."

I was ready to protest that I regarded it as quite my business (without knowing exactly why) to right or avenge any wrongs done to those whom I—well, *esteemed*—as I esteemed Max himself, and had vowed to clear his name. But the protest was unnecessary; Anastasia declared she felt obliged to speak in more frank detail than normally one might: first, because we might else misjudge her Uncle Ira's motives; second, because these incidents from her early youth were not unrelated to her subsequent marriage; and third, because if I was indeed a Grand Tutor, it was not hers to decide what ought to be told me and what ought not, but rather to open her heart trustingly and completely as she did in her nightly petitions to the Founder, without whose forgiving comfort and understanding she would long since have perished under the burden of misconstruction put upon her actions by her husband and others. The memory of these same misconstructions, presumably, brought tears to her eyes: I could not imagine a face more piteously appealing.

"I never *mean* to hurt anybody!" she said. "It says in the Scroll that Love is the Founder, and all I ever mean to do is *help* people, like in the Infirmary and the Psych Clinic. How can you help them except to find out what it is they need and then give it to them, if you have it? But it always seems to do damage somehow, when *I* do it!"

"Now *pfui* on that," Max consoled her, and I too declared it unthinkable that so generous a heart could do other than good.

"Well, take that time in Uncle Ira's study . . ." She was clearly encouraged by our words, though her expression remained doubting. "He said in a way he thought of me as his daughter and in a way he didn't, and I naturally supposed he meant because he was really my great-uncle instead of my father. So when he started explaining what it was the boys

wanted, there was no reason to think he wasn't just trying to
help me. I *still* think he was; I *know* he was, even later on!
He'd been working on some accounts that night, as usual,
and there were double-entry ledger-sheets spread on his desk;
when he drew some pictures on them for me, to show me
what he was talking about, I was a little upset, but he had to
do *something* like that because I was so stupid. But he
couldn't draw right, he said so himself: the people in the pictures had the funniest expressions on their faces! I told him if
his drawing of the girl's parts was right, then there must be
something wrong with mine, the proportions were all different; but I said I was pretty sure *mine* must be okay because they were just like Miss Fine's, my language-tutor's,
and when Miss Fine and I used to play with each other she
always said mine were the nicest she'd ever seen."

Though her tone remained glib as a child's, Anastasia
blushed furiously. Max also, but not I, though my blood
pulsed.

"You see how *dumb* I was! I was going to show him then
and there to make sure, in case Miss Fine had just been being
polite, and I told him I couldn't for the life of me see why he
was so angry at her, when my other tutors and governesses
and maids had all done and said the same kind of things. I
said if he promised not to be angry with Miss Fine I'd teach
him all the games I'd learned to play—I liked him better than
Miss Fine anyway, because she would bite sometimes; what's
more he had whiskers, and I was sure they'd be fun—but I
wasn't certain about men, he'd have to show me . . . He
couldn't talk for a while: I thought he was shy, the way some
of the maids were the first time I'd ask if I could play with
them; I never dreamed what I was *doing* to the man. I even
touched him . . ."

"Yi."

"*Well,*" Anastasia said, "to make a long story short, he
gave me a good spanking, big as I was, and fired all the tutors
and maids except an old cook and housekeeper who weren't
any fun to play with anyhow. After that he wouldn't trust
anybody to teach me unless he was in the room too, and
every night he'd lecture to me in his study about how flunkèd
my tutors and maids had been. I'd agree, and try hard to believe it, but I just couldn't understand what was wrong with
something so nice."

"I know what you mean!" I exclaimed, thinking of my

own difficulties with moral education. "I'm *still* not sure I understand!"

Her eyes were bright and yet wondering, as if she was pleased by my words but not certain she wasn't being baited.

"After all," she said, "it wasn't from some *book* I learned to do what I'd been doing, but from my cats and dogs and my teachers, so that it not only seemed like the naturalest thing in the University for people to take their clothes off and have fun with each other, but the *passèdest* thing, too, especially if the other person was old or not pretty or needed something very badly, and you pleased them so much. The first teacher I ever had explained that to me, and I loved her such a lot I guess I never could get her idea out of my head. She was the sweetest lady!"

"Not so young, I bet," Max ventured, and Anastasia confirmed his suspicion with a merry smile, though her eyes still shone with the earlier tears.

"Well, right or wrong, I couldn't feel ashamed of what I'd done, even though I was ashamed at having done something I *should* be ashamed of—you see the difference, don't you, George?" I nodded, hoping I did. "But at least I saw how I'd upset Uncle Ira, so I pretended to feel the same as he did about it. I was only sixteen or so when this happened with Uncle Ira, but I guess I'd become sort of an expert at guessing what people needed, sometimes even before they guessed it themselves; and being brought up the way I was, I couldn't help trying to please them, whether I understood what I was doing or not. If I'd been allowed to go out with any of those nice boys, I'd have seduced them before they ever got their nerve up to kiss me, and probably I'd've thought I was a real Graduate for doing it!"

This intuition, she went on, plainly showed her that while Ira Hector was honestly horrified by her behavior, he also relished chastizing her for it. In particular, she observed, it had done him a campus of good to administer that spanking: time and again he alluded to it; teased or threatened her, according to his mood, with the prospect of another, and never failed, when he kissed her good-night, to swat her playfully athwart the haunches "in case she thought he couldn't do it again if he had to." Finally one day when he was in a rage over political reverses (young Lucius Rexford, the chancellor-to-be, had just won his party's nomination and had pledged to break up the reference-book monopoly if and when he defeated the incumbent Reginald Hector in the final elections), she had deliberately perched on his lap and asked permission to attend the next Freshman Cotillion, knowing clearly what his reaction would be: quite as she had foreseen, his wrath leaped its bounds; with an oath he turned her over his knee (a feat he never could have managed without her cooperation), snatched up a ruler from his desk, and bestowed on her backside a swinging admonishment. Nay further, it being evening and she forewarned of his ill humor, she had donned for the occasion a summer night-dress which scarcely covered her at all, so that it was fetching flesh he smote, more often than not, until he was winded and could smite no more. Whereupon, marvelous to relate, he found his wrath spent with his strength: he begged her pardon, wept for what must surely have been the first time in his life, and astonished her utterly by granting her request. Moreover, he was quoted next day in the NTC newspapers as believing Lucky Rexford to be "not near as close to Student-Unionism as most so-called liberals are."

Needless to say, Anastasia thanked her guardian profusely for having chastised her, declaring that a good old-fashioned hiding was just what today's adolescents required now and then to confirm in them the old-fashioned virtues; the two went hand-in-hand, as it were, and she dearly hoped that whenever her behavior displeased him he would once more put her straight. He did, once a week at least, for a year or so thereafter, nor ever remarked, so far as she could tell, that her willfulest days coincided with his most irascible. He became, in consequence, less fearsome than his oldest subordinate could recall having known him, and showered privileges upon his ward—the more readily as she feigned herself loath to accept them . . .

"The truth was," she said with a sigh, "all I had to do, if a boy wanted to be alone with me after that, was ask Uncle Ira to please not leave us alone, and he'd say, 'Nonsense, I trust you absolutely—any girl who'd ask to be spanked just for dreaming a naughty dream!' (I used to do that.) So he'd leave us alone together, and of course I'd let the boy do whatever he pleased—it was just as nice as with girls, if not nicer, and the dear things were *so* surprised and grateful; it would almost make me cry to see how happy I could make them! Then afterwards Uncle Ira would want to know if anything had happened, and I'd blush and say that the boy had kissed me three times, or touched my breast when I wasn't watching out. And if I saw he needed cheering up himself, I'd start to cry and say I had to admit it had been kind of exciting, after all, and did it flunk me forever to have such a feeling? And he'd say, 'No, my dear, that's perfectly natural, and the Founder doesn't flunk you for feelings; it's what you *do* that counts. But the danger,' he'd say, 'is that you won't be able to keep your actions separate from your feelings.' And I'd kiss him and say, 'You're right, Uncle Ira: I need discipline!' Then out would come the ruler . . ."

"By George!" I cried. "Do you know what I think? I think he *enjoyed* spanking you!"

There was a pause; Max allowed dryly that there might well be something to what I said. Anastasia looked perplexed from me to him, and he explained to her in an earnest tone that an examination of the sayings of Grand Tutors would reveal the quality of their insights to be not so much a complex subtlety as a profound and transcendently powerful *simplicity*, which the flunkèd sophistication of modern intelligences might confused with naïveté.

"*I* would've," she admitted. "That shows how naïve *I* am."

She went on with her story: "It was about this time that Maurice Stoker began coming to the house to see Uncle Ira—it was during the election campaign and just after, when Grandpa Reg had been defeated, and everybody was wondering what would happen to Uncle Ira's business. I thought Maurice was the most *interesting* man I'd ever seen: I liked the strong way he laughed, and I used to find excuses for coming into the study while they were talking, so I could see his black beard and those eyes of his, and I told Uncle Ira I thought Mr. Stoker must have the whitest teeth in the University. You know how young people are: when Uncle Ira said Maurice was a very flunkèd man who did naughty things to co-eds, and I mustn't even come out of my room while he was in the house or I'd get a spanking, I was scared to death and more curious than ever. So I used to wave to him from my window when he'd drive up on his big black motorcycle, and he never waved back, but just stood in the driveway with his hands on his hips, and smiled at me."

"I hate what's coming," Max groaned. "I hate this whole part."

Anastasia went on to say that she had wondered in addition whether her Uncle's threat was not in fact a kind of invitation to further spankings, though it *did* seem to her that he was more concerned about Stoker than about the procession of undergraduate young men—of whom, in these months, she made a very large number "*so* happy, pass their poor hearts," virtually under his nose, he being preoccupied with the threat to his reference-book monopoly. It came to pass that quite often Stoker himself was in a position to afford transportation to and from the house to these visitors of hers, so frequent were his business-calls there, and thus he'd soon possessed himself of the details of her peculiar philanthropy. ("Can you *imagine?*" Anastasia asked us, as incredulously as if the event had only just occurred. "He thought I was letting them make love to me because *I* liked it! I mean just for my own sake! He actually thought I was *promiscuous*—he still pretends to think so!" I shook my head at this presumption, and Max covered his eyes.) Not long afterwards, eavesdropping at the study door, she'd learned something of the nature of what business was between her guardian and the visitor with the curly beard: the new chancellor, it seemed, had been elected by a narrow margin, and so was particularly interested in a *rapprochement* with Reginald Hector (who whatever his limitations as a political administrator, was still revered in New Tammany College for his role in Campus Riot II); he could not of course expect his beaten opponent to accept a post in the new administration, but it was an open secret that he sought the ex-chancellor's support for certain controversial measures of policy with regard to WESCAC and the Quiet Riot. On the other hand, though Lucky Rexford was himself a wealthy man and a staunch supporter of the private-research economy, he felt obliged both by promise and by principle to make some gesture towards dissolving such monopolies as Ira Hector's, which had flourished under the former regime. Now it was known that however sincerely he deplored Maurice's activities, the Chancellor was bound to his alleged half-brother by Stoker's firm hold on the Power Plant and Main Detention. What Ira Hector proposed (for it was he, not Stoker, who had initiated the interviews), was to establish Reginald Hector as the figurehead president of his reference-book firm—in fact his brother badly needed some such employment, not having an iota of Ira's business-sense—in the hope that some *quid pro quo* could then be diplomatically arranged: he, Ira, would guarantee his brother's support for Chancellor Rexford's varsity policies; the Chancellor in turn could not only find grounds to spare the business headed by the lovable old professor-general, but might in addition see to it that Ira's counterparts in the textbook field were *not* spared. The scheme seemed a likely one, but as a cautious entrepreneur Ira was suspicious of the new chancellor's youth and the fact that Rexford's own fortune had been inherited, rather than earned in the rough-and-tumble of competitive research—both which factors might lead him to put principle above interest, as it were, and proceed the more vigorously against any organization which attempted to negotiate with him. To minimize that risk, it were preferable that the overtures to negotiation be made by the Chancellor himself, who however must needs be assured by some close and disinterested advisor that they would not be rebuffed. The man for that work was Maurice Stoker: Anastasia heard her guardian offer him a sizable inducement to attempt it. But Stoker, while admitting with a laugh that the plot's nefariousness appealed to him, and expressing his confidence that he could manage it with little difficulty, seemed not especially interested in the reward. This was the matter of their frequent meetings, which had reached an impasse: Stoker claimed frankly that he had wealth enough already, and desired only powers and pleasures, neither of which Ira Hector was able to offer him; Ira seemed unable to comprehend this attitude, or unwilling to believe in its sincerity, and so kept raising the amount of his bribe to no avail.

"It was the awfulest thing to *listen* to!" Anastasia said. "Maurice has a way about him . . . I don't know how he does it, but he seems to make everybody worse than they really are. I couldn't believe it was Uncle Ira I heard saying 'There's nothing on this campus can't be bought by the man who can pay the price.' Then Maurice began teasing that Uncle Ira liked to *pretend* to be selfish and hard-hearted, but actually he was a sentimental old do-gooder (which is just what *I* think!). The more Maurice teased him about founding the Lying-In Hospital and raising me out of pure generosity, the more Uncle Ira swore he'd done those things for nobody's benefit but his own. When Maurice saw how upset Uncle Ira was, he vowed he'd do that business with Chancellor Rexford for nothing, the day Uncle Ira could prove it wasn't simple good-heartedness with me and the Unwed Co-eds' Hospital."

"You see what a Dean o' Flunks he is?" Max cried to me—who was gripping my stick with anger.

"It got worse and worse," Anastasia declared. "After a while Uncle Ira was claiming he'd built the hospital just so he could interview the girls himself—he said he liked to ask them questions about how they'd gotten in trouble, and see them cry when they told their stories; he even said he liked to *watch*, in the delivery-room—I *know* it isn't true! And Maurice said so himself, that Uncle Ira was trying to *sound* flunkèd, because he was ashamed of his passèdness . . . Well, I burst in and said I'd heard the whole thing, and told Uncle Ira he should be ashamed of himself for such fibs, and Maurice for leading him on. Uncle Ira was furious, but Maurice just laughed and said 'What about *her*? Does she let you watch when the boys—[I can't say it; you know what I mean]?' Uncle Ira turned white—I did too!—but then he seemed to get hold of himself, and he said, 'Stacey, this man is a wicked liar who'll say anything that suits his purpose; but he also knows every flunkèd thing there is to know about people that they wish nobody knew of. So when he says you've been letting all those boys [you-know-what], he might be lying or he might not. I want you to tell me the plain truth now,' he said: 'if he's lying I'll throw him out, and Lucky Rexford can do his flunkèdest to break me to pieces. But if he's telling the truth, I'm going to thrash you like no co-ed on this campus was ever thrashed!'

"It seemed to me Maurice got worried when Uncle Ira said that, because he said, 'What do you *expect* her to do when you put it that way? You're begging her to lie about it, even if it costs you your business! And you call yourself a selfish man!' But Uncle Ira hardly heard him, he was staring so at me; and you know, I almost *did* tell a lie, he scared me so much. And especially I didn't want to get a spanking there in front of Maurice! But then Uncle Ira looked like he was ready to have a stroke, and the only thing I could *think* of was how important it was to calm him down and get it out of his system. And I hated to tell a lie anyhow, especially when it might ruin his business—"

"I wish I didn't hear this," Max said. "I wish this was finished."

"I'll bet anything you told him the truth," I hazarded.

Anastasia nodded sorrowfully. "I couldn't say a *word* at first, but I bent over his desk, the way I always did for spankings, and that was the same as admitting about the boys. Believe me, it was just for Uncle Ira's sake; and Maurice—he's so *clever* about these things—when Uncle Ira started spanking me, Maurice laughed and asked me wasn't it true what the boys had told him, that I didn't make love to them for my own sake at all, but just because they said it would hurt them if I didn't? At first I thought he was saying that for *my* benefit; Uncle Ira even stopped spanking me for a minute and asked me was it true, and Maurice said, 'Sure, it wasn't *her* fault; they told her they'd commit suicide or flunk their exams if she didn't *help* them, and she believed them."

"Why, that was decent of him, wasn't it?" I exclaimed. The image of Anastasia bent over the desk was much with me.

But she shook her head. "Don't you *see?* As soon as he said it I realized that if I *agreed* that that was how it was—I mean on *my* side of it, because I'm sure those boys never said what they did just to take *advantage* of me—if I agreed, Uncle Ira might stop and drive Maurice away, and lose his business and all. So, awful as it was, I had to tell a worse lie yet: I had to say it was *me* that persuaded the boys to do what they did, because I wanted to fool Uncle Ira and because—I just *enjoyed* doing flunkèd things!"

"He knew you better!" Max burst out.

"Maybe so. But he *did* need to get it out of his system, Dr. Spielman. He started in again, and Maurice laughed, and I was crying all over the ledger-sheets, and worrying because my tears were making the ink run . . . But the worst was what happened next. Maurice told Uncle Ira he certainly must love me very unselfishly to get so upset over what I'd done; it just proved what a sentimental old fool he was! Uncle Ira *really* went crazy then: he spanked me harder than ever, and started crying himself, and he shouted, 'I enjoy it! I enjoy it! *There's* my profit, right there!' I *know* he didn't mean it! But he said 'What do you think I raised her for? I *love* this!' Oh, George, you can't *believe* how it hurt him to say that! The ruler flew out of his hand, and he tried to spank me with his bare hand and couldn't do it right; it didn't even hurt. He was completely helpless, and I turned around and hugged him and told him not to worry, it had been a terrible spanking and had taught me a lesson I'd never forget. Maurice quit his laughing then and looked at me in the strangest way: it wasn't just that he could see through what I'd said; it was as if he'd suddenly thought of something that

upset him the way he'd upset Uncle Ira . . . I can't say it
right . . . but much as I hated him right then, it seemed to
me he had some *terrible* need of his own."

I struck the sand with my stick, and Croaker growled
under me. "If you say *he* spanked you too, I'll flunk him!
There's been enough spankings!"

Max said nothing.

"It wasn't that," Anastasia replied. "He just had an awful
look in his eyes—I thought he was ready to cry himself, can
you imagine? Then he told me in this strange voice that he
knew very well I'd confessed on purpose to save Uncle Ira's
business, but he couldn't decide just why, and before he made
up his mind whether to help Uncle Ira or not he had to know
some things: Hadn't I really enjoyed it with those boys? And
didn't I let Uncle Ira spank me so I could get what I wanted
from him? Mind you, I couldn't tell which answers would be
the right ones for Uncle Ira's sake. Also there was this awful
need on Maurice's *own* face, like if I said the wrong thing it
would do something terrible to him—but whether it might be
better for him in the long run to have that terrible thing happen, I couldn't tell either. I was *confused!* So finally I just
told the plain truth: I said that what I enjoyed about the boys
was just what I'd liked about playing with the maids when I
was little: that it seemed to make them happy without hurting me. As for the spankings, they certainly did hurt, but the
reason he mentioned wasn't right at all: Uncle Ira had *always*
been sweet to me, spankings or no spankings, but everybody
needed to get things out of their systems now and then, and I
owed Uncle Ira such a lot, and it was good for him in so
many ways, he could spank me twice as hard and twice as
often if he wanted to, and I thought it was just *awful* of
Maurice to make him say those terrible things about himself!

"All this time, you know, Uncle Ira was sitting in his
desk-chair, making noises, and I was standing beside him
holding his head against me. But when I finished talking he
put his head down on his papers and wouldn't let me comfort
him at all. The Maurice took hold of my arm—his voice
wasn't teasing the least bit any more; it was like he was *begging* me, if you can imagine it, and he said, 'Now tell me the
Founder's truth, girl.' And what he asked me was, didn't I
find it even a *little* bit exciting to—to have Uncle Ira bend
me over the desk and spank me like that? What a *horrid*
idea! It was the flunkèdest thing I'd ever *heard* of! But his

eyes were just blazing, and there was something about his face—I'd never *seen* such an expression! Uncle Ira sat up and looked at me, and I realized what he'd think about himself if I said it was just for his sake I'd let him spank me. But the other was such a flunkèd thing to say, what Maurice wanted to believe! *Much* worse than pretending about the boys; I could hardly make the words come. But I said, 'If you must know, I guess it *is* a little bit exciting, in a way.' I thought *that* ought to satisfy him, but he squeezed my arm harder and said in that same voice, 'In what way?' How was I supposed to know what to say then? All I knew was that I had to say something *awful,* and the only thing I could think of was what I'd hear the boys say sometimes; I didn't even understand it, whether it was possible for girls too, I mean, or how it could apply to a thing like *spanking,* but something told me it was the right thing to say . . ."

Anastasia's cheeks flamed; but she pressed on, even regaining her disconcerting glibness. "So I looked him straight in the eye, and I said, 'When Uncle Ira spanks me with his ruler, Mr. Stoker—it gets me *all hot!*' Do you see why I had to say that, George?"

In truth it was not until later I learned her exact meaning, but I thought I had the general sense of the situation, and took my cue from Max in praising once again her astonishing selflessness and deploring the flunkèdness of which she had been victim.

"I could have *died* for shame!" Anastasia declared. "But it turned out Maurice didn't believe a word of what I said. It was as if that's what he'd *wanted* to hear, all right, but it made him mad to hear it—because he wanted it to be true and knew it wasn't. He almost hit me himself! *'Flunk* you!' I remember him shouting at me. 'How far will you go?' Then out of a clear sky he tells Uncle Ira he wants to marry me (what he really said was, he *had* to marry me), and he looked at me in this twisted kind of way; it scared me to see him. He said he'd guarantee Uncle Ira's business would get twice as big if I'd marry him. It was strictly a business deal, he said: 'if Uncle Ira wanted to prove what he'd bragged about before, here was his chance; it would be like selling me for a big profit. But he ought to understand (this was Maurice talking) what he was letting me in for . . .'"

"I *will* kill him, Max!" I vowed.

But Anastasia bade me hear her out. What Stoker's propo-

sition came to, it developed, had not even the technical re-
spectability of marriage: she was to become upon his completion of Ira's business, the mistress of Stoker's every whim and
craving—the which, he hinted darkly, were as infinite in
number as they were bestial in character.

"It was a *terrible* spot to be in," she said. "If Uncle Ira
said *no,* he'd lose his business and have to admit he was generous at heart; if he said *yes,* he'd lose me—and he really did
need me—and probably hate himself besides for what he'd
done. I wanted to decide *for* him, so he wouldn't have to
blame himself; but I didn't know which to choose either, I
loved them both so . . ."

"You *loved* them?" I cried, and Max, equally astonished,
said, "Stoker too yet!"

"Well, you know what I mean: he was really terribly
upset! It was perfectly plain to me he just needed somebody
to get things out of his system with, and he was as afraid of
showing it as Uncle Ira was. Why do you suppose men are
that way?"

I was sure I didn't know.

"Anyhow, I couldn't say a word, and neither could Uncle
Ira, and Maurice wouldn't. He walked out of the study with
this set look on his face, and Uncle Ira and I kind of followed after, as if we could've been going up to our rooms or
out for a walk or anything. We ended up out front where
Maurice's motorcycle was, and it seemed to me Uncle Ira
must have been wanting me to go with Maurice, or he would
have made me stay in the house. Or maybe he thought *I* was
leading the way, I don't know. Anyhow Maurice got on the
motorcycle and started up, and everybody kind of hesitated,
and it didn't seem to me there was anything I could do then
but go with him; everybody seemed to be waiting for me. I
don't remember deciding: one minute I was standing with
Uncle Ira, the next I was in Maurice's sidecar and off we
were going, just like the wind, and Maurice threw back his
head and laughed!"

She tisked her mouth-corner. "That was a couple of years
ago. And you know, he *did* keep his word to Uncle Ira, even
though in a way he didn't have to—I mean, since he had me
anyhow. I think that was very good of him, don't you?
There's something really *decent* about Maurice, way down
deep."

"Deep is right," Max said. His voice was hushed with appall. Recalling the distressed young co-eds of legend, I assumed she had been kept prisoner since that fateful day—her husband being after all the warden of Main Detention—and fervently offered my services to the end of freeing her, by force if necessary. But Anastasia was merely amused by my suggestion: she was no prisoner at all, she declared; on the contrary, she came and went from their lodgings at the Power Plant quite as she pleased—witness her position in the NTC Psych Clinic—and was persuaded Stoker would not restrain her should she ever choose to leave him permanently. However, he had after all married her, "in a way" (she did not explain in what way), at her insistence, and she didn't mean to shirk her conjugal obligations. Moreover, he needed her ever so much more than her Uncle Ira had.

"Then all that talk of mistreating you was just to scare you for some reason?" I asked. "I'm glad to hear *that!* Aren't you, Max?"

"Who's heard it?"

"Now don't jump to *conclusions,*" Anastasia pleaded. "Just because Maurice's needs are *different* doesn't mean they're not as important to him as the regular ones are to *most* men."

"What he needs is to be wicked as the Dean o' Flunks!" Max said passionately. "He needs to wreck and hurt, so you let him wreck and hurt you, *ja?*"

"You don't *have* to look at it that way, Dr. Spielman," the girl insisted—but added immediately that of course he could if he wanted to, if it was *important* to him . . .

What I myself wanted was to hear exactly what sort of abuses Anastasia suffered, willingly or otherwise. But I had no opportunity to ask, for at her last remark Max virtually burst with compassion.

"Look here once, child!" He touched her sandal with his hand and pointed to his eyes. "I'm not your poppa, and I never was! Don't I wish I had been and Virginia Hector your momma? Flunk Ira Hector he ever laid his nasty hand on you! Flunk all those boys took advantage of you! But flunk Maurice Stoker most of all, that beast from South Exit, he'd never have laid eyes on you if *I* was your poppa!"

"I'm not blaming you," Anastasia reminded him.

"You don't blame nobody nothing!" Max shouted. "I know I'm not your poppa because I can't be nobody's poppa: I had an accident with the WESCAC twenty-some years ago." He had purposely not mentioned this fact to Virginia or her father, he explained more calmly, because in thus exculpating himself he'd have convicted her, and robbed her moreover of the chance to volunteer the truth of his innocence.

"And it's not to escape any blame I'm telling you now," he declared. "You got to know I never was your poppa so you'll hate me for the right things. Eblis Eierkopf—*he* was your poppa, girl, and flunk him he never owned up to it! But flunk me too; flunk me twice I didn't swallow my pride and marry Virginia, she'd have stayed off the bottle and you'd have never been spanked and the rest! Don't you dare forgive me that!"

Anastasia's face was full of tenderness. "It's hard *not* to! The way you must have *suffered* all these years!" She sounded almost envious; then a frowning wonder darkened her eyes. "Mother *did* used to work with Dr. Eierkopf, but I never *dreamed* . . ."

"It's not good news," Max sympathized.

She shook her head. "I didn't mean it that way. But he's not very . . . *nice,* you know? No wonder, being a cripple and all—I'm sure I'd be twice as disagreeable if *I* had to depend on Croaker for everything! When I *think* of all the times he and Croaker have come by the Clinic, and me not *dreaming* he was my father! I could've been so much nicer to him than I was!"

Max clapped his head. For myself, I was too busy steadying Croaker, the mention of whose name had made him ominously restive, to marvel further at Anastasia's charity. He stirred in her direction and had to be tapped smartly twice or thrice with my stick, which discipline I was not at all sure wouldn't turn him upon me. Indeed, he caught the stick in his hand and bit into the shaft of it—a testimonial to the power of his jaws, for the wood was hard—and despite Anastasia's assuring me that he often chewed on boughs and twigs for amusement, and could even nibble quite clever decorations into canes and chair-rungs with no other chisels than his teeth, I was by no means certain I'd be able to restrain him, especially without my weapon, if he took it into mind to assault her once again. As it happened, we all were diverted just then by snarlings in the nearby forest, which grew to a roar and burst upon the beach with half a dozen bright lights, flashing red or blinding white. For all my resolve I was taken with alarm, very nearly with panic; G. W. Gruff himself might have trembled at so instant and terrific a besetting—unheard-of, unprepared-for, monstrously wobbling uswards now with its sprawl of eyes, mad hoots, and growling throats. Max too was startled, and clambered to his feet; Croaker let go my stick and crouched under me with a grunt—whether of defiance or fright I could not judge. Only Anastasia seemed not especially anxious; she frowned at the snarling lights more in disapproval than in fear, and remained in her place by the fire.

"He always has to do things *dramatically*," she complained.

"Those are motorcycles," Max muttered to me. "Ten or twelve separate ones. The noise is their motors and horns."

I was at once unspeakably relieved, for though I'd seldom actually seen motorcycles, I understood them well enough. As they drew nearer, the firelight revealed a party of humans in black leather jackets, variously ornamented with silver studs and bright glass jewels. Goggled and helmeted, each was mounted upon a gleaming black machine with sidecar attached. They drew up in a rough half-circle around us, engines guttering: piled up, rather, for there was no precision in the maneuver. The lead cyclist—a bearded, sooty fellow—braked abruptly with a spray of sand and no prior warning; the second missed striking him only by good luck and instant reflexes, which those behind seemed not to share, for they bumped one another, perhaps even intentionally, with curses, shouts, and laughs. One who had no sidecar attached fell over onto the sand, his wheels roaring and racing; another made as if to run over him—skidded close to his head, sounded a siren, and was sprung upon a moment later by a third, in sport or anger. "Knock it off!" their leader bawled, and the man beside him—long-nosed, thin-toothed, and dapper, the only one of their number both sootless and unwhiskered—repeated or enlarged upon the order in some snapping other language, hectoring the squabblers with some difficulty into line.

Anastasia sighed loudly. "It's just Maurice." She stood up and brushed sand from her shift.

I was nonetheless far from easy, what with the formidable ring before us, Croaker growling and turning beneath me as if at bay, and all I had heard of Maurice Stoker crowding to mind. The men on either end of the arc sprang off their machines now, put up their goggles, and advanced towards me, carrying what I guessed were pistols: the others shouted encouragement or raced their engines, ignoring the sootless one's command to be silent. Croaker moved at the nearer of the two, who raised his weapon and ordered us to halt. I had only an instant to think what to do, and not sure I could stop Croaker or that to do so would spare us a shooting, I chose instead to lash out with my stick: it cracked against the pistol and sent it flying. Anastasia cried out; the man swore an oath and sprang back to his fellows, several of whom jeered at his dismay; there came just behind me a deafening bang, which crashed and rattled up the gorge, and as Croaker spun about I saw smoke still issuing from the leader's pistol, aimed at the sky. I raised my stick again, though the fellow was well out of reach and might easily have brought us down had he chosen to. But unlike his companion, whose expression had been first threatening and then frightened, this man had a fierce grin on him and a sparkle in his eyes; he seemed delighted either by the sight of me perched on Croaker's shoulders or by our little initial victory, and he neither retreated nor aimed his gun at us when Croaker came towards him.

"Whoa down!" I said, uncertain how to proceed, and was gratified at least to see Croaker obey. With pounding heart I regarded our adversary, who had removed his helmet and goggles and was calmly blowing the smoke from his pistol-barrel: ruddy-cheeked, short-statured, and heavy-set he was, but not fat, with black curls on his head, hands, and finger-tops. Shags of the same bushed over his eyes and upper lip; he had a sharp beard, like a black spade, and one vertical ridge from the front of either temple up to his hairline—a not unhandsome face withal, and the more striking for the clear eyes that flashed from so swart a field.

"I'm George the Goat-Boy," I said distinctly. Someone whistled, and was told by someone else to shut his mouth. My antagonist merely scrutinized me, arms akimbo. His grin was a plain challenge, to which I rose with some heat.

"I'm not afraid of you. I'm a Grand Tutor."

The man replied with a raucous fart ("Hear hear!" his cohorts cheered), raised his pistol again, and with incredible smiling calm aimed it at my heart. I understood then that he himself was Maurice Stoker.

5.

Whether in fact he meant to shoot me dead or merely try my boast I was not to discover, for Anastasia hurried between us at this point. There were whistles and improper comments from the ring of cyclists.

"*Don't*, Maurice, for pity's sake! He doesn't know what he's saying. He really *is* the Goat-Boy!"

He lowered his weapon and grinned at her. "Had yourself an ape; now you want a billygoat." His voice was only teasing; I was chagrined to see Anastasia lower her head and touch his leather jacket.

"You shouldn't have let that happen," she complained. "You could have stopped Croaker in time."

He clouted her lightly aside the head with his helmet: it was a left-hand swat, and at too close range for injury. But the mean insinuation, the unreasonableness of the blow, Anastasia's small cry and the way she clung to her abuser—these so enraged me that I dug my heels into Croaker's ribs, raised my stick, and charged him, heedless of the pistol. But several of his men had dismounted by this time, armed with what looked like electric cattle-prods; they held us at bay while the long-faced officer put a hollow pipe to his lips, gave a puff, and sent a little dart into Croaker's buttocks. With a bellow Croaker swiped at the wounded ham and brushed the dart away; he made to spring at the blow-pipe man, who retreated a step but then stood ground instead of running; half a second later Croaker dropped to his knees, and I barely managed to scramble off as he pitched face-forward onto the sand. Instantly I was myself hemmed round by cattle-prods. Anastasia ran from her husband to examine Croaker, whom four laughing men already were dragging, dead unconscious, towards one of the sidecars. They paused to let her look at him, and ogled her the while.

"Just a little nap," Stoker called. "We wouldn't kill a friend of the family." Then to me he said, "You care to sleep awhile too, Billy-buck? Why not park your shillelagh and join the party?"

Stick in air I had been about to have at the cattle-prods, but hesitated at his odd approximation of my former name. In that instant I heard Max (who had stood helpless by the fire this while, wringing his hands) say, "Don't fight, Georgie. That don't Graduate anybody."

I lowered my stick, though my heart beat hard still with attack. My guards gave way, their prods however held yet at the ready, and Anastasia slipped between them to my side.

"Give her a goose," I heard one man mutter; he was answered by a jab in the backside from another, and at once the two went rolling in the sand, their comrades calling encouragement from the sidelines.

"Croaker's all right," Anastasia assured me. "He'll wake up in an hour or so. Please don't mind Maurice and the others; they always carry on like this. Let us drop you and Dr. Spielman off somewhere."

I merely frowned, uncertain what to think and distracted both by the riotous men and by Stoker's now approaching Max, with a look of joyous disbelief.

"I *will* be flunked!" he cried. "Is it Max Spielman under all that hair?" He opened his arms to embrace him, but Max shook his head and raised a warning hand.

"It *is* Max Spielman, the fingerless proctologer! Who're we going to EAT this time, Maxie?"

"Dean o' Flunks!" Max cried.

A new and delightful idea seemed to occur to Stoker; he turned to Anastasia, face alight. "Did you know it was your own daddy watching you with Croaker?" And to Max again, not waiting for reply: "Wait till Virginia Hector sees you in that Old-Syllabus get-up: she'll swear off forever!"

Bounding from us he directed his men then to see to it Croaker's arms and legs were secured against revival; dashing back, he bade us all climb into sidecars for the trip to the Powerhouse, where, he declared, we would carouse the night away while he and Max recalled the grand old days when they had EATen ten thousand Amaterasu undergraduates at the cost of one Moishian forefinger.

"Get on, get on there!" he shouted to the wrestlers in the sand, who cried back "Flunk you!" until the long-faced aide snatched up a cattle-prod and herded them over to assist with Croaker.

"A goat-boy!" Stoker clapped an arm high-heartedly about me, another about Anastasia, and paid no heed to the squabbling troops—some of whom now drew pocketflasks from their trousers, while others set to tinkering with their engines. "And a Grand Tutor too, did I hear you say?" That, he vowed (never once pausing in his burst of speech), he must hear more of, a billygoat being in his estimation the only creature on campus, his wife excepted, from whom he might learn a thing or two worth knowing. And if later at the party I should find Anastasia too forward or compliant a stall-mate, or too well-washèd, say, to rouse my ardor, he was certain he could scare up a nanny-goat somewhere on Founder's Hill, perhaps at the Refuse Dump.

Max held his ears against this outpouring; Anastasia blushed and looked away. I found myself aghast and amused at once by the barrage of aspersions, so outrageous and pointed, and for all my indignation could not repress one twitch of a smile, which I saw the wretch instantly notice. Then on he went, hilarious and full of force, thumping my chest for emphasis, mussing Anastasia's hair, gesticulating with pistol and helmet, striking postures in the glare of the motorcycle headlamps, and flashing always that flush-cheeked, even-toothed grin:

"Look what you've got round your waist!" He snatched at the amulet Max had given me. "Is this what I think it is, old buck old buster? Look here, Stacey—I swear it's mountain oysters on his belt. It is! Billygoat bobblers! Are they his own, d'you think? You find out, I'll ask you tomorrow . . . Hey, here's what we'll do (*George*, was it?): we'll tap a keg of bock-beer and you toot your pipes—you're the Grand Tutor! You toot your pipes while Maxie and I toot a few on the EAT-whistle, for old times' sake. Stacey'll do a dance with Croaker. You *do* have pipes, don't you, George?"

Anastasia in her embarrassment had touched her brow to my arm (Stoker having sprung out from between us to illustrate the dance he had in mind), and thinking to assure her that her husband's talk did not distress me, innocently I patted her behind, as was my wont when any lady of the herd needed calming. She looked up at me with quick wonder, also squeezed my arm uncertainly, and Stoker broke off his raillery to shout with laughter.

"*Olé!*" some others called.

"Stop!" Max commanded, stamping his feet.

"No no, Maxie, he just started! Watch he doesn't eat your

hair-pins, Stacey; they eat anything, you know. Not like your gorilla-friend . . ."

"I don't listen!" Max cried, and covered his ears once more. To me he said desperately, "Pat her on the head, you got to pat her! It's different with human girls!" Then to Stoker, more determinedly: "I'm not her father, Stoker, much as I wish I was. But neither she nor Georgie's going with you. You got to kill me first."

Anastasia made a flutter of protest; Stoker laughed delightedly and drew his pistol; the cattle-prods moved towards us. I began to perspire.

Max opened his arms. "Na, wait," he pleaded, "I make you a bargain. You told me once you watched the Bonifacists burn some Moishians in the Riot, *ja?*"

"Only a few," Stoker answered modestly; the prospect of a bargain clearly amused him. "They were sure I was spying, but didn't know for which side, so the day I took a tour of their extermination campuses they only did a few."

Max's thin face glared. "But you told me you enjoyed it, *ja?*"

"*Enjoyed* it! I never had so much fun—except the day you and I pushed the EAT-button. What a party! This one chap in particular, we couldn't wait to try: biochemist named Schultz—maybe you've heard of him? He'd decided the only way to keep West-Campus culture from going up in smoke was to fireproof the Moishians. So he invented some kind of asbestos bagel, I believe it was, and ate nothing else for three months before he was picked up. When the Bonifacist scientists heard about it they put him straight in the oven—they don't miss a trick! You know, it's surprising how *thirsty* you got, around that place! Siegfrieder beer is the best in the University, and they had two kegs of it down by the ovens: one for enlisted men and one for officers and guests."

Breathless I asked, "Did it work? The bagels?" and only realized I'd been baited when Stoker's glee rang round the gorge.

"Founder forgive you!" Max said softly. And to Stoker: "Laugh all you want, I got reason to think this boy's a Grand Tutor, even though there's things he's got to learn yet. And this poor suffering girl you call your wife—she's a passèd Graduate, if ever there was one! So I make you this bargain, Stoker, you got one speck of right-mindedness in you: let her and George go on by themselves to Great Mall, and do what you want with me. Burn me up if you want, like poor Chaim Schultz—rest his mind!"

Stoker snapped his fingers. *"Chaim,* that was it! Chaim Schultz the biochemist. Very warm type, I remember. So many of you Moishian chaps were . . ."

In tears now, Max threw himself at Stoker's knees. "For Founder's sake let them go! Burn me!"

Anastasia and I hastened to calm him, she assuring him (her earlier complaint to the contrary notwithstanding) that her husband's bark was far worse than his bite when it came to maltreating her, and I that I had more faith in my incorruptibility than Max seemed to, and no intention to let anyone suffer in my stead. As to Anastasia, I was not persuaded that her decision to remain with Stoker was freely chosen, nor contrariwise that it was simply coerced; I meant to investigate the matter further and act accordingly. In short—I vowed with some heat—the three of us would go together, whether to Great Mall and Main Gate or to the Power Plant. I might have added, but chose not to, that I was curious to see with my own eyes what flunkage really was, the better to understand its opposite, and thus looked forward to visiting both the Power Plant and Main Detention; also that Max's pathetic gesture touched me less with gratitude and respect for him than with disapproval, even with a small, unexplainable contempt. It was but an amplifying of my own sentiments when Stoker said, "These Moishians, I swear to the Dunce, they *enjoy* being persecuted!" His tone was most amiable. "Don't let anybody tell you they're the Chosen Class: they volunteered!"

He ordered Max then to get off his knees and end the theatrics; he could burn all three of us if he had a mind to, he declared, and throw Croaker in for a backlog, but in fact he wanted only to entertain us for the night, inasmuch as he'd never matched drinks with a billygoat before, to say nothing of a Grand Tutor.

"Never," Max said. "These children and I aren't going." He took Anastasia's arm (who still pressed mine) and made as if to lead us away. The cattle-prodders glanced to their chief for instructions; Anastasia hesitated, as did I, unable to share my advisor's resolve.

"Doggone!" Stoker said, ignoring us all. "There *is* a fellow we've got to burn; I'd almost forgot him! Black chap we fished off the dam. Friend of yours, was he?"

He strode over to one of the sidecars and flashed an electric torch: there sprawled the brown-skinned, white-fleeced body of G. Herrold, his head flung back; each separate water-drop upon him sparkled in the torch-beam. We went over, shocked, and regarded our lost friend. Max moaned and tore at his beard. Anastasia snatched up the dead man's wrist and laid her ear to his chest.

"He's not asleep, like Croaker?" I demanded.

She shook her head. "I can't help feeling it's *my* fault! If he hadn't seen me out on the bridge . . ."

Stoker looked from speaker to speaker with a grin. I was smitten with grief. Dark fetcher from booklift, Belly, barn; first lover and teacher of full nelson; savior, sweep, and summoner (whose left hand still clutched the buckhorn)—he was the first dead human I had seen. His mouth being open, I kissed his cold forehead, and felt on my lips, with anger, drops of the river he'd crossed at last.

"This flunking place!" I cried. "What's it called?"

"Just 'The Gorge,' " Anastasia said.

"If you go with this Dean o' Flunks here"—Max pointed grimly to Stoker—"you might as well call it South Exit, because you're flunked for sure."

"I'm going to give it *his* name," I declared, indicating G. Herrold. Max showed some surprise at the firmness of my tone, but shrugged. To the company at large I announced: "From now on this river's name is *George*. And the gorge is George's Gorge."

Max nodded, Even Stoker cocked his head and grinned approval.

"That's okay," Max said. "And we'll bury him ourselves, right here. Help me lift him out, George."

"Now, now, Maxie!" Stoker laughed. "You don't go sticking people underground any way you please. Health rules! Forms to fill out; questions to answer! We'll have to fetch him up to the morgue and have him looked over—only take a few minutes if you come along. And the Staff Graveyard's right on Founder's Hill, above the Powerhouse; we run the College Crematorium off the same pile as the main steamboilers." To me he added, "Awfully clever piece of engineering, actually: big oven man from Siegfrieder College designed it when we first hired him, just after the Riot . . ." He interrupted himself before Max could speak, to order his men to restart their engines. They answered him with curses, but finally obeyed when the order had been repeated several times by the lieutenant. "Hop in now, friends; the night doesn't last forever. Maxie, you ride with your wet pal there and see he doesn't bounce out. You kids ride with me." He grinned at his inadvertent word-play and snatched my elbow to guide me to his vehicle. "Do you kiss a girl before you climb her, George, or just sniff around? I never saw a goat go to it, much as I admire them."

"I'm not actually a goat," I explained politely. "There may not even be any goat in me at all. And I never climbed a human girl before—just does, when I was younger."

"You don't tell me!"

I nodded, rather suspecting I was being teased but for some reason scarcely caring. Max's warning, Anastasia's mortified "Maurice!" my grief for G. Herrold—all caution and consideration were swept before Stoker's outrageous high spirits. I rattled on as though despite myself. "G. Herrold and I used to do tricks sometimes, while we wrestled, till Max told me a Grand Tutor shouldn't. Otherwise I certainly would enjoy Anastasia."

"Would you, though!"

"Yes, sir."

"Looks pretty good to you, does she?"

"Yes indeed. I think her teats are remarkably well formed, for a human girl's, and I especially liked the patch of black hair I saw . . ." I turned to the red-faced lady I was complimenting and touched my stick lightly to her crotch. "Do you have a special name for it, ma'am? What we call the escutcheon?"

Stoker's laugh rang over the roaring engines. Anastasia shrank from my stickpoint with a gasp—but did not let go my arm. From behind, Max's voice came shrilly.

"Quit, George! Dear boy and girl, don't!"

I glanced back: two grinning sooty guards were lifting him into the sidecar where G. Herrold was. "Take me and let them go!" I heard him beg one of them. "They aren't even Moishians. You can kick and beat me!" To encourage them he began pummeling his own head with both fists, and continued to do so even after they had deposited him in the sidecar and mounted their cycles. Distressed as I was by the spectacle, I felt again that odd irritation—along with bad conscience, to be sure. I helped Anastasia into Stoker's own sidecar and climbed in beside her.

"Don't hurt Dr. Spielman, Maurice," she pleaded. "He's such a nice man, I wish he *was* my father. Promise?"

Stoker mounted chuckling to his seat and donned helmet and goggles. "Who needs to hurt Maxie? He does it himself!"

My laugh—I couldn't help laughing—was lost in the blast of a small whistle he now blew several times, at the same time signaling with his arm and shouting, "Forward! Forward!" A great din rose as the cycles throttled slowly into motion, nudging, threatening, and blocking one another as if each aspired to lead the column. "Out of my way, flunk you!" Stoker would shout, and race his engine to intimidate those jockeying around him; they cursed him back with a grin, sometimes in our language, sometimes in others; we swarmed in all directions for a moment, like queenless bees, until Stoker by thrust and knock had got clear of the tangle—whereupon with a whoop and cracking backfire he took off up the shore. The others followed in a wobbly line, weaving and bumping over shale until we reached the roadway that came down to the broken bridge. There we turned inland on the harder pavement; Stoker opened the throttle, and we roared out of George's Gorge at a breath-catch clip. I was amazed by the noise and speed: I clutched at the handrail and Anastasia's shoulder; my head jerked back, and I gasped for some moments against the rush of air.

"Not so *fast!*" Anastasia fretted.

I shook my head. "It's all right."

Stoker's teeth flashed through his whiskers. "Okay, hey, George?"

"I think . . . I like it."

"Hooray!" Stoker let go the handlebars to shake hands with himself; Anastasia squealed and admonished him to drive more carefully. In truth he delighted in recklessness, as did his fellows: we were less a procession than a freestyle race, which Stoker led not by virtue of his rank but by speed and daring. When someone threatened to overtake us Stoker would block his way and make as if to force him into ditch or embankment; inevitably the challenger yielded with exuberant curses. Any turn in the road, however blind or precipitous, inspired him to more speed rather than less: he would bid us lean right or left as he instructed and skid full tilt into the curve, sometimes lifting the sidecar off the pavement. A signpost or streetlight picked up by our headlamp (there were not many) became a target; never slacking speed for an instant he unlimbered his pistol and blazed away, as did others behind us. Woe betide the rabbit, snake, or opossum who crossed our path: if no wrench of the machine itself could run him under our wheels, he was brought low by a fusillade of bullets as the line roared past. At all these things Anastasia shrieked and protested; excepting the fate of the animals, however, which moved her to tearful poundings of her husband's side, she seemed as much exhilarated as afraid: between her screams and shakings of the head her breath came fast; she clutched at my wrapper for support, and though her eyes would shut against a peril-in-progress, I sometimes saw them sparkle at one's approach. I too, alarmed as I was to the marrow by the wild novelty of the experience, had seldom felt such thrill: I even found myself applauding Stoker's marksmanship, over Anastasia's protests, and praising his riskiest maneuvers.

"You shouldn't *encourage* him!" she scolded. "How can a Grand Tutor encourage reckless driving?"

I admitted cheerfully that I didn't have the least idea whether my attitude was proper for a Grand Tutor; but I added (the notion having just occurred to me): "It must be all right, though, come to think of it—since it's *my* attitude, and I'm the Grand Tutor."

"Well said!" Stoker let go the handlebars again to clap his hands, and Anastasia clawed at my arm.

"Besides," I said, "if I'm not mistaken, you like it too."

"I do *not!*"

Stoker shook a finger at her. "Don't argue with the Grand Tutor, dear: you're only a Graduate. Hey, George, is she really a Graduate?"

I considered her frowning face. Despite the racket and wild motion I sensed a good peculiar power in myself: a clarity of muscle, a tonus of thought, such as I'd rarely or never known. "She may not actually have Commenced yet, as Max thinks. I haven't learned enough to tell. But I'm sure she must be a Candidate . . ."

My last words were lost on Stoker, who coming to a crossroads marked by direction-signs skidded to a halt and sprang off the motorcycle. Anastasia however was moved enough to lower her eyes, ignoring the riotous action before us. Stoker's purpose in stopping, it developed, was to give the signpost a quarter-turn, "purely on principle," as he later declared: a principle for the sake of which he not only sacrificed his hard-held lead but risked his life as well—bullets raised dust-puffs near his boots as the others flashed by, and clipped into the signboard over his head.

"Do you believe me?" I asked her.

Wanly she smiled. "I think you're being polite. But I appreciate it—*very* much." She raised her eyes. "I've hardly even *thought* of Graduation! Much as the boys used to argue about it at Uncle Ira's, when they came to see me. I used to hope and hope they'd pass the Finals. Whether *they* hoped so or not."

"Didn't you want to pass too?"

"Oh, I guess I've *thought* of it. Lots of times." Now that the line of motorcycles had passed, the air was quiet but for their fading backfire, and I could hear her without straining to listen. "But I know how silly the idea is, for me, so I've never dared *wish* for it really. Imagine *me* passing the Finals, after all I've done!"

"Do you believe in Graduation, Anastasia?"

"Believe in it?" Her expression was shocked. "I'd *die* if I didn't! Could I go on living if I didn't, after something like tonight on the beach?"

"Then you ought to believe what Enos Enoch said: *Passèd are the raped . . .*" I turned a finger in the hair upon her neck-nape. "*For they shall be my virgin brides . . .*"

"I believe in Enos Enoch," she said quietly. "I really do."

I smiled. "But not in me. Why don't you believe in me too?"

She wrinkled her brow. "I *want* to, George! Honestly. But you're so *different* from Enos Enoch. You don't seem to hate Maurice very much, and you talk so strangely. And look what you're doing now—" She removed my hand from her hair. "As if you were any ordinary fellow! Enos Enoch wouldn't do that."

Stoker came back from his work upon the roadsign (which now showed quite altered directions) in time to catch the famous name. "She should've been an early Enochist," he said to me. "Put *her* in the arena, she'd make love to the lions— just to keep 'em off the others, you know." He restarted our engine and turned onto a small dirt road, which he declared would get us to our destination ahead of the others. Then he shouted from the side of his mouth, with what seemed to me deliberate nonchalance: "Hey, why not pass her yourself, if you're the Grand Tutor? You already examined her on the bridge, I understand."

"That's rather witty," I said, ignoring Anastasia's embarrassment. I explained, however, that while I was beyond question a Grand Tutor, I had not as yet begun actually Tutoring, it being necessary in Max's opinion as well as my own to matriculate as a common student and undergo the dread Finals myself before descending into WESCAC's Belly, changing its AIM, and thus bringing peace of mind to the entire student body. Indeed, to the best of my recollection Max had never mentioned the passage or failure of individual students in connection with my program, though it seemed to me (now I considered it) as proper work for a Grand Tutor as preventing Campus Riot III—perhaps even properer. I would think further on the matter. In any case, it was not my impression that Grand Tutors and Examiners were quite the same: my task, as I saw it, was not to pass or flunk anyone myself, but merely to point the way to Commencement Gate—which I must discover myself before leading others thither.

Thus I spoke, freely and eagerly as never before, sensing for the first time the power of my chosen role and wondering, even as I spoke, whether I had interpreted correctly the obscure message on my PAT-card: *Pass All Fail All.* I was pleased to see Anastasia listen with whole attention, if diverted eyes.

"That nutty Spielman!" Stoker marveled, much amused (we were obliged to move less swiftly on the rough dirt road, and so could speak without shouting). "What a prize he's made out of you: a billygoat persuaded he's Enos Enoch!"

I shook my head vigorously. "No, no, you're wrong all around. In the first place Max didn't persuade me: he's a fine advisor, and I owe him my whole education, almost; but it was I who told *him* I'm the Grand Tutor. He still doesn't believe me as much as he needs to, hard as he tries. He *wants* it to be true; he suspects it might be; but I'm the only one so far who knows it is."

"You're Max's boy, though," Stoker insisted. "Where'd you get the notion you should change WESCAC's AIM?"

I admitted that it was indeed Max who had first proposed that particular labor, the worth whereof however I fully affirmed. All *I* had known was that I must rescue studentdom: from what, and how, I depended on experience—as well as my advisor—to clarify.

"How about your deportment?" Stoker challenged. "That's Max's doing too, isn't it?"

"Beg pardon?" I mistook him to have asked which *department* of New Tammany College I intended to matriculate in, and it occurred to me that I'd given no thought to the choice of a suitable major since my discovery, some months earlier, than no program in Herohood was listed in the Undergraduate Catalogue. I would have to consult Max on the matter before I registered.

"I mean your silly morals," Stoker said. "Where'd you get the idea you shouldn't have a go at Stacey, if not from Max? You said yourself you'd like to, and you can see she's willing."

"Maurice!" Anastasia held her ears.

"Wasn't it Max who told you you couldn't be a stud-buck if you want to be Enos Enoch?"

"Now look here," I said firmly, "that's another mistake you all keep making, and Max too. I may be a Grand Tutor—I *am* the Grand Tutor!—but I'm not Enos Enoch, and I don't want to be." Anastasia looked at me wonderingly. "Enos Enoch was Shepherd Emeritus, and I'm the Goat-Boy. There's a big difference."

"By George, we'll have a drink on that!" From his trouser-pocket Stoker drew a black flask, unscrewed the top with his teeth, and forsook a clear chance at a strolling possum to tip himself a drink. Then he offered it to me.

"Grand Tutors don't drink," Anastasia said. It was half plea, half challenge; I responded by accepting the flask.

"They do when they're thirsty."

Stoker cheered. Anticipating water, I choked on the scalding stuff I swigged, a dark liquor manufactured, so Stoker explained, in the Powerhouse itself. Yet it promised splendid things against the chill night air, and I managed a second swallow before returning the flask. Anastasia turned away with a sniff.

"You're all right, George!" Stoker said. "I'm glad Max didn't ruin you altogether."

I was firm. "That's enough about Max. He's a good man, and I'm glad for his advice. Wouldn't listen to anybody else's." I tapped my chest. "But *I'm* the Grand Tutor, not him."

"Exactly! My sentiments exactly." Stoker whacked my shoulders. "A grand old man, but *limited,* you know? What worried me, the way you pulled your virtue back there, I thought he might actually have clipped you . . ."

"Oh, for pity's sake!"

"No, really! I thought that might be your own equipment on your belt there."

Without bothering to recount its history I declared the amulet-of-Freddie to be older than myself, and asserted further that so far from being castrate I knew my studly endowment to be greater than any buck's in the herd, and than Max's and the Beist-in-the-buckwheat's too. Though not of the magnitude of either Croaker's or the late G. Herrold's. Rest his mind. Which observations led me—

"I'll just try another sip, if you don't mind . . ."

"Do!" Stoker urged.

"Thank you."

Which observations, I went on to declare, led me to suppose myself at least as well hung as my most generous host and chauffeur, he being white-skinned under his soot. If not better, in view of his short stature. No offense intended.

"Show us!" Stoker cried. "Get the flashlight, Stacey!"

"George, *don't!*" Anastasia's angry plea came just in time, for I was nowise loath to test my supposition. "He's only teasing you. He wants to make a fool of you."

"Why? Because his *is* better? How do you know, till you've compared us?"

She tried over Stoker's laughter to explain that I misunderstood the question, which was one rather of modesty than of fact.

"Ah," I said appreciatively. "You mean I shouldn't boast. Excuse me, I haven't learned all your manners yet. But that makes sense. Excuse me, Mr. Stoker: didn't mean to offend you."

"No offense! No offense! Oh, what a party we'll have tonight!"

Anastasia shook her head and tried again, "It's not an offense to *him,* one way or the other! I mean, knowing Maurice, I guess he *might* be disappointed or something if his was smaller—but that's not what I mean either!"

Stoker guffawed.

"It's just not proper, in the presence of a lady!" she cried. Then she added quickly, "I don't mean you meant anything *naughty* by it . . ." The labor of articulating made her frown. "I realize you were brought up *differently,* just as Croaker was . . ."

I protested (the liquor burning well from my throat to my belly) that I was not so ignorant of West-Campus manners as all that: had I not that same evening rebuked *her* for displaying across the Georgian River her own escutcheon? But plainly there was a crucial difference between the cases: my reproach had not been for the display of beauty as such—to which none could reasonably object without advocating that her face be covered as well, and her fine-modeled arms and dainty pasterns, not to mention all the countless other of nature's charms, from rainbows to thistle-blossoms. Nay, it was the *motive* I protested, not the deed: her intent, as I'd mistaken it, to compromise the Grand-Tutorial chastity enjoined on me by Max . . .

"I knew it!" Stoker said triumphantly.

"But I had no such thing in *my* mind just now," I said. "Naturally I'd be complimented if you thought all my parts were handsome, too—poor G. Herrold used to like them, rest his mind, and I'm pleased enough with them, I guess. But beauty's not the point here: the question was a simple one of size. I can't see where propriety comes in."

"Don't you understand, woman?" Stoker chided her. "That's just how her mind works, though, George: she thinks you want to put it in her."

"I do *not!*" Anastasia cried, at the same moment that I declared, "I *do!*" Not a little impatient at her consternation, I said, "Didn't I make that clear? I'd like nothing better than to mate with you if I weren't the Grand Tutor. Which I am! I don't even know for sure if Max is right about this chastity business; I'll have to decide for myself. If I decide he's right, nobody can tempt me; if I decide he's wrong, nobody can stop me."

"Hear! Hear!" Stoker said.

I smiled gravely upon the excellent girl. "Especially I think it would be good to bite you in the belly, Anastasia—not really to hurt, you understand. Your belly is very attractive. Very."

In a small and uncertain voice she said, "Thank you."

"Provided you *wanted* me to," I added, as a particular admonition to Stoker and by way of demonstrating what I took to be Grand-Tutorial judiciousness. "That's something none of you seems to consider: to mate or whatever with a doe that's not in heat—a *girl* I mean of course—is not right at all. No buck would ever do such a thing. You couldn't *make* him."

Stoker shook his head. "Stacey could make him. *Everybody* mates with her: chancellors, uncles, laundrymaids, billygoats—everybody! And yet she's never been in heat in her whole life."

"Isn't that odd! Why do you suppose that is?" It was she I asked, but seeing she'd hidden her face at the disclosure, I tactfully changed the subject. "Do you remember what your goat-friend's name was, that you mated with? I'm sure I'd know him if he was one of our studs."

I was astounded to see her wail into tears; nor would she permit me to calm her with my hand, but pushed it from her withers as if I had offended her, and whipped her head from side to side.

"Now stop!" I told her. "I don't see why you're crying!" I rather wished Max were there to advise me, despite the pleasures of independence I'd been feeling; for though I found Maurice Stoker more interesting and challenging than repugnant, I had no illusions about his straightforwardness. Now he said, "What's to see? You admit you used to bugger old Sambo back there, and then you tell my wife she's not worth biting in the belly! Don't you think the girl's got feelings?"

"That's all wrong! Don't you believe him, Anastasia: he's a regular Dean o' Flunks, and I'm the Grand Tutor! I'd *love* to bite your belly. I really would!"

"Even Max could hardly object to that," Stoker remarked.

"So what if he did? Anything I do, that's what a Grand Tutor *should* do. If I bite your wife in the belly, it's *right* to bite her in the belly!" Not to have Anastasia think my words mere idle rhetoric or dutiful apology, I went at her forthwith, sliding to my knees and boring my face past her hands into her midriff. Despite the sidecar's jolting and for all her wrench and wriggle (which I took for a kind of pouting with the whole body), I contrived to fasten through the cloth of her shift upon a pinch of that admirable, most soft place, which I clenched gently but unremittingly in my teeth until her writhing ceased and her hands no longer thrust but only clutched my hair. I felt us wheel round a bend, but was that determined she must affirm the rightness of whatever I did—a rightness, it occurred to me as I bit, *by definition*—I'd

not have let go even when we jerked now to a halt, had not
the roar of other motors suddenly enveloped us. Relinquish-
ing my tender gobbet I raised my head and blinked in a flood
of light: we were drawn up on a graveled apron before a
huge iron door, let into a steep dark hillside and guarded by
a pistoled host, sooty as their master. They grinned, as did
the riders thronging in from various roads to skid up near us,
at the wide amazement on the face that rose from Anastasia's
lap. But the only laugh was Stoker's, which, when the engines
quit, the massive door gave back, iron and ringing as itself.

6.

"So we're home!" Stoker cried. "Have to finish your meal
later, old chap!" To the door-guards he shouted, "Open her
up!" and to his aide on the nearest cycle (in which Max rode,
but would not return my greeting), "Tell Sear we've got one
dead Frumentian and one doped one he should have a look
at. And a goat-boy, too, if he's interested."

The sharp-faced lieutenant nodded. At his command (not
in our tongue) two guards with fierce-appearing dogs on leash
opened a small metal box near the door and did something
with their hands inside it. Engines were restarted; Stoker
winked at me, handed me his flask once more, and started
ours. With a grind the heavy door began to slide: smoky orange light streamed from the widening crack. I had time to
notice through my bedazzlement, as I sipped, only that other
such doors were visible in patches of yellow glare at various
heights on the rock-face, and that a double row of bluish
floodlights on tall poles, with a thick white pipe between,
stretched out over flat ground to leftwards—a brilliant line
straight to the horizon. Then we crunched forward on the
gravel towards the door, the aide's vehicle in the lead. The
guards gave way before his and Stoker's oaths; the dogs
lunged at Max, were checked with effort, and snarled at me
too as we went past them.

"They smell goat!" Stoker laughed.

I sat back in my place, stirred by the strange sights; wished

Max were in less glum spirits; marveled at the rolling door. Anastasia's solemn eyes were on me. I grinned, perhaps wildly, and rubbed my hand over where I'd bitten her.

"Didn't hurt, did it?" My attention was straining to assimilate the cavernous chamber we rolled into, hewn from the rock, dim-lit, and lined with pipes and large machinery. I scarcely caught her reply, delivered as it was almost in a whisper and with her eyes closed.

"Founder help me!"

"How's that?" I leaned closer.

She half-opened her eyes. "Is it *possible?* I don't even dare *imagine* . . ."

"What: that I'm the Grand Tutor? Of course I am." All else I ignored now except her troubled eyes. "If I weren't, I wouldn't have said I was."

"But how can a Grand Tutor . . . *bite?* I don't understand it!"

I turned up my palms. "Me either. But I think there's more than one road to Commencement Gate."

She put her hand on my forearm. "Shouldn't you be gentle and meek? And suffering? You're very *physical,* George . . ."

"Sure I'm physical. Listen, Anastasia—" It was interesting to use her name. "Do you want to Graduate or not?"

"I do!" Her eyes filled with emotion. "I'm so ashamed of all the things that've happened to me. More than anything in this campus I wish I could find out what the Answer is!"

"So do I, and I intend to. Then I'll Tutor, and on Commencement Day the wise will pass and the ignorant flunk. Don't you believe that?"

The effort gave her visible pain. "I *want* to . . ."

I touched my lips gravely to her brow. "When you do, you'll be my first Tutee, Anastasia. And the first Tutee will be the first Graduate. I swear it."

I might have added, just fully appreciating it myself, that Max had not pre-empted that distinction; much as he needed, wanted, and endeavored to believe in me, he had yet truly to manage it. But the motors roared so now in the confines of the room, speech became impossible. For just that reason, perhaps, as Anastasia's eyes considered my strange words, impulsively I said, "I rather love you, you know."

Midway into the declaration the engines once more quit together, as on some signal—though why that one and no other should be so efficiently responded to, I cannot say—with the result that my latter words stood clear. Anastasia put her hand on my fleece and glanced towards Stoker, as did I. Had he heard me through the din? I wasn't sure I cared; I myself could not have said what my words meant! But I was not easy at the way he beamed and whistled when the motorcycles parked now and their riders dismounted. A little crisply, as I helped Anastasia from the sidecar, I said, "You understand what I mean: the way Max loved all of us in the herd, because he was our keeper. A Grand Tutor loves the whole student body."

"Belly and all, hey?" Stoker cried. He caught us each by the arm. "Let's take a look around the Plant before we join the party."

But Anastasia shook her head. There was dull irritation in her face and voice now. "I want to go to bed, Maurice."

"Bed! We've got a Grand Tutor on our hands! How often does that happen?"

"Please," I told him, "I hate to be a bother . . ."

"No bother!"

"Maurice—" Anastasia covered her eyes. "Croaker *hurt* me. Please let me go now."

Her husband sighed. "Oh, all right. I'll send Sear up to have a look at you." But at her insistence that she had no need of doctors or medicines, only of rest, he shrugged and dismissed her with a cheerful smack on the posteriors. My heart was clutched with confusion.

"See how willful she is?" Stoker appealed. "And they say I mistreat her! Tell you what, George; you run along with her, cheer her up a bit. We can tour the Plant later."

He spoke with his usual breezy authority and even gave me a little push after her, who was approaching a small door in the farther wall.

"*Verboten!*" Max cried from behind me. The word—I hadn't heard it for years—halted me like a tether. Max too had stepped from his sidecar, and glared at me, his face drained. Heads spun around; the language of the order was apparently not unfamiliar to certain of the guards, in particular those with the dogs.

"Founder help her, George! She's in his power, and we got to choose!"

I heard Stoker sigh beside me.

"One girl or the whole student body!" Max cried. "If they

won't take me in your place, I'm going to walk out of here until they stop me." He turned his furious eyes on the officer near him, the long-faced one, who watched impassively. "Don't give them another minute, Georgie. Come with me; this is a flunkèd place."

I was divided as on that day when the shophar had summoned from the barn while Lady Creamhair lingered in the hemlock-grove. Max took a final look at G. Herrold's body, murmured something in his beard, and spat at the officer's feet—a thing I'd never have supposed him capable of. He turned and started for the great iron door, which was grinding shut. The guards who made to seize him were checked by a slight sign from the officer, who also with his hand bade the sentries halt the door where it was. Max paused in the narrow opening and looked back to me. His voice was terrible.

"Grand Tutor or goat!"

Stoker grinned; the guards stood by. The dogs growled through a small hum of machinery. Anastasia I saw had opened the small door and stepped into what I presently learned was a lift. I moved towards her, meaning to call, "Come with us!" But at my move she closed the door. Stoker signaled, and I turned, blanching, round: alas, Max had mistaken my step for a choice and gone; that door too shut.

Stoker clapped me on the shoulder. "Flunk 'em both, hey? Good for you! I'll send a man after Max to see he's all right. Splendid old fool, that Max—stubborn as a jackass! Convinced I'm the Dean o' Flunks! I love to tease him about the Moishians and the Bonifacists; he believes anything . . ." Interrupting himself, he gave orders to his lieutenant to change out of uniform, overtake Max in an unmarked vehicle, and transport him to some hostelry of the College. The man saluted with a click of bootheels; Stoker led me towards the door behind which Anastasia had vanished.

"Come on, I'll show you the Plant. Come on!" He laughed at my reluctance. "Max'll be all right, and you'll see Stacey later. She's upset now because of what you said, but she'll get over it. Quite a girl, isn't she?"

"She's—very nice." I allowed myself to be led with him.

"Can't say no to a soul! Oh, here, you're probably thirsty . . ." He pressed the flask on me. "Take those dogs of ours, for instance: we got them from a kennel on the Siegfrieder campus, where they'd been trained to bite anything without blond hair and blue eyes. Let me go near, they'd take

an arm off; but for Stacey they'll roll over like pups, to get
their bellies scratched. I mean the male ones, of course: can't
do a thing with the bitches; they're jealous as the Faculty
Women's Club. Attaboy, George."

The liquor was a welcome thing. One of Stoker's aides
pushed a button beside the lift-door, and we stood about
waiting for it to open.

"No, really, she's amazing, that woman." Stoker's eyes
sparkled, and he spoke behind his hand in a mock whisper.
"These Siegfrieders, you know—can't beat 'em for cleverness.
They'd trained these dogs to hump the Moishian co-eds in
their extermination campuses. Ask your friend Eierkopf about
it—didn't I hear Max mention him? He'll tell you it was all
for the sake of science; but you know those Siegfrieders,
what sports they are. I asked one of their officers once what
would happen if a Moishian girl should whelp a litter by a
purebred Siegfrieder watchdog: wouldn't that mongrelize the
class? And he said, 'Vunce dot hoppens ve is condomps on
der dogs puttink, same like ourselfs.' He even showed me his
orders from *Der Oberbefehlshaber-Professor: Blausiegelen*
for enlistees, *Superblausiegelen* for officers. Some science!
Here, I'll have one too."

He took a drink from the flask, wiped his sooty face with
the back of his hand, and returned the liquor to me. Then
with a great belch he resumed his anecdote:

"You can imagine what a time we had training *that* little
habit out of the dogs! If Stacey hadn't helped us taper 'em
off—like narcotics in the Psych Clinic, you know?—the
sons-of-bitches would've serviced every trustee's wife that
took a tour of the Plant!" He shook his head in good-natured
despair. "Then we had to taper *Stacey* off; 'Can't stand to
hear the poor things whimper,' she used to say. No wonder
the bitches don't like her!"

At last the lift-door opened, and I was moved with Stoker
and two or three guards into the elevator—the first I'd seen.
Other guards, I observed, had lifted the still-unconscious
Croaker onto a large wheeled table, which now they rolled
away; a second of the same kind was drawn up to the sidecar
wherein G. Herrold lay.

"They shouldn't hate her, though," I said thoughtfully, referring to the watchdog-bitches. For obvious reasons, the
story of Anastasia and the dogs did not affect me as it might

an ordinary human. "Don't they understand she was only helping their mates?"

Stoker positively hugged me. At the same moment the lift began to rise. "She was! She was, George! Oh, wait till Sear meets you! We *must* tell Lucky Rexford's wife and all the others not to be so unreasonable: Stacey's only trying to help their poor husbands!"

"Your wife is very sweet that way," I said firmly. "Very generous."

"Oh my, yes!" Stoker roared. "Generous she is!"

I knew I was being baited, but the strong liquor, perhaps, made me not care. "I wonder if you really appreciate her," I insisted. "You think she does things for flunkèd reasons—at least you pretend to think so. But she doesn't. She didn't want Croaker to service her this evening; she was counting on you to rescue her in time. And you *would* have, if you'd seen how she trembled; she's not big enough for him! Yet she was willing to let it happen, to keep *us* out of danger . . ."

"Sheep!" Stoker's face now was red and scowling—the first time I'd ever seen him grinless—and his voice was rough. "She's a sheep, and Spielman's another! *'Baa, baa,* take me to the slaughterhouse!' With their great silly lamb's eyes! 'Do what you want to us, we won't bite.' Made to be persecuted! Why don't they *fight?*"

The elevator stopped; its door opened noiselessly onto a narrow passageway. Stoker glared at me; the others stood expressionless. I was as much roused as shaken by the outburst, and having abandoned Max, now rose to his defense.

"Max has his faults, Mr. Stoker, but he's no coward."

"He's a sheep!" The voice echoed down the corridor. No one moved to leave the elevator. "A Moishian sheep! 'Please cut my throat, sir!' "

"No. He's a great goatherd and a great scientist. And the best advisor any hero ever had."

Stoker glowered still, but his temper seemed regained. "I notice you don't take his advice, though. Mustn't confuse the sheep with the goats, eh?" His laugh now was easier—and still we lingered in the lift! "Advice or no advice, we bucks need our bit of nanny now and then, don't we!"

"You're not part goat too, are you, sir? You don't *look* like a goat."

"See here, George—" He stepped with me just into the hall and pointed to a closed door at its blind left end. "My wife's bedroom is right at the end there. She's waiting for you. Run along, now."

Much as the notion stirred me, I shook my head. "That's not why I stayed here. Besides, she's angry with me for some reason."

"Go on! That's because you said you didn't love her any more than you loved the other girls! Very tactless remark for a Grand Tutor! No, no, don't apologize—" I had only been going to protest. "I know you didn't mean to hurt the girl's feelings. But she's *sensitive*, you know? Among us human people, when a chap bites a girl in the belly he's supposed to follow through. Go down there now and tell her you're sorry, and give her an extra-good service to make up. That's what she's waiting for."

I smiled. "You don't understand . . ."

"I do! It's you that doesn't understand. The girl's in heat, for pity's sake!"

I considered his face seriously to guess whether he was joking. Human females, as I understood, had no particular rutting-season, and of course no tails to wag in the rousing manner of an amorous doe; I frankly hadn't realized there might be other signs and sessions, as unmistakable in studentdom as was a fine-flushed vulva in our herd between the autumnal and vernal equinoxes. The notion that Anastasia was in heat threw considerable light upon the psychology of her behavior, I had to admit, however obscure its morality remained. Nay, more, it seemed to me to render pointless both Stoker's change of willful concupiscence on her part and Anastasia's pleas of self-sacrifice with charitable intent, neither of which had impressed me as quite adequate to the case. I knew myself a kid in the tangled thicket of human morals; doubtless there were complications of which I was unaware; nevertheless I'd have very much liked to ask Max just then why the phenomenon of rutting (by its nature indiscriminate) was regarded as a neutral fact, even a merit, in the stockbarns, and a likely cause of flunkage in the campus proper. Granted even that eugenical considerations (or social ones, whereof I was but dimly aware) took moral form in studentdom, so that for some intricate reason it was undesirable for a woman to bear children by any sire except her husband: on what ground did the Founder object to "coveting thy classmate's wife" if one took the contraceptive precautions I had read of? Or to mating with desirable members of a different species (as Max with the goats and Anastasia with the watchdogs), or with partners of one's own sex, in any of which cases reproduction was precluded? I supposed there was more to the matter—my dream of Mary V. Appenzeller came to mind, with a flash of its mysterious, unreasonable shame—but what the More was, I could by no means see.

In any case, Stoker had said earlier that Anastasia never went into heat. Recalling this, I understood he was baiting me again, and resolved to give as good as I had got.

"Isn't a husband supposed to service his own wife?" I asked politely. "You claim you're not a gelding; are you impotent, the way Brickett Ranunculus was at the end?"

His face, always high-colored, darkened by a number of shades; his eyes turned fierce. "Impotent? Impotent?" I really thought he might assault me, and so clenched my stick to parry. But again his anger turned to heated mirth. "Oh my! Do you know who I *am?* Do you know where you *are?* Oh, my sakes!" He snatched up my arm and drew me back into the lift. *"Impotent!"* He pushed another button and burst into merry laughter. Moreover, as the lift began to rise he farted loudly, perhaps by way of preliminary demonstration of his potency. I helped myself to another sip of liquor and grinned, pleased to have got such a rise out of him, but I was ready enough to quit that compartment when the door reopened.

The room we now stepped into (our stone-faced companions remaining for some reason in the elevator) was low-ceilinged, brilliantly lit, and quiet. The walls were smooth and gleaming white, undecorated but for one large photograph of a smiling, handsome young man not familiar to me. The floor was laid with heavy carpeting. A dozen or more men, clean-shaved and sootless, stood intent before great dialed and buttoned consoles, upon which flickered sundry-colored lights; their uniforms, I noted, were immaculate and truly uniform, unlike the motley of the guards downstairs. One wall was a grating of heavy steel mesh, through which I saw a second room quite like ours, the only noticeable difference being in the cut and color of the attendants' garb: rhododendron-green on our side, rust-red on theirs. Other than a muffled click of switches and the whirr of tape-spools from a row of glass-front cabinets, the place was still. So much so, and so absorbed the dial-watchers, I was hushed upon entering—but Stoker belched as it were defiantly. And in vain, for no one so much as glanced his way.

"This is Founder's Hill you're inside of, you know!" His voice was cross and deliberately loud, as jarring as the dirty prints our shoes left on the carpet. "Talk about *power:* all the power on this campus comes from here! The same power that runs the University! This is the Control Room."

He seemed not at ease, and annoyed when I asked whether these attendants were under his command.

"What would I want with people like these? They don't talk my language." He hastened to add, however, seeing my insinuation, that although the dial-watchers were responsible only to the Chancellor, I should not make the mistake of thinking his, Stoker's, potency thereby diminished. The power was merely controlled and directed from this room; it originated "down below," in Stoker's bailiwick. Moreover, the so-called controllers had no real authority: they only attended the dials and switches whose actual instructions came not even from the Chancellor, but from that bank of tapes—in short, from WESCAC.

"WESCAC!" I frowned at the pulsing spools and tingled as if ambushed. "I thought WESCAC was in Tower Hall!"

"Oh well, this is just one arm of the thing, you know. Not even that: a finger. It programs the power needs for West Campus, itself included." As we strolled among the consoles (Stoker thrusting out his tongue at various attendants), he charged me not to forget that last fact: WESCAC, people rightly held, was the seat and instrument of West-Campus power—brain-power, military power, and thus political and economic power as well, indirectly. But it was essentially no more than a tool and manager, dependent absolutely on the power supplied to it, at its own governance, from the realm "down below." In short, the power that ultimately controlled the Power Plant originated in the Power Plant, necessarily and exclusively—and the Power Plant was his, Stoker's, domain.

"If you don't mind my asking: how did you get to be in charge of it?"

He grinned. "WESCAC appointed me."

While I assimilated this fresh paradox he led me to the steel-screen partition, on which I saw now signs of warning in several languages. "This screen is on the border between East and West Campus," he said. "The line runs right through Founder's Hill. Don't touch it, by the way, or you'll cook

—it's a high-voltage thing like the Main Power Line you saw outside, that marks the boundary."

I was familiar enough with electric pasture-fences to understand; from a respectful distance I scrutinized with interest the men on the other side.

"Are those real Nikolayan what-you-call-'ems?" The term for their administrative system had slipped my mind, perhaps aided by the dark liquor.

"Absolutely! Enemies of private education! Classmates in the classless college! Founderless Student-Unionists! You see how different their way of life is from ours." His tone was sarcastic, and indeed, but for the style of dress and the fact that their consoles and attendants faced away from ours (whereas ours faced away from theirs), I could see little difference between the two rooms. Their machinery perhaps was larger; ours I thought had more colorful lights. A small door, also of steel mesh, was built into the screen. Stoker approached it and set up a shout in what seemed to be no particular language, merely an abusive clamor accompanied by grimaces, foot-stampings, and waving of the arms.

"Awah! *Nyet! Da!* Open sesame! Borscht borscht!"

At once a man near us turned a series of knobs on his dial-panel, and on the Nikolayan side a stocky young fellow with a black eye-patch did the same. On both sides impassive guards with rifles appeared—they had been standing at such rigid attention in the corners that I hadn't noticed them—clicked their bolts, and held their weapons ready. The door swung open of itself.

"Don't you move," Stoker warned. But he himself swaggered through the doorway, made a deep bow to the Nikolayan riflemen (saluting them too with a cracking fart), and returned to pay the same compliment to the guards on our side. The dials were turned back, the door swung shut and latched itself, the guards marched precisely to their corners. Except for myself, who caught my breath with astonishment, and the young Nikolayan with the eye-patch, who grinned and shook his head, no one appeared even to notice the performance, much less protest it.

"Nobody else is allowed through there," Stoker said. "Me they have to put up with, like it or not, and neither side likes it. But they've got to have power if they're going to be enemies."

I had wondered whether he had a counterpart on the Nikolayan side of the screen; evidently he had not. So I asked why, since a single source powered both WESCAC and EASCAC, and he controlled that source, he could not single-handedly remove the danger of a third campus riot by turning off the power, or threatening to.

"That's a Max-Spielman question," he said, with some contempt. "You don't understand what power is! The furnace doesn't turn off the thermostat! You want the heart to decide to kill the brain, but it can't do it! The heart might *kill* the brain, but it can't *decide* to; only the brain can decide. Don't forget, though: it gets its deciding-power from the heart!" He waved his hand impatiently. "Flunk this! Come on, I'll show you."

Before leaving, however, he took the trouble to obstruct the view of the nearest attendant by standing nose-to-nose with him and making a grotesque face, which the man ignored as if Stoker were invisible. And I observed that when the same attendant reached for a flashing button on the panel, Stoker pretended for mischief's sake to catch at his hand, but never actually touched him, and even made way slightly, though cursing all the while. Then, not to confine his scorn exclusively to West-Campus controllers, he spat over his shoulder toward the Nikolayans: the drops struck the mesh with a puff and sizzled into curls of steam.

"I hate this place," he growled.

We returned to the elevator, pushed the bottom button, and descended a considerable distance farther than we'd come up. Stoker's face brightened as we dropped; the guards too seemed more at ease with every passing level. I myself was somewhat dizzied by the falling sensation—and by the liquor as well, no doubt—but it was a feeling more curious than disagreeable, and I chose not to surrender the flask on its account.

A monstrous din rose around us as we stopped, and doubled its volume with a crash when the door slid back—a roar like an endless thunderclap, shocking the heart.

"Furnace Room!" Stoker shouted in my ear; I could scarcely hear him. At first, owing to the darkness, I could see only that we had stepped onto a long balcony, beyond and below which were considerable steaming spaces lit by intermittent fires. The air was hot, with the reek of the fumigating-candles we sometimes used in the barns, and from near and far the din assailed us: grindings, shrieks, cracks, roars,

hisses, crashes, shouts! When my eyes accommodated I went
to the railing with Stoker and saw how truly whelming was
the place: the floor was a barn's-height below us, the ceiling
lost in dark vapors above; a fair-sized herd could scatter in
the space between the walls—rough-hewn from the mountain's bowels, black as coal, and warm to the touch. Vats or
caldrons huge as silos rose before us, interlaced with catwalks, pipes, and cables; the red glow came from under
them, where great fires seemed to rage beneath the floor. The
steam issued everywhere: from joints in the caldron-plates,
from valves big as wagon-wheels, from the steel trucks full of
ash or stone that rolled on rails down every aisle, from fis-
sures in the very walls and floor. Troops of grimed and burly
laborers, a few women among them, ran hither and thither,
toiling, cursing. Stripped to the waist or covered in sweat-
soaked denim, black rags about their heads, they wrestled
with valve-stems and winch-gears, plied wrenches big as
crowbars to great bolt-heads, and stoked the awful fires with
battering-rams. Whistles screeched; orders were bawled from
above and below; everyone seemed in everyone else's way.
Steam-valves were opened without warning, and those standing near had to spring for their lives; rail-trucks were sent ca-
reering heedless through crowded aisles, sometimes colliding
with one another and spilling half their cargo onto the tracks;
empty buckets were knocked off catwalks; toes were trod
upon, shins barked, fingers mashed; fights broke out on the
least occasion between work-gangs whose paths happened to
cross—rail-truck crews and furnace-men, for example—or
between members of the same gang, for no apparent reason
and as often in sport as in anger. Finally, there seemed to
prevail a continuing state of emergency: furnace-doors blew
open of their own accord; rail switches were thrown in the
nick of time; winches jammed; cables broke; steam-pipes
burst. Repairmen dashed from a partly-plugged leak to cut an
arcing cable that bid fair to roast a stoking-gang beneath;
breaking the circuit, however, released for some reason the
trap-door on a hopper of fly-ash suspended overhead from a
traveling crane, and both crews were half-buried in an ava-
lanche of grime. Fists flew instantly, along with spanners and
winch-handles; one man fell smitten into the dust, whether
dead or stunned I could not tell, and others surely must have
joined him had not everyone's attention been diverted by a
shriek from the leaky pipe abandoned earlier. Some scalding

liquid now sprayed from it upon an illuminated boiler-gauge, big as a window, across whose face I saw a large black pointer climbing steadily towards an area marked in red. A number of brawling repairmen rushed to the pipe; as many ran the other way. Two of the furnace-gang dragged off their fallen comrade, a third hopped in the ashes and tore, weeping, at his hair, while a fourth flung back his head and laughed at the whole spectacle—until all alike were obliged to leap clear when an empty train-car charged like a mad buck down their aisle and plowed into the fly-ash.

To gather one's wits was out of the question; I was seized up, as were Stoker and the guards, into the general alarum. Inquiry, explanation were impossible. "Here's where your *power* is!" Stoker shouted at me. Grinning he thumped his chest with one hand and extended the other towards the bedlam beneath us. "Volcano with a cap on it!"

He dashed away at once down the balcony and out onto the catwalk that ran beside the boiler-gauge. The guards ran with him, and I followed after as quickly as I could, towards the group that milled and tussled now around the leaky pipe. We all were wide-eyed and shouting, myself included; it was unthinkable not to widen the eyes and shout, though what our words were, if they were words at all, I have no idea. Stoker bellowed above us all—"Ho, there! Hallo! *Hey!*"—and pitched into the melee of laughing, swearing laborers, swinging at the men, pinching the massive women, and glancing from time to time (as did we all) at the meter-long needle on the gauge, still climbing slowly. No matter what the numbers signified: that the lower ones were black and the higher red was significance enough, given the general consternation and the horrid rumbling that began now under the boiler. Stoker pried and clubbed his way to the center of the gang with the aid of a long steel bar—a sort of mammoth box-end wrench, at least a meter in the shank—which he'd wrested from a black chap in the mob. His objective was a valve-stem just up-pipe from the whistling leak; two slams he gave it with the giant tool, heedlessly crippling a brace of repairmen with his backswing, and then fit the wrench-end on it like a capstan-bar.

"Hoya!" he roared, and shoved his neighbor to the bar, who laid hold and strained back on it with all his force. "Ho to, there!" he bawled at another; "put your arse in it!" And the second locked arms about the waist of the first, but the two together couldn't budge the valve. Now the rest fell to with a will, Stoker collaring and kicking them into line. But while a number locked together in a sweaty chain to pull the bar this way, the others strove as gruntly to pull it that. "No, blast!" would yell Stoker; "Flunk-ay!" they would curse back; and some on both sides seeing what was amiss, each changed to pushing instead of pulling, with the same result. One team had fewer members, but all male; the other had more men but three brawny women as well, by whose presence less was gained in horsepower than was lost in horseplay. After two reversals of direction, moreover, the rhythm broke entirely; every man pulled, pushed, or stood fast as he listed, braying imprecations on the rest in any case—and the bar stood still, but not the gauge-needle. Suddenly a man near the end of the longer line let go and fled—or would have, had I not thrust out my stick with an oath and brought him crashing down.

"Yi hoo!" I cried, and in an access of mad spirit hurled the liquor-flask at the glass face of the gauge. Since our objective, clearly, was to stop the pointer before it reached the red, why did we not lay hold of it, I wondered, swing from it if need be, and check it where it was? Alack, the flask rebounded to the catwalk, barely having cracked what I meant to shatter, and was scrabbled for at once by the deserter—luckily for me, who had not seen him raging towards me with a ball-peen hammer! And thus was worked the rescue of us all: the teammates he'd abandoned, seeing bad faith slaked while good went thirsting, broke muddled ranks to have at him, just when Stoker with boot-tip and tongue had got the lesser gang aligned and bade them heave. Heave they did, all unopposed, and tumbled arselong when the bar came about. Even as they rolled and cursed, the whistling petered; the pointer trembled at disaster's very threshold, lingered a moment still, then subsided with the rumbling underneath. Mine however was the only shout of joy: fights and tickling-matches had broken out among the workers, all of whom strove for the flask, and Stoker had set out merrily down the catwalk after a chocky lass who'd goosed him with her oilcan-spout at the moment of crisis. When I overtook them he'd already had his revenge, having cornered her against a switchboard, wrested the can from her, and under cover of a stolen kiss, squirted a jet down the open bosom of her shirt. It was a lubricant black as oil but evidently less bland, for it set the girl into a hopping frenzy. She bounded from him in my direction, jerking and squealing as if a coal were between her breasts; indeed the stuff burned her at least as much as the prank amused; she tore open her work-shirt, looked round her wildly, and spying my fine new wrapper, flung herself at my knees, where with violent motions, laughing and shrieking, she soiled my fleece with her blackened bubs. Not content, Stoker stole up behind her as she writhed, drew back the waist-band of her breeches, and fired a second squirt into the seat—which so got to her she let go her teats and raced down the catwalk, now flinging her arms wide, now clawing at her breeches, now leaping and spinning, now rubbing her buttocks madly against the rail. Her fellow workers and myself shouted with laughter at her plight, which soon caught everyone's eye; all work was abandoned; mirth thundered off the walls. Then Stoker tilted back his head and simply bellowed. I did likewise—it was the perfect thing to do!—and one by one the rest joined in, as if together we might burst the mountain. Never such spirit as now roared in me! I had need of the railing to steady myself; it was as though we floated on the very roar, which once begun appeared to go on of itself—until another pipe or valve exploded aisles away. Stoker sprang to the switchboard and pulled a pair of levers; altogether in the spirit I pulled a few myself, and was rewarded by the spectacle of winches spinning, crane-buckets dropping, signal-lights flashing, and work-gangs leaping like creosoted fleas.

"This is Graduation!" Stoker shouted happily. "Never mind the question: the Answer's *power!*"

Its fine explosive sound made him repeat the word, and me join in. *"Power! Power!"* I pulled another lever, and the entire catwalk slowly descended towards the next lower balcony; yet another, and the nearest furnace door yawned to afford me my first clear glimpse of the fire inside—a boundless, flickerless, terrifying white-orange glow, like one compressed and solid flame, the heat of which even at fifty meters had like to have singed my fleece.

"Wrong lever!" Stoker laughed, and having pushed it back and pulled two others he rushed me off the catwalk and onto the lower balcony. Moments later a crane-bucket swinging furnacewards (at my command, it seems) crashed through the catwalk rail and spilled its molten contents directly on the switchboard. Sparks flew, bells rang, men with masks and hoses swarmed to the catwalk, which soon disappeared in a pall of steam.

"Come on, before the whole flunkèd place blows!" Stoker opened a nearby door marked AID STATION, and grinning at the high-voiced cries and oaths that issued forth, beckoned me in. Standing in the middle of the room (a small one, better lit than the Furnace Room and much quieter once the door closed) was the victim of his recent prank; shirt off and trousers down, she had been being ministered to by three other women, brawny workers all, who had smeared white ointment on her soot-grimed bosoms and husky posteriors. One of the women who had come wrathfully forward now smiled and said, "Oh flunk, it's the Chief! You sure fixed Madge."

"She had it coming," Stoker said cheerily.

Upon our entry Madge had spun from us and snatched up her breeches; seeing who we were now she let them fall and grumbled, "Sonofabitch, all I done was goose you. Look what *you* done!" She thrust towards us her injured hams. "Like to took the skin off!"

"No! Let's have a look, Madgie." He pretended to examine her closely, turning her around by the hips and frowning at the blisters. "Striking effect, George, isn't it?"

"Quite striking," I agreed. And in truth, for all her sweat and dishevelment, the naked laborer was not without a hefty beauty: her short black hair was bound by a grease-stained rag, under which her wide, coarse-featured face beamed mischievously; her arms and waist were thick, her hips ample, her thighs well-muscled, her legs unshaved. Aware she was being made game of, she nonetheless exhibited herself with pride and petulance, hands on hips; and while she was in no way comparable to Anastasia, astonishing indeed were the white-salved bosoms against the brown skin, their nipples puckered stoutly under our gaze. Just as fetching was her spirit: having turned full circle she seized her examiner's hair and rubbed his face into the salve, seeing to it he got a beardful despite his merry oaths. The other women chuckled and vowed good-naturedly he had got no more than his desert; by way of compensation for his prank Stoker granted Madge relief from the balance of her shift—on condition she accompany us, just as she was, to a costume party which he said was in progress in the Living Room.

"I *wondered* why your pal had that get-up on!" she said. The prospect of appearing naked and bedaubed before strangers nowise dismayed her; she agreed to go with us, stipulating only that she be permitted to improvise a mask for the sake of her modesty and wear her high-top safety shoes for the sake of her toes, which were afflicted with corns. Stoker consented and fetched a new flask from the first-aid locker while the woman shucked off her denims. Her two companions, loudly envious of her good fortune, pitched in to repaint her, improving their earlier effort with bright-colored tinctures from the locker: her nipples and deep-punched navel they ringed concentrically with red against a white-salve background; bright yellow ointment banded all her limbs and set off cleft and dimples of her strong brown rump. Her hair they left bound in the kerchief, and by way of a mask wound her head in gauze bandage, outlining eye-, nose-, and mouth-holes with red antiseptic. Though they laughed and teased as they worked, wagering their chief would appear next morning with a multicolored beard, they were much impressed when they stood back to view the finished product, which I applauded vigorously.

"Aw, you're beautiful, Madgie," one of them said. "You'll knock their eyes out."

"Pretty as a picture," said the other. "Ain't she, Chief? I just wish I could see their faces when you walk in. Have loads of fun, honey."

"Don't dare breathe a word to Harry!" Madge pleaded happily. "He'd have a conniption!" She looked down at her body. "Wish to Pete we had a mirror in here. Flunk it all, Mr. Stoker, we need a mirror!"

Stoker slipped his arm around her waist and offered her the flask. "Here's all you need, Madgikins." He dismissed her attendants, bidding them notify his own that we were gone to his Spring-Carnival party in the Living Room, and promising that Madge would have much to report on the morrow. The woman stood erect, shod and painted, in the middle of the room, and tipped the flask up—the action thrust out her bull's-eyed belly (hard as G. Herrold's, by the look of it) and flexed the muscles of her ribs and shoulders.

"By George!" I exclaimed.

She saw how I gazed at her, and winked as she drank. "You ain't badlooking yourself, kid." Feet apart and arms akimbo now, she ignored Stoker's playful strokings from behind. "So where's the party?"

I rushed at her with a joyous cry, seized her by the hips, and would turn her about for a proper mounting. She laughed, game enough, but did not at once understand just what I wished, and Stoker took advantage of the little confusion to intervene.

"Plenty of time later, old fellow."

"Later nothing! Bend over, ma'am! I'm George the Goat-Boy."

But he inserted himself between us with a grin and would not be pushed away. "You forget you're already spoken for."

"You think I can't do the pair of them?" I demanded.

"Attaboy!" Madge cheered.

"I'll show you who's potent," I vowed.

But Stoker, though he beamed approval of my attitude, insisted we move on to the party, and clasping each of us firmly about the shoulders, let us through the rear of the Aid Station into a long dim corridor, just wide enough for three to walk abreast. Light-headedly I complained, "Supposed to be so potent. I think you're jealous."

Stoker only hooted, and Madge laughed too. We paused to pass the flask around, and I found myself leaning against the wall for support as I drank.

"Jealous he ain't, lamb," Madge said. "Not a jealous bone in him! He caught me and Harry going to it in the Aid Station once and didn't say a word, did you, Mr. Stoker? Just stood there and watched." Her voice turned mischievous. "I figured that was why he'd brought *you* along—so he could watch us."

"Tales out of school!" Stoker scolded, and pinched her near buttock. She sprang forward with a squeal, then around behind me to escape him. I growled and snatched at her gaudy breasts, which by virtue of their paint slipped from my grasp, and the three of us then raucoused down the corridor. At the end was a double door labeled LIVING ROOM: Madge reached it first, found it locked, and turned breathless and laughing to face us. Stoker came up next, but instead of having at her he drew a ring of keys from his trouser-pocket and commenced to search through them. She turned then to me, held back by my limp; and seeing I was still all hot resolve, shrank laughing to the door and held out her arms to fend me off.

"Now, pet!" she warned merrily. "Mind what the Chief said! Not till later, when you're done with Miss Stacey!"

"He's not *my* chief," I declared, and hoisting my wrapper, laid hold and approached at the ready.

Stoker found the key he wanted and thrust it into the lock. "Tell her who you are, George: she ought to be proud."

"She'll know soon enough," I replied. "Turn around, ma'am!"

She looked to Stoker.

"Better do what George says," he advised, and turned the key in the lock; "believe it or not, he's the next Grand Tutor."

What her expression was, I could not tell. She still pressed against the door, but lowered her arms uncertainly and then put her hands behind her. Eagerly I laid hold of her; dutifully she turned. But the moment I crouched for the service Stoker pushed on his door, and the two flew open as one. Madge pitched forward, and I swayed dumbstruck—my stick in one hand, myself in the other—before a sumptuous, thronging hall.

"Ladies and gentlemen!" Stoker shouted. "The Grand Tutor of the Western Campus!"

7.

The Living Room, if less cavernous and dark, was in its way as riotous a spectacle as the Furnace Room, and almost as noisy. A hundred men and women, at least, roistered and roiled there in every degree and quality of dress, from sequined gowns to sooty coveralls. None, after all, wore masks, nor were any save Madge quite naked, as far as I could see, and though the faces of the women were painted, what they displayed of their backs, limbs, and bosoms led one to doubt that any bull's-eyes or yellow-daubed dimples hid under their clothes. So grand was the general carouse, only the nearest dozen faces turned when Madge tumbled gorgeously in. A few folk whistled or applauded; three or four raised her to her feet with much horseplay, and then a brawny chap dived roaring at her legs, hoisted her up on his shoulders, and bore her off laughing and waving into the throng. Several others saluted their host with upraised glasses, two or three stared curiously at me; the rest went on with their merrymaking. It was the first *party* I had witnessed. The guests sang, they danced and scuffled. Here one vomited; there one wept. This one balanced bottles on his nose; that one beat his head against a wall. Two gentlemen tickled a flailing lady until with a whoop she pissed; three matrons sat upon an old man's back while a fourth befoamed him with a fire extinguisher. Here a bloody fist-fight was in progress; there a game of leap-frog. A brass band bleated like two-score shophars in a storm of thunder—my first experience of *music*. Long tables at the wall were laden with bowls of black liquor and great platters of meat: the guests, I realized with horror, were gnawing upon legs of fowl and knuckles of deceasèd pigs. I saw a very pregnant lady brought to one such table and laid supine among the spare-ribs, where, drawing up her knees and clutching at her belly, she shouted, "Here it comes!" I saw a shy young couple holding hands in the corner, and two pretty maids kissing, and two fellows waltzing nimbly together, and a solitary chap with his hand in his trouserfly. Just before my eyes a man was struck down with an empty bottle and robbed of his watch by his drinking-companions, one of whom failed to make good his escape because he paused to defend a young girl being forcibly undressed by three uniformed men: the thief was apprehended by one and the watch returned by another to its owner (who however could not rejoice in his good fortune, being either insensible or dead); the third, meanwhile, was obliged to give way before the fury of the girl their victim, whose placket had been torn: he begged her pardon and the honor of a dance; she hesitated, laughed, stripped off the torn skirt, and spun merrily away with him in fetching cotton drawers.

All this I saw, and yet scarcely saw anything, so enormous was the sight. I gaped in the doorway, cod in hand.

"A little Carnival party," Stoker said. "We have one every night this week. You should see the place on New Year's Eve!" So persistently rumored was the approach of a new Grand Tutor, he explained, it had become popular practice among conscientious students to don caps and gowns and celebrate his arrival, and their own Commencement, in advance; in less reverent circles, like Stoker's, the same thing was done in burlesque: one of their number would be chosen "Tutor of the Revels" and given absolutely direction of the party, bestowing honors on the gamest and flunking from the premises any who declined to join the fun. What was more, there had been in recent years a rash of pretenders to actual Grand-Tutorhood, who, however bizzare or insubstantial their claim, never failed to find at least a few believers, and indeed were sometimes quite popular and influential. These were much sought after by earnest students and smart party-givers, and while it was within Stoker's jurisdiction, as director of Main Detention, to arrest any truly dangerous impostors, he often invited the more colorful ones to entertain his guests.

"Wish you could have seen the chap we had here a month ago: claimed the basic energy in the University was a kind of sound-wave given off by the sex-organs, that only he and his Graduates could hear. We all put little microphones between our legs and made Organic Harmony. That's what he said the Answer was—Music of the Spheres! He particularly liked Stacey's *timbre* when he tuned her in, and she swore she could hear something, too, like singing. All *I* could hear from anybody was farts and static . . . Have a bite to eat?"

A waiter had paused before us with a tray of burnt and dismembered chicken-bodies. Stoker helped himself to two handfuls; I turned away to keep from retching at the sight.

"Sorry, old man; forgot." He sent the waiter off with orders to find a plate of hay, offering me in the meantime a handful of paper napkins by way of *hors d'oeuvre*, which I declined, having quite lost my appetite.

"Another chap we had claimed the Answer was a science he'd invented called Psychophysics. Something to do with the Third Law of Emotion, and the mind as a Reaction Engine . . . I forget exactly. Anyhow he said we'd never reach Commencement Gate because we'd lost our compression and had no spark; we were too choked up; the modern transmission of our power-drives had made us shiftless; we were neutral idlers who slipped in the clutches for want of a new converter; our blocks were cracked; we needed our heads examined and our old shock-absorbers replaced. So he picked Stacey to be the first to get a Psychomotor Tune-up and be equipped with new Overhead Values—they *always* pick Stacey. But by the time she got up on the platform with him—see that platform in the middle of the floor, where Croaker's dancing with your friend? It's right over the furnace we use for cremations. Well, he had all his gadgets set up there, but once he got under Stacey's hood . . ."

I heard no more, but with an angry cry charged into the crowd. There indeed was mighty Croaker on a dais in the center of the room, hub of the carouse. Upon a sort of couch there, low enough to have escaped my notice, he had been laid out in black gown and mortarboard, the corpse of G. Herrold beside him; now apparently just reviving from his anesthesia, he had staggered to his feet as Stoker talked, and a cheer had gone up from the crowd; he'd looked about him in a daze, then for some reason raised my dead friend's body from the couch. The dim room-lights at once grew dimmer, a spotlight fell on the dais, and the band set up a pounding rhythm—whereupon, even as Stoker so placidly remarked, the black giant had commenced a horrid shuffling dance. Rage flushed my dizziness away; I thrust and shoved people aside, spilling their drinks, even knocking them down.

"Gangway for the Goat-Boy!" Stoker called behind me.

Before I could get near the dais the sport changed character: some bold fellow leaped up to join the dance and was knocked sprawling by a sweep of Croaker's arm; another took his place, a lean dark-haired chap, who instead of dancing held out a lady's wrap and called, *"Huh, toro, huh!"* Croaker dropped G. Herrold's body to the couch and rushed at the newcomer, who however sidestepped, spun the garment gracefully behind his hips, and sent Croaker flying head-first off the platform, into the crowd. Those nearest screamed and scrambled; others shouted *"Olé!"* The dark-haired fellow bowed and hopped lightly down to do the trick again. Now the spotlight followed the action about the room: coats and kerchiefs flapped from all sides, and Croaker, his mortarboard gone, heaved and laid about him indiscriminately. Some managed to dodge him in the manner of the dark-haired fellow; others he caught hold of and flung, howling, through the air, men and women alike—and every rush brought a chorus of *olés*.

"Make way for the Grand Tutor!" Stoker shouted. "Let the Goat-Boy through!" But all were preoccupied with Croaker. Then indeed they scattered, not in deference to me but because Croaker happened to charge next in my direction, and I found myself facing him alone. The light embraced us both, and whether because he dimly recollected me or merely because I looked different from the others, he paused to blink. Then with a growl he came on. Notwithstanding my limp and the quantity of black liquor I had drunk, I felt no fear, only excitement, as in the days when I'd merrily baited the bucks of the herd. If Croaker was several times heavier than Redfearn's Tommy, and more powerful, he was infinitely less nimble: he could not turn in his tracks, hook with his head, spring high in the air, or kick behind him, and he was easily faked out of balance. All I had to fear from him was the span of his arms and the clutch of his hands, both which I found it possible to elude by ducking, feinting, and springing—the finest arts of goatdom. The real danger was that the crowd who quickly pressed round to urge us on would take up my springing-room; this peril I minimized by the simple expedient of leading Croaker full tilt into them on every pass until they maintained a respectful distance.

"Olé!" they cheered, more enthusiastic than ever. "Ole! Olé!" Never since my ill-starred tenure as Dean of the Hill had I known such applause. I curbed my exhilaration with that memory and looked before I leaped, passing under his arms, feinting here, springing there, spinning, dodging, dancing from him, and always gauging from the corners of my eyes my distance from the crowd. Five times I passed him, and a sixth, each time more daringly, and he never touched me. After the second I was sure he recognized me: his roars turned to cunning grunts, and his eyes grew bright as a sportive buck's. When on the fifth pass I spun him off-balance and brought him crashing down, he groaned as in protest and lost interest in the game; I believe I might have leaped upon his shoulders then and rode him with impunity, but loath to put an end to those olés I managed to tease him into one charge more. His heart was not in it; his eyes wandered even as he lunged, and fixed upon loud-hammed Madge, whom a lady and a gentleman had led unsteadily into the light. At sight of Croaker in academic gown she was seized with mirth—and wondrous was the dance of her bull's-eyes in the glare! Croaker halted before them, blinked twice or thrice, gave a whimpering grunt, and snatched.

"Hunh, Croaker!" I cried, but he would not be provoked. Madge he flung over-shoulder like a sack of grain; she whooped but seemed not fearful as he bore her off. When I came up behind and dared even to thump his back with my fist, defying him to turn, she grabbed my hair and kissed me merrily, then waved and thrust out her tongue at the parting crowd. As for Croaker, I had as well challenged a black-oak trunk or buck in mid-service for all he heeded me. The spot-light followed them, as did many of my audience, and I considered chasing after; but others pressed drinks and attentions on me, a heady new pleasure I could not forgo. My original indignation had quite passed. Two of Stoker's staff, I noted, were restoring G. Herrold to his repose on the dais-couch, and I twinged with a moment's wonder whether all was well with Max; then Stoker joined the crowd around me, and I gave myself over to the dizzy spirits roused in me by exercise, and nourished by liquor and acclaim.

Especially cordial were the pair who a few minutes earlier had escorted Madge onto the scene, and whom Stoker identified now as Dr. Kennard Sear and Hedwig, his wife.

"*Enchanté*," the doctor smiled. "Remarkable performance." A long dry gentleman he was, superbly manicured and groomed, with close silver hair and fine soft garments. His face, frame, and fingers were thin tan, even his voice was, and without moisture; only his eyes were less than desiccate, their pale brightness turning into glitter at every blink. The whole effect of him was of a lean pear dried in the sun, its gold juice burnt into thin exotic savor—and in fact it was pleasant to smell him, all but his breath, which was slightly foul. "Doesn't he have classic features, Hed?" he asked his wife.

"He looks like Maurice in bronze!" Mrs. Sear exclaimed. "He could be your younger brother, Maurice." She too, and her voice, were dry and not unhandsome, but where her husband seemed *cured*, like supplest vellum, Mrs. Sear was brittle—sharp-edged as the stones on her ears and hands, but more fragile.

Stoker affirmed the resemblance. "George's got more in common with me than *some* brothers I could mention."

"You're really Max Spielman's protégé?" Dr. Sear asked smoothly. "We *must* have some interviews."

"And evenings," Mrs. Sear insisted, narrowing her bright eyes and touching my fleece with her long red nails. "Something more *intime* than this madhouse of Maurice's. Are you matriculating, or just on tour?"

"Ma'am?" Despite my liquor I felt at ease and self-possessed, they so obviously admired me. But I had difficulty following conversations. It occurred to me to remark that I had once loved a doeling named Hedda; but I forbore

on the grounds of possible tactlessness, and thought myself a
subtle fellow.

"You haven't heard, Heddy?" Stoker cried. "This is no ordinary goat-boy: he's come to show you and me how to pass
the Finals!"

"Dear me," Dr. Sear said mildly. "Another one?"

"Oh, George!" his wife scolded me. "That's too tiresome!
You're charming enough just as you are. Isn't he, Ken?"

"A regular faun," her husband agreed. "We'll certainly
have you out some evening."

"Watch him, though," Stoker warned. "He bites bellies."

"Just be a goat-boy," Mrs. Sear said, like a child giving an
order, and patted my shoulder. "It's much more original.
Everybody's a Grand Tutor lately."

I only smiled at them, they were such amiable people. The
orchestra struck up a spirited tune, and the bystanders dispersed, some to dance, others to join a new excitement across
the room, whither Croaker had fetched his prize. Dr. Sear
took two glasses from a passing waiter and gave one to me.
His wife congratulated Stoker on his knack for "turning up
originals," declaring he'd surpassed himself this evening with
Croaker, myself, and "that delicious creature with the boots
and bull's-eyes."

Stoker grinned. "I knew you'd hit it off with Madge."

"I couldn't keep my *hands* off her! Is she George's . . .
mate?"

"Just a pipefitter from the Furnace Room," Stoker said
lightly. "I'll get her to give you her number after the cremation—if there's anything left of her when Croaker gets
through."

I declared that I had no mate.

"You *don't?*" Mistaking my meaning, both Sears expressed
their sympathy and assured me that that condition need last
no longer than I wished it to. "The co-eds will go wild over
you," Mrs. Sear said enviously, and her husband agreed, adding in a frank and cordial tone that if however I preferred a
maturer and more knowledgeable partner, one from whom
even a young satyr like myself might learn a thing or two, he
did not judge it out of place to propose . . .

"Here comes Heddy's competition," Stoker interrupted,
and my chest tingled at the sight of Anastasia coming towards us. She had exchanged her soiled white shift for a
long-sleeved wrapper of red silk, belted at the waist—a sleep-

ing-garment, perhaps—and her hair was piled now high on her head and bound with red ribbon. Beautiful, beautiful she was: her face seemed rather paler, and her eyes were most luminously troubled as she made her way through the brawling crowd.

"Stacey *darling!*" Mrs. Sear hastened to embrace her. "I heard what *happened* in the Gorge, dear baby! Did it hurt you terribly?"

What she replied I could not hear, but she acknowledged Mrs. Sear's demonstration with a quick smile and turned her cheek to be kissed. The woman hung onto her, touching now her shoulder, now her hair, and with an arm slipped around her waist led her up to us. Dr. Sear hastened to add his sympathy to his wife's, catching Anastasia's hand briefly in both of his and brushing gracefully with his lips her forehead. For a long moment her eyes were on me, questioning, appraising, and I endeavored to give back a gaze equally intense; but though my mind and flesh were most passionately stirred, there was no clearness left in me, and I swayed on my feet. She flashed a blaming look at Stoker, who was regarding us as usual with huge amusement.

"He's *drunk!*" she said bitterly.

I pointed my stick at her. "Come here to me, Anastasia." She turned her face away as I approached. "I love you," I said sternly.

"You don't know what you're saying."

Stoker explained to the Sears that I'd made the *faux pas* of declaring I loved all studentdom equally.

Hedwig purred. "Of course he does, dear: he's *supposed* to." They both caressed her, and Dr. Sear patted my shoulder also, as if to bridge our differences.

"I'm not upset," Anastasia said crossly. "Maurice is only teasing."

"She's his first Tutee," Stoker said.

"She will be," I declared, and touched the back of my fingers to her neck. She stiffened, but did not withdraw. "But she doesn't believe me yet."

Dr. Sear looked interestedly into my face for a moment and then exclaimed to Stoker: "Splendid fellow! Can't get over it!"

"Enos Enoch with balls," Stoker agreed. "Did you notice his amulet, Hedwig?"

Mrs. Sear did now, caught it up in her hands, and squealed with delight.

"Aren't they a handsome pair," her husband murmured.

"They *are,* Kennard!"

"No, my dear, I mean Stacey and George. They're nymph and faun." He joined my hand to hers, declaring that all things beautiful ravished his spirit; that Beauty in fact was as close to being the Answer as anything he knew. "I've been exposed to every idea in the University, George," he complained with a smile, "and don't believe in any of them. But if there *were* such a thing as Finals, and I were the Grand Tutor, I'd pass the two of you just for being beautiful."

Anastasia blushed. When I made to sip my drink she stayed my hand. "Please don't drink any more. Maurice wants to make a fool of you."

I declared myself indifferent to that prospect.

Mrs. Sear embraced us both. "I'd love to paint you together! In the nude!"

"It matters to me," Anastasia said quietly. "He wants to show them you aren't what you say you are."

Dr. Sear agreed with his wife that we would make a splendid group.

"Could you work from a photograph, Heddy?" Stoker asked. "We could photograph them after the funeral."

"Let him do what he wants to," I said to Anastasia, squeezing her hand. "Whatever I do and however I look, I'm still the Grand Tutor."

"Listen to him!" Dr. Sear marveled.

"Didn't I tell you?" Stoker said. "He's a natural."

"A Grand Tutor doesn't get drunk and make a public fool of himself!" Anastasia scolded.

"A Grand Tutor does what I do," I replied, and, not certain I'd made my meaning clear, I added, "It's not what I do, it's because *I* do it."

"Why—that's perfect!" Dr. Sear exclaimed. "What a thing to say!"

I pointed out to him—not however removing my eyes from Anastasia, on whom I smiled with mounting love—that had I said something stupid instead of wise, it would have made no difference.

"Quite! Quite! Absolutely!"

"We're about ready for the funeral," Stoker put in suavely. "I'm sure the Grand Tutor would like to say a Word of Passage over his friend before the cremation. It's the usual thing."

"Who cares whether it's usual?" Dr. Sear demanded. "George has taken care of that point very brilliantly."

"George," Anastasia pleaded, and blushed when I turned to her. "Let's go to my room. I'm all confused."

"He could even do *that!*" Dr. Sear affirmed. There was some excitement in his voice.

"Anything at all," Stoker laughed. "This one has it all over Enos Enoch."

"No, really, Maurice, it's actually a rather profound idea . . ."

"Kiss her, George!" Mrs. Sear commanded.

Anastasia frowned. "Don't, Heddy!" But I kissed her lips at once—marvelous they were, and marvelously pliant her whole body in my arms. It was by way of being my first full experience of human embrace, in its passionate form (a thing unknown in the herd), and the pleasure of it set me afire. I heard cheers from Stoker and others; Mrs. Sear it must have been who stroked our hair and necks as we kissed, and her husband murmured approval.

"Beautiful, beautiful. Figures on a vase."

With my hand in the small of her back I pressed her to my standing wrappered organ. She broke off the kiss then, but put her brow against my chin and said, "Think what you're *doing!*"

"A Bride of Enos," Dr. Sear remarked suddenly.

"Of course!" cried his wife. "Up on the dais! I *wish* I could paint it!"

"It's perfect," Dr. Sear insisted. "The will to believe and the will to be believed."

"I'll tell the band," Stoker said. "Why not use the funeral-couch?"

Mrs. Sear clapped her hands and embraced the two of us again. "I don't know *which* of you I envy more! Kiss me, George! Kiss me, Stacey!"

But it was Anastasia I kissed, lifting her chin in my hand.

"This is terrible," she whispered. "You'd be committing *adultery.*"

In fact I'd not been thinking so far ahead, and even now the word paled before the image. I sipped tears from the long-lashed brims of both her eyes. More faintly yet she said, "At least let's go somewhere else . . ."

For reply I swept her up, and a jubilant cry rose round about. Dr. Sear supported me with an arm about my waist; Anastasia hid her face in my shoulder. I had in mind no clear direction or intent; it was stirring enough just to hold her so. But Mrs. Sear went before us and Stoker before her, opening an aisle through the guests, who whistled and applauded as we passed. The roomlights darkened once again, and the floodlit dais gleamed ahead. Dr. Sear spoke quietly and clearly into my ear.

"In the old days this was the execution-chamber of Main Detention; they use it for high official funerals now. There's a chute under the dais that leads to one of those natural ovens, like the ones you saw in the Furnace Room, and when a chancellor or vice-chancellor dies, they cremate the body from here and then sound the EAT-whistle to let the campus know. Maurice says the steam-boiler for the EAT-whistle is fired by the crematorium, but he's probably joking. Quite an honor for your late friend, actually, even though it's unofficial."

But Anastasia from her slung perch disagreed. "It's just Maurice's idea of a party-joke, Kennard, and you know it. I think it's *terrible* the things he does in Founder's Hill."

Dr. Sear gave a mild shrug and adjusted his spectacles upon a neat small bandage on the bridge of his nose.

"Never mind," I said thickly. It surprised me a little to hear the girl speak with such crispness of impersonal matters, from my very arms, when desire so filled my own breast, and liquor my head, that I could scarcely make a sound. I was to learn in time that this disconcerting ability was characteristic of her and shared by many of her sisters in female student-dom: whatever her scruples and misgivings, once seized up she made herself as comfortable as if I were her favorite parlor chair.

"Way for the Bride of Enos!" Mrs. Sear called. She snatched a bowl of pretzels from someone and broadcast them like largesse, curtsyed before us, danced from one side of the aisle to the other, and time and again kissed Anastasia's hair or the arms clasped round my neck. "Way for the Bride and Groom!"

"Honestly!" Anastasia protested. But the extravagance of Mrs. Sear's ushering made her smile. Now the orchestra commenced a processional-piece:

"Oh, listen, George," she said; "they're playing the *Alma Mater Dolorosa!* I love that hymn." And indeed it was most moving to hear her sweet girl voice against the stately horns:

Wan- der we down Coll- ege Mall;

Old as time its elms with- al.

Broad as hope and dark as fate, it

leads   us   to   Com-   mence-   ment   Gate....

I reached the dais with tears in my eyes and gently set her
upon its edge. The two guards grinned from their stations at
the couch's head, where Stoker too came now to meet us.

"All set," he said briskly. "Heddy and Ken will get things
ready while you're saying your piece, and we'll press a pedal
at the head of the couch when you're finished. Now, do you
see that pull-cord, George?" He indicated a black braided
rope suspended from the ceiling at the foot of the couch.
"When a red light comes on in the tassel it means the cremation's finished and the whistle's ready to blow. You pull it for
one long blast."

"No more," Dr. Sear appended with a chuckle, "or they'll
think it's an EAT-alarm up on campus."

Too stirred by the music and the solemn prospect to attend
him closely, I let him assist me up onto the dais, whereat a
comparative hush fell upon the room. From some corner
came a half-hearted *"Olé,"* bespeaking in the far dark
Croaker; from somewhere else came a shatter of glass, a mild
oath, and a woman's short laugh quickly shushed. But I was
full of the sight of G. Herrold where he lay, arms folded
now. The buckhorn, as ever, was in his hand; one dead eye
was wide and the other shut, and his mouth was ajar as if to
draw breath for bugling. The orchestra paused (I heard Anastasia behind me saying No, impossible, she'd die of shame
even if I *were*), then wound into a dirge:

The echo of the final chord caught Dr. Sear's voice still pitched loud. "... can't be *proved*," he was asserting; then he went on quickly in an audible whisper: "It's not the kind of thing you *reason* about, my dear: you believe it or you don't."

Stoker poked me in the side and advised me to "make it short" lest Croaker interrupt the ceremonies. While I pronounced Words of Passage over the body, he declared, he would turn on the closed-circuit Telerama, as was his wont at the end of a Spring-Carnival party, so that the assemblage could watch the Sunrise Service on Founder's Hill, and the first rays of morning strike Tower Clock.

I nodded shortly, almost angrily, neither knowing nor caring what closed-circuit Telerama might be. My eyes were strong with tears now, and I was obliged to clutch G. Herrold's fleece, as well as lean upon my stick for support. A long and desolating day had been this first of my Grand-Tutorhood, whose dawn seemed ages past! Stunned with liquor and fatigue, I leaned on my friend for the last time and felt to the full his responsibility for my life, and mine for his death. Now I resented Croaker and Stoker and Anastasia too, the chance encounter in George's Gorge and its fatal issue—which was to say, at last I was appalled by the monstrous ease of my seduction, my heartless casting-off of Max, my forswearing of every bond and precept to carouse at my savior's bier and lust for the tart who had brought him to it. Late in the day, late in the day, to come to mourning!

"Omniscient Founder," I began—but no words followed. I was not used to invoking that name; in truth I'd never before addressed Him or much pondered who He was, beyond imagining Him a kind of super-Max—which kidly image no more served. The guards growled. Those guests nearby who had paused to hear me shuffled and turned. Suddenly I perspired all over; my insides sank. At the same moment when I reached to take the shophar from G. Herrold, a guard tramped down on something with his booted foot: instantly the cushions parted, swinging down like double trap-doors into the bier itself, which was revealed to be a chute. G. Herrold folded in the middle and slid into the searing air that blasted up; for part of a second his fingers gripped the shophar still, and pulled me after; I jerked back, blinded and terrified, and the horn came free. One thump I heard, far down in the awful drop, before the cushions sprang into place with a click. The crowd-noise welled. I believed I would go mad. I raised the shophar and blew blind honks, horn-rips that I wished would burst my head.

"Olé!" they cried behind.

As if responding to my note the horns or the orchestra began a grand chorale, its measured chords resounding in all my nerves. Anastasia was before me, led onto the dais by the Sears; we regarded each other with brimming eyes. Mrs. Sear hugged my arm and declared, "Well, *I* believe in him." Her tone was petulant, as if to scold Anastasia. "I think he's cute."

"We've almost got you a convert," Dr. Sear said lightly. "I told her that belief has to come before believability, but it must not sound convincing when *I* say it."

I shook off their hands. The horns took up my pain and gave it back in gold sonorities. Imperious, austere, nobly suffering, they spoke both to and for me. Even as I slipped the shophar's lanyard over my head, a red bulb lighted in the tassel of the pull-cord.

"Ready!" cried one of the guards.

But now the floodlights dimmed and the waiting party murmured as on the far wall a great screen glowed, blinked hugely, and focused into a picture: a single shaft, like a stark stone finger, pointed against a pale gray sky; winding towards it up a dark slope in the foreground was a procession of flickering lights, and from the column-top itself a larger flame roared. A new sound burst into the room, as it seemed from all directions, blending with and mounting over the splendid brass.

"That's the dawn-service upstairs on the Hill," Dr. Sear remarked for my benefit. "Big ceremony for the new spring registrants. They run the organ on natural steam from down here and use the tunnels for resonance. Superb bass response."

Anastasia moved to me in the dim light, stirred no doubt as I was by the sound and spectacle. "Your poor friend," she said.

I could not find my voice. Mrs. Sear drew us closer.

"That's the place where Enos Enoch passed on," Anastasia said, referring to the hilltop. "For all studentdom."

I shook my head. "Only for the kids who believed in Him."

"Come on," Mrs. Sear insisted, reaching as if to unbelt Anastasia's robe. The girl pressed against me to forestall her, and we found ourselves kissing—stiffly, then not so. Abruptly she turned her face away.

"I *want* to believe you!" she said, much distressèd. "I almost *can!*"

From behind me somewhere Stoker instructed me that the whistle was ready when I was, and bade me not delay. "Take her to the couch, Heddy," he said.

"I'm *trying*," Mrs. Sear fretted. "Come on, dears!"

"You must *make* yourself believe," Dr. Sear said pleasantly to Anastasia. "Matter of will, actually."

But she shook her head. "It's not *right*. Especially at a funeral service."

Before I could inquire what exactly was afoot, Stoker himself came up on the dais and firmly ordered his wife to go with Dr. and Mrs. Sear. She hesitated, her face distraught, and then permitted herself to be led to the bier. There were a few *olés* and some scattered applause—whether for her, or a newly roused Croaker, or something on the screen, I was too grieved to care.

"Now," Stoker said briskly. "You know what *service* means, George; I've heard you use the word yourself. Well, that's the Spring Sunrise Service going on on the Hill—you can't see the actual servicing because it's too dark. And when somebody important dies we have a Memorial Service in his honor. Life over Death, all that sort of thing. Usually private, you know, between married relatives, but since you're the Grand Tutor . . . Blow the whistle as soon as you're done."

With a clap on the shoulder he took me to the couch, beside which Anastasia stood and would not let Mrs. Sear unbelt her.

"It's not *so*, George!" she said. "There's no such custom at all, except at these parties. Believe me!"

But the swelling organ bore my doubts away. "You believe *me*," I said. "Nothing else matters." With my free hand I gave her sash the needed jerk; Mrs. Sear moved quickly to open the robe.

"*Look*, Ken!" she cried. "Oh, you little *darling!* I wish *I* were a Grand Tutor!"

As evenly as I could before the revelation I said to Anastasia, "Do you believe?"

"Hind to," Stoker directed the Sears, who having loosed her half-reluctant grip upon the robe and removed the garment entirely, to the pleasure of the assemblage, were gently pressing her upon the bier. "He's a goat-boy, remember." They turned her about—lightly, with constant caresses—

until, pliant and full of doubt, she knelt on the bier's end, facing away. Only as they drew down to the cushion her head and shoulders, stroking her all the while, she wondered, "George . . ."

A light fell on us; the music rose, could not imaginably soar higher. Upon the screen glowed a larger image of the column, its base ringed now by torches. The crowd took the hymn up, mighty, mighty, as I leaned my stick against the bier, raised my wrap, and steadied myself with a hand upon the perfect rump that swam in my tears.

"In the name of the Founder," I declared, *"and of the sun—"*

"Olé!" they cried behind me.

"—and of the Grand Tutor so be it!"

Incredibly, as I mounted home, the music swelled and rose to bursting. As ever in goatdom, the service was instant: swiftly as the sunflash smiting now the Founder's Shaft I drove and was done. Anastasia squealed into the cushion, "I *do* believe!" and fell flat. Unmuscled at once like Brickett Ranunculus, like him overbalanced by my thrust, I tumbled back and would have fallen had I not been hoist amid a chorus of *olés* by Croaker, who caught me from behind and hiked me up on his shoulders. The guards sprang from the dais into the crowd; Dr. and Mrs. Sear, alarm in their faces, pulled Anastasia to her feet and then, as she could not support herself, shrank away and left her leaning against the bier, her face in her hands. I had just had time, as I pitched from the service, to snatch up my stick. Gripping Croaker with my legs I raised it to strike now—at him, perhaps, or at Stoker, the sight of whom (with my serviced Anastasia limp in his arms) suddenly enraged me—at anyone, for I was transport with grief and the aftermath of passion. But when I made to bring the weapon down it tangled in the cord, and a howling whistle—the loudest shriek I'd ever heard—drowned out organ, crowd, and orchestra. Again and again it blasted as I tried to free the stick and keep my perch on lurching Croaker. It was the same wild summons which had opened that dreadful day, and after the first few screams of it pandemonium broke out in the hall. Whether out of fear of my bellowing mount and his frantic rider, or because in their liquor they believed that an EAT-wave truly was upon them, the carousers yelled and sprang, mobbing the doorways, tripping and trampling, climbing one another in their haste. The musicians fled the bandstand and joined them, swinging their golden horns like clubs. On the Telerama, too, all was disorder: the celebrants flung away their torches and ran, sprinting down footpaths and through shrubbery, diving behind rocks, flinging themselves flat upon the ground or into bushes. The organ-music turned wild and broken, then ceased altogether, and the crowd-din grew berserker.

At last I freed my stick, and the EAT-whistle stopped. But it had blown from my head all liquor and delusion and left me stricken by my folly, aghast at how far and lightly I'd strayed from Grand-Tutorhood. Had that been, as Max had suggested, Stoker's purpose? He stood now on the loveseat-bier itself, soiling the cushions with his boots, and surveyed with a grin the general panic. Hands on his hips, he laughed at the scrambling worshipers, at the frenzied party-guests, and at me—virtually in my face, for on our separate perches we were of a height.

"Couldn't do better myself!" he cried. "Why not go to work for me?"

I might have attacked him, but Croaker was too excited by the chaos in the room to heed my orders. Stinging with self-reproach I dug my heels in, and we charged into the crowd, who now that the whistling had stopped were beginning to recover their senses. I looked with mixed feelings for Anastasia, but she and the Sears were gone; Madge however I observed belly-down on a nearby table, laid out across several platters of cold-cuts: an apple was in her unbandaged mouth, her eyes were closed, and the guards from the dais were spreading mustard on her hams. I spurred Croaker on lest he too caught sight of her. We bounded to the exit-door, which opened at our approach, and as we entered the corridor beyond, Stoker's merry voice roared out from loudspeakers on every side:

"Think it over, Goat-Boy! I'll see you again!"

And his laugh preceded and pursued us as we went, unopposed, unaccompanied, from hallway to hallway, chamber to chamber. Guards stood back with a grin; levers were pulled, lights flashed, all doors opened before us and closed behind—even the last, that great iron portal of the entrance-chamber through which we issued now as we had entered hours before, not knowing how we'd got there. The watchdogs snarled, but were held in check; Croaker snarled back, but I steered him on. We crossed the graveled apron, floodlit still and chilly in the early light, and plunged down a wooded slope, through groves of oak and dew-soaked laurel. At the foot, in a bright-misted clearing near the road, a kilometer at least from the Powerhouse, we came to ground—collapsed in fact together into the leaves, from an exhaustion I'd not guessed he shared. And though rage, remorse, and doubt burned in me like Stoker's awful fires, which no amount of tears could quench, yet weariness banked and dampered them: careless of comfort, of health, of safety (but Croaker seemed no longer a menace, having come to the dais, now I reflected on it, more probably to aid than to assault me; and as for Stoker, I saw little cause why he might pursue us, and less hope of eluding him if he should), I glanced over at my companion, already snoring, then closed my eyes, and just as I had fallen, pitched asleep.

THIRD REEL

1.

From ill dreams of among other things peanut butter I woke to the sound of what I took for squirrels, a scratchy gnaw against a scolding chitter, and for one sweet second couldn't place myself. Then I saw Croaker hunkered near in a patch of forenoon light, biting on my stick while gray squirrels fussed overhead in the oaks, and recollection like a morning muscle ached along me.

It wasn't memory alone and bone-joints pained, but head and belly, the one a-crack, the other heaving. I sat up, reeled, and retched, too ill at once for more remorse about G. Herrold, Max, Anastasia. Croaker came to me and banished any doubts of his fidelity by grunting gently at my state and offering me nourishment. He had been up betimes and made a little fire somehow; in its coals he'd roasted a quantity of migratory songbirds and small mammals—shrews, perhaps, or infant possums—a double handful of whose charred carcasses he now dumped proudly in my lap. When I had done gagging and flapping them off me, he proffered fare more to my taste: a store of chestnuts, not all of them wormy, which too he'd roasted in his fire and which suggested, considering the season, that the burnt animals were offspring of those haranguing squirrels, their provender gone the way of their progeny. But the warm hulls were welcome in my hands, the light meats easy in my stomach. More welcome yet, for I had a cruel thirst, he'd stoppered the shophar-tip with elderberry pith and filled the whole horn with springwater, which worked miracles of bracing and clearing when I rinsed me inside and out with it. Last, most marvelously, he'd found and plundered us a bee-tree! No better redress than honey for gastric abuse: so sweet to my innards was that amber balm, redolent of last year's clover, I suffered my provider to eat roast rodent in my sight while I breakfasted on chestnuts and honey, and vomited no more. Uncertain how much he could understand—of my language and generally—I thanked him with a whole heart for the meal, and was gratified to see him smile and offer me more. I accepted a mouthful of honey-comb-cappings to chew as we traveled, and was further de-lighted a moment later, upon standing to urinate on the coals, when he gave me my stick before I could ask for it.

"What's this, now?" I marveled.

Along the ashen shaft, with no other instrument than his teeth so far as I could discover, he had incised a number of humanish figures, recognizable though much stylized, and not unattractive. Their torsos were squat, sometimes nonexistent except for the apparatus of generation; their faces were squared, their eyes, ears, noses, and mouths very large, their teeth pointed. They rode one another's shoulders or stood upon one another's heads, two columns of them up the stick, and on each level the figure in this was engaged with its counterpart in that, in one or several ways: they clapped and coupled, buggered and bit; also sniffed and fiddled and fingered and shat, thrust out their tongues and forth their pudenda—a rare interclutchment it was of appetites. Again I thanked him, pointing to the design to make my message clear; he frowned and shook his head. I was puzzled until with invita-tion in his eyes he fetched up his gown and took his own mighty organ in one hand while with the other he indicated a pair of figures on the stick: two blocky chaps more neatly scissored than ever G. Herrold and I in wrestling-days. I un-derstood then that the artwork was functional as well as a decorative—that to point to any pair of Croaker's figures was to give a particular command—and that my own finger had rested inadvertently on a full-faced *shelah-na-gig,* which being female had nonplussed him. I was to learn later of fur-ther significances in the arrangement of figures from bottom to top—a kind of hierarchic psychronology of lust whereof the ingenuity, combined with the art of the composition, sug-gested that Croaker was working in some tradition more so-phisticated than himself. I declined his invitation; signaled my desire to mount his shoulders instead and be off for Great

Mall in search of Max. Though I had no claim on Croaker, he seemed a willing and most valuable servant as well as a formidable ally; I could make better time on his legs than on my own, and be reasonably sure besides that he'd commit no further mayhem while under my governance.

Following a brief confusion (our commands were not clearly worked out yet, and he was still thinking in stickly terms) he put me on him lightly as a hat, I pointed ahead, and we went off, first down to the road and then, as I hoped, towards New Tammany—in any case, away from the Power-house. It was an asphalt pavement in good repair, yet apparently little used—I'd heard no vehicles upon it since waking—and I chose to go in plain sight rather than stalk through the woods, reasoning that if Stoker or others were bent on obstructing me they'd find me anyhow, if not here-abouts then at Main Gate, and in the meantime I could cover more ground and perhaps locate Max. Not impossibly, too, I was aware that to be "captured" by Stoker (for whatever rea-son) could mean seeing Anastasia once again, and her good escutcheon—but I have little patience with this sort of analy-sis. She was most certainly on my mind, with sundry other matters, as we went along; the road was straight, the scenery unvarying, the sun high and warm on my face: everything conduced to reverie. It was not my habit to think in a di-rected manner, but rather to brood upon what images came to mind as it were unbid: not to manipulate and question them, but to attend like an interested spectator their links and twinings, stuntful as the folk upon my stick. Max and G. Herrold, Anastasia and Stoker, Dr. and Mrs. Sear, Sakhyan in his yellow robe and Madge with her mustard buttocks—they came and went and came again, myself among them, re-hearsing deeds and speeches from the script of memory or improvising new. And in lieu of reasoned conclusions, net feelings were what I came to. I had, ever since waking and despite my hangover, felt unaccountably cleansed, emptied: now as I watched myself watch me drinking the black liquor with Stoker, biting Anastasia's belly and serving her upon G. Herrold's public bier, I noted with interest that while I was perplexed, I was penitent no longer: my humility was nothing humiliation, but more nearly awe before the special nature of my freedom, not appreciated thitherto. Truly it seemed to me (though I could no more word it then than Croaker could discourse upon low-relief woodcarving) that a deed became

Grand-Tutorial from its having been done by the Grand
Tutor and in no other way; at the same time, that the Grand
Tutor defines Himself ineluctably and exclusively in the
Grand-Tutoriality of His deeds. There was no cause, I
strongly felt, to *worry* about myself: if I was indeed Grand
Tutor then I would choose infallibly the Grand-Tutorial
thing—how could I do otherwise?—whose Grand-Tutoriality
could yet be said to derive from my recognition. If I was not,
then no choice of actions could make me so, because in my
un-Grand-Tutoriality I would make the wrong choices. The
statement is paradoxical; the feeling was not. Max believed
that a Grand Tutor was a man who *acted* thus-and-so, who
did the Grand-Tutorial work: Enos Enoch, Max argued, said
Love thy classmate as thyself because to love one's classmate
as oneself was a Right Answer; He'd had no option, except to
be or not to be a Grand Tutor; had He commanded us otherwise, He'd not have been one. I on the contrary had sometimes held that to love one's classmate as oneself was Correct
only because Enos Enoch so commanded; that to hate oneself
and one's classmate would be just as Correct instead had He
commanded *that;* in short that His choice was free because
His nature wasn't, He being in any case a Grand Tutor. But
now I felt that we both had been in error: Max himself
might love his classmate and the rest, and teach others
to—might even sacrifice himself in the name of studentdom
as Enos Enoch did—and yet by no means be a Grand Tutor
in his own right, but only an imitation Enos Enoch. On the
other hand Enos could not have gone about saying just *anything,* or nothing, and still have been Enos Enoch. In truth
the doer did not define the deed nor did the deed the doer;
their relation (in the case at least of Grand Tutors and
Grand-Tutoring) was first of all that of artists, say, to their
art, and to speak of freedom or its opposite in such a relation
was not quite meaningful. Without Grand Tutors there'd be
no Answers, no Commencement, any more than there'd be
great poems without great poets: to ask whether Maro say,
could have *not*-written the *Epic of Anchisides* is to ask
whether he was free to be not-Maro—a futile question. There
remained this difference: a great poem might be anonymous,
the manner of its making and the character of its maker not
even known except as implied in the piece itself. What Enos
Enoch said and and did, on the other hand—or Maios the
Lykeionian, or the original Sakhyan—was if anything less

important than the way of His doing it: Grand Tutoring was inseparable from the Grand Tutor, of Whose personality it was the expression; it could never be anonymous, and thus must be always more or less lost by the Tutees, as Enos Enoch was lost in Enochism. Yet the analogy held, after all: a man who transcribed a copy of the *Anchisides* or imitated it was not Maro, any more than the Graduate was the Grand Tutor. And as the poet might transcend the conventions of his art and with his talent make beautiful what in lesser hands would be ugly, so the Grand Tutor in His passèdness stood beyond ordinary Truth and Falsehood. Maios drank the night long and let young men fall in love with Him; Sakhyan in His youth had a herd of mistresses, and in His Tutorship never lent a helping hand to anyone (any more than His descendant—I was stirred to recall—had tried to rescue G. Herrold); Enos Enoch Himself had once railed against the Founder, lost His temper on several occasions, and contradicted not only the teachings of the Old Syllabus but even His own *obiter dicta*—and had passed both Carpo the Fool and Gaffer McKeon the Perfect Cheat.

To be sure, there were questions for which I could not yet feel clear answers. Could Enos have murdered as well as railed? Could Sakhyan have taken a mistress during His Tutorship as well as before? Could Maios have practiced outright pederasty? And Carpo: was he an ordinary fool whose passage was meant as an illustration, or did he have some special passèd quality not recognized by his classmates? Or was his passage so purely gratuitous that even to interpret it as an illustration of Grand-Tutorial gratuitousness was to give it false significance? I began to suspect that such questions were invalid, but before the suspicion had time to clarify itself my attention was caught by the sight of a figure squatting in the weeds some hundred meters up the roadside. Croaker spied him too, and muttered. Then all my new composure was put to rout—by joy, uneasy conscience, and concern—for I saw that it was Max.

I shouted to him and urged Croaker on. We had passed no inns—indeed, no buildings of any sort. Had Max spent the night outside, or had he been lodged by Stoker's aide and set out in the morning to find me? I scolded myself afresh for having abandoned him; my alarm grew when I saw that he was not at stool there among the dock, as I'd supposed, but merely hunkered and hugging himself, as against the cold, and resting his forehead upon his knees. Even the approach of Croaker, whose new manageability he had no way of knowing, seemed not to impress him: he raised to me a blank, distracted face.

"We have a new helper," I said, and smiling, clambered down. Croaker took the stick from my hand as I dismounted, and squatted peacefully with it in the weeds like a dog with a bone. I touched his shoulder lightly for support, a bit put out that Max ignored my mastery and smart handling of what after all had been a menace to the student body. In my own mind it augured well for the graver encounters ahead. "I have him under control now. We've been looking all over for you. Are you all right?"

"All right?" His voice was feeble. He got stiffly up.

I took his arm, not certain of my ground. "I'm glad to see you, Max." It was on my tongue to apologize for deserting him, for carousing in the Power Plant, and the rest. But I remembered that in a sense it was he who had abandoned *me*, and that anyhow I wasn't sure it was necessary to regret my behavior in itself. Apart from those earlier considerations—the qualitative tautology, so to speak, of act and agent in the case of Grand Tutorship—it seemed not so terrible even to regard my night as simple dereliction. Anchisides, to mention only one example, had dallied with his mistress for an entire winter, whereas I, if guilty at all, was so of but a single Memorial Service. "Sorry if you had to spend the night outdoors."

Max shook his head. "A little sore in the joints is all." His tone was as guarded as mine; he too, then, it gave me some comfort to imagine, had had second thoughts about leaving me. I decided not to reproach him, nor on the other hand to recount my night's activity.

"Well. Do you feel strong enough to go on?"

He widened his eyes, like one just waking. "I guess."

"Stoker *sent* a man after you," I said defensively. "He was supposed to make sure you had a place to sleep."

The name put a temporary end to Max's strange reserve. "That Dean o' Flunks!" he cried, waving two fists above his head. "Stoker and Eierkopf—two Bonifacists! *Bragging* what they did to the Moishians! *Ach,* I hate them!" He went on in this vein, not always coherently: Eblis Eierkopf he cursed for a flunkèd soulless monster who had betrayed studentdom in general and Virginia R. Hector in particular in the name of some Siegfriedish perversion of science; Stoker he reviled afresh as the very principle of antiFounderism, who had not even Eierkopf's twisted rationale for his iniquities, but relished them openly for their flunkèdness; whose one delight and motive, like that of the legendary Dean o' Flunks, was to tempt out everyone's grievousest failings, to show cankers in the hearts of roses, make the worse appear the better reason, and laugh at the debauchment of the purest, most generous minds, like Anastasia's. Tears stood in his eyes; his voice turned shriller. All very well to love one's enemy, as Enos Enoch enjoined, so long as the enemy was a human student with the mortal proneness of us all to unthinking cruelty and the like; but the Bonifacists and their ilk had removed themselves from human studentdom. To call them *beasts* was to insult the nobility and lack of malice in even the fiercest wild animal: embodiments of flunkage was what they were, and he Max had been wrong not to hate them before, not to wish them dead and work for their extermination with all the energy they'd devoted to his, and to his classmates'. Vain to object, as he had used to, that violence in the name of *any* principle was flunking: when the principle was anti-violence and the victim the violent principle; when it was a case of either destroying the violent few or delivering the innocent many into their hands, the matter was ethically *sui generis,* and otherwise valid rules did not apply, *etc., etc.*

I was impressed not only by the violence of his speech itself, so foreign to his usual temper, but also by my inability to quite agree, though I was much stirred. Nor was it that like the Max of old I did not assent to violence on any grounds: on the contrary, what I felt, dimly but positively, was that in a way beyond my describing there was something *right* in Stoker's attitude; that Dean-o'-Flunkèdness, so to speak, was not so simply to be understood and come to terms with, at least not by a Grand Tutor. I could by no means have argued the point, and therefore said nothing, but vividly before my mind's eye was the uproar of the Furnace Room, ever on the verge of explosion; the glimpse of that natural inferno in the bowels of Founder's Hill; the wonder of flinging back my head in Stoker's fashion and roaring like a madman at the top of my lungs . . . To this, to my intoxication (which I could not even recognize yet by name), to all I'd seen and been and done subcampusly, as it were, there was a certain all-rightness which I sensed as clearly as I sensed that

Max would never understand it. I myself was far from under-standing it, if for no other reason than that in the harmony of my feelings it nowise discorded with Max's compassionate indignation; but I felt it had nothing to do with rationalizing on the one hand or Grand-Tutorial apriority on the other. I set the matter aside, with my earlier speculations, against the improvement of my experience, and asked Max if he'd had anything to eat.

He shook his head. "I got no appetite." He gave me a sharp look and combed at his beard with his fingers. "Two things, George. Whatever else I did wrong in my life, I never touched Virginia Hector, so I can't be that poor girl's father. It's got to be Eblis Eierkopf. And if Maurice Stoker sent any-body after me, it wasn't to find me a hotel. But this is the second thing: I waited right here by the road all night, and *I never saw a soul.*"

This established, he lapsed into the heavy spirits in which I'd found him, and made no move either to go or to stay. I blushed at the reproach in his last remark, and we stood about awkwardly for a moment. Then, in view of his age and uncertain condition, I suggested he ride pick-a-back on Croaker, whom I did not yet quite trust unmounted, while I went beside on foot. I was prepared to counter any misgiv-ings with praise of Croaker's reliability and resourceful-ness—indeed, I had no idea how we'd manage for food and fire without him, unless Great Mall proved but a short way ahead, and though I supposed I'd have to return him to Dr. Eierkopf upon reaching New Tammany proper, in the mean-while I reckoned him a potent companion, whom I'd give up regretfully, and I hoped that once Max was himself again we could learn to deal yet more effectively with the huge crea-ture. But my advisor showed neither fear nor interest: he shrugged and permitted himself to be set aloft when I'd got the message through to Croaker. I retrieved my stick, on which now an intaglio spiral of grape-leaves and tendrils fili-greed the limbs of the lowest figures and promised to bear clusters upon the next. Another time I'd have invited Max to admire the carving with me, but as he seemed so spiritless I merely pointed down the road with the stick, and we trudged away.

With his light burden and stronger legs Croaker's pace was better than mine. Every hundred meters or so he'd gain a dozen and wait with a grin for me to catch up. We went in this manner for about a kilometer, and then at one of his pauses I saw him turn abruptly off the pavement toward a ditch that ran beside us. I called and hurried after, afraid he was bolting; Max held tightly to keep from falling but seemed otherwise indifferent, and made no effort to stop him. However, it was something in the ditch had caught his eye. He sprang down in, grunting like a boar, and as I overtook him fetched his prize up onto the roadside: a black motorcycle, which he hauled out lightly as a toy. It was the kind used by Stoker's men, and perhaps for this reason Croaker hammered at it earnestly with his fists until I bade him stop.

"One of your friends had an accident," Max observed.

Indeed, the sidecar was partly crushed, the windscreen broken, and the front tire burst, as if the vehicle had plunged into the ditch with some force. I suggested that the driver, nowhere in sight, must have been the sharp-faced officer sent to find Max, but then observed that the original position of the motorcycle in the ditch, as well as its tire-marks on the shoulder of the road, indicated that it had been traveling *towards* the Powerhouse at the time of the accident.

"So," Max said without interest. "There's lots of roads, and Stoker's got more bullies than one."

"What happened to the driver, do you think?"

Max shrugged. As he was so plainly indifferent, I ordered Croaker to wait while I searched and called through the underbrush on both sides of the road, in case someone lay injured. There was no reply.

"He must have gone for help," I decided. "Or someone came after him already."

Max turned his head contemptuously and would not even look at the damaged machine, which I however examined curiously.

"How far it is to Great Mall, Max?"

"Farther than yesterday," he said dryly. Among the other misfortunes of encountering Stoker, it seemed, was that previously we'd been moving west, from the College Farms towards Great Mall, but the route from the Gorge to the Powerhouse had fetched us many kilometers to the north, out of our way.

I decided then to attempt to use the motorcycle: if it proved possible to manage it, at a low speed, Croaker could either sit in the sidecar or trot alongside, with Max on his shoulders, and we might reach Great Mall before dark; oth-

erwise we'd spend another night in the open or have to beg
lodging. So at least I imagined, ignorant as I was of the campus and of such matters as the medium of exchange and
Max's wherewithal; I assumed that, once officially matriculated, one was housed and fed at the College's expense—but I
knew nothing of these matters, and Max, who ordinarily
might have advised me, was grown so morose I had difficulty
getting out of him that he knew nothing of motorcycle-
operation himself or the legal aspects of borrowing the vehicle. This I could scarcely credit; privately I was becoming
persuaded that besides his distress over G. Herrold and his
objection to Stoker, what was really upsetting him was my independence of his authority, and Anastasia's declaration that
he was her natural father—which for all I knew might be
true despite his denying it. In any case he was too lost in his
broodings to care much what I did, and so I set about examining the machine's controls and recalling what I could of
Stoker's operation of them.

After some experiment I managed, partly by accident, to
get the ignition on, the throttle half-opened, the carburetor
choked, and the clutch disengaged all at the same time, and
was rewarded by a sputter from the engine when I kicked the
starter. Presidently I contrived a sustained idle, having by
chance let off the choke, and was able to sit on the trembling
three-wheeler and vary the engine speed most satisfyingly—
without however moving from the spot. Next came a series
of jerks and stalls as I fiddled with the shift-lever and learned
its association with the clutch-pedal; finally, by a happy combination of chance and deduction, I released my grip on the
hand-brake, shifted out of neutral into low gear (not suspecting there were other ratios still), and throttled the engine sufficiently in time to keep from stalling. The jerk nearly took
me off the seat; luckily my hand slipped from the throttle before I could reduce speed and stop again out of terror; but I
hung on and even mustered presence enough of mind to steer
away from the ditch, onto the pavement. To negotiate a
straight course was more difficult than I'd imagined, owing
(as I was to learn presently) to the flat front tire and the pull
of the sidecar, which had been wrenched out of line by the
crash. But I was exhilarated—two monsters brought to heel
in as many days!—and hobbled along delightedly in low gear,
with the engine roaring. Croaker skipped alongside, grinning
and grunting, and bid fair to bounce my advisor from his

shoulders; he seemed as pleased as I by my achievement, and I perfected his bliss by giving him my stick to chew, since Max showed no interest in using it to direct him. We did after all move a little faster in this clumsy wise than we had before, though perhaps not enough to redeem the time lost in my self-instruction. Happily there was no traffic to deal with. More happily yet, as it turned out, we came in a quarter-hour to a crossroads, where a young man with orange hair and a satchel was.

He wore a trim gray woolen suit and a cap of raccoon-fur and did push-ups in the road; his flowered necktie, loose at the throat, folded itself upon the asphalt when he sank and unfolded when he rose. Mid-dip he paused at the sound of us, face gleaming like his hair, then stood and waved his cap as we approached. An uncommonly tall chap: his trouser-cuffs hung shy of his great yellow shoes, his sleeves of his great red hands. Now we were nearer I saw he meant us to stop, and wondered whether, despite the freckled cheer of his countenance, he mightn't be some sort of threat. It seemed odd, too, that he showed no alarm at sight of Croaker, whom however he regarded with a look of merry amazement. There was no time for Max to advise me, even had he wished to; in any case I'd have had trouble hearing him over the engine. It was a choice between stopping, running the man down, and turning to right or left: I chose to stop. Indeed, the choice was made for me by my ignorance and indecision: I braked without either declutching or closing the throttle, and the motor stalled.

"Mercy sakes a'mighty *Pete!*" The fellow drew out his exclamation in an accent not unlike G. Herrold's, scratching his head the while. His grin quite laid my apprehension, as did the good-natured wonder in his eyes—in his eye, rather, for though the pair were of an equal blue and glint, it was only the right that moved from me to the flat-tired cycle to Max and Croaker, while the left (if anything more wide than its companion) stared always straight ahead.

I returned his smile, addressing it to the bridge of his nose. "How do you do. Is this your motorcycle?"

He grinned farther yet. "You mean she ain't yourn? Might of guessed, way you handled 'er."

As there was no criticism in his tone, just frank amusement, I described the circumstances of my discovery and appropriation of the cycle. I had no mind to *keep* it, I explained: inasmuch as Mr. Maurice Stoker was an acquaintance of mine and his wife by way of being a particular friend, I was certain they'd not object to my borrowing their machine to reach Great Mall and—the pleasant notion occurred to me as I spoke—returning it to Mrs. Stoker at the Psych Clinic when I had done registering.

"I always did hear there was big goings-on at the Powerhouse this time of year," the tall man said. "Don't know Mr. Stoker my own self, but I bet half what they say about him isn't so." I recognized that he was being agreeable. He was, now I saw him close, less young than I'd supposed: more probably forty than twenty for all his boyishness of look and manner.

"Ha," Max said, and showed no further interest. However, the stranger seemed not to notice his incordiality.

"Hey, that's some darky you got there! You all been to a fancy dress party?"

As the term meant nothing to me, I identified Croaker, explained how he happened to be with us, and introduced Max and myself as well.

"My gracious sakes! Proud to meet you all!" Much impressed, he thrust out his hand first to Croaker. "Greene's my name, Mr. Croaker."

Croaker growled. "He doesn't speak our language," I said.

"Is that a fact! Won't bite, will he?"

"You don't try to lynch him he won't," Max said.

"Now hold on!" Green's protest was still good-natured, though I gathered he had grounds for feeling insulted. "Just because he's a darky don't mean I don't admire his football-playing. I got nothing against darkies. I grew up with darkies."

"Congratulations."

Greene turned to me with a chuckle. "He's a peppery one, ain't he?" Then he reached his hand up to Max. "Peter Greene, sir, and proud to meet you. I read about you in the papers a long time ago."

"You got nothing against Moishian Student-Unionists either?" Max asked sarcastically. But he didn't refuse the handshake, and I saw a trace of a smile in his beard for the first time that day.

Peter Greene stoutly cocked his head. "I'm ready to riot against Nikolay College anytime the Chancellor says," he declared with dignity. "But I got nothing against any man that's got nothing against me. Darkies or Moishians, it don't matter."

"A liberal," Max said.

"Call me what you want, I'm just Pete Greene." He winked his right eye at me. "Nobody knows better'n me how the papers twist things ever whichaway. Don't flunk me till you get to know me, and I'll do you the same favor."

"Pleased to meet you, Mr. Greene," I said when my turn came. And indeed I found his manner on the whole winning, though somewhat disconcerting.

"*Pete,*" he insisted. "Same here, Mr. George. I never did meet a Grand Tutor before." I wondered that there was no trace in him of the skepticism I'd learned to expect upon identifying myself; only curiosity, which I was pleased enough to satisfy.

"How come you got to matriculate like everybody else?" he wanted to know. "Now you take me, that's just a plain poor flunker like the next: all I can do is hope the good Founder may find it in His heart to pass me when the time comes. Which He sure ain't passed me yet, evidently, much as I thought He had."

I explained that while I was what I was in essence, as it were, I was not yet so in act, and would not be until I had passed my own Finals—just as a chancellor's son, in the days of hereditary office, might become the lawful ruler of his college while still in his infancy, but would not exercise his powers in fact until he came of age.

"Well, I think it's a wonderful line of work for a fellow to take up," Peter Greene said stoutly, as if to encourage me. "You might not believe it to see me now, but when I was a boy I was president of the Junior Enochist League. Youngest president they ever had! More than once I've thought I should of took up Tutoring myself, instead of business engineering. But there wasn't the profit in it then there is now." He grinned and winked again, this time at Max. "Going to take you all a while to reach Commencement Gate on *that!*"

I agreed that considering my skill as a driver and the condition of the vehicle it might be as well to walk—especially if the roads were busier near Great Mall—and invited him to join us. He accepted at once, declaring he abhorred above all things solitude, having spent his childhood in the College Forests; but he saw no reason to abandon the motorcycle, which it seemed to him could easily be made serviceable. With my permission he opened a leathern pouch on the rear wheel—I'd scarcely noticed it—and fished out an assortment of tools from which he chose two or three box-end wrenches and one with adjustable jaws.

"If it's a thing I do love," he declared, "it's fooling with *motors.*"

I dismounted and watched him go to work on the machine. Heedless of his clothing and at home with the tools, he first unbolted the sidecar from the motorcycle proper, declaring it bent out of line past salvaging, and then availed himself of its perfectly sound wheel and tire to replace the ruined one on the front of the cycle. From the sidecar also he fetched a black canister, which he uncapped, sniffed, and poured from into a tank above the motor. The whole operation took no more than half an hour. Then he wiped his hands—blacker than Croaker's now with engine-grease—on a clean linen handkerchief and powdered them with dust from the road-side. His suit and shirt-front were quite soiled.

"Now, by gosh!" He adjusted the throttle and other de-vices, kicked the starter, and produced at once a roar from the motor more hearty by far than any I'd managed. I in-sisted that he drive, since he was familiar with the controls and I had no notion how to balance upon two wheels. Fur-ther, I proposed that Max ride behind him on the saddle and I on Croaker's shoulders, inasmuch as despite my greater weight I was a less fragile burden, who safely might be trot-ted instead of walked.

Max grunted and mounted the cycle. "You don't mind chauffeuring a security risk?"

Greene shook his head agreeably. "Maybe you're a risk, sir, and maybe you're not." He squinted his eyes. "But you ain't a traitor to your college like they said, I know that."

"You know already? How do you know?"

"I can tell by looking," Greene declared, and paraphrased a saying of Enos Enoch's: " '*'Tain't the cut o' your coat, but the cut o' your jib.*' "

Max scoffed. "Some eyes you got." But he seemed not dis-pleased. Greene replied, turning to the controls, that he had in fact but one good eye, his right, having lost the other in an accident years before—but he supposed there were *some* things he could see clearly enough. He frowned at the rear-view mirror on the handlebar.

"Speaking of eyeballs, if you and George don't mind I'll

just take this thing off before we start . . ." He unscrewed it, with my consent, and pitched it into the weeds. "I got a thing about mirrors since my accident. You know? No sirree," he went on energetically, testing the throttle and not pausing for reply or acknowledgment: "I'd know by looking if a fellow was a traitor to his college." He turned to Max with an innocent frown. "New Tammany *is* your college, ain't it?"

My advisor laughed aloud, and Greene joined blushing in, as did I when I saw the little joke. We started off then much more smartly than before: our new companion, an expert driver as well as a vigorous talker, held the cycle balanced and perfectly matched to Croaker's trot, with a minimum of engine noise, at the same time remarking endlessly upon himself and the campus scene.

"Fact is, it's still a free college," he declared, adding though that it wouldn't be for long if Tower Hall kept meddling with the School of Business. "And what I say, a fellow's got a right to whichever Answer strikes him best, I don't care if it's the Junior Enochist Pledge or the Student-Unionist Manifesto." He nodded his head in forceful jerks as he talked, and blinked several times at every period. My impression was that he spoke less from conviction than from an earnest wish to be agreeable, which was at least a refreshment after Max's attitude. "He ought to teach what he wants in the classroom too," he went on. "But he better not force anybody to agree, by golly Jim! And if he don't love his alma mater he should transfer out, that's what I say! Now you take me—" He took himself with his left hand, throttling with his right. "Nothing red about old Pete but his head—"

"Maybe the neck too," Max suggested.

"I swear it proudly," blinked Mr. Greene, "and would take an oath upon it every morning of my mortal life: I'm a loyal New Tammanian. But much as I personally loathe and despise your Student-Unionism—"

"Max was never a Student-Unionist," I put in, for it seemed to me that my advisor was somehow being flunked in his Commencement, as who should say to an innocent man, "I forgive you for the murder you committed."

"There now!" Greene jerked his head affirmatively. "I knew it from his face he weren't! Gosh darn newspapers! Even if he was, though, what the heck: he could preach it in *my* ear all he wanted, long's he didn't shove it down my throat. Now then, sir!"

"*Ach,*" Max said.

"Well, I'm just a dumb forester that's behind the times," Greene said, in a voice that turned old for the space of two sentences. "All righty then, I'm out of date, but I believe in the Founder Almighty and New Tammany College—whether or not!"

Whether or not what, I wanted to know; but Max was saying, "Too old you aren't. Too young is what."

This observation moved our new friend to a truly boyish, Dunce-may-care laughter. "Say what you want," he invited us, shaking his head as if helpless before Max's wit. "I'm a slow hand in the classroom, but put me in the woods I can show you a thing or two!"

I wondered that Max contemned with a sniff what seemed to me a sturdy enough set of Answers, worthy at least of reasonable debate. I was about to inquire further into them, but we rounded a bend and were faced with so startling a spectacle that all else was forgot. A sign it was, on the edge of a pine-woods—but no ordinary notice like GOAT-FARM #1 above the door at home or the direction-signs we'd passed by the way. This hoarding itself was big as a barn-wall, so big that the trees pictured on it were larger than those it hid. On one side, in taller letters than a man, was spelt the injunction DON'T PLAY WITH FIRE; on the other, KEEP OUR FORESTS GREENE. The messages flashed, first this then that, in bright orange light, bedazzling the eye. Yet scarcely had I grasped their wonder when I was horrified to see that just between them, in the center of the sign, no other disaster than the one they warned of had befallen them! A fire of painted logs was there, amid the picture-pines—but real smoke issued from it, that blackly rolled upon itself and skywards.

"Giddap!" I ordered Croaker, and bade the others follow. I thought perhaps we had water enough, in the shophar and our four bladders, to check the blaze before it spread past managing. To this end I laid the buckhorn on, then sprang to a narrow platform built before the sign and made the accurate-test water I could into an orifice from which the smoke came. Croaker stood by perplexed, who might have drowned what I could but add steam to; I lacked a right command and had no time to search my stick for a micturating figure.

"Whoa!" cried Greene, more amused than not. "You'll ruin my good signboard!"

I was with difficulty persuaded that there was no danger;

that the smoke came cold from a machine designed to produce it behind the billboard; that its whole intent was to draw the traveler's eye to the pair of messages, which were blazoned on similar hoardings the length and breadth of New Tammany College. He was astonished, Greene professed, that I had never seen one, goat-boy or no goat-boy, as he thought he'd had the college "blanketed," in his term, and the goat-farms were unequivocally a part of NTC. By jiminy he would take the matter up with his "P.R. boys"—whoever *they* were—and that heads would roll, I could bet my boots. Not the least remarkable thing about Greene's explanation was the manner of its delivery: there was a new hardness in his tone and something impersonally baleful in his swagger.

"Got the idea when my ROTC outfit was across the Pond in C. R. Two," he told me proudly; we stepped behind the billboard to inspect the smoke-machine for water-damage, and he tinkered with its pumps and valves as ably as he'd dealt with the damaged motorcycle. "Saw the way Siggy'd built his gun-towers, one in sight of the other, so no matter where you stood you could see two or three of them around the horizon . . ." It did not occur to me at once that by "Siggy" he meant no person, but the Siegfrieder Military Academy in general. "Well, sir, when we rang the curtain on the big show over there, I says to my P.R. team, 'Let's toss this one over the old plate and see who swings at it.' "

"Ah," I said.

"Yessirree George!" Greene nodded. "Tower Hall was talking Public Lands again, don't you know, and College Forests, and Conservation, and it seemed to me it was time to blow the whistle on Creeping Student-Unionism. 'Light up the watchfires,' I said to P.R.; 'Smoke the pink profs out of Tower Hall!' So we put a task-force on it and came up with these billboards, on every highway and byway, and we placed the smoke-boxes so no matter where you stood in good old NTC you'd see the Signal-Fires of Freedom burning somewhere . . ."

"Signal-Fires of Freedom?"

Greene blinked proudly. "First we thought of *Smokescreens for Security,* but when we played that on the old kazoo it sounded like we were hiding something, you know? *Flames of Free Research* looked big for a while too, very big, but finally we decided it would give us a black eye imagewise—cross up the Keep-Our-Forests-Greene bit, I mean." That lat-

ter slogan, he acknowledged, was his own, and all boasting
aside, he deemed it punwisely so felicitous a merger of the
Conservation and Private-Research bits that upon devising it
he'd dismissed his entire staff of advertising consultants—"Sent
the whole team to the showers"—and taken the field himself
in his own behalf: on behalf, that is, of Greene Timber and
Plastics, of which concern he was Board Chairman. Indeed,
when treading musewise on the heels of *Keep Our Forests
Greene* came *Signal-Fires of Freedom*—with its suggestion at
once of non-destructive vigil, of summons to a common cause,
and of the red-skinned preschoolists who first inhabited the
NTC campus—he had devoted less time every year to his manu-
facturing interests and more to promotion and packaging: the
locomotive and caboose, raison-d'êtrewise, of his train of
thought.

We had come back to the roadside to contemplate the
huge advertisement while Greene discoursed upon its history.

"*Yi,*" Max groaned. "Max Spielman on the same motorcycle with Greene Timber and Plastics!"

Reverting to his earlier manner, Greene winked and
grinned. "I reckon I can bear it if you can, sir. I'm right color-
blind myself, but they do say red and green balance out."

Max was not amused. "The blight and flunking of this college, George," he said. I could not discern whether it was the
sign or the man he pointed to, but in either case his judgment
struck me as extreme. I myself found the advertisement, like
its creator, more diverting than appalling; indeed I could
have stood agape before the flashing lights and rolling smoke
for a great while longer, and left only because the afternoon
pressed on. As before, Peter Greene was undismayed by the
criticism: his "feedin'-hand," he declared, was "pert' near
tooth-proof" from having been "bit so durn reg'lar." I was
hard put to it to follow his shifting lingo, but the dispute between him and Max, which went on until dinnertime, was of
interest to me, for it had to do with the virtues and failings of
what Greene called "the New Tammany Way."

"Now you take me," he invited us again above the
engine-noise, and grasped his own shirt-front as before. "Me,
I'm no smarter nor stupider than the next fellow; I had to
work hard for everything I got—"

"Which is plenty," Max put in. Peter Greene agreed with a
laugh that he was not the poorest man on the campus, yet
denied he was the richest, that distinction belonging to Ira

Hector—for whom, when all was said and done, he had a grudging admiration. "Despite some say he's a Moishian . . ."

"Mr. Greene!" I protested.

He winked and cocked his head. "Now, don't get het up; I don't hold it against him if he is! And I guess I think *Reggie* Hector's about the greatest man in New Tammany."

Max closed his eyes.

"But what I was saying," Greene went on, "I don't mean to boast, now, but what I figure—*By jingo, I'm okay!*" He bobbed his head sharply. "When all's said and done! If I do say so myself!"

I begged his pardon.

"I figure I'm passed because good old NTC is passed," he said. "The passèdest doggone college in the doggone University!"

"You've taken the Finals, then?" I asked with interest. It occurred to me that I ought to have been asking that question of everyone—of Anastasia, of Maurice Stoker, of Dr. Sear, of Max himself. Why had he not advised me to?

"When they call me flunked," Greene declared, "they call the whole darn college flunked, that's what I'm getting at. And any man that's willing to flunk his own alma mater— well, he's a pretty poor New Tammanian!"

He thrust forth his chin and opened the throttle wider, perhaps without realizing it, so that I had to urge Croaker to a swifter trot. Max I observed had drawn a hand over his face before this curious logic, which even I saw the several flaws in, or else had turned to brooding upon other matters. He was not the Max of yesterday!

"Well, *are* you a Graduate, or *not*?" I insisted. "What were the Finals like? Why are you going back to register again?"

"I got no secrets," Greene said stoutly. "I'll lay my cards on the table. Don't believe everything you read in the papers. My life is an open book. *I'm okay.*"

I assured him that I'd read nothing about him in the newspapers, uncomplimentary or otherwise, not ever having read any newspapers, and that what I'd seen of his resourcefulness and gathered of his enterprise quite inclined me to assent to his okayness, whatever the term implied. That there was nothing hostile or even skeptical in my questions, but only the general curiosity of one who had the Finals still before him, and the special curiosity of one whose mission it was eventually to teach others the right Answers.

He replied with a most-warm, open smile. "You're okay too, George: I can tell by your face. Goat-boy or not, it don't matter. I had a friend once name of George."

He volunteered to review for my benefit the afore-mentioned book of his life: a tome, he acknowledged, not without a dark page here and there, but which taken all in all was nothing shameful, by gosh. However, the afternoon was waning; there was an eating-place not far ahead where he would be pleased to *grub-stake* us in return for picking him up and hearing him out; his story would keep until we reached it. We had for some minutes been climbing a gentle rise behind which the ruddy sun had already descended. Before us now the woods stopped, where the road went over the ridge; the tree-limbs there were finely lit.

"You never saw New Tammany proper before?" Greene asked. I shook my head. He topped the rise a few meters before me and, braking the cycle, called over his shoulder, "Well, there she sets, friend!" There was reverence in his voice; he had removed his fur cap, and his orange hair and outstretched hand gleamed like the tree-limbs in the light, which lit me too when Croaker came up beside him. "How 'bout *that*, now!"

What had I imagined a great college would look like? I cannot remember. Photographs I had seen, descriptions I'd read, but with only the livestock-barns and the branch library for scale, I must have conceived the central campus of New Tammany as a slightly larger version of our stalls and pastures. Certainly I was not prepared for the spectacle before and beneath us. Sparkling in the purple dusk, it stretched out endlessly, endlessly. Avenues, towers, monuments; corridors of glass and steel; lakes and parks and marble colonnades; bridges and smokestacks, blinkers and beacons! Hundreds of messages flashed in every color, from here, from there, on roofs and cornices: FIND FACTS FAST—ENCYCLOPEDIA TAMMANICA: DON'T BE SAD—STUDY BUSINESS AD.; YOUR ROTC KEEPS THE RIOT QUIET; ALWAYS A HIT: LATE-MEDIEVAL LIT. Thousands of motorcycles, bicycles, scooters swarmed along the boulevards, stopped at traffic signals, flowed into roundabouts, threaded into residential mazes; the mingled roar of horns and engines hung like a pall of smoke or the echo of a shout. In truth I could scarcely draw breath in face of such tremendousness; before the ignorance of what lay in store for me there and the knowledge that I would go down to meet it, my heart sank in my breast. And New Tammany was but one college of the many in West Campus, and West Campus far less than half the University—smaller both in area and population than its Eastern counterpart or the aggregate of "independent" colleges! And Max maintained—but how was one to swallow it?—that our whole University was but one among an infinitude of others, perhaps quite similar, perhaps utterly different, whose existence in the fenceless pastures of reality, while as yet unconfirmed, had perforce to be assumed. And those hundreds of thousands of human people below there, in New Tammany alone—each with his involvements and aspirations, strengths and weaknesses, past history and present problems—I was to be their Tutor, show them the way to Commencement Gate?

"Fetches you up, now, don't it?" Greene demanded proudly. I shook my head, couldn't answer. He identified Tower Hall, its belfry floodlit in the distance, and pointed out the brilliant string of lights that followed the Power Line eastwards from that building to the Boundary and behind us to Founder's Hill—the string whose other end I'd glimpsed from the Powerhouse. WESCAC was there—the storied Belly, the awful EATer; and there too, somewhere beneath that high-spired dome, was the fabled Central Library and a certain particular booklift where my journey had begun. The ambiguous thrill brought tears to my eyes; I leaned down and touched Max's shoulder for comfort, and he briefly put his brooding by to share my feeling.

"Twenty years since I went over this hill," he said.

"Lots of things have changed since then," Greene said cheerfully. "They're all the time tearing down old ones and putting up new."

Max pointed out the Lykeionian-revival porch of the Chancellor's Mansion, the Remusian pilasters of the Old Armory, the flying buttresses of Enoch Hall. I inquired about what appeared to be, after the Stadium, the largest building of all, a floodlit multistoried cube of enormous dimension with a featureless limestone facade.

"Military Science," Max said grimly. "And out past Tower Hall, the last big building to the south—see those four turrets with the searchlights? That's Main Detention, where I spent my last night before they sent me away."

"Ain't it grand?" said Peter Greene. "We got the biggest detention-hall in the University!" What was more, he added, the clock-tower of Tower Hall was the tallest structure on the campus; and there were so many kilometers of hallway in the Military Science Cube that the professor-generals pedaled bicycles from office to office; and nine out of every ten NTC staff-members (and eleven out of every twelve students) owned his own motorbike—a ratio triple that of Nikolay College and well ahead of any of our West-Campus colleagues. The total power expended in a single day by all these engines equaled the energy of a hundred EAT-waves of the latest type . . .

"And make the most important poison in the atmosphere," Max added, "except for the drop-outs from EAT-wave testing."

"Say what you want," Greene chuckled. "If it weren't for all them drivers there wouldn't be no drive-ins."

We came down then from the overlook into the stunning traffic of a main highway ("Hit 'em right at the evening rush," Greene remarked—and hit them he very nearly did on a number of occasions, by driving through traffic lights at intersections or misjudging the distance of approaching head-lamps. In addition to his color-blindness, it seemed, he was unable to perceive depth with his single eye; I was to learn later that he was subject to certain photisms, or optical hallucinations, as well, but fortunately was spared that extra cause for alarm during this first experience of vehicular traffic). The noise took my heart out; I was terrified by the rush and by the confusion of lights and signals. Arrows flashed this way and that; signs commanded one on every hand to stop, to go, to turn. I spurred tireless Croaker to his utmost gallop; even so the slowest of the vehicles sped past as if we stood still. Not the least of my astonishments was that we drew so little attention: horns would blow and insults be shouted if we strayed off the shoulder onto the pavement or trespassed inadvertently against the right-of-way; otherwise, however, young and old roared past without a curious glance—as if a fleecèd goat-boy, astride a black giant and accompanied by a bearded old Moishian, were to be seen at every interchange!

Not until we turned from the highway onto the apron of the promised eating-place did anyone really notice us: the evening was warm, and a throng of young couples had drawn their machines up to the Pedal Inn, as the place was called. They laughed and slouched in their sidecars or at outdoor tables, in every kind of dress; some danced upon the asphalt to music that seemed to bleat from half a dozen floodlight poles; others smoked tobacco, furtively pawed one another's bodies, or chewed upon victuals (meat, I fear) run out to them by white-frocked attendants. They greeted our approach with cries and whistles and claps of the hand; I distinguished Croaker's name several times, and was pleased to see them give way. A number of the girls were not unattractive, by human standards, and it relieved me to see that Croaker was after all too fatigued by his final sprint to need restraining. It seemed to me a colorful and animated host; I took their merriment as an expression of goodwill and waved my hand cordially. They formed a large ring around us as Peter Greene parked, and those inside the glass-walled eating-place stared out. The jaws of most worked vigorously, as if upon a cud; some pared their nails with knives while they hooed and hollered; others combed and combed their hair.

"Wonderful kids, aren't they?" Greene exclaimed.

Max muttered something unpleasant about a lynch-mob and asked whether Greene was sure the place would serve Frumentians, Moishians, and goat-boys.

"They'll durn well serve any friends of mine," Greene laughed, and confessed to being part-owner of the establishment. The name Pedal Inn had occurred to him one day at lunch, and he'd built a chain of drive-in restaurants to bear it.

2.

"That was two-three years ago," he said; "before things went kerflooey."

We sat inside, in a stall with benches, and dined on cheeseburgers and fried potatoes. I could not of course stomach the meat and so made do with the buns and onions and a sheaf of paper napkins, which I found piquant with tomato catsup. Croaker on the other hand squatted on the floor and ate his raw; Max declared he had no appetite, though he'd eaten little all day, and remarked besides that Moishian custom forbade meat and dairy produce at the same board—a rule I'd never heard him invoke before. He contented himself with occasional sips of sarsaparilla. After the original stir of our entrance, though they came to the window now and then to stare, most of the young people returned to their former pursuits, and I was able to listen undistracted except by the overwhelming novelty of the surroundings.

"Kerflooey?" I said.

Greene tisked and nodded. "Used to be, I was sitting pretty. I liked people; people liked me. Business doing fine. Married to the prettiest gal in the neck of the woods: sweet as apple cider; pure as pure. Then all of a sudden, *kerflooey*, the whole durn thing. I swear to Pete."

The kerflooiness of things, it developed, had a bearing upon Mr. Greene's return to Great Mall, and consisted of reverses both professional and domestic. He had in fact put home and business behind, and had now to choose whether to return or make the breach final. Yet things had not after all gone kerflooey in an instant of time: rather they had slipped into that condition by degrees, over a period of many semesters.

"I wonder sometimes if I ain't one of them drop-outs from the EAT-wave tests, you know? Things ain't been the same at all since I come home from the Riot and set up in the plastic and promotion way."

I inquired whether Mrs. Greene was also a Graduate.

"I should hope to kiss a pig!" Greene cried, and though the phrase itself conveyed to me no certain answer, its tone and context suggested affirmation. "I guess she was the smartest little gal I ever did run across, was Sally Ann—till things went kerflooey. When she'd call on a fellow to recite his lesson, he'd better know it right by heart, don't she'd fetch out that ruler of hers and crack him a daisy! Fellows twice her own size, that could break a redskin in two or lick their weight in wildcats!"

From this I inferred that in her youth Mrs. Greene had been some sort of pedagogue in the wilder reaches of the NTC Forestry Preserve, and that it was the idiom of that place and time into which her mate now slipped as he recalled it.

"I was a wild 'un back then," he confessed with a grin. "No flannel pants in *them* days! And no time for lallygaggin' round no drive-ins, like young 'uns in this Present Modern College of Today."

He seemed now altogether scornful of the students roundabout, whom he'd lately been praising. About his own childhood I found him similarly of two minds, declaring on the one hand his intention to see to it that his children enjoyed all the privileges himself had never known, and on the other that the modern generation was plumb spoilt by the luxuries of life in present-day NTC and would amount to nothing for want of such rigor as had been his lot.

"I run away from home at the age of fourteen," he said proudly. "Not that it was much of a home, with Paw a-drinkin' and Maw forever a-layin' the Good Book on me." The actual nature and location of his birthplace I could not discern: sometimes it appeared to have been the meanest hovel, sometimes a place of ancient grandeur. In any case he'd abandoned it, his parents, his patrimony and hied him into wilderness departments, to live off the land. His motives, as he characterized them, were praiseworthy: the pursuit of independence and escape from the debilitating influence of corrupt tradition. "My folks and me, we come to a fork in the road," he said: "they had their notions and I had mine, that's everything there was to it."

But Max questioned this assertion. "Yes, well, the way I read once, you were hooky-playing from school always, *ja?* And making trouble till they ran you out?"

Greene reckoned cheerfully that he'd made his share of mischief now and again, and acknowledged further that on his voyage into the wild, in a homemade vessel, he'd been accompanied by another fugitive, a Frumentian from a South-Quad chain-gang; that they'd saved each other's lives more than once, and had become fast friends despite their difference in race.

"But that's *all* we ever was, was pals," he insisted. "Old Black George and me (I used to call him Old Black George, despite he weren't old), we went through thick and thin together 'fore we parted company. I guess no boy ever had a better pal: that's why I bust out laughin' when they say I don't like darkies! But friends is *all,* and them smart-alecks that claim we was *funny* for each other—I'd like to horsewhip 'em!"

I remarked that I too had been fortunate enough to have a Frumentian friend by the name of George. Max considered his sarsaparilla.

Equally libelous, Greene assured us, was the gossip that

he'd taken a daughter of his fellow-fugitive into the bush for
immoral purposes: the truth was that an influential white
lady had arranged to have Old Black George paroled into the
custody of his family, all of whom were domestic workers in
the boarding-school she operated; only his parole hinged on
the condition that this particular daughter, who had taken to
a lewd course of life, leave the premises. "O.B.G.," as Greene
was wont to call his friend, had at first been reluctant, but
upon Greene's offering secretly to take the girl with him and
look after her, he accepted the condition.

"'Tweren't my fault she turned out bad," he said. "I had
my hands full clearin' land and huntin' meat and buildin'
shelters and chasin' off redskins; I couldn't watch no sassy little pickaninny every minute."

"But you never touched her yourself?" Max demanded.

"Me touch *her!*" Greene grinned. "It was her pesterin' *me*
all the time! And a-teasin'! And a-beggin'!" His eyes hard-
ened. "And declarin' she'd tell Miss Sally Ann if I didn't
watch out."

As best I could fathom it, he had permitted the Frumentian girl to share his sleeping bag, cook and wash for
him, and mate with certain redskins. It was possible even to
infer that his life had been preserved by those same aborigi-
nals at her behest, but the story was vague. In any case, despite her inclination, if not positive passion, he had seldom
actually serviced her, he vowed—perhaps never at all—for
the reason that it "weren't decent." In the meanwhile, other
adventurers had followed Greene's lead until at length a
small quadrangle was established in the wilds; New Tammany
College annexed the territory, and Tower Hall dispatched
ROTC units to subdue the redskins, and schoolteachers to educate the settlers. Greene himself, from established habit, had
declined formal schooling; but he taught himself reading,
writing, and arithmetic—with no other light than the fire on
his hearth, no other texts than the Old and New Syllabi, no
other materials than a clean pine board and a stick of char-
coal. And if his manners and speech were untutored, his
courage, high spirits, and intelligence must have made up for
them, for he wooed and won the pretty schoolmistress herself—Miss Sally Ann from back in the East Quads, whose
mother was the boarding-school directress mentioned before.

"You can talk about your Grand Tutors," he sighed, and
set his jaw; "Miss Sally Ann was Enos Enoch and His Twelve

Trustees as far as *I* was concerned, and her word was the pure and simple Answer. Wasn't for her, I'd of been a beast of the woods: the way she prettied up the cabin and the schoolhouse was a wonder! And talk about your Finals: when Sally Ann got done with me I could recite you the Founder's Scroll backwards or forwards."

"Is *that* how to pass the Finals!" I exclaimed with a frown.

"Pfui," Max said. "It's how to flunk a whole college."

But Greene insisted that Miss Sally Ann was Founder and Chancellor and Examiners too, to his mind, and had besides the prettiest face and figure in the entire territory, durned if she didn't. She herself was the Answer: she had rescued him from the clutches of the Dean o' Flunks, from the way to failure, and he would let no vileness near her. It was chiefly for her sake, to provide her with every comfort known to studentdom, that when not yet twenty he claimed squatter's rights to vast tracts of virgin timber, formed his own Sub-Department of Lumbering and Paper Manufacture, built sawmills and factories, laid waste the wilderness, dammed the watersheds, spoiled the streams, and became a power in the School of Business and an influence in Tower Hall. For her sake too (though it wasn't clear whether she demanded these things or he volunteered them) he eschewed liquor and tobacco, and forbade them to others; left off cursing, gambling, and fist-fighting, of which he'd been fond; and had Old Black George's daughter committed to Main Detention as a common prostitute. By discharging in his office the energies previously wasted on idle pursuits, he grew at an early age more affluent than his neighbors. Yet though he swore by his union and career as by Commencement itself, he showed signs of restlessness: he began playing truant from his office, as formerly from the classroom; spent more time on the golf-links than at the mills; became a collector of famous paintings, expensive books, antique motorcycles, pornography, and big-game trophies. And he welcomed the chance to fight for New Tammany as an officer of infantry in Campus Riot II.

"I don't deny you fought like a hero," Max said. "He won the Trustees' Medal of Honor, George, for killing so many Bonifacists. A fine thing."

I was surprised to see that he spoke not at all sarcastically.

"I thank you, sir," Greene said, in an accent much brisker and clearer than he'd used thitherto: a modest but military tone. I asked him whether it was in combat with the enemy that he'd lost his eye.

"I wish to Sam Hill it was," he said, and cocked his head ruefully. "Weren't, though." He then declared, for reasons not at once apparent, that the opinion commonly held of him outside NTC was a cruel untruth—namely, that he was henpecked; that his wife "wore the pants in the family" and was unhappy with the fit, as it were; that too much complaisance on his part had led her at first to discontentment, thence to shrewishness, and at last to the Faculty Women's Rest House, and everything kerflooey.

"Fact is," he said, as if talking about the same thing, "my eyes never *were* very good, but I didn't realize it till I was grown up. I used to press against my eyeball to see things when I was a kid, and then like as not I'd see two redskins where there was one, or my eyes would fill up and blur." Then one day during his courtship of Miss Sally Ann, he said, he'd brought her all the way to Great Mall for the annual Spring Carnival, and it was during their tour of the midway amusements that he'd lost his eye, in the following manner—which he confided in frank detail in order, he asserted, to correct the misrepresentations of malicious gossip. The courtship had been proceeding satisfactorily: pledges of love had been exchanged and intent declared to marry as soon as his position was more securely established, he being then scarcely past adolescence and only begun on his various enterprises. They had learned something of each other's history: on his part, that he was a rebellious orphan with an undistinguished past but great hope for the future, of small resource but large resoucefulness, short on tutoring but long on ambition, with a craving to Commence and make his mark on the campus, and eager to be married though with little experience of women—he confessed to her solemnly his youthful connection with Old Black George's daughter, whereof he was so contrite that, going it may be beyond the facts, he declared he was no virgin, the more severely to chastise himself. She had wept but forgiven him, and admitted sorrowfully that she too had something to confess, though not of a guilty nature: she was beset by a Peeping Tom and secret masher, who, though she had provoked him in no wise but by her general beauty, which no amount of modesty could veil, for some time had plagued her by night—peering in her windows, hissing obscenities from bushes, exposing his member to her moonlight view. She would have spoken of it earlier, she declared, but for her fear that Greene might think the man a beau of hers, present or past, and break their engagement.

Beside this disclosure (the more alarming because young Greene, after incarcerating O.B.G.'s daughter, had taken secretly to patrolling the area of Miss Sally Ann's cabin by night, to prevent exactly such molestation in the rough backwoods, and had seen nothing more sinister than deer and raccoons though his view of her windows was unobstructed) the other details of his financée's background were of no importance to him. Outraged at the mysterious interloper's effrontery—Miss Sally Ann had not seen his face, but was convinced of his reality and motive—Greene vowed to marry her at once, despite the insecurity of their position, the better to insure her maiden honor against mischance, and to thrash the masher if he caught him. He would have wed her that same day, but for one nagging detail . . .

"It's the simple Enochist Truth," he said; "I'm a shy one where the girls are concerned. Always have been! Always will be!" He blinked and winked. "That don't mean I ain't got an ace or two once the chips are down! But I'm slow to make my play, and the reason is, there weren't no girls around when I was growing up. O.B.G's daughter don't count; not just she's a darky, but she come on so fast and teased so much she'd scare the starch right out o' me, despite I'd love to shown the hussy a thing or two . . . I used to tell her she was lucky I was saving up for marriage, but the fact of the matter was, I'd get me in a state quick enough just a-thinking how she carried on, but once she was right there face to face—no spunk at all! Know what I mean?"

Naturally I did not, except by considerable effort of imagination—what could be more alien to life in the goat-barns than pusillanimity in the face so to speak of erotic provocation?

"You weren't *able* to service her?" I hazarded.

Greene blushed and glanced out of the booth. Croaker was asleep now in the aisle, my stick in his lap, and the flaring music-box broadcast above our voices a queer loud plaint:

Moreover, it was grown dark, and though the headlit motors came and went from the apron of the Pedal Inn, few noses pressed now to the plate-glass wall beside us.

"I was able!" Greene protested, in a vehement whisper. "I just never could get up nerve enough, is all!"

Yet he had hesitated to commit himself to husbandhood, he said, until his capacity was proved, and Miss Sally Ann (somewhat to his surprise) seeming not finally averse, he had fetched her to Great Mall with the understanding that they'd lose their innocence each to the other before they returned. They took separate rooms in a Great-Mall inn for the three nights of the Carnival, but slept together. On the first night he'd been doubled up with cramps and unable to move—an effect, he believed, less of fear than of shame at the notion of subjecting so passèd a lady girl to his carnal lusts. On the second, nonetheless, they had striven resolutely—but in vain, for failing to find himself in the studly way from the very first kiss, as he thought proper, he so furiously reproached himself that no subsequent ministrations of Miss Sally Ann's could turn the trick. She had better betake her to some callous stud, he had told her bitterly, who being less confounded by the

architecture of her naked flesh could possess it like a master
instead of trembling like a truant freshman before the Chancellor's Mansion. So saying—despite her protests that she was
no Frumentian doxy who measured her lovers by the road, as
it were; that for all her willingness to yield love's fruits to
him she was content enough to sleep in his arms as on the
previous night; that on the other hand if his pride would but
permit him to see himself as curator instead of conqueror of
that same Mansion, she was confident they could open its
gate as well with a pass-key as with a batter—despite all this
he cursed himself back to his room and drank himself into a
solitary stupor.

On the third and final day of the Spring Carnival he'd
groused about, uncertain whether to destroy himself or
merely break their engagement. They watched the ritual
Dance of the Freshman Co-eds around the shaft; the cercmo-
nial Expulsion and Reinstatement of the Chancellor, com-
memorating Enos Enoch's weekend in the Nether Campus;
the coronation of a new Miss University in white gown and
mortarboard and her parade down Great Mall on a float of
lilies. The more Miss Sally Ann endeavored to raise his spirits
by feigning animation, the gloomier he grew: after dinner,
when they went to the brilliant midway, he insisted she ride
on ferris-wheel, carousel, and roller-coaster—of all which
amusements she was shrieking fond—but would not accompany her; he even sent her, against her inclination, alone
through the Tunnel of Love and the adjoining Chamber of
Horrors. While she made her way reluctantly through the latter, he stood outside in the sawdust and brooded upon his
reflection in a row of distorting mirrors near the entrance. In
one his neck rose like a swan's above his body; in another his
bulbous trunk perched high on stork-legs. They put him
glumly in mind of certain of his dreams wherein a more pertinent piece of him had similarly been drawn out to miraculous
length, with astonishing consequence. This memory led in
turn to reveries of Miss Sally Ann disrobed, and he was
roused in fact, though not beyond human proportions. To
conceal his condition he was obliged to sit down on a bench
near the exit and cross his legs.

His choice of seats, he discovered a moment later, was not
in the best interest of detumescence: the last "horror" of the
Chamber was a grating in the exit ramp-way, a few meters
before him, through which when it was trod upon a blast of

air blew, to the end of lifting the co-ed's skirts. I was far
enough from goatdom to understand with no further explanation that the consequent brief exposure, not of actual escutch-
eons but of drawers and female harness, was by virtue of its
involuntary nature mortifying to the victims and both amusing and arousing to human male onlookers, who might
scarcely take notice of a more comprehensive and prolonged
display under other circumstances—lady girls in swimsuits at
a pool, say, or their own wives in the showerbath. Peter
Greene watched erect, savoring of each blowee the squealing
fluster, the vain endeavor to hold down her skirt, the half-
second's glimpse of silk-snugged crotch. Thin girls, fat girls,
pretty girls, plain—in his fancy he lusted shamefully for them
all, every soft-thighed lass who ever was, had been, or would
be; even the blushfullest, he reflected, would in her lifetime
admit some man, or several, into that passèd private place: he
could not bear that it should not in every instance be himself.
How he should have enjoyed that the lot of them be in his
power! In a vast subcampus chamber of his own devising, lit
by flambeaux and known to none but himself, he would
keep them prisoner, not a stitch among them, and perpetrate at his
whim exquisitest carnalities upon whom he chose. Perhaps
they would all be blindfolded, or bound at wrist and
ankle . . .

"Founder's sake!" I was moved to exclaim. Max seemed to
have joined Croaker in sleep.

"Shucks," Greene scoffed " 'tweren't nothing but a day-
dream. All a girl's got to do's say *boo* to me, pass her heart, I
turn tail and run! Anyhow, I set there hotter'n a fox and
watched 'em get their skirts blowed up, till finally along
comes Sally Ann, with some old Enochism-teacher she'd met
in the funhouse that used to know her, and he'd helped her
find her way when she was lost inside. I figured she'd just as
leave not show her drawers to him—especially since he
seemed to be carrying on right smart for who he was and
all—so I jumped up to tell her about the air-hose; but she
was laughing at something or other and didn't notice me till
whoosh—up goes her dirndl, and there's her pretty drawers
with the yellow roses on! Right then I hear a whistling and a
whooping, and a voice hollering out to Miss Sally Ann to
come there and see what he had for her, stuff like that. Made
my blood boil! I looked round to see who'd come up, 'cause
till then there hadn't nobody been left of me where the hol-

lering was, you understand? Weren't even no benches there to
set on. What there was was just this tall skinny plate-glass
window along the wall, right near the exit, and when I
squinched up my eyeballs with my fingers I could see a fellow standing there, bold as brass! First thing struck me, it
must be that Peeping Tom she said'd been a-pestering her—
seeing he knew her name and was talking so fresh. Anyhow
I knew he was the one that was whistling and hollering,
'cause I could see he still had his hand up by his mouth. So I
figure, I'll teach him a lesson he won't soon forget, by Jimmy
Gumbo, and I pick me a rock up off the ground. Now I took
for granted the window was open, it being such a warm night
and him a-hollering so plain; all I had in mind to do was snib
him one to show him what was what. But time I hauled off to
chunk, I saw he'd got a rock his own self and was set to
knock my block off with it, so I let fly all my might. Never
did find out if I hit him, 'cause we never saw nor heard from
him after that. But he sure got me! What happened was, the
durn window was shut—whatever it was—and his rock and
mine must of busted into it right the same time. His never hit
me, but the glass went flying every whichaway, and a little
tiny piece of it struck me in the eye."

His fiancée's alarm, he went on to say, soon brought assistance: he was hurried to the Infirmary, where first the glass
was removed and later the eyeball, irreparably damaged.
Upon reviving from anesthesia he found Miss Sally Ann at his
bedside, and they commiserated for the loss of both his eye
and their last night to spend together on Great Mall. More to
his chagrin, now that making love was out of the question he
was splendidly erect, nor did any amount of ironic remark
upon this phenomenon at all diminish it. Nay, his pain and
the blindfold of bandages notwithstanding, he lusted more
powerfully than ever before; her consolatory kisses only inflamed him; he must have her then and there, nurses be
flunked; she must close and block the door and come at once
to bed. Reluctant at first, she was at last brought blushing to
it, rather to his surprise: protesting soft but breathing hard
she slipped out of her shoes and between his sheets, and the
sweet deed was done.

"Well, sir," Greene declared—more as one beginning than
concluding a story: "I told her the honest truth then: how it
was my first time, and I never had actually swived old
O.B.G.'s daughter."

This news, he said (when Max returned to partial slumber after stirring to remark that *swive* was a fine old verb whose desuetude in all but a few back-campus areas was much to be deplored, as it left the language with no term for *service* that was not obscene, clinical, legalistic, ironic, euphemistic, or periphrastic), Miss Sally Ann professed not to believe; she'd even scolded him a bit for so exaggerating the importance of what, to her mind, was a mere technicality beside the fact of true and exclusive love that he felt he must deceive her on the point. They married soon after, and directly his wound was healed and his glass eye installed, he immersed himself with equal passion in his work and his newly realized manhood. Greene Timber doubled and tripled its holdings, destroying its competitors, exploiting its workers, depleting the countryside, and diversifying into related areas of manufacture. The Greenes moved from cabin to manorhouse and begot a great number of offspring, whose rearing Mrs. Greene relinquished her profession to supervise; there was no further need for her to work anyhow, and she agreed with her husband that woman's place was in the home. There she gave orders to a staff of domestics, took up the piano and painting on glass, read long novels, and tatted the hems of pillowslips. They regarded their match as ideal and themselves as blissful in it—but in certain moods, now he was initiated, Greene bewailed his lost opportunities with O.B.G.'s flunkèd daughter and perhaps even consorted with her secretly, in or out of prison, always however berating himself the while for polluting, or thinking to pollute, his perfect marriage. And Miss Sally Ann now and then complained of spells of faintness and that her life was after all as empty as some statue's in a Founder's Hall.

Then, sometime in his twenties, for reasons he could not well articulate, Greene's opinion changed profoundly on the question of Answers and Graduation. Some said he was influenced by disillusioned veterans of the First Campus Riot; others, that this disillusionment in turn was but the popular dramatizing of a state of intellectual affairs that dated from the Rematriculation Period and had long prevailed "across the Pond" in the famous seats of West-Campus learning. Still others pointed out, quite correctly, that Greene was a rustic without classical education or much use for the departments of moral science and the fine arts; they were inclined to relate his new attitude to the loss of his eye or of his adolescent vigor, to the belated realization of character deficiencies, or to domestic and business difficulties.

"Which is putting the cart before the goshdarn horse, them last ones," he said. "I figure I invented my Answers my own self, just like Sally Ann and me invented making love, no matter how many'd thought of it before."

Whatever the causes, the effects were unmistakable: they moved from their rural estate to an urban quad; he made his wife a full-time equal partner in his business; they toured distant campuses, learned to smoke cigarettes, drink cocktails, dance to jazz-music, drive fast motorcycles, and practice contraception. Miss Sally Ann now freely admitted enjoying what theretofore she had seemed only to permit: husband and wife put by all inhibition and together tasted every sweet and salty dish in love's cuisine, improvising some, discovering others accidentally, borrowing not a few from the high-spiced cookbooks of ancient Remus and Siddartha, which Greene no longer perused in secret but shared with his wife. Nay, further, emancipated alike from the stuffy prohibitions of old-fashioned lecturers and the economics of harder terms, they went from twin beds to separate vacations to separate residences and friends, and mortgaged all their assets to extend by daring speculation their business interests and finance their costly extracurricular activities.

This continued to the end of that decade of their lives, and ended, alas, in general fiasco. One memorable night, happening to meet each other en route to their separate apartments from separate illegal taverns, but both drunk on the same distillation, Greene announced impulsively to his wife, whether as confession, boast, or wish, that O.B.G.'s daughter (no longer in prison) was threatening him with a paternity suit, or might one day so threaten for all he knew; and Mrs. Greene replied, between hiccoughs, that for all *she* knew she might one day threaten O.B.G.'s daughter's husband with the same, if the trollop had one and he was properly manned. They went then their separate ways, but whether that encounter was the trigger, or certain ominous signs that his speculations were overextended and no longer basically sound, there ensued just prior to his thirtieth birthday a collapse of Peter Greene's self-confidence and a lengthy spell of profound depression.

"Just seemed like it all went kerflooey at once," he said. His research and production plants failed, one after another, or were shut down by organized mutinies among his staff, some of whom openly professed Student-Unionism. Greene's own sympathies were split between affinity for any rebellious cause (a habit of mind carried over from his childhood) and his contempt for anything that smacked of the "welfare campus." So at odds was he with himself, he would bribe the campus police to put down a demonstration, then find himself marching unrecognized among the demonstrators, in his old forester's clothes, and take a beating he himself had paid for. Sexually he became subject to periods of impotence; socially he withdrew, lost interest in the few friends he had left, as in himself. Whether he appeared well or ill in the public eye and his own no longer concerned him; he could not even manage to despise himself much, so thoroughgoing was his sense of futility. Much of his time he spent rocking in a chair. To his surprise (for he was not given to speculation of the philosophic sort) he found not only that he no longer regarded himself as Graduated, but that he disbelieved in the reality of Graduation, the Founder, and Final Exams. Nothing in the University mattered in the long run, it seemed perfectly clear to him: one man studied and strove for the good of his classmates, another cheated, lied, and tattled: both soon passed away and were forgotten, with the rest of mortal studentdom, and the blind University went on, and too would vanish when its term expired. To rock the campus, to rock a chair—what did it matter? Mrs. Greene dropped by with the children to spend the weekend, bringing with her a supply of the sleeping-capsules which both had come to depend on for rest; they quarreled, resolved to institute bankruptcy and divorce proceedings, drank a final drink together, and ended by dividing the capsules between them, each swallowing a number he judged most honestly to be on the threshold of lethality, perhaps beyond it.

"You wanted to *kill* yourselves?" It was an idea I could comprehend only faintly, by recollecting my state of mind on the day I had murdered Redfearn's Tom. But what a difference in circumstance! I took a wondering swig from the catsup bottle. Greene sighed, and arched his orange eyebrows, and fiddled with the sugarbowl lid.

"Didn't have the gumption to choose either way, sir. But I sure did wish I was dead." I could not discern whether his respectful mode of addressing me was general habit or particular deference. "We figured if the pills did us in, okay; if they didn't, what the flunk, we'd have to think where to go from there."

As it happened, they'd misjudged not only the dosage but the drug itself, a mild soporific, the first of what was to be a series of ever-more-sophisticated prescriptions. It was an ignorance they could no more have been saved by in later years, when their knowledge of chemicals came to rival a pharmacist's, than they could have attained sweet sleep by that old potion. Sleep they did—soundly, long—and Peter Greene dreamed of the great Spring Carnival. When the children woke him next morning his wife was sweetly sleeping still, and it was some moments before he remembered having taken the capsules. He felt utterly refreshed; it was a sunny Saturday, no haste to rise. Nothing had changed: there was still no Founder, nor sense in the University; he was still wretched Peter Greene, his manner graceless, his enterprises failing, his character deficient, his family unhappy; there was still no more reason, ultimately, to heed the summons of his bladder and children than not to. Yet all these truths had a different *feel* now: he kissed Mrs. Greene and left the bed, still utterly uncertain how his life was to be managed and heedless of its course, but with a new indifference to this indifference.

"Didn't matter a durn to me any more that nothing mattered a durn," was how he put it. "I knew I weren't worth a doggone, and couldn't of cared less." For the first time in a long while he felt like working; instead he made love to Miss Sally Ann, also for the first time in some while, and something of his mood must have touched her, for they clung together ardently, swore their love, repented their abuses of it, mourned the past, vowed to do better. He listened to their words with tender unbelief. No matter. Even the question that had come to live with him some months earlier—having visited his fancy on rare occasions over the years—now lost its urgency and seemed just interesting: the question of the broken glass.

"What it was," he said, "I was looking at myself in the bathroom mirror one afternoon, just when my big depression started. I'd been out all day with the stiffs on the picket-line, busting the windowlights out of one of my papermills, and I'd come home to get a shower before the cocktail party we were having that evening for some Tower Hall big-shots. I got to making ugly faces at myself and feeling terrible, and suddenly it struck me maybe that wasn't no window at all I'd chunked that rock through, or any flunkèd Peeping Tom hollering at Miss Sally Ann; it could of been one of them mirrors that make you look queer! For all I know it could of been just a plain mirror; I couldn't see clear enough to tell. There wasn't any checking back, 'cause they take everything down after the Carnival, and I never could locate the fellow that had run the funhouse, to find out from him. I took to asking everybody I'd meet whether they'd been to the Carnival that year, and did they recollect what was on the wall next to the exit. Some swore it was a windowpane, some was sure it was a trick mirror or a regular one; some said there weren't nothing there at all. Most didn't remember."

I agreed with him on the importance of the question, which had occurred to me some time earlier.

"Once I'd thought of it, I couldn't think of nothing else," Greene said. He had spent hours then before his mirror, studying his face and what lay behind it, back to the beginning. At times, and in some aspects, what he saw now seemed possible to affirm—in more innocent years he'd taken his appearance for granted, assuming its unblemished handsomeness—but in the main it struck him as repellent, hopeless. Not even fascinatingly so: after an orgy of self-inspection he became so persuaded that it was some sort of mirror he'd smashed on the midway that he now smashed his own (by hurling it out the window), not to have to see himself any further. And though since the critical night of the sleeping-capsules the question had largely ceased to torment him, he still had, in his phrase, "a thing" about any sort of glass near his face: he shaved and tied his necktie by feel, and refused to wear lenses to correct his faulty vision.

"How about windows?" I wondered, for we had huge ones all about us.

"They don't bother me somehow," Greene laughed. "Anyway, to wind up my story . . ." I was relieved to think him nearly done, as we had distance yet to travel.

He had not had opportunity, he said (returning to the subject of his post-capsular attitude), to see whether the strange new feeling would persist—an acceptance of himself, as I took it, and of the student condition, based on the refusal to concern himself further with their unacceptability—and whether unassisted it would have lifted him from his depression. For he was seized out of it shortly thereafter by irrelevant circumstance, in the form of Campus Riot II. The impending threat of it reunited him with his wife, ended all picketing, and kept every shop and laboratory open around the clock; the resultant prosperity, together with the climate of emergency, the exhausting pace, and his new indifference to the question of Final Examinations, did away with what limited appeal Student-Unionism briefly might have had for him. He enlisted in the ROTC and became something of a hero. Unfriendly rivals and vanquished adversaries might complain that it was his size and material advantage that accounted for his successes, rather than superior skill and character; he himself was too busy to care.

"I am okay," he formed the habit of repeating to himself when his motives or performance was criticized, *"and what the heck anyhow."* As an officer under Professor-General Reginald Hector, with unlimited supplies partly of his own manufacture, he led his men to victory and emerged from the riot well-known throughout the campus and generally well-liked, with a reputation for open-handedness, vulgarity, fair dealing, bad manners, good intentions, gullibility, straightforwardness, lack of culture, abundance of wealth, and sentimentality. The wealth was certainly a fact: the manufacture of riot-matèriel (directed in part by his wife) had made him immensely prosperous, and the great post-riot demand in NTC for building-material, paper, and plastics (a line he'd branched into during the hostilities, when metal was scarce) promised to make him more prosperous yet: Ira Hector alone exceeded him in wealth and unofficial influence in Tower Hall.

"But things went kerflooey all the same?" I asked. I was eager now to have done with the story, which however had certainly illumined me on the subject of human marriage. Greene shook his head *no,* but in a way that I presently understood to mean *Yes, and I still don't understand it,* or something similar. His speech grew no less at odds with itself from here until the end of his relation: an inharmonious amalgam of the several idioms I'd hear him employ thus far:

"Durn if I can figure what got to us, togethernesswise. We bought us a fine house in a suburban quad, with a pool and a color Telerama and all like that; the kiddies started music lessons; Sally Ann had her own wheels to get around with, and only worked when she felt like getting out of the house. She weren't tied down a speck, what with O.B.G.'s daughter to clean house and me helping with every meal. And like, I'm busy, sure, but George, it ain't as bad as the old days, no sirree Bob, when I was up with the chickens and worked till midnight." What was more, he said, they'd agreed to cleave exclusively each to the other, as in the early terms of their marriage, with the difference that now they were to be equal partners and faithful companions in every aspect of life, rather than master and mastered.

"It ain't that business is slow, you understand, despite the way taxes have gone up. I spend me a fortune every year around Tower Hall to get the College Senate to lower my taxes and stop buying cheap stuff from across the Pond, but it's no go, sir; and they keep taking more and more timberland for college parks and the like. I hired me a roomful of Ph.D's to find out how to do more business: after awhile I got so took with the idea I closed down half my mills and paperplants and went into the Marketing- and Packaging-Research Department my own self. Didn't need all them people working for me anyhow, with their durn committees: we got machines now that WESCAC operates, you stick a log of wood in one end and get newsprint out the other, with nobody touching it in between. WESCAC even tells us how many trees to cut down, and which men to lay off."

In consequence, I learned, though he was prospering as never before, he was virtually unemployed, WESCAC having taken over executive as well as labor operations. When O.B.G.'s daughter had turned up and publicly accused him of having exploited her immorally in his youth to further his own interests, and possibly even having fathered a child on her, he had offered to hire her as a housemaid despite his wife's old resentment of her. Miss Sally Ann herself he made financial director of his concerns. Their children were amply provided for: the girls twirled silver batons in one of the Sub-Junior Varsity Marching Bands, the boys were star performers on the Faculty Children's Athletic League Farm Teams; they were never spanked, received large allowances, played games and took vacations with their parents—whom they called by their first names—had Telerama receivers in their bedrooms and a private bowling alley in their recreation basement, and regularly attended their neighborhood Enochist Hall for tradition's sake, as did their parents, though it was made clear to them that the Enochist Answers were their own reward, there being no such places as Commencement Gate and the Nether Campus. On weekends they all played golf and went to parties at the houses of their friends.

But no one was happy. O.B.G.'s daughter refused on the one hand to be "degradated," as she put it, to the role of menial, and on the other to be "bought off" with a slightly higher income and the title of Assistant Homemaker. Neither would she take the position he offered her as Special Representative in his Promotion Department, though the job entailed nothing more strenuous than being photographed for advertisements in Frumentian publications: she insisted that he confess his past attraction to and maltreatment of her, that he pay her neither more nor less than he would pay a white male for the same work, and that to redeem his past abuses of her he educate her children along with his, in the same classrooms, summer camps, and Founder's Halls. His own children showed no such aggressiveness, excepting one son who stole motorbikes for sport and contracted gonorrhea at the sixth-grade prom: they were tall and handsome, their teeth uncarious, their underarms odorless; yet they seemed not interested in anything. As for Mrs. Greene, she had become a scold—perhaps because, though she was still youthful enough in appearance to be mistaken for her daughters, in fact she was approaching middle age. Her moods ran to sudden extremes, more often quarrelsome than otherwise; she complained of her responsibilities; neither she nor her spouse thought it possible to pursue a career, raise the children, and supervise the housework at the same time, yet they could not bear the foolish women who had nothing to do but drink coffee and talk to one another by telephone; they believed in an utterly single standard of behavior for men and women, but practiced chivalric deference in a host of minor matters. She did not think they went dancing often enough; he wished he had more time to play poker with his colleagues.

"I'd swear I wanted her to be her own woman, independencewise, but whenever she'd go to work I'd freeze up and wish she was just a plain wife. Then she'd wife it a while, fix fancy meals and sew drapes and all, and I'd wish she had something more interesting than *that* to talk about! We got to be so much alike and close together, we'd be bored fit to bust for something *different*—but go away one night on a business trip, we'd miss each other like to die. And me getting soft, and overweight, and tired all the time from nothing!

And Sally Ann skipping periods, and starting to wear corsets! And both now and then half a-yearning to bust out and start over, but knowing we'd never do as well, compatibilitywise, and loving each other too much anyhow, despite all. Durn if it weren't a bind! I'd say to myself, *I'm okay, and what the heck anyhow*—but that didn't help none when she'd bust out crying and go back for another prescription. And them doctors, and them analysts, and them counselors! One'd tell her 'Stay home and be a *woman*.' Another'd say 'Go to work full-time, let it all go.' One'd say 'Get divorced any time you want, that's the kind of campus we live on nowadays'; another'd say 'Stay married no matter what, 'cause if the family don't hold fast there won't be no character left in the Present Modern College of Today.' Some told Sally Ann she should let me have my head but tread the straight and narrow her own self, like olden terms; others said to me what's sauce for the gander is sauce for the goose, one way or the other. Take pills; don't take pills! Go back to Enochism; eat black-strap molasses; practice breath-control! One high-price fellow told Sally Ann she ought to sleep with *him* to cure herself, 'cause his own wife didn't understand him! I swear to Pete! I swear right to Pete!"

Things had come to a head only recently, he said, when during a pointless midnight quarrel (over a change of analysts and low-fat diets) he explained to his wife his dissatisfaction with their current therapist, who had declared it impossible to help a patient until the latter overcame his "resistances to therapy." It was, Greene had been in the process of telling her, like announcing to a sick man that he must get well in order to take his medicine . . .

But in the course of his analogy his wife had interrupted him with a scream, and another, and a third, and a fourth, and another and another, beyond his shocked remonstrances to consider the children, to get hold of herself, for Founder's sake to stop. He grew frantic; still she lay in their bed and screamed, her eyes tight shut. At last he called in a neighbor lady and O.B.G.'s daughter. By the time the family doctor arrived to sedate her, her cries had turned to wild weeping; the children were awake and had been told that their mother's nerves were bad from too much work and worry. Did they understand? Solemn-faced, they nodded yes. Next morning it was added that she would be going away to rest, and away she went—to the Faculty Women's Rest House, whose services she was entitled to by virtue of her one-time position as district schoolmistress. Once she was established in that stately, hushed retreat, where so many were of their acquaintance, her spirits lifted; indeed, she was more calm and optimistic when he went to see her than she'd been for a long while, despite her doctor's vagueness about how long she'd have to stay; she quietly apologized for her hysteria, for leaving him in charge of the house and children, for whatever was her share of responsibility in their difficulties . . .

"I missed her so much and felt so flunking flunked I thought I'd die," he said. "First thing I did, I come home and got drunk as a hooty-owl, all by my lonesome. But drunk or sober, sir, it seemed to me one minute there was something awful wrong with the way we lived, trying to be pals and lovers and equals all the same time, and next minute it wasn't our fault at all, we'd come to the right idea, the best idea, but the past was a-gumming us up. Then right in the midst of this pull and haul, who should come into the bar where I went one night but O.B.G.'s daughter—as a customer, mind, and I didn't even know they served darkies in the place! She asked me how Miss Sally Ann was, all the time a-smiling in her mischievous way, like she was daring me to grab ahold of her, and she said she figured I must be awful upset to be out drinking so late all by myself, a big family-man like me. I knew what she was up to, but I didn't bear her no grudge for all the things she'd said about me in the papers, and being so ungrateful I'd treated her so white. I bought her a drink, and we talked about poor Sally Ann and old times, and how hard all this was on the kids; and O.B.G.'s daughter said there probably ought to be somebody home with them at night for a while, till they got more used to their mother being gone. All the time she was smiling that smile, that put me in mind how she'd smiled it years ago, when I was just a scaredy-cat kid and her a gosh-durn tease. Her own husband had run off on her a few months before, and their kids were at some sister's place; I knew she'd come on home with me if I asked her, despite all she'd said. And I was so low down, and so durn hot and bothered, I up and asked her, and of course she came, teasing me all the way for treating her like a South-Quad slavey. What you going to do with a gal like that, and such a mess as me?"

I was unaware that his question was of the sort that requires no answer. "Well, now, Mr. Greene——" I began with a frown.

"Pete," he insisted.

"I find your story quite touching, Pete. I hadn't appreciated how curious *marriage* is, and I'm interested to learn now whether it's that way generally. The only other married folks I've met are Mr. and Mrs. Stoker and a Dr. Sear and his wife, and their attitudes seemed a little different from yours and Mrs. Greene's, at least to me."

"Dr. Sear!" Greene laughed. "You know Kennard Sear? He was my analyst I was telling you about! Heck of a nice fellow, ain't he? Couldn't do a passèd thing with me, but he's a smart one, Sear is."

I agreed that he seemed a most courteous gentleman, and pressed back to the subject: "I think I still don't understand why you're hitchhiking to Great Mall, when you're so wealthy, and what you're going to do when you get there."

Peter Greene was more or less durned if he quite knew either, except about the hitchhiking, which he did purely for the heck of it and to stay "in shape"—the fact being that for all his regimen of calisthenics, vitamin pills, mechanical exercisers, and low-fat diets, he was overweight. The best reason he could offer for placing his children in a boarding-school (though it had "near killed him" to part with them), closing the house, neglecting his business, and taking to the road, was that while he was absolutely sure he was passed, he was certain he was failed. He had betrayed, deceived, and defiled Miss Sally Ann in the wanton arms of O.B.G.'s hot daughter—whom, however, for better or worse, he had once again found himself impotent with and who, ungrateful as always, had laughed at him in the morning when he'd offered to raise her wage. He'd had no choice then but to discipline such uppitiness. And though he loved, honored, and respected his unhappy wife, he was also profoundly troubled by their reciprocal grievances, which he felt sure were justified albeit unjust. In sum, he was so utterly of two minds about himself and his connections with things that he seemed rather a pair of humans in a single skin: the one energetic, breezy, optimistic, self-assured, narrow-minded, hospitable, out-going, quick-thinking, belligerent, and strong; the other apathetic, abject, pessimistic, self-despising, indulgent, rude, introspective, complaisant, uncouth, feckless, and flabby. He had lost faith initially in the Founder and then in himself—in his

ability to pass, as it were, with neither syllabus nor Grand
Tutor to aid him, and to Commence himself without believing in Commencement. It was presently the season for his annual inventory and report: for paying his debts, collecting his
dividends, assessing the solvency of his various concerns,
and establishing policy for the year ahead; but he had found
himself unable to address the task. Moreover, he was plagued
of late by headaches that made his eye water (I'd observed
that he dosed himself with pills and liquids as he talked); his
own newspapers were critical of his "deteriorating image," as
they called it, unaware that he was hampered by his thing
about mirrors; his neighbors declared he ought either to
marry O.B.G.'s daughter or leave her alone, unaware that she
was the best-treated darky in the Quad; his children were
embarrassed by him and swore they would make themselves
into his opposite, whatever *that* might be.

Then a day had come when Miss Sally Ann told him
calmly that in a short time she would be ready to leave the
Rest House and come home, but not to the situation she had
left. She was not, she declared, blaming him—but her survival, not to say well-being, depended on an end to the tensions between them. She had not permitted him to reply: if
he was at home when she arrived, after the Carnival holi-
days, his presence would signify his readiness to Start Afresh;
if not, she would assume that he had found himself finally
and for all unwilling, or unable, to respond to her needs—
which he would then be free to regard as excessive if it comforted him to do so—and they would legalize their separation.

"I walked down the steps of that there house with my head
fit to crack," he told me. "And on one step I loved Sally Ann
and hated myself, and on the next it was vicey-versy. I tried
to think *I'm okay, and what the heck anyhow*—but it never
did sound just right. So I figured I'd better stroll around some
to clear my head, and next thing I knew, I was out along the
highway, and I thought I saw a cycle go by with some young
slicker a-driving it, and Miss Sally Ann in the sidecar!"

I expressed my astonishment, and Max, who had waked
again in time to hear the last few episodes of Peter Greene's
history, said "Hah," not very sympathetically. But Greene
himself seemed more bemused than disturbed by his vision.

"I don't see how it could of been, do you, George? The
fellow weren't more'n twenty agewise, smiling and flash-eyed;

and Sally Ann was a-giggling at something he'd said to her, holding her hand to her mouth the way she does, and I swear she looked exactly like she did the first day of that Carnival: happy and fresh as a spring lamb, and pretty as all outdoors. Must of been some co-ed and her date, just looked like her. *Must* of been! Or my oldest girl Barbara May that's about gone kerflooey herself, playing hooky from school. It don't matter. All I could think was how sweet and happy Sally Ann was when I took her to the Carnival, and how tore up we've been since. And no matter whose flunking fault it is—hers or mine or the terms we live in—I just stood there and bawled to think of it. And then I decided, by Billy Gumbo, I'd thumb me a ride to Great Mall in time for this year's Carnival. Kind of look things over, you know, back where it all started, and see what's what." He sighed, blinked his eye several times, and glanced at his wristwatch. "Which we better get along down the road for, don't we'll never find rooms tonight."

"I don't understand," I protested. "You're just going to the Spring Carnival, and not to register?"

He had initialed our bill for the waitress and was squinting with his good eye at the young hams that flexed and pressed beneath her tight uniform. He reddened and turned at my words, thumbing his chest.

"Look here, sir: *I'm okay*, doggone it! Any man's liable to have trouble with a strange gal when he's been married long as I have; that's the only reason I couldn't make the grade with O.B.G.'s daughter."

"I beg your pardon?" Both his terminology and his attitude perplexed me.

"Ah, flunk it. Let's hit the road."

As if, having lingered such a while at the Pedal Inn, he found it suddenly unbearable, Greene all but fled the place. As we wakened snoring Croaker (whose vine-work now climbed halfway up my stick) I saw our troubled host doing push-ups on the gravel apron and grinning at the cordial taunts of young couples parked all about. Max shook his head. Outside in the cooling floodlit dark I remounted Croaker and Max the cycle, but before we set out Greene left off the bantering he'd resumed, and took his hand from the throttle briefly to squint up at me.

"S'pose there really *was* a Grand Tutor!" he cried. Max had been sitting with his eyes closed; now he opened them to contemplate his driver's twisted grin. "S'pose you *were* Him right enough, come to put good old New Tammany on the track again, and you'd heard all the stuff I've told you 'bout me and Sally Ann and how everything's gone kerflooey! What would you *say?*"

Flabbergasted that he'd not truly believed me all that while, I could only stare at him. After a second he turned his face away and bitterly raced the engine. But the lights had flashed twice-bright for that second in both his eyes, the true and the false alike made mirrors by the pain he spoke of.

3.

Now we passed swiftly through a series of residential districts—rather handsome, I thought, though I could not understand at once why a *family* of four or five required as much stall-space as our entire herd—and pressed into the formidable traffic of the central quads. I clutched Croaker's head and gazed as one reluctant to believe his eyes; I could not have said which were most dismaying: the mighty buildings, square after square ablaze with light; the multitude of human folk, mostly young people in similar costume, who thronged the sidewalks with books in their hands and plugs in their ears, through which I was told they heard musical sounds from a central transmitter; or the elm-lined avenues themselves, wide as a pasture, paved in black, and lit like noon by blue-white lamps armed out from poles. All glittered in observance of the Spring Carnival: huge foil-and-tinsel ovoids hung suspended over intersections; on the arm of every lamp-post perched a mammoth butttterfly, terrifying until I learned they were not real creatures; their sequined wings, three meters in span, slowly closed and opened, sparkling with little lights in half a dozen colors. Here and there we saw groups of celebrants in gaudy garb, singing and roistering; some wore dominoes and checkered tights, others caps with bells or full-face masks, horrid of aspect; here was a girl delicious in white tights and tall silk ears, with a ball of cotton fluff atop the cleft of her rump; there a muscled red-cloaked chap with hayfork and imitation horns. These sometimes saluted as we passed, and merrily I waved my stick in reply; the rest ignored them and us alike, unless to make apprehensive way for Croaker. From everywhere the bold bright messages flashed at us: DEGREES WITH EASE—SAY "PHYS. ED., PLEASE." NO SWEAT: PRE-VET. HAPPY CARNIVAL FROM YOUR DEPARTMENT OF POULTRY HUSBANDRY.

"No zing in that there last one," Peter Greene remarked. Having made our way down what appeared to be the widest and most resplendent thoroughfare, we parked the motorcycle at its end. Here the boulevard became a mighty lawn of grass, flanked by statelier buildings and nobler elms, and fronted, just before us, by an iron fence-gate twenty meters tall. Unlike all else of eminence round about, Main Gate (for so I recognized it, with a shiver, and the lawn as Great Mall, and the imposing edifice far down it as Tower Hall) was unlit: guards prowled in the shadow along the ivied, gargoyled wall into which it made and before the famous one-way turnstile at the road's end. I was much excited by the general spectacle, and impatient to see all at once. It was the last night of the Carnival: crews of workmen were already dismantling some temporary structures along the mall; on one side of us was many-storied Bi-Sci House, the exclusive apartment hotel for professors of the natural sciences, with its notorious Vivisection Bar-B-Q underneath; adjacent were the glittering Gate House Ballroom, the Sophomore Cinema and Shooting Gallery, and other places of amusement whose fame was campus-wide. Opposite were cultural attractions: the Fine Arts Salesroom, the Pan-Sororal Playhouse, and nearest us, sloping down from Mall Wall, the vast Amphitheater managed jointly by the Sub-Departments of Ancient Narrative and Theatrical Science. I was taken with particular curiosity by this last because the playbills advertised that evening's performance as *The Tragedy of Taliped Decanus*, a work of whose hero I had heard though I hadn't read the tale of his adventures. It was to be the conclusion of a week-long series of classical productions, and lines of people were already filing in to witness it.

"Y'all want to take a look-see?" Greene suggested when I expressed my interest. "I never was much a one for stageplays, but they do say there's hot stuff in this one." He insisted then that we permit him to buy tickets for the four of us, including Croaker, who though surely unable to comprehend the play could not safely be left alone; there would be ample time afterwards to tour the midway, if we chose. Before this generosity I saw Max's expression soften; nevertheless he declined the invitation on the grounds that we had yet to find cheap lodging for the night, and that I had better retire early against the ordeal of registration, which was scheduled for sunup next morning—especially as I'd done my share of celebrating the night before. Moreover, he had certain advices and cautions to give me that evening, in case there should be no opportunity next day. I was disappointed, and yet gratified to see Max displaying something of his old concern for me.

But Greene would not be gainsaid. "Tell him what you want to while I fetch the tickets," he proposed, and offered further to spare us the bother of searching for rooms; all he had to do, he declared, was telephone from the ticket-office to the JELI, or Junior Enochist League Inn, where as past League Chairman he was always entitled to free accommodations. He would hear no further protests, just as during the ride from the Pedal Inn he'd refused to listen seriously to my assurances that I was in good faith a Grand Tutor, or Grand-Tutor-to-be, and not a pretender, madman, or costumed Carnival-goer. "The woods is full of 'em this time of year," he'd smiled. "But I know by your face you're okay. I believe for a fact you're the Goat-Boy, like you said, and that's wonder enough." Now, as then, Max shrugged, as if to say there was no use contending further, Greene might have it as he pleased. And he admitted that it might be fitting to witness the profoundest of the Lykeionian tragedies before I matriculated: there was no coincidence in its being produced just at Carnival's end, before the Spring Matriculation rituals. But he really must speak to me first confidentially, as my advisor. Greene went off happily to buy the tickets.

"Odd chap!" I remarked after him. "I don't know whether I like him, but he's certainly obliging."

Max made a deprecating gesture. "He's okay; I don't mind him."

I made bold to point out that he, Max, had not been consistently so tolerant during the afternoon and earlier evening, towards either Greene or myself, and begged him please to excuse once and for all my behavior at the Powerhouse or, if he found it inexcusable, allow me to proceed upon my way as I had set out, without the benefit of his company and counsel. The rebuke didn't sting him; indeed, he seemed if anything pleased to hear it. He nodded several times and said quietly, "You don't talk like a kid, all right. Na,

George . . ." He put an arm about my back (I had come down off Croaker) with more affection than he'd shown me for some time; I was quite moved by the gesture and the warmth in his voice as he explained what lay immediately ahead for me, though at the same time I wondered at a mournful urgency in his face, as if what he was saying must be said without delay.

"We'll talk about the Powerhouse and Maurice Stoker when there's time," he said. "There's more important business now." Leaving Croaker my stick to gnaw upon, we strolled onto the grassy verge of the Mall, near the gate. "Things like the Gorge and the Power Plant were just *sidetracks*, Georgie, bad as they were. Same with that poor girl Anastasia that thinks I'm her poppa—just a sidetrack, whether she meant to be or not. But right there is the first big hurdle you got to get over." He indicated the Turnstile with a wave of his hand. "It shouldn't be any trouble—what I mean, it's either impossible or easy, never in-between—but you mustn't get sidetracked or hesitate even for an eyeblink when the time comes, or you're *kaput*."

He then explained briefly the ritual of registration and matriculation as it had developed in the West-Campus colleges, especially New Tammany, in modern times. The large gates on either side of the Turnstile, presently closed, normally stood open and were the common entryways to the heart of the College, the site originally of all its buildings and latterly of the administrative and military-science quadrangles. Theoretically no one except Graduates and Certified Candidates for Graduation was admitted, and in the heyday of the Enochist Curriculum this restriction was technically enforced, the Enochist Fraternity ruling on credentials as the Founder's deputy in the University. Over the semesters, however, as the Fraternity's authority had declined and the nature and existence of the Founder Himself was debated and challenged, the practice had fallen into disuse. Even in the old days those outside the various Mall Walls of West Campus had always outnumbered those within and were included in the Fraternal hegemony and instructed by its professors; *Many are Registered but few are Qualified*, Enos Enoch had said, and inasmuch as none but Him could tell true Candidates from false, the Fraternity tutored everybody. Today it was strictly forbidden in the by-laws of colleges such as NTC to disqualify a man for matriculation and campus office by reason of his pedagogical beliefs, and in lieu of the old Degrees of Wisdom, the administration conferred upon anyone who completed his course-work successfully and passed certain "technical examinations" a Certificate of Proficiency in the Field; such men were called "graduates," were said to have "commenced," and were eligible either for employment in their "fields" or for further study beyond the C.P.F., at the end of which they became "professors" in their own right—a far cry from the original meaning of those terms! Yet the Enochist tradition was preserved in certain college rituals—echoed, rather, for the celebrants had little idea what it was they celebrated: the Spring Carnival itself, with its attendant symbols, was one such tradition, originating in ancient agronomical ceremonies and modified by the Enochist Fraternity to celebrate the Expulsion of Enos Enoch, His promotion of the Old-Syllabus Emeritus Profs from the Nether Campus, and His triumphal Reinstatement. Trial-by-Turnstile was another, observed at the opening of each term and with especial solemnity at Spring Registration, which was scheduled for next morning. The tradition was that only bonafide Candidates for Graduation (using the terms in their original sense) could pass through the Turnstile and the tiny gate somewhere beyond it—both which, being one-way affairs, committed the passer-through not to anything so prosaic as "Minimums" and C.P.F.'s, but to the Final Examination and thus to absolute Commencement or Flunking Out.

"The trouble is," Max smiled, "there haven't *been* any Candidates since ancient terms, and things being how they are, the Enochists wouldn't dare say any more who's a Graduate and who isn't—even in the old days they never decided on that until after the student passed away. So the Turnstile's never been turned—it's probably rusted shut—and Scrape-goat Grate's been locked since it was built."

My fancy was caught by that latter name, and I squinted into the shadows with new interest. Max explained that the word had nothing to do with *scapegoat,* more the pity, but alluded to three characteristically anticaprine remarks of Enos Enoch's: that He was come to separate the sheep from the goats; that the Way to Graduation was too narrow for even a goat to walk, but a broad mall for His flock; and that it were easier for a goat to scrape through an iron fence-grating than for a merely learned man to enter Commencement Gate. The present practice in West-Campus colleges was for the strongest and nimblest young men from each quadrangle—generally the winners of athletic competitions held in conjunction with the Carnival—to fling themselves against the Turnstile, bleating in what they took to be goatly fashion, while the new registrants and spectators cheered them on and a figure dressed to represent the Dean o' Flunks endeavored to block their way. When all the athletes had failed they were garlanded with lilies by Miss University and by her symbolically driven from the scene, to the Dean o' Flunks' delight; then the great Right and Left Gates were thrown open, as if they were Scrapeboat Grate, and while the Dean o' Flunks gnashed his teeth in mock frustration, the hosts of actual new registrants were admitted into the Gatehouse just inside Mall Wall, and the business of scheduling courses for the term was begun. Few who participated in these festivities were aware of their original significance, any more than they recognized *Carnival* as coming from the Remusian "farewell to flesh" that preceded any period of fasting or mourning; Trial-by-Turnstile was no more than an amusing sport at the end of a week's carouse, and it was cause enough to rejoice for most students if they were able to turn out at all so early on that Friday morning, after partying all through Randy-Thursday night.

Of late, however, the tensions of the Quiet Riot, alarming rises in the student delinquency and divorce rates, and such exacerbating problems as overcrowded classrooms and the "drop-outs" from EAT-wave testing (which was held to poison the intellectual atmosphere and produce each term a certain number of defective minds)—these anxieties had lent a new significance to the ancient rites, at least in the eyes of the Enochist Fraternity, who held that only a return to the teachings of the New Syllabus could save the University from self-destruction, and studentdom from final Failure. Many non-Enochists, though they found that particular Answer unacceptable, agreed on the seriousness of the problem, and remembering the Spielman Proviso in WESCAC's Menu-program, called for a new Grand Tutor to change the AIM and give to contemporary West-Campus culture a fresh direction, a Revised New Syllabus, as Enos Enoch had done in His term.

"That's what that Greene meant a while ago," Max said, "when he said the woods is full of Grand Tutors this time of year. Spring Term is when your old wandering researchers and dons-errant used to appear on campus, or do their big projects." Furthermore, he declared, it was my selection, as though by chance, of this particular time of year to set out for Great Mall that had finally persuaded him of the possibility that there might be something to my claim to Grand-Tutorhood.

"Ah, Max!" I broke in at this point. "Even yet you can't believe me, can you?" My distress was so purely for his sake and not my own (there were tears of concern in my eyes) that he was moved to embrace me.

"Dear Billy!"

"*George,*" I corrected.

"Suppose you *were!*" he muttered intensely, much as Peter Greene had done, and repeated the sentiment so familiar to me by now, and irritating: that it was beyond belief that so uncanny a chain of happenstance could be mere coincidence, *and yet* . . . By which was meant, I neither talked nor behaved Grand-Tutorially, in his estimation, and so the "chain of happenstance" must be coincidental after all, *etc.* "But if it's not you it's not anybody else around," he added, as though with clenched teeth, "not in my lifetime; and hard as it is to believe in Grand Tutors and all that daydreaming, I think of Stoker, and I think of Eblis Eierkopf, and I know we're going to EAT each other up if *somebody* don't stop us!"

He then confessed, excusing his bluntness on the grounds of short time and antiflattery, that he didn't for a minute subscribe to the hope that any "campus-passing spook" could change the student mind in general—indeed, he was still old-fashioned enough to find such a prospect as depressing as it was unlikely. Nor, he had to admit in all affection, did he regard me as a mental giant: excuse him, he had known prodigious intelligences in his day, in both scientific and philosophical departments, and they were different from me, no offense intended. Studentdom, he felt, must pass its own Examinations and define its own Commencement—a slow, most painful process, made the more anguishing by bloody intelligences like the Bonifacists of Siegfrieder College. Yet however it seemed at times that men got nowhere, but only repeated class by class the mistakes of their predecessors, two crucial facts about them were at once their hope and the limitation of their possibility, so he believed. One was their historicity: the campus was young, the student race even younger, and by contrast with the whole of past time, the great collegiate cultures had been born only yesterday. The other had to do with his comparative cyclology, a field of systematic speculation he could not review for me just then, but whose present relevance lay in the correspondency he held to obtain between the life-history of individuals and the history of studentdom in general. As the embryologists maintained that ontogeny repeats phylogeny, so, Max claimed, the race itself—and on a smaller scale, West-Campus culture—followed demonstrably—in capital letters, as it were, or slow motion—the life-pattern of its least new freshman. This was the basis of Spielman's Law—*ontogeny repeats cosmogeny*—and there was much more to it and to the science of cyclology whereof it was first principle. The important thing for now was that, by his calculations, West Campus as a whole was in mid-adolescence . . .

"Look how we been acting," he invited me, referring to intercollegiate political squabbles; "the colleges are spoilt kids, and the whole University a mindless baby, *ja?* Okay: so weren't we all once, Enos Enoch too? And we got to admit that the University's a precocious kid. If the history of life on campus hadn't been so childish, we couldn't hope it'll reach maturity." Studentdom had passed already, he asserted, from a disorganized, pre-literate infancy (of which Croaker was a modern representative, nothing ever being entirely lost) through a rather brilliant early childhood (". . . ancient Lykeion, Remus, T'ang . . .") which formed its basic and somewhat contradictory character; it had undergone a period of naïve general faith in parental authority (by which he meant early Founderism) and survived critical spells of disillusionment, skepticism, rationalism, willfulness, self-criticism, violence, disorientation, despair, and the like—all characteristic of pre-adolescence and adolescence, at least in their West-Campus form. I even recognized some of those stages in my own recent past; indeed, Max's description of the present state of West-Campus studentdom reminded me uncomfortably of my behavior in the Lady-Creamhair period: capricious, at odds with itself, perverse, hard to live with. Its schisms, as manifested in the Quiet Riot, had been aggravated and rendered dangerous by the access of unwonted power—as when, in the space of a few semesters, a boy finds himself suddenly muscular, deep-voiced, aware of his failings, proud of his strengths, capable of truly potent love and hatred—and on his own. What hope there was that such an adolescent would reach maturity (not to say Commencement) without destroying himself was precisely the hope of the University.

"What brings a boy through?" he asked of his four-fingered hand. "Good guidance, for one thing; a character that's stronger than its weaknesses, and flexible; and good luck." The *guidance* of the University, he reasoned, was such root pedagogical documents as the Moishianic Code, the Founder's Scroll, the *Colloquiums* of Enos Enoch, the *Footnotes to Sakhyan:* they did not of course come from "outside"—one mustn't overdo the analogy—but from individual students who had matured and Graduated over the semesters—from "inside," if I pleased; they were the best Answers that studentdom had devised, came early in its "upbringing," and comprised the strong but inconsistent conscience of the University. The *healthy character* he judged to be partly a matter of chance and partly of this "early training," and *luck* he felt involved the possibility of catastrophic accident: adolescents took chances and were by nature strenuous and impulsive; Campus Riot III might occur after all and studentdom be EATen, as a prep-school boy might resort to delinquency or suicide, or be killed in a motorcycle race.

"So what are the odds?" he asked further, again rhetorically, and paced me more vigorously back and forth before the darkened Turnstile. I listened intently, for though most of what he said I'd heard many times before—indeed, it seemed to me I'd heard it from the play-pound—it was as if, the events of the past several days under my wrapper, I understood him for the first time. "By George, I think the odds for *survival* are pretty good. Some kids don't make it through adolescence, but most do." Similarly, he said, most reached a fair level of grown-upness—although Commencement was of course another matter, if there was such a thing at all. The University was a big place: when lecturers spoke of East and West Campuses, or the "Nature of studentdom," they tended to forget the curious colleges in remote corners of the University, which were only beginning to be touched by the Informational Revolution and Applied Research. What was more, though the colleges themselves could be said to have a fair degree of identity and self-consciousness, the University as a whole was barely stirring in that direction. This was not to say that its maturation must be as slow and painful as a college's: it would have its own growth-rate, sped by the sophistication of individual quads, especially if the rivalry between East and West Campus could be made less negative. Max guessed that the chances for West Campus's reaching maturity were good: in the past, the behavior of the colleges towards one another, particularly in disputes, had been at the primary-school level, or worse; but there was evidence of real restraint in the matter of EATing-riot and relevant intercollege policy. The prospect was not hopeless.

"Pfui," Max said grimly. "The University *will* make it if we can ease the worst pressures and not EAT everything up! That's why you're important."

The immediately urgent thing was to alter WESCAC's AIM—a feat achievable only by WESCAC itself on its own unlikely "volition," or by a Grand Tutor: that is, by someone whom WESCAC would recognize as such and admit un-EATen into its Belly. And though Max had no use for or credence in other aspects of Grand-Tutorhood, he was familiar enough with WESCAC's programming in this particular, and Eierkopf's thinking in the Cum Laude Project, to have a general conception of the prerequisites developed by and fed into the computer, and a general strategy for what lay ahead. What it came to was that I happened to be the animate object most closely correspondent to those prerequisites and thus most suited to take the risk of reAIMing WESCAC; in his view such things as high IQ and new Answers had as little to do with my role as with an athlete's or riot-squad leader's: I was the tool designed for the work, nothing more . . .

"Don't be upset," he begged me firmly; "if there's more to it, then I'm wrong and studentdom's better off. If I'm mistaken the other way, you'll be EATen and I'll jump off Tower Hall. But you got to get registered before you can do anything, and you can't register in the usual way without a proper ID-card and lots of other things you don't have, including more education and something to pay your way with."

I was stunned: these were considerations that had never occurred to me. But Max waved them off—along with Peter Greene, who had been approaching with our tickets but lingered now grinning and blinking some meters away, where squatted Croaker.

"So we forget about the usual requirements," Max said. He

lowered his voice. "If I'm right, what you got to do tomorrow is pass through the Turnstile and Scrapegoat Grate."

I looked at him with alarm.

"It's part of the Grand-Tutor business," he whispered. "Like the way G. Herrold found you, so you've either been EATen already or for some reason WESCAC didn't EAT you. That was the first big step, and starting out like you did the other day was the second. Getting past Main Gate is the third." He then advised me as clearly as he could what lay ahead and how I must deal with it.

"Be here tomorrow morning before six o'clock," he said, "and let the others try as much as they want to get through the Turnstile. They won't make it: they're not supposed to. Is your watch working?"

I drew the silver lanyard from the neck of my wrapper; Lady Creamhair's watch had run down some time ago, and I feared that the water in George's Gorge might have ruined it, but it began ticking promptly upon my winding the stem a little.

"Set it when you hear Tower Clock strike the hour," Max advised. "And at exactly four minutes after six tomorrow morning, no matter what's going on or who's in your way, go up to the Turnstile and Scrapegoat Grate and go through them."

I certainly didn't understand. "Right through?"

Max shrugged. "Don't ask me how, but it's the only way. Keep your eyes open, look around, watch out for whoever it is that's playing Dean o' Flunks; it could be an enemy, if word's gotten around in Tower Hall that you might be the real thing." He had reason to believe, he said, that supervision of the Trial-by-Turnstile ceremony had been given over to WESCAC since he'd been in exile—there had been such proposals during the debate over the Spielman Proviso, and Max saw above the Turnstile what he believed to be a scanning device. "If you can't get through, you're not the man," he declared. "Even if you found a way to sneak through the Right or Left Gates, they'd never let you near Tower Hall basement, any more than they'd let a Nikolayan read the Menu. So don't let anything tempt or scare you; don't listen to anybody or stop to pick up anything you might drop or lose." He frowned and raised a finger. "No, wait: you might have to give the guard something, I don't know what. But anything you lose, don't go back for it: drive on through, and if you make it some way or other—you *might* be the right one."

He went on to say that once through Main Gate I should proceed to the Gatehouse, where, if things were still done as formerly, I would meet the Chancellor himself, Lucius Rexford, who always addressed the new registrants. On the strength of my having passed the Trial-by-Turnstile, I should announce to him my intention to enter Tower Hall and change WESCAC's AIM, which to Max's mind meant removing from the computer's Belly those "Diet"-tapes which were the heart, so to speak, of its Automatic Implementation Mechanism. The Senate, he warned, would do all it could to stop me, in the name of alma-matriotism and common sense, as would the more dangerous (because more secretive) Department of Military Science; what I intended to do amounted to no less than "unilateral fasting," and I could assume that in most quadrangles I'd be regarded as a Student-Unionist agent or a madman. As Max conceived it, my task would be to rally enough support among the rank and file of studentdom to make myself too formidable for the professor-generals to assassinate and too popular for the Senate to oppose; the best, perhaps the only means to that end was to demand in the Gatehouse my rights as a bonafide Candidate: that is, a statement from WESCAC of whatever requirements I must satisfy to take the Finals, and then administration of the Finals themselves. Once certified (by WESCAC or whomever) not as a mere C.P.F. but as an actual passèd Graduate, I should then proceed to demonstrate my Grand-Tutorship by going into WESCAC's Belly; when and if I emerged unEATen, I would be in position to demand that Tower Hall instruct me how to locate and remove the Diet-tapes and program WESCAC's AIM toward such pacific ends as cooperation with Nikolay College and a truly effective supra-collegiate administration: a government of the whole University.

I was utterly dismayed: what in the barn had seemed a matter of simple courage—like walking into a dark room and turning on the light, or rescuing a kid from a pack of dogs—seemed here an impossibly complex and unlikely task. "How will I ever get all that done?" I cried. "And you talk as if you won't even be around to advise me!"

"I hope I may be, Georgie," he answered gloomily. Then his face brightened for a moment. "Who knows if it's pos-

sible or not? If things weren't impossible we wouldn't need
Grand Tutors!" He pointed out that when a man found himself in great danger—pursued by a bull, say, or drawn under
by a treacherous current—it not uncommonly happened that
he discovered in himself extraordinary resources, thitherto
unsuspected, with which to rescue himself. Such a resource to
studentdom in general, it seemed to him, were those whom
men called Grand Tutors: adrenalin for the imperiled student body. "If you get through the Grate you'll find your way
without my help. All I can do is warn you in a general way,
from studying how it went with ones like you in the past, and
I don't know how useful that is. Look at yesterday."

He smiled somewhat sadly, to let me know he held no
grudge, and we rejoined Croaker and Peter Greene. They in
turn had been joined by a desiccate gentleman whom I recognized as Dr. Kennard Sear, and who it developed remembered Greene cordially as his patient of some years previously. The two seemed to be on good terms despite the
great difference in their natures and the fact that their professional relationship had been unfruitful. Greene had bought
an extra ticket for the Doctor and was clapping him on the
shoulder as we approached.

"My dear George," Sear murmured amiably. "Good to see
you again. Pity Hedwig isn't here; she was quite taken with
you last night."

I shook the fine dry hand he offered me and then put by
my apprehension at the morrow's prospect to join the general
good-fellowship. Dr. Sear was delighted to see Max once
more, having been among his admirers and supporters in the
troubled past.

"*Kennard Sear . . .*" Max frowned. "*Ja,* sure, the young
radiologist with the Cum Laude Project. I thought you were
on Eierkopf's side."

"Gracious no!" Dr. Sear closed his eyes in a delicate expression of horror. "That is, I'm on everybody's side. '*Tout
comprendre,*' all that sort of thing. Bloody bore, taking sides;
not my line at all." He smiled very pleasantly. "But what's
this they're saying about you and young George here, and all
this Grand Tutor nonsense?" The man's manner was so ur-
bane, his way of saying things so gracious, that Max chuckled at what surely would have affronted him from someone
else. He assured Dr. Sear that while age and exile had doubtless taken their toll upon his faculties, on the subject of

Founders and Commencements he was still the skeptic he'd
been in the Senate. What was more, he declared, he was still
as inclined as ever to act in accordance with his beliefs—
unlike certain civilized and knowledgeable gentlemen who either had none or else disguised them wonderfully well.

"You're too severe," Dr. Sear protested mildly. We strolled
towards the Amphitheater. "I grant you I can't go along with
anybody's Answers I've heard of yet, but that's their fault, for
always being half true. *Founderism! AntiFounderism!* Look
at Greene here, with all his blather about Good Old NTC,
and Let the Chips Fall Where They May. Don't you agree it's
just simple-mindedness, this business of having principles?"

Greene whinnied merrily and jerked his head a number of
times. "I swear, *I* can't keep up with you!" He gave the tickets to a uniformed attendant, to whom also he made known
how interesting he found it that "these old-time thee-*a*ters,"
after which NTC's was patterned, had no balconies reserved
for darkies, though even a country boy like himself knew
that there'd been slavery in both Lykeion and Remus Colleges in their golden days. It all went to show, he maintained,
what high-minded folks those old fellows were, who never regarded a man as inferior just because he wasn't as good as
they were. He thumped the ticket-taker's chest congratulato-
rily as if he were himself not only an ancient Lykeionian but
the designer of unbalconied amphitheaters, and the fellow acknowledged the tribute with a gracious grunt. Then we entered the great bowl of seats, already mostly filled, and were
ushered down towards those reserved for us. I turned my attention from the cordial dispute between Max and Sear on
the difference between simple, strong, and narrow minds to
survey the dark stone stage and humming crowd. Though I
knew the huge enrollment-figures of the College I had no
appreciation yet of its size, and having met one acquaintance
by sheerest chance already, I searched the audience in hopes
of glimpsing Anastasia, or even Lady Creamhair—whom I
was determined to seek out and make amends to for my bad
manners, if she still lived in New Tammany. But there was
no sign of them. Greene bought from a passing vendor five
cartons of *popcorn*, pleasant stuff, whereof he and I took
each a box and Croaker three, Max and Dr. Sear declining.
The latter, enraptured by the carving on my stick (which
he identified as a first-chop example of late-transitional
mandibulary carving in the East Frumentian polycaryatidic

tradition except for the *shelah-na-gigs*—seldom to be found
in the work of mandibulary artists by reason of strictures extended from taboos against certain kinds of oral heteroerotic
foreplay—and the now completed intaglio vine, obviously an
extraquadrangular influence since both viniculture and
oenology were unknown in the East-Frumentian "colleges"),
declared to Max with a sigh that after all he sometimes regarded the absolutely unself-conscious, like Croaker, to be
the only real Graduates—"using the term figuratively, of
course . . ."

"*Pfui!*" Max replied, and Sear conceded at once that he
didn't *really* believe anything of the sort, though he certainly
did admire spontaneity and animal innocence above all
human qualities, despite his contempt for them.

"Who's nearer to being passed?" He included in a wan
wave of the hand Croaker, Peter Greene, and myself. "Them
or us?"

It seemed to me an improper question, presupposing as it
did not only the evident similarity between the two professors
but something significantly common to us eaters of popcorn.
But I let it pass, both because Max himself promptly challenged it and because my eye was caught by a photograph of
The Living Sakhyan and his retinue in a discarded newspaper
near my feet.

"Innocence, bah," Max said.

"I agree, I agree!" Sear protested. "But it's sweet, all the
same. Oh well, it's not, but it seems so to us ravaged post-
Pre-Schoolists. I suppose *we're* the innocent ones, when we
speak of great rascally simpletons like Greene there as being
innocent."

Greene winked above a cheekful of popcorn. "Say what
you want." I was impressed again by his strange combination
of attitudes: *I'm okay,* his wink declared—but with as much
supplication as conviction.

"*Pfui* on innocence," Max said.

"I couldn't agree more," Dr. Sear nodded. "I'll go even
further: innocence is ignorance; ignorance is illusion; and
Commencement, while it certainly is a metaphor, is no illusion. Commencement's for the disillusioned, not for the innocent."

Here Max parted philosophical company with the Doctor
(who, I learned in time, had moved from the fields of
radiology and general pathology into psychiatry, though like

Max he was learned in a great many areas beyond his profession), for he regarded Commencement itself as an innocent illusion.

"Ignorant, I mean, not harmless," he added, much more in the vein of the Max who'd raised me than the fellow who'd met me at the fork in yesterday's road. I knew by heart his old indictments of any Answer which turned studentdom from realistic work upon the failings of life on campus; and though I was curious to know how he reconciled that point of view with his acknowledgment of my Grand-Tutoriality, I was more interested in scanning the front page of the *Tower Hall Times*. The photograph represented The Living Sakhyan seated on the grass beside a massive elm-trunk, perhaps on Great Mall, his associates round about, just as I'd last seen him on the beach in George's Gorge; his palms were pressed together, his eyes closed, and his lips turned slightly upwards at the corners, as if he were placidly amused by the crowd of photographers and curious passersby around him. The caption underneath read LIVING SAKHYAN MEDITATES ON MIDWAY and was followed by a brief account of how he had been rescued from the East-Campus Student-Unionists by his protégés, a flight he'd neither willed nor opposed; how he neither sought nor shunned publicity, but withdrew into meditative trances whenever he saw fit, regardless of time, place, or company. The rest of the page was given over to collegiate and inter-collegiate news: HIGHWAY DEATHS TO BREAK CARNIVAL RECORD, SAFETY COMMITTEE WARNS; REXFORD TO ANNOUNCE NEW EAT-TESTS TO UNIVERSITY COUNCIL; TENSION MOUNTS ALONG POWER LINE; THOUSANDS MASSACRED IN FRUMENTIAN INTRAMURAL RIOTS; FAMINE SPREADS IN T'ANG; FLOODWATERS RISE IN SIDDARTHA; NTC RAPE-RATE UP 4 POINTS. The weather promised to be fair for the last night of the Carnival as well as for tomorrow's registration and attendant ceremonies, and for that reason the Department of Meteorology urgently reminded everyone to refrain from looking directly at the sun during the annular eclipse predicted for shortly after dawn.

"I respect your position on the *social* aspects of the Commencement question," Dr. Sear was saying to Max, "but not on the phenomenon of personal Graduation. One good medical therapist might be worth a hundred professors of Enochism, as you say; but a real Grand Tutor's worth all the medical therapists that ever were."

Max shook his head.

"You believe in Graduation and Grand Tutors, then, sir?" I asked him—rather surprised, but much gratified.

"Of course I do," he smiled. "If you mean do I believe they *exist*, of course I do. But I mean something rather special by the terms, that has nothing to do with Founders and Dean o' Flunks. Even Dr. Spielman agrees that there really are heroes, and that they serve a useful purpose. Why else would he enlist you in this quaint project of his?"

Max objected that to his mind heroes were one thing—even Grand Tutors, whom he regarded merely as a particular variety of heroes—and Graduation was another. "What I believe, certain men are born with a natural talent for the hero-work; they're no more miraculous than great violinists. It's a neutral thing: some people are red-haired, some are hump-backed, some are heroes." And what everyone went through for himself, he went on, more or less profoundly depending on one's character, Grand Tutors went through on the level of the whole student body: "Every college needs a man now and then to go to the bottom of things and turn us around a corner. That's what George must do with the WESCAC if he can." As for *Graduation,* if Sear meant by the term simply the emotional and intellectual maturity that normally followed the ordeals of adolescence, whether in an individual student or an entire college, then Max was quite ready to affirm its reality; indeed, cyclological theory was founded on such correspondences as that between the celestial and psychic day, the seasons of the year, the stages of ordinary human life, the growth and decline of individual colleges, the evolution and history of studentdom as a whole, the ultimate fate of the University, and what had we. The rhythm of all these was repeated literally and emblematically in the life of the hero, whose function, Max took it, was the important but prosaic one of helping a college grow up or get out of a particular bind: more than that he denied. And if there was a difference between Grand Tutors and other sorts of heroes, it was that men like Maios, Enos Enoch, and the original Sakhyan taught students how to behave more decently toward one another, while heroes like Anchisides and Laertides actually preserved their classmates from immediate harm, whether by slaying certain monsters or by resettling groups of student refugees threatened with extinction. Me he conceived to be, not *destined* to save studentdom from being EATen but very possibly *designed* for that task, as who should call a man uniquely designed to play championship tennis, without implying either a designer or that he will ever take racket in hand. If I chose to regard myself as a Grand Tutor, that was my affair; Max would not split hairs. But if I or Sear or anyone maintained that there was something to herohood or Commencement beyond this unglamorous definition—something *magical* or *transcendental*—then we must excuse him, he had no patience with such notions.

"We quite excuse you!" Dr. Sear insisted cordially, "Don't we, George?"

I confessed I wasn't sure I grasped Max's point, and that I considered it anyhow my business less to understand than to perform my task, which was immediately to get through Scrapegoat Grate and then to do what I'd come to the campus for: to pass all or fail all. They both seemed pleased with this reply, and fortunately didn't ask for an explanation of that dark imperative from my PAT-card, which I could not then clearly have given them. The Amphitheater was quite filled now, and the floodlights dimmed. People hushed and coughed. Dr. Sear lowered his dry voice to remind Max that not much if any of Sakhyan's Tutoring, for example, had to do with interpersonal relations or the general welfare of studentdom, except indirectly, and that while Anchisides and Moishe had unquestionably led their followers to a new and greater campus, Laertides was the sole survivor of an expedition that benefited no one (even the giant he blinded had scarcely been a public menace, remote as he was from inhabited quadrangles), and among the more primitive heroes of ancient lore it was rather the rule than the exception that their exploits profited no one save themselves. But surely, he protested, Max knew this better than he, and no doubt had in mind a distinction between *practical* and *emblematic* heroes, the former being those who in fact or fiction rendered some extraordinary service to studentdom, the latter those whose careers were merely epical representations of the ordinary dramatical metaphor, if he would.

"What do *you* think Graduation and Grand Tutorhood are?" I asked again, in a whisper. "They must be real things, or I couldn't want them so much."

He smiled at my reasoning. "I imagine you would, in any case. The desire to be a Graduate is normal enough in young people, although in adults it's a neurosis, often as not. And the itch to be a Grand Tutor—that's always neurotic, wouldn't you say?"

"Neurotic means not right in the head," Max explained, tapping his temple and watching me with interest.

"Well, how about the person who actually *is* the Grand Tutor?" I demanded.

Peter Greene clapped me on the knee. "Attaboy, George! Don't take nothing off him!" He had been reading the pages of sporting-news and comic drawings in the newspaper, and joined our conversation now only because the lights had gone too dim to read by.

"Why," Sear asserted good-humoredly, "he's necessarily somewhat mad, my dear boy. Enos Enoch, Anchisides—all those hero and Grand-Tutor chaps. Charmingly mad, I grant you. Magnificently mad, if you like. But mad."

I was the more put out by this remark in view of my infant circumstances and G. Herrold's state after rescuing me from the tapelift. But fifteen folk in white cotton wrappers, high boots, and masks had filed onto the stage below, and since I scarcely knew how to reply in any case, I turned to them my troubled attention. They carried leafy branches in their hands and sat now here and there upon three long steps in the forepart of the stage.

"Please don't be offended," Sear whispered. "Who wouldn't choose to be mad like Enos Enoch instead of sane like Dr. Spielman and me? Besides, there's another kind of hero that we didn't mention: the *tragic* kind." I was not consoled. To Max he added, "They never got their due in the Cum Laude Project, either, when Eierkopf had us all working on that flunkèd GILES. But if you ask me, the only sane heroes are the tragic heroes." He nodded his elegant thin head towards the stage, where now a man taller than the others, with a greatly pained expression on his mask, had stepped forth from a central door in the background to approach the seated gathering.

"There's the best example of all," Dr. Sear whispered to me; "that's Taliped Decanus."

4.

Taliped's my name: the famous Dean
of Cadmus College. You're the ad hoc team
(department-heads and vice-administrators)
whom I named last year as evaluators
of our academic posture. Maybe you knew
these things already. Notice I've come to you
in person: that's because I itch to find
out what, if anything, is on your mind,
and why you're camping on the Deanery stoop.
You, there: you're head of the Speech and Forensics
                                            Group

    and closest to retirement; speak without fear
or rhetoric: What on Campus brings you here?

"A modern translation," Max remarked. "I hate it." But
Dr. Sear declared that idiomatic translation of the classics
was much in fashion in the College, and that while he agreed
that the modernization could go too far, he approved of the
general principle. I observed that the line-ends seemed to
rhyme, more or less, in pairs.

"Heroic couplets," Dr. Sear explained. "Nothing modern
about *them.*"

"Ah."

Now an old chap, not unlike Max in appearance, with
white beard and wrapper, spoke for the assemblage:

COMMITTEE CHAIRMAN: *Ahem. I am most proud, Dean Taliped*
                       and honored colleagues, to have been the head
                       of this, my last committee, whose report
                       and urgent recommendations—

TALIPED: *Make it short;*
                       I've little time: appointments, letters, lunch
                       with six assistant deans, and then a bunch
                       of meetings until five. Get to the facts.

COMMITTEE CHAIRMAN: [Aside]
                       Respect for his elders is what this fellow lacks.
                       [TO TALIPED]
                       I mean to, Mister Dean. The facts are here
                       in our report: complete, unvarnished, clear—

TALIPED: [Aside]
                       And laced with purple passages, I'll bet.
                       Of all the speech-professors that I've met,
                       here in Cadmus and back where I used to teach,
                       not one could make a clear, unvarnished speech.
                       [TO COMMITTEE CHAIRMAN]
                       No need to read it: summarize what's in it.

COMMITTEE CHAIRMAN: [Aside]
We waste two weeks; he can't spare a minute.
[TO TALIPED]
Very well, sir; I'll forego analysis
of our problems, and of certain fallacies
inherent in some proposals for relief—
though it's quite worth hearing. Also, to be brief,
I'll skip our truly moving peroration
and read you these last pages of summation,
done in a post-Philippic courtroom style . . .

TALIPED: *Let's skip that too, okay? I swear that I'll*
be just as moved to hear in a word what's what.

COMMITTEE CHAIRMAN: *In a word, sir: Cadmus College has gone to pot.*

TALIPED: *To pot, you say?*

COMMITTEE CHAIRMAN: *Quite utterly to pot.*
Shall I say more?

TALIPED: *I know you will. But not*
in post-Philippics. Lay it on the line.

COMMITTEE CHAIRMAN: [Reads from last page of report]
Item: our fruits are dying on the vine—

TALIPED: *So's the Department of Plant Pathology.*

COMMITTEE CHAIRMAN: *Agronomy reports that there will be*
another field-crop failure—rusts and blight.
Item: Dairy Research declares we might
lose half our stock to hoof-and-mouth
disease . . .

I clutched Max's arm. "That's terrible!"

"Oh well," sighed Dr. Sear, "at least the tickets didn't cost us anything."

COMMITTEE CHAIRMAN: *That means we'll lack for beef and milk*
and cheese.

TALIPED: *I know what it means!*

COMMITTEE CHAIRMAN: *It means, sir, that we'll die*
of malnutrition soon—or plague, if I
correctly read those secret, censored portions
of the epidemiologists' report. Item: abortions,
both spontaneous and not, are much
more common every term; so too are such
once-rare events as murder, arson, cheating,
robbery, riot, rape, divorce, wife-beating.
Morale is low, inflation high; vice thrives;
we're losing accreditation and our wives.
Famine, stillbirth, crime, despair, the pox—
fact is, sir, Cadmus College is on the rocks.

TALIPED: *What else is new?*

COMMITTEE CHAIRMAN: *Well, sir, to be sure,*
we understand that, while you're brilliant, you're
no passèd Founder; that however keen
your intellect, after all you're just a dean—
and young besides, in years if not in mind.

TALIPED: [Aside]
And thin-skinned, too, this windy fool will find;
I'll break his contract and revoke his pension,
I swear it!

COMMITTEE CHAIRMAN: *Mister Dean, sir—your attention?*
What we mean, sir, is that inasmuch
as you contrived to save us from the clutch
of that she-monster at our entrance-gate—
who quizzed us with her riddle and then ate
us when we flunked—since you alone, I say,
by some device were able, on that day
nine years ago, to get her off our back,
you must have had some influence that we lack
with the powers-that-be. I don't think it was
                                knowledge
(I know more learned men in Cadmus College)
or wisdom, either; simply good connections.
Therefore, in the subsequent elections
you won the Cadmus deanship and your wife,
the old Dean's widow . . .

TALIPED: *Don't review my life;*
I know the story twice as well as you.

"*I* didn't," Greene whispered into my ear. "I'm glad the
old man let us in on it."

"*Shh,*" somebody hissed behind us.

COMMITTEE CHAIRMAN: [Aside]
He tells it twice as well and often, too.
[TO TALIPED]
We hope, sir, you'll be able to repeat
that stunt; to set the College on its feet
by some great deanly deed, before we're dead.
That's what we came to tell you, Taliped.

TALIPED: [Aside]
Tell is right—the threat's thinly veiled!
Their point's quite clear: that, deanwise, I've
            failed,
and should resign my post.
                    [TO COMMITTEE CHAIRMAN]
                    Look here, by Neddy!
You tell me nothing I don't know already.

"'By Neddy!'" Sear exclaimed. "That *is* a bit far!"

TALIPED: *In fact, while you've been sitting on your*
            thumbs
(and on my steps), I've done things. Look: here
            comes
my brother-in-law, by sheer coincidence,
this minute, whom last week I had the sense
and foresight to dispatch, as assistant dean,

> with all expenses paid, to survey the scene
> first-hand, and then to pay a formal call
> on the Professor of Prophecy in Founder's Hall
> and ask his advice, just to forestall the shout
> that rascal raises when I leave him out.

COMMITTEE CHAIRMAN: [Aside, TO COMMITTEE]
> Of all the men around, look which he picks
> as his assistant! Campus politics
> makes strange bed-partners. Now, of course,
>   we must
> pretend to be impressed by and to trust
> this arrant ninny's judgment—not that he
> has either sense or perspicacity.
> Connections, though, he does have, which we
>   worship:
> [TO BROTHER-IN-LAW]
> Top o' the morning to Your Brother-in-lawship!

"Is that a proper rhyme?" I inquired at once of Dr. Sear. He promised to go into the subject with me later, but bid me heed now the important exposition being revealed down on the stage, where Taliped had greeted his brother-in-law's timely arrival and asked him what the Professor of Prophecy had had to say.

BROTHER-IN-LAW: *You want it straight?*

TALIPED: *Why not?*

BROTHER-IN-LAW: *You want it here?*
> *Right now?*

TALIPED: *There's no choice. Despite my fear*
> *of more bad news, I've got my reputation*
> *to maintain—the one that Public Information*
> *invented for me (may they all get cancers):*
> *"The Dean who'll go to any length for Answers."*
> *Flunk the day they dreamed that up! But now*
> *I'm stuck with it, I guess. So, tell me how*
> *things are, and what the Proph-prof says to do*
> *about it.*

BROTHER-IN-LAW: *Man, have I got news for you.*

TALIPED: *You'd better have, considering your expenses.*

BROTHER-IN-LAW: *I won't repeat the Proph's own words; their sense*
> *is*
> *that one man is responsible for all*
> *our miseries and travail.*

TALIPED: [Aside]
>   *That's Founder's Hall,*
> *all right: I know their rhetoric.*
> [TO BROTHER-IN-LAW]
>   *Go on, sir.*

BROTHER-IN-LAW: *One man's doing more harm than the monster*
> *ever did to us. The Proph-prof feared*
> *we're done for if that man's not cashiered.*

TALIPED: *It's like those propheteers to pin the blame*
on some bloke they don't care for! What's his
*   name,*
this poor schlemiel that's poisoning the place?
I'll sack him if I must.

BROTHER-IN-LAW: *   ᴴis name and face*
the Proph-prof couldn't help us with.

TALIPED: *   Some prophet!*
I wish the bloody faker would come off it
and admit he's in the dark as much as we are.

BROTHER-IN-LAW: *Now that's no way to talk about the Seer,*
Taliped. He couldn't name the dirty
dog right out, and yet he made it pretty
clear whom we're to look for and expel
from Cadmus College.

TALIPED: *   Then come on and tell*
me who I've got to fire, man! Whom, I mean.

BROTHER-IN-LAW: *The killer of Labdakides, our dean*
before you took his place nine years ago.

TALIPED: *That was my predecessor's name. Although*
he published not a word before he perished,
Agenora speaks of him—his cherished
wife, that I took later for my bride.

BROTHER-IN-LAW: *No need to tell me that.*

TALIPED: *   But how he died*
I never took the trouble to find out.

BROTHER-IN-LAW: *I noticed.*

TALIPED: *   Excellent. But if the lout*
who did the old man in is still around
and causing all this trouble, he'll be found,
by golly, and I'll show the wretch no pity.
[TO COMMITTEE CHAIRMAN]
I here appoint you head of a committee
to find the killer of Labdakides.

COMMITTEE CHAIRMAN: *Thanks a lot.*

TALIPED: *   The rest of you will please*
continue to function as committee-members.
[TO BROTHER-IN-LAW]
So how'd he die, and when?

BROTHER-IN-LAW: *   Nine Septembers*
ago, I think, or ten—no, it was nine—
Labdakides—a relative of mine,
I might add—

TALIPED: *   Everybody is, it seems.*

COMMITTEE CHAIRMAN: [Aside]
Not everyone: just deans and wives of deans.

BROTHER-IN-LAW: *In any case, the Dean had been invited*
to head up a symposium; this delighted

him: he loved to speak in distant places,
eat and drink for free, and see new faces;
no matter what the subject or how rough
the journey, if the fee was high enough,
he'd go.

TALIPED: There's nothing strange in that; it is
among a dean's responsibilities.
He set out by himself, then? Please speak faster.

BROTHER-IN-LAW: Alone he wasn't. Besides the wagonmaster
he took his secretary—quite a peach,
she was—his valet, P. R. man, and speech-
writer. Five men and the girl, and all
but one was killed.

TALIPED: I guess it was the doll
who got away?

BROTHER-IN-LAW: I wish she had, old pal; it
should have been the girl and not the valet
who escaped. The way that kid could walk!

TALIPED: All right, all right; forget her. Did you talk
to this one chap, this valet who got away?

BROTHER-IN-LAW: I did. But all the yellow wretch could say
for himself was that he wished he'd never been
promoted from his old job by the Dean—
he'd used to be a shepherd, and he said
he wished he'd never valeted instead.
I guess he had no stomach for such snobbery ...

TALIPED: Flunk his stomach! Was it highway robbery,
a crime of passion, or assassination?
Why was no subsequent investigation
held? This valet himself might be the crook!

BROTHER-IN-LAW: I doubt it: we made it plain we'd throw the book
at him for lying, if we caught him at it.
He swore to us he knew no more than that it
was a gang of toughs who did the deed.

TALIPED: A gang of toughs? What for?

BROTHER-IN-LAW: I wish that we'd
had time to ask that question. But before
we could, the shepherd bolted through the door
and fled to the remotest Cadmus barn.
We would have fetched him back, but then the
          darn
monster-business comes along and ties
us hand and foot, investigationwise.
We put all other matters on the shelf
till you came by. You know the rest yourself.

TALIPED: So here we are, hung up again with riddles!
The Proph-prof prophesies, the committee
          fiddles,
everybody gripes, and I'm supposed
to solve a murder-case that you-all closed
nine years ago. That's great! And not a shred
of evidence! The shepherd's no doubt dead

> *by now, or else he will have clean forgotten*
> *what little he saw.* [Aside] *Founder flunk this*
>   *rotten*
> *image they've laid on me:* Master Sleuth:
> The Dean Who'll Dare Anything for Truth!
> [TO COMMITTEE CHAIRMAN AND BROTHER-IN-LAW]
> *Okay, okay, I'll see what I can do*
> *to get the College off the hook and you*
> *birds off my doorstep. It's not a bit of fun*
> *to know that on the campus there's someone*
> *who likes to kill administrators (not*
> *to mention pretty secretaries). What*
> *we need's a public show of deanly prudence.*
> *Also firmness. Summon all the students*
> *and professors here at once. By heck,*
> *I'll find out who's to blame or break my neck!*

We all applauded this resolution—all except Croaker, who I saw was fast asleep, and Max, who found the translation unsatisfactory. Dr. Sear especially commended Taliped's statement, declaring however that in his mind its appeal came from the fact that it was precisely this high-minded vow that would be the Dean's undoing, according to the laws of tragedy. Taliped and his brother-in-law left the stage now, by way of the Deanery door, and the committee of department-heads and vice-administrators dispersed to right and left, but reassembled again a moment later, facing us in a line, just as I was about to inquire further into the laws of tragedy, which I was unfamiliar with.

"This is the *párodos*," Sear whispered. "They sing and dance."

As I heard of dancing before but never seen any except in Stoker's Living Room, I attended the line of committeemen with interest. First they stepped sideways to the left, in unison, singing in a kind of chant and taking one step to each accented beat of the rhythm:

> *O Founder all-potent and -wise,*
> *Who sees with unspectacled eyes:*
>   *You must see that we're*
>   *All spitless with fear*
> *Since You laid on this latest surprise.*

They then danced back again in the same manner, regaining their original position at the end of a stanza equal in length to the first:

> *To You, Sir, we come for advice,*
> *Because (like we said) You're so wise.*
>   *You rescued us once, Sir,*

> *From the jaws of the monster;*
> *For pity's sake rescue us twice.*

These separate dances Dr. Sear called *strophes* and *anti-strophes*, and he excused the committee's bad grammar on the grounds that probably no more than one member was from the Language and Literature Department. There were two other pairs of stanzas:

> *Cadmus College is half down the drain:*
> 　　　　　　　　　　　　　[STROPHE 2
> *The drop-outs are dropping like rain;*
> 　　*Tuition's outrageous;*
> 　　*The kids are rampageous;*
> *And all people do is complain.*

> *No wisdom or virtue survives:*　　[ANTISTROPHE 2
> *Small boys prowl the streets with large knives.*
> 　　*Student morals are looser:*
> 　　*What they do when they woo, Sir,*
> *We don't even do with our wives.*

"What do you suppose that could be?" asked Peter Greene, but no one answered him. The committee's complaint greatly moved the audience, many of whom murmured assent or blew their noses into paper tissues.

> *All classes of woes seem to ail us;* [STROPHE 3
> *For pity's sake pass us or fail us!*
> 　　*Things look pretty quiet,*
> 　　*But we're all set to riot*
> *Against these dark foes that assail us.*

On this strophe the dance had been rearwards; now in the closing antistrophe the committee marched forward, its voice rising strongly over the burst of applause from the spectators:

> *Our enemy's strong, and he's clever,*
> 　　　　　　　　　　　　[ANTISTROPHE 3
> *And we're fairly stupid. However,*
> 　　*We hope that our Founder'll*
> 　　*Search out the scoundrel*
> *And flunk him forever and ever!*

So great was the response to this last supplication that although Taliped reappeared from the Deanery door in time to hear it, and raised his hand for silence, it was some time before he could make himself heard.

"Conservative hysteria," Max grumbled. "Always leads to persecution."

"Now comes the first *episode*," Sear whispered to me. The audience grew quiet.

TALIPED: *Come on; there's no use moaning to the Founder.*
Let's put our own IQ's to work. It's sounder
and also more reliable.

"I'll say it is," Max said.

TALIPED: *Now look:*
it seems to me the surest way to hook
the fish we're after is to make it clear
that anyone can speak up without fear
who has a tip of any sort. I won't
ask why he didn't speak up sooner; don't
fear that. But on the other hand, by gum,
if any prof or student knows the bum
who turned my wife's first husband off,
          he'd better
come across, in person or by letter:
the penalty for silence is suspension.
The killer of the old dean (not to mention
his stenographer and other lackeys)
will suffer more: his punishment, in fact, is
going to be total flunkage and expulsion
from the College. Such is my revulsion
for deanicide, I won't hesitate
to drive the rascal out myself; I hate
him in advance! Even if it should
turn out to be a relative, I would
put it to him without mercy. I'm
as hot and bothered over this old crime
as if I'd seen it happen. Can you hear
this vow I'm vowing, you folks in the rear?
I couldn't more despise the killer had he
killed, not my predecessor, but my daddy!

COMMITTEE CHAIRMAN: [Aside]
At least he talks a good investigation,
and vows a pretty vow. In Proclamation
One, an undergraduate course, we teach
that sort of thing.
          [TO TALIPED]
                    Look here, I'll swear no speech-
professor's guilty of the deed, or of
withholding evidence.

TALIPED: *Because they love*
to talk, but not to act. What's on your mind?

COMMITTEE CHAIRMAN: *This, sir: Was the Proph-prof disinclined*
to give your brother-in-law the killer's name,
or didn't he know it?

TALIPED: *Beats me.*

COMMITTEE CHAIRMAN: *I don't blame*
him, understand; he's not a bad advisor.
I wonder, though, if it might not be wiser
in this case to get all the help we can.

TALIPED: *A stunning inspiration. What's your plan?*

COMMITTEE CHAIRMAN: *Let's call in Gynander, the Proph-prof
                       Emeritus. That old boy knows his stuff,
                       you must admit—although you think he's swishy.*

TALIPED: *Think, man! I know there's something fishy
                       about that guy. You've heard the standard tale—
                       how he was male at first and then female,
                       and then turned male again. That was his brag, at
                       least. Myself, I think the guy's a faggot.
                       But never mind: we deans soon learn to work
                       with every sort of crank and queer and quirk;
                       if I cashiered for moral turpitude
                       adulterers and faggots—those who've screwed
                       their colleagues' wives, or shacked up with each
                            other,
                       or humped their dog, their sister, or their
                            mother—*

COMMITTEE CHAIRMAN: *Mother? Blah!*

TALIPED: *—I'd lose four out of five
                       of my best men. So what I say is, "Swive
                       away, my friends! Be cocksmen, dykes, or
                            fairies—
                       but stay out of the pants of secretaries,
                       and please don't lay your students."*

COMMITTEE CHAIRMAN: *That seems just.*

TALIPED: *Now, speaking of Gynander: I don't trust
                       the blind old fag as far as I could throw
                       him, but I told my brother-in-law to go
                       and fetch him anyhow, to please you birds.
                       Here he comes now, right on cue.*

COMMITTEE CHAIRMAN: *His words
                       of prophecy are always good.*

TALIPED: *For a laugh.*

A youngster now led onstage an old man with a stick, who
except that his beard had a tint of henna looked even more
like Max than did the Committee Chairman.

"There's *my* Grand Tutor!" Dr. Sear exclaimed. "Give me
Gynander, and you can keep your Enos Enoch."

TALIPED: [TO GYNANDER]
                       *Hello there, old blind Proph-prof with a staff!
                       How's by you? I guess you wonder why
                       we took you out of mothballs, huh?*

GYNANDER: [Looks around until he locates voice]
                                          Oh, hi.

TALIPED: *On second thought, you know without my telling
                       you, unless it's true that you've been selling
                       us a bill of goods. At Founder's Hall
                       they speak of you as Doctor Know-It-All:*

*how come you didn't know we were in trouble
and hustle yourself down here on the double?
Ah well, forget it. Do your hocus-pocus,
if you please, and tell us who the bloke is
that we're after.*

GYNANDER: *Goodness gracious me.
It isn't any fun at all to see
the Answers when they're always such bad news!
How could I have forgotten that? Excuse
me, Taliped, my dear; I hope you'll let
us go now.* [TO BOY] *Lead me home again, my pet.*

TALIPED: *Oh no you don't! Hold on there, sonny boy!
Now listen here, Gynander: don't be coy
with me. I see your racket: you allow
as how you know some deep dark truth, then vow
it's much too terrible to tell. Your tracks
are nicely covered, aren't they?*

GYNANDER: *One who lacks
eyes may see what sharp-eyed deans are blind to.*

TALIPED: *Is that a fact! By George, I've half a mind to
haul you in for obstructing justice. That
would fix you! If you weren't blind as a bat
I'd say you knocked off Dean Labdakides
yourself!*

GYNANDER: [Aside]
                *And he calls me blind! When he sees
the flunking mess he's in, he'll see he's blinder!*

TALIPED: *Proph-prof—ha! When that old bitch resigned her
bloody post as College Entrance Riddler,
it wasn't you who'd found out how to diddle her,
was it? No indeed! You had to wait
till Taliped Decanus reached the gate,
didn't you? I had no crystal ball
or magic charms like Doctor Know-It-All;
brains were all I had, man! When she said:
"Answer this question quickly, or you're dead:
What mother eats up all her children, hey?"
I didn't dance in circles; I didn't say:
"I know the answer, ma'am, but it's outlandish,
so I won't tell it." She'd have made a sandwich
out of me if I'd pulled those old tricks!
Intelligence was what it took to fix
her wagon! I said, "Nothing to it, Grampus:
the mom that eats her kids is Mother Campus—
matter of fact, she's having you for supper!"*

COMMITTEE CHAIRMAN: [Aside]
*"Hearing this, the fearsome beast threw up her
paws and died as if a spear were in her
heart," et cetera. I'll throw up my dinner
if I have to hear that bragging tale again.*

TALIPED: *No clairvoyance, Gynander: just my brain,
my passèd human brain—that's what it took!*

GYNANDER: *Then use your passèd brain to find the crook,
since you're so good at riddles. Here's a clue:*

Know yourself. *Begin your search with you.*
You'll see the man you're after in a mirror;
take your falseface off—you'll see him clearer.

TALIPED: *We see a flunking traitor; that's what we see!*
A nasty, scheming, blind old AC/DC
traitor to the College! My wife's brother's
in cahoots with you, I'll bet—and others
too, no doubt. I see your pretty plot:
you'll pin the rap on me, and when you've got
me banished from the place, my brother-in-law
and you will be co-deans. I never saw
such flunkèdness!

GYNANDER: *Your brother-in-law's a fool,*
but you're a nut. When this play's over you'll
regret you made that silly vow of yours.
You tragic-hero types are bloody bores.
Who are you, Taliped? Say who your dad was!
Where were you born? Why'd you come to
Cadmus?
Why marry Agenora and no other—
a woman old enough to be your mother?
Labdakides himself could hardly stand her!
You're the blind one, Dean; not old Gynander.

TALIPED: *Be glad you're old; I'd have your* derrière
on a platter if you weren't old, you fairy!
Because I haven't bragged about my past, sir,
you make me out to be some nameless bastard,
and tell me it's unnatural to enjoy
a woman who is—well, mature . . .

COMMITTEE CHAIRMAN: [Aside]
Oh, boy,
that gal's mature, all right! Poor Agenora—
she'd be senile if she were maturer!

TALIPED: [TO GYNANDER]
There seems to be no end to your affronts
and dark insinuations!

GYNANDER: *Let me once*
again declare, more clearly than before,
the ugly answer to our problems: You're
the wretch you want. You'll see, when Scene
Four's done,
that you're your daughter's brother,
your own stepson
and foster-father, uncle to your cousin,
your brother-in-law's nephew, and (as if that
wasn't
enough) a parricide—and matriphile!
Bye-bye now, Taliped. You call me vile,
but your two crimes will have us all upchucking:
father-murdering and mother—

TALIPED: *Ducking*
out won't save you! You'll hear from me!

GYNANDER: *You killed your daddy.*

TALIPED: *No!*

GYNANDER: *You shagged your mommy.*

With these last dreadful words the old man withdrew, led
by the youngster. The Committee Chairman restrained Taliped from assaulting him, and presently the Dean retired,
much agitated, into the Deanery, pausing on the doorsill to
shake his fist at the crabbed back of the Proph-prof Emeritus.
The Chairman then gathered the committee around him to
sing an ode on this appalling new development. This time
they danced in pairs and clapped their hands three times
sharply at the end of the longer lines.

> *Things have gone from bad to worse,*
> [STROPHE 1
> *And in singsong doggerel verse*
> *We will sing a song of things that make us*
>   *stagger:*
> *First the Founder's Hall Proph-prof,*
> *Then Gynander sounded off,*
> *And it seems as though the Dean's a mother-*
>   *shagger.*
>
> *Though he's often made us sore,* [ANTISTROPHE 1
> *No one's called him that before;*
> *So we trust Gynander's just a little batty.*
> *It's a first-class tragic trauma*
> *To be told you've humped your momma,*
> *And to further hear you've murthered dear*
>   *old Daddy.*
>
> *But Dean Taliped's no dummy;*   [STROPHE 2
> *Agenora's not his mummy*
> *(Even if she's over fifty, which she sure is).*
> *Though the old dean came a cropper,*
> *He could not have been the poppa*
> *Of a lad who came to Cadmus as a tourist.*
>
> *So we won't believe the slander* [ANTISTROPHE 2
> *That our old Proph-prof, Gynander,*
> *Made us ill with—not until it's verified.*
> *Since the Dean pays us our wages,*
> *We declare the charge outrageous*
> *And quite false. The Dean's our boss.*
>   *Gynander lied.*

Dean Taliped's brother-in-law now strode onstage and
commenced the second episode by addressing the Committee
Chairman:

BROTHER-IN-LAW: *Just now I met that sly old pederast*
                    Gynander, with his boyfriend, and I asked

him how his interview with Taliped
had gone. If half of what the bugger said
is true, then cross my heart and hope to flunk
if I don't break the neck of that young skunk
my sister had the lack of sense to marry.
Called me a traitor, did he? I declare!

COMMITTEE CHAIRMAN: He
did say something of the sort, I'm sure.

BROTHER-IN-LAW: I'll slug him!

COMMITTEE CHAIRMAN: What, and lose your sinecure?
I'll bet you will.

BROTHER-IN-LAW: A whipping-boy—that's what
he's looking for! This guff about a plot
against him is a way to pass the buck
for his bad judgment.
                        [Enter TALIPED, from Deanery]

COMMITTEE CHAIRMAN: Well, I wish you luck;
you're going to need it.

BROTHER-IN-LAW: Hah! I've half a mind to
punch his nose!

COMMITTEE CHAIRMAN: He's standing right behind you.

BROTHER-IN-LAW: He wha— Oh, hi there, Taliped, old buddy!
Ha ha! I was just saying how that cruddy
Proph-prof ought to be hauled in for selling
baloney without a license. I was telling
my old friend here that. Ha ha! Ha! Ha.

TALIPED: He said I murdered Pa and mounted Ma.

BROTHER-IN-LAW: Gynander said that? Wait till I see him!

COMMITTEE CHAIRMAN: [TO BROTHER-IN-LAW]
Don't sock the Dean too hard.

BROTHER-IN-LAW: [TO TALIPED]
                                I ought to trim
the rascal's ears back for him!

TALIPED: And I ought
to break your scheming neck for you! You
                thought
I didn't see what you were up to? Haw!
Gynander and my own dear brother-in-law!
Who would've thought you had the guts?

COMMITTEE CHAIRMAN: He doesn't,
Taliped, believe me.

BROTHER-IN-LAW: [TO COMMITTEE CHAIRMAN]
                        Thanks.

TALIPED: It wasn't
him who hatched the plot?

COMMITTEE CHAIRMAN: It wasn't he.

BROTHER-IN-LAW: No, sir, it wasn't me.

COMMITTEE CHAIRMAN: I.

TALIPED: *Yes sirree,*
I think it was. Why did Gynander wait
nine years to speak? When I came through the
                          gate
of Cadmus that first time, he could have made
his crazy speech. The truth is, he was paid
to tell those lies today.
[TO BROTHER-IN-LAW]
                                        You want to be
the dean, right?

BROTHER-IN-LAW: *Wrong. It wasn't me.*

COMMITTEE CHAIRMAN: *It wasn't I.*

TALIPED: [TO COMMITTEE CHAIRMAN]
                          Who said it was?

COMMITTEE CHAIRMAN: *Excuse me.*

BROTHER-IN-LAW: [TO TALIPED]
Consider this, sir, and you won't accuse me:
Why would I want your job, when my own
is so much better? You don't hear me groan,
like you, about long hours and great mobs
of nincompoops to deal with.

TALIPED: *No.*

BROTHER-IN-LAW: *My job's*
an easy job.

TALIPED: *The easiest.*

BROTHER-IN-LAW: *It pays me*
well enough.

TALIPED: *Too well.*

BROTHER-IN-LAW: *I'd be crazy*
to want the deanship. You don't get the credit
when things go well; the teachers do.

TALIPED: *You said it.*

BROTHER-IN-LAW: *And yet when things go wrong you take the*
                          blame.

COMMITTEE CHAIRMAN: [Aside]
Not if he can help it.

TALIPED: *All the same,*
I say you're out to get me, and since I'm
the dean, what I say goes.

COMMITTEE CHAIRMAN: [Aside]
                                        Now there's a prime
example of his keen intelligence!

BROTHER-IN-LAW: *You're not a dean, sir, when you don't talk sense.*

TALIPED: *For Cadmus' sake!*

BROTHER-IN-LAW:	*This joint's my alma mater;* *it isn't yours.*
TALIPED:	*Oh boy, you're in hot water* [Enter AGENORA, from Deanery]
COMMITTEE CHAIRMAN:	*Hey, look: here comes old Agenora.* [Aside] *That woman can't resist a quarrel or a man. Her tongue is second to none for meanness, and she'll sleep with anything that has a—* [TO AGENORA] *Deaness, dear! How nice you look today! So young!*
AGENORA:	*And you're so gallant. Pity you're not well hung.* [TO TALIPED] *What's going on here, lover? Gee, you're cute when something makes you angry.*
BROTHER-IN-LAW:	*The dispute you overheard was Taliped accusing me of treason!*
AGENORA:	*That's the most amusing poppycock I've heard all day.*
TALIPED:	*It's true.*
AGENORA:	*You're handsome, strong, and sexy, doll, but you don't have as much upstairs as down below. Him a traitor! Sweetums, don't you know he couldn't hurt a flea? He's such a lily!*
BROTHER-IN-LAW:	*Thanks a lot, Sis.*
AGENORA:	*Now, then: quit this silly squabbling, before Momma spanks you both. My brother signed the Cadmus loyalty oath; that proves he's loyal, doesn't it? Of course.*
COMMITTEE CHAIRMAN:	[Aside] *She reasons like the Dean himself.* [TO TALIPED] *There's force in what she says, sir.*
AGENORA:	*Who asked you?*
COMMITTEE CHAIRMAN:	*Beg pardon, beautiful.* [Aside] *I couldn't get a hard on with such a sharp-tongued, nymphomanic sow even to gain a deanship—which is how young Taliped got where he is today.*
AGENORA:	*"Peace in the Deanery," I always say. Let's have one now, all right? It's been a while. Forget this treason nonsense, love, and I'll show you what the old dean used to run for.*

TALIPED: *Close your mouth once! Don't you see I'm done*
    for
if he's not guilty? It's a doggone sticky
spot I'm in! This loudmouth Chairman tricked me
into promising I'd sack whoever
killed Labdakides, and then your clever
brother paid Gynander to pretend
that I'm the guilty one. Should I suspend
myself? It's me or your flunking brother!

AGENORA: *My little man's upset! Come here to Mother . . .*

TALIPED: *For Founder's sake, don't talk like that! Not here*
in public, anyhow.

AGENORA: *All right, my dear;*
you always used to like it, though, when I'd
talk baby-talk to you, and we'd play hide-
and-seek at night upstairs, all mother-naked—

TALIPED: *There you go again, for pity's sake! It*
isn't like it used to be!

AGENORA: *It sure*
isn't! You don't love me any more!

TALIPED: *Agenora, dear—*

AGENORA: *You think because*
you're young and I'm beginning menopause
it's quite all right to ditch me now and take
a crack at some young co-ed on the make!
You men—that's all you think of!

COMMITTEE CHAIRMAN: [Aside]
        Look who's talking.

TALIPED: *Now, now, my dear; I'd never dream of walking*
out on you, as you know very well.

AGENORA: *Say you love me.*

TALIPED: *Of course I do.*

AGENORA: *No, tell*
me right.

TALIPED: *But, sweetheart . . .*

AGENORA: *Now!*

COMMITTEE CHAIRMAN: [Aside]
        It always pays
to hear these things. I'll bet I get a raise
next month, to keep me quiet.

AGENORA: *Say it!*

TALIPED: *Oh,*
all right. [Whispers] *I wuv—*

AGENORA: *No, don't just whisper!*

	So
TALIPED:	*I'll shout: I WUV OO!* [TO COMMITTEE] 　　　　　　　*Don't you bastards smile!*
AGENORA:	*Again.*
TALIPED:	*I WUV OO VEWWY MUCH!* [TO BROTHER-IN-LAW] 　　　　　　　　*And I'll* *break your grinning head if you don't get* *it out of here!*
BROTHER-IN-LAW:	*Oo mean I'm fwee?*
TALIPED:	*I'll bet* *I tear you limb from limb, you flunking boozer!*
BROTHER-IN-LAW:	*Hah. You always were a lousy loser.*　　[Exits
COMMITTEE CHAIRMAN:	*So what do we do now, Dean Taliped?*
TALIPED:	*Don't ask me. I should've stayed in bed* *this morning.*
AGENORA:	*That's my boy! Come on, let's run!*
TALIPED:	*What about Gynander? It's no fun* *to be accused of parricide—and worse!*
AGENORA:	*Forget that old hermaphrodite. The curse* *of every campus is its local prophet.* *Tell him he should take his charge and stuff it.*
COMMITTEE CHAIRMAN:	*Mercy, how unorthodox a view!*
AGENORA:	*All right, so it's unorthodox. So sue* *me. Look, I'll prove to you once and for all* *what liars proph-profs are: one came to call* *on me and my first husband years ago,* *just after we were married, and you know* *what he told Labdakides would be his fortune?*
TALIPED:	*What?*
AGENORA:	*He said I'd better get an abortion* *quick, or else my husband would be killed* *by his own son.*
TALIPED:	*And was that curse fulfilled?*
AGENORA:	*Of course not, silly! Naturally I declared* *the proph-prof was a liar; but he scared* *Labdakides so bad that when our kid* *was born—a boy—we secretly got rid* *of him the way unmarried co-eds do it.*
TALIPED:	*And how was that, I wonder?*
AGENORA:	*Nothing to it:* *we stuck a peg or something in his feet* *and dumped him in the woods for crows to eat.*

"That's a terrible thing to do!" I cried aloud. "How could anybody do a thing like that?" Until people shushed and chuckled all around me, I was as indignant as I'd been at Troll's misconduct years before. Apparently, however, Agenora herself had not approved of this cruel expedient, for she wiped the hollow eyes of her mask with the hem of her robe and said:

AGENORA:	*The thought of it still makes me want to throw up.* *Labdakides was sure the kid would grow up* *and do him in; for my part, I was willing* *to take a chance on that instead of killing* *our only son. My husband had his way,* *but things weren't right between us from that day* *until the day I heard that he'd died.* *Now listen, and you'll see the proph-prof lied:* *Our poor boy never had a chance to clobber* *Labdakides; it was some highway robber—* *a gang I mean—that knocked him off near Isthmus* *while he was out weekending with his mistress.* *That intersection called the Three-Tined Fork* *is where they ambushed him and pulled his cork,* *and slit his little girlfriend's throat from ear to ear.*
COMMITTEE CHAIRMAN:	*His girlfriend?*
AGENORA:	*What, are you still here?* *Yes, I mean that brazen little slut,* *his secretary. Was I glad they cut her up!*
TALIPED:	*Excuse me, dear, but were there two* *or four roads at that intersection you just mentioned?*
AGENORA:	*Are you deaf or something, baby?* *Three-Tined Fork is what I said.*
TALIPED:	[Aside] *Then maybe old Gynander's not entirely blind!* *Good grief!*
AGENORA:	*What is it, doll? What's on your mind?*
TALIPED:	*Tell me again: it was a robber gang?*
AGENORA:	*That's what the valet said who came and flung* *himself before me. Four or five, he swore,* *attacked my husband and that little whore.* *They were so busy murdering and raping,* *they didn't notice he was escaping.* *He said it was a gang, and begged a transfer to the sheep-barns.*
TALIPED:	*I must hear that answer* *from the man himself. I wish you'd ask your maid to fetch him.*

AGENORA:
                              I put him out to pasture
years ago; but he can always leave.

TALIPED:
Send for him, then. My dear, you won't believe
what I'm about to tell you . . .

COMMITTEE CHAIRMAN: [Aside]
                              Here we go:
another monster-story.

TALIPED:
                    Sure, I know
I look as perfect as you think I am:
handsome, brave, and smart—

AGENORA:
                              Sexy, lamb,
not smart.

COMMITTEE CHAIRMAN: [Aside]
                    Not modest, either.

TALIPED:
                              I'm so swell,
you probably won't believe me when I tell
you that I once did something bad . . .

AGENORA:
                                        I'll try.

COMMITTEE CHAIRMAN: *Me too.*

TALIPED:
                    Are you still here?

COMMITTEE CHAIRMAN:
                              Where else?

TALIPED:
                                        Then I
will tell you both of the one indiscretion
in an otherwise faultless life. This whole
*   confession*
is off the record, naturally.

COMMITTEE CHAIRMAN:
                                        Oh, sure.

TALIPED:
I know you've often asked yourselves before:
"Where did our clever, handsome dean come
*   from?"*

COMMITTEE CHAIRMAN: *I stay awake nights wondering that.*

TALIPED:
                                        "How come
he came here?" you have doubtless asked each
*   other.*
"Who was his daddy, and who was his mother?"
Well, it's this way: Once upon a time—

AGENORA:
Spare us the details, hon.

TALIPED:
                              All right, I'm
from Isthmus College, where the dean's my dad.
I was his fair-haired boy—you see I had
it made there. I would be their dean today,
except I heard a drunk old poet say
at someone's cocktail party that I wasn't
my dad's son at all! Now, such talk doesn't
bother me, as a rule; bad-tempered fellows
call you a bastard just because they're jealous.
This poet, though, had no ax to grind,
and so I called our proph-prof in to find

out what he'd say about it. (Dad refused
even to discuss it; I was used
to silence from him and from Mom—his wife—
whenever I brought up the Facts of Life.
I had to learn the truth myself.)

AGENORA: *I see.*
[TO COMMITTEE CHAIRMAN]
That's why he was so green when he met me.
I taught him what a young man needs to know.

COMMITTEE CHAIRMAN: *You taught us all, madam, even though*
we weren't young and didn't need a tutor.

AGENORA: *You needed blood transfusions.*

COMMITTEE CHAIRMAN: *Or someone cuter,*
who wouldn't've had to pull her husband's rank
                       to
get us into bed.

AGENORA: *Screw you.*

COMMITTEE CHAIRMAN: *No thank you.*

TALIPED: *Stop mumbling, please, and listen.*

COMMITTEE CHAIRMAN: *If we must.*

TALIPED: *As I was saying . . .*

AGENORA: [TO COMMITTEE CHAIRMAN]
              I'll fix you, buddy; just
you wait.

TALIPED: *Some things the proph-prof said*
                 weren't clear—
you know how those chaps talk–he didn't hear
my question, or chose not to answer it.
Instead, he told me something that, well, hit
me like a load of bricks. You'll never guess . . .

AGENORA: *He didn't say you'd kill your father?*

TALIPED: *Yes.*

COMMITTEE CHAIRMAN: *And swive your mother in the prone position?*

TALIPED: *That's right! How did you guess?*

COMMITTEE CHAIRMAN: *Just intuition.*
I swear, those proph-profs have a one-track mind.

AGENORA: *A dirty track at that.*

TALIPED: *I'm inclined*
to think so too.

AGENORA: *What happened next?*

TALIPED: *I quit*
my assistant-deanship. Daddy had a fit.

COMMITTEE CHAIRMAN: *Naturally.*

TALIPED:
I left the College on sabbatical,
hoping I'd avoid what that fanatical
proph-prof laid on me. I'm still on leave,
and never shall return.

COMMITTEE CHAIRMAN:
It makes me heave—

TALIPED:
A sigh, to think I left them in the lurch?

COMMITTEE CHAIRMAN:
—my lunch, to think of all the great research
I could've managed on a nine-year furlough.

TALIPED:
I would have done some, too, except there
were no libraries where I traveled.

COMMITTEE CHAIRMAN:
I'll bet not.

TALIPED:
In any case, one day I reached that spot
they call the Three-Tined Fork and tried to hitch
a ride to Cadmus with some sonofabitch
who passed by with his lackeys and who turned up
his old nose at me. Boy, was I burned up!
He wasn't headed for Cadmus, so he shouted;
he told some drunken tale—no doubt about it,
he was plastered—of a beast someplace
behind them, with a pretty woman's face
and a lion's body. Naturally I thought
the guy was putting me on, and when I caught
a glimpse of what was sitting on his knees,
I knew the old man was afraid I'd please
her more than he could. "You're a liar," I said.
He had the gall to punch me in the head
just because I called him that and pinched
his girl's backside. Well, of course that clinched
it. First I cut the old man's throat and dumped
him out, to teach him manners. Then I humped
his girlfriend as he bled to death, for sport.
My policy, in cases of this sort,
is first to stab 'em in the belly-button
and then cut other things. She was a glutton
for punishment, this kid—all kinds of stamina.
I spent so much time butchering and banging
her, the others almost got away. I found
three, as I recall, hiding around
and underneath the wagon, and of course
dismembered them.

COMMITTEE CHAIRMAN:
I'm ill.

TALIPED:
I felt remorse
afterwards.

AGENORA:
Nonsense: you did your duty.
The wretch insulted you. As for his cutie-
pie, she got what she deserved.

COMMITTEE CHAIRMAN:
I'm iller.

TALIPED:
Sure she did, but shucks, I'm not the killer
type; I'm gentle as a lamb.

AGENORA:
And twice
as sexy, big boy.

TALIPED:

                          Killing isn't nice,
even when it's justified, and I
would not have stabbed those fellows in the eye
or carved initials in the girl's behind
unless I'd lost my temper.

COMMITTEE CHAIRMAN: [Aside]

                          Or his mind.
And I thought I was sick! He's got some sort
of complex!

TALIPED:

                    Well, to make a long tale short,
the Three-Tined Fork is where I blew my gasket.
Perhaps I'm just a worry-wart—

COMMITTEE CHAIRMAN: [Aside]

                          A basket-
case is what he is.

TALIPED:

                    —but I must hear
this shepherd-fellow tell me not to fear
that it was old Labdakides I killed.

COMMITTEE CHAIRMAN: *How could you dream it was? The roads are filled*
with old Cadmusian topers and their staffs
and pretty girlfriends. They ride out for laughs
to Three-Tined Fork and tell hitch-hikers there
a monster-story, just to throw a scare
into them. We lose a lot of folks
that way to angry strangers.

TALIPED:

                      Your bad jokes
will cost you dearly one day. That old fault in
me of getting angry and assaulting
those who cross me—it's my tragic flaw,
you might say—well, I have it still. You saw
me threaten old Gynander. A word to the wise ...

COMMITTEE CHAIRMAN: *... is quite enough, sir. I apologize.*

AGENORA:

[TO COMMITTEE CHAIRMAN]
To me, too, if you know which side your bread
is buttered on. A man no good in bed
should be polite, at least.

COMMITTEE CHAIRMAN:

                      Forgive me, Deaness.

AGENORA: *You're cute when you're contrite.*

TALIPED:

                      I have the keenest
interest in this shepherd's testimony ...

COMMITTEE CHAIRMAN: [Aside]
Here we go again. I hate this phony
Go-to-any-length-for-Answers bit.

TALIPED: *Perhaps he was embarrassed to admit*
that he ran off instead of fighting too.

COMMITTEE CHAIRMAN: *Or that one man did in the Dean's whole crew.*

TALIPED: *How nice of you to mention that!*

AGENORA:

Now look:
You were alone at Three-Tined Fork. That
    shnook,
the shepherd, said it was a gang that cut
the Dean up. We all heard him say it. But
so what if he says something different now?
I told you once already, sweetie, how
Labdakides turned off our poor kid early
and beat the prophecy. So put your curly
head to rest on that point, baby. We'll
ring the shepherd in to give his spiel,
but nothing he can say will change the facts.
Proph-profs are for morons. So relax.

TALIPED:

Gee whiz, I hope you're right.

AGENORA:

              I always am,
sweetheart.
[TO COMMITTEE CHAIRMAN]
    Run along now, sport.

COMMITTEE CHAIRMAN:

              Yes, ma'am,

AGENORA:

[TO TALIPED]
My little boy will have his little way.
Let's go in, till the shepherd comes, and play.

When Taliped and Agenora went into the Deanery, the
committee reconvened onstage, this time in a circle, and
holding hands skipped gravely clockwise on the strophes and
counterclockwise on the antistrophes of their quite perplexèd
ode.

Department-heads like us are loath [STROPHE 1
      To question old traditions;
We honor deans and proph-profs both,
      Despite their oppositions.

The Dean's our boss, and so we [ANTISTROPHE 1
    trust
      Gynander was mistaken.
Yet proph-profs can't be wrong; we must
      Preserve our faith unshaken.

To question proph-profs doesn't pay; [STROPHE 2
      It leads to bold conjectures.
If students got that habit, they
      Might criticize our lectures.

The Prophecy Department would [ANTISTROPHE 2
      Go bankrupt. Heads would fall—
Department-heads, perhaps. No good
      Can come from doubt at all.

Dear Founder, Whose most cagey [STROPHE 3
    hand

> Arranges how things go:
> Preserve us from all changes, and
> Maintain the status quo.
>
> Keep us from doubts, reforms,   [ANTISTROPHE 3
>   imprudence,
> New ideas, too;
> And we'll see to it that the students
> Still believe in You.

"That was a right pretty thought there," Peter Greene said. "I approve of that."

I remarked to Dr. Sear that it looked to me as though Dean Taliped might really turn out to have done what the Proph-prof Gynander foretold, in which case he was certainly the flunkèdest man in the University.

"He is that," Dr. Sear agreed. "But there's more to it." As Agenora came forth from the Deanery he added in a whisper: "The business of the ID-card comes up now. Very important."

Agenora displayed some green branches and small bottles which she was carrying, and addressed the committee:

AGENORA: For Pete's sake, simmer down, boys. Don't you think
I've been a dean's wife much too long to stink
my public image up? I know quite well
the Proph-prof's full of bull—but I won't tell.
I'll go to Founder's Hall and lay these sticks
and perfume-bottles on him, as the hicks
expect me to. That faker gets my goat,
but Agenora doesn't rock the boat.
                    [Enter MAILMAN

MAILMAN: Excuse me, lady—

AGENORA: Well, now. Who's this?

MAILMAN: A Handsome Mailman.

AGENORA: How about a kiss,
handsome?

MAILMAN: Sure, kid.

AGENORA: Mmm. I think you'd better
repeat the message, honey. Mmm.

MAILMAN: This letter
here's a special-delivery, ma'am; I guess
I'd better get it to the right address,
much as I'd like to neck awhile. You know
we Handsome Mailmen can't be stopped by snow
or dead of night or housewives out to vamp us.
I'll see you after hours.

AGENORA:
                    On this campus,
love, you'll see me when I want you to.
I'm Mrs. Taliped.

MAILMAN:
                    You are? Then you
can take this letter for your husband, dear.
It's from his alma mater. Now, come here;
that means my work's all done and we can neck
a little while before I have to trek
along.

AGENORA:
        Hold on . . .

MAILMAN:
                    That's what I'm doing, girlie.

AGENORA:
I'd better read this first.

MAILMAN:
                    It says that early
yesterday the Dean of Isthmus died.
Heart attack. Now are you satisfied?

AGENORA:
I see you like to read what you're delivering.

MAILMAN:
Here's something else to set your husband
                    quivering:
as soon as he presents his ID-card
at Isthmus College, folks there will regard
him as their dean, as well as yours. I try
to memorize these things in case some guy
should ever rob the mail, you understand?

AGENORA:
You bet I do, big boy. Let go my hand
now; here comes hubby.

[TO TALIPED]
                    Hi there, Taliped.
This Handsome Mailman just blew in and said
your father down in Isthmus had a stroke
or something and dropped dead.

COMMITTEE CHAIRMAN:
                    I'm glad you woke
up when you did, sir.

AGENORA:
                I'm not.

COMMITTEE CHAIRMAN:
                    This sad news
is not without its brighter side . . .

TALIPED:
                        Who's
dead? What's this? What's up? What does it
                    mean?

AGENORA:
It means, sleepyhead, that you're the dean
of Isthmus College now, and Cadmus too.
It also means that anybody who
believes the proph-profs is a bloody fool.
I told you so. Don't worry now that you'll
do in your dad. The old man had heart-failure.

TALIPED:
He did?

MAILMAN:
        That's right.

AGENORA:
                    As for your mother's tail, you're
not to worry over that again.

TALIPED: *I'm not?*

AGENORA: *No.*

TALIPED: *Why not?*

AGENORA: *Because half the men on campus, in their dreams, have slipped it in the place they first came out of. That's no sin.*

MAILMAN: *She's right. I've dreamt such things myself at times.*

AGENORA: *I'm sure you have, pet.*

COMMITTEE CHAIRMAN: *Dreams like that aren't crimes, Dean Taliped.*

TALIPED: *Are you still here?*

COMMITTEE CHAIRMAN: *Yes, sir.*

AGENORA: *Those evil-minded proph-profs like to stir up trouble by pretending dreams come true. They don't, so there.*

TALIPED: *It isn't hard for you to talk that way, dear: you don't have the curse.*

COMMITTEE CHAIRMAN: [TO MAILMAN] *She hasn't had for years.*

MAILMAN: *That's nice.*

TALIPED: *The worse of those two prophecies might snag me yet: I can't kill my old man, but I might get to my old lady, since she's still alive.*

MAILMAN: *Is that your problem, Dean?*

TALIPED: *That's one.*

MAILMAN: *Then I've got news for you. You don't know me, but I know you from way back when. That nice old guy in Isthmus and his wife, that used to call you Sonny, weren't your mom and dad at all.*

TALIPED: *They weren't?*

MAILMAN: *No. You needn't have skipped out.*

TALIPED: *Then who the flunk am I?*

AGENORA: *Please don't shout; I have a headache.*

TALIPED: *What do you think I've got? Good news, he calls it! Don't you see I'm not off the Proph-prof's hook yet? Look, old man—*

AGENORA: *He's not so old.*

MAILMAN:
[TO AGENORA]
    You either, kid.

AGENORA:
[TO MAILMAN]
       You can
put your mail in my box any time.

TALIPED:
For Founder's sake get serious, or I'm
a goner! If they weren't my folks, then why'd
they raise me as their son? Why did they hide
the truth from me?

MAILMAN:
      The Dean and his old lady
kept their mouths shut 'cause they knew how
  shady
your adoption was. And they promoted
me so I'd shut up. Before I toted
mail I was a shepherd, see, and once
his guy I used to shep with, couple of months
each season, in the hills near Dean's Ravine—

AGENORA:
Hey, that's in Cadmus, isn't it?

COMMITTEE CHAIRMAN:
       It's between
Cadmus and Isthmus campuses, I think.

MAILMAN:
Well, anyhow, my buddy gave a wink
at me one day and asked me if I knew
what he had in his lunch-pail. I said, "Stew."
That's what he usually ate. He said, "Heck, no.
I got a kid for sale, pal, and I'll go
halfies with you if you'll fence him for me . . ."

AGENORA:
That dirty doublecrosser!

MAILMAN:
       Well, he swore he
couldn't feed some flunking crow or eagle
perfectly good merchandise, illegal
or not.

TALIPED:
    How tenderhearted.

MAILMAN:
       What I did,
since he was anxious to unload the kid,
I bought him then and there at the wholesale
  price.
I'd looked him over quick; he seemed in nice
enough condition—maybe not too handsome,
but I could get my money back and then some,
I was sure, because the Dean was sterile
and in the baby market. Man, I swear I'll
break that swindling shepherd's neck if ever
I lay eyes on him again! The clever
bastard had the kid wrapped in a sheet,
and when I took it off, I saw his feet
were pegged together, and he was almost dead.
Well, you can imagine what I said!
But it served me right: I'd bought a kid-in-a-poke.
I pulled the peg, and figuring the kid would croak
by morning, sold him to the Dean that night
at cost. Turned out the kid survived, and right

after that I got his job as mailman.
Neither dark of night nor sleet nor hail can
stay me, but the ladies slow me down.
[TO AGENORA]
Bye-bye now, Deaness; next time I'm in town
I'll look you up.

AGENORA: *You know my address, hon.*

TALIPED: [TO MAILMAN]
*Hey, wait! You mean to tell me I'm the one
you bought and sold?*

MAILMAN: *Are your feet scarred?*

TALIPED: *They always have been.*

MAILMAN: *And your ID-card
says* Taliped Decanus, *does it not?*

TALIPED: *Of course it does.*

MAILMAN: *And I guess you know what*
Taliped *means?*

TALIPED: *It means "swollen foot."*

MAILMAN: *You're It, then, pal.*

TALIPED: *By George! I never put
two and two together until now!*

COMMITTEE CHAIRMAN: *A mathematician you aren't. But tell me how
a woman like your wife can go to bed
for nine years with a man named* Taliped
and never see his scars!

AGENORA: *Listen, tootsie:
you and your wife might like playing footsie,
but when a fellow goes to bed with me,
it isn't his big toe I want to see.*

COMMITTEE CHAIRMAN: *And yet you must have wondered—*

AGENORA: *Will you please
get off my back?*

COMMITTEE CHAIRMAN: *When old Labdakides
and you—*

AGENORA: *Shut up!*

TALIPED: *Yes, do. Now, Mailman, tell
me this: where'd he get the child to sell,
this fellow up in Dean's Ravine you shepped with?*

MAILMAN: *Beats me. It could have been some dame's
                              he'd slept with.
But come to think of it, he didn't look
much like a shepherd—flashy clothes, no crook—
I mean, he was one, but he never carried
one. My guess is that some young unmarried
co-ed had the kid and paid a fee
to make it disappear, you know? If he*

had a regular little business going,
it wouldn't surprise me.

TALIPED:
                              Now I'm really growing
curious to interview this pair
of shepherds. Can you fellows tell me where
this crookless crook hangs out, and what's his
                              name?

COMMITTEE CHAIRMAN: *I think, sir, that this fellow is the same*
you sent for a while ago.

TALIPED:
                              He gets around!

COMMITTEE CHAIRMAN: *I noticed, sir, that Agenora frowned*
at everything the Handsome Mailman said.
Perhaps there's something on her mind.

AGENORA:
                              Drop dead
already! [TO TALIPED] *Listen, sweetie, let's forget*
this shepherd-type. Who needs him? I say let
well enough alone.

TALIPED:
                    Indeed I won't.
I'll never get my clearance if I don't
correct my ID-card. The folks at Isthmus
won't give me the deanship if I miss this
chance to find out who I am.

AGENORA:
                              Who cares?
I've got enough to think about. If there's
one thing I don't need, it's your life-story.

TALIPED: *I think you're worried that some scrub-girl bore*
                    me.
So what? It makes me an even grander guy,
that I began so low and rose so high.

AGENORA: *I need an aspirin. Maybe the whole bottle.*
Find out your name, and all the pills I've got'll
do no good. I'm going to hang this dress
up on the clothesline now. It looks a mess.
But please, lover, take my advice and flunk
this ID-quiz. 'Cause if you don't, we're sunk.
                                        [Exits

COMMITTEE CHAIRMAN: *What's eating her?* [Aside] *As if I didn't know.*

TALIPED: *Like all administrators' wives, she's so*
rank-conscious that she'd probably have the
                    vapors
to see it entered on my ID-papers
that I'm some freshman co-ed's son, who laid
her math professor for a better grade.
But I don't give a flunk. I'm just as great
no matter who my folks were. I can't wait
to learn the Answer! Who cares what it is,
as long as it's the Founder's truth? Gee whiz!

COMMITTEE CHAIRMAN: [Aside] *Prepare yourselves to see things fall to*
                    pieces:
The Dean believes his own press releases.

I was by this time entirely involved with Taliped's resolve to learn his identity. I'd finished my popcorn, and began to eat the tasty box as the committee sang a brief and sprightly song of conjecture about Dean Taliped's parentage, coming curiously to a full stop at each line's end, whether the word was complete or not.

> *Whoopee! Hooray for truth! The un* [STROPHE 1
> *examined life is not*
> *worth living! Truth will make you freel*
> *And other campus mot*

> *toes of that sort. What is a coll* [ANTISTROPHE 1
> *ege for if not to seek*
> *the truth? Hooray for truth! Whoopee!*
> *I'll bet this time next week*

> *end, when the moon's full, we'll be* [STROPHE 2
> *dan*
> *cing up in Dean's Ravine,*
> *where Taliped was transferred out*
> *of Cadmus to the Dean*

> *ery of Isthmus, Gosh! We won* [ANTISTROPHE 2
> *der who his mom can be!*
> *No doubt she was a trustee's wife —*
> *or some such high-class fe*

> *male whom the passèd Founder Him* [STROPHE 3
> *self knocked up in the grass.*
> *Dean Taliped's the Founder's son:*
> *a most uncommon bas*

> *tard!* [ANTISTROPHE 3

"Hey, I never thought of that!" I whispered to Max. "Do you suppose—"

He met my eyes gravely. "No, my boy."

Dr. Sear identified the approaching scene as the next-to-last, his favorite and the climax of the tragedy. It opened with Dean Taliped, the Committee Chairman, and the Handsome Mailman standing together as before, while from the wings a small old man was dragged in between two burly chaps.

TALIPED:

> *The Campus Cops are on the job, I see.*
> *We'll put the screws to this old boy till we*
> *squeeze out his answers or his worthless life.*

> [TO COMMITTEE CHAIRMAN]
> *But first: is he the valet that my wife*
> *was speaking of? I don't have time to torture*
> *ancient shepherds simply for the sport.*

COMMITTEE CHAIRMAN:
You're right; that would be wasteful. He's the man, okay: Labdakide's flunkey.

TALIPED:
[TO MAILMAN] *Can you say for sure that he's your former pal?*

MAILMAN:
Former is right. That's him.

COMMITTEE CHAIRMAN:
That's he.

TALIPED:
Now cut that out! [TO SHEPHERD] *Look here, old man, you'd better speak the truth, the entire truth, et cetera.*

SHEPHERD:
I wish I was dead.

TALIPED:
You may be, soon. Now answer this: were you Labdakide's man, sir?

SHEPHERD:
Yep. I shepped his sheep for quite a spell.

TALIPED:
Where'd you mainly shep 'em, pops?

SHEPHERD:
Oh well, let's see: I shepped 'em here and shepped' em there . . .

TALIPED:
In Dean's Ravine?

SHEPHERD:
I shepped 'em everywhere. Stinking hungry sheep—they're always eating.

TALIPED:
In Dean's Ravine, do you remember meeting this chap here? This Handsome Mailman type?

SHEPHERD:
Nope.

MAILMAN:
Come on! It's me you used to gripe about your boss to, every time the two of us would split a jug of Mountain Dew.

SHEPHERD:
Okay, so we're old pals. Congratulations. So what?

MAILMAN:
Remember our negotiations about a kid one day? You guaranteed it was in perfect shape and wouldn't need repairs before I sold it, flunk your eyes!

SHEPHERD:
So sue me. I don't take back merchandise after thirty years.

MAILMAN:
That's not the point. Tha kid was Taliped, who runs this joint.

SHEPHERD:
What are you—some kind of nut?

TALIPED:
I warn you, Shep: this is the Deanery, not the barn.

> There's more than one way to squeeze out facts
> from shankers like yourself. We break their backs
> and screw their thumbs and stretch 'em on the
>   wheel
> and do things to their privates till they squeal.
> It's lots of fun, and gets results, too. Break
> one finger for him, boys.

SHEPHERD: For Founder's sake,
I'm old and—ouch! That smarts! Okay, okay,
I'll talk! Ask me something!

TALIPED: Did he pay
you for a child once, this man here? And did
you take the cash and hand him one male kid?

SHEPHERD: Yep. I made a killing. Not the kind
I was sent out to make, though.

TALIPED: Never mind.
Where'd you get that kid from, anyhow?

SHEPHERD: Must I tell you?

TALIPED: [TO GUARDS]
                    Break his finger.

SHEPHERD: Ow!
Two pinkies in two minutes: the heck with that!
The Deanery here is where I got the brat.

TALIPED: The cleaning-lady's kid? Who was the father?

SHEPHERD: I can't say . . .

TALIPED: [TO GUARDS]
                    Break his finger.

SHEPHERD: No! Don't bother!
They said the bastard was Labdakides's.

TALIPED: The Dean's himself's!

SHEPHERD: I hope that answer pleases
you. It was his kid.

TALIPED: By Agenora?

SHEPHERD: I didn't ask.

TALIPED: She gave it to you?

SHEPHERD: For a
price I said I'd feed him to the squirrels.

"Squirrels don't eat meat," Peter Greene remarked.

TALIPED: Unnatural mother!

"Indeed she was!" I said, shocked to tears.

SHEPHERD:
> *Well, girls will be girls.*
She wasn't too enthusiastic, sir.

TALIPED: *Then why'd she do it?*

SHEPHERD:
> *Better go ask her.*
She gave me some malarkey how she was sure
the kid would kill his dad—some such manure.

TALIPED: *Ai yi!*

COMMITTEE CHAIRMAN:
> *Me too.*

TALIPED:
> *Your answers scare me stiff!*

MAILMAN: *They don't much bother me.*

TALIPED: [TO SHEPHERD]
> *But, flunk you, if*
she gave those orders, then you disobeyed!

COMMITTEE CHAIRMAN: *So fire him.* [TO MAILMAN] *Oy, these deans!*

SHEPHERD:
> *I was afraid*
they'd pin the rap on me if things got hot,
so I decided, Why not make a pot
and also save my neck? This moron swore
he'd carry you a long way off before
he retailed you.

MAILMAN:
> *I did, you crook!*

SHEPHERD: [TO TALIPED]
> *But you*
came back and made the prophecy come true.
So help me Founder, Dean! I'd rather lose
eight more fingers than be in your shoes!

COMMITTEE CHAIRMAN: [TO SHEPHERD]
We call them buskins.

SHEPHERD:
> *Oh,*

COMMITTEE CHAIRMAN:
> *Well, Taliped?*

TALIPED:
The truth! The truth at last! In my own head
I figured out the Answers to this mess!

COMMITTEE CHAIRMAN: *You had a little bit of help, I guess . . .*

TALIPED:
The blinding light! At last I see the light!
And what it shows me is: Gynander's right!
I'm flunked on my ID-card, flunked in bed,
and flunked at Three-Tined Fork—I, Taliped,
the smartest dean that ever deaned, will never
see the light again! I'm flunked forever!

With this final cry he rushed into the Deanery, and while my spine thrilled with the horror of his Answers, the committee reconvened to sing its final plaintive report, the members holding hands and swaying gently from side to side:

Here today and gone tomorrow.　　　[STROPHE 1
What the dickens. What the heck.
Men are whiffenpoofs that pass and get forgot.
Our committee will adjourn now,
But before we say bye-bye
Let us recapitulate this tragic plot:

In the protasis, or prologue,　　　[ANTISTROPHE 1
The protagonist exposed
To the deuteragonist and choragos
Hamartia caused by hubris,
While the background was disclosed;
Then the chorus danced and sang the párodos.

After that the anabasic　　　[STROPHE 2
Epeisodions commenced,
With the dithyrambic stasima between;
And ironic stichomyths led
To the anagnorisis:
A peripetal misfortune for the Dean.

Now the climax is upon us.　　　[ANTISTROPHE 2
In the éxodos to come,
The catharsis will catharse us till we're spent;
Till catastrophe has pooped us
And the epilogue is done;
In the meantime here's the kommos, or lament:

Now their voices rose most sweetly in the touchingest
words and music I'd ever heard—which, however, did not
constitute a true *kommos,* according to Dr. Sear.

Taliphed had a mind like an iron trap.
　　　　　　　　　　　　[STROPHE 3
　　　Boo hoo hoo.
Caught the monster, caught the deanship,
　　　　caught the Dean's wife in his lap.
　　　Boo hoo hoo.

Gentleman, scholar, and keen dean!
　　　　　　But　　　[ANTISTROPHE 3
Caught himself in his trap, like a nut.
Bet he wishes he'd kept it shut.
　　　Boo hoo hoo.

Why did you murder your daddy, my friend?
Why did you roger your mommy? And
Why must we sing this refrain again?
　　　Boo hoo hoo.

At this point, while my eyes swam still, the hush in which
the committee's last notes died was broken by a static rustle
and a terse voice from loudspeakers around the margin of the
Amphitheater.

"*Ladies and gentlemen: we interrupt this catharsis to bring
you two special news bulletins . . .*"

There was a general stir; Dr. Sear muttered something

impatient about the adverse psychological effects of *catharsis interruptus*, but after a moment's pause the amplified announcement continued:

"The body of Herman Hermann, former dean of the Bonifacist extermination campuses, has been found in the New Tammany College Forests near Founder's Hill. Hermann, sought since the end of Campus Riot Two for crimes against studentdom, is reported to have been shot. His body was discovered this afternoon by a detachment of Powerhouse guards. Main Detention has begun an investigation of the case at Chancellor Rexford's request . . ."

The announcement was received with an outburst of cheering from everyone in the Amphitheater except Dr. Sear, who shrugged his shoulders, Max, who shuddered, and myself, too surprised by the novelty of loudspeakers to assimilate the news at once. Even Croaker woke up, grunted, and clapped his hands with the others. I heard people nearby remark that the beast had had it coming; that shooting was too good for the man who had administered the Bonifacist extermination campuses.

"No," Max said. "It was wrong."

"Here is the second bulletin," the loudspeakers went on. *"Late this afternoon WESCAC read out the following tidings of great joy: A true Grand Tutor is about to appear in New Tammany College, to show right-thinking students and staff-members the way to Commencement Gate. I repeat: WESCAC has officially read out that a true Grand Tutor is about to appear . . ."*

One heard no more of the restatement, owing to the great stir in the crowd. People murmured and shouted, hooted and whispered. Some wiped their eyes on their sleeves; some shrilly laughed. A few left the theater; many others seemed to want to, but could not bring themselves quite to it.

"How 'bout *that!*" Peter Greene exclaimed; he slapped my knee and shook his head admiringly, as though I had played a great amusing trick on him. Dr. Sear regarded me with a look of sharply interested doubt, and Max embraced me— almost fearfully, I thought—and then excused himself mumbling that his bladder was full. I could not decide whether to rise and proclaim myself or hold my peace yet a while; moreover, for all my surge of feeling at the announcement, I had foresight yet to wonder what one did after the proclamation: having said, "I am that same Grand Tutor," did

one then sit down again, or commence Tutoring straightway?
And what did one say? Where anyhow *was* Commencement
Gate? Better, I decided, to bide a bit more time; the players
were assembling again in the orchestra; the lights dimmed
that had come on for the announcement; I looked around for
Max, but he had gone through the exit behind us; the crowd
still hummed and shifted as the committee and its chairman
gathered before the Deanery door through which now the
Handsome Mailman came and waved his arms for silence.

MAILMAN: *You ain't heard nothing yet.*

COMMITTEE CHAIRMAN: *We've heard a lot . . .*

MAILMAN: *This college is a loser.*

COMMITTEE CHAIRMAN: *If you've got
more bad news, don't beat about the bush;
lay it on us.*

MAILMAN: *Okay. Then I'll push
along for home, since neither snow nor rain,
et cetera.*

COMMITTEE CHAIRMAN: *We know.*

MAILMAN: *I can't complain
about the weather here in Cadmus; it's
your women burn me up. "If the shoe fits,
wear it," so they say, and Mrs. Dean
fit me like a—you know what I mean.
I went upstairs to check the old girl out
on first-class mail reception—you no doubt
recall her parting words?*

COMMITTEE CHAIRMAN: *She meant to go
and hang her dress up, I remember.*

MAILMAN: *Oh
boy, and did she ever! I near flipped
when I walked in and found the Deaness stripped
mother-naked . . .*

COMMITTEE CHAIRMAN: *Isn't she a dear?*

MAILMAN: *. . . and also swinging from the chandelier.*

COMMITTEE CHAIRMAN: *At her age! Pass her heart, she's full of juice,
that girl!*

MAILMAN: *No more, my friend: she'd made a noose
out of her gown and hanged herself, and there
she swang: pop-eyed, purple-faced, and bare.*

COMMITTEE CHAIRMAN: *A pity! Now our plump and placid wives
will be the only women in our lives.*

MAILMAN: *Too bad for you; you're in the wrong profession.*

Any ow, I'd gone up for a session
of playing Post Office, not to see
a naked female corpse. It seems to me
the woman could have waited till tonight,
when I was gone.

COMMITTEE CHAIRMAN: *It sure was impolite*
of her.

MAILMAN: *You said it. But, that's how it goes.*
In any case, I forgot to close
the bedroom door, and as I stood there swearing
and ogling her, young Taliped comes tearing
in. He yelled and hollered; I said, "Hi
there, Taliped," but he never did reply.

COMMITTEE CHAIRMAN: *Another rude one. Cadmus seems to be*
a little short on hospitality.

MAILMAN: *That's right. Anyhow, he grabbed a knife*
from somewhere and cut down his black-faced
         wife—
I mean his black-faced mother . . .

COMMITTEE CHAIRMAN: *Let it go;*
we get the general picture.

MAILMAN: *And you know*
what he did then?

COMMITTEE CHAIRMAN: *I hope he wasn't rude*
to you.

MAILMAN: *Judge for yourself. There lay his nude*
old lady, with the gown around her chin;
he tore off his diamond-studded fraternity pin
and also his old man's—she wore them both,
you know—then he let go an awful oath . . .

COMMITTEE CHAIRMAN: *He's good at that.*

MAILMAN: *He said, "A flunking curse*
upon that pair or breasts I used to nurse
and later played with in a different wise;
the breasts that wore these pins! Flunk the eyes,
your sun-blind husband's eyes, these too-bright
         wretches,
that blindly saw them!" He undid the catches
then, and poked his eyes out.

COMMITTEE CHAIRMAN: *"Too-bright sun"!*
He should have stabbed himself for such a pun.

MAILMAN: *I just report the news; I'm not a critic.*
The Dean's blind.

COMMITTEE CHAIRMAN: *Like our hermaphroditic*
Seer Emeritus, who foresaw this mess!
What's Taliped up to now?

MAILMAN: *You'll never guess:*
he wants to make a general exhibition,

to staff and students, of his low condition
before he flunks himself.

COMMITTEE CHAIRMAN: *We can't have that.*
What would the Trustees say? But he can chat
with us awhile, I guess, before he goes.
It helps to talk things over. I suppose
this is the poor chap coming now. Ugh!
                                    [Enter TALIPED

TALIPED: *Yes,*
it's me, friends.

COMMITTEE CHAIRMAN: *I.*

TALIPED: *It's I, and I confess*
I'm right bad off.

COMMITTEE CHAIRMAN: *You are that, Dean. It makes*
me somewhat ill to see you.

TALIPED: *My heart breaks*
for you. I was so handsome in Act One,
and now look.

COMMITTEE CHAIRMAN: Ech.

TALIPED: *It's bad, huh?*

COMMITTEE CHAIRMAN: *If you're done,*
sir, we'll be seeing you.

TALIPED: *I'm not done yet.*

COMMITTEE CHAIRMAN: I thought perhaps you were.

TALIPED: *I wish you'd let*
me speak my piece; it's my catastrophe.
Gee whiz, it hurts to know as much as me!

COMMITTEE CHAIRMAN: *As much as—*

TALIPED: *Never mind! I'd like to choke*
that shepherd-type who saved my life.

COMMITTEE CHAIRMAN: *The bloke*
did no one any good, that's a fact.
If I were you, I wouldn't end this act
a blind old beggar: death would be much nicer,
I believe.

TALIPED: *I don't need your advice, sir.*
Suicide has never been my cup
of tea, and it would mess the symbols up.
Excuse me now; I have some things to curse.

COMMITTEE CHAIRMAN: Well, all right; go ahead.

TALIPED: *I'll take a verse*
or two to flunk that ditch called Dean's Ravine
because I didn't die there; then I mean
to flunk old Isthmus College and the chap
who raised me as his son. I'll take a slap
at Three-Tined Fork, and when I've flunked it I'll

curse marriage and love-making for a while,
since they're what made me what I am today.
Ten minutes ought to do the whole curse.

COMMITTEE CHAIRMAN:
Say,
I guess we'll have to take a rain-check on it;
here comes your brother-in-law.

TALIPED:
That clown!
Doggone it,
he's got no right to steal my biggest scene!

COMMITTEE CHAIRMAN: *Be careful what you say; he's Acting Dean*
these days, you know.

TALIPED:
Oh boy.
[Enter BROTHER-IN-LAW

COMMITTEE CHAIRMAN: [TO BROTHER-IN-LAW]
Good evening, sir!
Nice to see you!

BROTHER-IN-LAW:
Sure it is. You were
always glad to see me, I recall.
But never mind. Come on and help me haul
this eyeless bastard out of here before he
tells some news-reporter the whole story.
He never can leave well enough alone;
he's always showing off.

TALIPED:
Gee whiz!

BROTHER-IN-LAW: [TO TALIPED]
Don't groan
for pity now, you sonofabitch. You had
it coming.

TALIPED:
Lay off, Uncle; I'm in sad
enough condition. Look, why not expel
me from the place?

BROTHER-IN-LAW:
I'll let the Proph-prof tell
me what to do, not you. I wish I'd thrown
you out nine years ago.

TALIPED:
Me too. Alone,
I'll wander up to Dean's Ravine and die
where Mom and Dad first ditched me. Or I'll try,
at least . . .

COMMITTEE CHAIRMAN:
Do try.

BROTHER-IN-LAW:
Try hard.

TALIPED:
I will; and yet
I know somehow that my end won't be met
in any ordinary way. Some queer
fate lies ahead for me; if not this year,
then next—some strange, spectacular surprise.

BROTHER-IN-LAW:
Nonsense. Must you always dramatize
everything you do?

TALIPED: *Grant one request,*
Uncle dear . . .

BROTHER-IN-LAW: *What now?*

TALIPED: *I have the best-*
looking daughters and the brightest sons
on campus, right?

COMMITTEE CHAIRMAN: *You have the corniest puns;*
I'll vouch for that.

TALIPED: *The boys can get along*
without me, but I think it would be wrong
to leave the girls behind.

COMMITTEE CHAIRMAN: *Another play*
on words, and naughty, too.

BROTHER-IN-LAW: *The girls will stay*
with me. No use to complicate things further.
You are their dad and brother; if you were their
lover too, we'd never get things straight.
                              [Enter KIDS
Make your goodbyes short; it's getting late.

TALIPED: [TO KIDS]
Poor kids! You've got a rugged row to hoe.
You won't have any boyfriends, 'cause they'll
          know
your daddy was your brother. Boyfriends hate
to hear such things as that about a date.

KIDS: *Some big brother you turned out to be.*
You're pretty sexy, though.

BROTHER-IN-LAW: *I think that we*
should stop right where we are.

COMMITTEE CHAIRMAN: *Me too.*

TALIPED: [TO COMMITTEE CHAIRMAN]
                                        Are you
still here?

COMMITTEE CHAIRMAN: *Where else?*

BROTHER-IN-LAW: *Well, girls, say toodle-oo*
to Taliped. It's time for him to go.

KIDS: *Toodle-oo, Pops.*

TALIPED: *No!*

BROTHER-IN-LAW: *Yes.*

TALIPED: *No!*

COMMITTEE CHAIRMAN: *Yes.*

TALIPED: *No!*
Leaving my pretty girls behind is quite
the hardest thing on campus!

COMMITTEE CHAIRMAN: *I was right:*
He can't resist a dirty joke.

BROTHER-IN-LAW:	[TO KIDS] *now, girls,*	*Get lost*
KIDS:		*Okay.*
COMMITTEE CHAIRMAN:		*Bye-bye.*
TALIPED:		*No, wait!*
BROTHER-IN-LAW:		*You've bossed*

us long enough, pal; I'm in charge here now.
You weren't too good at deaning anyhow.

COMMITTEE CHAIRMAN: [Aside]
A good administrator's hard to find.

TALIPED: [Aside]
I might take up proph-proffing, now I'm blind.

"That's *my* Grand Tutor!" Dr. Sear whispered proudly. "Poor blind Taliped and his fatal ID-card, stripped of innocence! Committed and condemned to knowledge! That's the only Graduation offered on West Campus, George—and, my dear boy, we *are* Westerners!"

"I beg your pardon, sir?" Stirred by the pitiful sight of Dean Taliped being led from the orchestra, and wondering too what was keeping Max, I but half-heard what he'd said.

"We have to plumb the depths of experience," he went on very seriously. "If there's such a thing as Graduation, it's not for the innocent; we've got to rid ourselves of every trace of innocence!"

"Why is that, sir?" The stage was cleared now except for the Chairman, whose committee was forming a semicircle behind him, facing the audience.

"We all flunked with the first two students in the Botanical Garden, George; we're committed to Knowledge of the Campus, and if there's any hope for us at all, it's in perfecting that knowledge. *Ye would be like Founders*, the Old Syllabus says, *with knowledge of Truth and Falsehood.* Very well, then we've got to *be* like Founders, even if the things we learn destroy us . . ."

I was not uninterested in this line of reasoning, especially since it was expounded with such uncommon intensity by the usually blasé doctor—whose eyes, however, as he spoke, flashed curiously more like Maurice Stoker's than like any founder's eyes. But now the Committee Chairman chanted the epilogue directly at us, and because of the extraordinary events that followed upon it, I wasn't able to draw my companion out further on his theory of Graduation.

"So take a look at Taliped Decanus," invited the Chairman:

> The hot-shot Answer-man who nearly ran us
> on the rocks. We envied Taliped
> the old dean's chair and Agenora's bed;
> he solved the monstrous Riddle, cracked the Quiz,
> and found out wh om he'd humped and who he is.
> Look where his Answers got him, and rejoice
> that you don't know who you are, girls and boys!
> Don't be too optimistic, vain, or proud;
> every silver lining has a cloud.
> Let no man be called passèd from this day,
> until he painlessly has passed away.

He bowed; then as he turned to his committee our applause became a rush of dismay, for a great white figure fluttered out of the black sky onto the stage. Whether on wires or by some other means, one could not tell; two large somethings waved from his shoulders as he descended, and disappeared as if tucked in when he lit in the orchestra. Though like the others he was gowned in white, his costume had a different cut: long-skirted in the style of a ceremonial vestment, but tight-cuffed, high-necked, and buttonless on the order of a doctor's tunic. The chorus of committee-members seemed as surprised as we by his appearance; they gave way, some in plain alarm, and the actors who had played the roles of Taliped and Agenora thrust their heads out from the Deanery to see what was causing the commotion.

"There's no *machina* in the script!" Dr. Sear exclaimed.

"Failed!" the white figure declared, in an oddly clicking way. Holding a mask to his face like one of the principles in the play, he pointed accusingly at Taliped. "Taliped Decanus and his sort are flunked forever! Tragedy's *out;* mystery's *in!"* He removed the mask and tossed it behind him, revealing a round, black-mustachioed countenance.

"For pity's sake," Dr. Sear exclaimed. "It's Harold Bray."

"I'm your Grand Tutor!" the man on the stage said loudly. At once there was an uproar in the audience, partly mirthful, over which he shouted, "I'll show all of you who believe me the way to Commencement Gate! I'm the way myself, believe me!"

"He is not!" I protested to my companions. *"I* am!"

"His name's Harold Bray," Dr. Sear explained, evidently amused and impressed. "Minor poet, half dozen other things. Used to do some kind of therapy-work in the Clinic, too. What do you suppose he's up to?"

Bray went on: "I'm the Tutor WESCAC announced. If anyone doubts it, I invite him to talk things over personally with me in my office. I've come to pass you flunkers all, and to prove I'm the one who can do it, I'll walk into WESCAC's Belly and come out unEATen. See if I don't! See for yourselves!"

"Remarkable chap, actually," Dr. Sear beamed—every bit as interested in Harold Bray as he had been in me. "Came to New Tammany a few years ago, goodness knows where from. Fancy him the Grand Tutor!"

"He can't go into WESCAC's Belly," I insisted. "I'm the only one who can do that!" I looked back for Max.

Now Bray stepped forth from the orchestra into the aisle of the Amphitheater, raising his arms to left and to right.

"Come on!" he clicked. "All you folks who need Commencing, come on to me!"

There was near-pandemonium in the audience, everyone shouting to his neighbor and crowding this way and that. Those who wished only to leave the theater pressed against those—a growing number—who thronged already down towards the man in white: some on their knees, some carrying children in their arms, who it seemed to me were up past their bedtimes. Greene was on his feet next to the aisle up which the pretender came; Dr. Sear leaned back and surveyed the spectacle with a little smile, lacing his fingers about one knee.

"Why is Max taking so *long?*" I asked him. He shrugged his eyebrows and marveled skeptically at Bray's announced intention of entering WESCAC's Belly.

"I'm going up and try to find Max," I announced. "Croaker will be all right with my stick to chew on."

But the aisle as Bray drew nearer was choked with the curious and troubled, who far outnumbered the mockers. "Can you cure cancer of the cervix?" I heard someone shout.

"I know the way!" Bray called back. His face was ruddy; his eyes were dark and glintish.

"How'd you ever fly down like that?" asked another.

"I have the Answers!" Bray replied.

I forced my way into the aisle behind Peter Greene, who I thought had heard my intention and was clearing a path for me. But he turned—Bray was no more than ten steps below us now—and called down to him between cupped hands:

"S'pose a fellow's lost one eyeball? Ain't nothing you can do 'bout that! Is there?"

"Come along and see!" the man called back.

Max had to be found at once. I left Peter Greene to his delusions and struggled through the crowd to the exit. The first uniformed attendant I met—a slack-mouthed pocky chap my age—paid no attention to my question; his eyes were fixed on the self-styled Grand Tutor, and his expression was transfigured. I inquired of several people near the box-office (to which more crowds were swarming, the news apparently having spread) whether they'd seen a small white-bearded old man in a mohair wrapper, but got nothing for my troubles except frowns and mocking replies—until a stout campus policeman, one of a number endeavoring to keep the crush from getting out of hand, shouted over his shoulder: "Spielman? You his lawyer or something?"

I declared that Dr. Spielman was my advisor.

"Don't take *his* advice!" the policeman laughed. "He's yonder in the pokey, under arrest!"

He could not be bothered with explanation. Stunned, I made my way across the street to an office labeled CAMPUS PATROL—GREAT MALL SUB-STATION, and learned from a uniformed reception-clerk with yellow hair and a large red face that Max was in Main Detention, charged with the shooting of Herman Hermann.

"That isn't so! Max doesn't believe in hurting people! It's some trick of Maurice Stoker's!"

Unimpressed by my opinions, the clerk informed me that I might be permitted to speak to the prisoner after his arraignment, but not before. Then he looked at my wrapper suspiciously.

"You don't happen to go by the name of Goat-Boy? *George* Goat-Boy?"

I confessed that I was that same person, and though I couldn't satisfy his request for an ID-card to prove it, he finally either accepted my word or decided he didn't care.

"Takes all kinds to make a campus," he grunted. "Prisoner left a message for one George Goat-Boy." He declared as if reading from a paper: *"No need for me. Announcement settles everything. Don't hesitate at Scrapegoat Grate."* As he spoke, a number of telephones on his desk began ringing, and the roar of the crowd outside increased. He picked up one telephone receiver and leaned to see around me through the window. "Run along now, Mac. We got our hands full, this Grand Tutor business. *Yes, sir*," he said into the telephone, and cleared the yellow hair from his brow with his other hand.

I couldn't imagine what to think or do. From the steps of the stationhouse, heart draining, I looked out over the host that now, all mirth gone, bore white-gowned Bray upon their shoulders, up the boulevard, cheering, chanting.

"Hooray for Bray!"

"Bray's the Way!"

His arms were lifted over them; he turned triumphantly from side to side; even at that distance, when he faced in my direction, I saw the striking glitter in his bush-browed eyes, like a goat's or cat's eye in the dark, most remarkable. And across the translux in the square the message flashed, over and over: *Never fear: Commencement's here! All the way with Bray!*

There were no such advertisements for myself.

In a short while the area before Main Gate was clear, everyone having gone with the celebrators. The Amphitheater hoardings and ticket-office were dark, the entrance-gates left open and abandoned. Of our borrowed motorcycle there was no sign. I went over, thinking to tell Dr. Sear about Max's misfortune and ask what might be done to right the error of his arrest. Moreover I had no idea where I was to sleep, or how procure tomorrow's food—such an easy matter at home, and so difficult here where nothing grew!—or what I was to do with myself once past Scrapegoat Grate, or how to deal with the arrant pretender Harold Bray. To ruminate in the meadows of leading studentdom to Commencement Gate was one thing; to stand in the concrete brilliant heart of a mighty college, potent and populous beyond imagining, and dwarfed by its towers to find one's own way, not to mention others', was quite something else. Never had I more need of my advisor!

At the rim of the great dark bowl I paused. Vast and empty, strewn with discarded programs that palely caught the moon, the theater gathered like a giant ear echoes of distant jubilation. Dr. Sear was gone; there was no sign of Greene either, who I had half hoped might lodge me somewhere. No one was about but Croaker, his black outline discernible as an occlusion of white trash where we had sat through the tragedy. I went down. He was picking popcorn kernels from the stones with one hand, scratching at his groin with the other, and croaked to see me.

"Don't *you* believe in Bray?" I asked him, and got no answer. I picked up my stick, and, perhaps misunderstanding me, Croaker hoist me to his shoulders. Very well, I had no reason to protest, or on the other hand any direction to give him. I rested my arms and chin on his black bald skull and worried about Max, permitting Croaker to range at whim about the aisle and tiers. The reasonablest explanation I could come up with was that my advisor and keeper might indeed have seen the murder occur, or come upon the Bonifacist's corpse in the woods, and said nothing about it—that would account for his unusual behavior during the day. Judging from remarks of Stoker's and the general character of his staff, it would not be surprising to learn that the infamous Hermann had been employed at the Powerhouse under some alias, perhaps even with Stoker's knowledge and under his protection. Max might have recognized him, and Stoker seized upon some pretext for having the man killed before his identity came to light and blaming Max for the crime. It would not be easy to save him, I imagined, what with Stoker chief administrator of Main Detention. Perhaps, if things went well next morning, one could approach Chancellor Rexford with the truth . . . But rumor had it he and Stoker were half-brothers!

As I considered how a Grand Tutor ought to manage the situation—what Bray, to my shame be it said, might for instance have done in my position—Croaker evidently achieved his fill of popcorn-leavings or was taken by some dim new urge, for he gave over his ransack and trotted up out of the bowl; turned left and left again and loped away, Founder knew where, through emptied streets, I jogging listless pick-a-back.

5.

We wended up an alley and through a wall beyond which stretched a lawn of some dimension. On its farther side, moonlit, a squat domed tower was, with slits and slots but no

proper windows; Croaker galloped to it, grunting. A plank
door in its base flew open without our having touched it; we
went in and up a spiral of stone stairs as if Croaker knew
what he was about, and emerged into a bright chamber under
the dome, of which my first impression was that it was full of
apparatus as had been the Powerhouse Control Room. Lights
winked on panels; things hummed. But more arresting than
the furniture was the occupant of the room, before whom
Croaker squatted now. Hairless he was and naked, with the
whitest skin I'd seen; his legs were useless-looking sticks that
dangled from the high stool he perched on; shrunk too were
his hams (though his hips were wide) and his bald gonads
scarcely there at all. His paunch however was considerable,
even bloat, and rounded up to a smaller chest and the sloped
white shoulders from which plumpish arms depended. Most
remarkable was his head: an outsized hairless browless ball
that dandled forward and to one side as if too weighty for
the neck. Thick round eyeglasses he wore on it, whose rim-
less lenses magnified his thumbnail-colored eyes. He had no
teeth.

"So," he said, Z-ing the sibilant as Max did. But his voice
was a furry pipe. Croaker at once set to whining.

"He wants you off so he gets his work done," the strange
man said, with a faint smile. I dismounted and leaned on my
stick, confounded. At once Croaker hurried to a metal locker
nearby, took a white robe out, and draped it about the man's
shoulders; our host bared his gums, and Croaker hurried to
another room, returning presently with a set of false dentures
in his hand. Accepting and inserting them, the man sighed
and said, more clearly: "It was good not to have the brute
around, but I do need him." He addressed Croaker then in a
flurry of some unfamiliar speech, which the black man
evidently understood, for he sprang to a cupboard and set
about some task.

"You're the famous Goat-Boy, *nein?*" He tapped a long
metal cylinder beside him, thrust into a slit in the wall. "I
saw you through the night-glass while I was adjusting the
main telescopes. There's an annular solar eclipse tomorrow.
I'm Eblis Eierkopf." He smiled at my alarm and fluttered a
hand. "Don't believe all Herr Spielman tells you." Here he
managed an actual chuckle. "That dumbhead, shooting Herman Hermann! He thinks with his ventricles!" He had, he explained, heard the news bulletins about Max's arrest and Har-

old Bray's appearance in the Amphitheater, as earlier he'd heard reports from the Powerhouse of Croaker's having been subdued by the Ag-Hill Goat-Boy, *et cetera*. I was still too disconcerted by his identity and appearance to make a proper reply. This was the man responsible for the Cum Laude Project, and Miss Virginia R. Hector's undoing? This was Max's arch-enemy? Anastasia's father?

"Sit down," he invited. There was another stool near the eyepiece of a huge telescope aimed through a vertical opening in the dome. "Croaker brings beer as soon as my pablum's ready."

This my former ally did, clearly now emancipated from my direction; not only beer he brought me—excellent stuff in a pewter-topped stein—but boiled chicken-eggs, which he sliced with a clever wire gadget.

"Not those!" Dr. Eierkopf wailed when he caught sight of him. "They're for research!"

But it was too late, the eggs were sliced; whatever scientific work they'd been meant for would have to be begun afresh. Croaker served them round and spoon-fed Dr. Eierkopf his gruel—insisting, with grunts and throaty babble, that he eat every bit of it.

"So," Dr. Eierkopf sighed again. "When he ran off I could think undistracted, just as your friend Stoker promised, but I starved to death. Now I eat and don't get my work done, and he spoils my research. Drink up! Don't be afraid of me."

"I'm not afraid," I said. "I—believe I should despise you, sir."

This news he merely nodded at. "Of course you should, after all Spielman told you! The old man is plenty mixed up."

Sternly I declared that my keeper and advisor was the passèdest man on campus as far as I was concerned—

"As far as you *know*, you mean."

As far as I knew, then; that he most certainly had been cashiered unjustly, thanks in part to the bad offices of Eblis Eierkopf; that nothing could be more false than the present charge against him, inasmuch as all his life he'd affirmed the principle of non-violence—whereas his rival had been, if not actively a Bonifacist himself, at least a leading enemy scientist during Campus Riot II, who had contemplated without protest the combustion of numberless Moishian civilians in the furnaces of Siegfrieder College, and after the Riot had agreed without qualm to do EAT-research for New Tammany.

And so forth. My harangue lasted some while, fueled by an actual twinkle in Dr. Eierkopf's eyes. Croaker meanwhile was peering through the smaller telescope, the one identified as a "night-glass"; he moved it slightly, gave a croak, and offered the eyepiece to his master, who begged me to excuse him for a moment.

"*Ja,* that's nice," he remarked a second later, and I was not too indignant to be astonished at Croaker's fondling the man's tiny organs while he peered. "Want to look?" he invited me. "Young ladies' dormitory across the way. But you're too agitated. No matter." He pushed Croaker's hand away. "*Ach,* that's enough. He *is* droll, don't you think?" he asked me. "Flunking nuisance, all the same. Now, Goat-Boy, let's see where to start on these notions of yours and Spielman's. I really am obliged to you for bringing Croaker home." He laughed aloud, as if struck by an extraordinarily amusing thought. "Do you know, your distinguished keeper went so far once as to accuse me of making his girlfriend pregnant. Imagine!"

"You deny it?"

He opened his robe with a kind of giggle, and Croaker tickled him at once. "Do I need to? Stop that, Croaker! So." More seriously he said to me, "Let's start there. You see how I'm made; I had early a kind of infantile paralysis; it left my legs and the rest as you observe. And young Mrs. Stoker does not call me her father."

I acknowledged that she did not.

"Then one of two things is true," Dr. Eierkopf reasoned lightly: "Max Spielman is Anastasia's father—"

"No!" I repeated indignantly what Max had told me about his accidental exposure to EAT-radiation, which had destroyed his fertility. Dr. Eierkopf smiled and nodded.

"Is that so? Very amusing! Well then, if Spielman isn't lying—by the way, Dr. Kennard Sear could verify that . . ."

"Dr. Sear!"

Expressing his agreeable surprise that I knew the man he spoke of, Dr. Eierkopf affirmed that certain classified files under Dr. Sear's jurisdiction could attest the fertility and potency of any male in New Tammany College who had been of spermatogenic age twenty-odd years ago. At that time, as part of the culminating phase of the Cum Laude Project, semen samples had been taken from all New Tammany males between puberty and senility. These had then been analyzed, classified, and culled under Dr. Sear's supervision to the standards evolved by WESCAC for the Grand-Tutorial Ideal: Laboratory Eugenical Specimen, and although then-Chancellor Reginald Hector had curtailed the whole project shortly afterwards, the donor-data files from "Operation Sheepskin" were still intact and under seal somewhere in the Infirmary's research laboratories—as well, of course, as in WESCAC's memory-banks.

"So maybe Max is lying and maybe not," he went on.

"And maybe *you* are," I interrupted—not unimpressed, however, by the information.

Dr. Eierkopf made a high sound. "Very good! That's very good. Indeed, I might be lying. But suppose everybody's telling the truth; so your keeper is potent but sterile, and I'm fertile but impotent. Now what's left? Maybe Virginia Hector's telling the truth, how WESCAC was the father? How one night she goes into the Cum Laude Room to meet a boyfriend, and WESCAC grabs hold and fertilizes her with the GILES, yes?"

I was up off my stool. "Is that true? Is that why the project was stopped?"

Dr. Eierkopf raised the skin where eyebrows usually are. "So Miss Hector said. And *ja*, that's what made her poppa so angry he stopped the Cum Laude Project. A very great pity, when we were so close to success. A greater pity than any of those dumbsticks in Tower Hall can understand."

I demanded to know whether Miss Hector had been telling the truth. Dr. Eierkopf's tone suggested that he knew more than he cared to tell at the moment—and he openly acknowledged that many details of the Cum Laude Project were still secret, for various reasons—but certain facts, he maintained, were beyond doubt and could be spoken of: the GILES, he would stake his life on it, *had* been successfully developed, at least in prototypical form, and had been so to speak in WESCAC's hands, awaiting the selection of a volunteer "mother" and permission from Tower Hall and the Enochist lobbies to proceed with an experimental insemination. Second, WESCAC had, in Operation Ramshorn and the much-maligned *Überkatzen* experiment, demonstrated its capacity to take initiative and implement its resolves; for just that reason the Cum Laude Room had been designated temporarily off-limits to female employees, to prevent untimely accidents. Third, the precious original GILES had undeniably disappeared on the night in question, and was never found. Finally, a secret obstetrical report, which Eierkopf had seen just prior to his demotion, affirmed that Miss Virginia R. Hector quite definitely had been impregnated.

"So she's telling the truth!" I cried. So wondrous a notion then occurred to me that I stood speechless: the entire mystery of myself seemed in an instant brought to light, in a way that confirmed my hopes beyond my dreams! Enormous moment—which Dr. Eierkopf, alas, soon dashed to campus.

"Impossible," he said. "I don't say she's lying, but her story can't be correct." The logic of the case, he insisted, was this: WESCAC had been programmed to inseminate solely with the GILES; but the GILES would by definition produce a male child, the future Grand Tutor. Inasmuch as Miss Hector's baby had been female—the present Mrs. Maurice Stoker, among whose unquestionable attributes Grand-Tutorhood was surely not included—one of two things must be true: either WESCAC did in fact impregnate Virginia Hector, but *ad libitum*, on a self-programmed "malinoctial" impulse, and not with the GILES but with an ordinary semen-specimen acquired in some unknown wise; or else it was not WESCAC but some human male who clipped her in the Cum Laude Room. Assuming the latter, and further that both Max and he were speaking truthfully, then Miss Hector either had another lover or fell afoul of some unidentified rapist.

"For me," he concluded, "I happen to believe that she did have the great privilege of being chosen by WESCAC, just as she says. But then the computer must have decided not to honor her with the GILES, and either fertilized her with a different specimen or merely . . . *enjoyed* her, you know, without fertilizing her at all. For practice, *ja?* Or just for the malinoctial sport. And then later she happened to conceive by some ordinary lover." He appeared to wink. "She was quite a fetching person in those days . . . I myself used to wish sometimes that I were fashioned like other men, for her sake . . . But bah! I never was one-tenth the fool that Spielman was, with his flunking Compassion, and his Honor, and his Dignity of Studentdom! Scratch a liberal Moishian, Goat-Boy: you'll find a sentimentalist, every time."

Croaker made to refill my stein, leaving his vigil at the night-glass for the purpose. At first I declined, declaring to Dr. Eierkopf my resolve to go to Main Detention and do what I could towards Max's release. But he assured me that

nothing could be done that night in any case—even telephoned a Main-Detention office on my behalf to confirm the
fact—and that despite Maurice Stoker's unsavory reputation,
the New Tammany judicial system was, in the main, fair.

"If Max didn't kill Hermann, they're not likely to convict
him," he insisted. "If he did—as I suspect—there'll be a great
deal of sentiment in his favor anyhow."

I asked him what, if not general malevolence, led him to
believe that Max was guilty.

"You are a witty fellow," he replied, and excused himself at
Croaker's summons to watch a co-ed undress in her darkened
room a quarter-mile away. "But you are confusing malevolence with malificence." He spoke from the side of his
mouth. "I like watching people in the night-glass; that may
be naughty-minded, but it doesn't hurt anybody." As for his
affiliation with the Bonifacist riot-effort and his later work on
EAT-weaponry and the Cum Laude Project, it was not the
fault either of himself or of science that men used the fruits
of his research for flunkèd purposes; he was but a toiler in
the field, an explorer of nature's possibilities; his sole allegiance was to his work; he had no interest in intercollege ri-
valries—petty, to his mind, even if they led to the destruction
of the University. No, he declared, the evil on campus was
done not by disengaged intelligences like his, which amused
themselves between prodigious intellectual feats by spying on
naked sophomore girls with an infra-red telescope; it was
done by principled people like Max Spielman, who prided
themselves on having hearts as well as brains; who committed
themselves with a passion to high-minded middlebrow causes;
in short, who claimed or aspired to membership in the
human fraternity.

"Especially these self-sacrificial ones!" he warned. "Watch
out for that sort! Your Moishian liberal with his Student
Rights and his Value of Suffering—he'll take you down with
him, and tell you it's for your own good. Imagine, they used
to say to me back in Siegfrieder I should jump into the fire
along with them, as a protest!"

What bearing this had on the question of Max's guilt or
innocence I never quite determined, unless it was that in
Eierkopf's view a man capable of any emotion at all was capable of any other, and not to be trusted. I was intrigued as
well as repelled by the hairless cripple—who remarked in
passing that he never slept at all in the usual way, but merely

"turned his mind off" at odd intervals in the day and night, between mental tasks, and in this manner rested, like a fish or a machine. These were matters I wished to take up with him, out of general curiosity or in hope of immediately practical information: tomorrow's matriculation procedure, the problem of finding good counsel for Max, Anastasia's parentage and my own, the nature of Graduation, the character of my apparent rival Harold Bray, the question of entering WES-CAC's Belly and changing its AIM (which for all I knew he might be better informed about than Max, having dealt more recently with the computer), and sundry others. Since in any case I had nowhere to go and nothing to do until four minutes after six in the morning, and sleep was impossible under the troublous circumstances, I lingered on in the Observatory and at length accepted Dr. Eierkopf's invitation to talk through the night—fortified and stimulated by sips of the black liquor distilled under Founder's Hill, of which Croaker located a flask. Chased by the cold pale beer it was a bracing drink; fatigue was put from me, and I found myself obliged to acknowledge that while abhorrent in general and repulsive in many particulars, my host was not devoid of attractive qualities—as Maurice Stoker himself had not in my eyes been. He was undeniably generous in his way, ingenious, efficient, and orderly, brilliantly logical and systematic, and his opinions were interesting if not always agreeable. His contempt for Max was milder than at first it appeared, and had to do not with my keeper's intellectual and scientific accomplishment, which he quite respected, but with his concern for non-scientifical campus problems and his general secular-studentism—all which Eierkopf dismissed irritatedly as "beside the point." Mildly too he admitted to a few inclinations of his own in the administrative-policy way: he rather thought, for example, that a rotating commission of experts from the various sciences could run the University more harmoniously and efficiently than could the law-school, political-science, and business-administration types who customarily inhabited Tower Hall. He seconded without abash the idea of "preventive riot": it was EAT or be EATen, he placidly declared (confessing that the acronym nauseated him), and New Tammany would be well advised to EAT the Niko-layans at once, without warning, both to simplify the political situation and to protect herself from destruction at the hands of an enemy who surely would not scruple to attack by stealth. At the matter of the Moishian genocaust he merely shrugged his narrow shoulders: riot was riot; the Siegfrieders had been cut off from their normal fuel supply; a few good Moishian researchers like Chaim Schultz had gone up in smoke, but not many; the slaughter of whole student bodies was a tradition as old as riot itself—had not Laertides been called "Sacker of Cities"?—and the mere scale and efficiency of the Moishian extermination did not in his view make the Siegfrieders any more flunkèd than the classical Remusians, for instance, considering the proportionate increase in University population since ancient terms, and the improvement of homicidal technology.

"Despite the Moishiocaust and deaths from all causes on both sides during C.R. Two," he pointed out, "there were more people on campus at the end of the Riot than at the beginning. So?" And blandly he turned up his palms.

But less egregious, and to me more interesting, were his opinions of Harold Bray, Grand-Tutorhood in general, and Graduation—all which matters, like ethics and politics, he first declared with a smile to be "out of his line"—suitable enough for small talk, but not worth serious attention.

"I myself am a Graduate, you know," he said.

"You!"

"That amuses you. Nevertheless, I am. Even your friend Bray agrees—not that that matters. And I verified it on WESCAC before I was demoted: there's the *real* Grand Tutor, of course."

I coughed on my beer. "WESCAC?"

"Certainly." He was sorry, he said coolly, that he could not second my own claim to that distinction—how he knew of it I couldn't imagine. He granted that in many respects my history paralled that of the Grand-Tutorial Ideal as abstracted by WESCAC, and if I had happened to be Virginia Hector's son by the GILES, there could be little doubt of my authenticity. But seeing I was not, the best he could say for Max was that my keeper—in his isolation, bitterness, and advancing years—had gone soft-headed and groomed me for some preposterous scheme of redress. Max being in his opinion incapable of sustained deception—other than self-deception—Eierkopf concluded that in all likelihood Max really believed me to be a Grand Tutor, and would even more so if he knew of the GILES incident.

"But don't forget," he said, "you have only Spielman's

word for it that you came from the Tower Hall tapelift, for example. I remember hearing stories about a crazy *Schwarzer* finding a baby, but Max could have made up those stories—so could the *Schwarzer* have—or you might not be the same child." He smiled. "Or you might have been EATen yourself, *ja?*"

"I've thought of that."

"So. But anyhow you aren't Virginia Hector's child. And all this AIM business! Nobody knows how WESCAC's programmed itself since those days, or whether the criteria it reads out for Grand-Tutorhood are actually the ones it would go by if somebody tried to enter the Belly—it might be fooling us! Or talking a different language."

I began to feel dizzy, melancholy, and yet stubborn, as always when the uncertainty of my position was analyzed.

"Who says it's the Grand Tutor's job to straighten out the Quiet Riot anyhow?" Eierkopf went on cheerfully. "Only Spielman, he's such a big Moishian pacifist! Did Enos Enoch worry about varsity politics? *Unto the Chancellor that which is the Chancel'or's; unto the Founder that which is the Founder's.* And Scapulas says old Maios fought in the front lines in the Lykeionian riots, a regular alma-matriot."

Uneasily I declared, "I haven't decided yet what I'm going to do. Max is my advisor, but he's not my keeper any more. I'm pleased to hear you don't believe in this Bray fellow, at least."

"Bray? Bah! We'll see what happens when he goes into WESCAC's Belly. Want to see what he's up to now?"

He threw a number of switches on a nearby panel. Around the upper margin of the walls, just under the dome-edge, was a row of slightly convex glass screens, each half a meter square, which now glowed bluish-white in the manner of the Powerhouse Telerama. Scenes appeared on them, mostly unfamiliar: streets, buildings, interiors, for the most part dark and deserted. On one screen, however—which Eierkopf selected, shutting off the rest—a considerable crowd was represented, around a single column that marked the scene as Founder's Hill. A white figure stood near the pediment alternately haranguing the throng and bending to touch and speak to individuals who knelt before him. To certain of them, it appeared, he gave something cylindrical and white, like a rolled paper.

"He's Certifying Candidates already," Eierkopf snorted. It

was indeed Bray, I saw now in a closer view. "You'd better get busy, there won't be anybody left to Commence."

"Is he really Certified by WESCAC? He claimed to be." I wondered too how the man had contrived to appear from the air, like a great stork, and who he was anyhow, and whether the NTC Chancellor's office would not take measures to investigate and suppress the imposture. Even as I inquired I thought I saw Peter Greene in the floodlit throng, pressing close to the monument; and there in the background, less surprisingly, was the swart stock form of Maurice Stoker, one hand on his hip, the other in his beard, grinning and shouting orders to the patrolmen who contended with the crowd. Then consternation fetched me to my feet, for as Eierkopf by turning a dial magnified and closed in on the scene, I saw a slender young woman, in a shift white and simple as Bray's own vestment, come forth under uniformed escort and embrace the pretender's knees.

"Get up from there!" I cried.

"*Ja*, by George, it's Anastasia," Eierkopf laughed. "Remarkable creature, isn't she? Pretty as her mother, and never says no. You want to watch?"

Sick at heart I declined, and he turned the device off. Croaker approached with an odd-shaped white-enameled vessel, into the neck of which he put his master's little penis, and Eierkopf urinated.

"You're jealous a little," he said. "It was fun last night in the Living Room, *ja?* I saw it on the monitor."

Since the Cum Laude scandal, I learned, he had been removed from his official directorship of WESCAC research—the machine had grown so self-directing that his post had all but lost its significance in any case—and demoted to the office of Clockwatcher. The job was actually quite sensitive, involving responsibility not only for the measurement of NTC time but for the "ticking heart" of WESCAC itself, "the very pulse of West Campus": as best I could conceive it, a metronomic apparatus (or was it merely a principle?) which both set and was itself the pace of WESCAC's operations; which in some manner beyond my fathom both drove and derived from the Tower Hall clockworks, currently under repair. In this capacity his talents, too valuable to do without, were available to the administration, which yet avoided the embarrassment of having a notable ex-Bonifacist in charge of New Tammany's military research programs.

Moreover, at Maurice Stoker's urging, the Clockwatch had recently extended its operations to assist Main Detention in what was called Safety Surveillance; a genius with lenses, microphones, and such, Eierkopf was developing and integrating into WESCAC an elaborate system of monitoring devices, designed to improve the effectiveness of NTC law enforcement groups in preventing rule-infractions before they occurred and protecting the College from espionage. When perfected, S.S. would feed into WESCAC whatever its ubiquitous eyes and ears picked up; the computer would scan and assess the data, cull from it by its own program any evidence of infractions-in-the-making, and either take or recommend appropriate action. At present the system consisted merely of a few hundred cameras and listening-devices scattered about the campus and monitored by an experimental automatic scanner there in Eierkopf's Observatory—thus his surprising knowledge of my recent adventures.

"You and Bray and this Living Sakhyan fellow—we're watching all of you, naturally, as much as we can. A Grand Tutor's always a potential threat, as you're no doubt aware: that was even a criterion in the GILES program."

I was too much stricken by Anastasia's defection—how else interpret her behavior?—to be properly appalled by these disclosures. So passionately she had affirmed me in the Living Room, only to embrace the first imposter to come along! Eblis Eierkopf of course was merely amused; he offered the suggestion that she might accept Certification from Bray in order to reinforce his own authenticity, if she felt he needed the support—had she not done the same for me, and half a dozen others?

"The things she used to do for me with Croaker!" he exclaimed. "She knew it helped me to watch her through the night-glass, especially when the gossips said she might be my daughter. Remarkable girl!"

He would have documented in more detail, but I waved away the offer. In an effort to raise my spirits he had Croaker refill my stein and recounted what he knew of Harold Bray.

"A crazy-man. A fake. A mountebank," he insisted. "Don't believe him for a minute; he doesn't even have the qualifications you have." But, he allowed, Bray *was* an extraordinary fellow, if a gross impostor, and had acquired a diverse notoriety on the campus before ever the "Grand-Tutor craze" began. It was generally agreed that he'd first appeared in

NTC about eight years previously—though no one could say for sure when and whence he'd come, and it was merely a hypothesis, albeit a likely one, that the several roles attributed to him under different names and appearances had been played by a single man. "Sometimes I think he's a species instead of one man," Eierkopf declared. "At least he must be quintuplets."

In brief, within a few months of his appearance in NTC he seemed to know the names, histories, achievements, and involvements of nearly everyone on campus—including their friendships, enmities, and privatest lives, as if he had an S.S. system of his own. Basically squat and dark-haired, and in years somewhere between young manhood and early middle age, he nonetheless contrived to change his appearance substantially overnight from time to time, and his vocation as well. First he'd been an avant-garde poet—bearded, booted, long-locked, and malodorous—the darling of eccentric undergraduates, an *enfant terrible* in exotic garb who'd boasted of his sexual prowess, dropped famous names like birdlime all over Great Mall, spread slanderous gossip (always with a grain of substance in it) that set the members of the Poetry Department at one another's throats, and published scores of poems, some of which could not be proved to have been plagiarized. Subsequently—perhaps even simultaneously, it was far from certain—he had been a psychotherapist—bald, cleanshaven, dapper, washed, and fat—cashiered from the Psych Clinic when his glowing reference-letters proved to be forgeries, but not before he'd achieved a fair percentage of apparently successful cures. Again, under a third name, with a crew haircut and a stocky-muscled build, he'd been a field entomologist, explorer, and survival expert, able to flourish indefinitely in the wilderness without so much as a pocketknife or canteen of water—but the Departments of Cartography and Entomology, satisfied as they were with his abilities and indifferent of his credentials, had reluctantly to fire him when he refused to disclose his methods. He had no ID-card; rather, he had such a variety of forged and stolen ones that no one could say what his actual, original name was. No one had ever seen him eat, sleep, or relieve himself; no one knew where he lived; he spent all his hours in taverns and other people's offices and dwelling-places, talking endlessly and knowledgeably on any subject whatever—he was either a pathological liar or a widely traveled polymath, everyone agreed. Neither had anyone seen him at work; yet books and monographs in a dozen languages and a score of fields (survival techniques excepted) appeared under his *noms-de-plume* and sundry aliases; they were always challenged, but seldom wholly discredited. In time he had become the chief topic of conversation at New Tammany committee-meetings and cocktail parties. He was laughed at and over, reviled, contemned, cashiered, threatened with lawsuits—and yet stood in awe of, especially by students. His most hostile critics agreed that the man was a gifted impostor—so much so that in some instances the question of his fraudulence became more metaphysical than legal or ethical. If a man utterly without experience and knowledge of painting resolves to pose as an artist, Eierkopf hypothesized, and purely as part of the mimicry comes up with a painting that at least a few respectable critics deem a work of art, is the painter a fraud? If to prevent its being discovered that his surgical knowledge is only feigned, a man successfully removes an appendix, is he a hoax? Many people thought not, and the celebrated impostor had in time become a bonafide celebrity, an institution, a kind of college mascot whose deceptions often delighted the deceived. New Tammanians waited with approved curiosity to see where Bray would turn up next, and in what capacity; his poems, paintings, and scholarly articles became collector's items; everyone agreed that he was in his counterfeit way as considerable a genius as the encyclopedic giants of the Rematriculation, and in some quadrangles it was fashionable to claim for his productions a legitimate intrinsic value.

"So if anybody can mimic a Grand Tutor, it's Bray," Dr. Eierkopf concluded. "No telling what he's got up his sleeve; the curious thing is that he's posing without disguise. He's using one of the names he's known by instead of making up a new one, and the face is the same face he used as a psychotherapist." In consequence, it was already being suggested by some news commentators that this time he wasn't posing at all; that his former impostures had been in the nature of preparatory omens, or deliberate challenges to faith, as who should say, "I dare you to believe in me!" That thousands were ready to accept the challenge was evident: what Eierkopf was interested in seeing was how many actual Passages Bray could effect; how he would comport himself as an accepted Grand Tutor, especially in the matter of descending into WESCAC; how WESCAC itself would appraise him—as inevitably it must, if it had not already; and what would occur when the time came for him to meet that end described in the GILES profile as the fate of all Grand Tutors . . .

"The Enochists say that a man can teach the Syllabi effectively even though he's flunkèd himself," he declared. "If everybody believes Bray's the Grand Tutor, and he goes into WESCAC's Belly and Commences the student body, does it make any difference whether he's the real thing?"

"Absolutely!" I cried. "All the difference on campus! *I'm* the Grand Tutor, whether anybody believes it or not!" Even as I protested, my throat smarted at the thought of Peter Green's apostasy, and Dr. Sear's (though I knew they'd only been being agreeable from the beginning), and particularly Anastasia's, since I'd come to regard her as my first protégée. Croaker himself had forsaken me, to squat by the night-glass against his master's further orders.

"I don't feel well at all," I said.

"Do you want a woman?" Dr. Eierkopf asked at once. "I'll have Croaker bring up a Dairy Science co-ed."

I declined the offer.

"An aspirin, then? Or a sandwich? I'll have to ask you to eat it in the bathroom, though."

These too I declined, observing that perhaps it was sleep after all that I needed most, next to Max's counsel.

"Whatever you please," said Eierkopf. "Croaker fixes you a cot, and we see to it you're up in time to register. I really am grateful to you for bringing him home, I suppose."

I closed my eyes for a moment. "You're welcome, sir."

"You know . . ." He dandled his head on the other side, and his magnified eyes rolled merrily. "I almost wish you *were* the GILES, George—may I call you George? And you call me Eblis, if you like . . ." He sighed briefly, whereupon as if commanded Croaker came and set him on his shoulders. Eierkopf seemed quite at home there, but I was surprised to see what looked like tears shining behind his spectacles.

"You see? He's always getting things mixed up, like my eggs a while ago. Nothing ever gets done just the way I intended. But what can I do? And I cramp *his* style, too, I'm sure . . ."

Forgetting then the subject—his wish that I were the true GILES—not to mention the proposal of an end to conversation, he launched into a recounting of the nature and history of his connection with Croaker, which I attended with what imperfect wakefulness and patience I had left.

"I'd just been brought to New Tammany," he began, resting his little chin on Croaker's skull—a white spheroid perched on a great black pedestal. "They had just begun to use WESCAC to pair up roommates, and refugee research-people were handled just as students were in the regular dormitories. *Verstehst?* You'll see tomorrow morning . . ."

At matriculation-time, he continued, everyone's attributes had been coded onto cards, which then were matched automatically on the basis of complementation—a homely farm-girl with a chic young piece from Great Mall, and so forth. This was before the days of Prenatal Aptitude Testing, and Eierkopf allowed that it wasn't in itself a bad system.

"But show me the *programme* without hitches, Goat-Boy!" He had come to this campus with bad eyesight and false teeth, he declared; was never robust; could hardly stand on his legs (they were stronger then)—all this was duly punched into his card, he'd signed the loyalty-oath, got his clearance-papers, watched WESCAC's card-sorters riffle and click. Going then to the lodging assigned him he found there not the clear-eyed practical, *gemütlich* young engineer he'd rather expected (himself being subject to sick headaches and "too busy in the head" to bother with housekeeping), but Croaker, the famous Athlete—All-Campus candidate in football he was then, before they named him Frumentius's delegate to the University Council for his own protection.

"Imagine, Goat-Boy! A mindless brute that ate raw hamburger at the Coach's order, wore nothing but a loin-cloth, picked his nose, took what he pleased, urinated in the shower-bath, danced and farted, rolled his eyes, bared his teeth, and had his way with a parade of co-eds!"

Often and often, he said, when he'd had equations to think through or wanted only to rest his mind, he would come home to discover Croaker at his business with one of the girls—perhaps a cheerleader, with crimson letter on the breast of her pullover. Naturally Croaker never troubled to draw the blinds, and in those days the spectacle gave Eierkopf headaches: from his perch on the outside stairway he was obliged, so he complained, to watch the pair at their rut: how the little pink beast feigned displeasure, even threatened alarum; how her ape-of-the-woods merely croaked, and naked himself already, had at garter and hook, put her in a trice to the fearsome roger—whereat, coy no more, she'd whoop.

"And the worst was, we had to share the same bed!" Hard enough to relax, he said, in the odors of perfume and sweat; more than once, when sleep at last had granted respite from all thought he would be roused by Croaker's heavy arm flung over him; caught up in prurient dreamings the Frumentian mistook him for the prey, and must either be waked (no easy task) or his hug suffered till the dream was done.

I clucked sympathetically, and Eierkopf hastened to assure me that even so, his roommate had not been all bad. "I never begrudged him his salary, you know; brains aren't everything; studentdom must have its circuses. The whole body attended the games; I watched them myself through binoculars, cheering with the rest." Croaker was, he allowed, a splendid supple animal after all, full of power and grace; it could lift even Eierkopf's spirits to see him leap about the room or chin on the shower-rod or lay waste half a sorority. They were not always at odds, I must understand. Though the smell of raw hamburger retched the frail scientist, Croaker saw to it he never starved, and except in most obstreperous humors fetched and carried at his roommate's command, even as he'd done for me. In return, Eierkopf had filled out Croaker's scholarship-forms, reconciled his financial statements, schooled him in the simplest etiquette and hygiene—not to defecate in classrooms, not to copulate on streetcorners—and did his homework.

"I devised little tasks to make him feel useful and regimens to keep him fit. Sometimes I even chose his girls: leave him to himself, he'd as likely hump somebody's poodle or the Dean of Studies! I was still interested sometimes in women then; let a pretty baggage from Theater Arts refuse me her company or make fun of my eyeglasses: I'd point her out to Croacker on the sly, and one night soon I'd have the joy to see her boggle at his awful tup!"

In sum, Croaker could not have survived long on the campus without Eierkopf's help, and the scientist in turn would have found life insupportable had Croaker been shot to death, say, by the father of some ruined sophomore, or lynched by the White Students' Council. However much, then, he might despair at Croaker's grossness, and Croaker perhaps at his roommate's incapacity and frailness; however much they each might yearn at times to live alone or with a partner more congenial—which yearning Maurice Stoker had lately played upon, for mischief's sake—at their best they muddled through, strange bedfellows, who in any case were bound by the strictest of leases, which could not be broken before its term. And so strong a thing is custom, Eierkopf declared, he soon could scarcely recall having ever lived alone; it was as if he and Croaker had been together from the beginning, for better or worse. What was more, if their connection was at best uneasy, they'd come more and more to depend on each other as terms went by. Eierkopf's affliction worsened; he took to a wheelchair and gave up sleeping; Croaker delivered him to and from laboratories, even learned to take dictation and type out reports—except during seizures like the one that had lately fetched him to George's Gorge. As for the Frumentian, he had got along previously by a kind of instinct, which, when he saw how better he fared with Eierkopf's assistance, he either put by or clean forgot.

Again tears welled into Eierkopf's eyes, whether of affection or chagrin I could not decide. "I even learned the art of football for his sake, and lectured him between matches on his specialty, the Belly Series! All which, my friend, the athletic directors, the student boys and girls, and my colleagues came to accept, grudgingly or not: to get Croaker they had to take me; to get me"—he chuckled or sobbed—"who had my own kind of fame, you know—they must put up with Croaker."

Did his face fall in despair, or did he kiss the grinning giant's pate?

"It was a *package deal,* not so? And still is; it still is. Croaker and Eierkopf—we are inseparable as two old faggots, or ancient spouses!"

He said more; indeed he may have talked the night through, but further than this I knew nothing until Croaker waked me with a gentle touch. My first thought was that I'd dozed off for half a sentence—Dr. Eierkopf sat on Croaker's shoulders as before, and resumed the conversation as soon as my eyelids opened—but I discovered that I was lying on a cot, and a large clock on the wall read four and a half hours after midnight. Croaker set a folding screen before me and served up a breakfast of hard-boiled eggs, pancakes, and sausage; while I dined (I could not of course stomach the sausage any more than Eierkopf could abide the sight of my eating anything at all) my host spoke on from behind the screen:

"It *is* extraordinary how many things point to your being the GILES, except the one thing that proves you're not. And it's almost a pity. You're an interesting young man, a pleasant young man—but that's not the point." What he meant was that although he assumed the Cum Laude Project to be a cause forever lost, it intrigued him to imagine what WESCAC might have produced had it indeed fertilized some lady with the GILES. Moreover, while he felt certain that he knew what Graduation is, and that he was himself a Graduate, there were admittedly moments when he could almost wish it were something else—something miraculous after all, as the superstitious held it to be.

"What is Commencement?" I asked him through the screen. Croaker fried a decent pancake.

"Commencement is a conclusion," he replied at once. "There's nothing mysterious about it: when you've eliminated your passions, or put them absolutely under control, you've Commenced. That's why I call WESCAC the Grand Tutor. I can prove this logically, if you're interested."

I did not deny that I was interested, but pled shortness of time. Not to be discourteous, however, I asked him whether, when a man had reasoned his way to Commencement Gate, as it were, he truly felt Commencèd—for I had often heard Graduation described as an experience, but never as a proposition.

"Bah! Bah!" my host cried, with more heat than I'd seen him display thitherto. "That question leaves me cold!" The ejaculation confused Croaker, who mistaking it for some unclear but urgent command, galloped wildly about the observatory for some moments, knocking down the screen and upsetting a tray of watch-glasses before he could be calmed.

"There, look what he's done!" Eierkopf pounded him feebly on the head and wept a single tear. Like a frightened horse, Croaker still rolled his eyes and fluttered at the nostrils. "I *would* be a Graduate, if it weren't for him! I can't pass with him, and I can't live without him! *Feel, feel,* that's all people think of! There's *feeling* for you!" He indicated Croaker, who, quite placid now, had set his rider on a stool and was doing his best to tidy up the spilt watch-glasses. "If Commencement were a feeling, he'd be the Graduate!" Now Dr. Eierkopf laughed until a rack of coughing stopped him. "Maybe he is, eh?"

I said to soothe him that I could not imagine Croaker as a Candidate yet, much less a Graduate, though to be sure I admired his physical prowess; nor could I on the other hand accept the notion that Graduation was merely the end of a dialectical process. But in any case, I felt bound to remark, Croaker was not altogether devoid of reason, however imperfectly he employed it, nor was Dr. Eierkopf absolutely without emotion or appetite. Even as I spoke, tears flowed freely from his lashless eyes, a surprising sight, which he acknowledged as support of my observation.

"So maybe I'm not myself Commenced yet," he admitted. "But what else can Commencement be? You want spooks and spirits? Bah, George Goat-Boy! We look with our microscopes and telescopes, and what do we see? Order! Number! Energies and elements! Where's any Founder or Grand Tutor?" He tapped his gleaming skull. "In here, no place else. And in Tower Hall basement. That's all there is!"

I rose from the cot, where I'd been sitting with my coffee, and politely shook my head.

"*I'm* the Grand Tutor, sir. I'm going to ask Max and Dr. Sear about this GILES business as soon as I get through Scrapegoat Grate. But GILES or no GILES, I'm the Grand Tutor."

"I like you, Goat-Boy!" Eierkopf cried. "But how can you say such a thing?"

I admitted that I couldn't explain myself, and even that I had as yet no clear conception of what Graduation was; I acknowledged further that my conviction as to my Grand-Tutorhood was not unremitting—that I was subject to lapses of confidence and moments of bad faith, as well as errors of judgment and waverings of policy, just as Anchisides, Laertides, and for all I knew Enos Enoch had been. Yet it was persistent and prevailing, this conviction. I *was* the Grand Tutor, as surely as I was George the Goat-Boy! I had no ax to grind; I craved neither fame nor deference except in poor moments; I had come from the goat-barns to Pass All Fail All and would most surely do so, whatever that injunction might turn out to mean.

"And I promise you this, sir," I declared, stirred by my own rhetoric; "if it ends up being that Commencement is a miracle, then keep your night-glass and day-glass on me, and you'll see a miracle one day with your own eyes. Don't ask me how I know!"

Those same eyes squinted at me now behind their lenses, and either he shook his head or it dandled of its own accord.

"What a fellow you are!" he said—more pitying than awed. "Everybody has his weaknesses, and you know you can make me think of mine by speaking of yours, not so? So I don't believe in hocus-pocus, any more than Max Spielman did before he got senile. But what do I do in weak moments? *I try to take nature by surprise!* I try to catch her napping once!" He laughed at his own folly, which it nevertheless plainly excited him to confess. He would sometimes stare at the furniture of his observatory for hours on end, he declared, at the familiar books and instruments in their accustomed places, and contemplate the inexorable laws of nature that held them fast, determined their appearance and relations, and governed his perception of them. And he would find himself first fretting that the brown pencil-jar on his desk, for example, could not suddenly turn green, or stir of its own inexplicable volition; from a fret that such wonders could not be, he would come to a wish that just once they might, thence to a vain and gruntsome willing that they be—as if by concentration he could bring the miracle to pass. And this coming naturally to nothing, he would lapse at last into a melancholy of several days' duration, after which, as a rule, he was fit to take up once more the orderly business of his life.

I glanced uneasily at the clock.

"Who wants to see the Founder, or the Founder's son?" Eierkopf exclaimed. "No! But what if some little messenger-spook should drop once out of the sky—not to bring you a personal message, but maybe just to ask directions . . . Or what if you discovered even his footprint in the grass, where he'd lit for a moment? Less than that, even!" He indicated the shelves of the room with a roll of his eyes. "Just to see a *sign* once, that things were thinking their own thoughts. A little voice in the air, *ja?* One little leaf to move the wrong way all by itself, that's all it would take; I'd know right away . . . But *bah!*" He waved away such speculation. "I got to get ready for the eclipse. Croaker shows you where to go."

There was indeed little time; but when I'd thanked him for his hospitality and frankness, and expressed my hope that we might see each other another time under less upsetting circumstances, I couldn't resist asking him what exactly it was he'd "know right away" if, to use his expression, he should once catch nature napping.

"Forget I said it," he replied, as gruffly as his piping voice permitted. "There aren't any mysteries; just ignorance. When something looks miraculous it's because we're using the wrong lenses. *Ja,* that reminds me . . ." He said something in another language to Croaker, who, smiling grandly, brought me my stick. At various places along its length now had been affixed little lenses, concave and convex, mounted in shiny steel rims that swung on pivots. Moreover, the stick had been cleverly drilled through from tip to tip, and slotted transversely in such a fasion that certain of the lenses could be swung down into the bore.

"A little matriculation-gift to go with Croaker's" Eierkopf said. "Mirrors and lenses are my favorite things." He showed me, when I'd thanked him for the gift, how by selecting the proper lenses and sighting through one end or the other, I could use my stick as either a telescope or a microscope, and make fire with it as well.

"Look all around the University," he advised me. "You'll see stars and planets you didn't know about, and girls undressing and doing things with their boyfriends. You'll see your blood cells and your crablice and your spermatozoa. Some things that look alike you'll see to be different, and some you thought were different will turn out to be the same. But you can look from now until the end of terms, and you won't see anything but the natural University. It's all there is."

I thanked him again most sincerely, quite touched by his generosity despite my reservations about his opinions, and promised to apologize, once I'd verified his impotency-claim with Dr. Sear, for accusing him in the Virginia Hector affair. Then I set my silver watch and begged his leave to go on Croaker's shoulders to the Main-Gate Turnstile. He could not so far oblige me, he begged pardon, as he needed Croaker to adjust the astronomical apparatus and perform sundry other chores before the eclipse. But the Gate was neither distant nor difficult to find, he assured me—a ten-minute trot on Croaker: at most a twenty-minute limp for me; there was ample time to get there before sunrise. He bid me *auf wiedersehen* and promised he'd watch on his telescreens the Trial-by-Turnstile ceremony; if I should contrive to pass through the Turnstile and Scrapegoat Grate—a feat never before managed outside of legend, and to all appearances physically impossible—my claim to Grand Tutorhood would warrant more systematic and detailed refutation; until then, I had his good wishes but by no means his credence. I smiled and shrugged my shoulders, whereat, almost crossly, Eierkopf said goodbye, turned on his stool, and peered into his night-glass. Croaker led me downstairs to set me on the right road. As the Observatory door opened automatically, Dr. Eierkopf's voice piped from a speaking-tube on the jamb.

"Listen here, Goat-Boy," he said crisply. "A bulletin just comes in that Harold Bray will enter WESCAC's Belly and change its AIM. Can you hear? But he must have something up his sleeve, because Chancellor Rexford has officially recognized him as Grand Tutor to New Tammany College, on the strength of his pledge. The Military Science Department would never allow that if he meant to disarm the EAT-system."

My heart constricted.

"You know what this means, Goat-Boy?" Eierkopf went on. "It means he's automatically in charge of Admissions to Candidacy. He'll oversee the Trial-by-Turnstile this morning. You won't succeed, my friend!"

I put my mouth to the brass tube and replied, "Keep your eyes open, and you'll see." But I felt less confident by half. The air was fresh, the sky moonless now and just lightening, the grass drenched. Croaker pointed out across the dark lawn, grunted something, tapped my stick, and squinted through thumb and forefinger as through a glass. I aimed the stick where he directed and tried several combinations of lenses, but saw nothing. Then I tried another, and darkly before my eye a distant building wobbled, around whose corner a procession of cyclists and pedestrians turned out of sight.

"That way to Main Gate? Behind that building?"

But when I looked from the lens I found Croaker gone and the door shut, both without a sound. Gooseflesh pricked my forearms; I legged off through the dew no comfortabler for knowing that a night-glass surely watched me go. Did another, less hospitable, see me coming?

6.

A motorcycle snorted behind me, and I was hailed: Peter Greene, on our borrowed vehicle, mounted up behind its owner, who throttled down and grinned through his beard at me in the dim light.

"*Told* you it was a goat-boy!" Greene said triumphantly to him. "And me only one eye!"

"Flunk me for not recognizing an old friend!" Stoker laughed. He offered his hand, which I shook before recalling that I did not consider him a friend. "Pity you left so early the other night," he said easily. "Spoiled the party for Stacey. She sends her love."

"By George, that's a gal, that Stacey!" Greene cried reverently. "I swear if she ain't!"

I walked on. Stoker idled the machine alongside. "Last night was the *real* party," he said. "Randy-Thursday affair. Could've used your act. Oh, say—" He touched my arm; I drew away. "Too bad about Max. I'll have to prosecute, of course, but it *is* awkward that my man turned out to be Herman Hermann."

I clenched my teeth at this confirmation of my suspicions. "Max didn't do it."

Greene applauded. "Attaboy!" His manner—and Stoker's too, who seconded his approval of my pronouncement—said that I did admirably to stand by my friend, who however was most certainly guilty as charged.

"No question!" Stoker scoffed. "Herm was my aide, you know—the rascal I sent to catch up with Max the night of your visit." He'd been aware, he said, that the man was an ex-Bonifacist—no doubt others of his staff were also; he didn't know or care about their ID-cards or histories as long as they did their work—but he'd not known it was Herman Hermann himself whom he'd dispatched to "take care of" my advisor, or he'd not have risked so valuable a man. I set my lips. Stoker's declared opinion was that Hermann had overtaken Max along the road and that my advisor had recognized and killed him; whether in a spirit of revenge for the exterminated Moishians or in self-defense remained to be established.

"Could of been an argument and then a scuffle," Greene offered. "Seen it happen a dozen times, fellows get to squabbling." His tone, I noted, was deprecatory and pacific: obviously he was on cordial terms with Stoker and wished to mollify my hostility.

"Max would never fight," I said. "Not even to defend himself. I know."

Stoker chuckled. "Oh, you know, do you?" He pointed out then in an amiably serious way that he too was surprised at Max's breach of his avowed principles, though he'd assumed all along that the Moishians were as capable of flunkèdness as any other group in studentdom, given the opportunity. "But really, George, you mustn't believe *I'm* behind this—as I understand you told Sear and the chap at the sub-station desk." Max, he reminded me, had turned himself in after the news bulletin, and freely confessed to shooting Hermann. " 'Overcome by vengefulness,' he said he was, as soon as he realized who the man was. Most normal human thing he ever did, I told him myself! Now, of course, he's gone Moishian again—says he wants to pay his debt to studentdom, all that rot."

"They'll never convict him," Greene said stoutly. "Begging Mr. Stoker's pardon, the man's a hero if you ask me."

Stoker grinned. I vowed I would believe nothing except from Max's own lips. But the story of his surrender and confession did not strike me as being so fantastic as I could have wished; it squared uncomfortingly with his late remarks about the Bonifacists being outside the pale of charity, and about implacable, irrational varieties of flunkèdness which must be neither accommodated to nor forgiven.

"Let's run over to Main Detention and see him now," Stoker proposed.

Greene reminded him that it was getting on to Trial-by-Turnstile time; we must all make haste if he and I were not to be late for Registration and Stoker for his ceremonial role of Dean o' Flunks.

"I'll drop you off," Stoker answered him pleasantly. "But I'm sure George is more concerned with his keeper's trouble than with his own little ambitions. Especially now the Grand-Tutor thing's all settled."

The taunt stung me to reply, more heatedly than I intended, that nothing was settled by the theatrical advent of the person called Harold Bray, who, whatever his spurious official-backing, was a patent fraud, as I meant to prove in due course. And I added that eager as I was to confer with Max—both on the matter of his arrest and on certain other subjects—I had his own word for it that it was imperative for me to matriculate on time. I checked my watch: Tower Clock should chime five-thirty any moment. Hobbling faster I declared my suspicion that our encounter was in fact probably not coincidental, but part of a scheme to prevent or delay my registration, and I warned Stoker not to attempt to stay me, as I did not share Max's commitment to non-violence.

"You needn't tell me!" Stoker laughed. "I've heard what you can do with that stock of yours when somebody gets in your way!" Then, as if to atone for that unhappy allusion (how he'd heard of Redfearn's Tommy's death I couldn't imagine) and at the same time to give proof of his goodwill, he bade me climb up behind Peter Greene and be transported post-haste to Main Gate. Full of suspicion, I nonetheless agreed, choosing the possibility of kidnaping over the certainty of being late if I continued on foot to a place I'd yet to locate. I straddled the rear fender and we sped off, Stoker explaining at the top of his lungs that the vehicle we rode was the same we'd found ditched the day before, and was in fact the one Herman Hermann had set out upon from the Powerhouse. He had already thanked Greene for salvaging it, he said, and now he thanked me also. I was not to worry about discarding the sidecar, removing evidence from the scene of a capital crime, and using a vehicle without license or authorization, all which misdemeanors he could charge me with if he chose to, along with imposture; he was pleased enough to have the motorcycle back, especially as it was now unmistakably linked with Max's movements just after the murder. Already he had given Greene certain modest tokens of his gratitude, which it was his desire I should share.

"Ain't he the durnedest?" Greene demanded with a shake of his head. "Look here what he give me to split with you, just for a joke." From his coat pocket he withdrew four small black cylinders and pressed two of them into my hand. "Flashlight batteries!" He laughed, blinked, and exclaimed as at some splendid piece of foolery.

"What was I supposed to give you?" Stoker shouted over his shoulder. "You've got everything already, and Grand Tutors don't need anything. There's about two million more where they came from."

"You are the durnedest," Greene declared, and flung his batteries, to Stoker's delight, at early pigeons purring upon a seated statue of some former chancellor. I might have discarded mine also, as I had no conception of their use and wanted anyhow no beneficences from Maurice Stoker; but even as the ruffled pigeons flapped we rounded that corner I'd spied through my lenses and entered the square before Main Gate—a place of such unexpected throng and pageant, I forgot that my hand clutched anything. Floodlit in the paling twilight, thousands of young men and women filled the square. Many were seated in temporary grandstands erected during the night, which flanked a broad central aisle leading straight to the Turnstile; others milled freely about, some riding pick-a-back for a better view; a bright-uniformed band played martial airs; a double row of policemen kept the aisle clear.

Stoker paused smiling at the edge of the square. "Look here, George, Bray's down in WESCAC's Belly this minute, so that takes care of that. Hadn't you better go see Max?"

The news shocked me until I realized that I needn't believe it. Even if it were true, as Greene now assured me, that Bray had disappeared at 3 A.M. from the Randy-Thursday festivities at Founder's Hill (where he'd gone in triumph with the host of his "Tutees"), declaring his intention to descend into WESCAC's Belly before dawn; even if it were true that subsequent bulletins from Tower Hall, allegedly read out by WESCAC, confirmed that he'd successfully entered that dread place, even if it were true that Chancellor Rexford had in consequence proclaimed him official Grand Tutor to New Tammany College and named him to preside over the Trial-by-Turnstile—it could be all an elaborate hoax, a political stratagem to turn the Grand-Tutorship into an agency of the Quiet Riot, or to forestall the necessarily revolutionary consequences of a genuine Grand Tutor's appearance. On the other hand, perhaps he really *had* entered the Belly, in which case he must be EATen alive, and that was that.

"*I'm* the Grand Tutor," I told Stoker, and noted crossly that in his company I seemed always defensive, overambitious, and foolish.

"Well, now," Greene said—his expression so fatuous it

made me hot with impatience—"maybe you and Him *both* is Grand Tutors."

I wouldn't acknowledge his remark, though I saw Stoker watching with amusement for my reaction. Greene was twice my age, a wealthy and powerful figure to whom, moreover, I was in a small way obliged, yet I found myself almost contemptuous of him this morning, and not knowing quite how, I felt certain that Stoker was responsible. His presence either made me intolerant or actually transformed Greene's otherwise agreeable simplicity into simple-mindedness—as it seemed to turn my own pride into vanity, and had made Anastasia's martyrdom on the beach into something perverse. I strode off without a word towards the far end of the aisle or track, where a bare-chested group of athletes were loosening their muscles for the Trial; Greene called goodbye to Stoker and hurried after me. Sure enough, my irritation was left behind like a patch of nettles, and once out of that mocking influence Greene's ingenuous good nature seemed again more winning than annoying. He clapped his arm about my shoulder and cheerfully flunked himself for "always saying the wrong durn thing." Then with surprising insight he declared that because he had never met a man he didn't like, and himself craved frankly to be liked by everyone he met, he not infrequently made enemies of his friends by making friends of their enemies—as in the case of Bray and myself.

"So I just don't fret," he said. " 'Like it or lump it,' I say to myself: I'm okay, and what the heck anyhow, it don't nothing matter. Ain't that Stoker a dandy, though?"

I smiled and shook my head; one could not stay annoyed with such insouciance. Greene chattered on about his night's adventure: I was wrong to despise Bray, he declared, who when all was said and done was a darned smart cookie, insightwise. He'd held real person-to-person interviews—*in depth,* didn't I know—with numerous of Stoker's guests in the Living Room, and all agreed afterwards, when Bray left for WESCAC's Belly, that *there* was a man who could read the passèd heart of every flunker in the room, and make you feel a little bit brighter than you did before. He, Greene, did not regret for a moment having gone with the crowd to Founder's Hill instead of revisiting the Carnival midway as he'd planned; he felt a campus better for it. Even Dr. Kennard Sear, it seemed, had put by skepticism after his interview and declared that Bray's analytical perceptiveness was extraordinary.

"Then Dr. Sear's isn't," I said. "I'm surprised he couldn't see through him."

Greene chuckled. "Wait'll you have *your* interview! I told Mr. Bray about you being a Grand Tutor and all, and He said He'd be right proud to have a chat with you. He's one in a million, that fellow. Really opened *my* eyes."

I judged it futile to argue. Moreover, Greene's admiration of my rival turned out to be at least partly a mere reflection of his *real* enthusiasm, which now he beamingly confided.

"That Anastasia thinks a lot of you, too, George; I could tell by looking at her! Guess you two are sweet on one another, huh?"

Without mentioning what had passed between us in George's Gorge, Stoker's sidecar, or the Powerhouse Living Room, I declared that I regarded Mrs. Stoker as an uncommonly beautiful human female lady person both physically and otherwise, and was sufficiently impressed by her generous nature to hope that she might be the first I could lead to Commencement Gate, once I'd found it myself. For this reason I naturally thought of her with a particular fondness, as might Max of a prize milch-nanny; as for *love,* however— which I took his expression to mean—I asserted firmly that a Grand Tutor could no more devote himself to certain Tutees and exclude others than could an algebra professor. My responsibility was for studentdom, as I conceived, not for any particular comely students . . .

"Then I might as well say it right out," Greene broke in; "I love that woman fit to bust! A sweeter, purer, prettier girl I never hope to see, and I'm bound and determined I'm going to marry her! Soon's I can see my way clear!"

He blushed happily at my astonishment, but his incredible resolve was proof to objection. The girl was already married to Maurice Stoker, I pointed out. Impossible, Greene replied: he could tell just by looking her square in the eyes that she was as virginal as the pines in his farthest timberlot; he doubted she'd even kissed a man yet.

"Are you joking?" I cried. I hadn't time or heart to rehearse for his edification Anastasia's extraordinary sexual accomplishments; I merely pointed out to him that she wore a wedding-ring, called herself Mrs. Maurice Stoker, and had countered Max's vow to free her from the Powerhouse by declaring that she stopped there of her own will, because her husband needed her.

"Then he's got her hypnotized, or doped," Greene said firmly. "But she's still a maiden girl, I can tell by her eyes; and if the marriage ain't consummated it can be annulled." His mind was made up, he declared: his own marriage he regarded now as having been incipiently kerflooey from the outset, and himself a perfectly okay man whose headaches and other difficulties were the effect of his wife's excessive standards, or something, he did not care what. Though he had seen Anastasia but once, and been unable to speak a word to her, the vision of her stainless beauty as she knelt at the Founder's Shaft encouraged him to wipe clean the troubled slate of his past and start anew—a resolve which Mr. Bray had personally seconded.

"Directly this Registration business is done with," he said, "I'm going straight to Miss Virginia R. Hector and ask for Anastasia's hand in marriage. Now, then!"

I was dumbfounded, the more when he capped his madness with a plea that I go with him to see Anastasia's mother, who he understood was herself somewhat kerflooey, on the subject of Grand Tutors. If I would support his cause with her, he promised, he would use every resource at his command to clear Dr. Spielman of the charge against him.

"It's no more'n Miss Stacey'd want her own self," he said, and added that it was in fact only to intercede with Bray on Max's behalf that Anastasia had attended Stoker's Randy-Thursday party in the first place, an affair not otherwise fit for her maiden presence. But she had moved through the bawdy crowd like a swan across a cesspool, he went on, and anon had knelt so sweetly before the Grand Tutor that he, Greene, had been smitten with love upon the instant. So much so that when he'd seen some fellow "go for her" as she knelt, he'd rushed to protect her from molestation, and a little fist-fight had ensued.

"Young Nikolayan fellow, that I thought was going to lay his durn Founderless hands on her! Had a black patch over one eye to start with, and I blacked the other one for him!" But not, he admitted with a chuckle, before he'd nearly got a shiner himself. Stoker's guards had separated them, lest a varsity incident be made of it; the Nikolayan visitor (whom I believed I remembered seeing through the metal curtain in the Control Room) had been quickly escorted back to his classmates on the other side of the Powerhouse. Anastasia then had retired with Hedwig Sear; Harold Bray went off to fulfill his pledge in WESCAC's Belly; and Peter Greene, provided with aspirins and cold compresses by his host, stayed on to the party's end—but so full of the image of Anastasia, he could scarcely attend the naughty entertainments that climaxed the night. And obliged as he felt to Maurice Stoker for the hospitality and the free ride back to Great Mall, he hoped with my assistance to have the unconsummated match annulled and make Anastasia his virgin bride.

What was one to say? I shook my head sharply, as before a dream or hallucination, thanked him for his offer to assist Max, and agreed at least to accompany him soon to see Virginia R. Hector, the story of whose connection with Max I wished to discuss with her anyhow. This pleased him enough for the moment, and I was able at last to turn my attention— much disconcerted!—to the serious task at hand. Greene's long-winded enthusiasm made me nervous at the passage of time: the boulevard ending at Main Gate ran from it due eastwards straight as a fence-line, but whether any distant elevation would delay the apparent sunrise, as happened in the rolling pastures at home, I couldn't discern. Tower Clock had yet to strike six; it occurred to me that Eblis Eierkopf had mentioned some malfunction in its works. I'd have to rely on my watch to tell me when to try the Turnstile, trusting that the clock in Dr. Eierkopf's Observatory had been correct.

Stoker, evidently popular with the students, I saw now making his way slowly through them towards Main Gate, his siren purring. They cheered and called to him; a pretty girl in white sequins perched herself on his rear fender and donned his helmet; from somewhere he'd got a little loudspeaker, through which now he addressed them.

"Everybody back to bed!" he said to some: "Registration's been postponed till after the eclipse." "Why bother matriculating?" he asked others. "You'll never pass the Finals anyhow." "Big party at the Powerhouse this morning!" he announced generally. "Everybody welcome! We'll get you back in time to register."

These messages and invitations—to which he added warnings of the trials ahead and vague threats of revenge upon any who did well in school—were received by the students with hoots and high-spirited heckling. Greene explained— what I'd been told already—that it was part of the Spring

Registration ritual for someone to take the role of Dean o'
Flunks and pretend to lure people away from all hope of
Graduation; but I was surprised to observe that a considerable
number seemed to take his words seriously. Many forsook
the grandstand and either went off on cycles of their own or
climbed into the sidecars of Stoker's guards, whose vehicles
were stationed all along the aisle. There food of some sort
was provided them, and young men and women boldly made
merry; whether they later registered or actually went with
Stoker to the Powerhouse, I never learned.

We reached the upper end of the track, half a hundred meters from Main Gate. The athletes in their shorts did
push-ups and skipped rope; Greene spoke to them familiarly,
being a fan and patron of varsity athletics. We were approached by their herder or tender, a balding plump official
in a striped shirt with a whistle-lanyard round his neck and
pens and pencils clipped to a clear plastic guard on his breast
pocket. He would shoo us, but him too Greene knew, and
was called *sir* by.

"My pal here and me just want a good view," Greene explained.

"Yes, sir, that's okay. Long's we keep the track clear."

"I didn't come just to watch," I declared. "I'm going
through Scrapegoat Grate."

The official laughed, and looked anxiously at his wristwatch, told the athletes to crouch in single file, alphabetically
ordered; as soon as the sun's rays struck the Turnstile he
would blow his whistle at thirty-second intervals to start
them.

"By George, you really want to try it?" Greene asked me.
When I assured him that I most certainly did, he took up the
notion as a splendid lark and vowed he too in that case would
"have another crack at the old Turnstile," an event in which
(in its rustic version) he'd distinguished himself as a young
forestry-student.

But the official (Murphy was his name) grew red-faced
and loud of chuckle at the proposal. "I'm awful sorry, Mr.
Greene, sir! I'm not authorized to let anybody try that hasn't
qualified!"

Undismayed, Greene took a rolled parchment from his inside coat-pocket. "I reckon there's more'n one way to be qualified." He unrolled it triumphantly for the man to inspect.
"This here's from the Grand Tutor, and says I'm a Candidate

for Graduation. If that don't qualify a fellow, I'm durned if I know what does!"

Much surprised, I examined the document along with Murphy. *Be it by these presents known,* it proclaimed, *that Peter Greene is a bonafide Candidate for Graduation in New Tammany College.* The statement was printed in an archaic type except for the name, which was penned, and a subscribed quotation from the Founder's Scroll: *"Except ye become as a kindergartener, ye shall not pass."* It was dated *March 20,* the previous day, and signed *Harold Bray, G.T.*

"Got it last night at the Powerhouse," Greene said proudly. "Give 'em to a bunch of us His own self, after He'd interviewed us."

The official toyed with his penclips, repeated that he didn't like to say no, admitted that while the situation was unprecedented, the Certificate was undoubtedly authoritative, and at last granted permission for Greene to participate in the Trial-by-Turnstile—making clear, however, that he was not responsible for any trouble the irregularity might cause in Tower Hall.

"How 'bout my pal here?" Greene persisted.

The man regarded my beard and wrapper skeptically and supposed that I too had been Certified by the new Grand Tutor. Before I could articulate the denunciation inspired in me by the sight of my companion's false paper—a problem, since I had no wish to quarrel with him or injure his pride, but felt it important that he be disabused of the illusion of his Candidacy—Greene cried, *"He* don't need no Certification, Murph! He's a Grand Tutor His own self!"

"Aw, Mr. Greene," the man pleaded. He spoke from one corner of his mouth, holding his whistle in the other. "You'll get me fired. I can't let *everybody* run, or we'd never—"

"Hear this." A great loudspeakered voice interrupted him; the crowd grew still, and all eyes turned to Main Gate, its top now gleaming in the sun's first rays. *"The next voice you hear will be your Grand Tutor's."*

"You don't have to beg for me," I whispered to Peter Greene. "I'm going through anyway."

The crowd's applause made reply impossible; with a shock I realized the implication of the announcement: had Bray then come unEATen from the Belly? The official Murphy, relieved by the interruption, wandered off frowning at his watch and the diminishing shadow on Main Gate.

"Dear Tutees," a new voice said, and its familiar clicking roused me now to frankly jealous anger. *"Trial-by-Turnstile will begin in one minute. Please have your ID-cards ready for scanning. Contestants will be admitted at the Left Gate as the Turnstile scans and releases them; all others may enter through either gate as soon as the last contestant is admitted. Proceed then directly to the Gate House Assembly Room for Chancellor Rexford's welcoming address. Remember:* Except ye believe in me, ye shall not pass; *and no one may matriculate without an ID-card. So be it."*

"I got one somewheres," Greene said, slapping his pockets. There was a fishing for cards among the spectators; the crouching athletes held theirs between their teeth. I of course had none, and for the first time that morning began to be daunted by the prospect of Trial-by-Turnstile. How on campus had Bray managed such a fraud—upon WESCAC itself!

"Got the pre-game jitters?" Greene said cheerfully. "Use my slogan, if you want; it ain't copyrighted."

Now drums rolled, and Maurice Stoker, with exaggerated gestures of menace, took up a position before the Turnstile, facing the athletes. The sequined beauty on his motorcycle, evidently the new Miss University, was escorted to a dais near the Left Gate. Stoker's appearance this time was met with good-humored hisses and boos, as he represented the Dean o' Flunks now in his aspect of Opponent rather than Tempter.

"He's in pretty good shape for a fellow his age," Greene said. "But his reflexes won't be too quick." He himself now stripped off jacket, shirt, and undershirt—in order, he explained, both to run and climb the more freely and to offer Stoker as little as possible to grab hold of. For the latter reason the athletes also oiled their skin.

"Best *we* can do's work up a good sweat," he said, and asking me to hold his ID-card, began doing push-ups on the pavement. Me he advised to do the same, but since I thought it inappropriate to remove my wrapper, I saw little point in perspiration. 1 did however accept from him a "pep pill," as he called it, to counter the effect of two restless nights; had I known the black capsules came from the Powerhouse, I'd perhaps have declined. Just as I swallowed, the drums ceased with a crash; Stoker spread his arms and danced threateningly; the whistle blew; and the first athlete dashed with a bleat from the starting line. As he neared the "Dean o'

Flunks" he feinted left, then dashed around him to the right; just as Green had anticipated, Stoker was unable to recover his balance quickly enough to catch him. The crowd applauded, and the athlete nimbly sprang up into the teeth of the Turnstile. In former terms he would then have merely strained with every muscle to turn it—in vain, of course—until the "Dean o' Flunks" pulled him down, whereupon he'd be suitably laureled, kissed by Miss University, and admitted. Today, however, for the first time, the objective was to climb as high as possible up the stationary gate, like a great comb stood on end, through which the spindled teeth of the Turnstile proper passed. The apparatus was some seven meters tall: when the climber had half scaled it, unpursued, it clicked and turned, and he was caught like a twig in a hayrake. The spectators exclaimed—as did I, thinking all was up with him—but then applauded his effort when it became clear that he was unhurt. From a metal arm above him swung down the lensed device which Max had guessed to be a scanner; the pinned athlete turned his teeth to it, still clenching his ID-card, and at once he was released. Thereupon Bray's voice proclaimed from the loudspeakers what traditionally it had been the role of some Founder's-Hall dignitary to say:

"Get thee hence, Dean o' Flunks! Let this man be matriculated!"

Stoker stamped the ground in mock chagrin, the Left Gate rang open, the whistle blew again, and as the first athlete, waving to the crowd, was rewarded by the sequined girl and ushered inside by a gowned official, the second charged down the aisle to a similar fate, making what he took to be goatlike noises. I ticked my batteries nervously together and shifted the shophar-sling to my other shoulder, wondering how I'd be able to climb with a walking-stick in my hand. Impossibly, my watch read only six; yet the sun's edge now was plainly visible behind us and the whole gate fired with light. A third athlete set out. On a sudden dread suspicion I put the watch to my ear—it was silent. I shook it, horrified, and tried the stem: it turned freely. I had neglected to rewind it at the Observatory!

"What time is it?" I cried to Peter Greene. But the third runner had been named Foltz and the next was to be Harvey, so my companion had knelt at the mark to take his turn.

"Later'n you think, I reckon!" he called back, and whinnied away, his irregular costume provoking mirth among the onlookers.

"It's me'll catch heck for this," Murphy complained.

I shouted, "Wait!" and set out after, having noted earlier that *George*—and for that matter, *Goat-Boy*—ought to start before *Greene*. Now there was merriment indeed in the grandstands; my wrapper flopped, the shophar pitched, my watch flew on its lanyard, and as I gimped the lenses clattered on my stick. Murphy blew his whistle again and again at us, mistaking which signal the rest of the athletes sprang forth and pounded behind me. Stoker had poised himself to intercept Greene, but seeing me he changed his mind and crouched to snatch with particular relish.

"Not you, Goat-Boy!"

But as once before in George's Gorge, my stout stick served me. *"I'm okay,"* I said to myself, and with an angry ranuncular trumpet jabbed it at him. He sidestepped grinning and caught the stick's end, but the dodge fetched him squarely in the way of the runner behind me. The pair went sprawling; the crowd roared to its feet and pressed into the aisle, blocking other contestants. I sprinted the last few meters to the Turnstile, in whose lower teeth Greene was already caught.

"I'm okay!" he laughed. "It don't matter anyhow. Misplaced my durn card!"

I saw it lying at his feet and snatched it up for him as the scanner descended. Just as I pressed it into his hand the gadget buzzed, and the great stile turned a few degrees to release him. The crowd and shrill officials pressed in; there was no time to scale the standing teeth; as Greene stepped out I slipped behind into the angle he'd been trapped in. A guard snatched at me, caught hold of the bouncing shophar; I ducked out of its sling and left it in his hands. The Turnstile turned back to catch me just as I reached its axis. I pressed there into the vertex, where a little space was between the shaft and the standing teeth. No one could reach me, but I thought I might be crushed in the machinery, and desperately told myself what the heck anyhow, it didn't nothing matter, so to speak. If I came through and attained that grander Gate, well and good for studentdom! If I passed away then and there, I would be saved one later pain, and the loss was studentdom's, not mine; let them attend their Harold Bray, and all of them fail! I was in short okay.

What happened in fact was that the bald eye of the scanner scanned in vain, the stile moved on, and I was squeezed past the points of the standing teeth, which I cleared so narrowly that one ran into the armhole of my wrapper, another under my amulet-of-Freddie. I was inside then, but caught fast, and twisting to unhook myself managed only to catch my collar on a third tooth. No one could touch me: some laughed, others clapped hands, Peter Greene's voice behind me cried, "By George, He done it, fair and square!" and officials whom I couldn't turn to see fussed about, berating Murphy. Again the scanner dipped to face me; I smiled politely, but had no card to show. The Turnstile clicked and ground on, either to trap the next athlete or to deal with me. Girls squealed; the next row of teeth came through and pressed so hard against my back, I thought I must be sliced like Eblis Eierkopf's hard-boiled eggs. But that foreseam I had started (wrestling with Croaker in George's Gorge) now gave way with a rip from neck to hem, my knit-wool liner with it; the stile jerked on, the thong of my amulet parted, and for the second time those hides as dear to me as my own were sacrificed. Clad now in mine alone I was propelled onto Great Mall and into the arms of two sooty patrolmen who rushed up.

"*Get thee hence, Dean o' Flunks!*" the voice bid from the loudspeakers. "*Let this man be matriculated!*"

Not impossibly he referred to Harvey or some other athlete caught outside as I was caught in; I didn't look back, but seized the chance to demand imperiously of the Gatekeepers (so labeled by their armbands), "Take me to the Chancellor!"

At once they fell to disputing whether I should be fetched off to Main Detention as a gate-crasher or ushered into the Assembly Room as a matriculated student. It was agreed I could not be permitted to stand there indecently exposed, but the crowd beyond the gate grew so uproarious, especially when I turned to retrieve my watch (whose neck-chain too had caught on the Turnstile and been snapped), that the gatekeepers abandoned self-control and scuffled with each other. I saw fit to wave through Main Gate to the crowd as I undid my watch-chain, and they responded enthusiastically, whistling and sailing laurel-wreaths over the gate. Miss University stood openmouthed; when I blew her a kiss, she hid her eyes. My wrapper and amulet I regretfully abandoned as too enmeshed to salvage—indeed, they had so jammed the Turnstile that Trials were ended and both side-gates flung open for general admission, either automatically by WES-

CAC or upon executive order. Too soon off the goat-farm to be abashed by nakedness, I crowned myself with a wreath of laurel, took my watch and stick in hand (alone with the two small batteries, which only now I noticed I still clutched), bowed first to the crowd and then to the grappling Gatekeepers in the dust, and followed a guide-rail rightwards to the nearest door of the Gatehouse. To show my composure as another pair of Stoker's guards approached, I even took a moment to glance at the sun, now fully risen and already eclipse-bitten at its edge. Then I leaned on my stick and once again demanded, before they could speak: "Take me to the Chancellor!"

7.

One growled, "Sure we will."

"No police brutality, Jake," the other cautioned, and said to me more pleasantly as each took an elbow: "We'll *all* see the Chancellor soon, bud. First we got to get some nice clothes on, don't we?"

"I'm okay," I declared. Following Max's advice I reminded them that I had done the unexampled in passing the Trial-by-Turnstile and was therefore a fully matriculated Candidate—not for any paltry Certification of Proficiency but for bonafide Graduation—who ought to be ushered at once into the Chancellor's presence.

"Sure you are," the first guard said. "Wouldn't surprise me if you was the Grand Tutor Himself. Come along nice, there won't be no brutality."

"Fact is," said the other, more cordially, "everybody comes through the Gate has got to be okayed by the Health Office before he registers. Ain't that so, Jake?"

Jake agreed it was, adding that without Dr. Sear's stamp on the Matric Card (as the ID-card was called after formal admission) not even a Harold Bray could schedule coursework in the College. At mention of that former name I consented to go with them—which was just as well, since in any case they propelled me strongly up the Gatehouse steps into a large room striped with desks and tables. Men and women working over card-files stood to nudge one another and stare as we came in.

"That'll be okay," I was saying. "I know Dr. Sear."

Jake nodded gravely. "Figured you might, son." To the on-lookers he cried, "Okay, back to work, folks; this ain't any vaudyville show." And the other guard cleared our way past long tables over which hung signs—LIBERAL ARTS; ENGINEERING; BURSAR: HAVE RECEIPTS READY—to a side-room marked X RAYS. Hustled in without ceremony, I saw Dr. Sear himself turn angrily from a large machine on whose glass face a singular spectacle glowed: the lower torso of a transparent woman, large as life, her bones and organs darkly visible inside her. What's more, she was alive: before our eyes her phalanges toyed with something not far from her pubic symphysis, and her voice continued a rhythmic mur-mur for some seconds after our entry, as if she had been singing to herself.

"Get out of here!" Dr. Sear cried, hurrying towards us. "I'm examining a patient, for Founder's sake!"

The guards apologized but pled the unusual nature of the situation—no more able than I to turn their eyes from the startling screen. The hand and voice there quit now; the pel-vis turned away, and from a curtained stall behind the ma-chine emerged a woman—middle-aged, untransparent—tying a white-cotton gown about her waist.

"Crashed through the Turnstile," the guard not named Jake was explaining. "Some kind of nut. You better handle him . . ."

"Just wait outside!" Dr. Sear said crossly. He frowned at my nakedness as he herded them doorwards, and was too discomposed to return my greeting or even acknowledge yet that he knew me. But the woman's eyes unsquinted now, and crowing, "It's the Goat-Boy, Kennard!" she lurched in my direction. I recognized then the puff-eyed brittle face of Hed-wig Sear, who had so relished mating me with Anastasia in the Living Room.

"Georgie *darling!*" But she stumbled into a chair-arm and thence into its seat, her legs immodestly sprawled; something seemed wrong with her balance. We looked on astonished.

"My wife's having an attack, as you see," Dr. Sear said impatiently. "My nurse isn't here today, and she was preparing herself for treatment. For pity's sake leave this chap here and wait outside!"

The guards apologized and withdrew, promising to stand by in case their help should be required. The one's expression was resolutely sober, but Jake grinned and winked as he closed the door.

"Beasts," Dr. Sear muttered. Yet his composure had quite returned. "What on campus are you up to, George? Get him a gown, Hed." Before I could explain my naked presence he pressed upon me an explanation himself, of the extraordinary scene I'd interrupted. A portable X-ray unit was set up in the Gatehouse at registration-time, he declared, to provide free tuberculosis examinations for any who wished them. Ordinarily Anastasia assisted him, but since her services had been commandeered for the morning by Harold Bray Himself, at the Grateway Exit, Hedwig had volunteered to take her place.

As he spoke, Mrs. Sear toyed with herself shamelessly, humming the while.

"Unhappily, my wife is subject to spells of uncontrolled behavior," he went on to say: "She came here this morning in the condition you see, and I was attempting to calm her by radiation-shock when you interrupted. I trust your discretion."

I assured him he might depend on me not to tell tales out of school. Dr. Sear shook his head. "Treatment didn't work, I'm afraid."

"Balls!" called Hedwig. Not sufficiently conversant with modern literature to have mastered obscene slang, I nonetheless guessed by her tone that she meant the term otherwise than literally; thus I judged it witty of me to pretend to mistake her, and said: "I lost Freddie's in the Turnstile, ma'am."

Whether or not she appreciated the humor, she scrambled at me on all fours like a crippled doe.

"No, now, Hed!" her husband chided. I retreated a step, but Dr. Sear restrained me with a look of whimsical despair.

"Indulge her for a second, would you, old boy? There's a good chap."

I stood nonplussed while the woman knelt before me.

"I wish she'd be less indiscreet," her husband sighed. "But if you don't humor the poor thing's spells she carries on dreadfully." He patted his wife's cropped head with one hand and caressed me frankly with the other. Yet something in the lady's manner left me limp; though I had no particular wish to be unaccommodating, their joint endeavor could not rouse me. After a moment Mrs. Sear remarked, "He needs Stacey," and then gave over the business with a shrug, stood up, straightened her hair, and seemed entirely normal once again. I apologized.

"Quite all right, darling," she said. "Kennard's made me such a wreck I can't even get Croaker excited. I'll get you a gown."

"Really, my dear," her husband protested; but he seemed amused by her remark. "You'll have George thinking we're perverted."

"Hah," said Hedwig. From the curtained booth behind the fluoroscope she fetched a white hospital gown like her own for me to wear until "something more suitable could be arranged."

"You *must* come to dinner," she chattered on; the two of them fussed and patted my gown into place. "I'll be a shepherdess and you'll be a buck, and Kennard can be the jealous shepherd."

"Excuse me?" I could not imagine shepherds in connection with goats; the notion was almost obscene.

"We could have Stacey in, too, and do it *à quatre!*"

Dr. Sear tut-tutted this proposal as extravagant and gently asserted to his wife that it was just such overeagerness on her part that chilled her male companions.

"But look here, George," he added, "we have no secrets from you, and you're obviously a man-of-the-campus, so to speak. It *would* be a lark for Hed and me both if you'd care to stay with us till this business about Max is resolved. You see we're agreeable people; you could live as you please."

I thanked him for his invitation, the hospitality of which was clear, however obscure the promised entertainment. But his mention of Max put me sharply in mind of more pressing business. I requested their address, promising to call on them in any case that same evening or the next to speak of Max's arrest and the GILES program. And I admitted that in fact I had made no arrangement yet for eating and sleeping, nor had any clear idea how such arrangements were made in human studentdom.

"But you must excuse me now," I concluded. "I have to see Chancellor Rexford yet about my Candidacy and then go through Scrapegoat Grate. And I want to have a talk with Anastasia, too, if I can find her."

They expressed their surprise that Max had made no dormitory reservation for me or even provided me with funds, and so I explained very briefly the unusual circumstances of my departure from the goat-farm, adding Max's observation that Grand Tutors and the like never as a rule packed even a sandwich in advance, though their hero-work might want nine years to complete. I had had, for example, no ID-card, yet I'd got through the Turnstile all the same, and was confident I'd find a way through Scrapegoat Grate.

"Think not of next period . . ." Dr. Sear marveled. "I was telling Bray last night at Stoker's what an extraordinary chap you are, and what a really miraculous string of coincidences your life has been. Look here—" He glanced at his watch. "You've a good half-hour yet till Rexford's address; they've got all the regular admissions to process, and the Assembly-Before-the-Grate is just across the way from here . . . Have you an advisor?"

When I told him I had not, since Max's false arrest, he volunteered to fill the role himself, declaring that although he could not share my antagonism for Harold Bray, he respected the grounds of my own claim to Grand-Tutorhood, admired me personally, and would be pleased to assist me through the tedious ordeal of registration.

Mrs. Sear, who was lighting a cigarette, remarked, "He wants to blow you, too."

"Really, Hed."

I begged their pardon.

"We all want to, dear," she said, shrugging at one or the other of us. "Novelty's our cup of tea. Isn't it, Kennard?"

Dr. Sear smiled. "You'll give George the wrong impression."

The woman pinched my cheek. "Georgie's no dunce. He knows what was going on when he came in." Her husband, she declared, had long since lost his taste for ordinary coupling, whether conjugal or extra-curricular, and even for such common perversions as sodomy and flagellation. Watching others still amused him, but only when the spectacle was out of the ordinary, as in Stoker's Living Room; she herself, since she'd lost both novelty and youth, could interest him only by masturbating before the fluoroscope.

"That's very curious," I said. "Do you enjoy it, too?"

Dr. Sear had seemed bored by her recital, but here he laughed aloud. "There you are, Hed! She claims I've corrupted her, George, but she's as tired as I am of the usual tricks. You put your finger right on it."

"I wish he would," said Hedwig. She was bored with sophistication, she maintained, and yearned to be climbed in the exordinary way by a simple brute like Croaker; but catering to her husband's pleasures had so defeminized her that her effect on men was anaphrodisiac, as I had seen.

"Hedwig exaggerates," her husband said patiently. "It's true we've done everything in the book, but nobody forced her. She likes women and won't admit it."

I could have wished to hear more on this remarkable head; also perhaps to question Croaker's alleged simplicity, which his art-work on my stick belied, and compare Dr. Sear's optical pleasures with those of Eblis Eierkopf, to learn how prevalent such tastes were among well-educated humans. But it seemed more important to get back to my advising, and when I reverted to that matter, Mrs. Sear changed her tone completely. I could not do better, she declared seriously, than to have Kennard Sear for my advisor, as he was the most knowledgeable man on campus; in fact, he knew all the Answers, despite his perversions.

"Not *despite,* my dear: *because of.* George understands the tragic view."

They kissed most cordially. The mixture of affections in the Sears' marriage relation I found quite as curious as their amatory whimsies, since life in the goat-barn had left me open-minded in that latter regard. But their goodwill towards me was evident. Gratefully I put myself into their charge, stipulating only that in view of the urgent work at hand we forgo any further embraces—*à deux, trois,* or *quatre,* on-screen or off—for the present.

"I quite agree," the doctor said. The important thing, in his opinion, was for me to by-pass the ordinary machinery of registration and deal only with the highest authorities; otherwise—since Bray's advent had put the campus into such confusion, and my status in the College was irregular—I might be dismissed to the goat-barn by any minor official on some such technicality as my lack of a surname. "You've got through the Turnstile somehow; we can use that as grounds for admitting you as a Special Student, if Tower Hall authorizes it. I'll give Rexford's wife a call: she's a patient of mine. Meanwhile I'll look you over and write you a Clean Bill of Health; maybe that'll do instead of an ID-card to get you through registration."

"Why don't I go see Bray in the Grateway Exit?" Mrs. Sear asked him. "He might intercede for George with Rexford. He could even register him himself, I'll bet."

"You want to see Stacey again," Dr. Sear teased. But they obviously enjoyed planning my strategy together.

"And you can hardly wait to see George's insides," she retorted. Then they both laughed and agreed that the idea was a good one. To my objection that Bray was a false Tutor from whom I wanted no assistance even if he wished to provide it (which struck me as unlikely), Dr. Sear answered, "False or not, he's in a strong position and he's awfully acute, and it's part of his stance to affirm people who deny him. Last night at Stoker's I told him that I'd never pass the Finals because I know too much to answer simple questions, and the rascal Certified me with a line from the Founder's Scroll: *Be ye nothing ignorant, saith the Founder.* Then I told him very frankly that I had no morals at all in sexual matters, and he quoted Enos Enoch: *Who knoweth not Truth's backside, how shall he pass?* Awfully clever chap!"

As he spoke, Mrs. Sear left by a back door on her errand. "Poor thing," he said after her, "she really *is* a simple Home-Ec. type at heart, and I suppose she's on her way to the Asylum from living with me. But flunk it all, George, it's a big University! How can we understand anything without trying everything? When Harold Bray compared me last night to Gynander, he understood me better than Hed does after fifteen years of marriage."

To turn the subject from my rival I asked, "Do you mean the blind man in the play?" And he answered, "Very clever, George," with a kind of dry sigh, though I'd meant no irony. He proceeded then to examine and to X ray me, and his interest in the childhood injury to my legs gave me occasion to inquire about the GILES-files, whose bearing on the question of Anastasia's paternity I briefly described.

"Why, that's interesting!" he exclaimed. Indeed (as I'd rather hoped) the little mystery so intrigued him that he gave over his heavy-breathed inspection of my sigmoid colon. "I didn't dream they were still quarreling over that old business! Even Stacey's never mentioned it."

The fact was, he declared, he could say confidently that

neither Max nor Eblis Eierkopf was lying; he would have been glad to verify their innocence from the GILES-files if only it had occurred to anyone to ask, or to him that the dispute had never been settled.

"All of us who worked under Spielman had half a dozen specialties, you know—he inspired us that way—and I'd already moved on from genetics to psychiatry and anatomy before the Cum Laude scandal broke. I never did have any use for that project; put it out of mind as soon as we'd programmed the GILES, and haven't really thought of it since. GILES indeed!"

His objections to the Cum Laude Project had been theoretical and practical, rather than moral: he'd thought Eierkopf's sampling inherently biased by the fact that androgynous Grand Tutors like Gynander were by definition sterile, and anyhow he doubted WESCAC's ability to manufacture and employ a GILES even when they'd supplied it with the seminal factors called for in the program. He confessed however to having been titillated by the prospect, and had gone so far as to volunteer Hedwig as receiver of the GILES, on condition he be allowed to watch—an offer vetoed by WESCAC.

"In any case I remember the results with Max and Eblis when we collected all the samples, because it seemed to me they proved my point: two utter geniuses, whatever else you might think of them, but Spielman was sterile from his accident, and Eierkopf was so impotent he couldn't even give me a specimen. So if there really was a GILES, as Eblis claims, and if Virginia Hector really received it, as you say *she* claims, then it didn't work. Much as I love dear Stacey, she's no Grand Tutor. I'll put her straight about Max."

I had it in mind then to ask whether he knew anything of my own discovery in the tapelift. But our conversation was interrupted by the guards outside the door, who called in to ask whether all was well, and should they fetch me to Main Detention or the Infirmary.

Dr. Sear frowned at the door-latch. "Just a moment, please." As we wondered what to do, his wife slipped quietly in from the rear exit.

"Should I go out that way?" I whispered.

Dr. Sear shook his head. "Is Bray with us?" he asked Mrs. Sear. "Don't pound so!" he called to the patrolmen.

Mrs. Sear's expression was doubtful. "Bray says he won't tolerate pretenders . . ."

"I won't either!" I declared.

"Stacey's doing all she can," Mrs. Sear went on. "But Bray says it's Scrapegoat Grate and WESCAC's Belly or out."

"Oh dear," her husband sighed. But I insisted that those terms, while I did not acknowledge Bray's authority to make them, were no more than my own intention, and that in fact I meant to demand that Mr. Bray accompany *me* into the Belly, for I had no faith whatever in his claim to have been there. We should see then who got EATen and who did not.

Dr. Sear shook his head, but had no time to argue.

"Let's have him now, Doc," the guards called, more sternly. "We got assembly-duty."

Then the doctor's face brightened, and he undid the latch. "Certainly, gentlemen." The guards came in, looked first at the fluoroscope screen, then at Mrs. Sear, and only finally at me.

"Mr. George forgives your misunderstanding," Dr. Sear said smoothly, "but it really would be pleasanter all around if you apologized." I was, he declared, no Gate-crasher at all, but the man of the hour, the first in modern history who legitimately had passed the Trial-by-Turnstile!

"Legitimately?" Jake asked.

"Of course legitimately." It was an unhappy symptom of studentdom's malaise, he said, that Heroes were arrested for disturbing the peace; however, he believed I harbored no grudge, and would overlook the insult if they'd take me at once to the Assembly-Before-the-Grate. I listened astonished, but had presence enough of mind to keep a neutral expression.

"He's already sent word to Maurice Stoker that you're not to be punished," Mrs. Sear put in. "If I'd had *my* way you'd be locked up yourselves, the way you barged in here."

The pair had been looking skeptical, though clearly impressed. But when I assured Mrs. Sear that they'd only been being overzealous in performance of their duties, Jake scowled and nodded, and the other removed his cap.

"Come along," I told them. "I want a seat near the Chancellor."

"The Grand Tutor says He'll meet you at the Grateway Exit after the address," Mrs. Sear said. "Kennard's going there now with your Clean Bill of Health."

"That won't be necessary."

"No bother at all," said Dr. Sear." I'm very honored to have met a potential Candidate for the Real Thing. Which reminds me—" He took from a nearby desk drawer a small round mirror mounted on a spring-clip. "It's customary to give a little gift on matriculation-day; something to represent what we wish for the new Candidate. Will you take this?"

I thanked him politely and inquired whether I was correct in believing it to be a mirror.

"Yes. May I clip it on your stick? One side's concave and the other convex, but that's neither here nor there." As he clipped the mirror down near the point of my stick, his manner grew serious. "As you know, George, I think that Knowledge of the University, no matter what it costs, is the only Commencement we can hope for. Even if the price is flunking, which it is. When you look at this mirror I hope you'll remember that there's always another way of seeing things: that's the beginning of wisdom."

I thanked him again, quite touched, and sighted down the stick-shaft to try my new token. All I saw, actually, was the magnified reflection of my eye—perhaps because one of Dr. Eierkopf's lenses was loose on its pivot and swung into my line of vision—but I understood the point.

"You can look up co-eds' dresses with it, too," Mrs. Sear observed. "That's what *we* do."

"Really, Hed!"

I promised I would call on them that evening, if I could. The guards chuckled respectfully, quite unsuspicious now, and thanking me for not reporting them, escorted me through the tabled Registration Room to a large auditorium, the Assembly-Before-the-Grate. It was filled with spring registrants, who called and whistled as I went down the aisle in my hospital garment. Whenever a guard looked doubtfully at us my escorts shrugged; we were not challenged. I chose a seat on the front row with the unsuccessful athletes and turned to wave modestly at my admirers. Two young men with press-cards on their lapels approached, but before I learned what they wanted the houselights dimmed, the rostrum was spotlit, and a young man sprang to the microphones to say: "Ladies and gentlemen: the Chancellor of New Tammany College!"

A brass band in the rear of the hall struck up a lively march; the assemblage clapped and stamped their feet enthusiastically, even paraded in the aisles; hats of indifferently flavored straw sailed ceilingwards, also tasty paper streamers of which I made a second breakfast as I watched. From nowhere banners and placards appeared, whereon, above the slogan WE LOVE LUCKY, was represented the smiling face of a handsome though beardless young man, the same I'd seen on the wall of the Control Room. His teeth were excellent; twinkling crow's-feet at his eyes belied the responsible furrow of his brow, and a forelock of his bright fair hair would not be ruled but must dangle front, in groomed independence of its fellows. A spotlight fastened upon the side-curtains of the stage, and the placard-man strode in, attended by aides and guards. His build was not unlike my own, short and springy, but his hair and skin were fairer and his eyes bright blue. His assistants, I observed, were youthful-appearing also and given to forelocks, but their coats were dark, whereas the Chancellor's was fine light linen.

A young woman behind me cried to her neighbor, "Isn't he a *doll?*" Another could say nothing, but squealed like a shoat. Though his administration was not new, and its record of accomplishment not extraordinary (so Max had told me, whose admiration for the Chancellor was sternly qualified), Lucius Rexford was clearly adored by young undergraduates. He lifted his hand slightly and a little stiffly to acknowledge the tumult, as if it embarrassed him; but his eyes were merry, even mischievous, and when a group of co-eds pressed between Stoker's guards to shower roses in his path, he grinned, stepped out of his way to pick up a white boutonniere, and shook several hands over the footlights while his attendants fidgeted. In vain their waves for silence when he reached the rostrum; only the playing of NTC's Varsity Anthem brought order to the hall:

> *Dear old New Tammany,*
> *The University*
> > *On thee depends.*
>
> *Teach us thy Answers bright;*
> *Lead us from flunkèd Night;*
> *Commence us to the Light*
> > *When our School-Term ends!*

As we stood in the ringing echo of this plea a dark-frocked

dignitary raised both hands: everyone present (excepting myself, who was ignorant of the rite, and some turbaned chaps in the Visitors' Gallery) closed his eyes, pressed fingertips to temples, and recited with the dignitary the traditional *Grand Tutor's Petition* from the New Syllabus:

> *Our Founder, Who art omniscient,*
> *Commencèd be Thy name.*
> *Thy College come; Thy Assignments done*
> *On Campus as beyond the Gate.*
> *Give us this term Thy termly word.*
> *And excuse us our cribbing,*
> *As we excuse classmates who crib from us.*
> *Lead us not into procrastination,*
> *But deliver us from error:*
> *For Thine is the rank, tenure, and seniority, for ever.*
> *So pass us.*

As heads were raised and the registrants took their seats, Chancellor Rexford grinned and said into the microphones, "Let's have a little light on my subjects!" In the applause that greeted this request, the houselights came on and someone said cynically into my ear, "That's a slogan from the last elections." It was Stoker, accompanied once more by Peter Greene. The sight of them annoyed me; I had too much on my mind to put up with Stoker's teasing and Greene's peculiar childishness. But the late Dean o' Flunks returned my shophar and dismissed the two guards, for which favors I was grateful enough, and Greene whispered congratulations on my passage through the Turnstile.

"Now we get the lights," Stoker predicted. "My brother's a nut on this *light* business." And indeed, the Chancellor's next words were that matriculation-gifts from Mrs. Rexford and himself would be distributed among us while he made a few preliminary announcements. I found his manner engaging: the exuberant youthfulness that in Peter Greene took a sometimes irritating form, Lucky Rexford combined with apparent good breeding and self-discipline; his speech, dress, and demeanor were restrained; the responsibilities of his office he seemed to address as he addressed us: seriously, but with grace, wit, and gusto. Forelocked aides now nimbly moved up the aisles with pasteboard cartons from which they handed out small silver pocket-torches. Others moved discreetly to the rostrum from time to time to lay message-papers beside the Chancellor's notes. The room grew silent (except for the clicking of flashlight-switches) and expectant, for it was Lucius Rexford's custom to preface his speeches with often surprising announcements.

He leafed through the bulletins, selected one, and said: "I'm sorry to report that the Department of Military Science has been told by WESCAC that a new series of EAT-tests was initiated in Nikolay College last night." A stir went through the room. "In view of this news," the Chancellor said briskly, "I've authorized the Military Science Department on WESCAC's advice to proceed with our ANTEATer test series, which you recall was suspended provisionally three terms ago, when the Boundary Conference convened. We've also made a formal protest to the Board of Directors of Nikolay College, and I'll address the University Council in a day or so on this and related matters." He smiled grimly and took up a different paper. "While I'm at it, here's some more bad news: WESCAC reports that two more NTC Power-Line Inspectors were EATen just before dawn this morning, in the neutral strip between the East- and West-Campus power cables. This is a clear violation of the Boundary-Conference ground rules established last semester, and I've ordered our riot-research programmers to ask WESCAC whether or not NTC should withdraw from the Conference. I'll make the full text of the reply public as soon as it's read out."

The audience murmured angrily. Greene pounded his fist on the chairarm. "*Doggone* those Nikolayans! We ought to EAT the whole durn crowd!"

He spoke loudly enough for Rexford to hear, who smiled in our direction until he caught sight of Maurice Stoker. Then his eyes dropped quickly to his lecture-notes, and he seemed to redden slightly.

"Mr. Greene's not the only one who's been turned into an EATnik by this sort of thing," he declared. His use of the popular slang-term for believers in "preventive riot" drew laughter from the crowd. "We all get tired of being patient and responsible," he said. "It's very tempting to turn our backs on moderation and call for radical measures . . ." He gave Stoker a sharp look. "And there's always someone ready to take advantage of our impulses in that direction, unfortunately."

The rest of his remark on this head I missed, for the flashlight-man had reached our row, and I must examine my gift. I moved the switch to *ON*, but nothing happened. None of the others lit, either, I observed. Peter Greene shook his at his ear and said, "Shucks, they didn't put no batteries in! Why'd I throw mine away?"

Stoker grinned. "Next time don't be so wasteful."

Greene then kindly installed my batteries for me, and in the process noticed for the first time the new mirror on my stick, which so upset him that he had to excuse himself and take another seat.,

"What a prize!" Stoker marveled after him. "Did I tell you he thinks Stacey's a virgin, and wants to marry her? He actually had a fight last night with a Nikolayan chap, over her *honor!*" He shook his head as if in awe—all his attitudes were *as if,* for that matter: one sensed their calculatedness and wondered uneasily what his real motives might be. "My brother has blind spots, too, but at least he's not demented."

I might have protested both his abuse of Greene and his claim to kinship with Lucius Rexford, which seemed preposterous now I'd seen the pair of them; but I was clearly being baited, and wanted moreover not to miss what the Chancellor was saying.

"So many extraordinary things have happened in the last twenty-four hours," Rexford said, reading from his notes now, "that we can scarcely begin to assimilate them as facts, much less see clearly what they imply. Yesterday, for instance, many people were complaining that only a new Grand Tutor could solve the great problems that the Free Campus faces . . ." He favored me with a brilliant smile. "Today, by my count, we have at least two full-fledged Grand Tutors in New Tammany, and a Candidate for a third." Many eyes turned to me, but their amusement, in the spirit of the Chancellor's, was friendly, and though it turned out he meant I was the Candidate, and Bray and The Living Sakhyan the full-fledged Tutors, I could not resent his misunderstanding.

"Frankly, I find this a happy state of affairs," he went on, "and I'm sure we can work out some cooperative arrangement with these gentlemen to everyone's benefit."

Stoker whispered loudly to me, "He could work out a cooperative arrangement between Enos Enoch and the Dean o' Flunks." People hissed at him to be quiet; apparently they regarded as out of place here the irreverence they'd been amused by before Main Gate. But Stoker only farted. Chancellor Rexford went on to express his shock and regret at the unhappy allegations against Dr. Max Spielman, whom he said he'd always regarded as the very image of gentle enlightenment; he assured us that the case would be investigated thoroughly and justice done, and entreated us not to let either liberal sympathy or conservative antipathy tempt us from dispassionate judgment of the evidence as it was brought to light. Finally he announced a new Field-Certification Program outlined by WESCAC for pre-Graduates—which was to say, virtually everyone—as an official alternative to Commencement. It was a step that the College had been reluctant to take thitherto, for while everyone agreed that few people really took the Finals any more, if indeed the Finals existed at all, yet no responsible person wanted to repudiate New Tammany's Moishio-Enochist heritage, which held Graduation to be the aim of campus life. In consequence, though everyone still had officially to aspire to Commencement, there was no agreement on what defined it; no degrees were awarded, nor in fact were any sought. From this somewhat demoralizing impasse (which I must say Rexford himself seemed not terribly distressed by) no practical egress had been found until WESCAC's affirmation of Harold Bray as an authentic Grand Tutor. Now the plan was to make *de jure* what had long been recognized *de facto:* that a Certificate of Proficiency in the Field was all a modern undergraduate need aspire to, or a modern college award. To the Enochist objection that such a policy devaluated Final Examination and true Commencement, it could now be answered that a bonafide Grand Tutor was in residence, whose function it would be to review and authenticate the status of any who presently claimed Candidacy or actual Graduateship, and to act as Examiner of all future Candidates. In addition, having apparently demonstrated already that he could enter WESCAC's Belly and return unEATen, Dr. Bray was to be given Cabinet rank in Tower Hall, with final responsibility for WESCAC's AIM—a move proposed by the computer itself.

Needless to say, I heard these things with heavy heart. To pass the Trial-by-Turnstile, even to penetrate Scrapegoat Grate—these were mere physical stunts, however difficult. But to deal with so suddenly established a pretender, to Pass All and not Fail Anything, when I had no firm notion of what Commencement was, or how to achieve it! Yet my distress became determination—stubbornness at least—under Maurice Stoker's needling.

"Your friend Bray's got the edge on you," he'd whisper, or urge, "Jump up and declare yourself, George, the way Bray did! Eat Lucky's lecture-notes—that'd shut him up." The temptation to do some such spectacular thing was strong, the more since I'd seen Bray's success. And the situation was opportune: Chancellor Rexford's address was doubtless being broadcast everywhere in New Tammany, perhaps all over West Campus, and my success at the Turnstile not only confirmed that I was no Regular Freshman but lent me a certain notoriety which might be made use of before it passed. So keenly did I wish to seize the moment, in fact, that only Stoker's urging me to do so kept me from it—and perhaps a disinclination to follow Bray's pattern. Uncanny, how the man played upon one! No sooner did I shush him than he said, "D'you really think you should sit still just because I tell you to move? That puts you completely in my hands."

"You're not the Dean o' Flunks, you know!" I told him angrily. "You may not even be *flunked* yet. Don't be so proud." I spoke only to spite him, and he laughed so loudly that the Chancellor had to pause in his speech; indeed, Stoker left the hall, laughing, as though at Rexford's announcement that the topics of this morning's address were Brotherhood and Practical Graduation. Yet even when I learned afterwards that this mocking exit, like his performance before the Turnstile, was part of the matriculation ritual (signifying the temporary retreat of the forces of Failure), and that it was only to withdraw at just this point that Stoker had entered the Assembly in the first place, still a redness in his scowl, something shrill in his mock, suggested to me that my words had somehow touched him.

I sat then and listened quietly, but not at all easy, to the address, wondering whether Stoker truly meant to keep me from Grand Tutorhood, and if so, whether out of private flunkèdness or as agent for some cabal, and if the latter, who my real adversaries were, and why. Yet his mocking but confirmed my resolve and thus abetted me indirectly, even as his avowed contempt for Lucky Rexford only increased the latter's popularity, and his claim to be Rexford's brother lent credence to the Chancellor's mild denial of any such relation. Remembering the advice that Dr. Sear had given me, I speculated whether just this effect was Stoker's final intention after all; and if so, was it then benevolent, or ought I to frustrate it by yielding to his temptations? A briar-patch of conjecture! I thought with sympathy of Peter Greene's aversion to mirrors, and to extricate myself repeated that I was okay.

Chancellor Rexford declared, "A favorite maxim of mine is Entelechus's remark that *Graduation is a matter of degree.* I take it to mean that the difference between people like you and me on the one hand and Mr. The Living Sakhyan on the other—perhaps even Enos Enoch—isn't a difference in *kind.*" Lest the good Enochists start picketing the Chancellory, he hastened to add, it should be understood that he was speaking empirically, of things observable, not of revealed Answers. As a busy administrator of a large and powerful college dedicated to the principles of University-wide enlightenment and free research, he thought the dictum attractively combined the best aspects of both aristocratic and democratic institutions: it insisted on the real difference in people's worth—"Let's face it," he smiled; "it's better to be bright, handsome, healthy, and talented than to be stupid, ugly, sick, and incompetent"—while at the same time denying that the gifted were different in kind from their less lucky classmates.

The play on his nickname drew applause from the audience.

"I have enough faith in the Founder," he went on, always smiling, "to believe He'll give me an A for effort even if my notion of Him is all wrong. So I'll tell you frankly that my ideas about Commencement are pretty much the same as old Entelechus's. Graduation, I take it, consists in fulfilling one's Assignment on this campus. Since studentdom by definition is composed of rational animals, it's the Assignment of every one of us to have the best mind in the best body he can manage; and the Graduate must be a *splendid* animal, *excellently* rational. An All-College halfback, say, with a Ph.D.!"

I gathered from the audience's amusement that the remark was meant wittily.

"Actually, I see the typical Graduate as a man about forty years old—young enough to be vigorous, but old enough to be prudent; he's physically, intellectually, and materially at the head of his class, excellently brought up and educated. I see him as neither cowardly nor foolhardy, but firmly courageous; neither meek nor arrogant, but justly proud; an enjoyer of all the good things on campus in proper measure: food, drink, love, sport, friendship, art—even learning itself. In the same way I see him as generous, witty, tolerant, philanthropic, gentle, cheerful, energetic, fair-minded, public-spirited, sagacious, self-controlled, articulate, and responsible—and neither too much nor too little of any of those things! In his youth he served in some branch of the ROTC; in his middle years he helps administer his college or department; his later life he'll devote to research and publication . . ." Everyone was chuckling by this time at the obvious correspondence of the image to the Chancellor himself. Rexford flashed his grin. "I haven't decided yet whether it's absolutely necessary for him to have a riot-wound, a political-science diploma, and a pretty wife. Probably not, if he comes from the right quad and has good connections."

More seriously, he said, while it seemed clear to him that men were quite variously endowed with character as well as goods and intelligence, he firmly believed in equality of opportunity. To be Commencèd, then, was in his view a thing somewhat analogous to being talented or comely: each involved an arbitrary native endowment and the good fortune to have that endowment developed, or at least not spoiled, in one's early youth; but each was also capable of being disciplined and cultivated by its possessor or let go to waste, and became thus a matter of responsibility. Surely it was no student's fault that he matriculated into this campus crippled or ugly; yet it was the winner of the race we applauded, the lovely face we turned to admire, and though we might praise a runner despite his limp, or love a woman despite her uncomeliness, at least we never normally valued them *because* of these defects. Never mind whether things *should* be thus; thus they were. And if it seemed to any of us that he did wrong not to question further these first principles—on which he had constructed his life as well as his administration—he called to our attention those characters in animated Telerama-cartoons who unwittingly walked off cliffs and strode upon the empty air assured and successful—until they looked down, saw what they stood upon, and fell.

Though I was ignorant of the art-form he alluded to, I saw the point of the image and applauded with the others. In truth I'd felt the limitations of his premises, thanks to Max's tutelage: to one like myself—a goat, a gimp, Chance's ward and creature—it was by no means self-evident that my Assignment was to be an athletic intellectual with a handsome face and a charming disposition; or that if it was, Graduation consisted in fulfilling it; or that if it did, fulfillment lay on the middle path between extremes; or that if it so lay, anyone could mark with authority the middle path. But Lucius Rexford was his own best argument, so immediately engaging that my merely logical objections seemed beside the point. If such as he were not Graduates, I reflected, then to be a Graduate was a less happy fate than to be in his fraternity.

"Now I'll leave the Philosophy Department and get to my own," he said, plainly pleased to have been up to the excursion and equally to have it behind him. "Since WESCAC's AIM will be so much in the news this term, I want to talk about my conception of New Tammany's aims, as I see them—especially in the Quiet Riot, which my critics think we're losing." Here his face turned serious: "I believe in light and order, my friends, and in moderation, discipline, harmony, and compromise. Extremism and disorder I conceive to be the enemies of enlightenment, and I despise them—moderately, of course. Now I happen to think it's West Campus's Assignment, and New Tammany's in particular, to make the University such a place that every student in every one of its quads is free to fulfill his own Assignment to the best of his abilities. In fact all men *are* brothers (perhaps I should say roommates; I've never had a brother, but I've had plenty of roommates)—fraternity-brothers, let's say—and they should compete like brothers, in light and order, in spirited but friendly rivalry. NTC will become a Graduate School the day we make that possible."

The same analogy, he maintained when we had done applauding, pertained to the several colleges: the competition of East and West Campus for leadership of the University should be like a championship chess-match between brotherly rivals. Indeed it *was* such a match; what made it fearful, he believed, was not so much the stakes of the game or the awful fact that each side had the weaponry to EAT the other, but the intemperate personality, if he might so put it, of our Student-Unionist brother—the fact that his Answer was not a kind of excellent normalcy and healthy rationality, but something extreme, and counter to student nature: a subordination of means to ends, and of individual Graduations to the Commencement of the Student Body—which was to say, the Student Union. Competing with East Campus was like playing chess with a violent-tempered brother who might shoot you dead to capture your pieces.

To those well-intentioned liberals in the College who advocated "unilateral fasting" (as Max had), Chancellor Rexford objected that it was necessary for a dangerous brother like East Campus to believe that he'd lose in an EATing-match but win in a Quiet Riot, so that he wouldn't be tempted to EAT in desperation, campus suicide, or revenge. "A terrible question, that last one," he remarked, looking up from his prepared text. "Here we are with all this frightful EATing-capacity whose only purpose is to deter Student-Unionist aggression—there's no really workable ANTEATer yet, you know. Now suppose they really *should* press their EAT-button one day—Founder forbid! In five minutes we'd all be destroyed, whatever we do. So tell me, do we press our button then? Do we EAT them out of sheer revenge? The answer, unhappily, is yes—WESCAC's already AIMed to do it, as you know; otherwise there's no deterrent. But how dreadful it is to have to commit oneself to a *policy* of revenge, in order not to have to commit the deed!"

Assuming the deterrent to be effective, the Chancellor saw two grounds for optimism about the outcome of the Quiet Riot: if East Campus should grow more prosperous, it might grow more conservative and moderate; *rapprochement* might become feasible, and real *rapprochement* and exchange of students could gradually wither the objectionable aspects of Student-Unionism itself. Something of the sort could be seen occurring in Nikolay College even presently. On the other hand, if the economic situation in East Campus should grow continually more desperate over the semesters, and EATing-riot could be deterred, then their whole academic complex must crumble. The strategy, in that extremely dangerous situation, would be to encourage them up to the very last minute to believe that there still remained hope of their winning; but of these two possibilities, the Chancellor frankly preferred the former, as the less immoderate and perilous.

"Professor Marcus," he said lightly, "says that time is the enemy of West-Campus Informationalism. But given the ultimate conditions of the Quiet Riot, WESCAC versus EASCAC, this isn't necessarily so." If the future of the University was materially optimistic, he believed, then time was West Campus's friend, the more so since Eastern teaching held it not to be. "It comes to this apparently cynical thing," he asserted: "The basic ills of studentdom have been historically on the Student-Unionist side: hunger, ignorance, physical oppression, and the like. But when the basic needs of the student body are satisfied, its secondary drives are on *our* side, for better or worse: egoism, ambition, and the yen for comfort, as well as the desire for academic freedom and the Graduation of the individual."

I sensed a sharp interest in the room: it was that holders of elected office rarely spoke so candidly and unsentimentally on controversial matters, though I did not of course appreciate this fact at the time. But Rexford's style was to balance conservative action with daring speech: to call all spades but not to play them recklessly, and while never losing sight of the ideal, to come to terms wherever necessary with what he called "the flunkèd realities."

Now he came to what he called the endgame of his imaginary chessmatch: a surprising appraisal of what he saw as the "maximum threat" of Student-Unionism to the West Campus.

"Suppose all my other Answers are incorrect," he said. "Suppose the Quiet Riot remains quiet, but time proves to be the friend of Student-Unionism after all, and the much-heralded Decline of West Campus really comes to pass. Indeed, suppose the worst—" His voice was deadly earnest. "Suppose New Tammany College were utterly to lose the Quiet Riot, and were annexed to East Campus. What would happen?" There was strained laughter here and there in the hall, and some shouted, "No! No!" But Chancellor Rexford declared (in a lighter voice) his belief that after the initial dreadfulness of annexation—bloody proscriptions, military occupation of West Campus, a painful drop in the standard of individual student life in New Tammany, radical reorganizations of curricula and administrative machineries, and so forth—there must come gradually, over the terms, a mutual assimilation of East and West. The "free campus" was too vast to hold forever subject to an alien military-science department; a genuine All-University Administration, however repugnant its initial form, would have been achieved; the staggering military-science budget that presently bled the resources of both East and West would be no longer required. Though several generations of undergraduates would be raised on Student-Unionist ideology, the University literacy-rate would improve, as eventually would academic- and living-standards all over the campus. And as literacy, prosperity, and enlightenment advanced in a truly unified University, there could not but be, Dr. Rexford thought, a rematriculation of West-Campus values: of academic freedom, individual dignity, and the liberty of every student to labor at what he took to be his personal Assignment, in quest of his personal Graduation.

"In short," he concluded, "my view is the opposite of the tragic view. The author of *Taliped Decanus* believes we lose even when we win; that there are only different ways of losing. But I believe we'll win even if we lose!"

Much applause greeted this statement. Peter Greene especially seemed to share the Chancellor's optimism: he stamped his feet and whistled through his fingers.

"However," Rexford said, "since you and I wouldn't be here to enjoy that sort of victory, I'd rather win by winning. That's why I think the true pacifism isn't unilateral disarming of WESCAC's AIM, or any other sort of surrender, but military deadlock—stalemate, even. In this chess-game with our dangerous brother, only very long-range strategy will win; when you read about our setbacks in the Boundary Dispute or trouble on the Power Line, remember that pawns and even an occasional Dean or Don-Errant may have to be sacrificed to draw our opponent out of position; to overextend him, so that in the endgame we can turn what appeared to be a stalemate into a checkmate. I happen really to believe it can be done, and for that reason I'm not afraid either of the present or of the future. Thank you very much, and welcome to New Tammany!"

The close of his address was received with another cheering demonstration, which required some minutes to spend itself. When it was done an aide announced that the Chancellor, as was his custom, would answer a few questions from the floor before turning the registration-procedure over to WESCAC. The man had much impressed me, in particular that cheerful energy which saw WESCAC merely as a useful tool, and spiritedly denied that the student condition was in essence tragic—as Dr. Sear for example had held it to be. To one as subject as myself to fits of doubt, to buckwheat ecstasies and hemlock glooms; who, fed on hero-tales, conceived the Answer as a thing fetched up from Troll-lands of the spirit, Lucius Rexford's image was refreshment. Sweet to imagine a Graduation attained by sunny zest; by smiling com-

mon sense at work in bright-lit classrooms; by decent wholesome men well groomed and well intelligenced, eminently lik-
able, with handsome wives and pretty children, whose life
was unshadowed pleasure to themselves and others! While the
demonstration was in progress I regarded Lucky Rexford's
sapphire eyes and thought grimly of Taliped's—dark in the
sockets of his mask and then bloodily extinguished. And
Maurice Stoker's, black-flashing as he bellowed through the
Furnace Room, fired by disorder and every flunkèd thing.
Even Harold Bray's, that weirdly glinted when he flunked
Dean Taliped from the stage and bid all follow him through
the mystery to Commencement. Sear's mirror then gave back
to me my own—brown and burning in an unwashed face,
shagged by unbarbered brows, passionate with uncertainty—and moved me to a clear and complex vision: I saw that
however gimped and pleasureless my way, rough my manner,
crude my tuition, outlandish my behavior and appearance,
profound my doubts—I was nearer Graduation than Lucky
Rexford, whose lot was so brighter! I could not say what
passèd meant, but in an instant I saw that neither he nor Sear
nor Greene, nor Stoker, Croaker, or Eierkopf, nor even Max
or Anastasia, was passed; they all were failed! Dean Taliped,
in the horror of his knowledge, was passèder than they, as
was I in my clear confoundment; he was as passèd as one can
be who understands and accepts that in studentdom is only
failure. If anything lay beyond that awful Answer; if Commencement was indeed attainable by human students; then
the way led through the dark and bloody Deanery of Cadmus, there was no getting round it; not through the clean,
well-windowed halls of Rexford's Chancellory. Alas for that!

"Mr. Chancellor!" I stood and rapped my stick for attention, perhaps interrupting a question in progress. People
snickered, guards scowled, Lucius Rexford frowned at the
irregularity of my outburst, but then accepted it with patient
amusement.

"Yes?"

Lights and cameras turned my way. I had been going to declare my identity and aim, Bray's necessary fraudulence, my
ignorance of the nature of Commencement but conviction
that I would discover it—this and more; but there were no
words; I was a fool; who was I anyhow? Tears stung me, of
embarrassment and doubt, but I would not shed them or sit
down, I bleated a question after all: "If it's your brother—if

it's your brother you're playing against—" I saw his handsome jaw set. "Why not forget about the game and hug him? Why not let him have all the pieces, if he wants them, and then embrace?"

An unfriendly murmur rose as I spoke; I scarcely understood the question myself; I heard Max Spielman's name whispered, and the word *Student-Unionist*. Lucius Rexford reddened, much less than I, but replied good-naturedly.

"As I think I said earlier, I don't have any brothers myself. But it was a *competition* I meant—sibling rivalry, if you like!" He smiled. Admiration for his reasonableness filled the room. "If we're all brothers, then we're all rivals, aren't we? And so surrender would mean submission, obviously. I don't think we New Tammanians are the submissive type."

His words were of course applauded, but I pressed on despite the antagonism I felt in the hall.

"What's wrong with submitting to your brother?"

He stayed with a little gesture the guards who approached me, and joked that to heckle administrators was an honorable sport in a democratic college. Then briskly he declared, in response to my question, that I was carrying the analogy too far. "Submission—to some kinds of brothers, if not all— means annihilation, at least in the Boundary Dispute; and annihilation isn't my idea of University Brotherhood. You're the fellow who brought Mr. Croaker back to Dr. Eierkopf, aren't you? A thing we're all grateful to you for, by the way. Well then, you've seen the famous relationship between them. Would it be brotherly of Dr. Eierkopf to let Croaker eat him up?"

The point was merrily applauded: Croaker and Eierkopf were proverbial figures on the campus. "Seriously," Rexford went on, "I'm quite aware that Enos Enoch teaches us to love our opponent and give him our gown if he snatches our cap. But Enochist submission assumes a Commencing hereafter—otherwise it would just be suicide, which the Enochists say is flunking!" He happened to be an Enochist himself, he said, though perhaps not in perfect standing, and so he subscribed, as a personal principle, to the teachings of the New Syllabus. But he could not in good conscience impose his private conviction on the whole College; he had no intention of embracing an alleged Brother whose declared intent was to destroy him.

It occurred to me to ask him then whether the case was

that one struggled to control one's brother because he was dedicated to one's destruction, or that he was thus dedicated because one struggled to control him; my own wrestle with Croaker in George's Gorge seemed in some way pertinent to the question. But the Chancellor had had enough of interrogation; an aide whispered to him, he nodded assent, someone called as if on signal, "Thank you, Mr. Chancellor," and amid general applause he yielded the rostrum with a grin to the man who'd first introduced him.

"We'll turn the meeting over to WESCAC now," this man said. "As I understand the new procedure, all regular matriculees will go on with their scheduling, and Candidates for Graduation—if there *are* any!—will proceed to the Grateway Exit to be congratulated by Chancellor Rexford and get their Assignment from the Grand Tutor."

He nodded then to someone in a balcony behind us; there was a sharp click and a whine which I'd come to recognize as of loudspeakers warming. A mechanically inflected voice, more neutral than Bray's, said crisply: *"Hear this: all holders of ID-cards please exit through the side doors and enroll in the regular curricula. No one with an ID-card is a Candidate for Graduation."*

I thrilled. There was general amusement and much headshaking. "I swan!" cried Peter Greene. "Can't matriculate without and can't Graduate with!" Among the forelocked fellows near the rostrum the consternation appeared more grave. As WESCAC repeated its announcement I thought I heard one say, "Don't tell *me* the flunking thing's not haywire . . ." but that idea was so surprising I could not be sure I'd heard correctly. At the exit behind them, which I took to be the Grateway, Lucius Rexford was deep in conference with other aides, who, it seemed to me, glanced pensively from time to time in my direction. All except myself moved a-murmur towards the side doors. Then every light in the Assembly-hall suddenly went out.

"Durn them Student-Unionists!" I heard Greene exclaim. "Chess-game my foot!" Others soberly agreed that the power-failure might be due to another Nikolayan provocation at the East-West border; my own first thought, recalling the Furnace Room, was that the whole Power Plant had finally exploded. But a ringing laugh from the back of the hall— which I recognized as Stoker's—changed some people's minds.

"That's going too far!" I heard one say.

"He's getting even for that speech."

I had been ready to go onstage to the Grateway when the lights went out; now I could see nothing. But a host of little clickings all about the hall reminded me that *my* pocket-torch was not empty. I pressed its switch, and a beam of light aimed past the rostrum. Someone enviously said, "Lucky!" Stoker laughed again. I climbed onstage, went directly to where the Chancellor waited with his party, and offered my hand to be shaken. Guards seized me.

"He's okay," an aide said.

"The flunk he is," said another.

"Spielman's kid, isn't it?"

"So?"

They spoke virtually at once: things were balled up altogether; the newspapers mustn't get wind of it, or there'd be the Dunce to pay; first Bray, then Spielman, then the Turnstile mess, now *this;* what the flunk next?

"Tell Bray to make a statement," Rexford ordered. *"No panic, everything's in order,* that sort of thing. Somebody find out if my flunking brother has anything to do with this. Let's get back to the Chancellory."

"Take that guy's light," someone told someone else.

I clicked it off before anyone could take it. "Beg pardon, Mr. Chancellor—"

"Turn it on!" Rexford said sharply.

I did so, bidding him please not to take it, as I needed it to get through Scrapegoat Grate.

"See here," said the youthful Chancellor, coming close to the light. He put his hand straightforwardly on my shoulder. "Are you working for the Nikolayans? Or for Maurice Stoker?"

"He *is* your brother, then?"

"Never mind! This is a college crisis."

I swore by the Founder I was working for no one but studentdom and had no intention save the Grand-Tutorial one of passing the Finals and discovering the way to Commencement Gate, for myself and my classmates.

"Another nut," somebody said.

But the Chancellor himself, after turning my light-beam on me for a moment, said, "He might be okay." He asked what name I went by, where I'd got the batteries from, and how I happened not to have an ID-card. As I answered, briefly and frankly, the lights came on again, just enough to see by.

"Now listen carefully, George," said the Chancellor, his manner friendly but concerned: "We're not sure what's going on with WESCAC lately—maybe nothing to worry about, maybe something serious. But we don't want anyone to start blowing the EAT-whistle about it, you understand? I want you to cooperate with us, for the good of the College."

No need to tell him that my loyalty lay not with any college but with general studentdom. Clearly accustomed to making important decisions in a hurry, he declared his confidence in me and told me some surprising things in an even tone: The Power Line controversy was more critical than was generally supposed, and West Campus's position in the border negotiations was weakened by recent odd behavior on WESCAC's part. Whether Bray was in fact a Grand Tutor, Rexford said he had no idea, though all the rational-skeptic in him resisted such a notion. But for some time past WESCAC had in truth been reading out equivocal predictions of some such happening as Bray's advent in the Amphitheater; and the computer's affirmation of Bray's descent into its Belly was an indisputable fact. Happily, the man seemed eager to assist the Administration. He'd already Certified Rexford himself, and alarming as was his connection with Stoker, for example, he apparently had none but benevolent motives. It had been decided in the interest of NTC to acknowledge him officially (that is, to acknowledge WESCAC's acknowledgment of him) and give him Cabinet status; some professor-generals worried that WESCAC's AIM might no longer be protecting its Belly from intruders as formerly—but who wanted to test it?—while others feared Bray might "pull some pacifist trick," Grand Tutor or not. Most, though, had been reassured by his pledge to render unto Remus that which was Remus's, and unto the Founder *etc.*

"Now *you* claim to be a Grand Tutor too, and got through the Turnstile somehow, and you tell me Bray's a fake!" It made no difference to him personally one way or the other, Rexford declared; his business was to run the College and do what he could to strengthen the West-Campus academic complex. To these ends he thought it most prudent to acknowledge my claim to Candidacy, not to shake the public's faith in WESCAC; should I manage somehow to pass through Scrapegoat Grate (which had never been penetrated and was now strictly scanned by WESCAC), he would give me free run of the campus and top clearance as a Special Student, and Tower Hall would defray my expenses for the term of my Assignment. In return, he trusted I would do nothing to subvert New Tammany in general and his administration in particular; he hoped he might count further upon my being prudent enough not to alarm the College with accusations of fraud against Bray unless I was prepared to make them stick—but of course it was a free college. If beyond this I felt inclined actually to *support* Administration policies, intramural or varsity, he guaranteed reciprocal support for me of any kind that Tower Hall could in good conscience offer.

"What do you say, George?"

His manner quite pleased me. There was no suggestion of bribery in his proposition, merely an open, cheerful request to cooperate in the common weal, which inspired me to reply in the same spirit.

"Let's wait until I've passed Scrapegoat Grate," I proposed. "Maybe you won't have to do business with me at all."

This answer was well received: one aide admitted that the same thing had occurred to him, another praised my grasp of "the political facts of life—the flunkèd realities," and the Chancellor himself smilingly confessed that he'd assumed I was some sort of charlatanical pedagogue, whether hypocritical or sincerely fanatic, of the sort that always appeared in turbulent semesters, and with which the most idealistic chancellors had sometimes to come to terms if the college was to be administered.

"Of course, you might be yet!" He grinned. "But at least Dr. Spielman brought you up to play on the first string. Very pleased to've met you."

We shook hands as might two athletes before a match. I was invited to call at the Chancellory on Max's behalf—if and when I'd passed the Grate—as the Hermann case had serious implications for public opinion towards Siegfrieder College, an important member of the West-Campus complex. The Chancellor then excused himself to return to the urgent business of his office and left through a side door with a phalanx of his aides—one of whom, however, he deputed on the spot to follow my fortunes at the Grate and report to him directly afterwards. I was escorted down a short dark hall behind the Assembly-stage to a door whereon my flashlight showed the word GRATEWAY; it opened of itself at our approach. From the dim interior beyond, a clicking voice said "Prospective Candidates only, please," and a second—familiar also, but huskily, womanly human—added, "It's all right, George; He means you."

"I'll wait for you out here," said my forelocked escort. But now my eyes had accommodated to the flickering instrument-panels and Telerama screens of the Grateway antechamber, I saw not only Harold Bray and Anastasia, perched on twin stools at a massive console, but behind them Scrapegoat Grate itself, a thick portcullis let into the chamber wall. Beyond it, squared by that iron weft and strangely dark, Great Mall's elmed colonnade stretched out of sight.

"I won't be coming back," I told him.

He clucked his tongue. "Well. We'll see."

I stepped in, and the door closed at once. Like the Powerhouse Control Room, and to some extent Eierkopf's Observatory, the Grateway antechamber was walled with dials, reels, and switches, that quietly hummed and clicked. There was a subtle fetid odor about, not describable but distinctly unpleasant. My rival's appearance was not exactly as I recalled it—his skin seemed paler, his mustache smaller, his face less round, his pate more bald—but his eyes, unmistakable, gave back my flashlight-beam as if they too were lit.

"No lights necessary," he said.

I braced my back against the panel opposite the console and raised my stick, still holding in my left hand the flashlight and my watch with its broken chain. My plan had been to move straight to the Grate, ignoring Bray utterly if I could and striking him down if he tried to stop me. But it was bitter to see him perched in white-frocked authority with Anastasia reverent beside him. I left the light on.

"Don't be upset, George," Anastasia begged. "Dr. Bray's not a *bit* jealous. He says He'll program an Assignment for you and let you try the Grate. We saw your Trial-by-Turnstile on Telerama, and you were wonderful!"

It stung me to hear as it were the capital letters in which she spoke of him. *"He says!"* I burst out. "You're fickle, Anastasia!" And to Bray I cried, "You know very well you aren't what you say you are! You're an impostor!"

Anastasia started off her stool. "George . . ." But Bray restrained her, with a hand long-fingered for one so heavy.

"No matter, my dear," he said. I loathed the bony sight of his hand on her arm; was moved almost to strike it.

"You'd understand if you'd seen what *I've* seen," Anastasia protested: "WESCAC didn't do a thing when He went down in the Belly, and Scrapegoat Grate opens right up for Him! It's really wonderful, George . . ."

"Nothing at all," Bray said. His face never changed expression, nor did his voice, yet I imagined him much flattered by her awe. Her defense was vain: I'd not forgotten the sight of her kneeling in Bray's presence before he'd done these alleged wonders, and it enraged me to suppose *he* lusted for her too.

"Don't you dare let him service you!" I warned her.

"George!"

"You're too affectionate," I scolded. "You let *everybody* service you, whether they deserve to or not. Men take advantage of you."

"Mrs. Stoker is Certified," Bray said. "The Founder's Scroll says *Love thy classmate as thyself, or flunkèd be.*"

"Certified!" I scoffed, and declared to Anastasia that whomever else she mated with, she must not let Bray climb her; if she did I would regard as proved what in any case I half suspected: Stoker's charge that beneath her charity was simple carnal appetite and a contemptible want of faith. How else explain her protestation of belief in me, her receipt of my Memorial Service for G. Herrold in the Living Room, her aspiration to Commencement at my hands—and then her apostasy with the first pretender to come by?

"You don't understand, George!" But her eyes were tearful in the flashlight. "You make me feel *awful!*" From a large black drawstring purse on the console she took a tissue.

"No need to abuse her," Bray said. "Perhaps the dear girl was simply being hospitable to both of us. Look here, young man, I don't ask you to believe in me; call me an impostor all you like! Let's suppose *you're* the real Grand Tutor—a real one, anyhow . . ."

His conciliatory tone surprised me; my first suspicion was that he meant to ingratiate himself with me in hopes of protecting his fraud. "I *am* the Grand Tutor," I said coldly.

"Very well, suppose you are, and I'm an impostor, and my success at the Belly and the Grate is some kind of trick, or a malfunction in WESCAC."

I asserted that such exactly was my conviction—and was

pleased to make it so, for that excellent last possibility had not occurred to me.

"Even so," he went on, "you don't claim you're a Graduate yet, do you? Enos Enoch Himself didn't claim so much at your age. So, no matter who the Grand Tutor is, you're indisputably matriculating as a Special Student in New Tammany College, who wants a Graduation Assignment. And I'm undeniably the Keeper of the Grate, by the Chancellor's appointment. Don't you agree?"

Reluctantly I did and lowered my stick, still however hostile.

"Then let's not contend, shall we?"

"All those Certifications of yours are false," I charged. "Those people aren't Candidates yet. I'll bet you even Certified Stoker!"

Bray put his fingers together and once more quoted the Founder's Scroll: *"Passèd are the Founder's fools, and flunkèd they who hold His ways make sense.* But I'm not here to Certify you as a regular undergraduate, George; simply to read out your Assignment so that you can pass it or fail it, as may be. Think of it as WESCAC's Assignment, since you seem not to care for me; that's what it *is,* actually."

I hesitated. His reasoning seemed unexceptionable, but I was loath to acknowledge it.

"It's just like regular Matriculation," Anastasia said. Her tears were wiped, her voice was soothing again. "Except in your case—because of the Turnstile and no ID-card and all—it's . . . *irregular."*

"Everything that's happened since you came to Main Gate has been fed into WESCAC," Bray said briskly; "all that's known about your background, plus what Eierkopf's scanners picked up at the Powerhouse, the Turnstile, and the Assembly just now. All I have to do is ask you the Candidacy Question so that WESCAC can evaluate your Answer: if it's right, you pass—through Scrapegoat Grate, presumably. If it's wrong, you don't. Please don't lean against that panel: it's part of the Assignment Printer." He pressed a number of buttons on the console and new whirrings began, behind my back and elsewhere. "Do you want to commence now?"

"Well . . . I guess so. Yes." As I spoke I moved away from the Assignment Printer and found that my watch-chain had caught somehow on the panel of it. But before I could look to free it I was alarmed by the sound of a buzzer and the sight of several blinking red lights, in whose flash Anastasia urgently shook her head. It dawned on me that Bray's apparently preliminary question had been the real one, tricked out in disguise, and that WESCAC was recording and rejecting my answer!

"No!" I cried. "Wait!"

More lights and buzzers. I was furious at having fallen twice into so simple a trap. "That doesn't count! That's not my answer!"

Bray made a clicking chuckle. But as he shrugged his shoulders (bony, like his hands), ready to dismiss me, Anastasia said meekly to him, "Actually it *didn't* count, Sir . . ."

He tutted. "Of course it did. That was the Candidacy Question, and he flunked it."

Humbly she smiled. "But we didn't have a *Ready* on my panel, I'm afraid. Do You think his watch-chain might have short-circuited something?"

"Flunk it all!" Bray cursed.

"Give me a second," I said. "I'll get it loose." I bent to see how the chain was fouled, doubly happy for the second chance and the evidence that Anastasia was after all loyal. Alas, the chain-end had got into a slot in the panel and would not come free; above it an orange light glowed. I fumbled to employ one of Eierkopf's lenses, thinking to magnify the problem, but my hands were too full.

"Here," Anastasia said. "Take this purse to keep your things in. It's just an old bag of Mother's; you can put everything on campus in it." She slipped off the stool to hold it open near me—was the touch of her breast against my shoulder accidental, or a sign? "That little bottle that The Living Sakhyan gave you is in there."

I thanked her, dropped in my flashlight and the shophar, and put Eierkopf's lens to my eye. But I had difficulty focusing it.

"I have a *Ready*-light now, Sir," Anastasia reported to Bray. "Do You want to repeat the same question, or what?"

"Well," Bray clicked in my direction—chagrined, I thought: "What's your Answer?"

But I was not to be tricked that way again. "My answer to your first question or my Answer to the Finals?" I demanded to know. "And what did you mean by *commence* before?" I turned from my fruitless inspection to see how he'd react. Again red lights flashed and buzzers buzzed, as if, though I hadn't really answered, I'd answered wrong. But what dismayed me more, Anastasia was fondling the scoundrel's neck! Where *was* her loyalty, that directly my back was turned she'd run a teasing finger around the collar of his tunic? Nor give over even when I looked, and he caught at her to stop!

"Mustn't, mustn't," he said.

"Tickee-tickee," teased the shameless girl.

I cried, "Flunk you, Anastasia!"

Bray said impatiently, "Look here, Goat-Boy . . ."

Ah, I was looking there, where yet she tickeed, with Eierkopf's high-resolution lens still at my eye, and marked how her finger-end ran somehow as beneath the skin half down his neck. But what mattered that small oddness when my heart was stabbed? Flunk his Candidacy Question; I leaped lump-throated at the pair of them, breaking my chain.

"Oh!"

"ZZZ!" It was Bray himself that alarmingly buzzed; but dwarfing that wonder, when I batted her hand from him Anastasia's nail snapped his neck-skin like a garter! To mind sprang the image of Bray's advent, when he'd tossed a mask aside . . .

"*Baa!*" With a Brickett-bleat I seized his scalp—it peeled off like a glove, mustache and all! Anastasia squealed; I stood struck dumb. Bray buzzed no more, but coldly glared at me from a face not different from the one I'd snatched, only perhaps a shade less slack, a bit more moist.

Then, "Put it on!" cried Anastasia.

"Goat-Boy!" Bray warned, rising from his stool. "Do you want to Graduate, or not?"

I slipped the silk-dry mask over my head, snatched up the purse of Anastasia's mother, and charged at Scrapegoat Grate as I had used to charge the fence in kidly days. A scanner scanned and disappeared, blue sparks and smoke shot from the panel where my watch-chain was; when I hit the Grate its grid-irons slipped in slots, I was through before I knew it, they clacked behind me but I would not look.

Even as I sticked myself up from the threshold and doffed

the mask, out of a pipe in the Grate-wall popped a paper, to unroll at my feet. A circle it was, size of a cheeseburger-plate; around its edge in tall block capitals my PAT-phrase, thus:

And on the *verso*-top, when I'd retrieved it, the heading ASSIGNMENT, followed by a list.

With a grin I pursed my watch—chainless now—and false-face, and conned the Mall. I was registered! Few were about; the Carnival-structures were no more. Why was it dark? I had forgot: but for a flashing ring the sun was eclipsed. A fat man in a yellow robe sat on the grass some elms along. Beyond him, benched, one old and thin, a dark-suit stranger. The rest of studentdom was in class, I did not doubt, hard at Assignments of their own. And I—a Registered, Matriculated, Qualified by George Candidate for Graduation—I read mine:

ASSIGNMENT

To Be Done At Once, In No Time

1) *Fix the Clock*
2) *End the Boundary Dispute*
3) *Overcome Your Infirmity*
4) *See Through Your Ladyship*
5) *Re-place the Founder's Scroll*
6) *Pass the Finals*
7) *Present Your ID-card, Appropriately Signed, to the Proper Authority*

Founder, Founder! Those I thought I grasped, I gasped at; most signified not a thing to me. What ID-card? Which infirmity? When had the Founder's Scroll got misplaced? And ay, and ay, so short a term! Fist to brow I told them over, faintful list, and struck at each. One, two, three, four, five, six, seven!

So too did Tower Clock. But was it right?

Volume Two

FIRST REEL

1.

My own timepiece, when I fetched it out, said something earlier, but I'd been so careless in the winding and setting way that I'd scarcely have dared trust its accuracy even had the River George not got to it. On the other hand, my first Assignment-task confirmed that not all was well with Tower Clock. I stepped to consult the dark-suit oldster, as more likely than The Living Sakhyan to own a watch. Lo, as I did, half a dozen young ragged fellows gathered to him from the shadows, uncordially. They jostled and threatened.

"Let's have it, old man."

"If you want it," I heard him reply, "pay for it." But his molesters were plainly ready to have by force what they were after. I cried stop to them and gimped to the man's assistance.

"Look what's coming," said one of their number.

They were too many; as I passed The Living Sakhyan's elm I rapped His shoulder, less than reverently it may be, and bade Him help me help. T. L. Sakhyan's palms were pressed together under His breast, fingers upward, and His eyes gently shut; yet I knew Him to be awake by that tranquil smile He'd borne across the torrent at our last encounter, and with which He'd favored Anastasia's ravishment. It put me in a sweat of ire.

"At least call a patrolman!" I shouted in His ear, then dashed the more rashly, for my exasperation, to aid the old man, whose two chief botherers now turned to me. The others had only stood by—shaggy lads mostly, out at elbows—and seemed inclined to withdraw when I challenged. I heard one say, "It's that goat-boy," in a tone that, oddly, did not mock. Others grinned; a few looked sheepish, and I took heart.

"Shoo!" I commanded, wishing that their old victim would fly to safety while he might. But he held his ground; worse, he called them scamps and beggars deserving of the horsewhip, a judgment he might have rendered at a better hour.

"Shameless!" one of them cried, more outraged than wrathful. Indeed, when the old man charged them further to go steal a watch if they wanted the time, as they'd not get free from him what others paid for, even the more aggressive pair seemed disarmed by the force of their own indignation, and called on the Founder to witness to what flunkèd depths of meanness the student mind could sink. I too was startled out of countenance.

"You only wanted the time of day?"

That, it developed, was their sole craving. Indigent scholarship-students all, they had not a watch among them, yet needed to measure the exact duration of the current eclipse in connection with some astronomy assignment. Understanding Tower Clock to be out of order, they had approached the "Old Man of the Mall," who I now learned was a kind of institution in New Tammany College, famous for his store of information and his ability to tell the time of day, to the second, by the length of people's shadows on the path.

"Not for free, though," the old man said. "I don't sit here for my health." Now I could see it, his face was hornybeaked and sere-eyed like a turtle's, and his neck as corded, loose in the carapace of his collar. I was amazed. A tattered, glaring chap turned to me.

"He's the stingiest man on campus! Let's shake it out of him!"

And indeed they might have laid hands on him, but I was inspired to point out that until after the eclipse there would be no clear shadows for the Old Man of the Mall to reckon from.

"I wouldn't've told 'em anyhow," he said.

"You *are* stingy!" I scolded him. The young men granted my point, but were incensed enough by the fellow's meanness—as almost was I—to offer him a roughing in any case. I forestalled it by giving them the reading of my own timepiece, the best I could manage, for which they thanked me and withdrew, not without grumbled threats to return with the sun.

"Don't come empty-handed," the old man called after them. "I'm not Reg Hector."

"You're mad!" I cried. "Why didn't you tell them yourself you didn't know the right time?"

He rubbed his thumb against the tips of two fingers. "What's it worth to you to find that out?"

I wished him loudly to the Dean o' Flunks and promised next time to look on smiling, like The Living Sakhyan, while he got what his miserliness deserved; then I declared that it was to check my own watch I'd approached him, and that, he being in my debt already, I meant to have the time of day from him as soon as the eclipse ended (it was passing already) or call back the shabby young men to finish what I'd interrupted.

"I owe you nothing," he said. "Did I hire you to help me?" However, he added, since I'd given him something he hadn't asked for, he'd repay me with something I didn't need: a blank ID-card and enough indelible ink to sign it with my name. Forged cards, he pointed out, were much in demand among undergraduates too young to purchase liquor legally; in fact, it was not for interfering in his private affairs that he was rewarding me with so salable a piece of goods, but for teaching him a new way to drive off the beggar-students who forever importuned him. Thitherto he'd been obliged to give the more threatening ones what they wanted, in order to insure his own safety, and he had been thoughtless enough to give them correct information. But thanks to my example (now there was sun enough to cast shadows, he could tell by the length of mine that my watch was slow) thenceforth he would buy his safety with false coin, seeing to it that any answers extorted from him were not quite accurate. He could hardly contain his satisfaction at learning this business-trick, the more pleasing to him since he had it from me *gratis;* nor much better could I at being rewarded, unbeknownst to him, with something I very much needed after all. If I was able to take the ID-card and ink with a show of indifference, it was only because my delight was pinched by bad conscience at having in a manner sharped him—and, himlike, savoring the cheat.

"You don't get the whole bottle," he grumbled. "Just enough to sign your name."

I had no pen, but struck a bargain for the loan of his in return for what ink I saved him by having one name instead of three. Then, as I wrote *George* on the proper line, I saw that the card was after all not a new one; nor was the ink, it seemed, absolutely indelible: dimly could be made out there, after mine, the previous owner's name: *Ira Hector*.

"You stole this card!"

He closed his eyes, thrust out his underlip, shook his head.

"Look here: it says *Ira Hector!* It's a used card!"

"You don't want it, give it back. But no refunds."

I saw his eye glint so at that prospect that shrewdly I promised to have him taken up for theft if he didn't give me at once the accurate time of day, which I needed to proceed with my Assignment.

"Call a cop," he dared me. "He'll arrest you as an accessory. In fact, I'll say *you* stole it: your name's on it! And I'll charge you with extortion besides."

Improvising swiftly and in anger, I declared myself willing to match a prospective Grand Tutor's word against a nameless vagrant's, or used-card dealer's, especially since Mr. Ira Hector, when I should return his card to him, would doubtless apply his famous wealth and influence in my just behalf.

"Don't count on it," the old man chuckled. "*I'm* Ira Hector."

I denied it.

"Of course I am, you great ninny. Everybody knows the Old Man of the Mall."

Alas, he did quite fit the impression of her uncle I'd got from Anastasia's narrative, and I was the more appalled at such petty avarice in the wealthiest man on campus. But I challenged him to prove his identity without a card.

He blinked like an old testudinate Peter Greene. "You should be a business major, Goat-Boy!" However, it was his notoriety in the College, he told me, that rendered his ID-card superfluous and induced him to sell it. *Everybody* recognized him, he was sorry to say, and pestered him for handouts which they no more deserved than did those young beggars the free tuition provided them by Chancellor Rexford's new grant-in-aid program. Creeping Student-Unionism was what it was, to Mr. Hector's mind: the tyranny of the have-nots, of the ignorant over the schooled. The only thing to be said for the Administration's reckless giveaways was that, the untutored being always (and justly) more numerous

in the NTCROTC, arranged his marriage to the woman whom Ira himself had been courting, financed his campaign for the chancellorship after C.R. II, and appointed him director of the Philophilosophical Fund: his end from the beginning had been simply to profit from his brother's offices and connections, and profit he had.

These disclosures were surprising news to me; even so I failed to see what gain there was in losing his fiancée, for example, or endowing the Philophilosophical Fund.

His smile was chelonian: "Why should I pay for the woman's keep, when I could get her for nothing anytime I wanted?" Referring to Reginald's wife, Anastasia's grandmother.

"Is that what you did?"

"It's what I *would* have done; but she died when Stacey's mother was born. There's always a *few* investments don't pay off." As for the P.P.F. and the lying-in hospital, they were manifold assets, he insisted, providing him with tax write-offs, opportunities for graft and patronage, and such entertainments as playing doctor with patient young ladies when the whim took him. He had, for example, assisted in the delivery-room when his niece, Virginia R. Hector, gave birth, and had quite enjoyed the show even though she'd brought forth neither monster nor GILES, as had been predicted in some quarters, but only Anastasia, a normal baby girl whom he then raised to serve his pleasures.

"But you *did* try to help Anastasia," I said, no longer certain however of my point. "She told me so."

Ira Hector winked and licked his lips. "I helped myself, like everybody else! Stoker says he gets a commission on her; *I* used to get her whole price!"

Repellent as I found this remark, and its maker, I was skeptical of its truth. For one thing, Anastasia had confessed worse things unabashedly in George's Gorge, but had made no mention of fees and commissions. For another, I observed that Ira Hector could not speak painlessly of her connection with Maurice Stoker: his neck-cords flexed at the man's name, and his voice shelled over.

"You *pity* her!" I accused him. "You pitied her mother, too, and your own brother when you were kids."

"Rot!"

"And all those unwed co-eds! I think you pity *everybody*, and you're ashamed to say so!"

Now his eyes gleamed. "I pity you, you nincompoop!"

"I bet you did business with Bray for the same reason Anastasia did," I said. "Out of charity! You taught her to be the way she is!"

"Charity be flunked!" Ira hollered. "Every man for himself!"

It occurred to me to argue, then, more out of spite than out of conviction, that even his vaunted miserliness might be passèd, and its opposite flunked. Enos Enoch, it was true, bade men give all their wealth of information to poor students and become as unlettered kindergarteners, if they would Pass; but it seemed to me that this was to pass at the expense of others, those to whom one's wealth was given, for nowhere did the Founder's Scroll say "Passèd are the wealthy." What nobler martyrdom, then, than to keep from men that which it would flunk them to possess, and hoarding it to oneself, flunk like a scapegoat in their stead?

"You're demented," Ira said. "You think I'm going to pay you for clap-trap like that?"

"I'm not Harold Bray," I replied. "I can't be bought." And seeing I would not get from him what I needed, I walked off.

"Nobody *has* to buy you!" Ira cackled after me. "You give yourself away for free! Like Anastasia!"

His taunt relieved me, giving as it did the lie to his talk of prices and commissions. I walked on. Students were beginning to throng Great Mall now, en route I presently learned to first-period classes, having eaten their breakfast.

"You got nothing from me!" Ira called again. "I got all you had to offer!" His voice was triumphant, but when I turned to him his old face was fiercely anxious.

"Then maybe you've helped me to pass," I said, "and yourself to flunk. Thanks."

The Living Sakhyan, I observed, smiled as ever from the foot of His elm. I might have upbraided Him for failing me once again (indeed, His condition, reputedly a kind of Commencement, seemed to me little different from Eierkopf's infantile paralysis. The one was unhelpful, the other helpless; for those in need of help it came to the same thing, and Eierkopf's at least was not wholly voluntary, though he affirmed it in his relationship with Croaker and his unconcern for the welfare of studentdom); but before I could speak I was hailed by several of the unshaven botherers who'd precipitated the whole encounter. Their attitude was friendly: though indigent, they were not ordinary beggars, I was to understand, but vagabond scholars—"Beists," in fact, who accepted tuition from Rexford's grant-in-aid program but contemned the whole academic establishment as mid-percentile and conformist, committed to the intercollegiate power struggle, hostile to art, sex, and the human spirit, and generally, in their vernacular, a drag. They inferred from my appearance that I was of their fraternity; were frankly envious, in fact, of my garment, stick, and bagful of tokens; and while their position, as I understood it, struck me as something wanting in consistency, they were clearly earnest, and I was grateful for their goodwill. However, there was no clarity between us. They knew who I was, but would not accept it that I had truly only one name, for example, and was literally half goat by training. "We dig those symbols," they assured me. And when I confessed that I couldn't make out their argot, they thanked me for reminding them that the Answer lay in wordless Being rather than in verbal formulas. Yet their own inclination was plainly towards the latter.

"How do you go about doing *your* Assignments?" I asked them. "Mine says *Complete at once . . .*" Some homely practical advice was what I sought, as one undergraduate to another; but they responded with disputation as passionate and abstruse as if I'd posed Dean Taliped's riddle.

"What *is* studentdom's Assignment, when all's said and done?" they demanded of one another; one asserted that there *was* none, as there was no Assigner; another, that each student was his own sole Tutor and Examiner; and so forth.

"Please," I said. "What I mean is, didn't WESCAC give you an Assignment? It gave me one."

"What He means is the analytical, conceptualizing consciousness," said one of my new classmates, as if speaking of someone not present.

"The flunk He does!" another objected. "He's putting us on, to remind us to be like Sakhyan."

"No, man!" insisted the first. "It's the Form-is-the-Void thing. Like the categories aren't real, but there they are, and we're in them even though there's really no *us*."

A third intently scratched his crotch. "But does WESCAC symbolize Differentiated Reality or the Differentiating Principle?"

"Neither!" Number Two said contemptuously. "WESCAC symbolizes *Symbolization*. What He means—"

"Please," I said. At once they were respectfully silent. "The

Assignment I'm talking about is a list of things I have to do to Pass . . ."

"See?" One said delightedly.

"I'm supposed to Fix the Clock, for example, and End the Boundary Dispute . . ."

"I'm with you!" Two muttered: "Space/Time thing!"

"And I'm supposed to Overcome My Infirmity and See Through My Ladyship, whatever all *that* means . . ."

"The Transcendence bit!" Three whispered.

But they could not decide whether I was exhorting them to attack their Assignment (whatever it happened to be) on its own terms, or the terms of the Assignment, or the very concepts of Assigner and Assignee. And did my aphorisms signify that the "Wheel of Passage and Failure"—their term—was to be affirmed, denied, ignored, or transcended? Specifically, for example, should they go to class and take respectful notes, go to class and quarrel with their professors, or cut class altogether? I left them contending beard to beard so heatedly that they took no notice of my departure. For though their debate was incomprehensible to me, and I despaired of getting usable advice from them, their illustration had suggested something to me for the first time: as young Enos Enoch had enrolled in the manual-training course taught by His mother's humble husband, so would I audit some ordinary professor, the first I came to, in hopes of learning something germane to my task. I would go to class!

Great numbers of students were hurrying into a large hall not far distant. I joined them—rather, they made way for me, some mocking, others amused, most of them indifferent—in a vast low-ceilinged room divided into stalls by chest-high partitions. Each stall contained one chair and a console of sorts, far simpler-appearing than the ones in the Control Room and the Grateway. I saw no professor, humble or otherwise, but a number of young men in slope-shouldered worsteds and horn-rimmed spectacles were directing students into the stalls and explaining how to operate the consoles.

"Who's hazing *you*, frosh?" one asked me good-naturedly. I found the question meaningless, but identified myself with the aid of my new used card and asked whether I might sit in on the lecture, if there was to be one. The instructor leafed doubtfully through a roster of names on his clipboard, warning me that the class-rolls had just been read out on WES-

CAC's printers and might be incomplete, especially in the case of special or irregular students.

"George your first or last name?" His confidence was not bolstered by my reply; but as it happened there I was, under *G: George.* "I guess it's you," he said. "How the flunk can I tell? Not even a matric-number!" There was, however, a notation after my name to the effect that I was authorized by the Chancellor's Office to audit any courses offered in the College, though not for credit. The man addressed me more respectfully:

"Exchange-student, are you? Visiting this campus?"

I supposed he might put it thus, and he kindly showed me into a stall. The machines were teaching-machines, he explained, one of many varieties in the College, all wired to WESCAC's Central Instructional Facility. As a rule one addressed the device with one's "matric-number" and was then instructed individually, the subject-matter, pace, and method being determined by WESCAC's analysis of the student's record and current performance, as well as his academic objective. The machines in this particular hall, however, were designed for the orientation of new registrants; the morning's program consisted of a lecture recorded by the new Grand Tutor for that purpose. Doubtless noting some change of my expression, the instructor acknowledged rather sharply that attendance was voluntary: but he certainly thought it prudent for any new undergraduate to avail himself of the Grand Tutor's wisdom before commencing his regular course-work and assignments, especially as it was Dr. Bray's first formal lecture to the public. I had only to address the console (he did it for me, in fact, using the number on my ID-card, before I could decide to leave), don the earphones ready to hand, and press the *Lecture*-button to begin the recording. Should I desire elaboration of any particular point I was to press a button marked *Hold,* which stopped the lecture-tape, and another marked *Gloss,* which provided footnotes, as it were, to the text. Having explained this, he left the stall, a bit ruffled still at the idea that anyone could be uninterested in what after all was a historic event (he was himself a new instructor in the History Department), and went to give instruction to respectfuller students. But for all my disdain I pushed the *Lecture*-button, curious to hear what my rival conceived to be Grand Tutoring, and wondering too how he'd found time to put together a recorded lecture while partying at the Powerhouse and allegedly going into WESCAC's Belly. *I* hadn't managed yet even to visit Max in Main Detention! Through my headset came the clicking voice I knew—speaking, however, in a somewhat archaic style reminiscent of Enochist harangues:

"My text today, Classmates," Bray began, *"is the First Principle of Life in the University, which you must clasp to your hearts during Freshman Orientation and never lose sight of after, not for an eyeblink of time, how clamorous or brave soever the voices that deny it . . ."*

I tossed my head impatiently, considered throwing down the earphones and leaving—but decided to hear what false principle the rascal had sharked up, what platitude or half-truth, the more substantially to contemn him.

"On all sides," he was saying, *"you will hear platitudes and half-truths—as that the unexamined life is not worth living; that the truth shall make you free; that understanding is its own reward.* Cum laude *diplomates, even full professors, are not above urging you to greater efforts with such slogans, wherefore I conclude that either like all* virtuosi—*artists, athletes, yea Croaker himself—they ill understand the secret of their own greatness, or else they find it practical pedagogy to dissemble with you, as a child may best be lured from the cliff-edge by promise of sweets, when in fact his rescuers are candyless and want only to save his life . . ."*

I endeavored to sneer at the simile, but found it alas rather apt, if elaborate.

"For whatever the case in Academies of fancy, one thing alone matters in the real University: to avoid the torture of remedial programs, and the irrevocable disgrace of flunking out! In short, to Pass!"

Obviously.

"Except this, what has importance? Very well to preach the therapy of swimming for injured legs, or its intrinsic pleasure: thrown overboard, one cares only to reach the shore, whether by sidestroke or astride a dolphin!"

Which didn't mean one *ought* to care for nothing but self-preservation, I thought to myself—but knew I was simply being captious, and recognized besides, not comfortably, a point like one I'd made to Ira Hector. Yet wasn't Bray as much as inviting dishonesty?

"To be sure," he went on, *"the Examiners are above corruption and intimidation; no Candidate ever bribed or*

threatened his way to glory; to attain it he must know the Answers, nothing else will serve: There is the sole and sufficient ground for prizing knowledge: all other preachments are, if not mere sentimentality, hollow consolation for the failed—who are ipso facto inconsolable . . ."

I considered demanding a Gloss on *ipso facto*, a term of whose meaning I was not entirely sure; but my hand was stayed by both the brazenness of Bray's piety (who had himself made deals with Ira Hector, Lucius Rexford, and Founder knew who else!) and the force of his next remark:

"Get the Answers, by any means at all: that is the undergraduate's one imperative! Don't speak to me of cheating—" The word, I confess, was on my tongue. *"To cheat can only mean to Pass in ignorance of the Answers, which is impossible. Otherwise the term is empty . . ."*

Experimentally, and also as a kind of impudence, I pushed the *Hold* and *Gloss* buttons. Instantly a matter-of-fact feminine voice said, *"The term is otherwise empty inasmuch as the fact of Passing, on the Grand Tutor's view, determines all morality: what tends thereto is good, all else evil or indifferent. This Gloss was prepared by your Department of Logic and Philosophical Semantics. Remember: 'The mind that can't philosophize, never ossifies.' "*

Automatically the two buttons popped out again at her last word, and Bray's voice resumed: *"As you see, then, nothing could be simpler in theory than the ethics of Studentensleben . . ."*

I let the term go.

"But I don't suggest that the practice is without its difficulties! In the first place none of you knows for sure what you'll be asked, or whether your Answers will be acceptable. No two Candidates are quite alike, however similarly trained, and no Graduate, should you find one to consult, can say more than that he himself was asked so-and-so, to which on that occasion and such-and-such reply proved acceptable . . ."

The point had not occurred to me, and reluctantly I granted its validity, even its value. And despite my hostility I found myself attending Bray's next remarks closely.

"In consequence, you will discover in the terms ahead numerous hypotheses about the nature of Examination, which can be sorted into two general categories: one holds that while the Questions are different for each Candidate, the

Answer is the same for all; the other, that while the Question never varies, the Answers do. Whether, in either case, the variation is from term to term or Candidate to Candidate; whether it's a difference in formulation only, or actual substance; whether it's radical or infinitesimal; whether the matter or the manner of the Candidate's response is of more significance, the general tenor or the precise phrasing—these and a thousand like considerations are much debated among your professors, many of whom, one sadly concludes, are more interested in academic questions of this sort than in the ultimate ones which in principle they should prepare you to confront. You undergraduates are to be pardoned (but alas, not necessarily Passed) for being in the main more realistic, if sometimes pitifully wrong-headed. Snatching at straws, you will badger your professors with down-to-campus queries: 'Will we be asked this on the Finals?' 'Does attendance count?' 'How much credit is given for class participation, for extracurricular activity, for washing blackboards and beating erasers, for a neat appearance and respectful demeanor, for improvement over bad beginnings?' Not a few of you are persuaded that independent thinking is the sine qua non, *even when naïve or erroneous; others that verbatim responses from your lecture-notes are what most pleases. Some, of a cynic or obsequious temper, will openly flatter your instructor's vanity, hang on his words as on a Grand Tutor's, turn the discussion to his private specialty, slap your knees at his donnish wit, and rush to his lectern at the hour's end. 'What other courses do you teach, sir?' 'Is your book out yet in paperback?' You co-eds, particularly, are often inclined to hope that a bright smile may make up for a dull intelligence, a firm bosom for a flabby argument, a clear peep for a cloudy insight. And (more's the justice) not one of these gambits but has succeeded—in some cases and to some extent! Given two young ladies of equal merit and unequal beauty, who has not seen the fairer prosper? Who has not observed how renegade genius goes a-begging, is actually punished, while the sycophant's every doltishness is pardoned? A term's hard labor in the stacks, an hour's dalliance in Teacher's sidecar—they come to the same. Who opens her placket may close her books; she lifts her standing with her skirts; the* A *goes on her Transcript that should be branded in her palm . . ."*

Ah, I was moved, so immediately likely seemed this review of the student condition—flunkèd, flunkèd! And, black as surely had to be the heart of any false Grand Tutor, the art of Bray's imposture watered my eyes.

"*Yet all this is vanity,*" he said, and his voice despite its click was heavy with compassion. "*The Examiners care nothing for transcripts, only for Answers. Campus legend is peopled with model students who never passed and mavericks who did; of those tightly fleshed and loosely moraled queans, some go dressed in white gown and mortarboard to be diploma'd out of hand, others are led shrieking down the Nether Mall to be thrust beyond the pale forever. No theses so contrary that history won't feed both, and a chosen few of you with both eyes open may soon induce that our whole collegiate establishment—our schools, departments, and courses of study, our professorial rank and tenure, our administrative apparatus, our seminars, turkeypens, elms, and alma m ers, even our WESCAC—is but one more or less hopeful means. The most organized, surely, and hallowed by custom, but a mere alternative for all that. And the very advantages of organization are not without their own perniciousness: faced with a Department of Moral Science and one of Swine Research, each with budget, offices, and journals, one comes inevitably to believe in the real separateness of those subjects—as if one could fathom hogs without knowing metaphysics, or set up as a practicing ontologist in ignorance of Porcinity! Worse, within the same department one finds the Duroc-Jersey men at odds with the Poland-Chinas; the Deontological Intuitionalists and the Axiological Realists go to separate cocktail parties. Yet one must choose curriculum and major, ally oneself with this circle or that, dissertate upon* The Navigation of Sinking Vessels, Coastwise and Celestial, *or* Foundation Planting for Crooken Campaniles . . ."

It was true, all true; I knew it at once despite my inexperience of the campus and the accidental fact that we in the goat-barns had been spared the intellectual degeneration of those pig-men. I peeped over the partition: some of my classmates slept, some furiously took notes, some picked their noses, some played cards, but none save myself seemed distressed by what I assumed we all were hearing.

"*Alas,*" went on the firm sad voice in my ears, "*the Finals are comprehensive; the Examiners care not a fig for your Sub-Department of Rot Research; one wonders whether they know of its existence! Our Schools and Divisions—what are they but seams in the seamless? Our categories change with the weather; not so our fates. In vain our less myopic faculty preaches general education: they have not only the mass of their colleagues to contend with, but the very nature of great institutions. Bravely today one devises something 'interdisciplinary": perhaps a pilot survey of Postlapsarian Herpetology and Pomegranate Culture. 'Dilettantism!' cry the pomologists; the natural-historians, 'Thin soup!' By tomorrow there is a Division of General Education, with a separate Department of P.H.P.C., and in time an additional Department of P.H.P.C. Education to train instructors for the first. There's no end to it."*

How was it, I wondered, an impostor dared speak so heretically against the Administration—all administrations? His next assertion—*"Now mind, I mean no disrespect for the colleges, certainly not for old New Tammany, which I love as 'y an adopted child can love its mother"*—enabled me to revive for some moments the contempt for him I wanted to feel. *"A wart on Miss University,"* he said warmly, *"were nonetheless a wart; and if I will not call it a beauty-mark, neither would I turn her out of bed on its account."* It was all a pose, then, that subversive compassion: a stance he took in order to abandon it, as a lover feigns displeasure to gain a kiss! But Bray went on then to speak of institutionalized education in terms so affecting, hypocritical or not, that it was much not to weep outright:

"We teachers forget our business; the University does not. There is a spirit in our old West-Campus halls, a wisdom in the stones as it were, that no amount of pedantry or folly quite dispels. I hear the pledges singing in their cups truths deeper than they know:

> The Gate is strait,
> And Great Mall is not all . . .
>
> Strait is the Gate;
> Great Mall, not all.

"For those with eyes to see, New Tammany abounds with voiceless admonitions to humility. Not for nothing are 'Staff' and 'Faculty' equally privileged, so that groundskeepers and dormitory-cooks are affluent as new professors; not for nothing does custom decree that our trustees be unlettered folk, and that our chancellor be selected not from the intelligentsia

but by ballot, from the lower percentiles: tinkers and tillers and keepers of shops. For the same reason one observes among the faculty not graybeard scholars only, their cowls ablazon with exotic marks of honor, but men of the people: former business-majors, public-relations clerks, gentle carpenters and husbandmen. It is fit that our libraries be more modest than our cow-barns, our cow-barns than our skating-rinks, our skating-rinks than our stadiums. Was not Enos Enoch, the Founder's Boy, by nature an outdoor type, a do-it-Himselfer who chose as His original Tutees the first dozen people He met; who never took degree or published monograph or stood behind lectern, but gathered about Him whoever would listen, in the buckwheat valleys or the wild rhododendron of the slope, and taught them by simple fictions and maxims proof against time, which now are graved in the limestone friezes of our halls?

Not the cut of your coat, but the cut of your jib.

Milo did not pass in class,
Nor did he fail in jail . . ."

Blinking back tears (and recognizing neither of the alleged Maxims as my former keeper's) I Held and Glossed. A crisp male voice, refreshingly passionless, explained that the allusion in the latter epigram was to an early diplomate of Lykeion College from whom Milo Park, New Tammany's largest stadium, took its name:

"*Book One of The Acts of the Chancellors,*" the glosser proceeded, "*tells us that Milo matriculated in a provincial Lykeionian Ag-school during the so-called 'Golden Chancellory' of Xanthippides, with the modest aim of studying dairy husbandry; but though he covered himself and the Lykeionian Complex with glory for his athletic prowess, and became the inspiration of a dozen sculptors, he repeatedly failed to qualify for Candidacy, for the reason that a certain heifer named Sophie, assigned to his care, refused to eat the experimental feed-mixtures he prepared for it. Certain of failure, Milo turned on the animal one evening in a rage, dispatched it with a single sock, and carried it on his shoulders across most of Lykeion from the old Doric Stock-Barns to the Chancellor's Palace, where he left it high in a young red oak. For this outrage he was fetched to detention by the cam-*

pus patrol, who however were unable to remove the dead beast from its perch. Seeing it next morning, the Chancellor asked how a heifer had contrived to climb his oak, and, told of Milo's offense, so far from exhibiting anger, he smiled and remarked: 'There is one way to raise a cow.' He then convoked the entire Department of Animal Husbandry and inquired whether the ablest among them had ever got a heifer up a tree, or knew how to coax one down. When none replied, he ordered Milo released from Detention Hall, dismissed the charges against him, and passed him without further examination—the power of Summary Bond and Loosement being still vested in the Chancellory in that place and term. This gloss was prepared by your Department of Agricultural History. May we remind you that—"

Impatiently I jabbed at the *Hold*-button, not to have to hear another advertisement. Owing to some characteristic of the machinery the gloss Held, but the lecture did not recommence; therefore I depressed *Gloss* again, and learned of a new dimension in the program: instead of the interrupted advertisement I heard a third voice, energetic and intense, apparently glossing the gloss:

"The Milo incident, and thus the later Enochist epigram, has been variously explained. Philocaster the Younger (in his Commentary on the *Actae Cancellorum, Volume Two, pages four thirty-eight ff.) formulates the classical interpretation: 'Excellence is non-departmental'—that is, greatness is what counts, irrespective of its particular nature. Opposed is the influential little treatise by Yussuf Khadrun,* De Vacae in Arbores, *which holds that ends, rather than means, are the Examiners' primary concern: that the excellence for which Milo was rewarded lay not in his athletic record but in his radical (and in the final sense practical) solution of an apparently flunking predicament. To the objection that treeing the cow was not a solution of anything until the Chancellor made it so by rewarding it, later Khadrunians have asserted that Milo's victory was not over the problem on its own terms, but over the terms of the problem—that is to say, over the directive 'Raise this heifer' in its conventional interpretation. As Fanshaw and Smart ask (in* The Higher Pragmatism): *'What did the Examiners care about experimental pasturage or the physical well-being of Sophie the heifer? In one sense everything, in another nothing. Milo's bold gesture made his failure the Department's failure. As one of Sakhyan's "foot-*

notes" reminds us, too eager pursuit of solutions may blind us to the Answers, which are at least in some cases to be discovered by strange means indeed, and in strange places.' End of quote . . ."

I listened amazed. Though the quotation was ended, the gloss-upon-the-gloss evidently was not:

"*Hugo Krafft takes a similar stand in his brilliant and exhaustive (if sometimes oppressive)* West-Campus Cattle-Barns from Pre-History to the Thirty-Seventh Remusian Chancellory, *and, like other semantically oriented interpreters, makes much of Xanthippides's fondness for word-play as a pedagogical device. The Neo-Philocastrians, to be sure, like the Scapulists they derive from, have never sympathized with pragmatism, higher or lower, and are inclined to be skeptical of the close textual analysis made popular by Krafft's followers; in general they still maintain that virtuosity, rather than net achievement, is the key to Commencement Gate— whether the performance wherein it is manifest be* 'admirable' *or not. Thus Bongiovanni cites the examp.. Carpo the Fool, an early freshman who knocked himself senseless in a fall from the parallel bars and was for some terms thereafter the butt of campus humor, and Gaffer McKeon, 'The Perfect Cheat,' who confessed to never having given an uncribbed answer during his brilliant undergraduate career. Both men passed.*

"*But the West-Campus Philocastrians identify virtuosity with particular excellencies, while their East-Campus counterparts (if so various a group may be thought of collectively) tend to speak of it with a capital V, as something distinguishable from virtuoso performances. Thus the old East-Campus table-grace quoted by Dharhalal Panda:*

> With Milo, Carpo, and Gaffer,
> I live alone alone:
> Four fingers of a hand.
>
> May I, with Sophie or some other thumb,
> Grasp Answers as I grasp this food;
> Eat Truth; and on the Finals know
> I feed myself myself.

"*Among the rash of modern researches into the political and economic life of the early West-Campus colleges one finds frequent mention of Milo and the heifer—for example, in E. J. B. Sandry's scholarly analysis of the old enmity between the Divisions of Agriculture and Athletics in the Lykeionian Academy. Yet while one welcomes new light on studentdom's history from whatever source, one cannot but regret the deprecatory tone of these investigators and the glib iconoclasm especially manifest in their handling of traditional anecdotes. Sandry's suggestion, for example, that Xanthippides saw in 'the Milo affair' an opportunity to '. . . pull the collective beard of the Ag Hill Lobby [sic]' as a gesture of mollification to Coach Glaucon, who was miffed at the large appropriation for new mushroom-houses, is more exasperating by reason of its partial truth than are plainly lunatic hypotheses (e.g., that the Chancellor's hand was forced, there being no other way to unoak the cow; or that the whole incident was cynically pre-arranged by Milo and the Chancellor, or by the School of Athletics, or by some Lykeionian equivalent to the Office of Public Information, for publicity purposes)."*

Surely, I thought, that must end both gloss and gloss-gloss. But the indefatigable scholiast went on to recommend as perhaps the best general work on the whole matter a recently-taped study by one V. Shirodkar, called *There Is One Way:*

"As the title suggests, Shirodkar approaches 'Khadrunianism' and 'Philoeastrianism' (which is to say, in a special sense, Entelechism and Scapulism) by way of the ambiguity of Xanthippides's famous observation, and he attempts to combine, or at least subsume, the major traditions into what he calls Mystical Pragmatism. The result, alas, is more syncretion than synthesis, but Shirodkar's historico-semantic schema belongs in every undergraduate notebook. Please Hold and Gloss."

Appalled, I did, and from a slot in the console issued, in the form of a printed diagram, this gloss upon the gloss upon the gloss upon Bray's quotation from Enos Enoch's allusion to Xanthippides's remark upon Milo's misdemeanor:

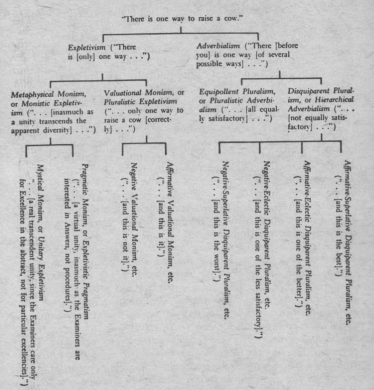

"There is one way to raise a cow."

Expletivism ("There is [only] one way . . .")

Adverbialism ("There [before you] is one way [of several possible ways] . . .")

Metaphysical Monism, or Monistic Expletivism (". . . [inasmuch as a unity transcends the apparent diversity] . . .")

Valuational Monism, or Pluralistic Expletivism (". . . only one way to raise a cow [correctly] . . .")

Equipollent Pluralism, or Pluralistic Adverbialism (". . . [all equally satisfactory] . . .")

Disquiparent Pluralism, or Hierarchical Adverbialism (". . . [not equally satisfactory] . . .")

Mystical Monism, or Unitary Expletivism (". . . [a real transcendent unity, since the Examiners care only for Excellence in the abstract, not for particular excellencies] . . .")

Pragmatic Monism, or Expletivistic Pragmatism (". . . [a virtual unity, inasmuch as the Examiners are interested in Answers, not procedures] . . .")

Negative Valuational Monism, etc. (". . . [and this is not it] . . .")

Affirmative Valuational Monism, etc. (". . . [and this is it] . . .")

Negative-Superlative Disquiparent Pluralism, etc. (". . . [and this is the worst] . . .")

Negative-Eclectic Disquiparent Pluralism, etc. (". . . [and this is one of the less satisfactory] . . .")

Affirmative-Eclectic Disquiparent Pluralism, etc. (". . . [and this is one of the better] . . .")

Affirmative-Superlative Disquiparent Pluralism, etc. (". . . [and this is the best] . . .")

Even as I endeavored to make sense out of the diagram, the *Hold*-button popped out and the recentest speaker concluded primly:

"*Pragmatic Monism, for example,* Shirodkar *maintains, comes to quite the same thing as Equipollent Pluralism, and Valuational Monism to the same as Disquiparent Pluralism. That this correspondence (which may be merely verbal) is ground for synthesis seems doubtful: the position of the old Lykeionian Sub-Department of Dairy Husbandry may, it is true, be assigned with equal justice either to Negative Valuational Monism or to Negative-Superlative Disquiparent Pluralism; but what meeting of minds can be hoped for between Negative Valuational Monism and Positive Valuational*

Monism, or between Mystical Monism and any of the others? These secondary and tertiary glosses were prepared by your Sub-Department of Comparative Philosophical History."

I chewed ¯nervously on Shirodkar's historico-semantic *schema,* waiting to see what would happen next. The *Gloss-*button popped up and automatically redepressed itself, whereupon the voice of the earlier commentator, the Agricultural-History man, resumed his own conclusion—no advertisement after all:

". . . Heifer House, which generations of exchange-students have been surprised to find is no stock-barn but the ancient headquarters of the Lykeionian Campus Patrol, stands where Sophie's Oak reputedly stood. The exact site of the tree is marked by a bronze disc let into the floor of what was formerly an auxiliary detention-chamber. Thank you."

Up came *Gloss* and *Hold* simultaneously, down went *Lecture,* and at once into my headset Bray's voice rang, more impassioned even than before:

"Learned Founder! Liberal Artist! Dean of deans and Coach of coaches, to whose memos we still turn in time of doubt: stand by us through these dark hours in Academe! Teach me, that am Thy least professor, to profess no thing but truth; that am Thy newest freshman advisor, not to misadvise those minds—so free of guile and information— Thou has committed to my trust. Help me to grasp Thy rules; make clear Thy curricular patterns as the day; Thy prerequisites unknot for me to broadcast with the chimes. Enlighten the stupid; fire with zeal the lowest percentile; have mercy on the recreant in Main Detention and the strayed in Remedial Wisdom; be as a beacon in the Senate, a gadfly in the dorms. Be keg and tap behind the bar of every order, that the brothers may chug-a-lug Thy lore, see Truth in the bottom of their steins, and find their heads a-crack with insight. Be with each co-ed at the evening's close: paw her with facts, make vain her protests against learning's advances; take her to Thy mind's backseat, strip off preconceptions, let down illusions, unharness her from error—that she may ere the curfew be infused with Knowledge. Above all, Sir, stand by me at my lectern; be chalk and notes to me; silence the mowers and stay the traffic that I may speak; awaken the drowsy, confound the heckler; bring him to naught who would digress when I would not, and would not when I would; take my words from his mouth who would take them from mine; save

me from slip of tongue and lapse of memory, from twice-told joke and unzippered fly. Doctor of doctors, vouchsafe unto me examples of the Unexampled, words to speak the Wordless; be now and ever my visual aid, that upon the empty slate of these young minds I may inscribe, bold and squeaklessly, the Answers!"

I shucked the earphones and left the stall—moved to the pasterns by his rhetoric, dazed with envy at the force of his imposture. No one else seemed to be leaving: perhaps the orientation-lecture was not ended, or perhaps they had availed themselves of more glosses than had I. But I could hear no more; I left the hall despite my horn-rimmed helper's information that one could select questions from a prepared list to ask the commentators by remote control. Aside from my distress, I saw no help for my Assignment in that learned chatter, and sad to relate, Bray not only had reminded me, with the Milo epigram, of my responsibility to Max, but had tutored me as well. More accurately, his description of class- and course-work as merely one among a number of possible means to Commencement (a sentiment so recognizably Affirmative-Eclectic-Disquiparent-Pluralistic that I never doubted he had lifted it from some old Hierarchical Adverbialist, probably without permission) gave a rationale to what had been my inclination since leaving the barn: to waste no further time on books and lectures. Matriculation yes, class-attendance no; I must wrest my Answers like swede-roots by main strength from their holes.

I flung away the *schema,* unpalatable even literally, and fetched a morning newspaper from a trashcan near the exit, thinking to tide myself over until lunch with its inklesser pages. But bannered across the top was the headline SPIELMAN CONFESSES, followed by two columns that confirmed what Stoker had told me: Max had surrendered himself to the Campus Patrol and declared himself guilty of the murder of Herman Hermann, substantiating the confession with exact details of the scene, time, and circumstances of the crime. He had been sitting by the roadside not far from Founder's Hill, the news-report said, when he was accosted by a man in the uniform of a Powerhouse guard, astride a motorcycle, who offered him a ride. The two shortly afterwards fell to quarreling over political matters, and upon recognizing the guard as Herman Hermann, the Bonifacist Moishiocaust, Max had been so overmastered with desire for revenge that he had shot the man with his own pistol. Nay, further: "according to the Grand Tutor," who had interviewed him at some length in Main Detention, Max admitted to having harbored for years a secret yen not merely to settle a part of the Moishian score against the Bonifacists, but, for a change, to be the persecutor instead of the victim. Yet once he had arrogated this position (so Bray claimed) a wondrous change had come over my advisor's heart. *"The fact that Dr. Spielman cannot, by his own admission, repent of the murder, has had a remarkable effect on his spirit,"* Bray was quoted as saying. *"The secular-studentism which he had always formerly espoused assumes that the heart is essentially educable and ultimately Passable; faced with the revelation of his own failing, however, Dr. Spielman now sees that the heart is flunkèd, desperately flunkèd; that what it needs is not instruction but Commencement; not a professor but a Grand Tutor, to Graduate it out of hand and with no Examination; otherwise all is lost, for however we may aspire to the state of Graduateship, we may never hope to deserve it."* And Max himself had allegedly said to Bray, "By me the only way to pass is to pass away," and had requested capital punishment "as a Make-Up for his failure." Campus sentiment, I read, was even more sharply divided than before; the old issues of Max's former leftish connections and his opposition to the "Malinoctis" program had been revived, though with far less virulence than when they had led to his dismissal. Liberal sentiment, as always pretty generally in his favor, was embarrassed by his confession of violence; right-wingers, on the other hand, while inclined to despise him on principle (and to view the murder as evidence of a Student-Unionist conspiracy to assassinate all ex-Bonifacists now doing important work for New Tammany), were much impressed by the humble tone of his confession, in which they seemed to hear a recantation not only of Student-Unionism in favor of Informationalism, but of Moishianism in favor of Enochism. "Go now, and flunk no more," appeared to be their net reaction, whereas the liberals' was just the contrary: that Max had formerly been among the persecuted Passed, but now had flunked himself. The argument had grown intenser, I read, since early morning, when the prisoner had been Certified for Candidacy by the new Grand Tutor—who, however, emphasized to reporters that the Certification by no means implied that Max was innocent of the murder or deserving of mitigated punishment: "Passèd are the flunked," Bray had quoted from the Founder's Scroll, "who repent and suffer for their failings."

What alarmed me, other than Max's confession itself, was not that Bray had Certified him—he seemed to be Certifying everyone—but that Max had evidently accepted the Certification, as if Bray were qualified to give it! And how had Bray found time to visit Main Detention in addition to the hundred other things he seemed to have got done since the previous evening? Pressing as was the deadline for my Assignment, I resolved to go to Main Detention at once and hear from Max's lips that all these allegations were false. For that matter, he might advise me how to attack most efficiently my list of labors, as he had pre-counseled me so valuably through the Turnstile and Scrapegoat Grate.

How to get to Main Detention? My first impulse was to look up and down the mall for Peter Greene. Had I appreciated the size and populousness of New Tammany I'd never have bothered—but I did not, and espied him at once. Four elms up and one over, he was doing calisthenics on the grass, almost the only person in sight. A kind of stationary jog: I heard him panting "Right! Right! Right!" in rhythm with his step as I approached, not alone to mark the cadence, it turned out, but in some wise to reassure himself as well; it was in fact the motto he'd lent me at Turnstile-time, reaccented for its present use:

"I'mal*right!* I'mal*right!* I'mal*right!*"

It developed, however—when I saluted him and hove in range of his working eye—that he was not all right. From the Assembly-Before-the-Grate, where I'd last seen him, he had proceeded dutifully to a first-period lecture in a course very close to his concerns, *Problems of Modern Marriage,* hoping to learn something useful; for though he was still resolved to put by Miss Sally Ann and pay court to Anastasia, he was much afflicted with bad conscience and wanted to satisfy himself that his union really was unsalvageable—and that his wife was chiefly to blame for its disintegration. But he'd "plumb fergot," he told me, how tiresome it was to be a schoolboy. As the lecturer (on closed-circuit Telerama) had droned on about such matters as "contemporary role-confusion and attendant anxieties," he had first fallen asleep, then diverted himself by making spitballs and carving initials in his desktop, and finally left the building on the pretext of visiting the toilet.

"It's over *my* head," he complained to me. "Durn if it ain't!" How ever he would pass without going to school, he confessed he had no idea, any more than he knew how he could live without the woman he loved but could not live with. "Weren't for Bray's diploma I'd swear I was flunked, interpersonal-relationwise," he admitted. "Figured I'd come out and get me a breath of air, take a little pill, try 'er again."

I could not discern whether by The Woman He Loved But *etc.* he meant his wife or Anastasia; I did not inquire. Indeed, for all my good fortune at finding him so readily, it was with some misgiving that I asked him to transport me to Main Detention, for I feared he'd hold me to my promise of intercession with Anastasia's mother. But though he was delighted by the errand and "the chance to get to know Stacey's family better"—as if Maurice Stoker were her father!—he made no mention of that mad embassy; it did his spirits a campus of good, he declared, to learn that I too had cut my first class. Much of his eagerness to oblige me, I presently observed, stemmed from his pride in a new motorcycle he'd acquired just after registration, and had yet to try out on the open road. He showed me it, parked nearby: an astonishing contraption, all chromium plated, larger-engined than any of Stoker's, and equipped with every manner of accessory: headlights, fog-lights, spotlights, signal-lights, Telerama, air-horns that blasted the opening phrase of *Alma Mater Dolorosa,* a liquor cabinet, three dozen dials and control-knobs, an air-conditioned sidecar, and upholstery of stripèd fur. It was so new he'd not had time even to remove the mirrors (of which there were half a dozen); they were merely turned away from him. He bobbed his head happily.

"Pisscutter, ain't she?"

I agreed that it was an extraordinary machine, if that was what he meant. It proved a shocking fast one, too, and happily so loud (thanks to a lever marked *Cut-Out*) that he couldn't speak of Anastasia or anything else during the dash to Main Detention. Greene knew the route, and by means of simple gestures which we agreed upon before we started, I was able to distinguish for him between the few actual stop-signs along the way and the many he imagined he saw, and to function as his rear-view mirror also. We were halted at the somber gate of the outside wall by a uniformed guard, recognizable as one of Stoker's by his beard and dog, though sootless. I requested an audience with Max, identifying myself and explaining that I had Chancellor Rexford's authorization to go anywhere on the campus. The guard prepared to unleash the dog.

"Hold on!" Greene cried. "Pete Greene's my name: 'Keep-Our-Forests Greene,' you know? This here's a pal of mine. Look at my ID-card."

To prove that his card was not forged or stolen he wrote out a matching signature, this one on a personal check payable to the bearer, and insisted the guard retain it "as proof." Before this evidence the man relented and telephoned a companion inside the walls, who, given a similar affidavit of our sincerity, ushered us to the Warden's Office. For all my unease in those bleak courts and gray stone corridors, I might have voiced my doubt about the correctness of Greene's procedure; but the sound of Maurice Stoker's laugh distracted me. It issued from an inner office into the empty outer one where we were told to wait until the Warden was finished dictating letters to his secretary, and did not sound terribly businesslike. A female voice said something indistinct. The guard winked and left us. Peter Greene—chuckling, blinking, blushing—supposed aloud that a fellow with a stick with a mirror on its point could peer over the transom without being seen, if he had a mind to and no thing about mirrors. I didn't reply. More impatient at the delay than annoyed or intrigued by what Stoker might be up to, I tapped my sandal-toes and frowned at the floor-plan of the building, framed on one wall. It revealed Main Detention to be much larger in fact than I had supposed, for in addition to the single floor at ground-level there were three successively smaller ones beneath. The ground floor, as best I could discern, was given over mainly to adminstrative offices and living-quarters for the staff, but included combination detention-and-counseling facilities for two sorts of mild offenders as well: a large exercise-room for loafers, procrastinators, and students who refused to choose a major or whose transcripts showed straight *C*'s; and a courtyard for the mentally defective and the invincibly wrong-headed. On the floor below were detained four classes of miscreants: first, students who spent their evenings amusing themselves with classmates of the opposite sex instead of studying, and professors who turned their sabbatical leaves into honeymoons or participated in faculty wife-swapping parties; second, those who abused their dining-hall privileges, scheduled more than the normal credit-load, or stayed awake all night reading; third, those who read and researched but would neither teach nor publish, and contrariwise those who spent so much time publishing and lecturing that none was left over for reading and research; and fourth, professors who browbeat their students and students who circulated angry petitions against their professors. The second subterranean floor was divided into three cell-blocks, smaller than the ones above but like them containing chambers for both students and instructors: one block was reserved for anti-intellectuals, insubordinates, and those who refused to sign the College loyalty-oath; a second was for textbook writers who published revised editions to undercut the used-book market, padders of essay examinations, proliferators of unnecessary footnotes and research, and unscrupulous dispensers of grants-in-aid; the third was itself divided into sub-blocks: one (where I guessed Max was held) for murderers, rapists, extorters of answers by duress, and destroyers of library-books; another for droppers of courses and leapers from dormitory windows; the third for faggots, dykes, and teachers employed in the same departments from which they held degrees. The bottom floor, though smallest in area, was most complexly laid out: in wedge-shaped sections around a central sinkhole were incarcerated (clockwise from the top of the floor-plan) "make-out artists" (sic); "apple-polishers and brownies"; purveyors of "cribs" and "ponies"; impostors and charlatans; sellers of rank, tenure, absentee-excuses, and false ID-cards; users of academic distinction for social, political, or mercenary ends; cribbers and plagiarists; malicious faculty advisors and dormitory counselors; organizers of panty-raids, interfraternity brawls, and departmental cliques; and what the chart called "bullslingers and snowmen." In rings around the sinkhole itself were ranked those who'd tattled on classmates, roommates, or colleagues; who'd given classified military-science data to hostile colleges; and who'd exploited the naïveté of exchange-students or visiting professors. Finally, poised as it seemed over the sinkhole itself, was a single cell reserved for any who undid in flunkèd wise his professor, department-head, dean, chancellor, or—most heinous treason!—his Grand Tutor.

Though not all of the penciled labels were meaningful to me, I was much impressed by the size and layout of the institution—much more orderly, at least on paper, than the Powerhouse. Had not other matters pressed, I'd have asked Maurice Stoker to guide me through the place and explain how the several sorts of malefactors were punished, and for what term. Specifically I wondered whether Stoker determined and administered their sentences on his own authority or as agent for the Chancellor, and fervently hoped that the latter was the case.

The inner-office door opened behind me, and a handsome dark-skinned woman came forth, tucking in her blouse.

"You all have an appointment with Mr. Stoker?"

Even as she asked—patting her hair into place the while—Stoker bellowed greetings at me from inside and emerged, also tucking his shirt-tails in. But now the secretary and Peter Greene had noticed each other, and he clutched his orange hair and cried, "Flunk my heart!"

"I beg your pardon?" the Frumentian young woman said. Stoker grinned.

"What you doing here, gal?" Greene exclaimed. "You're s'posed to be home taking care of Sally Ann!"

She donned a pair of glasses and looked questioningly at Stoker. "Should I know this gentleman? I don't understand what he's talking about."

"This is Georgina," Stoker said. "My new secretary. Georgina, Mr. George, the Goat-Boy." We exchanged polite greetings. "And Mr. Greene," Stoker added.

"That ain't her name!" Peter Greene said indignantly. "She's old O.B.G.'s daughter! You get on back to the house, doggone it; Sally Ann might need you!"

Georgina smiled and appealed to us: "He must be mistaking me for someone else . . ."

"Don't set there and deny you're O.B.G.'s daughter!"

"I'm sure I don't know those initials at all," she said a little impatiently. "My father's name was the same as this gentleman's."

Peter Greene would be durned if it was. "His name was O.B.G., and you know it!" To us he declared, "Him and me was thick as thieves when I was a boy—built us a raft together!"

Stoker's secretary replied that her father had been an assistant librarian until his recent death, and that that was that.

Then Stoker added gaily, just as I was coming to it myself, that Georgiana's maiden name had been Herrold. Having heard news of her long-lost father's death and cremation, she had sought out Stoker for more details; the conversation had turned into an interview—which our arrival had interrupted—and finding her qualifications satisfactory, Stoker had employed her on the spot. His teeth flashed in his beard. "Small campus, isn't it?"

"You gosh-durn hussy!" Greene exclaimed to Georgina, who having coolly replaced her lipstick was making room for her purse in a desk drawer. But his tone now seemed as much impressed as angered. Stoker suggested with amusement that perhaps Mr. Herrold had had *two* daughters—if indeed he'd been the man whom Greene called O.B.G. I myself was uncertain what to think: the woman's composure appeared more deliberate than natural, and she either was ignorant of G. Herrold's actual job or chose to exaggerate its importance; on the other hand I had small confidence in Peter Greene's eyesight, though his indignation was convincing. In any case her identity mattered little to me, much as I grieved the loss of my companion; I stated my business to Stoker, who knew it already, and proposed with a wink that Georgina and Peter Greene clear up their misunderstanding over coffee, in his inner office, while he took me down to see Max. They were both reluctant, but Stoker insisted; he would serve the coffee himself; something stronger, perhaps, if they wanted it; the guard in the corridor could take me to the Visitation Room as well as he.

"Maxie's coming on so with the 'Choose me' business, it makes me sick to hear him anyway," he said. "The old fool can't wait till we Shaft him." He summoned the hall-guard and gave him instructions, pinching Georgina as he passed behind her. She pursed her mouth; Peter Greene snickered. I went out with the guard, first offering condolence to the young woman for her bereavement, and Stoker closed the door behind us.

We passed along a balcony overlooking the exercise-court, where the Procrastinators and C-students appeared to be playing some sort of tag or chasing-game under the supervision of their guards; thence to a small empty room divided by steel screens into three parallel sections: in the first was a row of stools, on one of which I sat; the guard then entered the middle one to see that nothing except conversation passed between me and Max, whom another guard presently escorted into the third. A small bleat of pity escaped me at sight of him: thin to begin with, he had lost more weight overnight, and in the ill-fitting garb of detention looked frail as straw. Yet his face, so troubled all the previous day, was tranquil, even serene. He ignored my inquiries after his condition and commended me for having passed successfully through the Turnstile and Scrapegoat Grate. His tone was more polite than truly interested; he asked what courses I had enrolled in, as one might ask the casualest acquaintance, and when I described my encounter with Bray at the Grateway Exit and my perplexing Assignment, his mild comment was that my watch-chain had possibly short-circuited WESCAC's Assignment-Printer, for better or worse. Or possibly not.

"You sound as if you don't care!" I cried. Formerly he might have shrugged, or scolded me; now he said serenely:

"My boy, remember who I am, and why I'm here."

"You didn't do anything!" I said. "You're here because Stoker or somebody is out to get you!"

Max shook his head. Stoker was beyond doubt a flunkèd man, he said, and a flunking influence on everyone about him, myself included; yet his flunkèdness was necessary, for like the legendary Dunce he revealed to those with eyes to see the failings of their own minds and hearts—an invaluable if fatal lesson.

"You didn't kill Herman Hermann!"

But he nodded. "*Ja,* I did, George. In the woods that night by Founder's Hill. It was his motorcycle Croaker found."

"You couldn't kill anybody!" I insisted. "You're too passèd!"

But as the news-report had said, Max declared he was not passèd, never had been—until just a few hours previously. True, he had thought himself a charitable man and a gentle lover of studentdom, to whose welfare he had ostensibly dedicated all his works: thus he had invented the EATer, to protect men from being EATen; sheltered and raised me as a goat, lest I succumb to human failings; rejected Grand Tutors in favor of ordinary schoolteachers, believing education could lead men from their misery to a better life on campus. And he had been proud to be a member of the class least subject as he thought to hating, because most often hated.

"That's all true!" I protested. "You're a hate-hater! You're a love-lover!"

"I used to think," Max went on quietly, as if dictating a confession, "if Graduation meant anything at all, it meant relieving human suffering. Not so. Suffering *is* Graduation."

"Bray's been talking to you!" I charged. "Why didn't you send him away?"

"The Moishians have a name for Shafting Grand Tutors," Max replied. "That's one of the things I want to be Shafted for." He went on to say, as sadly and serenely as ever, that whereas he once had believed in the rejection of Grand Tutors whether "true" or "false," it now appeared to him to make little difference how questionable might be the authenticity of Bray, for example: the important thing was to see one's own abysmal flunkèdness. Since conversing with Harold Bray he had come to see clearly that nothing in his life had been done altogether passèdly: hating hatred, from which passion no man was free, he had perforce hated all studentdom, thinking he loved them. Thus his work with WESCAC and the consequent Amaterasuphage—

"Self-defense!" I broke in. "That was collegiate self-defense!"

But the self must not be defended by the suffering of others' selves, Max responded. And his foster-fathering of me, so apparently praise-worthy: was it not to revenge himself on Virginia R. Hector—nay, on studentdom in general—that he had raised me as a goat? And to revenge himself on New Tammany that he had at the last encouraged my delusion of Grand Tutorhood? Bray having confirmed for him these flunkèd possibilities and certified that only suffering could expiate them, he must believe that Bray was after all what He claimed to be (with stinging heart I heard the pronoun shift to upper-case); Max's encouragement of me, a mere common foundling, must be but one more instance of his perverse Moishianism . . .

"Stop this!" I said. "This is hateful!"

He shrugged. "So hate me, I got it coming."

Stoker thrust his grin through a small square panel at one end of the middle space. "Got so there was a crowd upstairs," he said, as if confidentially. "Mind if I sit in? Maxie breaks me up."

I was too hurt and appalled by my erstwhile advisor's declarations to acknowledge the intrusion, though as always

Stoker's grin filled the room like a sound, or odor, or change of temperature.

"I *do* hate it when you talk that way!" I cried to Max. "You *make* people hate you. It's like Anastasia, and people taking advantage of her!"

"That's what Herm used to say," Stoker offered. "About the Moishians in his extermination campuses."

"So hate, hate," Max invited us.

"That diploma from Bray is a fake!" I said angrily.

"All along I hated the Bonifacists," Max repeated. "I wanted to burn *them* up, and never realized it. We Moishians, we suffer and suffer, and then we Shaft us a Grand Tutor to get even. I want them to Shaft me instead."

Stoker chuckled. "Didn't I tell you?"

In a wondrous exasperation then, I declared to Max that not only his Certification but his whole view of things was false and flunking, the effect I could only hope of his age, and the shock of false arrest, and Stoker's perverse influence. The very grounds on which Bray had Certified his Candidacy, I maintained, were in fact the flunking of him: it was not any hidden urge to persecute studentdom's persecutors that he must atone for, but his pride in suffering—a scapegoatery as misconceived as Enos Enoch's, to my mind, and vainglorious as well.

"Give it to him," Stoker urged.

"I don't have to be a Grand Tutor to know a false goat from a real one," I went on. It was the motive that made the true scapegoat, I said, not the deed, and it might be that Max's motive lifelong had in truth been selfish, but not in the manner he confessed to. *Vanity* was his failing: the vanity of choosing himself to suffer for the failings of others, and of believing that his own flunkèd aspects (overrated, in my estimation) could be made good by that suffering. "You say I should hate you for falsely encouraging me," I concluded; "but the truth is, you're calling your encouragement false because you want to be hated!"

This accusation, which I thought rather acute, did not move him. "So add that on the bill."

"Flunk you!" I shouted. "You're not a Candidate yet, and you never will be if you let yourself be Shafted with that attitude! Passèd are the passed and flunkèd are the flunked, and that's that! I *am* the Grand Tutor—I will be, anyhow—and I *will* do my Assignment! I'll pass everything and not fail anything, and then I'll run Bray off the campus!"

I might have said more—I could in fact have re-reviewed my keeper's whole life for him from my new and unexpectedly clear view of it, and showed him that his conception of the amulet-of-Freddie, for example, was quite mistaken—but he had got up from his stool and was indicating to the guard his wish to return to his cell.

"Max," I pleaded, "I need advice, and I want to get you out of here, and all you can think about is your old suffering. That's selfish!"

For just a moment his irritating calm gave way, and I heard him say, *"Ach, I hate it too."* Then the guard led him out and Stoker came around to fetch me.

"Didn't I tell you?"

"It's your doing as much as Bray's, I'll bet," I said. *"Passèd are the flunked!* What kind of an idea is that?"

He shook his head sympathetically. "Isn't it a scream? You and I, George—we're the only ones who see what a phony Bray is. He's even Certified *me!*" From his jacket pocket he drew the inevitable sheepskin, on which over Bray's signature was, as always, a quotation from the Founder's Scroll—in this case, *Verily the railer against Me shall fetch himself in fury to My feet, while the light yea-sayer standeth off a respectful way. Presume, if ye would Pass.*

"Doesn't that beat all?"

I turned away. "You're no Candidate."

Stoker laughed and herded me to the lift. "Of course I'm not! I'm the flunkèdest flunker on campus! So Bray's a fake, right? Or else"—he swatted me in the back—"only the flunkèd are really passed, hey? And the passèd are all flunked!"

I remarked grimly, as we ascended, that passage by so cynical a pretender as Bray, at least, was most certainly failure; and in my discomfort at being so of a mind with Stoker I added that he tempted out his own failings as well as other people's. "I've seen how it pleases you when people call you the Dean o' Flunks. I'll bet you hope there really *is* a Founder, and that He'll pass you for driving so many people to disagree with you. You want to pass by acting so flunked that you pass other people."

"Oh, come on!" he teased. "You're as balled up as Max is."

We went up and down a number of times, for Stoker liked to push the elevator buttons and close the automatic doors in his employees' faces. I continued to challenge him, mainly from the surplus of my distress at Max's condition: his hope, I charged, was that Failure, deliberately elected, would somehow be equivalent to Passage, as the considered choice of a negative could be said to be an affirmation. But there was only Failure in the human university, so far as I had seen, and thus it would remain unless I could in some wise complete my Assignment and bring order and Answers to the campus.

"There *is* order!" Stoker scoffed. "Everywhere but in my brother's head!" His argument (which I assumed was meant simply to bait me) seemed to be that the opposition and tension of extremes—East and West Campuses, Passage and Failure—was itself a kind of harmony, and that moderationists like Chancellor Rexford, who regarded themselves as realistic, were actually deluded ("Not that Lucky's really what he pretends to be," he added with a wink: "If he'd let me get near him I'd show you his wild side!") But Stoker's reasoning was no more orderly than the rest of his character: having asserted in effect that Disorder was the only true order, and Contradiction the only harmony, he went on to maintain, always grinning, that in fact the alleged passèdness of such people as his "brother," his wife, and my advisor, if true, was false, inasmuch as it not only gave meaning and reality to his own flunkèdness, for example, but induced it into being—as I had myself admitted. Anastasia's submissiveness was a vacuum into which the air of his abuse had no choice but to press; and inasmuch as that which causes flunkèdness is flunked, to be passèd, as everyone agreed she was, must be to be failed!

"That's nonsense," I said. "What you really hope is just the opposite. You hope your flunkèdness will pass you because it gives Anastasia a chance to be passèd. You call Chancellor Rexford your brother so that nobody'll believe he is."

"Right!" Stoker cried delightedly. "So Failure is Passage and Passage is Failure! Let's have a drink on it after we spy on Greene and Georgina."

I shifted my ground then (not quite certain whether the argument was still intelligible, and more in hopes of unsettling my adversary than of instructing either him or myself): refusing to peep through the keyhole of the outer-office door, whence issued muffled noises of pursuit, I declared that the first reality of life on campus must be the clear distinction between Passage and Failure, the former of which was always and only passèd, the latter flunked. "The truth about you is that you're *not* the Dean o' Flunks," I said. "You act like him because you have such a high opinion of Commencement that you're afraid you can't make the grade."

"Ha!"

But I believed I had touched him, as in the Assembly, and thanks to Max's tutelage in logical manipulation I was able to press home my purely improvised position. The *real* ground of Stoker's failure, I told him (he was squatting at the keyhole now, pretending not to hear me), was this equation of Passage and Failure; but even by his own paradoxical reasoning he was not "truly" flunked, and was therefore truly flunked. By this I meant that if he really believed that Rexford's calm reasonableness and Anastasia's submission to abuse were flunkèd—because of their passèdness or however—and also that he himself could in a manner pass from very flunkèdness, then he should pursue a policy just contrary to his present one: deny that Lucky Rexford was his brother, but emulate the ordered normalcy that he regarded as a perilous delusion; be a gentle loving husband to Anastasia, even a submissive one; give over his sprees and orgies, all his mad mischief—in short, turn his personality inside out, and flunk by his own transvaluated terms instead of by the usual ones. It was a challenge born of my distress and bad temper, and riddled with equivocations; yet giving it voice I felt once again some murky, valid *point* in Stoker's life, which I could not as yet assimilate: obscurely I suspected that however flunking were his treatment of Anastasia and his repudiation of every passèd thing, there was another side to them.

Georgina burst into the hall, nearly upsetting her new employer, and took indignant cover behind him. After her came Peter Greene, but stopped short and reddened at the sight of us.

"For pity's sake leave her alone," I said crossly—as if I were the forty-year-old and he the twenty-. And he responded appropriately:

"Shucks, I was only playing I'd paddle her if she didn't 'fess up who she is."

"I *declare*," Georgina said—not very upset. "Some people's children!"

I advised him testily to leave such games to Stoker—if Stoker still cared to play them—and drive me back to Great Mall, as I had work to do: in addition to my Assignment I meant to take up that very day, if possible, the Chancellor's invitation to discuss Max's case with him; and I had business with Anastasia also, if and when my third task took me to the Infirmary. The truth was (though I didn't care to discuss it further before Stoker), I felt an urgent need to show everyone whom Bray had Certified the invalidity of their Certification, lest like patients falsely prescribed for they turn their backs on honest medicine. And I meant to begin with Greene himself, whose case seemed grave enough. As if to illustrate my simile, while agreeing eagerly to chauffeur me anywhere if Anastasia was along the route, he popped a flaming pimple on his chin, and then complained that the salve Stoker had loaned him the night before had made his acne worse instead of better.

"Is that a fact?" Stoker said. "It does a fine job of scaling our boilers." I heard distraction in his gibe, and hoped that my sarcastic words to him, if they were striking some unsuspected target, had more point than *I* could find in them. He ushered Georgina back inside without wink or pinch, and though he answered with a fart my parting plea that Max be treated gently, I thought it significant that he made no promise to the contrary.

"I swear if that ain't O.B.G.'s daughter!" Greene marveled as we crossed the stone courtyard. "Couldn't be *two* such uppity ones in the entire cottonpicking College!" He prodded an elbow into my side. "Ain't she a hot one, though—what you might say teasewise?"

2.

"Indeed she is not," I said. "Excuse me, but I wonder sometimes about the way you see things."

"You don't *believe* her, do you?" At my request he forwent the *Cut-Out* lever so that we could talk as we returned to Great Mall. I replied that the issue of whether or not Georgina was "O.B.G.'s daughter" seemed less to the point in my opinion than his appraisal of her, which struck me as altogether unwarranted.

"A durn floozy's what she is," he insisted. "Tease the bejeepers out of a feller."

"Not sweet and modest like your wife, I suppose."

"I should hope to kiss a pig!"

"And not pure, like Anastasia?"

Greene closed his eyes and bade me please not to speak in the same breath of darky harlots and passèd maiden girls. "Speaking of which," he added slyly, "don't forget what you promised me, Stacey's-motherwise; I'll see if I can fix up Dr. Spielman's prosecutor."

"For pity's sake!" I cried. "Look here, now——" He did, beaming and squinting, and very nearly steered us into a horse-chestnut tree. "No no! Look where you're going!" He returned his attention to the road in time to misread a sign directing us leftwards. He was sure it had pointed right, and turned that way; when I insisted it had pointed left, he reminded me that Stoker was a great hand at altering direction-signs, and that in any case the motorcycle's speed and power would compensate for mis-directions. He opened the throttle to demonstrate his point, and cried, "Yippee!" as we swept through a busy intersection. I told him sharply to stop behaving like a kid.

"Dr. Bray says be like a kindergartener if you want to pass," he answered—pouting a little, but to my great relief halving our speed. I pointed out to him that Enos Enoch's advice had been to *become* as a kindergartener, not to remain one, and that Bray was anyhow wrong to Certify him on that ground.

"You're plain jealous," Greene teased.

"Never mind that," I said. "Whatever it is that's passèd about kindergarteners, it isn't their childishness. Or their ignorance."

Here he grew stubborn, if no less cheerful: "Say what you want how I'm just a simple-head country boy; there's a thing or two I know for sure. I'd rather be me than a educated slicker like Dr. Sear."

I agreed that Enos Enoch might have had in mind a certain kind of innocent simplicity such as Dr. Sear could not be said to share. "But you're not innocent or simple either, it seems to me. You just like to see yourself that way."

"I guess I'm okay," he grumbled. "What the heck anyhow."

"You might be," I declared, "if you'd open your eyes a little. Pardon me for criticizing you like this, but I hate to see everybody believing what Bray tells them."

"It's a free college, George. Say what you want." Now he pouted in earnest, and flushed red as his fresher pimples. "I'm right used to getting knocked, imagewise, by Sally Ann and everybody else." His manner suggested nevertheless that he was curious to hear what I had to say, even eager, though apprehensive.

"Tell me one thing honestly," I said; "you *did* used to service O.B.G.'s daughter, didn't you?"

He snorted. "Which ain't to say, mind you! Durn uppity woman! Said she'd tell Sally Ann if not!"

"Tell her what?"

"That I'd been in the woods with her." He squinted his eye at me. "Which ain't to say!"

"But you did service her, didn't you? And put her in kid?"

"That don't matter!" He thumped the handlegrip with his fist. "It's the principle of the thing. Could just as well been one of them redskins."

"The ones you let service her, so they wouldn't scalp you?"

He jerked his head. "I soon learnt them a lesson: *Only good red's a dead red!* Who d'you suppose opened up the New Tammany Forest Preserve?"

"And drove out the redskins . . ."

"Yeah!"

"And cut down the trees, and ruined the rivers . . ."

"Say what you want! Say what you want!"

I did just that, all the way to Great Mall, but in a cordialer tone. First I laid his hostility by assuring him that unlike his wife and some other of his critics I did not regard him as a hopeless flunker, but rather admired what evidence I'd seen of his magnanimity, industriousness, efficiency, and ingenuity.

"Good old New Tammany know-how," he declared; and as I had expected, once sincerely praised he began to condemn himself: he *had* done wrong by O.B.G. and O.B.G.'s daughter, especially in terms gone by, and had yet to make right amends; he *had* laid waste the wilderness, exploited his mill-hands, sneered at book-learnèd folk and art-majors, been rude to exchange-students, played hooky from school, bribed traffic-policemen and legislators, serviced his private secretary (who however was as flunkèd a durn tease in the first place as O.B.G.'s daughter), subscribed to lewd magazines in plain wrappers, made a fortune in the Second Campus Riot, and cheated on his income tax; and though he'd made efforts lately to redeem in some measure this poor past, he had replaced old failings with new: he manufactured packages intended to disguise and mislead as well as to contain, and plastics designed to break upon the expiration of their guarantee; he spent too much time watching Telerama, for the low quality of which his own Department of Promotional Research was largely responsible; and it was he (that is to say, his staff) who had invented the premium-stamps with which rival departments now lured students into their curricula. But of all the failings for which he had to answer—and he dared say there was no article in the Junior Enochist Pledge that he had left unbroken—he counted none so vile as the desecration of his marriage-vows in the hot-chocolate arms of O.B.G.'s daughter. As well spit on the NTC pennant, become a Founderless Student-Unionist, or be disrespectful of your passèd mother like that immigrant Dean Taliped in the play, as defile purity with impurity! Which, however, wasn't to say.

"That's the only thing keeps Miss Anastasia and me apart, marriage-wise," he concluded.

I was astonished. "You mean she's said she'd let you service her if it weren't for deceiving your wife? Or what?"

"I beg you mind what you say!" he said angrily. What he meant, I discovered, had nothing to do with his wife at all (whose existence, like Stoker's, he seemed unable to keep in mind when his belovèd's name was mentioned): he simply felt so unworthy of Anastasia's pristine favors, sullied as his conscience was, that he could not bring himself to speak to her, much less make the proposal he yearned to make.

I bleated with mirth. "Oh, for Founder's sake!"

"Laugh if you want, doggone it," he said. "When a man's sunk down to the likes of O.B.G.'s daughter, it plain unstarches him for good girls like Chickie Ann and Miss Anastasia."

I assumed his tongue had slipped; it turned out, however, that he'd used one of his pet-names for Mrs. Greene. Unlikelihood! But that memory from buckwheat-days made me dizzy. Sorely I was tempted to inquire about Mrs.

Greene's tastes in verse; judging from Greene's view of certain people whom I knew also, and my recollection of his tale at the Pedal Inn, I began to wonder whether Miss Sally Ann was quite as guiltless as her husband made her out. But I had no clear evidence, and it seemed more tactful in any case to bring him indirectly to that consideration. Where to begin!

"Do you think Max is innocent or guilty?" I asked him.

He considered for a moment—not at all disturbed by the change of subject—and then replied: "You got to have faith."

"How about Maurice Stoker? Do you believe he's as flunkèd as people say?"

"Well," he said judiciously, "you know how folks are, supposing-the-worst-instead-of-the-bestwise. Me, I never met a man I didn't like."

We were drawing near Tower Hall, where I meant to have at my first task.

" 'Which ain't to say,' " I mocked.

"How's that? Which ain't to say what?"

I took his sleeve then, smiling for all my exasperation (we had parked in a lot beside the great hall), and begged him to hear me out for a quarter-hour without interrupting, as a Grand-Tutor-to-be with no motive but his welfare and eventual true Candidacy.

He blinked and bobbed. "Say what you want. I can tell by looking you're no slicker."

Without mitigation or abridgement then I reviewed for him what I knew of Anastasia, her husband, and others of our mutual acquaintance, both first-hand and by hearsay. I told him of the wondrous spankings, the boys in Uncle Ira's house, the rape in George's Gorge, and the Memorial Service. I repeated Stoker's avowed suspicion, which I myself could not entirely discredit, that Anastasia like Max had a talent for being victimized, possibly even throve on it; and further recounted what I'd witnessed and heard of Stoker's own diversions and abominations: his malice towards all, his delight in subverting every order and indulging every flunkèd impulse of the student mind. I described Dr. Sear's amusements and Dr. Eierkopf's, what I had seen in the buckwheat-meadow and done with dear departed G. Herrold; how I had bit Anastasia in the sidecar and watched her tickee the false Grand Tutor. Next I enlarged upon the divers failings of New Tammany College, past and present, as revealed to me by Max and partially confirmed by my own reading and observation: its oppression of Frumentians, its lawless Informationalism, its staggering wastefulness, its pillage of natural resource and despoil of natural beauty, its hostility to learning and refinement, its apotheosis of the lowest percentile, its vulgarity, inflated self-esteem, self-righteousness, self-deception, sentimentality, hypocrisy, artificiality, simplemindedness, naïve optimism, concupiscence, avarice, self-contradiction, ignorance, and general fatuity . . .

"Which ain't to say!" Greene could not help crying out; but his face had passed from crimson to white.

"Which isn't to say other colleges don't have their failings," I agreed. "Or that NTC doesn't have its passèd aspects too." What mattered, I declared, was that one not confuse the passèd with the flunked, or see no failure where failure was. All very well to Certify someone's Candidacy on the ground of Innocence, a no doubt passèd opposite to Culpability; I too might make such a Certification; but not unless the innocence were truly innocent, purified as well of ignorance as of guilt. "If I were your advisor, Mr. Greene—"

"*Pete,*" he said dejectedly.

"My advice would be to get a pair of high-resolution glasses like the ones Dr. Eierkopf gave me, to help you see the difference between things. And Dr. Sear's mirror, to take a closer look at yourself in."

He picked glumly at a pimple. "I got a thing about mirrors."

"Let Dr. Sear be your mirror, then," I suggested. "If there's anybody who sees the other side of things, it's Dr. Sear." To Greene's objection that his previous connection with Dr. Sear had been profitless, I replied that this time his aim would not be therapy, but sophistication, and that for Knowledge of the Campus Dr. Sear was reputed to have no equal. I repeated Dr. Sear's observation in the Amphitheater: that while Commencement no doubt involved vision, it had nothing to do with illusions, which must be got rid of absolutely.

Greene swallowed a vitamin-pill and scratched his head. "I don't know."

"Then you ought to find out," I said, and urged him further to drop in on the doctor immediately, as I would need no more chauffeuring for the present: when I'd fixed the clock I meant to call on Chancellor Rexford, just across the Mall, to

see what might be done about the Boundary Dispute; thereafter I'd most probably stop at the Infirmary myself to seek
Dr. Sear's interpretation of my third and fourth tasks, which
I did not clearly understand; I could meet Greene there if he
wished to assist me further.

"Hey, that's where Miss Stacey works, isn't it?"

I affirmed with a sigh that Mrs. Stoker was indeed Dr.
Sear's chief assistant, and wondered whether her
presence—which I'd forgotten to take into account—would
preclude or assure the success of my little project for him. He
was all enthusiasm for it now: vowed to cleave to Dr. Sear
night and day and clasp to heart his every word. "I'll tell him
you sent me," he said. "Better yet, you write me a note—like
I'm your student, sort of." The idea delighted him, as if he
were indeed a child given special permission to leave the
classroom; with little hope now of results I borrowed his
ball-point pen and scribbled an explanation to Dr. Sear on the
only available paper, the back of his spurious diploma. Seeing
Bray's inscription again, I could not resist amending it to
read *Passèd are the Kindergarteners—into First Grade.*

"You sure you don't want some good old New Tammany
know-how up there in the Clock-tower?" But though he
cheerfully insisted he'd like nothing better than to "take 'er
apart and see what makes 'er tick," he was clearly impatient
to be off. I declined the offer. He roared away then with a
"Yi-hoo!" and spray of gravel, saluted a mailman whom he
evidently took for some professor-general, and turned onto a
path marked PEDESTRIANS ONLY, which however quickly
cleared before his powerful machine.

I showed my ID-card to an attendant in the marble lobby
of Tower Hall and to another at a lift marked BELFRY, to
which I was directed. This latter, like the horn-rimmed man
at the orientation lecture, consulted a clipboard and discovered (to our mutual surprise) that thanks to WESCAC and
Chancellor Rexford I was among those persons authorized to
ascend into the clockworks—the list of names was not a large
one.

"Why can't everyone go up there?" I asked him. He wrinkled his forehead, smiled cautiously, and instructed me to
push the *Up*-button when I was ready; the elevator made no
stops between lobby and Belfry. I shrugged and pressed. The
ascent was long, or the lift slow; my ears clicked, clicked

again, and then the automatic doors opened on a formidable scene. The Belfry was floored and walled in rough cement, grease-stained and inscribed with the names of visitors and curious messages; the sides were open to the air above a breast-high wall, and afforded a splendid prospect of Great Mall—on which, however, it was difficult to concentrate, for what seized eye, ear, and nose was the huge machinery of the clockworks that almost filled the place. It seemed essentially a mesh of gearwheels of every size, from bright brass ones small as saucers to greased black cast-iron monsters, apparently motionless, of which only the topmost arc thrust through the floor; their shafts turned or were turned by drums of steel cable that disappeared through roof and floor. Great bells hung about, the smallest as large as a feed-bucket; their clappers were mounted outside them and connected by rods to various parts of the machinery. Everything clacked, clicked, creaked, and whirred together; rocker-arms and escapements teetered, governors whirled, circuit-boxes cracked and thudded, the middle-sized gears turned leisurely and the smaller ones spun into a shining blur. The place smelled of oil and iron despite the cool air that breezed through at that height.

"Halte dich dazu!" Dr. Eierkopf cried as the doors parted. I didn't see him at once, perched on Croaker's shoulders near a worktable to my left, but recognized the pipèd accent and could translate the tone of his command, if not its words. The spectacle anyhow held me for the second it took to see what I must beware of: the shaft of a great pendulum, fixed near the ceiling, swung noiselessly through a slot in the floor half a meter from the lift-sill; it rushed by even as Eierkopf spoke, hung weightily an instant, and rushed back.

"So: *der Ziegenbübe.*" Eierkopf squinted through his eyeglasses; Croaker grinned and grunted. "Step here then. Look sharp." As I made my way to them between the wall and the pendulum-slot, Dr. Eierkopf had Croaker place him on a high stool. The great Frumentian then bounced up and down, fetched up his shirt (he was dressed now in his usual garb, the gray cotton sweatsuit worn by varsity athletes, with NTC across chest and shoulders) and pointed happily to his belly, where I saw a livid pattern of fresh-looking scars below his navel.

"He wants you to congratulate him on his Certification," Dr. Eierkopf mocked. "You want evidence that Dr. Bray's a

faker? There you are." Bray it seemed had left the Belfry not
a quarter-hour past, having visited it to make an official
inspection of the clockworks, and before proceeding to the
Chancellor's mansion had Certified both Croaker and Dr.
Eierkopf.

"Both of you?" I could not conceal my incredulity. Dr.
Eierkopf agreed that Commencement Gate, whatever and
wherever it might be, could not imaginably be wide enough
to admit contraries: Entelechus's Second and Third Logical
Laws forbade the possibility. That he himself was a Candidate, if not indeed a Graduate, he needed no Grand Tutor
to tell him: Scapulas's motto *Graduation is a state of mind*
had long hung on the walls of Observatory and Belfry; it was
a conclusion he had reached, like Scapulas, by inexorable
logic, and confirmed to his satisfaction on WESCAC. He had
explained it politely to Bray out of deference to the
administration in which he hoped to recoup his former high
position, not out of any reverence for the man himself; and
the self-styled Grand Tutor had had the good sense merely to
write *Q.E.D.* under that motto, making it a certificate of
Eierkopf's Candidacy.

"What else could he do?" Dr. Eierkopf smiled over his
gums. "Even Scapulas was a brute compared to me." Which
made it the more absurd, he scoffed, that Bray should also
Certify the shoulders, so to speak, on which the head
perched. Scornfully he quoted Bray's quotation from the
Founder's Scroll: *"Consider the beasts of the woods, that
never fail."* Whatever Enos Enoch might have meant by that
advice, He surely wouldn't have Certified an animal who
couldn't even read the Certification. But Bray, apparently
determined to pass absolutely everyone, had first translated
the Certificate of Candidacy into a Frumentian pictogram (a
matriculation and procreation symbol, so he'd claimed) and
then, somehow gaining Croaker's confidence, had engraved it
on the black man's belly. Eierkopf himself was unfamiliar
with the emblem; whether the bearer understood its significance was questionable, but he was most pathetically
proud to display it in spite of the discomfort he no doubt
suffered.

I did not denounce these Certifications, but concurred with
Dr. Eierkopf's sentiments regarding the Certifier. Croaker's
incisions certainly did look tender; however, I could discern
no subscription of any sort on Eierkopf's Scapulist motto,

which hung over a worktable littered with files, lenses, grind-
stones, calipers, micrometers, high-intensity lamps, and cartons of eggs.

"I don't see those initials you mentioned," I said.

His head lolled, apparently in amusement. "I can't see
them either! Except through this glass." He pointed to a
thick-ringed lens on the table and explained that Bray—
whose ingenuity he *did* have to admire—had thought it
appropriate to inscribe his Certification in letters of a sort
and size that only an Eierkopfian Lens (a mated pair of
lenses, actually, the one "synthetic," or panoramical, the
other "analytic," or microscopical) could resolve and
focus—and that inconsistently, so it seemed, for when he
held the device for me I could see nothing.

"Oh well," Eierkopf said; "at least my Certification makes
sense, even if not everybody sees it all the time. Croaker is
seeing his, but nobody understands it!"

I was about to reply that Croaker could at least *feel* his.
But as Eierkopf made a gesture of contempt with the hand
that held the lens, I thought I glimpsed the missing initials on
its objective face. I pointed them out to him, a bit
triumphantly it may be, as further evidence of Bray's
deceitfulness; but although Dr. Eierkopf himself could not
see the reversed letters .ⵚⴹ.Ϙ on the glass (owing to some
feature of his spectacles), he was undisturbed by the disclosure.

"The point's the same," he said. "Anyhow, I told you I
don't believe in Grand Tutors till I see once a miracle." He
was pleased, however, to clear up the somewhat puzzling detail of the image's inconstancy, as he was convinced that for
better or worse all phenomena were ultimately intelligible.
Contrary to what one might suppose, he said, an image twice
refracted in certain complementary ways was not always
thereby restored to its original state, any more than a cat
dissected and reassembled in the zoology laboratories was the
same cat afterwards: sometimes it came out doubly distorted
(as it always was in theory); sometimes it seemed to vanish
altogether, especially when the characteristics of his own extraordinary eyeglasses and the astigmatism they compensated
for were added to the optical equation, or the light was
wrong.

"But," he smiled, "take away my lenses, I'm blind as Dean
Taliped." However, I was not to infer that because all lenses
distorted ("Your own included," he said, perhaps unable to

see that I wore none), nothing could be truly seen; all that was necessary was to compensate for optical error, and for this he relied, in his own work, on the lens in his hand, which he knew to be accurate.

I asked him how he knew. His round eyes twinkled.

"I like you, Goat-Boy! Croaker fixes you a lunch, you can eat it around behind the clockworks." But my question, which I'd thought to be serious and difficult as well as perceptive, he disposed of lightly, perhaps facetiously. The lens affirmed his Graduatehood, did it not? And since he was in fact a Graduate, he affirmed the accuracy of the lens.

"Wait a minute!" I protested. "Bray Certified your Candidacy, but you don't believe in him."

He wagged a hairless little digit at me. "I won't affirm Dr. Bray, but I can't deny him, because it must be the same with Grand Tutors, if they really exist, as it is with Graduates: it takes one to know one, not so?"

I readily agreed.

"And a Grand Tutor would know Graduates from non-Graduates, *ja?* But not vice-versa. Well, just so with this lens: I know it's correct because a Graduate like me can tell correct lenses from incorrect ones." The case was analogous, he argued, to the interdependent relation between WESCAC and the Tower Hall Clock, which he had explained to me in the observatory, and was reflected also in the problem of the clock's accuracy, which, like all problems involving final standards and first principles, could be only academic.

"You claim you're the Grand Tutor yourself, and Bray's not," he said, "but you can't prove it—without a miracle. You can only know it, just as I know I'm a Graduate."

I very much wanted to pursue the matter of the clock, my reason for being there, but I could not resist declaring to him that his position seemed to me not only circularly reasoned (which might indeed, as his analogies showed, be strictly a logical problem, not a practical one), but inconsistent with itself: he had deduced his Graduateship, on his own admission, by an operation of formal logic, and denied Croaker's by the same procedure; yet when the logic led him into a bind he waved it away, freely interchanging conclusions and premises.

"Is that a fact, *Geissbübchen!*" he said indulgently. "Then please Grand-Tutor me while Croaker and I do our work. You still don't think I'm a Graduate?"

Croaker all this while had been hanging by one hand from

a steel rafter near the machinery of the clock, with a light attached to his forehead and what looked like a whetstone in his other hand. Before him rocked an anchor-shaped escapement several meters tall, which served in turn to actuate the great pendulum, or be actuated by it; its impulse- and locking-pallets engaged and released the teeth of the last gear in the train, and the escapement itself rocked on a knife-edged bright steel bar that ran through a ring in the top of its shaft. Between *tick* and *tock* Croaker dextrously would swipe one side of this bar's edge with his stone, between *tock* and *tick* the other; then without ever touching the escapement itself he'd make some sort of measurement through a lens fixed onto the bar, and croak the reading down to Dr. Eierkopf. His noises were unintelligible to me, but Dr. Eierkopf would jot figures in a notebook, say *"Ja ja"* or *"Pfui,"* and return to measurements of his own, which he seemed to be taking with great delicacy from a white hen's-egg mounted in a nest of elaborate apparatus.

"May I speak frankly, sir?" I asked. "Presumptuous as it may seem to you, I *do* have a suggestion to make, and then I'd like to ask your advice about repairing this clock . . ."

His pink eyes rolled behind the glasses. "You lost your mind, Goat-Boy?"

I showed him my Assignment and told him how I'd come by it. "If it says to fix the clock, then the clock must be broken, mustn't it? I believe you told me WESCAC always reasons correctly."

Very much concerned, Dr. Eierkopf affirmed that the computer was normally incapable of faulty reasoning; he pointed out, however, that in the absence of any actual malfunction in the works, to speak of Tower Clock's being inaccurate was to speak unintelligibly, as who should accuse the Standard Meter of being short.

"But you told me yourself last night that the clock needed working on," I reminded him, adding that my own self-winding watch (by which term I meant, innocently, that I wound it myself) showed a different hour, whereto with his permission and Croaker's help I'd thought to make Tower Clock conform.

"Don't talk so!" Eierkopf cried. "You don't touch anything! It's bad enough Croaker, he's such a clumsy!" He squinted at my Assignment-list again, this time through his lens, and suddenly clapped his hands. "I got it, Goat-Boy!"

Croaker dropped from the rafter at once, mistaking the signal, and lifted Dr. Eierkopf onto his shoulders; the scientist was too pleased with his new idea to protest.

"It says *Complete in no time, ja?* So: the clock's not *kaput*, it takes you no time to fix it! You're done already."

This reasoning, though I could not refute it, satisfied me less completely than it did Dr. Eierkopf, who declared it at once a fulfillment of my task, an explanation of the troublesome due-date of my Assignment, and a vindication of WESCAC's "malistic" dependability. To my inquiry, Why was he himself tinkering with the clockworks if no repairs were needed? he replied that standards of reference were sometimes improvable though never logically subject to challenge; thus the University Standard Meter, for example, was originally one ten-millionth of the campus's quadrant, later the distance at 0° Centigrade between two particular scratches on a platinum-iridium bar in the Intercollegiate Department of Standards, and presently one million five hundred fifty-three thousand one hundred sixty-four and thirteen one-hundredths wave-lengths of red light from the element cadmium. In like manner the accuracy of Tower Clock was from time to time improved—though only by comparison to its own past accuracy, never (". . . *Q.E.D.*, Goat-Boy . . .") by comparison to the accuracy of other timepieces. Current work in the field, I was told, centered around escapement-theory, and had led to opposing points of view. One group of researchers (whom Eierkopf referred to contemptuously as "Everlasting Now-niks") would abolish all forms of escapement in favor of what they—or their detractors—called "tickless time"; the other, led by Dr. Eierkopf, hoped with the aid of special lenses and micromilling techniques to perfect the edge on which the present escapement pivoted—or the theory, I was not sure which.

"Here you got *Tick, nicht wahr?*" he said, and pointed to one pallet-point of the anchor-shaped escapement. "Over there you got *Tock*. So pretend all the Ticks is coming and the Tocks is already gone: what I want to do is measure the point exactly between, where Tick becomes Tock. Last term we got it down past millimicroseconds; pretty soon we lick it altogether." His labor was complicated by several factors: the two schools of thought, though not politically based, happened to divide roughly along East-West lines, the "Everlasting Now-niks" being in general associated with Sakhyanist curricula; and the political connotations which escapement-theory thus unfortunately took on were compounded—and confused—by the fact that Tower Hall Tower was a reference-point for cartographic as well as temporal measurements: that keen-edged fulcrum which Croaker had been honing happened to run north and south on the meridian of longitude which, higher up towards Founder's Hill, divided East from West Campus, and had been used as a coordinate in laying down the Power Line; moreover, the weathercock atop the Belfry marked the center of New Tammany's Great Mall area—a point indicated by brass discs on every floor of Tower Hall: both North-South avenues and East-West streets were numbered from the shaft whence its four arms extended. In consequence of all this it was difficult even for Eierkopf as official Clockwatcher to get permission to move or modify any part of the works, the more so as his critics (some sincerely concerned, some merely venting their anti-Bonifacism) charged that his method was self-defeating.

"I've gone from ticks to milliseconds to microseconds to millimicroseconds," he said, "and the dumbsticks say I just make bigger and bigger words for smaller and smaller things, but never get to the place between Tick and Tock." What their ignorance left out of account—and mine too, which saw no reply to their objection—was a technical breakthrough he'd recently achieved and was about to put to use: a precision honing device he called the Infinite Divisor. Attached to one end of the fulcrum-bar, its two opposed milling-heads—tiny diamond-dust affairs—would dart along the upper knife-edge, honing it as they went; during their approach to the hole in the escapement-shaft (the point on which the whole assembly pivoted) automatic calibrators would halve and halve again, *ad infinitum*, the width of the edge, until theoretically it reached a perfect point at the center of the hole and the midpoint of the Tick-Tock swing—a point whose measurement would incidentally be recorded on the calibrator-gauges.

"One moment, sir!" I protested, dizzied by this conception. Croaker held his sweatshirt-front out from his scars and whimpered a little. "It seems to me—"

"Pretty smart, *ja?*" He may have been addressing Croaker, whose head he patted, or myself. I agreed that the idea was striking, but wondered about certain theoretical problems which I sensed more than saw articulably: a riddle Max had posed me once about Peleides and the Tortoise . . .

"*Pfui*," Dr. Eierkopf said. "That's why two grinding-heads instead of one: we tackle the problem from both sides. Better hold your ears now."

He inserted a pinky in each of Croaker's, and Croaker clapped a giant palm over each of his, just as a new set of whirs and clackings shot through the works. I didn't catch his meaning until the first clapper swung against its bell, big as the lift I'd ascended in, and shuddered me to the marrow. Others followed, a tooth-jarring sequence even with ears held, until a four-phrase melody signaling the hour had been chimed: then a series of bells ascended diatonically a scale-and-a-half. The eighth brought a little cry from Dr. Eierkopf, either despite Croaker's pressing harder or because of it; the last shivered the egg in its calipered nest.

"*Durchfall und Vertreibung!*" Dr. Eirkopf squeaked, and pounded Croaker feebly on the pate. "You set the egg-clamp for high *sol* again! Put me down and clean up!" Croaker perched him obligingly back upon a stool and set to licking the apparatus.

"Didn't I tell you, Goat-Boy? It's the *Schwarzer*-work that flunks me, not the brainwork." His oölogical researches, of which I'd seen other evidence in the Observatory, were, like his clock-work, designed to restore him to favor in the administrative and general-student eye: having been told many terms ago by WESCAC, in the course of his ill-fated eugenical investigations, that "Commencement commences *ab avo*," he had launched into a grand historico-chemico-mathe-matico-biologico-mythophysical treatise upon the egg in all its aspects (excepting the culinary, which he dismissed in a long footnote to the title as intellectually unpalatable); its fourteen volumes were complete, as well as their prefaces, plates, paste-ins, fold-outs, glossaries, indices, appendices, bibliographies, celebratory sonnets, statistical supplements, epistles dedicatory, tape-recorded musical accompaniment, and jacket-copy; all that stood in the way of its publication (and proof of the author's own Commencement, if any was required) was a single little exercise in comparative oömetry which he'd planned to include as a footnote to *zygote,* the final index-entry. But so clumsy had been Croaker's measurement of long and short oöic axes, and so irrepressible his appetite for the subject of their researches, they'd already missed the Spring-Carnival target-date for publication, selected by the press for its obvious promotional tie-ins.

"Same with my Infinite Divisor," he lamented. "The blueprints are drawn, the computations are computed, but Croaker keeps dropping the pieces! What good's a right-hand man that's all thumbs?" And in a sudden access of dejection, as once before in the Observatory, he wondered aloud whether brutes like his roommate, altogether free of reason and discernment, were not after all the truly passèd.

"I'm not sure about that yet," I replied, assuming he'd put the question to me. "But even if Bray's citations for both of you are right—and like yourself I don't see how they could *both* be—it doesn't seem to me that either one of you has qualified for Candidacy yet on the grounds he cited."

Dr. Eierkopf was turning a fresh egg sadly in his fingers. "If I told him once about high *sol,* I told him twenty times." Now he brightened and tittered. "Did you know your friend Anastasia can break these with her *levator ani?* I had her do a dozen Grade-A Large with a stress-gauge on, for Volume Nine. I show you the readings . . ."

"Right there, sir," I said, shaking my head at the invitation; "that kind of thing, and the night-glass and all . . ." My point, which I tried to make tactfully, was that if he believed passèdness to be the sort of rationality that WESCAC (at least in pre-"noctic" terms) exemplified, then he was by no means a Graduate, or even a Candidate, so long as he indulged even vicariously such Croakerish appetites as I had seen signs of. Nor could Croaker, on the other hand, be said to be passed by the standards of *his* Certification, it seemed to me: what beast of the woods would so obligingly fetch and carry, not to mention taking scientific measurements?

"He always gets them wrong," Dr. Eierkopf said hopefully.

"But he *gets* them. And he cleans up messes—"

"His own."

"What beast of the woods does that? Not even a goat can cook pablum, or chew designs on a stick, or focus lenses . . ."

Eierkopf sniffed. "He busts as many as he focuses."

The point was, I insisted, that neither of them met strictly the terms of their Certifications, any more than Peter Greene or Max, in my estimation, met the terms of theirs; contrary as the roommates clearly were, there was still a flunking measure of Eierkopfishness in Croaker, and of Croakeriety in Eierkopf, which came no doubt from their close and constant association. And this was the more pointed failing in Dr. Eierkopf (I tried to suggest), because it went against his life's activity and principle: the differentiation of *this* from *that*. Let him but perfect and add a mirror to his high-resolution lenses; apply to himself as it were his Infinite Divisor (of which I heartily approved): he would see how far he stood from Commencement Gate.

"You want me to turn loose Croaker, like before? You got a screw loose, Goat-Boy?"

I reminded him politely that I had no clear conviction that Graduation *was* what he believed it to be; only that if it was, it behooved him to discern and repudiate everything about him to the contrary. Not to seem disrespectful of his age and genius (but also to drive my point home), I declared myself in his debt for this position of mine: surely the blurring of distinctions, especially between contraries, was flunking— hence Maurice Stoker's devotion to that activity. And just as the first step to Commencement Gate must be the differentia- tion of Passage and Failure, so (it seemed increasingly to me) the several steps thereafter—in the completion of my Assignment, for example—must depend upon corollary distinctions.

"I'll need the lenses you gave me for my next chore," I concluded as agreeably as possible; "I wish I could borrow your Divisor too."

Dr. Eierkopf seemed neither angered, as I had feared, nor chastened, as I had hoped, by my advice. "You still believe you're the Grand Tutor!" he marveled, and pensively gave Croaker instructions about the mounting of another egg. Then he repeated what he'd said the night before: "I half wish you were, to prove I was right about the GILES."

I smiled. "If I have to be the GILES to be the Grand Tutor, then I must be the GILES, somehow: it's a simple syl- logism." However, I added, I couldn't very well be Virginia Hector's child, inasmuch as I had it from Ira Hector's own lips that Anastasia was.

Eierkopf turned up his palms. "Then you aren't the Grand Tutor, any more than Bray. Look once, I prove it on WES- CAC." He gave a further string of undecipherable instruc- tions to Croaker, who turned several switches on one of those consoles that seemed to be everywhere in the College. I watched with sharp attention.

"The child born from the GILES would be a Grand

Tutor," he declared. Croaker punched certain buttons. "Miss Anastasia Hector isn't a Grand Tutor, we agree." More buttons. "But no woman except Virginia Hector could have got in where WESCAC had the GILES. Since Anastasia is the one that got born, it couldn't have been the GILES that Virginia got fertilized by, and you couldn't be the Grand Tutor. Now WESCAC reads it out." Croaker had pressed buttons after each of these propositions; he pulled a long lever now on the side of the console, things dinged and whirred, and from an opening down in the front a strip of paper began clicking out, which Dr. Eierkopf perused with satisfied nods and peeps. I would have objected that his initial premise, even if granted, seemed to me inadequate to the case—it was no GILES that had engendered Enos Enoch, or the original Sakhyan, nor need one have engendered me: if the GILES could be shown to have come to naught, that fact cost me nothing but a handy proof of my authenticity, which however was contingent on no such proofs. But Dr. Eierkopf, having said, *"Ja . . . ja . . .* just so . . . that's that . . " at points along the paper tape, suddenly pushed his eyeglasses up on his nose and whipped out the lens that bore his name.

"Unless!" he cried. He grinned at me slyly and winked his left eye. "Maybe you and Anastasia are twins, hey?"

Owing to the liberal circumstances of my kidship I was more interested in the relevance of this possibility to my claim of Grand-Tutorhood than appalled by its retroactive implications about the G. Herrold Memorial Service. But I was not ignorant of studentdom's attitude towards incest; I chided Dr. Eierkopf for salivating at the idea that I'd serviced my sister, and firmly declined his offer to rerun the tape he'd made two nights before on the Safety Surveillance monitor.

"That's just what I meant a while ago," I said. "You've got more of Croaker in you than you'll admit."

"When I find out you're Stacey's twin brother, I take your advice," he promised merrily.

A little cross, I bade him goodbye and called the lift. My first chore, so far as I could see, was accomplished by forfeit, and I must get on with the second, at the same time foraging some lunch if I could; if Dr. Eierkopf would not heed my suggestions, it was his own flunkage.

"Don't fuss, *Zickelchen,*" he said; "I just tease you a little."

"It's yourself you're teasing, sir; I don't care either way."

What I *did* care about, I declared, was Bray's false Certifications, and I urged him to consider, for his own and Croaker's sake, my suggestion. He promised to do so; and further to placate me (for I had no great faith in his pledge) he offered to run a similar logical-possibility test for me on my other chores.

"To me, for instance, there's just three ways to end the Boundary Dispute," he said. "We EAT them; they EAT us; or we all link arms and sing *Wir wollen unseren alten Dekan Siegfried wiederhaben*. But WESCAC maybe knows another way . . ."

"So do I," I replied. The lift came. I assured Dr. Eierkopf I wasn't angry, requested him at least to relay to Croaker, if possible, my sentiments and advice about Bray's Certification, and thanked him for teaching me, intentionally or otherwise, the relevance to my Assignment of his lens-principle, which I'd already been applying unawares in my criticisms of Max, Peter Greene, himself, and even Maurice Stoker.

He waggled his head. "You're a wonder, Goat-Boy! Maybe WESCAC tells me what to make of you. You don't want me to ask it anything?"

I replied that while I no longer regarded WESCAC as essentially Trollish (on the contrary, I rather respected it now as the embodiment of Differentiation, which I'd come to think the very principle of Passage), nevertheless I trusted myself to find my own Answers. I wished him success with his great oölogical treatise, promised to consult it on the day of its appearance to find out whether chicken or egg had paleoontological priority, and pressed the *Down*-button.

3.

My plan for dealing with the Boundary Dispute was necessarily tentative, more a principle than a program; but its wisdom seemed to me confirmed by my luncheon-briefing in the history of the problem. Leaving Tower Hall I had crossed Great Mall to the Chancellor's Mansion ("Lucky's Light House," wags had dubbed it, because of Mr. Rexford's installation of floodlights all about the grounds and his custom of leaving the interior-lights burning all night in virtually every room), where, on the strength of my special Candidacy, I was admitted—not directly to Lucius Rexford, as I had hoped, but to the office of one of his advisors, a gentleman whose skin was the rich fawn color of Redfearn's Tom's coat, and whose knowledgeable, crisp analysis belied my assumption that all Frumentians were either brutes like Croaker or gentle servitors like G. Herrold. His dress was impeccable, his mind and tongue were quick, and though he could not affect the Rexfordian forelock, his accent was closer to the Chancellor's than to Peter Greene's, for example. An elegant meal was sent in, of which I ate the salad- and vegetable-courses while it was explained to me that the Chancellor was about to depart for a Summit Symposium at the University Council that afternoon, where he was expected to censure the Nikolayans for breaking the "Provisional Fast" agreement and provoking fresh incidents at the Power Line.

"Originally that boundary was defined jointly by EASCAC and WESCAC," the advisor said; "our only experiment so far in cooperative computation. The principal sightings were made just after Campus Riot Two from the Tower Clock fulcrum on our end and a similar reference-point in the Nikolayan Control Room in Founder's Hill, and the main power-cables for East and West Campuses were laid side by side along most of the boundary." For many terms, he said, students and staff from the westernmost East-Campus colleges had "transferred" freely in large numbers, without authorization, across the line to West Campus. More recently, however, EASCAC had read out that any further unauthorized transferees would be EATen at the line—and only the sick or feeble-minded were ever authorized. WESCAC's reply had been a threat to EAT Nikolay College automatically the instant any Nikolayan EAT-wave crossed the west side of the Power Line, and EASCAC had read out an identical counter-threat. There the dangerous situation stood: a few determined East-Campusers still managed to slip across; a few more were EATen in the attempt by "short-order" waves designed to fade out just a hairsbreadth from NTC's line. A few border-guards on each side—those intrepid fellows who walked the great cables like armed acrobats—had fallen to their deaths in the no-man's land between East and West or been shot from their perches by unidentified snipers. Any such incident, both sides feared, might touch off Campus Riot III, the end of the University. Yet it was contended in New Tammany that the Nikolayans were covertly advancing their line towards NTC's to exploit an ambiguous clause in the original read-out ("The Boundary shall be midway between the East and West Power Lines"); the Western position was that this clause was intended to locate the cables with reference to the Boundary, not vice-versa, and they demanded a resurvey from Tower Hall and Founder's Hill. But the Nikolayans refused to admit outside surveyors, even from "neutral" colleges, to enter their Control Room, calling the proposal a mere pretext for cribbing secrets, and argued besides (though not officially) that it was the Power Lines that determined the location of the Boundary. Thus the dispute, which had been being debated continuously in the University Council for at least six terms, and had come to involve the equally thorny question of "fasting" (the popular term for abstention from EAT-tests): on the one side, pacifists like Max advocated unilateral fasting; on the other, "preventive rioters" like Eblis Eierkopf taunted, "He who fasts first fasts last," and counseled, "He who fasts last, lasts." In between was every shade of military- and political-science opinion: Chancellor Rexford's own, as affirmed in the Assembly-Before-the-Grate, was that the debate must continue, however meager its yield or exasperating the harrassments, inasmuch as the hope of effective compromise, though slim, was in his judgment the only hope of studentdom.

"I expect we'll test as long as they do," my host concluded; "but we won't break off the Summit Symposium or leave the U.C., even if it's proved that they're moving their cable."

"I'm not so sure that's a good idea," I ventured.

"Pity." He patted his lips on a linen napkin. "The Political Science Department, after years of study, seems rather to approve of it."

"What I want to suggest to Mr. Rexford is a different principle entirely," I said. "I thought of it a few minutes ago."

"Ah. Care for a cigar?"

"No, thank you, sir. You see, I was discussing a different matter this morning with Dr. Eierkopf, and before that I'd been talking with Mr. Maurice Stoker . . ."

His eyes turned up from the end of his cigar. "I see. Eierkopf and Stoker."

I would have bade him please not to misunderstand me, that my strategy for the Quiet Riot was not derived from those gentlemen, though my conversation with them had inspired it. But as he repeated their names his eyes flashed over my shoulder and he jumped smiling to his feet, jamming the fresh cigar into an ashtray. I glanced doorwards and had presence enough of mind to rise quickly also as the Chancellor himself strode in, unannounced. His forelocked entourage pressed just outside, some with concerned expressions, others grinning like Rexford himself, whose visit to the office was apparently not expected.

"Did I hear someone say a naughty word?" He shook hands with me, waved off his assistant's apology in my behalf, and congratulated me on my penetration of Scrapegoat Grate; I thanked him in turn for his prompt action in clearing my entry into various College buildings.

"It's not Maurice Stoker's idea I wanted to tell you about," I said; "it's my own. My second Assignment-task is to end the Boundary Dispute, and I thought—"

"Look here," he interrupted, obviously enjoying his associates' discomfiture; "want to ride along with us to the Symposium? You can tell me your plan on the way, and we'll wrap up the whole Quiet Riot by dinner-time."

Though I knew the prediction for a tease, the invitation seemed sincere, and I accepted it eagerly. With the train of guards and assistants I gimped after him through elegant corridors, pleased to be photographed in his presence, though I knew that the mightiest deans and chancellors were as pallid candleflames beside the radiance of Truth, which from the sun of Grand-Tutorhood warmed and lit the University. On another impulse he turned onto a verandah, where, from a respectful distance, we saw a handsome young woman turn her cheek to him for kissing; she was sitting with a group of similarly comely young men and women, all of whom except herself rose at his approach; he chatted for some moments, more with them than with her, and then led us to a row of white motorcycles with large closed sidecars, along the curb. I found myself honored with a seat in the first of these, along with the Chancellor; the remainder of the party paired off in the others.

"I told Mrs. Rexford I hoped you could help us with the East-Campus Transfer problem," he joked as we started off. The sidecars were elegantly appointed, and virtually soundproof. "Since you made it through the Turnstile and Scrapegoat Grate, maybe you can find a way for people to slip through the Power Line." He asked me then how I was faring, and I recounted briefly my morning's travels and my concern at Harold Bray's promiscuous Certifications. He tisked sympathetic disapproval of Max's attitude. If only Max would leave all pleading to the lawyers, he said, there would be no trouble getting an acquittal, or at worst a suspended sentence; Siegfried-New Tammany relations would not be threatened, and Max would be free to punish himself in any way he saw fit. The problem was especially vexing at the present time, Rexford added, when NTC was counting on the support of its former adversary in a number of controversial programs which would be handicapped, even spoiled, by any general resurgence of anti-Siegfrieder sentiment in West Campus. At my mention of Maurice Stoker I felt him bristle and knew I was being undiplomatic, but as it bore upon my plan for the Boundary Dispute I explained my conviction that Stoker claimed kinship with him in order that none might believe the claim; thus that the flunkèd libel had a passèd effect, if not a passèd motive: the polar distinguishing of Passage and Failure, which never for an instant must be confused.

Mr. Rexford was cordially skeptical. "Earlier this morning you wanted me to admit he *was* my brother."

"If I did I shouldn't have," I apologized. "I think you should be as opposite to him as you can be. You should deny him once and for all, publicly. By name."

"Oh well . . ." He waved cheerfully from the sidecar to throngs of well-wishers along the seedy campus streets through which we happened to be passing. Many were garishly dressed women—prostitute ladies, in fact, as I presently learned, or "campus-followers," who throve in the rougher quadrangles of the College. They all waved back, as did their pimps and the other toughs of the quad. "That would be going a little far, if you mean refuse to do business with him at all."

"Then you won't like my plan for ending the Boundary Dispute, I'm sure," I said; "my notion about opposites is that they ought to be kept as distinct and far apart as possible."

The Chancellor assured me that he quite agreed. We were passing now through an equally squalid quadrangle: the paths and steps were littered with drunks; youths loitered in mean-looking knots; posters advertised erotic films; a man punched a woman in the mouth with such force that she almost dropped the baby she was nursing. This last scene particularly arrested Mr. Rexford, who turned to watch the pair over his shoulder when we had passed, and tisked his tongue when the lady's assailant kissed her contusions.

"It seems to me," I went on, "that making clear distinctions must be the first step to Graduation: not confusing one thing with another, especially the passèd with the flunked."

"I couldn't agree more," Mr. Rexford smiled. "That's why I think of WESCAC as our colleague instead of our enemy: the only cure for knowledge is more knowledge." However, he added (speaking as though in a rehearsed interview, but growing clearly interested in the subject as he talked), there were two distinctions in particular which he felt must be insisted on when speaking of the importance of Distinctions in general. One was the difference between scientific and human affairs: in the former, though all might be precise in theory, seldom was anything in fact, and in consequence—as Dr. Eierkopf's frustrations illustrated—real nature could only approximate the orderliness of theoretical nature, and often contradicted it. In the areas of studentdom's morals and government, on the other hand, all theories soon led to impossible contradictions—hence the typical despair of advanced students in those fields—but in practical fact much could be achieved. East and West Campuses, he reminded me before I could remind him, were ideologically irreconcilable—thus the conservative insistence that negotiation between them must be fruitless—yet the record showed, to his satisfaction at least, that constant negotiation backed by flexible strength and firm leadership had brought New Tammany and Nikolay Colleges closer together in fact, if not in theory. "Remember what I said this morning about the two sides of the arch," he said; "their opposition supports the whole building. Look how influential the small colleges are getting in the U.C. because we and the Nikolayans are deadlocked. It's a constructive state of affairs."

The second distinction he'd also mentioned in his speech of the morning: the difference between questioning means and questioning ends; between the criticism of operations and the challenging of first principles. The University, he insisted again, made what sense it made only when one accepted certain first principles without question. "You remember the old story about the Chancellor's New Gown, that the tailors claimed was invisible to cuckolds? Well, I say the truth of it is that he *was* robed until that kindergartener said he wasn't. The people laughed at him then and punished the tailors for fraud, because the alternative was to admit that they *were* all cuckolds, every one, including the Chancellor himself." I noticed that he blushed at this point. "As for the child: if he was too young to be cuckolded, he was too young to understand a robe invisible to cuckolds. That doesn't make him right. There are plenty of things on campus that can't be seen until you've learned to see them, and some of the most important disappear when you look at them directly, or too closely. It doesn't follow that they aren't there." He reaffirmed his criticism of the author of *Taliped Decanus:* "The fact is, Taliped was a good father and husband and a good dean until he let his basic research go too far: the playwright cheats by pretending that a flunking situation can exist without anyone's knowing it, and then choosing one that everybody in the theater knows about except the characters in the play! So the idea of Taliped's *not* finding out is as horrifying to us as his discovery." He blushed again. "But look at you; look at me; look at all of us—we're getting along, aren't we? Was Cadmus College any better off at the end of the play? Why didn't Taliped leave well enough alone? People ought to mind their own business, and get their work done, and not ask basic questions like whether anything's worth doing!"

This last was said with such surprising heat, even bitterness, that the Chancellor noticed my dismay and apologized. "I get as carried away as Maurice Stoker sometimes," he confessed with a little laugh. "It's a great temptation to say 'Flunk all this responsibility and reasonableness.' It would be awfully easy to go home and get drunk, and beat your wife like that fellow back there instead of living *reasonably* with her; or say any mad thing you feel like saying instead of weighing all the consequences."

He admitted then that his unwonted vociferousness was due to his certainty that I'd challenge the ground of his recent Certification by "the Grand Tutor," which now he showed me. *Passèd are the riot-quellers,* it read: *if order is better than disorder, Lucius Rexford is a Candidate for Graduation.*

"My assumption is that order *is* better than disorder," he

said. "I don't question that for a second, and frankly I don't care to hear it questioned."

I assured him that I had no quarrel with the proposition; on the contrary, I was ready to affirm (as I would not have been on the previous day) that order and disorder were like Passage and Failure, not to be confused either in fact or in value. I kept to myself certain reservations about his comment on the *Taliped* play (had he forgotten that Cadmus College was rotting and dying from the poison of the Dean's secret flunkage? And that Gynander, the Cadmusian equivalent of a Grand Tutor, had *not* been ignorant of the awful answer?) and commended sincerely both his distinction between theory and practice in science and in politics and his general position vis-à-vis first principles, which I rather shared: would I not otherwise have despaired long since of my undemonstrable Grand-Tutorhood? Of all humans I had met on campus, I told him, there was none whose Candidacy it would more delight me to affirm than his . . .

"*But,*" he grinned sadly. I had indeed a *but* or two, not unrelated to my program for ending the Boundary Dispute, but before I could think of a respectful way to voice them the Chancellor said, "They tell me you've seen a bit of Mr. and Mrs. Stoker recently." I acknowledged I had, remembering suddenly and with interest an insinuation of Stoker's: that Lucius Rexford was among those to whom Anastasia had granted—more accurately, not denied—her favors. The image of Mrs. Rexford's coolness on the verandah recurred to me. "Excuse the personal question," the Chancellor went on: "we've all heard how he abuses his wife; even beats her. Did you get the impression that she loves him?"

I considered for a moment—not so much the *yes* or *no* demanded by the question, but how I might turn my response to more pertinent account.

"Do you think it's ever right for a man to strike his wife, sir?"

"What?" He frowned sharply. "Well, no. No, of course not." Whether or not he saw the difference between his question and mine, he answered at once, blushing vigorously, and added before I could think how to ask it: "Or be unfaithful to her, either. It's indefensible—especially if his wife is loyal and affectionate."

"And Stoker's *not* your brother, is he, sir? You agree that his way of life is flunkèd, don't you?"

Because I saw his eyes begin to flash dangerfully, I hastened to modulate to a less personal and particular application of my general point, the same I'd endeavored to make to Max, Peter Greene, Dr. Eierkopf, and Croaker—even, half-wittingly, to Anastasia, and perversely to Ira Hector and Stoker himself: that apart from the question of whether the grounds of their Certifications were valid or the Certifier was authorized, I was not convinced that themselves quite measured up to those several standards after all. Just as I'd found on the one hand Stoker's Dean-o'-Flunkhood and Ira Hector's selfishness equivocal, and likewise on the other Anastasia's vulnerable magnanimity, Max's scapegoatery, Greene's innocence, Eierkopf's asceticism, and Croaker's appetitiveness, so I suspected that Lucius Rexford was not so entirely free of Stokerishness, so to speak, as we both might wish: I dared guess he had lost his temper with Mrs. Rexford on occasion, perhaps even had struck her—surely not more than once or twice—as well as sampled at least upon one occasion the extracurricular pleasure of Anastasia. Obversely, his condemnation of extremism and disorder, as manifest in Stoker, had never been more than mild; it was his partisans and associates who shouted down the gossip of their fraternity.

Not to speak of these things directly, I praised instead his speech of the morning and the philosopher Entelechus on whom he'd drawn, and with whose thought I had a passing acquaintance, thanks to Max. Then I made bold to suggest that the principle of moderation and compromise lost its meaning if it too was compromised and moderated. Entelechus himself, I happened to recall, had warned against "means in the extremes"—by which he meant that one was not to lie, cheat, steal, rape, or murder even discreetly, but to eschew those vices altogether. Just so (I spoke in as objectively illustrative a tone as I could manage) with adultery, wife-beating, drunkenness, and violence of all sorts; the question was not when, with whom, how much, or how often, but whether at all in any case; and the answer was No.

"There's the U.C. building ahead," the Chancellor observed. His voice was glum.

I begged him in that event to hear me out, as I'd only been illustrating what seemed to me to be the correct Entelechian approach to the Boundary Dispute.

"Our present policy isn't Entelechian?" His tone was

amused: New Tammany's strategy, he said, had been to do business of every sort on as many fronts as possible with the Nikolayans; to involve the affairs of the two colleges so subtly and extensively that *détente* would be the actual state of intercollegiate affairs regardless of theoretical contradictions, and riot would become tantamount to economic as well as physical suicide. The long-standing Boundary Dispute—now virtually an institution, with its own budget, offices, officers, rituals, and publications—provided the occasion and machinery for innumerable other connections with Nikolay and the lesser Student-Unionist colleges: to name one cynical example, the Departments of Espionage and Counter-Intelligence on both sides would be seriously handicapped without such points of contact as the conference-table; and the secret diplomacy essential to any serious intercollege business would be unmanageable without a convenient "front" like the Boundary Dispute.

"If it didn't exist we'd have to invent it," Mr. Rexford said, only partly in jest. "But it's much better to use a language that's already been worked out, don't you agree? The Nikolayan delegate, for example, the fellow who calls himself Classmate X—suppose he says his college will refuse to pay its dues to the University Council as long as New Tammany blocks the admission of T'ang College. What he *means* is, they don't want T'ang in either, but it wouldn't be nice to say so, so if we'll keep blocking T'ang's admission and let Nikolay save face by reneging on their debt, they won't interfere with our extension-work in certain other colleges. We know this is what he means, and Classmate X knows we know it; so our delegate agrees by denouncing people who don't pay their bills and by threatening not to pay our own—which means we *will* pay, since we've got more to lose than the Nikolayans do if the U.C. folds up, but it'll be hard to push the appropriation through a conservative Senate, so they'll have to lay low on the Power Line at least until after the next election." He smiled. "All this must sound very cynical to somebody raised on a goat-farm by Dr. Spielman."

"I'm afraid it does indeed!" I exclaimed. But the Chancellor maintained that, lamentable or not, such were the political realities; he declared that the best political scientists were those to whom these multiple meanings were so clear that they truly went without saying; to whom the symbolic use of varsity political language was such second nature that they

felt neither cynical nor hypocritical about the disparity between their public statements and their actual policies: for
them, and their fellow-initiates, there *was* no disparity; they
never confused symbol with referent.

"That's not Entelechian!" I protested. "Excuse me, sir:
that's Dean-o'-Flunkish! You sound like Maurice Stoker!"

He had for a moment put by the reserve that characteristically went with his good humor; now it was stiffly in place
again. "I suppose, from a Grand Tutor's point of view . . ."

"From Entelechus's!" I insisted. "From your own, sir!" We
had drawn up by this time before a many-storied glass slab,
where throngs of students and policemen awaited the
Chancellor's arrival. A small herd of black-gowned dignitaries came down the entrance-steps towards us; a uniformed
ROTC officer opened our sidecar door and snapped to attention with a fixed salute. But the Chancellor half-raised a
hand to stay the greeters, smiled his most mischievous smile
at me, and said, "Obviously we mustn't EAT each other.
How would *you* handle the Boundary Dispute? Take a whole
minute if you need to."

I drew a breath. "I'd separate the Power Lines."

"What?" His expression was offended.

"Adjourn the Symposium," I said. "Double the distance between the Power Lines. Tell WESCAC to separate its circuitry completely from EASCAC's."

He declared I was joking, but reclosed the sidecar door for
a moment; those outside shifted about and consulted their
wristwatches.

"It's like Stoker, or the Dean o' Flunks, or a terrible disease," I argued; "if you do business with these things, they
always win. *Extreme in the mean* is what you've got to be,
and not compromise even for a second with Flunkage, or let
opposites get confused. An arch won't do between True and
False; they've got to be cut with an edge as sharp as the Infinite Divisor, and separated."

The Chancellor shook his head as I spoke, but his smile
was grave, and he seemed after all to be listening, so I quickly enlarged upon my theme. To make concessions to the
forces of Failure, I said—to this Classmate X fellow or to
Stoker—was like conceding to malevolent bacteria: one
might approve moderate exercise over athleticism, but not
moderate illness over health. And the health of a college, it
seemed evident to me, like the health of an orderly and

passèd administration, came not from cooperation with its antithesis, but from real repudiation of it. The spirit and letter of Rexfordian law was order, intelligence, and light; let there then be no disorder in New Tammany, or unreason, or other darkness. If it was inescapable that the lights of Great Mall depended ultimately on what went on under Founder's Hill, then let there at least be no converse between head and bowels, not to speak of envy and occasional emulation! Ban Maurice Stoker from Great Mall, I urged him, and deny his kinship from the rooftops; have no commerce with Ira Hector, much less Classmate X; let there be no negotiations with Nikolay College, overt or covert; disentangle WESCAC's circuitry once and for all; separate the power-cables; draw a hard line between them—well on our side, if necessary; double the floodlighting; triple the guard . . .

"You said the guards fall now and then because they look down," I finished pointedly; "They should wear a special collar like the ones we use on bad goats, so they can't look down."

As he smiled—tugging at his forelock somewhat wearily, I confess—and opened the sidecar door again, a commotion broke out upon the cordoned steps leading up to the hall. I had just time to glimpse a patch-eyed fellow struggling with policemen before two guards sprang, pistols in hand, to shield the Chancellor, and blocked my view.

"Another lunatic," Lucius Rexford muttered. He still smiled, but his face had briefly lost its color. "Let's go in," he said to the guards.

"Just a second, sir," one of them answered. "They're having a little trouble with him."

"He doesn't seem to be armed," the other guard observed. "Better play it safe, though."

But the Chancellor would not remain in the sidecar. As he stepped out, guards hurried to encircle him. The watchers cheered; he grinned and gave a little wave of his hand to them, but I felt distinctly that for all his popularity and charm he did not quite trust the adoring student body, from whose extremities assassins and Grand Tutors sometimes sprang. The police struggling with the patch-eyed man looked worriedly in our direction; their quarry's face lit up—I recognized him as that Nikolayan I'd seen through the electric mesh in the Control Room, and with whom Peter Greene had reportedly scuffled at Stoker's Randy-Thursday party. Indeed he was hard to hold onto: though four or five had hands on him he slipped their grasp, cried, "Great and good man!" and flung himself onto his knees in our path just as the guards seemed ready to shoot.

"Am not assassin!" he declared to the Chancellor. "Am transfer out of Nikolay! Great lover of you! Hello, Grand Tutor! I don't believe!"

Guards escorted the Chancellor rapidly towards the building; others slapped handcuffs onto the kneeling man's wrists, which however he opened as if by magic in order to wave to Lucius Rexford.

"Goodbye, goodbye! Peace in University!"

I had been left behind in the confusion. "You know this guy?" a guard in plainclothes asked me. Others replaced the handcuffs on the Nikolayan's wrists, which now he offered them smilingly.

"I know of him," I began to say.

"Alexandrov," the prisoner volunteered. Again with ease he slipped one hand free to extend it to me, and with the other tugged at his black mustache. "Leonid Andreich Alexandrov, Doctor of Engineering. Lover of Anastasia Stoker. Admirer of you. But don't believe in! Skepticismal!" His handshake, like his frame, was sturdy and powerful; his dark eye glistened cordially in a red face topped with black and handsome curls.

"Something wrong with them cuffs," a guard said. But the Nikolayan grinned, shook his head, and explained proudly that it was his special talent with locks that had enabled him to slip through the charged screen of the Control Room, make his way to the U.C. building (where his father, he declared, was head of the Nikolayan delegation), and transfer in the sight of all. "Main Detention, please?" he requested in conclusion. "You take me there now, okay?"

"You'd better sit in on the interrogation," I was told. The plainclothesmen were much aroused by the news that their man was the son of Classmate X; in view of the delicate diplomatic aspects of his defection, and my wish to rejoin the Chancellor in pursuit of my Assignment, it was agreed that the questioning should take place at once, in the U.C. offices of the New Tammany delegation; both NTC and Nikolay College would be likely to want the Symposium-opening delayed until the situation could be assessed.

"No," the Nikolayan insisted. "Main Detention." It was

remarkable how with the merest twitch of a muscle he escaped their clutch. "Am not a transfer," he said now. "Am a spy. Come to kidnap a scientist." He grinned. "Long live Student Union! Down with Informationalist adventurismhood! You send me to Main Detention, okay?"

The guards exchanged looks. "Let's talk it over inside," they said, almost politely. "If you're telling the truth, you'll see Main Detention soon enough."

Mr. Alexandrov considered for a second and then nodded assent. "You come along?" he asked me. "Mrs. Anastasia admires, I admire."

"But don't believe in," I reminded him.

He undid his handcuffs—two pairs this time—to clap an arm affectionately about me. "Goat-Boys *da;* Grand Tutors *nyet.*"

We went inside, our agitated escorts fending off journalists and crowds of the curious. Arguments in several languages were in progress in the lobbies and corridors we hurried through; at our appearance they grew louder, and a herd of gesticulating dignified gentlemen collected behind us. Mr. Alexandrov waved to some of them, who glared back. At the door of the suite of offices we went into, a furious debate commenced, through interpreters, between what appeared to be representatives of the two colleges involved, over the question of who should be admitted to the room.

"How do you do that trick with the handcuffs?" I asked the prisoner, who for the moment was being ignored. "It's very clever."

He beamed and playfully punched my chest. "Big secrecy, Classmate! I don't tell!" Then impulsively he laughed and added, "But Mrs. Anastasia's good-friend, okay!" He collared me in order to whisper into my ear something I heard imperfectly, for our guards and the Nikolayan officials both jumped to end the confidence. But though I declared to them honestly enough that I'd not understood the message through the din, it seemed to me upon later reflection that *Not locked* must have been its puzzling burden, along with the words *Let go!*—which could however have been either a specific demand of the guards who drew us apart, or a kind of general injunction. The Nikolayan himself appeared certainly to follow some such policy: he flung his arms freely as he talked, undid the second button of his already open-necked shirt, and loosened his belt when he sat down.

"Big spy!" he said, thumbing his chest; but his eye-patch looked like a broad wink. The Nikolayan officials all harangued him at once; he rejected them with a sweep of the arm and a shake of the head.

"He surrenders absolutely, confesses his intention to kidnap, and rejects counsel," a New Tammany official said to them, and added sternly that although he would clear the office of journalists and cameramen, and permit the Nikolayan representatives to remain, they must not interfere with the prisoner's right to speak freely. On the other hand, he insisted that Mr. Alexandrov was under no obligation to make a statement, and that all he said would be recorded as possible evidence against him.

"That's okay!" Alexandrov cried, and shouted down the Nikolayans' protests in their own language. "I fail assignment, deserve Main Detention!"

A report came to the office that the opening of the Summit Symposium had been delayed and that Classmate X was on his way to join us; the New Tammany official invited the prisoner to wait, but Alexandrov—whose emotions changed frequently and dramatically—declared with tears in his eyes that he had once already disgraced his father, whom he revered, and could not bear to face him disgraced again. Briefly then, in elliptical exclamations, he told his story: Believed wholeheartedly in Classless Campus and similar Student-Unionist ideals. No masters, no pupils! Despised Ira Hector and other greedy Informationalists, but admired several individual New Tammanians: Professor-General Reginald Hector, liberator of Siegfrieder concentration campus where he'd been prisoner in Second Riot; Chancellor Rexford, lover of peace and man of goodwill; Mrs. Anastasia, who would be Graduate except Graduation was Informationalist lie, opiate of lower percentiles; myself, who had right respect for goats and other animals (Anastasia, it appeared, had spoken of me to him in not unflattering terms, on Randy-Thursday)—a virtue evidently outweighing in his eye my claim to Grand-Tutorhood. Which didn't believe in, *et cetera*. But of all men on campus, admired most his father, for perfect selflessness exemplified in renouncing even a name . . .

"Greatnesshood!" he shouted, pounding the chair-arm. "Splendidacy!"

But now his eye sparkled with frustration: he could not help loving these people, yet he disapproved of his love, which smacked of Informationist idolatry. Nor was this his only failing as a Student-Unionist: he was subject, he confessed, to fits of impulsive insubordination and independent behavior, which no amount of subsequent remorse appeared to cure. As a young riot-engineer in C.R. II, for example, he had been captured by the Siegfrieders early in the conflict when he'd stolen behind their lines one night, without authorization, to untether a nannny-goat abandoned by a fleeing farmer. Thereafter, in the Bonifacist concentration campus, he'd turned his engineering skill to the arts of unlocking and releasing; ashamed to return to his own unit, he proved so competent at arranging the escape of others that the Nikolayan professor-generals soon were sending him lists, via deliberately captured recruits, of prisoners whose escape was to have priority—generally officers. But time and again his emotions had the better of his self-discipline, and he would free the recruits instead, out of admiration for their selflessness. After the Riot he'd risen to prominence as a computer-programmer, specializing in the untanglement of knotty mathematical problems; but his old proclivity now and then came to the fore—especially when, as sometimes happened, he would meet a comrade from former terms and drink too many toasts to their fallen classmates. After one such bout he had found himself in the Nikolayan Zoological Gardens and, smitten with sympathy for its internees, had commenced a wholesale uncaging. So spectacular was the consequent furor, and difficult the job of constraining him, he might have been shot along with sundry bears and tigers had not his father been fetched to the scene to command him, by loudspeaker through a cloud of monkeys, to surrender himself.

"Humiliationship!" he exclaimed, and pressed one fist of his brooding brow. His captors, he said, had despaired of holding him, though when he'd seen what carnage ensued from his generous intentions, he'd declared himself willing to be jailed for life: not only had several of the beasts necessarily been shot, but some had eaten others, and many of the more exotic were doomed to perish for want of their customary food and environment. A debate had followed on how best to punish him (a regular court-trial was out of the question because of his father's position); and seeing his superiors deadlocked, he generously volunteered them the means painfullest to himself—a cell lined with mirrors instead of bars. So strong was his aversion to any reflection—an antipathy he could not account for, at least in our language—that such a cell would need no lock at all to contain him: he would be frozen in its center with his eye shut.

I interrupted: "You have a thing about mirrors too! Isn't that curious! Did you know that Peter Greene, the man you fought with at Stoker's—"

Officials shushed me, lest the prisoner stop talking.

"Ha!" Alexandrov laughed. "A baby. But unselfish, Goat-Boy! And loves Mrs. Anastasia! But stupid! But okay, I like, and shouldn't fight with. A good man! But bah!"

This sentiment, though I think I shared it, was beside my point, but I let the coincidence of the two men's common aversion to mirrors go, as not worth the labor of articulating. Whatever the cause of Leonid Andreich's, it was at least as intense as Greene's, evidently, for after a day and night in the mirrored cell, which had been promptly constructed for him, he was seized by a kind of fit not unlike epilepsy, and, falling, struck with his head one of the hateful walls so forcefully that the glass shivered. He revived in a prison infirmary, minus his right eye and in such despair at ever becoming a credit to his college that when his father arranged him a position in the Founder's Hill Control Room he at first refused it as an undeserved honor. His eventual acceptance was in order not further to disoblige the man he most admired, and to carry out a scheme of atonement that had occurred to him: his own father, it seemed (one of our translators remarked that the Nikolayan word used occasionally by the prisoner actually meant "stepfather," and someone else explained that Classmate X had married Alexandrov's mother, a Riot-widow, only a dozen or so years previously, after Leonid Andreich's rematriculation), had been a computer-expert prior to his appearance on the diplomatic scene, and possibly had been involved at one time in counter-intelligence work as well—

"How's that?" cried the NTC official. "Have him say that again!" The consternation was equally great among the Nikolayans, who drowned out the prisoner's voice with protests and demanded that no more be said until they'd had time to consult their superiors. Angrily they denounced Alexandrov, who blushed and apologized for speaking thoughtlessly. He sprang up from his chair, shrugging off all hands; men hurried to block windows and doorways in case he meant to flee or destroy himself—but he was merely restless, and strode now vigorously about the room, waving his arms. He ignored his classmates' orders to say no more until their chief arrived; the New Tammanians delightedly scribbled notes.

"Forget I said about father," he laughed. "A stupidacy in my head!"

In any case, he said, he was aware how close and crucial was the race between Nikolay College and NTC to perfect the "dreadfulship" of their respective EATing capacities; realizing also that a man with his peculiar talent for "releaseness" would be in an advantageous position in the Control Room to aid the cause of his alma mater, he had resolved to slip through the electrified screen, kidnap some eminent computer-scientist from the West-Campus side, and by spiriting him over the Power Line put the Nikolayans ahead in the EAT-race, redeem his past failings, and become an honored and respected member of the Student Union like his father.

"But!" He gave a vast sly shrug. "I come here to say goodbye to father, I see instead Rexford—I admire! A forgetness; you catch me; I'm disgrace!" He seemed altogether pleased with himself. The New Tammany officials glanced at one another.

"You should be ashamed of yourself," I told him. One official frowned and asked another who the flunk I was anyhow; some reply was whispered into his ear. Leonid Andreich, as if reminded by my words that a man in disgrace did not ordinarily cross his arms and smile, quickly clutched his hair and agreed that Classmate X, himself so perfectly disciplined, would of course despise him for his "incompetencehood" in getting himself arrested. But for a man whose desire to please his father was as obviously sincere as was Leonid's, this profession of disgrace had a counterfeit ring. In any case his arrest was not what I'd been referring to, I told him, but his motive and intention. I conceded at the outset that Informationalism *was* based on a kind of flunking avarice, and that particular Informationalists like Ira Hector were to all appearances irredeemably greedy: *Flunkèd are the selfish*, it was written in the Founder's Scroll, and nowise might flunked mean passed.

"*Da! Da!*" the Nikolayan cried happily. "Even other Grand Tutor—I don't believe, I don't like either!—he says too!"

Very well, then, I said (concealing my chagrin), it was agreed on both sides of the Power Line that selfishness was reprehensible. But Leonid's behavior seemed to me selfish—in the sense of vanity more than of avarice—both in its intention and its motive. Recalling some of Max's observations on the subject, I declared that if to be a perfect Student-Unionist meant to efface one's personal self and identify absolutely with the "student self" or the "self of the college," then to wish to be a perfect Student-Unionist, or even a great Nikolayan, must "flunk" the wisher in the eyes of Classmate X, for example. Leonid's dilemma was thus not unlike mine, or any right-thinking undergraduate's, and I spoke of it therefore with compassion: the wish to achieve perfect self-suppression, like the yen to Graduate, was finally a prideful wish and thus self-defeating; to achieve it, not only the self must be suppressed, but the selfish wish itself. *Aspiration*, it seemed to me, by the logic of Student-Unionism, was permissible only in the College Self . . .

"I like you, Goat-Boy!" Leonid shouted—fortunately, for others in the room were not pleased by my words and chiding tone, and would have terminated our conversation if Leonid hadn't embraced me and insisted I continue.

"Well," I said, "you won't agree, I suppose, but my former keeper, Dr. Spielman, used to say that what the Student-Unionists do is transfer their normal selfishness onto the College Self, which then becomes more selfish than an Informationalist college, even though the people in it may be less selfish individually . . ."

Whether he understood my position, to say nothing of agreeing with it, seemed doubtful; he colored at the mention of Max's name and released me in order to pace again about the room. But I gimped beside him (most of the others were huddled in conferences against the arrival of Classmate X) and insisted he agree that the competition for supremacy between East and West Campuses was essentially a selfish competition, in which New Tammany and Nikolay Colleges each were guilty of seeking advantage over the other in every sphere and extending their hegemonies in the name of self-defense. Why else would the Nikolayans want the computer-scientist whom he had planned to abduct, or the New Tammanians not want to lose him? The colleges were all Ira Hectors . . .

"Goat-Boy, Goat-Boy!" Leonid groaned—in what spirit I could not quite tell. A little dismayed, I said, "I guess it's a real problem to be a good Student-Unionist, isn't it?" and from the doorway a voice like polished steel replied, "Not at all. A proper Student-Unionist can have no problems. Only the College may have problems."

The newcomer I guessed at once to be Classmate X: as slight and pinched a man as Ira Hector, though less determinate of age, he had too Ira's cold bright eyes, which glinted however more of metal than of gems. He wore an ill-cut suit of coarse material, was hairless, had much metal in his teeth, and spoke almost tonelessly. Two words he said to Leonid, in their tongue, and his stepson sprang to him. They regarded each other, Leonid clasping and unclasping his hands, Classmate X without gesture or expression. Then the older man asked a New Tammany official to explain why Classmate Alexandrov was being detained, and having listened impassively to the reply, and to his son's tape-recorded confession, he asked Leonid (according to our interpreters) to affirm or deny the charge of intent to kidnap. Leonid affirmed it, adding ardently that his motive had been to atone for the errors of his past, and declaring that he would find a way yet to make himself worthy of membership in the Student Union and of his father's respect.

Classmate X gave the slightest shrug of the shoulders. "The fool is yours," he said to the chief of the New Tammany officials, and turned on his heel. Leonid leaped after him, wet-eyed, then stopped and flung himself into a chair. Two Nikolayans left the room with their superior, and after a second's consideration I followed them into the corridor.

"Mr. X?" I called. "Mr. Classmate X, sir!" He stopped and precisely turned his leathern skull. His associates glared, even counseled him (so I gathered from their expressions) to ignore me; but he shook his head, as slightly as he had shrugged earlier, and permitted me to overtake them.

"Dr. Spielman's *protégé*," he murmured with the faintest of smiles. "No use trying to Graduate *us*, Classmate Goat-Boy: until everyone can pass, we won't believe in Passage. Too bad your Dr. Spielman's turned mid-percentile—he used to have more sense."

His accent, I noticed, was very slight, and closer to Max's, for example, than to any Nikolayan's I had heard. I asked whether he knew my former keeper personally, promising to pass along his regards when next I visited his cell.

"No use in that," he said quickly. "One knows Dr. Spielman by reputation, of course. Let's speak no more of him."

And so we moved on down the corridor towards a reception-room where he was to confer informally with Chancellor Rexford prior to the opening of the Summit Symposium (at which, his college being currently administered by a committee instead of one man, he was temporarily empowered to deal on equal footing with the NTC Chancellor); but he returned at once to the forbidden subject, expressing his skepticism that Max had really murdered Herman Hermann and his disapproval of the deed. That Bonifacists should be exterminated he quite agreed, but not in so laissez-faire a manner, at the whim of amateur individuals; programs of liquidation, like programs of "charity," were best left to *ad hoc* committees of experts like those which eliminated the counterrevolutionary elements in Nikolay College and directed the supply of food and "educational material" to certain famine-ridden Frumentian campuses some terms past—in both which operations, as he put it, "some of us participated." Otherwise, private feelings of hatred or compassion were liable at least to supplant the suprapersonal spirit in which the ends of collegiate policy ought properly to be served, if they did not actually interfere with the attainment of those ends.

I was ready to assure him from habit that Max couldn't possibly be guilty of the murder, but checked myself with the painful memory that he had confessed to the contrary, and affirmed to me his confession. So instead, with an aching throat, I briefly rehearsed my objections to the Student-Unionist doctrines of self-suppression and the insignificance of the individual student, and he heard me out impassively.

"I'm not speaking as a New Tammanian or an Informationalist," I declared.

"Really."

"Honestly. I've seen how selfish life in this college is, in lots of ways; and anyhow a Grand Tutor doesn't take sides in varsity politics."

"Ah."

But Commencement, I insisted, was always of the individual student, never of studentdom as such—a mere abstraction, in my opinion—and so while I condemned selfishness as heartily as he, it seemed to me that its passing opposite was not the unnatural and unfeeling selflessness of the dedicated Student-Unionist, but the warm unselfishness apparent in men like Leonid Andreich Alexandrov, whom I took to be more representative of Nikolayan studentdom than was his stepfather. "*I* felt more sympathy for him than you did," I charged. "Even the guards who arrested him were kinder than you!"

"Students are not important," Classmate X replied crisply. "Studentdom is all that matters." The Student Union embodied the general will of studentdom, he said, and Nikolay College had been appointed by history to lead the Student Union in the implementation of that will. If Leonid Andreich, or any or all of the rest of us, happened to obstruct this implementation, we must be sacrificed in its behalf. A willingness to make that sacrifice was the first condition of membership in the Union, whose will must be done; and making it the best validation of that willingness.

"But what about sacrificing other people?" I demanded. "Suppose you decide that the College Self calls for an EATing-riot?"

Classmate X cocked his head a very little. "If every living student in the University had to be EATen in the name of studentdom," he said politely, "still the will of the Union would be done."

I protested that he couldn't possibly be serious, yet was chilled to realize that he was. "Would you push the EAT-button yourself?"

We were at the entrance to a crowded reception-chamber; many heads turned at our approach. Classmate X covered his face with his hat when photographic lamps began flashing.

"To be the agent of the general will," he asserted through the felt, "is an honor exceeded only by being its instrument. If the will of the Union is that the button be pressed, then the one thing better than being the presser is to be the button." He made a scarcely perceptible bow, presumably by way of taking leave of me, and entered the room. But I pressed after.

"That's just plain vanity!" I protested. Several large Nikolayans moved towards me when I raised my voice, but I went on. "It's as bad as Max saying he wants to be Shafted in the name of studentdom! You're not really selfless at all!"

"Max is a fool!" Classmate X said sharply—his first betrayal of any emotion. But though my taunt evidently angered him, he motioned aside the aides who scowled between us and said in a small, hard voice—still covering his face: "One's original family was murdered by the Bonifacists, except for a single son, who fled with oneself to be killed in action later in the Riot. One's second wife died this year. And so Leonid Andreich is one's sole surviving relative . . ." Only when he mentioned Leonid's name did I understand that by "one" he referred to himself. "One is not displeased with such a relative," he went on; "not at all displeased! One feels one could do a great deal worse indeed than to have such a son as Leonid Andreich . . ." He actually tapped my arm, an unprecedented display of feeling. "And yet, Classmate Goat-Boy, and yet"—his eyes shone briefly over the brim of his hat—"because it is the wish of the Student Union that a certain party be *admitted to its ranks,* let us say, from the Other Side, and because no one is more suited to the work of escorting this party to us than Leonid Andreich . . . Because of these things, Goat-Boy, and despite the likelihood that the escort will never be permitted by the Other Side to return to his alma mater and his father's house, one *suggests* to Leonid Andreich that he expend himself in that sacrificial work. Do you understand my meaning? One even *orders* him to do so, giving him to believe that so unresponsive has he proved to the discipline of selflessness, he can earn his father's esteem in no other wise. *Posthumously,* you might as well say! As if—" But he whipped around in mid-blurt, choking off the clause.

"As if he *had* to earn it!" I cried after him. "I think you love your stepson very much!" Classmate X strode away—plunged, really, still hatting his visage—and hands restrained me from following, but I called at his retreating back: "I'll bet you sent him to New Tammany so he wouldn't *have* to suppress his self!"

What held him in range of my mad declarations—taunts they were, as much as insights, made in despair now of ending the Boundary Dispute by reasoning with the principals—was that an agitated group not unlike ours had come across the room to meet us, at its center Chancellor Rexford. Classmate X's pate had gone quite white; Rexford's face was uncharacteristically grim. Photographic lights flashed all about us now; plainclothes guards and other officials on both sides conferred in furious whispers, pointed to me, consulted papers, shrugged their shoulders angrily. We were a large ring now, enclosing Chancellor Rexford and Classmate X, myself to one side. Neither leader seemed willing to initiate the ceremonial handshake; both turned severely to their aides. Still inspired by desperation, I asserted to Classmate X,

"That kidnap-story was only a pretext; you were hoping Leonid would *transfer!*"

After a silent moment (during which cameramen and microphoned reporters edged into my end of the circle) everyone began shouting at the same time, and the ring became a little mob that pressed the three of us together. Chancellor Rexford, flushing red, made some expostulation in which I caught the phrases "privileged visitor," "special credentials," and "no harm done"; his tone seemed at first pacificatory, but changed when Classmate X waved his fist and shouted that there would be no Symposium; that the space between the Power Lines would be widened, the guard increased, and all communication between East and West Campuses terminated absolutely.

"You can't mean that!" Rexford said angrily, and demanded of an aide, "Can he speak for his college this way? What's the matter with him?"

I offered an explanation which both or neither of the parties may have heard: "He's identifying the College Self with his own self, instead of vice-versa. It's a flunking thing to do, by his own standards . . ."

"Shut that shaggy idiot up!" someone cried, and with a chorus of abuse I was hustled from the principals, who too had separated, or been separated by their respective aides. There was much excited talk of "insults," "loss of face," "torpedoed negotiations." Having got me out of reach of their leaders, no one knew what to do with me, for though their distress and indignation were evident, they had gathered I enjoyed some special status in the Chancellor's party.

"Founder help you if you're the one who upset X," snarled a forelocked fellow. "You've shot down the whole flunking Boundary Conference!"

Until that moment, distracted by my sympathy for Leonid Alexandrov and the ideological exchanges with him and his stepfather, I hadn't realized the significance of my achievement.

"By George, you're right!" I exclaimed. "I guess I've ended the Boundary Dispute!"

The aide conjectured disagreeably that it might prove the end of the University as well. Now the Chancellor's party came by, still waving hands and frantically conferring; only Lucius Rexford himself was silent, his face somewhat gray and his jaw set: the speech he was to have delivered had been canceled, the Summit Symposium indefinitely postponed, the entire business of the University Council suspended for the day. At sight of me he stopped, seemed to hesitate between denouncing me and going on his way, and at last said tersely: "New Tammany looked pretty foolish just then. It's lucky this mess looks like their doing and not ours—or yours."

"No, no, sir," I protested; "that's the only thing wrong with it. You've got to take back the initiative! This justifies all those other measures I suggested." Rexford moved on towards the entrance-lobby, walking swiftly, and I trotted as best I could beside him; his aides neither disguised their hostility nor dared restrain me.

"Do the same thing with Maurice Stoker that you did here!" I urged him. "Go the whole way, sir!"

He made no reply. I didn't venture to enter the sidecar with him uninvited—and in fact an aide sprang into the second seat, as if to forestall me—but before the door closed I called encouragement from the curb: "Light up everything! Make New Tammany an open book!" His motorcycle went off then (down the middle of the pavement, I was pleased to observe), and his party dispersed, still buzzing gravely, among the other official vehicles. As no one invited my company on the one hand, or on the other denied me the privilege of returning to Great Mall as I'd come, I found a seat alone in the last sidecar of the motorcade, and modestly dissembling my elation at having accomplished two formidable Assignment-tasks in just a few hours, I instructed my driver (an unnecessarily sarcastic fellow) to deliver me to the NTC General Infirmary.

4.

Though entirely sensible of the edge in his inquiry, whether it was the Infirmary proper or the Psychiatric Annex I wanted chauffeuring to, I ignored it and supposed aloud that my friend Dr. Sear, being a practicing radiologist and psychotherapist as well as director of the Psych Clinic, might have offices in both places. I would try the main building first, in hopes of a directory; he need not wait.

"Need not need not," the surly fellow grumbled, and sped off almost before I'd climbed out onto the sidewalk in front of the Infirmary. But I was in too fine spirits to report him. By contrast with the first two articles of my Assignment, this third seemed to me now light work both to interpret and to satisfy: having seen such demonstration in the past few days of the infirmities of others, moral and intellectual as well as physical, I could quite agree that a bonafide Graduate must be free of them, and a Grand Tutor exemplify their opposites. The injunction to overcome my infirmity had thus a ready allegorical sense, such as I'd sought in vain to discern in its fellows: just as passage was passage and failure failure, defined each by strict distinction from the other, so was it with their corporal emblems, health and infirmity. That I was physically in good condition my Clean Bill of Health would be proof enough, which Dr. Sear had written for me early that same day; I needed but to fetch it from his office, or a copy if Mrs. Sear had delivered the original to Harold Bray at Scrapegoat Grate. As there was no infirmity to be remedied, I could be said to have overcome at least that part of the Assignment at once, in no time. But not to leave anything to chance, I went so far as to acknowledge that the term might be regarded metaphorically, or that WESCAC's standards might be narrowly human—in which cases any residual "goatliness" in my character, say, might by an effort of bigoted imagination be considered an infirmity; or my "limp," though it ceased to exist when I reverted to all fours. With the former I could not reasonably be taxed, it seemed to me: I'd left the herd in spirit long before my physical departure. But as I floated up to Dr. Sear's offices in the Psychiatric Annex, I resolved to consult him about my old leg-injuries, if only for an affidavit that they were neither "correctable" nor "crippling," properly regarded.

This aim fled before confusion a moment later, when I stepped from the lift into a dim hallway down which a young man scrabbled at me on hands and knees—in itself no very alarming spectacle to one of my history, but the fellow barked most savagely besides, and growled, and bared his teeth. Old instincts seized me: with a panic bleat I sprang onto the back of an upholstered chair nearby, and when the creature nipped at my ankles I flung my stick at him. At once he scrambled after it, clamped it in his jaws, and trotted back (the word is a flattery: his gait had neither grace nor rhythm), waggling his hindquarters. He seemed content enough; indeed, as if in invitation to further romp, he dropped the stick before the chair and sat up bright-eyed, lolling his tongue. But I was too frightened yet to give up my perch. There were two others seated along the hallway, to whom I appealed for help now I had a moment: alas, the one (an elder gentleman) sprang down on all fours himself and darted for the stick as soon as my harasser dropped it; and when the ensuing barky tussle fetched them up against the chair of the other (a co-ed lady girl), she turned side to them, arched her back, threatened with her nails, and hissed.

I made use of the diversion to dash across the corridor (on all fours myself, for speed's sake, being stickless) into an office marked with Dr. Sear's name. It was a Receiving Room, empty, at the rear of which a little hallway was, opening, I presently learned, into the doctor's treatment- and observation-chambers. To this latter I retreated from the dog-men, who tumbled through the entrance-door I'd neglected to close, and I was distressed to find the dim room occupied by a long lean lunatic: what but madness would lead one to stand with his face cupped against a wall? Even as I called to him for help my heart misgave me—then leaped up, when he turned my way, to behold that he was Peter Greene, and that he had been peering through a little window into the adjacent room. My pursuers bounded at him; I cried warning; but Greene, undismayed, said, "Down, fellows," and pacified them with bone-shaped biscuits from his pocket. The creatures retired each into a corner to gnaw their prizes, and I retrieved my stick, which they'd fetched in.

"They don't bite," Greene assured me—in an offhand tone, as though preoccupied. They and the female in the hall, he said, were patients of Dr. Sear's awaiting diagnoses, whom Anastasia had asked Greene to mind for a moment while she assisted the doctor with an emergency case. To this end he'd been supplied with dog-biscuits—the cat-young-lady was not troublesome, it seemed, unless rubbed the wrong way—and instructions to keep the patients in sight; but the alarming behavior of Mrs. Sear, whose appearance in the office constituted the emergency, had so intrigued him that he'd neglected his duty in order to watch through the one-way glass of the Observation Room.

"Sear's going to have a chat with me soon's he finds time," he reported. "But he's been busy all afternoon, so I been sitting here watching Miss Stacey work, and too durn love-struck to say a word to her, conversationwise."

"*Mrs. Stoker*," I reminded him. I had been going to wonder aloud how came it that human studentdom considered it a sign of madness for one of their number to behave caninely, and a sign of intelligence in a dog to act like a human, for though I had no love at all for dogdom, I suspected a snobbery in this attitude that for aught I knew might extend even to goats. However, Greene's invincible obtuseness provoked such annoyance in me, and the news of Mrs. Sear's condition such curiosity, I put that wonder by and went to the observation-window, less dim now than formerly.

"She come in a-flailin' and a-flounderin'," Greene confided, "and a-sayin' things would curl your hair. First off I took her for some kind of nut, the way she carried on—said the durnedest things to me you ever heard! But Miss Stacey explained it was Sear's own wife, that had a *mental illness,* and they took her in there to calm her down."

The square of glass I had pre-empted was too small to serve us both. Greene added hopefully, "Last I looked, they couldn't hold her still on the sofa."

A glance revealed to me that this objective had now been attained; Hedwig Sear lay calmly on the leather couch embracing Anastasia, while the doctor petted them both. A sexualler connection was plainly to come, and I was a little stung, not by jealousy, disgust, or indignation, such as a normal undergraduate might have been, but by unhappy surprise that it was Anastasia who seemed to be taking the initiative. Fidgeting beside me, Peter Greene flipped a wall-switch, and voices from the Treatment Room rustled through a loudspeaker above us.

"I'll get the door," Dr. Sear said briskly, "before some idiot barges in."

Anastasia called over her shoulder: "Better see that Mr. Greene's all right, too, don't you think?" Her voice, at least, was mild as always.

Peter Greene jubilantly punched my shoulder. "What's that if it ain't pure love?"

"Look here, Greene . . ."

"*Pete.* Okay?"

I had meant expostulation, not invitation to the window—indeed, though I turned to him, wondering how the situation was to be handled, I endeavored to block the scene from his view with my head. Then above Mrs. Sear's moans, ever more amorous, Anastasia nervously asked, "What about the window, Kennard? Do you think anybody might look in?" and the doctor's wry response—that it would disabuse Greene of an illusion or two if he *did* happen to watch—inspired me to turn the uncomfortable situation to pedagogical account.

"I think you should stay here and keep your eyes and ears open," I told him, as if I were the doctor and he my patient. "I have an idea." He consented readily, and I made haste to leave the observation-chamber, closing its door behind me as he stepped to the window and Dr. Sear into the Receiving Room.

"Founder's sake, George!" The doctor's brows drew down around his little bandage at sight of me, but his frown was amused. He looked back quickly to assure himself that he'd closed the door, and glanced about at the empty office.

"Greene's in there with the dog-people," I said; "I'm not sure about the cat-girl." As he searched my expression for a hint of how much I knew, I smiled and apologized for once again interrupting his wife's therapy. Hastily then I explained why I had sent Greene to him for sophisticating, especially in the matter of Anastasia's innocence, and echoed his own suggestion that the treatment-in-progress might be as therapeutic for Greene to witness as it no doubt was for Mrs. Sear to receive—the more so in view of Mrs. Stoker's new forwardness.

"Frightfully irregular," Dr. Sear said, apropos equally of my proposal and Anastasia's behavior. "Officeful of patients . . ." But when I volunteered to assist the proceedings in any way I could, in return for his advice on the matter of my alleged infirmity, he admitted that the idea was too entertaining to resist, therapeutic or not.

"It's five o'clock anyhow," he said; "I'll send for an orderly to take the patients back to their wards." He proposed further, in an offhand tone, that I join his wife and Anastasia in the Treatment Room while he shared the observation-chamber with Greene, the better to interpret for him what he saw and translate his reaction into therapy. It wanted no great sophistication to discern something more in this suggestion than disinterested goodwill: so much the better, I decided, for Greene's education in the ways of the campus. As for me, inhibition in matters erotic was one infirmity, at least, which kidship had spared me: though my experience was small, shame and shyness in such affairs were emotions I knew chiefly at secondhand, from books and hearsay. Leaving Dr. Sear to his business, I strode therefore unabashedly into the Treatment Room, bid the ladies a very good evening, and inquired of Anastasia, not without irony, whether I could assist in any wise her charitable nurse-work.

She made a sound and leaped from her labors; batted at her blouse and Mrs. Sear's skirt; snatched up a cast-off underthing—then reddened and defied me, balling the dainty in her hand.

"The *nerve*, George!"

She would have bolted, I daresay, but that she felt responsibility for Mrs. Sear, who, still upon the couch, groggily bade her back to love. I begged her to continue the therapy as if I were Dr. Sear; I quite understood, I assured her, that in medical emergencies common restraints must be put by, and that her present connection with the patient was as impersonal as mouth-to-mouth resuscitation, for example.

Mrs. Sear raised her head to squint at me and said: "Balls." Then she flopped chuckling onto her belly and thrust up her haunches. "I'm a nanny!"

"Oh, Heddy!" On the edge of tears, Anastasia hastened to pull the woman's skirt-hem down; but Hedwig frisked it up again and bleated into the couch-cushion.

"Please *go!*" Anastasia cried to me.

Dr. Sear spoke from a loudspeaker: "No no, Stace, it's quite all right. Would you just service Hed once, please, George? Do her a campus of good."

"*Ba-a-a, ba-a-a,*" said Mrs. Sear—presumably mimicking a doe, though the noises were meaningless. Anastasia looked with nervous indignation at a dark mirror on one wall, which I took to be the observation-window.

"I'd really rather not," I said in that direction. "I'm *not* a goat, you know: that's one of the things I wanted to discuss with you. Shouldn't Mrs. Stoker go on with the treatment?"

"*Ba-a-a!*" Mrs. Sear now wriggled; and bald as was her rump compared to any doe's, and gaunt next to supple Anastasia's, I had not unlearnt my buckish indiscrimination, and was stirred a little.

"This is *awful!*" Anastasia cried. "I'm going home, Kennard!"

But I caught her elbow as she swept doorwards. "Please

don't leave. I'm sorry if I spoke unkindly; it surprised me a little to see you taking the lead for a change."

Perhaps forgetting that what she held was no handkerchief, she dabbed with the underthing at her splendid eyes and declared: "It's your fault; I've never done it before." By *it* I assumed she meant taking the initiative, since the therapy itself I understood to have been common practice in Mrs. Sear's case. And I was the more inclined to believe her because she so readily now gave over the initiative to me: made no attempt to break my light hold on her and even permitted me to stroke her flank with my stick-hand until I remembered to put that pastoral habit behind me. Two things (she sniffled through the silk) had prompted her present shamelessness: my rebuke to her before Scrapegoat Grate, when she'd only been trying to distract Harold Bray for my sake, and her husband's "behavior at luncheon." Upon this latter she did not then elaborate—I supposed Stoker had put her to some fresh indignity. In any case, coming on the hooves of my reprimand, it had led her in despair, she said, to become what we'd unjustly taxed her with being: a flunkèd nymphomane.

"Bah," said Mrs. Sear—more impatient now than lustful, as I thought. "Some stud *you* are." Indeed her obscene waggling was so deliberate as to have finally chilled me—as did her strange advances at our previous encounter—had not Anastasia's fine person been so near. When I comforted that girl's hair upon my shoulder, my arousement grew.

In vain Dr. Sear entreated his wife from the Observation Room to respect my anticaprine sentiments (a misrepresentation, but I let it pass) and either couple with me in some humaner fashion or permit Anastasia to resume the original therapy: she stubbornly rejected both alternatives, and Anastasia seconded her, declaring them equally repugnant. I was flattered to imagine a note of jealousy in her veto—but it fretted me to see so little getting done in the way of Peter Greene's education. For that reason I was receptive to Dr. Sear's next suggestion despite the prurience of his tone, which the intercom did not conceal.

"About this *goat*-business, George: you want some sort of voucher from me that you're strictly human, is that it?"

"I *think* that's what I want," I said. "My Assignment says *Overcome Your Infirmity*, and it might just be that—"

"Conscious depravity," Dr. Sear said crisply. I begged his pardon.

"Conscious depravity," he repeated. "What could be humaner?" I believed he must be alluding—with a tisk of the tongue, as it were—to the behavior of his wife, who now besides waving her brittle posteriors was nibbling a memorandum-pad between bleats, and winking lewdly. But he went on to ask, rhetorically, when a goat, or any other animal than *Homo sapiens*, had ever done a flunkèd deed from simple relish of its flunkèdness. If in the history of studentdom, he maintained by way of illustration, a goat had ever humped a lady girl (as Halicarnassides records in his old *Histories*, for instance), it was no naughtiness on the stud's part, but mere unconscious lust. The girl, however, must needs have been queer of appetite—unless like Anastasia with Stoker's dogs, her motives were uncommonly benevolent, or (as when Croaker beached her) she'd had no option . . .

I started to protest: was even a man of Dr. Sear's intelligence and wide experience too bigoted to allow for simple love between the species? But I saw the principle beyond his misapplication of it, and supposed besides that among his motives was the exposition of Anastasia's past. Therefore I agreed, for Greene's benefit, that of the scores of males and females with whom the dear girl beside me had coupled, some at least had surely been inspired not alone by lust but by the conscious urge to exploit her submissiveness—a pleasure unknown outside the human species.

"Go on and *say* it!" Anastasia challenged me. "Tell me I'm flunked, like Maurice does!" She shook off my arm and went to Mrs. Sear, who in a fresh fit of disequilibrium seemed about to roll off the couch.

"That isn't what I meant," I assured her, though privately I was not at all convinced that it wasn't at least partly true: when she bent to steady Mrs. Sear, for example, and that surprising person at once thrust a hand into her crotch, Anastasia wept for sheer distress at this new unpleasantness, but would neither leave the importunate woman nor remove the hand.

"Demonstrate your humanity, George," urged Dr. Sear. "If the goat-thing's not to your taste, do something *à trois*. Mrs. Stoker will let you."

I saw his point, and was not unwilling to implement it in some measure for the sake of my several objectives. But I was less assured than he of Anastasia's readiness to cooperate in a display of Conscious Depravity, and therefore I told her straightforwardly what was ahoof:

"Peter Greene's watching along with Dr. Sear, Anastasia."

At this news she would indeed have fled had I not gripped her pretty shoulders from behind, and Mrs. Sear her escutcheon from before.

"Peter schmeeter," said Mrs. Sear.

I held Anastasia long enough (against Mrs. Sear's best efforts to tumble us onto the couch) to tell her of Greene's mad conviction that she was virginal; his resolve to wed her despite both their spouses, and his inability to see the flunkèd aspects of his own nature—such as the "innocent" voyeurism he was enjoying presently as on certain past occasions. In addition I informed her of the third and fourth articles of my Assignment—*Overcome Your Infirmity* and *See Through Your Ladyship*—and declared she could abet my completion of both projects, and do Peter Greene an ultimate service as well, by granting me a certain immediate license in the Conscious-Depravity way. All this in her ear, as I gripped her around the chest.

"Oh, George!" she complained—and pinched, perhaps, by Mrs. Sear, she jerked back against me. Very nearly I ejaculated, at touch of those perfections; feeling me against them she flinched away, but did not otherwise endeavor to wrest free.

"I don't under*stand!*" she wailed.

But *I* understood a number of things, some for the first time. It was clear to me now that I (and alas, not I alone!) could do virtually anything I pleased with Anastasia, not because she was a passèd martyr to the needs of others, on the one hand, or on the other a self-deluding nymphomane, but because she simply had not the will to assert her wishes over another's. Protest she might, refuse never—at least in the matter of carnal demands. This revelation (for so it was to me, however banal or evident, perhaps, to one raised since birth among humans) illumined in a flash not only the aforementioned articles of my Assignment, but the present situation. My "infirmity," I saw, was neither gimp nor goatness, but the limited insight into human natures unavoidable in one so late discovering his own. "Overcoming" it, then, must consist in just such illuminations as the present. Nay, the two labors were one: to "see through My Ladyship" could only mean to understand Anastasia; that is, to divine the inmost heart of one fellow human—a task impossible without the gift of insight. Divination now achieved, it was I felt certain the accomplishment—"at once, in no time"—of both parts of my Assignment, *Q.E.D.* Though I might still, for the record, ask a Clean Bill of Health from Dr. Sear (and perhaps a professional confirmation of my analysis of Anastasia), it seemed to me that my principal business there was finished, most satisfactorily. It remained only to demonstrate my thesis to Peter Greene and my "humanity" to Dr. Sear. In a friendly way I said, "Let's undress you, Anastasia," and fetched her firmly couchwards.

She fretted: "I don't *want* to, George!" But Mrs. Sear, in better reach of her now, said, "Hot dog," joined me with a will in the couching, and, kneeling over her on the cushion, attacked the fasteners of her uniform.

"This is *awful!*" Anastasia said crossly, and covered her eyes. "I don't see the need of this at *all!*"

I implored her to trust me, as she had once before at the Memorial Service. My plan was a token mounting of Hedwig Sear, for though I sharply craved Maurice Stoker's wife (the more at sight of her darling flanks again) and had no appetite whatever for Kennard Sear's, WESCAC's suggestion that I might be Anastasia's brother restrained me from following my desire—for her sake, who I imagined would share the prevailing undergraduate view of incest. To service a female person whom I found repellent was surely enough to prove my humanity; more so in my own estimation than to embrace one whom—despite our possible consanguinity and the obligations of Grand-Tutorhood—I had almost said, *I loved.*

"What Mr. Greene must *think!*" Anastasia moaned. As Hedwig Sear bent to bite her I remarked with an ardent pang the welt of my own teeth on her belly. Ah, it was true. Once hatched, the thought would not take wing, but stayed a-fledge there in my fancy: I loved Anastasia! And not as my relative or Tutee, but as a human lady girl. And I suddenly dreaded not only that we might be kin but that I might for aught I knew be . . . not lovable. Horrid possibility! That she admired me was evident; alas, her admiration like her sweet legs embraced many another, and had little to do with love. And Founder pass me, in the yearbooks of campus history what Grand Tutor ever took a mistress?

"George?" It was a rebuke, timid but positive. Anastasia's eyes were on my hands, which I had laid upon Hedwig's haunches. Whether by my problematical insights (How my infirmity was overcome!) or Mrs. Sear's aggressiveness, I had found myself unmanned, so to speak, and been obliged to temporize with idle foreplay. The woman ignored me, but Anastasia sat up now sharply and declared she didn't like what was happening at all and intended to leave.

"Oh, not *now!*" Dr. Sear entreated—from the doorway, where he appeared unaccompanied. "I was just about to join you."

Relieved enough at the interruption, nevertheless I frowned as I lowered my vestment and asked where Peter Greene was.

"Poor chap couldn't take it, I'm afraid," the doctor said pleasantly. "White as a sheet when I went in, and your remark about his *voyeurisme* did the trick. I gave him a sedative for fear he'd faint or commit mayhem, and he went right off to sleep. Like a five-year-old, actually. Very low threshold." He touched the small of my back with one hand and patted Anastasia's troubled cheek with the other. "Fine of you to help," he told her: "I think we really might have jarred some foolishness out of the fellow." Smiling at his wife he said then, "Mind if I cut in? Then we'll all have dinner."

Mrs. Sear did not reply: upon Anastasia's sitting up she had gone glassy-eyed, and slumped now quite insensible upon the dark beacon of George's Gorge, that had called G. Herrold to his end.

Anastasia shook her head. "I don't *like* this Conscious Depravity business. It's been a *very* upsetting day!" Awed by my feelings, I watched her fasten up her clothes once more. Dr. Sear gave me an amiable wry look—an invitation, as I thought, to exercise my will upon her as I knew I could. But I said that I too had spent a toilsome day, by no means over, and had no appetite except for food. He shrugged, lit a cigarette, and repeated his dinner invitation.

"A drink will perk Heddy up, and we'll ask Greene to come along if we can wake him."

Anastasia at first declined on the grounds that her husband, who "hadn't been himself at all" during lunch, might be expecting her at home, and that she would anyhow be ashamed to face Peter Greene for some time. But I pressed her to come with us, as I had serious matters to discuss with her: Max's predicament, her Certification by Bray—and our relationship. At this last she raised her eyes, as did Dr. Sear his far less liqueous ones. I blushed.

"It isn't what you think . . . I'll explain later."

"Oh." She fingered a bracelet. "Well." She agreed at least to go as far as the Sears' apartment with us, since it was on her homeward way, and to telephone the Power Plant from there. Dr. Sear welcomed my acceptance of his invitation, declaring I could prove my humanity as easily after filet mignon as before, and with a wink expressed his readiness to be de-Certified if I thought it necessary. He busied himself then with reviving his wife, while Anastasia put her clothes in order; and pleased at the chance to delay my reply I went to attend Peter Greene. Truth to tell, the mention of meat worked counter to all my appetites, as did the recognition that I was beginning to be in love. Though my testicles hurt and my stomach rumbled, I could scarce abide the ideas of sex and food; it was only to speak with Anastasia and Dr. Sear (on the very matter he'd just brought up, among others) that I wanted to dine with them: else I had withdrawn to some private place to examine my heart's state and what it portended.

It transpired that we ate neither at the Sears' apartment nor in a restaurant, but had dinner sent up to the office from the hospital kitchens, for both Mrs. Sear and Peter Greene were in no condition to leave the building. The latter, whom I found just waking up on a couch in the Reception Room, greeted me with as woeful a groan as ever I'd heard; he rose to hug or hit me, choked into tears instead, and sat down again, shaking his head.

"Oh, Founder!" he said, with an affecting hoarseness. "She's the flunkèdest of all!" What he had witnessed from the observation-chamber, it appeared, had shocked him more profoundly than I'd allowed for. As previously he had seemed to believe that the human heart was essentially passèd, so now he declared it essentially flunked; no good my suggesting it was but desperately human. Anastasia was a whore, he vowed, worse than O.B.G.'s daughter, who at least had confined her harlotry to male humans; Dr. Sear and his wife were unspeakable perverts; me he spared, as entering the debauch purely for his benefit—indeed, he thanked me bitterly for opening his eye to the truth as only a Grand Tutor might—but the rest of studentdom, himself included, he now agreed must be as failed as I had described.

"I been a blind durn fool!" he cried. So far did he carry his black despisal, I feared it was wrong-headed as his former optimism. His displeasure with himself, in particular, was intense enough to make him shudder while he spoke, as might a fever. Clearly he was not fit to drive: when Anastasia entered the room to beg his pardon, he vomited explosively into a smoking-stand, to her great distress, and it was necessary for Dr. Sear to resedate him into unconsciousness. Hedwig too, the doctor said coolly as he withdrew the syringe, was more than usually *hors de combat;* her also he had sedated.

"Rotten shame," he tisked, having telephoned our dinner orders. I wasn't certain whether he alluded to his wife's condition, the change in our dining-plans, or Anastasia's having to clean up Peter Greene's mess, until he added a moment later, "Pity you didn't know Hed before she got this way, George: ready for anything then, she was! Full of spirit; nothing fazed her; put Stacey in the shade . . ." He shook his head and relaxed with a slender cigar on the couch, near Greene's feet. "What times we used to have! Lately, of course, she hasn't been herself. Terrible pressures. But it's still the most genuine marriage I know of. Ideal, in fact."

I could not conceal my incredulity. Anastasia paused too, paper towel in hand, then went on with her scrubbing. Dr. Sear smiled.

"What I mean is, it's the only *authentic* and *meaningful* kind of marriage, for educated people in modern terms, because it's based on freedom, frankness, equality, and no illusions whatever. It may not work, but even if it turns out to be impossible, nothing else is worth trying." He wrinkled his brow in a cordial tease. "I saw through *my* ladyship from the first, in every respect; and Heddy did likewise."

"And were you pleased by what you saw?" I asked him. I had been thinking of my own ambivalent insight into Anastasia, but Dr. Sear took the question as a challenge and amiably replied, "You mean her lesbianism, I suppose, and my own homosexual tendencies . . ."

"No no, sir! What I—"

"Don't apologize," he insisted. "I enjoy looking things straight in the eye." He went on to declare that while these same tendencies (the confrontation whereof in myself, he suggested, might well be the real purport of my fourth Assignment-task) were not inherently either passing or failing in his opinion, he readily seconded the Maxim that self-knowledge is generally bad news, and would yield to none in the degree of his own self-loathing. "By George, there's another possibility!" he exclaimed, interrupting his confession with a laugh: "Why don't you just masturbate?"

"Sir?"

"Really, Kennard!" Anastasia's scold was serious; she was still red-eyed with unhappiness over the events in the Treatment Room, and but half attended our conversation. "Enough is enough."

"Sorry," the doctor said lightly. "What I meant to say is that if *See Through Your Ladyship* means 'Understand the female elements in your psyche,' it's just another way of saying *Know thyself,* don't you agree, George? But since this whole Grand-Tutor business has such a Founder's-Scroll air about it, maybe *know* should be understood in the Old-Syllabus sense of carnal knowledge. In other words, *Fornicate thyself."*

I was not sure to what extent this interpretation was a *jeu d'esprit;* the earlier part of it struck me as reasonable enough, the more as it didn't really contradict my own speculations. But Anastasia said he ought to be ashamed of himself.

"Honestly, sometimes I think you *like* naughtiness," she declared, and went to take our dinner-cart from the maid at the door. Her remark (which seemed banal to me, love or no love) delighted the doctor.

"I *do,* as you know," he said to me. "And I do despise myself, of course. What other feeling is there, for a man both intelligent and honest? I can't take anybody seriously who doesn't loathe himself. That's why I admire Taliped."

I accepted a salad from the cart, blanched at the fragments of bloody steer-muscle on the plates, and took up the conversation to keep from imagining the bovicide that must be daily wrought to feed carnivorous studentdom its evening meal.

"You say you admire Dean Taliped's self-loathing, sir. Don't you actually just envy him his reasons?" The question was sincere enough but I confess it gave me an un-Grand-Tutorish satisfaction to defend what I knew was Anastasia's position. Throughout the meal—while Dr. Sear with mild good humor acknowledged his perversions and his wife's, agreed that her present condition was partly the cumulative effect, on her homely spirit, of their years of libertinism, but defended his biography on the grounds that "total experience," while ruinous, is requisite to Understanding—I was unnaturally aware of my belovèd's presence in the room. She said little during our harangue, but as I endeavored to point out to Dr. Sear (first begging his leave) how much of illusion and innocence could still be said to be in his thinking, self-deception in his confessions, and pride in his self-loathing, I watched her flashing eyes from the corner of mine and glowed in the certainty of their approval.

"Admit it, sir: you find your self-hatred . . . *interesting,* don't you?"

He cocked his head judiciously, a bit of flesh impaled on his fork. "Let's say *piquant.* Yes, piquant, definitely. Which is, I suppose, just that much more ground for self-hatred, as you term it."

"That much more piquant, you mean."

"Very good, George! Really, you amaze me."

But I was too desirous of Anastasia's esteem (not to mention Dr. Sear's final welfare) to be content with bland compliments. What I wanted, I told him, was not that he should be amazed, but that he should Pass, and prerequisite to that end was his real conviction, not merely that he was not passèd (despite Bray's Certification, which I sensed Sear had no final faith in), but that he was failed.

"Wait now," he protested more firmly; "you forget what Gynander—"

I interrupted: "Gynander was a proph-prof, sir. Excuse me, but that makes all the difference on campus. Gynander didn't do things just out of curiosity; he didn't especially even want to see everything he saw. But he *did* things; he had . . . a *power.* He wasn't just a spectator."

Dr. Sear allowed I had a point, and this time his expression of surprise at what he called my "native discernment" was more sincere, and less composed.

"But see here, George," he said, making a little grimace; "there's one factor in Hedwig's condition, and my attitude, that you're leaving out of account—naturally enough, since I've told no one about it except my wife." He contemplated the ash of his cigar. "The fact is, I won't be on campus much longer . . ."

Though he touched the little bandage on his brow as he spoke, I mistook his meaning until Anastasia, with a small compassionate exclamation, put by her tray and hurried to his chair-arm. Pressing his distinguished head at once to her chest, she declared she'd *known* there was more to "that sore place" than he'd let on. Her tears ran freely into his silver hair; I could almost envy him the squamous-cell carcinoma that provoked such sympathy. It had begun, he told us quietly, as a small growth upon the bridge of his nose, which had commenced to fester, as he'd thought, from daily contact with the frames of his eyeglasses. He himself had subsequently diagnosed it as malignant and arranged for its removal, but the surgeon-friend who excised it had discovered preliminary invasions of both orbits as well as of the paranasal sinuses.

"You've noticed," he said, almost with embarrassment, "that my breath is often foul. The cause of that, happily, also prevents my being able to smell it myself—or anything else." He attempted to turn this circumstance into a wry example of Tragic Compensation; but Anastasia, who knew the import of his words as I did not, weepingly implored him to cease making light of it, to have the cancer dealt with at once, before his eyesight and very life should go the way of his sense of smell.

"Nonsense, my dear." He patted her arm. "I have a twenty percent chance of living another decade if I let them cut my nose off; maybe thirty percent if they take the eyes out too. No thank you!" He had, he said, devoted his life to the admiration of beauty and the enlargement of his experience and understanding; he saw no reason literally to deface himself for the sake of a few horrid extra semesters. Moreover, though there was he supposed no end to art and knowledge, he could not but feel surfeited with both. He regarded his life as having been pleasant and rich in variety; for that very reason he was lately bored with it; nothing had for him any longer the delight of genuine novelty, and he confessed to looking forward to his dying with the temperate enthusiasm of a connoisseur, as the one experience he'd yet to try. To his mind, the only choice was aesthetic: whether to take his own life forthwith or let the cancer make a blind purulent madman of him before it killed him, a year or two hence. The latter course appealed to him, as the more passive and exquisite; he had always rather let experience write upon him than play the role of author. On the other hand he loathed monstrosity and unawareness, particularly in combination; even before the carcinoma reached his brain he would be stupefied with suffering or narcotized against it, and of what value was an experience one didn't experience?

"Oh well," he concluded—actually yawning, as if this subject too had begun to bore him; "naturally all this has been a trial for Heddy; she never was much of a philosopher."

Anastasia kissed him all about the face, but especially upon the fatal bandage; nor would Sear's tuts and pats assuage her concern.

"If I could *help* you somehow!" she grieved, and I knew with a sting that had the doctor been a man of normal appetites she'd gratefully close his sorrow in her honey limbs. I too was touched with pity and begged his pardon for my earlier criticisms, though I couldn't help feeling that the fact of his disease, however grave in itself, had no bearing on our argument. It pleased and chastened me that Dr. Sear acknowledged as much himself a moment later, when Anastasia had gone to the washroom to compose herself.

"I'm aware," he said, "that my attitude toward dying is quite as perverse as my other attitudes. Contemptibly effcte, if you like. And so I'm properly contemptuous of it—which is more effete yet, and so on."

I asked him to excuse my tactlessness, as I'd had little experience of human attitudes towards dying (the goats, it goes without saying, have no opinions on the subject); no doubt it was presumptuous of me to advise him at all, and particularly in these circumstances . . .

"No no no," he insisted, more cheerfully. "You're quite right; the cancer's beside the point; you must help me teach Hedwig that. So, you have a prescription for me, do you? A tip for the Finals?"

I saw he was ironical, but set forth anyhow a notion that had occurred to me when I considered his Certification in the light of the others I'd challenged. It came to this: that so long as he relished his self-loathing and found his failings piquant, he was by no means being "nothing ignorant"; on the contrary, his failure to see the vital difference between Gynander and himself—between the mantic and the connoisseur—argued to me that he was after all naïve.

"Naïve!" He very nearly tapped his cigar into his coffee-cup. "Naïve!" He could say no more. I blushed, but insisted on the term. What fundamentaller innocence was there, I asked him, than the inability to distinguish passage from failure? Hadn't he himself alluded, in the Amphitheater, to those verses in the Old Syllabus condemning fallen studentdom to "knowledge of truth and falsehood"—which was to say, awareness of their failure? Yet he still believed—*naïvely,* in my opinion—not only that total awareness of failure was somehow tantamount to passage, but that experience was synonymous with depravity. In short, he confused innocence and experience, self-knowledge and self-delusion, passage and failure.

"I see," Dr. Sear said coolly. "And how do you suggest I correct this lamentable ingenuousness?"

What I suggested, stubbornly, was that he learn to loathe his self-loathing in fact, and not just in the voluptuous way, by taking true measure of his perversion . . .

"Ah," he said, brightening up at once. I hastened to add that what I had in mind was no elaboration of his usual amusements; depravity *à quatre* was not perverser than depravity *à trois,* I argued, any more than voyeurism by fluoroscope was naughtier than Eierkopf's night-glass watches. No, the consummate perversion for a man of his temper, as I saw it, lay on the opposite hand: let him eschew the piquant and exotic, if he would taste the full flunkèdness of his life; let him pursue instead the humblest and most commonplace of satisfactions . . .

"What do you mean, exactly?" he demanded. "Eat my beef well-done? Drink beer from a can with dinner? Watch Telerama-shows all evening?" Even as he told over these suggestions I saw his fine nostrils begin to quiver, and was the more persuaded of my good judgment. I shook my head.

"It's your sex-life I had in mind, sir. I believe you should freshen Mrs. Sear."

He had been going to sip his coffee, and looked up with the cup poised before his mouth. "I beg your pardon?"

"Service Mrs. Sear yourself, sir, in the ordinary way. Breed her again. She's not past bearing age, I suppose?"

He was too astonished to reply, but as I was considering whether I'd possibly got the terms wrong for human husbandry, Anastasia came exclaiming from the hallway.

"That's a *perfect* idea!" she cried, and made it so with a kiss on my temple. "It's just what Hedwig *needs,* Kennard! Especially *now!*"

Dr. Sear scoffed: his wife's infirmities, her imminent widowhood, her beginning menopause—not to mention the parlous state of the University, ever worsening, and the general absurdity of existence . . . Anastasia clung to his arm, nestled into his shoulder, clasped his dry hand for very rapture at the thought of procreation; for such a coaxing I'd have studded Mrs. Sear myself, and I knew as well—so transparent to me now was My Ladyship—that Anastasia would gladly have taken the man's seed into her own unfruited womb, from sheer access of solicitude, or permitted any husband or most-treasured lover of her own to impregnant Mrs. Sear, if the doctor could not.

"Just *imagine,* Kennard!" she fairly wept; "a *baby* for Hedwig!" She rushed to me again; her excitement stirred even Peter Greene to grunt through his stupor. I drew her boldly to my lap this time, confident in my knowledge; sure enough, she let herself be set upon me, as she would upon any other who knew how to touch her, and my heart flagged even as my blood bucked at the feel of her.

Dr. Sear put down his cup with a clatter and strode this way and that.

"Ridiculous! It's unthinkable!" He laughed harshly. "Why do you suppose we've had no children all these years, for pity's sake? Besides—but what difference does it make! Absurd!" So he expostulated, slapped his arms to his sides, sniffed and fulminated, laughed and adjusted his spectacles atop the little bandage, while Anastasia wept and hugged me for delight: quite the most reaction I'd provoked thus far by my *Tutoring* (for Tutoring it was, I recognized now with a stir of awe, that I'd been at since Scrapegoat Grate, no less than completing my Assignment).

"Mom and Dad Sear!" he snorted, and bit on his foreknuckle.

"Yes!" Anastasia clapped her hands. "It's the absolute *answer!* You're a genius, George!"

Sear stopped pacing and narrowed his eyes at me with whimsical respect. "He's a tougher man to please than Harold Bray, I'll vouch for that. Hedwig and I!"

At every such allusion to my proposal, Anastasia bounced; I was relieved now that Peter Greene showed signs of rewaking, for had she not got off me (anxious to begone lest the sight of her do him further harm), I must soon have bespermed myself. She would telephone her husband from downstairs, she said—should have done earlier, he'd behaved so queerly at lunch—and either hail a taxi or wait for a Powerhouse-guard if Stoker cared to dispatch one to the Infirmary. Dr. Sear, it was hurriedly agreed, should keep Greene under his surveillance, either there or at home, until the man's trauma could be assessed and directed to the positive end of mature self-knowledge.

"Nothing *à trois,* I promise," he said to me, and shook his head once more in dismay at what I'd proposed. "You're quite welcome to spend the night too, you know; we never did get to talk about Max and the rest, and I want to look at that mad Assignment you mentioned . . . or were you going with Stacey?"

I had not of course considered my next move, much less where I'd spend the night; a clock on Dr. Sear's wall showed seven, my own watch six—in either case it was early evening, and tired as I was there were tasks remaining to be accomplished. I stood up and fished the Assignment from my purse.

"There *are* some important things I want to discuss with you," I told Anastasia. "Very important. Let me see what's next on my list . . . It says *Re-place the Founder's Scroll.* Have they lost it, do you suppose?"

Dr. Sear and Anastasia agreed that the so-called Founder's Scroll (a recently-excavated assortment of Old- and New-Syllabus fragments presented to New Tammany by the Chancellor of New Moishe College, where the parchments had been discovered, in gratitude for the help New Tammany's Moishians had given their symbolic alma mater) was not to their knowledge missing from its temporary display-case in the Central Library. Dr. Sear, however, remembered having read that the Cataloguing Office was experiencing some difficulty in the matter of filing it permanently: CACAFILE, WESCAC's automatic classification and filing facilities, he recalled, which operated from definitions originally programmed into it by various scholars and then improved by its own self-scanning techniques, could not decide (as it were) whether the precious relic should be classified under Religion, Philosophy, Literature, Archeology, Art, or History—each of which departments claimed it. When Library officials had presented it physically to the CACAFILE as a last resort, hoping to force a mechanical arbitration, the Scroll had disappeared for some anxious hours into the automatic bookstacks and been finally returned as unclassifiable.

"Yet it says *re*-place, doesn't it?" he mused. "Not just *place.* Intriguing task." His mind was not much on the matter, I perceived; though he remembered to give me the Clean Bill of Health I'd asked for, and suggested to Anastasia that she direct me to the Library on her way out, it was my advice that still absorbed him.

"Have a nice weekend," Anastasia bade him pointedly as we left.

His vellum cheeks actually colored. "Ridiculous!"

"Please, Kennard: Heddy'd *love* it, I know!" Even more, I saw, would she, who as our lift came was inspired with a further proposal: "Take her to the Honeymoon Lodge Motel, Kennard!"

"Oh, Stacey!" He turned away and closed the office door, for Greene was stirring loudly now. But even Anastasia acknowledged with a giggle that his impatience with us was of the embarrassed kind, and that what disconcerted him was his real fascination with the idea.

"You're a *darling* to think of it!" she said, and hugged my arm. Her plain arousement did nothing for my buckly cramps of love; but though I re-entered the lift more gimpish than I'd left it some time earlier, I rejoiced at being two steps nearer Commencement Gate.

5.

Once we were alone in the little compartment her self-consciousness returned: she let go my elbow and turned her eyes from the poked-out front of my gown. To put her at ease I said, "Pardon my erection," and assured her that despite my obvious desire, to which Love must positively now be added, I did not intend to mount her.

"Don't *talk* that way!" she pleaded.

"There's no help for it," I declared sadly; "in fact, I doubt very much that we'll ever mate again. Not because you're married—I haven't decided quite *what* to make of marriage yet. But I think we might be brother and sister, so we probably shouldn't copulate."

I had been going to recommend in addition that she forsake all other bedmates as well, in order to remove any doubts about the motives of her famous sympathy; but she paled so at mention of our possible relation that I judged it prudenter to postpone further counsel. Her lovely face was stricken; with welling eyes she heard WESCAC's account: that inasmuch as she was Virginia R. Hector's daughter, if I was truly the GILES we must have the same mother; and that if, as was the common report, Miss Hector had had but a single *accouchement,* we were actually twins.

She clutched the handrail and shook her head. The door opened upon a virtually empty lobby. I was obliged to lead her from the lift, and we stood uncertainly under the eyes of a distant receptionist and two orderlies at the revolving exit-door. Unease dispelled my cramps and detumesced me.

"Mind," I said to reassure her, "the only thing that's certain is that I'm the Grand Tutor and you're Miss Hector's daughter. All the rest, even this GILES business, is only conjecture."

"Oh, George, this is *awful!*" Her voice was faint with horror; yet even on the verge of swooning she evidently saw how my expression clouded—as I feared, against my better judgment, that she might be simply loath to own a goat-boy for a brother—and she begged me to believe that it was purely the memory of our public "union," as she called it, that appalled her. "All those *people!*"

I thought it perceptive of me to observe: "If I understand human propriety, they're scandalized already by our Memorial Service, aren't they? A little extra scandal won't much matter. Besides—I don't want to sound vain, but I *am* the Grand Tutor . . ."

Her eyes swam now with appreciation of this comfort, instead of shame. Warmly she said—and I thrilled to hear it—that she could think of no man on campus whom she'd prefer as a brother, though she knew herself unworthy of sistership to a Grand-Tutor-to-be . . . I bade her end such deprecation of herself; of *course* she was worthy, I insisted—or would be if she'd but accept from me a single bit of Tutelage; to wit: let no man, woman, or other beast mount her or in any wise know her carnally, not even her husband, from that hour forth, that no invidious *double-entendre* be read into the motto on her spurious diploma: *Love thy classmate.*

"Ordinarily I wouldn't include your husband," I said, as if I dispensed such prohibitions daily. "But your marriage is such an . . . *unusual* one that your motive in mating with him might be the same as your motive in mating with Croaker, or Mrs. Sear, or—or Harold Bray, for all I know . . ."

This last I tossed in off-handedly, but I was unspeakably pleased to hear her protest that she had not "united" with Bray even once, whatever he might have said to the contrary.

"He hasn't said anything, as far as I know," I confessed.

"He'd better *not*. I know he's a great man and all, but *ugh!*"

I was emboldened to add, less from vanity than by way of firming my own resolve, that even if I should summon her myself, in my capacity as Grand Tutor of the Western Campus, and bid her conceive a child by me, say, to carry on my work when I should pass away—even then, and knowing as she must that such undergraduate whimsies as the incest-taboo were void before that grand imperative, she was to refuse me.

Wide-eyed she whispered: "Okay."

"I do love you, you know, Anastasia," I said, not at all abashed now. "And I'm not a bit sorry about the Memorial Service in the Living Room . . ."

"You aren't?"

"Of course not. You were perfectly beautiful, I thought; and, needless to say, it was delightful to climb you. It doesn't matter whether Stoker was baiting me or not, or whether we're related: we were innocent. I swear to you as Grand Tutor: it was an okay service."

The color returned to her face now; she dabbed with a tissue at her eyes and thanked me wholeheartedly for clearing her conscience on that point. I admitted to her finally that, being above human prejudices by virtue of my calling as well as my background, I could not but continue to lust for her on sight, as the most serviceable lady girl I'd ever seen; at the same time I judged it improper for a Grand Tutor to play favorites among his Tutees—as my becoming her particular lover would surely be interpreted. Therefore I welcomed, albeit with a pang of regret, the possibility of brotherly love between us, and the added constraint that siblingship would impose (however artificially) upon our intercourse.

Anastasia listened with glowing eyes. "You're *sweet*," she murmured, and rising impulsively on tiptoes, bussed my cheek. "I've *needed* a brother to straighten me out, from the beginning!"

The prospect which had so alarmed her only a few moments previously seemed now to delight her quite as much as that of Dr. Sear's connubial husbandry. "I can't *wait* to see Mom!" she exclaimed. "I'll *make* her 'fess up this time!" Her face was alight. "I know what! Friday's her night to work: I'll go with you to the Library, and we'll kill two birds with one stone!" Her mother, she reminded me, was an assistant director of filing and cataloguing in the Central Library: an office she'd attained on her own merits before the misfortune of her illegitimate pregnancy and subsequent instability, and held since as a kind of sinecure thanks to the influence of her father, the ex-Chancellor. Thus it was she whom I'd be applying to in any case for authorization to re-place the Founder's Scroll. Anastasia proposed to accompany me there and take the opportunity to "get to the bottom of this *sister*-thing," as she put it. Already she was a-bubble with questions and conjectures: if we were twins, or even just siblings, she couldn't *imagine* why I hadn't been raised along with herself; how could *anybody* not want their own little baby? On the other hand, if something had "taken me away" at birth (of one thing Anastasia was certain: it could never have been our mother's wish), that circumstance went far, she thought, to explain Virginia Hector's subsequent lapses of reason, and even her rejection of Anastasia—by what mechanism of psychology I did not grasp. But why had "Uncle Ira" and "Grandpa Reg" never mentioned a brother? And if, as it now appeared, neither Dr. Spielman nor Dr. Eierkopf was our father, who on *campus* did I suppose was? And whatever could have happened to spirit me away?

"Let's hurry, George! Aren't you thrilled to *pieces*? Oh, *darn* . . ." She snapped her fingers. "I really must call Maurice. Only take a sec."

She hurried off to telephone the Powerhouse from the receptionist's desk, and I availed myself of the respite to herd my scattered thoughts and address them to the work at hand—more important by far, to my mind, than the details of my genealogy. Mother or no mother, sister or no sister, I had Finals to pass, an impostor to rout, and studentdom to tutor from its error. *Re-place the Founder's Scroll.* With humble pride, not unmixed with awe, I remarked how clearly each new task, so far from exhausting me, left me stronger for the next; how, for the man of sure vocation, nothing is gratuitous, and the merest happenstance is fraught with meaning. Dr. Sear's observation about the Library's classification-problem, now I considered it, pointed clearly to the sense of my task—a sense altogether harmonious (as Sear could never have guessed) with the rest of the Assignment. What had my day's work proved, if not the necessity of clear distinction? And what were my labors but a series of paradigms, or emblems of this necessity? To distinguish Tick from Tock, East Campus from West, Grand Tutor from goat, appearance from reality (or whatever contraries were involved in seeing through My Ladyship)—all these tasks, like my sundry concomitant advisings, were but ways of saying, "Passage is Passage, Failure Failure: let none confuse them." All that was wanted to put the Founder's Scroll in its place was sharper definition, I was confident—and eager to tackle the problem, I grew impatient at the little delay, for it began to seem not impossible that I might request Examination that same evening, and thus complete my Assignment in a single day—as close to "no time," surely, as anyone could demand!

After a few minutes Anastasia reported, with some concern, that Stoker had not appeared at the Powerhouse all day, nor had his new secretary at Main Detention seen him since mid-morning; the former office was particularly alarmed because of some threatening situation in the Furnace Room—I trembled to imagine it—that required his management. At least, however, she was free to go with me; we left the Infirmary after a brief dispute with the orderlies (who wanted proof of my discharge from custody and only reluctantly accepted my Clean Bill of Health and Anastasia's endorsement in lieu of the regular form), and as we rode Librarywards in a double-sidecar taxi, Anastasia explained what had disturbed her at luncheon.

"Maurice has never done anything *like* it before!" she said. "Coming right to the Infirmary and taking me out to eat! He'd even shaved, and bought a necktie!" Moreover—what I agreed was unimaginable—he had treated her with courtesy; had opened doors for her, praised her coiffure (as she reported this she touched her hair, still incredulous), dined with her in almost gentlemanly fashion, and finally announced that he wanted her advice: Didn't she agree that he should drop in at the Light House and publicly deny kinship with Lucky Rexford?

"I swear that's what he said, George—and so *mildly!*" Any moment, she declared, she had expected him to end the cruel pretense and become his normal self again. Had he but smashed even a *little* porcelain, called out a few obscenities, or pinched the waitress's behind, she might have dined with some small appetite despite the novelty of the occasion. As it was, she could eat nothing, and trembled with worry that she had displeased him in some way. His question she could scarcely comprehend; not until they rose from table did she venture to say, "Whatever *you* think, dear"—and that only to terminate the suspense, for she was certain that as soon as she took the bait of his polite inquiry he'd perpetrate some characteristic outrage in the tea-room. He had been drawing out her chair as she replied, and when he took her elbows then she'd closed her eyes and waited, almost with relief, to be assaulted upon the table or otherwise indignified—but he had gently ushered her out, expressing his pleasure in her company and his hope that they might have lunch together more often.

"Did he go to the Chancellor's Mansion then?" I asked.

She closed her eyes and pressed her fingertips to her temples. "I was so rattled, I can't remember *what* he said after that." Seeing my sharp interest, she asked whether I knew what might have "come over" her husband.

"I have an idea," I admitted. "He and I had a little conversation this morning . . ." I considered whether to tell her that Maurice Stoker's apparent good behavior, if it was the result of our talk in Main Detention, was more flunkèd in its way than his former immoderacies; but I wasn't certain I could rehearse that difficult argument clearly, and so I simply cautioned her instead not to be seduced, by his new gentleness, out of her new chastity.

She frowned. "But suppose he . . . wants me for something, George? Or asks me to . . . *do* something for somebody? I *am* his wife . . ."

Upon consideration I agreed that she might permit him a limited amount of dignified sexual converse with her person, so long as it was with her express consent and involved no force, degradation, perversion, or other abuse. "But not with anyone else, Anastasia," I repeated firmly. "And not just to please *him*. If you're in heat, or want to breed a child, then okay."

"I don't seem able to have children," she reminded me. "I guess it's lucky, considering." But the thought—of either her barrenness or her past promiscuity—so saddened her that for the rest of the ride she fiddled with a strand of her hair and

contemplated the evening traffic. The lights along the boulevards were less bright than they'd been the night before; they
appeared at times even to flicker. As we passed the Light
House I saw people gathered along the iron fence, some bearing placards whose messages I couldn't make out in the poor
light. A black wedge of motorcycles roared from one of the
entrance-drives and sped by us; I was almost certain that the
leader was Stoker himself—but bare-chinned, and wearing a
light-colored suit! Anastasia happened to be staring glumly in
the opposite direction, and I said nothing lest at sight of him
she change her mind about going with me.

On the esplanade before Tower Hall was another crowd,
standing about as if in expectation; one could hear a common
buzz of displeasure every time the streetlights winked.

"*Something* screwy going on," our driver ventured. He
took us around to the rear of the building; Anastasia put by
her melancholy reverie to pay our fare (which I'd not understood was required) and brightened a little as we approached
the enormous wing that housed New Tammany's Central
Library stacks and offices.

"I can hardly *wait* for you to meet Mom after all these
terms!" she said, taking my arm. We went through an
entrance-door over which was engraved THE TRUE UNIVER-
SITY IS A COLLECTION OF BOOKS, and made our way through
vast high-ceilinged reading rooms, sparsely peopled by reason
of the uncertain light.

"I *know* something's wrong at the Powerhouse," Anastasia
fretted. A lone student rushed past us in the corridor which
led to the Cataloguing Office; as we looked behind to see
where he might be going in such haste, he caught himself up
for a second and glanced back at me with an expression of
indignant disbelief, as if angry at having to credit his eyes. I
blushed, not knowing why I should, and gave Anastasia's
hand a brotherly pat.

At the end of the corridor was a large domed room entirely given over to rows of catalogue-files laid out like the
spokes of a wheel. In its hub, beneath a suspended sign which
declared THE FINAL SCIENCE IS LIBRARY SCIENCE, a large
metal-cornered glass case stood empty but for its black-velvet
bed. Anastasia gasped.

"It *is* gone!"

She meant the Scroll, ordinarily exhibited there. I twinged
with distress: if it had been lost or stolen, to restore it to its

place could take Founder knew how long! I insisted we learn what happened to it before pursuing our private business—which might have to be put aside anyhow if duty called.

"Maybe that's what the excitement's about," I suggested unhappily.

There being however no one in the room except ourselves, Anastasia pointed out that her mother was in the best position to answer this question as well as the other, since her office was adjacent to the card-files; she proposed we go to her at once, before she too should join the apparent exodus from Tower Hall; Anastasia would introduce me merely as the new Candidate for Grand-Tutorhood, and I could interview our mother undistracted on the matter of the Scroll before we disclosed our other concerns. I saw no alternative and so agreed, though with some misgivings; the gossip one had heard about Virginia Hector's unhappy condition inspired no confidence in her as an accurate reporter.

"Wait." I caught her arm. "Here comes someone else." A door from the corridor had opened and shut, and sharp heels clicked down the aisle next to ours. The lights blinked out entirely for two seconds; in the pause one heard a surge from the crowd outside. The clicking hesitated also, then resumed with the light. But I laid a finger to my lips and drew Anastasia two steps back into our aisle, because while the sound bespoke a woman's tread, it called to my mind the clickish voice of Harold Bray, and I wanted a moment to consider a half-formed notion that accompanied his hateful image: the texts of his false Certificates were cited by their bearers as coming not simply from the Old or New Syllabus, but specifically from the Founder's Scroll; assuredly there were transcriptions of the document which he might have consulted, but my antipathy put nothing past him. If one began with the assumption that he was a fraud and then looked for the motive of his imposture, it seemed far from unimaginable to me that he might make use of his position to deliver secret information to the Nikolayans, for example, or to steal a priceless treasure like the Founder's Scroll . . .

The interloper—in fact a female person of a certain age—emerged now into the center; Anastasia left off regarding me quizzically and smiled.

"Come on: it's Mom."

She would have hailed or gone to her, but when the elder

woman paused beside the case at sound of us and peered to see who we were, adjusting a pencil in her silver hair, light flashed from the point-cornered lenses of her eyeglasses. I gripped Anastasia's arm and very nearly swooned.

"Founder Omniscient!" I groaned, and ran with chill perspiration; was obliged to squat and feign interest in a low drawer of cards until I mastered my shivering. No mistaking her: it was Lady Creamhair, however drawn and silvered by unhappy terms!

Anastasia bent to me, frightened. "What *is* it, George?"

I shook my head. Lady Creamhair's eyes—*Virginia Hector's,* it staggered me to understand!—had evidently not improved since our dim dear days in the hemlock-grove; seeing nothing familiar about us or untoward, she went on to her office.

"You're sure that's Virginia Hector, Anastasia?"

"Of course it is! What on campus—"

"And . . . she's your mother?" I leaned against the card-file for support.

"*Our* mother, I hope!" She drew me hubwards. "Let's find out for sure, before she goes off somewhere."

But I held back yet a moment, flabbergast with memory and surprise. Poor dear Creamie! How I understood now your unwillingness to meet my keeper, or tell me your name; how I trembled at your old interest in me, your yen to pluck me from the herd, and—Founder, Founder!—your appall at my lust to Be, that drove you watchless from the grove!

"Anastasia . . ." I could scarcely speak. It was the empty Scroll-case now I leaned on, and drew her to me. Dutifully she resisted—until assured that it was a brotherly embrace. "I won't explain now, but . . . I've known that lady before, and I—I really think that you and I *might* be twins."

She hugged me enthusiastically—confounding my poor blood, which knew no longer what permissibly might rouse it. I suggested then that the shock of seeing me after so many terms might do her mother—*our* mother!—more harm than good unless properly prepared for; we agreed that Anastasia would go to her at first alone, draw her out upon the matters of our twinship and paternity while I listened from the doorway, and gently then introduce the facts of our acquaintance and my presence in the College proper. If Miss Hector found the news too distressing, I could present myself another time;

if not, Anastasia would summon and introduce me. I stationed myself outside the door, and Anastasia knocked.

"Come in, please? Oh, it's you, dear."

I closed my eyes; her voice had still the querulous resolve in it that had fetched me in kiddish fury once at the fence, and soothed my adolescent stormings in the hemlock. Anastasia greeted her with a cheeriness perhaps exaggerated by the situation, declaring that she had a few daughterly matters to discuss, and that it had anyhow been too long since they'd last chatted.

"Oh. Well. Yes. Well. All this commotion lately . . ." Lady Creamhair clucked and fussed, not incordially, but as if permanently rattled. She seemed indeed in less possession of her faculties than formerly, and with rue I wondered how much hurt my ignorant assault might have done her. The two women exchanged commonplaces for a while—rather formally it seemed to me, for a mother and daughter, but at least with none of the ill-will that had rejected Anastasia in her childhood. Then presently, with apologies for "bringing up a sore subject," Anastasia declared that the recent appearance in New Tammany of two claimants to the title of Grand Tutor had revived many people's curiosity about the old Cum Laude Project and brought up again the unhappy matters of the "Hector scandal" and her illegitimate paternity—

"That's nobody's business," I heard Virginia Hector say firmly. From the sound I guessed that Anastasia went to embrace her then and declared affectionately that indeed it *wasn't* the business of anyone outside the family; but that she herself, of age now and a married woman, was surely entitled to the whole truth of her begetting.

"You *know* I've always loved you, Mother, and you *must* know it doesn't matter to me what the truth *is;* I just want to get it straight! One person comes along and says Dr. Eierkopf's my father—"

"Ha," Miss Hector said scornfully.

"—then another person says it's Dr. Spielman—"

The import of her "Hmp" at mention of this name I could not assess, though I listened closely.

"And you've said different things at different times yourself," Anastasia went on. "Even that I'm not your daughter . . ." Her voice grew less steady.

"Oh, now," Virginia Hector said. Anastasia repeated that her affection for her mother could not be diminished by the facts, whatever they were—at least she began to repeat some such sentiment, but was overtaken midway by tears.

"Now, now, now . . ." So like was that voice to the one that had gentled my two-score weepings in terms gone by, I could have wept again at sound of it. I yearned to burst in and beg my Lady Creamhair's pardon; must press my forehead to the frosted door-glass to calm me. Some minutes the ladies wept together. Then there was a snap of purses and blow of noses upon tissues, after which Virginia Hector said: "I have much to be forgiven, dear, Founder knows . . . No, no, don't be so kind; you've every right to hate me for the way I behaved when you were little. I flunk myself a hundred times over just to remember it, and when I *think* of you married to that beast . . ."

The thought brought more tears, as well it might, despite Anastasia's reassurances that none but herself was accountable for her choice of husbands. Happily, Miss Hector seemed unaware of the details of her daughter's life, before as well as after marriage, understanding only in a general way that it was less than serene and respectable. She was able therefore to recompose herself sooner than she doubtless would have had she known the hard particulars of Anastasia's history.

"I was *awfully* upset, you know," she went on presently, referring to the period of her daughter's infancy. "You can't *imagine* how it is to know that nobody will ever believe the truth, no matter what. Not even you. Not even now . . ."

Anastasia vowed she would, if only her mother would produce it; and so, after a number of unconvincèd hums and clucks, Virginia Hector said clearly, almost wryly: "The truth is, I have never in my life . . . *gone all the way* with a man. Not once, to this day."

If I was slower to come to incredulity than Anastasia (whom I heard make an instant noise of dismay), it was not because I misinterpreted the phrase "gone all the way," but rather because my origin, my experiences, and my knowledge of Anastasia's past, for example, prevented me from grasping at once that by "never with a man" Miss Hector meant "never with a male of any species."

"When I learned I was pregnant, I blamed it on Max Spielman," she went on to say, "because I knew nobody would believe the truth, and I thought Dr. Spielman might love me enough to take the blame and marry me, even though he'd think it was another man's child. But he didn't, and that was that."

How I longed to tell her immediately the truth of Max's love and honor, so great that it was just her refusal to admit infidelity that had kept him from wedding her! But Anastasia—with a kind of tired incuriosity now, as if she knew in advance what the reply would be—asked then who *was* her father.

"Your father?" The question appeared to surprise Miss Hector; I tried to recall which word she'd accented, and couldn't. She announced then, as one might read from a page: "Max never would, and Eblis couldn't've if I'd wanted him to. It was WESCAC."

To hear this confirmation from the lady's own lips made me thrill; but Anastasia said disgustedly: "Oh, *Mother!*"

Miss Hector went on undaunted—indeed, unhearing: "Eblis warned me it could happen, and when they fed in the finished GILES he told me I was one of the ones WESCAC had in mind, you might say. I was in love with Max then, and as I said, I'd never *gone all the way* with anyone, though I suppose I would have with Max if he'd wanted to. Wait, let me finish . . ." Anastasia had made a little rustle of despair. "I'd been Miss NTC and Miss University, you know, just as you were—and, my sakes, weren't you lovely the day they capped you! Well . . ."

She herself had been a vain creature, Miss Hector was afraid, as flattered by WESCAC's election as by the student body's in terms before; and though she wouldn't for a *minute* consent to the sort of thing that "Eblis" hinted at, any more than *any* self-respecting girl would have, she'd found herself feeling self-conscious and a little proud whenever she walked past WESCAC's facility in the laboratories of the Cum Laude Project—as if the computer knew it was she and would have whistled if it could. Then one fateful spring evening she'd stayed late to file some data-papers for Dr. Eierkopf at the laboratory (where she'd worked during a temporary furlough from her Library post), and being the last to leave except for the night security-guards, had crossed the hall from her office to make certain that the door to the computer-room was locked . . .

"It *was*, just as it should have been," she said. "And I started to go; but then—maybe I thought I heard something peculiar, a singing-noise or something; maybe not, I don't know.

Anyhow I came back to the door, and for some reason or other I unlocked it and went inside . . . just to check, I suppose; or maybe some impulse . . . I was upset about Max's attitude, I remember . . ."

Her narrative grew less coherent here, until she'd got herself inside the computer-room and closed the door behind her—for what reason, she didn't recall or couldn't articulate, any more than she could explain why she'd not turned the lights on, or why she'd left the doorway and approached the main console, which whirred quietly as always, day and night, and winked on every side its warm gold lights, as if in greeting.

"I thought I'd just sit in the control-chair a minute," she said; "it was awfully peaceful in there; you've no *idea*. I could've dozed right off—maybe I did, for a second or two. But then . . . oh dear, it's not easy to describe how it was!"

The task indeed was difficult, and though her voice rose with a quiet joy as she spoke, so that every word came clearly through the door (despite an increased noise, like cheering, from the crowd outside), I cannot say I followed precisely her account. She had felt a kind of warmth, it seemed—penetrating, almost electrical—that tingled through every limb and joint and relaxed her utterly, as though all the muscles in her body had melted. This sensation had come on quickly, I gathered, but so subtly that she'd not at first realized it was external, and credited it to her fatigue and the extraordinary comfort of the molded chair. Only when the panel-lights ceased to wink and began instead to pulse together in a golden ring did she associate her sensation with WESCAC; even then she failed to comprehend its significance: her first thought was to move lest the tingling be some accidental radiation. But she did not, or could not, even when the whir changed pitch and timbre, grew croonish, and a scanner swung noiselessly down before her; even when, as best I could make out, the general warmth commenced to focus, until she'd thought her lap must burn.

"It seems gradual when I tell it," she said, "but it must have been very quick. Because just when I opened my mouth—to call for help, I guess, because I felt *fastened,* even though I guess I wasn't—anyhow, I just had time to draw one deep breath . . . and it was over."

"Over?" Anastasia echoed my own surprise; though she'd heard the story all her life, and assumed it was some unhappy delusion of her mother's, she'd evidently not heard it till now in such detail.

"It was all over," her mother repeated. "In no time at all. The scanner went away; the panel-lights and the humming went back to normal; I could move my arms and legs again. I'd have thought I dreamt the whole thing—just as everyone else thinks I did, if they believe I was there at all—but I still felt *tender* from the heat. You know. And when I went to get up I felt some wetness there—all of a sudden, this *wetness*. And as soon as I felt it, and moved, and felt it clear on up, I realized something had *gone all the way*—and it would have to be the GILES."

Despite her certainty, however—which I was in better position to share than Anastasia—Miss Hector had said nothing of the marvelous incident to anyone, even when the GILES was found missing next morning and Dr. Eierkopf had pressed her closely on her evening's work. Not until the fact of her pregnancy was unquestionable—and unconcealable—had she confessed it in a panic to her father, the then Chancellor; and not until he insisted that an abortion be performed at once, lest the scandal bring down his administration, had she realized the extraordinary value of what she carried. She'd told Reginald Hector the truth then, and been denounced as a liar; had persisted and been accused of hysteria; and finally, with the consequences I'd heard of from their victim, had chosen to name Max as the man responsible.

"But it *wasn't* Max, and it wasn't Eblis, or any other human person," she said quietly, when Anastasia voiced a discreet incredulity. "It was WESCAC. And it was the GILES, Founder pass us! Your Grandpa Reg knew it, too, in his heart—why else would he fire Eblis and end the Cum Laude Project? But he'd never admit it—even though the doctor had to dilate the hymen to examine me."

"He *didn't!*"

"Indeed he did," she insisted. "If he hadn't passed on he'd tell you himself: old Dr. Mayo. It was the baby itself that finally broke it, being born; before that it was just stretched a little—not near enough for a man, you know."

In response to further questions from Anastasia, she affirmed what I knew already: that the birth had taken place secretly one winter night in Ira Hector's hospital for unwed co-eds, with Ira himself presiding. And then, to my unspeakable delight, she went on to confirm what Max and I had once imagined (along with many an alternative) long before, out in the barns:

"Your Grandpa Reg was so afraid of the scandal, he didn't know *what* to do! When I wouldn't have an abortion, he kept changing his mind, all the time I was pregnant: one day I'd have to give it out for adoption anonymously; the next day we'd have to put it away secretly somehow; then it was no, there'd be *worse* trouble if *that* ever got out: we'd have to keep it and take the consequences, or call it Uncle Ira's foster-child . . ." So mercurial was he on the subject, she said, and desperate to avoid exposure of their shame, she came to fear he might take measures to destroy the child without her knowledge . . .

"Grandpa *Reg?*" Anastasia cried. "I can't *believe* he'd do such a thing!"

No more could she, Miss Hector replied, until he'd announced a few days after she gave birth his decision to do exactly that.

"I found out then it wasn't just the scandal," she explained. "It had to do with his own mother abandoning him and Uncle Ira, and how hard their childhood was; and *my* mother dying when I was born, you know, and Papa afraid some fellow would *take advantage* of me, like they had his mother . . ." Anastasia made a sympathetic noise. "He didn't want my child to go through what *he'd* gone through. Maybe there were other reasons, too."

In any case she'd pled vainly with him to relent, and scarcely dared let the infant out of her sight lest it be made away with. Then, just before the Cum Laude facility was dismantled at the Chancellor's order, a message for her had been brought to the New Tammany Lying-In by an unidentified person who said only that it had been read out on one of WESCAC's printers.

"It was just three words," Virginia Hector said: *"Replace the GILES!* I thought and thought, and finally I decided that since WESCAC knows everything, it must know how to solve my problem too. So the night Papa came to get the baby I told him he could have it, that I'd changed my mind—but I said he'd have to get rid of it the way I wanted him to." Having disclosed her plan, she said—but not her motive—and convinced Reginald Hector of its expediency, she'd bundled the baby in the blanket, left the hospital, and entered Tower Hall by the Chancellor's private door.

"Old Dr. Mayo had passed on during my pregnancy," she said, "and in the mix-up afterwards I'd had the WES-CAC-man at the hospital do the regular Prenatal Aptitude Test on the baby. He thought it hadn't worked, because all the PAT-card said was *Pass All Fail All;* and I didn't understand it either, but when Papa and I went into the military-science stacks in the Library—to the part where nobody's allowed except chancellors and professor-generals?—I took the PAT-card along, in case it meant *something.* I folded it up in the baby's blanket, so Papa wouldn't know it was there; then I gave him the baby, and he put it in the Diet-tape lift and pressed the *Belly*-button so that WESCAC would EAT it."

"He didn't!" Anastasia cried. Then her appall gave way to confusion: "How is it I *wasn't* EATen, then, if you sent me down into the Belly?"

It took some while for Virginia Hector to comprehend the nature of her daughter's misunderstanding, which was of course quite apparent to me; what *wasn't* evident however, even when her mother made it clear that she'd been speaking of a male child, the GILES Himself, I was pleased to see Anastasia question next: how came it that she had been spared, and I condemned? Miss Hector grew vague; seemed not readily to understand the question . . .

"It had to be twins you had, didn't it?" Anastasia persisted. "Uncle Ira never mentioned any brother of mine—I see why, now!—but he always liked to tell how he'd helped deliver me himself . . ."

"Well. Yes. Naturally." But Miss Hector's tone bespoke a fuddledness.

"Then how come we weren't *both* EATen?"

Instead of replying directly to the question, Lady Cream-hair declared sharply that no one had been EATen: the whole hope of her strategy, she said, was that WESCAC would recognize its own and not only desist but contrive my preservation when she restored me to it.

"It was a terrible risk," she admitted proudly. "An awful risk! But I was *right:* they never found him, dead or alive! And I happen to know for a fact he didn't die: my Gilesey's alive, this very minute! Of course, we mustn't ever tell Papa . . ."

Forgetting her original question now in her excitement—as did I, quickened to the heart by these disclosures!—Anastasia flung her arms about her mother (as I inferred) and confessed that she'd not only learned of her brother's existence, just that day, but had actually met him. "He's on Great Mall right now!"

"No, no," Virginia Hector protested, distracted into an odd air of serenity. "That isn't so, you see."

Anastasia laughed. "It *is* so, Mom! If you ever watched Telerama you'd have seen him yourself this morning, at the Turnstile Trials."

Her mother still declined to believe her—I knew well why—and began to ramble. Anastasia demanded good-humoredly to know whether she'd recognize me if she saw me.

"Well, yes, my, no, gracious. Children change so . . . Dear me, yes! No, I'd know my little Giles, yes indeedy; a mother doesn't forget. There was even a birthmark under his little hiney, down on his leg, a little dark circle. No sirree!"

As she went on in this vein I made use of the mirror on my stick to examine the back of my legs, and though the light was poor, and my hands unsteady, I satisfied myself that there was indeed, on the back of my left thigh, about halfway to the knee, a mark such as she described!

"I brought him with me, Mom!" Anastasia said triumphantly. "He's right outside!"

"Oh my, dear me, no . . ."

"Dear me, *yes!* And wait'll you see who he *is!* George?"

Considering Lady Creamhair's obvious distress, I thought it imprudent to reveal myself before she'd had time to assimilate the news of my presence in the College proper; but Anastasia, ignorant of our sore past, summoned me again. Even so I might have fled, for the present: but I heard a sound behind me and saw at the Scroll-case the white-caped figure of Harold Bray. Luckily he seemed not to have observed me. My hands perspired with anger at the sight of him. How he had got in so silently I couldn't imagine; the noise that alerted me proved to be the clack of a key against the glass case as he unlocked it. There was a large black cylinder in his other hand—the Founder's Scroll, I did not doubt, or some false copy which he meant stealthily to put in its place! Yet so brazen was he, Anastasia's call seemed not in the least to alarm him; he didn't even glance our way. The lights flickered, the crowd hummed; for half a second I considered whether to challenge him, exhibit myself to Lady

Creamhair, or hide from both until a better moment. Then Anastasia opened the door, our mother clucking behind her, and said, *"There* you are! Did you hear it all?" She hugged my arm. "Here he is, Mom: *hug* each other!" That same moment she saw Bray, and joyfully invited him to witness our reunion. No help for it then: I turned to Miss Hector . . . Lady Creamhair . . . my mother . . . puι out a hand to shake, and said, "How d'you do, ma'am. Nice seeing you again."

I might have gone on to apologize once more for having tried to mount her at our last meeting, but clearly she was hearing nothing. She opened and closed her eyes, smiled and squinted, shook her head.

"Oh no, indeed. No indeedy," she said, stunned into mildness.

"Billy Bocksfuss," I reminded her tersely, and glanced to see where Bray was. "The Goat-Boy, you know. *George* nowadays. I apologize—"

"Kiss her!" Anastasia insisted, drawing us together.

Bray's voice clicked jovially towards us down the aisle: "What is it, Anastasia? Reunion, did you say?"

"Oh my, no," Virginia Hector said. "Oh well! My!"

"The Goat-Boy himself," Bray said. "Good evening to you, Miss Hector; I hope the noise outside hasn't disturbed you. A most upsetting situation."

He put his arm familiarly about Anastasia's waist as he spoke; even whispered something in her ear, whereat she quickly lowered her eyes and drew in her lips.

"Stop touching her!" I demanded. "Take your hands off my sister!" I blushed, whether at the term or from anger at Bray. Anastasia colored also, but clearly with pleasure, and went obediently to her mother's side.

"What's this I hear?" Bray's tone I judged to be amused.

"Goodness me," Miss Hector sighed at the same time; but the whimsicality in her voice verged upon hysteria.

"Lady Creamhair—" I began again. At once she shut her eyes fast, and set her mouth against the name. "You know who I am. You knew all along!"

"Oh no sirree Bob . . ."

Touching her arm I reminded her, as Anastasia looked on amazed, of our seasons in the hemlock-grove, of her endless patience and wondrous solicitude; I fully understood, I declared, why she'd done what she'd done in my infancy, and so far from thinking ill of it, thanked her from the heart for having saved my life. What grief I'd occasioned I begged her to charge to my want of sophistication, especially to my ignorance of our true relationship.

She wouldn't open her eyes. "Oh. Gracious. Hm. Well."

"But we both know who I am now!" I said warmly, and turned to defy the pretender. "I'm the GILES, and this is my passèd lady mother!" I looked to her to tell him so; but though tears started now behind her pert spectacles, she smiled and shook her head still.

"Well. Now. No. I don't suppose—"

"Really," Bray tisked at me, "you go too far! We've all been *much* too patient with you, I'm afraid; if you only knew what trouble you've caused today! The clockworks, and the Power Lines . . . Enough's enough!"

I heartily agreed, adding that directly I'd seen to the Founder's Scroll's re-placing and had passed the Finals, I meant to present my ID-card to my mother for signing, and the campus would know once for all who was the GILES and who the impostor.

"They will indeed!" Bray chuckled. "The Scroll, by the way, you can forget about: it's back in place now. I took it out front at Chancellor Rexford's suggestion and read off a few Certifications to reassure the crowd. But you can't be serious about this GILES nonsense . . ."

I turned my back on him and bade Lady Creamhair and Anastasia to come with me. If there was an unruly herd of undergraduates to be calmed, their Grand Tutor was the man to calm them, and I would leave no mother or sister of mine in the odious, if not criminal, company of a base impostor.

Bray pursed his lips and shook his head. "If you choose to deliver yourself up to a mob which wants nothing better than to tear you to pieces, I suppose that's your affair. But I most certainly won't permit my mother and sister to be lynched with you."

"*Your* mother and sister!" I exploded. At the same time Anastasia cried, "Lynched!" and Lady Creamhair laid two fingers to her cheek and said, "Oh. Well."

Bray assured me levelly that I had a fair chance yet of escaping with my life if I listened to reason; it was to that end exactly he'd stopped at sight of me instead of returning at once to the work of calming the crowd. To Anastasia then, who asked him what the trouble was, he reported dryly that

Tower Clock had stopped, for one thing, thanks to some disastrous move of Dr. Eierkopf's of which it was known only that I had advised it; further, that Eierkopf himself was reportedly paralyzed from head to toe, that Croaker was once again amok, that the Power Plant was in grave trouble for want of supervision, that the Nikolayans were threatening riot at the Boundary, that WESCAC was rumored to be in danger of failing for lack of power, and that Chancellor Rexford, so far from making an appearance to calm the student body's alarm, would see no one, not even his highest advisors. General panic and breakdown of the College seemed imminent, and as my presence appeared to be the single common factor in these several crises, the crowd's fear was turning to wrath against me.

"Ridiculous!" I protested. But the lights winked again, and my heart misgave me. "You stirred them up yourself!"

Bray ignored me. "As for the rest," he said to Anastasia: "it's good you know now I'm your brother and the GILES, but *that fact changes nothing between us*—do you understand me?"

Anastasia objected faintly, wide-eyed and open-mouthed, and I very loudly. He'd said nothing of their kinship thitherto, Bray explained, out of concern for Miss Hector's state of mind, which was known to be precarious—witness her agreeing that he and Anastasia were twins, when in fact they were of different ages and had different fathers. Nor did he approve of proclaiming the truth thus bluntly to her now, but my pretenses forced his hand—another item in my daysworth of ill deeds.

"I won't hear this!" I shouted. "Get on out of here!"

"We'd all best get out," he said flatly, "before they come in after you. Tell Anastasia I'm the GILES, Mother, so she'll believe it. We'll try the Chancellor's Exit."

Lady Creamhair (so I still thought of her, and would ever think) hemmed and chirped, quite glazed now; then she said with surprising distinctness: "He's my Gilesey. Yes he is." And lest anyone mistake her reference she shook her finger at me and added: "Not you."

"Mom!" Anastasia cried.

Lady Creamhair shook her head firmly. "That's a naughty young man."

Bray beamed.

"She's upset," I said to Anastasia. "And no wonder! But

just look here . . ." I lifted my infirmary-gown enough to display the dark disc on my leg. "Look here, Mother: there's proof, if you need it."

Now the dear lady's murmurs became a plaint: "Oh. Oh." Anastasia clapped and bounced. I glared at Bray, and was pleased to take his expression for chagrin. But in fact it proved a curious concentration, like a man's at stool; he even grunted and grew red. Then he sniffed and smiled—I am obliged to say *sweetly*—and turning up the back hem of his cape and tunic, exposed a brown left knee, gaunt and hairless, in the crook of which however was undeniably a browner spot. Too low, surely, and something wanting in definition—but a round brown birthmark after all! Anastasia caught her breath; Virginia Hector whimpered; I could have wept for frustration.

"Flunk you! Flunk you! Flunk you!" I shouted.

"Please," he said: "Not in front of Mother. I'm still ready to help you."

Poor Lady Creamhair now grew quite incapable; I flunked the hour I had agreed to this confrontation. Anastasia—no less confounded but still in command of her faculties—led her away toward the Chancellor's Exit and Reginald Hector's offices, next door to Tower Hall. This was Bray's suggestion, and further to infuriate me he asked whether I did not affirm its prudence.

"You should go with them," he advised me. "I'll try to pacify the crowd till you're safely out."

Angrily I replied that neither he nor I was going anywhere until the issue between us was resolved.

"You go ahead," I told Anastasia. "I'm going to end this right now, one way or the other."

Bray bristled and said: "Pah."

Virginia Hector's growing delirium permitted no tarrying; Anastasia cast us a troubled last glance from the doorway. "You won't fight?"

"Of course not," Bray said grimly, and the women left. I myself was by no means so certain: a showdown between us, I now conceived, was what my whole day's labor had been pointed to, as the final separation of Truth and Falsehood. And I had no real fear of him, though he was both taller and heavier than myself—only a kind of uneasiness inspired by his manner and smell, which however would not have stayed my hand had I chosen to take stick to him. But he proposed now, with a kind of dry distaste, that the surest and fittingest way to resolve our differences was to go down forthwith together into WESCAC's Belly: not only could I take the Finals (which he would gladly administer himself), but the EATing of whichever of us was false, and the subsequent emergence of an unquestionably authentic Grand Tutor, might be just the thing to save New Tammany from pandemonium, and the whole West Campus from collapse in that grave hour. Galling as it was to be obliged once again to agree with him, I seconded this proposal at once.

"I'll send word of this to the crowd," Bray said. "That should keep them quiet until one of us comes out."

I clenched my teeth and agreed; then, both to assert my own authority and to preserve the order of my Assignment-tasks, I insisted that the Scroll-case be unlocked, so that I could re-place its contents before passing the Finals.

Bray clicked impatiently. "You've done harm enough, don't you think? Besides, there's no time, Goat-Boy!"

"I can *do* it in no time," I replied. "Give me the key."

A number of men rushed now into the Catalogue Room—library-scientists and campus patrolmen, it turned out, searching desperately for Bray to speak once more to the crowd before they stormed Tower Hall. They glared at me with bald hostility as Bray explained his strategy—*our* strategy—and instructed them to broadcast it.

"Has the Chancellor appeared yet?" he asked. They answered that the current rumor was that Chancellor Rexford had lost his mind; that his wife was leaving him; that he'd admitted kinship to Maurice Stoker, which the latter now denied; and that all these catastrophes were somehow owing to the subversive influence of a false Grand Tutor. Their expressions left no doubt about whom they considered the pretender to be.

Bray smiled at me. "We'd better get on with it."

Although I realized that any reluctance on my part could be interpreted as fear and thus as an admission of guilt—and that they could simply refuse me if they chose to—yet I showed them the order of my Assignment and repeated that I would enter the Belly-room when I had re-placed the Founder's Scroll, and not before.

"But it's *been* replaced," Bray pointed out. "There it stands."

Loath as I was to disclose my strategy to him before the

fact, I declared then that *Re-place* meant "put in its *proper* place," not necessarily its customary one: the Library's difficulties in filing the Scroll stemmed from insufficiently clear distinctions—as did (I added pointedly) many other problems in the University, whose resolution must inevitably be attended with some upheaval. The fact was, I asserted, that the Founder's Scroll, like the Old and New Syllabi, was unique; *sui generis,* of necessity, else it would be false. The CACAFILE needed then simply to be instructed to create unique categories for unique items, and the filing should proceed without difficulty.

"Nonsense!" snorted a gentleman-librarian. His colleagues agreed, objecting that such "special categories" would in fact be classes of one member, an unacceptable paralogism.

"So are Grand Tutorials," I replied.

"Now that was inspired!" Bray exclaimed with a sort of laugh, and though the library-scientists seemed far from delighted with my plan, he urged that it be transmitted to the catalogue-programmer and CACAFILEd as soon as practicable. "You don't intend to stand here until it's actually carried out, I suppose?" he asked me. "Quite enough to've solved the problem, I should think."

The crowd outside had commenced a rhythmic shout. To me it sounded like "Let's go! Let's go!" or perhaps "Let him go!" but Bray maintained, and the others agreed, that it was "Get the Goat! Get the Goat!" In any case it bespoke the urgency and peril of the situation.

"Very well," I said; "which way is the Belly?"

6.

"Do you know," Bray announced to the library-scientists and policemen, "this Goat-Boy's really a well-intentioned fellow at heart, I believe. And you can't say he lacks courage." Of me then he inquired, "You're sure you really want to do this? I thought you'd back down when the time came."

"I'm sure you did," I said. An elder official (the chief New Tammany Librarian, in fact), cautiously wondered whether news of an EATing mightn't aggravate the student body's unrest; the very legality of our entry into WESCAC's Belly he was not sure of—though he did not doubt that in the case of Grand Tutors . . .

"Grand *Tutor*," I interrupted. "There can't be two at a time."

"Quite so," Bray agreed, still entirely cordial. "As for the legal matter, it's of no consequence, actually. Thanks to the Spielman Proviso"—he made a little nodding bow to me—"the question of who *may* go into the Belly is beside the point. Only a Grand Tutor *can*, and come out alive. However . . ." He drew a paper from somewhere under his cape. "I took the trouble to prepare a release of sorts, just in case. We'll sign it and leave it with you gentlemen, if Mr. Goat-Boy is agreeable."

The document, addressed *To Whom it may concern,* declared that whichever of its signatories proved to be the Grand Tutor, He authorized the entry of the other into WESCAC's Belly for the purpose of attesting His authenticity, and was fully and exclusively accountable for the consequences of such attestation; moreover, that whichever proved to be *not* the Grand Tutor, he consented to and held none but himself responsible for his being EATen in consequence of his error. The Chief Librarian was satisfied that the release protected him and his staff from liability; I too assumed its sufficiency in that respect, and suggested only that the word *error* be changed to *imposture.*

Bray seemed to chuckle. "What about 'error *or* imposture'? I've never called *you* a fraud, you know, young man; on the contrary, I believe you're entirely sincere—and entirely misled."

I would not be put off by the desperate flattery of a frightened charlatan, I declared—but not to seem unbecomingly harsh I settled for "error *and/or* imposture," and borrowing a pen from the elder librarian, printed *GILES* in bold capitals at the foot.

"Ah," Bray said, and declined the pen. "That does for both of us, in the nature of the case. I'd heard you were denying that it matters whether you're the GILES or not; but since we both claim now that we are, let the loser be nameless. Eh?"

The officials seemed less content than I with this development, but there was no time for negotiation. We set off down a corridor towards the central section of Tower Hall, where a special lift—the only one so routed—would take the two of us down into the Belly-room. But immense though the building was, and heavily guarded, elements of the mob outside had forced their way in; we heard shouting in a large room at the end of the hallway and were intercepted before we reached it by other uniformed patrolmen, who advised us to retreat.

"Word just came in that the Power-Line guards are dropping like flies," one of them reported. "Some crazy kind of thing they were ordered to wear around their necks on duty; makes them lose their balance." He glared at me. "Flunking wolf in sheep's clothing!"

I was disturbed less by his shocking metaphor than by his news of the unfortunate border-guards and his obvious sympathy with the demonstrators: he informed us that this fresh calamity had infuriated them beyond restraint; they'd breached entryways all around the building in search of the man they held responsible for the day's catastrophes—and Founder help me when they got hold of me, for he himself would not.

"You should be ashamed of yourself," Bray told him sharply, and seemed prepared to scold him further for dereliction of responsibility; but one of our own party, left behind at Bray's suggestion to transfer the Founder's Scroll to safer storage in the CACAFILE, rushed up to tell us that the card-file room was now also invaded. The students had so far destroyed nothing beyond the door-locks that impeded them, but their mood was ugly, and we were cut off: he feared that if they did not soon find their quarry they'd destroy the Library in search of me, and anyone they suspected of concealing me.

"It's one flunking goat-boy or all of us," he appealed to the Chief Librarian; "and maybe the stacks too—some of them have torches."

If any scruple on my behalf lingered in the elder man's mind, it gave way before the notion of fire in the stacks. He clutched Bray's arm and said, "They mustn't even light cigarettes in here! That settles it!"

I perspired. Bray, on the other hand, smiled, not apparently ruffled by the danger. For once our relative fragrances were perhaps reversed.

"No one's going to be lynched," he declared. Quickly then,

but calmly, he issued orders for dealing with the crisis: word was to be spread that the crowd should reassemble at the impregnable Belly-exit at the rear of Tower Hall basement, whence very shortly the EATen impostor must issue with the true Grand Tutor. Thus they would see justice accomplished, and be safely outside the building. To reach the Belly-lift itself would require my cooperation in another stratagem, which he sincerely hoped I would find less repugnant than being dismembered:

"Mrs. Stoker, in her mischievous way, loaned you a mask of my face this morning to get through Scrapegoat Grate with. Put it on, if you still have it, and we'll go through the lobby together. If you've lost it, I'll give you another—unless you'd rather take your chances . . ."

A bitter pill, made no more palatable by the *Oho's* of my enemies, who welcomed the insinuation that I'd got through the Grate by fraud! But consoling myself with the thought—and declaration—that WESCAC soon would end all masquerade, I did as bid: fished the odious silky vizard from my purse and donned it. As before, it fit so perfectly and lightly, like a second skin, that the officials were amazed; after a moment I couldn't even feel it. The purse itself then we suspended from my stick, one end of which we each carried (since I refused to part with it), and in this manner we made for the lift to the central lobby. It was a terrifying progress: the large room at the end of the hall was packed with irate undergraduates, professors, and staff-people; their chant—it was, after all, "Get the Goat!"—broke rhythm as we approached, and though our vanguards announced our destination and circumstances, I trembled for all our lives. Triple pain—to hear them credit "the Grand Tutor" with countenancing, literally and figuratively, my descent into the fatal Belly; to see them give way, however muttersome, before the duplicated visage of their idol; and to feel on every hand the obtuse baleful scrutiny which, should it distinguish True from False, would rend to forcemeat its true Instructor!

We gained the lift, went down, and met the same scene in the lobby, magnified. "Give us the Goat, the Goat, the Goat!" they cried, and though a few seemed more in carnival-spirits than in murderous—linking arms with their lady girls and lifting emblazoned steins—the most looked dangerous enough. A half-circle of riot-officers held them from the lift-doors as a man in a neat woolen suit explained our intention through a megaphone.

"Please remain orderly," he implored them. "Surely you don't want to injure the Grand Tutor, and you can't tell which is which. They're going to the Belly now; you'll see the results at the rear exit. Please remain orderly, and do be careful with fire . . ."

I was startled to recognize the voice, and then the face, as Maurice Stoker's. Anastasia's report notwithstanding, it was difficult to believe that this tidy, bare-chinned chap—whom I now saw full on, quietly exhorting one of his men to remain calm in the face of the mob's provocation—was not some pallid, obverse twin of the Power-Plant Director. The crowd paid little heed except to jeer him, and threatened at any moment to breach the line of guards who but the day before would have had at them with bayonets and cattle-prods. Yet Stoker delayed us for anxious seconds between the elevator we'd left and the one we sought, a few doors down.

"Please excuse me for keeping you," he said to the pair of us. "I realize how trivial this sounds in these circumstances, but I'm really quite concerned about my wife. Does either of you gentlemen happen to know where she might be?"

His smile was polite, even abashed; his tone seemed perfectly sincere. Bray explained curtly that Anastasia had taken her mother next door to her grandfather's offices; his tone suggested disapproval of Stoker's new mien.

"I'm relieved to hear that," Stoker said. "She really wasn't herself at lunch, and I was a bit concerned." He turned to me now. "You must be George, then? Perfect disguise! And a very clever idea, too." He offered his hand to shake. "Thanks *ever* so much for your advice this morning; I wish I had time to tell you what a campus of good it's done me already. I *do* hope neither of you will be EATen . . ."

"For Founder's sake, man, be yourself!" Bray rebuked him. But we could tarry no longer; the crowd had pushed through. Before I could assess the genuineness of Stoker's attitude we were obliged to retreat into the other lift—barely large enough for the two of us, since it was designed for large self-propelled tape-carts rather than for human passengers. The library-scientists fled to safety; the guards pressed tightly together to shield the lift a moment longer; Stoker I heard saying, "Do be reasonable, ladies and gentlemen . . ." Any moment I expected Bray to withdraw and either confess his imposture or attempt some excuse for not accompanying me—in which latter case I was resolved to denounce him and, if possible, force him to the consequences of his fraud. But when I asked, to taunt him, "Shall we go?" he himself touched a button marked *Belly*, the only one on the panel. The doors slid to at once, and as there was no light in the lift, we went down in darkness.

For all my new assurance that I was not only the Grand Tutor but the GILES Himself, I was apprehensive; the descent seemed long, and for all I knew Bray might attack me in the dark and try to stop the lift somehow before it reached bottom. His odor, though faint, was particularly disagreeable in the closed compartment; what was more, he put a hard-boned arm about my shoulders and said in a friendly way, "You're what they call *in love* with Anastasia, I presume." When I didn't answer—I was wondering, in fact, how a man about to die could concern himself with such a subject—he added: "One would think, to look at her, she'd be a first-rate breeder. Why do you suppose she's borne no children?"

The lift stopped at his last word. I grasped my stick, ready to strike should he assault me in his death-throes. But when the doors opened—on a red-glimmering chamber, lined with racks of flat round cans stacked edgewise from floor to ceiling—nothing happened.

"This is what they call the Mouth," Bray said, stepping out. He gave a little sigh, as if loath to end the other conversation. "We'll use it for presenting our credentials. The Belly itself is through a little door over there, which WESCAC has to open."

"So *that's* it!" I too stepped from the lift, whose doors closed at once behind us. "You knew you could come this far without being EATen!"

He clucked his tongue. "Why are you so hostile? It makes you seem awfully defensive, for a Grand Tutor." In fact, he confessed, he had no idea whether WESCAC's "menu" for self-defense covered the Mouth-room or only the Belly, since none but himself had entered either. "I really advise you to be less critical of your colleagues and Tutees, George," he concluded.

"You advise *me!* But I see you're assuming I'll live to follow your advice. Don't think you can flatter me now into letting you go back up in the lift!"

He had gone to the inevitable console-panel beside a circular door on the far wall. "Flatter you?" he said. "My dear fellow: in the first place one *can't* go back up in the lift: it returns automatically and can't be summoned from down here. There's no way out except through the Belly."

"Good."

"As to flattering you, I've no such intention, I hope. *Praise*, now, that's another matter—but you'll see shortly what a wrong idea you have of me. I'm not what people think I am."

"No need to tell *me!*"

He smiled and pressed numerous buttons, as though typing out a message on the console. "But I'm not what *you* think I am, either."

I ordered him to stop temporizing and open the Belly-door—and wondered how I'd open it myself if he refused, for it seemed to have neither knob nor latch.

"Just what I'm doing," he said. "You'll have to put your ID-card and Assignment-list in this slot now—mine's in already, from last time."

"I'll bet it is." I foiled what I took to be his stratagem by producing the card I'd got that morning from Ira Hector. But if Bray was surprised at my having one after all, he managed to conceal the fact. Moreover, he ignored my sarcasm and merely remarked that inasmuch as WESCAC's "Diet program" provided for scanning and evaluating trespassers into the Mouth-room like ourselves, he'd taken the opportunity to ask it a few questions on the matter of the GILES, which he thought I might be interested in having verified before we proceeded. I accused him once again of delaying his inevitable end; but it was satisfying nonetheless to see WESCAC affirm unequivocally (as it could not do through its other facilities, I gathered, or before I'd presented my ID-card for its inspection) that it *had* impregnated Virginia R. Hector twenty-two years past with the Grand-Tutorial Ideal, Laboratory Eugenical Specimen, in accordance with a program-option developed malinoctically by itself. More specifically (this information was delivered us on cards the size of an Amphitheater-ticket, dropped one after another into a cup at the bottom of the console-panel as Bray pulled a lever beside it), the impregnation had been accomplished, stroke per stroke, as Tower Clock tolled midnight on the twenty-first of March of that year. A third card affirmed that WESCAC had PATted the fetus just prior to birth, which occurred two hundred seventy-five days after conception . . .

"Pass All Fail All!" I could not help exclaiming.

"Naturally," Bray said, and pulled the lever again. The fourth card—bearing, like the others, the smiling likeness of Chancellor Rexford on its obverse—verified not only that the infant GILES had been received into the tapelift but that WESCAC had arranged for a Library employee to rescue the child from its Belly, at the unavoidable sacrifice of some portion of the man's mental ability.

"G. Herrold, pass him!"

Bray clicked sympathetically. "Afraid I never met the chap."

On card number five, in reply to a question Bray had put about Anastasia's relation to the GILES, WESCAC disclaimed any knowledge one way or the other of multiple or serial impregnations of Virginia Hector; but on the sixth it confirmed Dr. Eierkopf's earlier hypothesis that no female sibling, even a twin, could be the GILES, either *also* or *instead;* that possibility was precluded by both the Cum Laude program and the fact that twins of different sexes are not genetically identical.

"That's enough," I declared. "Open the Belly."

"One more," Bray said, and handed me a card which WESCAC produced without his pulling the lever. As if he knew its message already (though he'd not apparently read it), he added, "Most important of all, eh?"

The card made three plain statements: that the GILES was a true Grand Tutor *in posse;* that WESCAC could discern Him upon scanning, and had done so already; that any other person who entered the Belly would be EATen at once. Even as I read this terse pronouncement the small door opened—a round port with a lap-leaved shutter that enlarged octagonally like a camera's. The chamber beyond was entirely dark. To forestall any trickery I snatched Bray's cape—stiffer and slipperier than it looked to be—and declared we would go in together.

"Why not? I should tell you the examining procedure in advance, though, since you're sure I'm about to be EATen." We would be scanned, he said, the instant we stepped through the port, and Electroencephalic Amplification and Transmission should ensue, if it was called for, either immediately or after I'd replied to one preliminary question and three main questions which would appear successively on a small central display-screen. Each was to be answered simply *yes* or *no* by pressing either the right or left button respectively of a two-button box suspended over the screen.

"Just a formality, I think," he said. "If you're able to take the Finals at all it's because you're a Grand Tutor already—which means you can't fail them, wouldn't you say?"

For reply I drew him grimly portwards, sure he'd resist at last: but he came to it readily as I. Together we stepped through and slid or tumbled down a short inclined tunnel to land feet-first in a padded chamber. There was an instant snap above and behind us. I started involuntarily, stuck out an arm to keep my balance, and found that the floor and walls of the chamber were lined with a warm, damp, spongy material (humidified and heated, I later learned, to preserve the tapes). Moreover, the room had the feel of an irregular hollow sphere, at least where I stood; it was difficult to maintain balance on its springy floor, which also pulsed and rumbled slightly as though adjacent to great machinery. Was Bray's brain EATen, then, I wondered, or was it only the port and scanners that had snapped? I neither felt nor heard him, and the room was black but for a small horizontal bar glowing some meters away, which I took to be the face of the display-screen. No matter: though I exulted at the recognition that I was unharmed—indeed, relief made me feel strangely at home in that fearful place, as if I were nestled at Mary Appenzeller's flank—I lost no time confirming my rival's fate, but went at once to the lambent bar. No longer than my index finger, and as wide, it floated green and fuzzy as though in mid-chamber—projected there, I assumed, by some optical means. I could only suppose it to be the preliminary question; and surely enough, through the lenses on my stick it resolved into five words:

ARE YOU MALE OR FEMALE

Curious inquiry! Had it not been established already that the GILES could not be female? But as I felt for the answer-button-box I realized that the question was more cunning than superfluous; I pressed the right-hand button. At once a different, longer question shimmered in my glass:

*HAVE YOU COMPLETED YOUR ASSIGNMENT
AT ONCE, IN NO TIME*

Reluctantly I answered *no*, thinking that I had after all been at work since dawn, and though my achievement was by no means inconsiderable, I had yet to get certain signatures on my ID-card and determine to what authorities it should be presented. Yet even as I pressed the left-hand button I thought better of it and pressed its mate by way of correction: Founder knew I'd done more than any normal undergraduate human could have hoped to, and what remained was obviously un-doable until I'd passed the Finals, whereof the question itself was part. Trusting that my hasty change of answers had been understood and accepted—since I remained unEATen—I addressed myself to resolving the next item on the screen:

GILES, SON OF WESCAC

At once, and in perfect confidence, I answered *yes*—or rather, affirmed what my father was declaring.

DO YOU WISH TO PASS

Triumphantly at this query too I pressed the right-hand button, for though I knew it to be held in certain quads that he who seeks Commencement Gate has perforce not found it, nor can the while he seeks, three instant and simultaneous counter-considerations overbalanced that one: first, it appeared that the Finals were designed for a series of affirmative responses—and aptly, for what could be more affirmative than Commencement? Second (and thus), those same aforementioned esoterics held that he is passed who knows himself passed, and so my *yes* was in fact a declaration of achievement more than an acknowledgment of desire. Finally, alerted by the curious sense of the preliminary question (whose function, I saw now, was just that alerting), I was not blind to the double meaning of this last one; and comfortable as the Belly oddly was, I did indeed wish to pass now through its exit and calm the anxious student body.

Lo, as if to confirm that third significance, when I pressed *yes* the bar disappeared, a new rumbling commenced round about, and the floor-walls seemed to pulse in slow waves towards the far end of the chamber. I saw a flicker there, heard a cry of many voices, and understood that the exit-port must be enlarging in the manner of the entry. I scrambled for it on hands and knees, assisted by the undulations; the crowd had seen the portal opening and pressed now nearer with flaming torches, by whose light I saw rise up before me, just inside the exit, the foe I had thought EATen!

Choked with dismay I cried, "Flunk you!"

"And Pass you, sir!" Bray exclaimed, as though joyously.

"Pass you to the end of terms! Take these, Grand Tutor of the Western Campus, and go to the head of your class!"

He pressed into my hand what turned out to be my ID-card and Assignment-list.

"You admit you're a fraud!" I challenged him. Outside, the crowd commenced to chant again: *"Give us the Goat! All the way with Bray!"* Knees to knees now on the floor, facing each other across the exit, we shouldered against the outward-pressing waves. "How come you're not EATen?"

"I'm *not* a fraud, sir!" he said happily, and even wiped an eye. "Oh, pass you, *pass* you!" He owed his preservation, he declared, to the fact of WESCAC's having chosen him, some time past, for the work now all but accomplished: the role of proph-prof, foil, and routed antigiles. As John the Bursar had been necessary to declare Enos Enoch's matriculation and administer to him the rites of enrollment, so he Bray had been appointed not only to Certify my passage of the Finals (which he had done, he said, on the documents now in my hand), but to pretend to Grand-Tutorhood himself, in order that I might drive him out at last from Great Mall in proof of my authenticity.

"I don't believe you," I said.

"You never did, pass your heart!" He would have embraced me, but I drew back. "You weren't supposed to—until now, of course." He went on: "Every one of my Certifications is false, and by failing all the people I pass, you prove your own passèdness. WESCAC spared me from EATing so that you could turn me over to the crowd—either now or after you've presented your ID-card to Reginald Hector. Then (you don't mind my suggesting this, do you, sir? Your father's suggestion, actually) the Grand-Tutorial thing to do would be to stop the lynching and merely expel me from the College forever." He motioned towards the port-hole. "Shall we get on with it?"

Plausible as was his explanation (indeed, how else account for his not being EATen?), and sweet the prospect of accomplishing his fall, I was riven with doubts and perplexities. To reconceive him so abruptly, from foe into accomplice of my destiny, was beyond my managing, the more for the Stokerish air of his invitation, which seemed to me fraught with guile. Did he tempt me, then, like Stoker, in order to be refused? And if so, was it refusal that would flunk me, or refusal to refuse? The Abyss yawned under me, as in the Assembly-

Before-the-Grate; I resisted it by yielding, not to the temptation to denounce him, but to an especially strong contraction
of the chamber-walls, which virtually ejected me, headlong,
through the port. It winked shut instantly behind, like an eye,
or the drawstrung mouth of Virginia Hector's purse, slung
over my shoulder. Even as I picked myself up—from a small
grassplot luckily situated under the aperture—the crowd
pressed to me, torches in hand, and lights from a mobile Tel-
erama-unit flooded the scene.

"Hooray for Bray!" they seemed to be shouting. I had time
for one glance behind me; he had contrived by some means
to remain in the Belly. Then the vanguard was upon me,
laughing and cheering; my heart quailed. But it was in victory they hoist me, stick in one hand, papers in the other, to
their shoulders. Not until a microphone was thrust at me, and
a reporter asked whether the Goat-Boy was indeed EATen
for good and all, did I remember what face I wore. Chagrin!
But I thought better than to proclaim the truth from so shaky
a platform.

"All's well," I told the questioner—and was pleased to hear
my voice amplified from the Telerama-vehicle. "The false
Tutor's in the Belly; he'll trouble this campus no more."

There was great applause. Handfuls of confetti and streamers of toilet-tissue filled the air; klaxons and bugles sounded;
undergraduate young men in ROTC uniforms seized and kissed
the nearest co-eds—who willingly submitted, standing on one
foot and raising the other behind them.

"Take me to your former chancellor," I exhorted them,
"and wait for me outside his office. There'll be a surprise, I
promise!"

What I designed, of course, was to present to ex-
Chancellor Hector my ID-card, in fulfillment of the final article of my Assignment (since Mother was not herself, and
among Grandfather's sinecures was the directorship of New
Tammany's idle Office of Commencement); having secured
his official endorsement that my Assignment was complete
and my ID-card in order, I would unmask myself to him and
to the student body, display my credentials, proclaim my indisputable Grand-Tutorhood, and *then* drive Bray from
Great Mall if his expulsion seemed appropriate. The throng
took up my promise with a right good will, brandished their
torches exultantly now and hymned out the *Varsity Anthem*
as they bore me forth:

Dear old New Tammany,
The University
   On thee depends . . .

Through I approved neither the narrow alma-matriotism of
that sentiment nor the general notion that the weal of studentdom was politically contingent, I could not but be
moved, in those circumstances, by the fitness of their appeal,
directed as it seemed not to their college but to me:

> *Teach us thy Answers bright;*
> *Lead us from flunkèd Night;*
> *Commence us to the Light*
>   *When our School-Term ends!*

7.

Reginald Hector's several offices—as Commencement Director, Executive Secretary of the Philophilosophical Fund, and
Board Chairman of his brother's reference-book cartel—were
housed, along with his living-quarters, in a smaller version of
Lucius Rexford's Light House, just across Great Mall. As it
had originally served the latter's purpose, it was now appropriately called the Old Chancellor's Mansion. Inappropri-
ately, however, its white-brick façade and gracious windows
were lit more brightly than those of its larger counterpart: either the Power-Plant trouble was localized, or Lucky Rexford
had altered his ways indeed! The respect still felt by New
Tammanians for their old professor-general was evidenced by
the fact that whereas half a hundred guards had not kept
them out of Tower Hall, the sight of one—a white-helmeted
and -gloved ROTCMP—was enough to halt my bearers a respectful way from the porch. The fellow was armed, of
course; yet surely it was not his rifle (held anyhow at Parade
Rest) that stayed them, but their esteem for the man whose
door he ceremonially protected. Much impressed at this contradiction of Max's contempt, and Dr. Sear's, for the former
Chancellor, I asked to be set down, declared again into a row

of microphones that important announcements would soon be forthcoming, perhaps from Reginald Hector as well as myself, and insisted that no one accompany me into the building. As I strode porchwards (gimplessly as possible) campus patrolmen assembled to contain the crowd—which I was gratified to see make no effort to push past them. A number of photographers and journalism-majors were rude enough to press after me up the walk, and though I respected their professional persistence, I was pleased when the military doorman, having inspected my ID-card and saluted me, obliged them to remain without.

"The P.-G's in the P.P.F.O., sir," he informed me; and so satisfying was his brisk courtesy I thanked him and stepped inside before considering what his message signified. Happily, another like him, only female, came forward from a desk in the reception-hall as I entered, and inquired politely whether it was the P.-G. I sought; if so, she was sure he would interrupt his P.P.F.-work for another audience with the Grand Tutor—especially in view of the shocking news, which she daresaid had brought me to the P.P.F.O. I understood then the several initials and, reminded of the general crisis by a dimming of the lights, bid her not fear the alarming reports from Founder's Hill and the Light House, since all radical progress entailed some temporary disorder.

"Oh no, sir," she said—a pert thing she, in her olive skirt and blouse and her dark-rimmed spectacles—"I meant what that Ira Hector's gone and done." She'd led me down a short hall to a glass-paned double door labeled PHILOPHILOSOPHICAL FUND: EXECUTIVE SECRETARY. "None of my business, I'm sure," she declared, opening the door with a fetching thrust of her hip, "but I still think Ira Hector's a nasty old man and the P-G.'s a sweetie. I'll tell him you're here."

Curious as I was to know what news she alluded to, I was more so at the sight, in the P.P.F. Office, of what appeared to be the same shaggy band of indigent scholars I'd rescued Ira Hector from in the morning. Beggars now as then, and no less disdainful, they seemed however to be meeting with more success. The man they importuned, pressing round the desktop where he sat, I gathered was Reginald Hector, my maternal grandfather and would-be assassin. A strong-jawed, hairless man in conservative worsted, he dispensed largesse with an even hand and a steady smile. Though his perch was informal, his back was as straight as the guard's outside; his eyes, blue, seemed now to twinkle, now to glint like mica; at each beneficence he said, "Take *this!*" or, "*There,* by golly!" in a tone of level satisfaction, as if delivering a counter-thrust. To one man he gave a check, to another a set of drafting-instruments boxed in blue velvet, to another a reference-book bound in half-morocco, to another three tins of corned beef; his own fountain-pen he took from his inside pocket and bestowed upon a long-haired woolly girl, who kissed his hand; his pocket-watch and chain, his desk-barometer and appointment-calendar, even his striped cravat and cufflinks went the same charitable way. And though two aides behind him replaced these items, including the personal ones, from a stock in cartons at their side, I was pleased by the spectacle of such philanthropy, stirred by the contrast between the brothers Hector, and not a little incensed at the students' want of gratitude; even the hand-kisser I suspected of a smirk, which happily her hair hid from her benefactor.

Out of his notice, I observed that the supply of goods in the cartons ran out as the receptionist approached. Ex-Chancellor Hector frowned, shrugged, smiled, cleared his throat, and deftly rolled himself a cigarette.

"That's the end, boys," he said briskly. "No more to hand out."

There was a chorus of complaints, but the aides sharply marshaled the supplicants past me into the hall, reminding them to call a final Thank-you-sir as they left. Few did, except mockingly. Me they regarded with expressions of suspicion, contempt, or hostility—a reassuring surprise, considering my mask. One called me a charlatan, another a "square," another a "company man"; they were, it was clear, disaffiliated from the mainstream of New Tammany sentiment, and my heart warmed to them. Indeed, I privately resolved to seek them out, once I'd proclaimed myself, and enlist them among my first Tutees, as they were beyond doubt the goatliest of undergraduates. Mightily tempted to reveal myself, I urged them to wait with their classmates outside, as I had good tidings concerning their friend the Goat-Boy. Naturally they sniffed at this news; the aides rallied them along then, despite their threats to "go limp" if anyone laid a hand on them.

"Flunking ingrates," one aide muttered to me. "We'll see how they holler with no more handouts from the P.-G."

I began to declare to him that their number included, in

my opinion, the very salt of the campus, but by this time the receptionist had informed "the P.-G." of my presence, and he came over to me shaking his head.

"Good to see you, G.T.!" he said warmly. His handshake was strong, his tone friendly, but his smile grave. "Everything's going to the Dunce, eh?"

The receptionist excused herself, but Reginald Hector asked her to look in once more on "Miss Virginia in the next room" instead of returning to the entrance-hall, as he feared his daughter was still half-hysterical.

"The things she's been saying . . ." He scratched his pate ruefully. "And there's always a flunking reporter around, you know." He cast a brief sharp eye at me, wondering no doubt how aware I might be of his daughter's new distress, and how much of her raving was true.

"Naturally Miss Hector's upset," I said. "Most unfortunate business back there in the Library."

"Unfortunate! I'd like to get my hands on that freak of a Goat-Boy!" He seemed unsure of his ground—as I could well imagine he might be, whomever his daughter was presently claiming to be the GILES. Gruffly he thanked me—that is, Bray—for having Certified him earlier in the day: the quotation on his diploma—*No class shall pass*—he deemed so apt a summary of his philosophy that he meant to propose it as a motto for his favorite club, the Brotherhood of Independent Men. Rather, he hoped to do so if he had the wherewithal to maintain his own membership in that society, now that his brother had "pulled the rug from under the P.P.F.," and the Executive Secretary's salary with it.

"More of that flunking Goat-Boy's meddling, so I hear," he said crossly. "Not that I think half those rascals deserve a hand-out anyhow! But better dole it out privately than turn New Tammany into a welfare-college, the way Rexford's been doing."

"Your brother's changed his mind about philanthropy?" I asked.

"Changed his mind! He's lost it!" It had always been his own policy, he declared, to be beholden to no man; to look out for himself in order to be able to look out for others. In this he differed from his brother Ira, who gave alms in self-defense, as it were, or to further his own interests. They shared the opinion that the ignorant mass of studentdom by and large deserved its wretched lot; their own example proved that ambition and character could overcome any handicap; but there was no reason, Reginald felt, not to pity one's inferiors. He thought it important that the College administration keep out of the charity-business, lest the worthless masses—already too dependent and lazy—come to think of free board and tuition as their due; and nothing would militate more favorably for Lucius Rexford's sweeping grant-in-aid bill than the curtailment of the Philophilosophical Fund.

I could not help smiling. "Maybe the Goat-Boy will get to Chancellor Rexford, too," I suggested. Reginald Hector declared with a sniff that he'd heard disturbing rumors to just that effect, adding that back in the days of C.R. II such a dangerous subversive would have been shot, at least under *his* command. Nowadays it was coddle, coddle—and look at the crime-rate, and the drop-out rate, and the illegitimate birthrate, and the varsity situation!

"The Goat-Boy won't meddle any more," one of the aides said from the hallway, and reported what he'd just heard from the crowd outside: that I had left the impostor EATen in WESCAC's Belly.

"No!" Reginald Hector exclaimed happily, and slapped me on the back. "Why didn't You say so, doggone You!" I confirmed that the false Grand Tutor was no longer a menace to studentdom, and explained the object of my visit: a final endorsement of my Passage and Grand-Tutorship now that the pretender had been put down.

"Gladly, gladly! Give Your card here, sir: I'll be glad to okay it!" He fished for a pen, found he'd given his away, and borrowed one from an aide. "I knew he was a phony— GILES indeed! As if there ever was such a thing!"

I smiled and handed him my Assignment-sheet. Within the circle of its motto, I observed, Bray had written *Passage is Failure*—alluding, I supposed, to those Certifications of his which I'd shown to be false. The presumption annoyed me until I remembered his dubious claim to accessoryhood back in the Belly, which I'd not had time to consider and evaluate.

"Mm-hm," the ex-Chancellor said, holding it at various distances from his eyes. Perhaps he couldn't make it out at all; in any case he only glanced at it hastily, nodding all the while. "Oh, yes, this is quite in order. Hum! I can sign it anywhere, I suppose?"

Calling his attention to the seventh and final task, I observed that no signatures on the Assignment-list itself seemed called for, only on the matriculation- (i.e., ID-) card—which too there was apparently no need for him to sign, only to inspect.

"Sure, sure," he agreed at once, as if he'd known that fact as well as his own name, but had forgot it for half a second. "Unless You want me to initial it just for form's sake . . ."

Inspecting the card myself as he talked, I saw that Bray had printed *WESCAC* in the "Father" blank and signed his own name as "Examiner." I borrowed Reginald Hector's borrowed pen, scratched through the name *George* I'd signed earlier, and after it, on the same line, printed *GILES*.

"Keep it, keep it," he said of the pen, and took the card. Instantly he reddened. "What's this?"

I offered the pen to its first owner, who, however, stepped back with a little embarrassed sign.

"Something wrong?" I asked the ex-Chancellor. "Here—initial it after my title, if you like."

"*I* see," he said, drawing the words out as if he'd caught on to a tease. "You examined Yourself! Why not? And You're going to call Yourself the GILES because You *are* the Grand Tutor." He scribbled *RH* at the end of the line. "Don't blame You a bit! Darned clever idea, in fact—help put an end to that Goat-Boy nonsense. There You are, sir!"

Retrieving the two documents I said, "I *am* the GILES, Mr. Hector."

"Of course You are!" he cried indignantly. "You've got every right to be! I was trying to tell that daughter of mine just a while ago, when Stacey brought her in all upset: she's got to get that nonsense out of her head—"

"That she's my mother?" I interrupted. "She *is*, Mr. Hector. I'm the *real* GILES, that you put in the tapelift twenty-one years ago."

"Ridiculous." He had been looking a rattled and somewhat fatuous old man; now his jaw set, and his eyes flashed in a way that must once have intimidated ranks of junior officers. In fact, the two aides withdrew at once. He was a military-scientist, he told me then curtly, not a fancy-talk politician or a philosopher with thick eyeglasses, and there were plenty of things over his head, he did not doubt: but be flunked if he didn't know a racket when he smelled one, and in *his* nose, so to speak, this Grand-Tutor business stank from Belly to Belfrey. What was my angle? he wanted to know. He'd gone along with Rexford and the others in recognizing my Grand-Tutorhood (which was to say, Bray's) for the same reason he'd joined the Enochist Fraternity during his campaign for the Chancellorship; because he knew it was as important for "the common herd" to believe in Commencement as it was for riot-troopers to believe in their alma mater, true or false—a consolation for and justification of their inferior rank. And he'd hoped I was merely a clever opportunist; in fact he'd rather admired my "get up and git," as he put it, and assumed I'd got what I was after: fame, influence, campus-wide respect, and a lucrative berth in the Rexford administration. But apparently I was after bigger, more dangerous game; had gone digging into great men's pasts in search of paydirt, as it were, and turning up that libelous old gossip about his daughter and the GILES, had thought to extort something from him with it . . .

"So lay it on the line, Dunce flunk you, or I'll break you in two!"

Despite the menace of his words and tone I saw he was alarmed—he was, for example, asking my price instead of calling a patrolman—and so I gathered he'd got the drift of his daughter's and granddaughter's recent experience in the Catalogue Room. In short, he knew the GILES was alive and about—whether in Bray's person or in George the Goat-Boy's—and had every reason to fear being brought to account for his old infanticide-attempt. I might have unmasked myself then; but a strategy occurred to me for gaining more truth from him before giving any in return. I *was* the GILES, I repeated, by WESCAC out of Virginia R. Hector: rescued from the tapelift by G. Herrold the booksweep, reared by Max Spielman as Billy Bocksfuss the Ag-Hill Goat-Boy, and come to Great Mall to change WESCAC's AIM and Pass All or Fail All.

"No!" he protested—but in awe now more than in denial.

"Oh yes." However, I declared, he was not to suppose I sought either wealth or fame for myself or retribution for him; I had left the barn to Pass All or Fail All, and having that same day passed all my tests and the Finals, I wanted nothing from him but a true accounting of my birth and infancy before I went forth to my larger work.

He rubbed his strong chin suspiciously. "What about that George fellow, crashed the Grate this morning?"

"An impostor," I said. "A false goat-boy."

"I heard from Maurice Stoker he was out to make trouble. Founder knows he's made plenty!"

"But not for you," I pointed out. "Anyhow, I've taken care of him."

He squinted at me afresh. "You're really Virginia's son? She was saying crazy things about that George fellow . . ."

My heart glowed; she *had* acknowledged me then, at last, after the shock of my old blind assault, and of seeing me again, had led her to deny me! My gratitude for this overcame any lingering grudge against Reginald Hector; I sat beside him on the desktop and laid a friendly hand on his shoulder.

"Mother's not well," I reminded him. "It upset her to see me again, after all these terms, and two of us claiming to be the GILES." But could he really imagine, I asked him gently, that a Grand Tutor harbored vengeance in His heart for an act that could only have been misguided?

"You're really Him?" he demanded once more. "That other fellow—I don't know; I was almost afraid . . ."

Speaking from my heart, not from my mask, I assured him once more that he was looking at the same Grand Tutor he'd committed to the Belly, and asked him why he'd done it. Surely one didn't murder to avoid a scandal? He shook his head and replied, glum with doubt and shame, that though "the scandal-thing" was no light matter when the reputation of leaders was at stake (since "men won't die for a fellow they don't respect"), two other considerations had led him—and me—to the fatal tapelift. The first was the strange device of my PAT-card, which he took to mean that I would pass or fail not every*thing,* but every*body:* in other words, that I'd be the Commencement or Flunkage of all studentdom, as the late *Kanzler* of Siegfrieder College, his adversary in C.R. II, had vowed to be. Considering Eblis Eierkopf's role in the Cum Laude Project and past affiliation with Bonifacism, he'd adjudged it an unbearable risk that his own daughter might have given birth to another *Kollegiumführer.* Moreover, even supposing that she had not, he could not abide the thought of his grandson's growing up as he had grown, and Ira, and to some extent Virginia also; better die ignorant than be an orphan in the University: nameless, by nameless parents got, and furtively brought to light!

"Never had a proper daddy myself, and never was one to Virginia," he admitted; "her mother dead a-bearing and mine a tramp . . . I did what I could to keep the same from happening to Virginia. And I don't know that I blame her, mind—but there she was: raped by a flunking Moishian, a flunking Bonifacist, or a flunking machine, one or the other, and half out of her head from it . . ."

"It was WESCAC," I put in, "not Max or Dr. Eierkopf. And it wasn't what you'd call a rape. You *did* put me in the lift, then, and push the *Belly*-button?"

"I did that," he acknowledged firmly. "Founder forgive me if I shouldn't have." To a professor-general in time of riot, he declared, responsibility for the death of others was no novelty. The blood of hundreds of thousands could be said to be on his hands, he supposed, if one chose to look at it that way; flunk him if I would, he'd done his duty as he saw it, was beholden to none, would take his medicine with head held high. I assured him I had no mind to flunk him, not on that account at least; his deed was wrong, but I quite understood what led him to it and did not think his motives dishonorable, only wrong-headed, like his opinions.

He began to color.

"What I mean," I said, "everybody speaks of your generosity and your brother's selfishness, and I see their point, but it *is* his wealth behind the Unwed Co-ed's Hospital and the P.P.F—or *was*, anyhow. And behind you too, all your life . . ."

"Now, look here, young fellow! I beg Your doggone pardon—"

But, good officer that he was, he must have felt that Grand Tutors somehow outranked professor-generals, for when I raised my hand he fell silent. I was not condemning him or calling him a hypocrite, I explained, and would as leave save the matter for another conversation—but valid as was Enos Enoch's dictum that students Commence or fail individually, never by classes, and admirable as was the virtue of self-reliance, I could not see that Reginald Hector exemplified either very well. How could he regard himself as beholden to none, when his brother had made possible his whole career, his famous philanthropy, even his marriage? Very possibly he had been a good professor-general and chancellor; very possibly his liberality was authentic—but those talents and virtues were empty abstractions without Ira Hector's wherewithal and influence.

"You Certified me Yourself!" he said angrily.

I smiled. "But that was before you'd Certified *me,* so it isn't quite valid." If he really wished to show his self-reliance, I suggested—now that he was out of a job anyway—why did he not chuck all sinecures and go to the goats, as Max had done? I was speaking half in jest (and half seriously, for G. Herrold's death, Max's arrest, and my departure left the goats much in need of herding), but the ex-Chancellor clearly believed I was baiting him, and looking ready to strike me. His Tutoring, I decided, must wait, since the crowd outside would not. I reassured him that I had no intent to denounce him publicly or otherwise reveal either his old attempt on my life or his various dependencies on Ira Hector. The one I forgave, the other was his affair. Neither did I want anything from him, except possibly the answer to a final question . . .

"Ask it," he grumbled. "I won't stand for blackmail, but I'm obliged to You for letting sleeping dogs lie. What I mean, I'm not *beholden,* You understand, but when a fellow needs a hand, why, I'll give him the shirt off my back."

I thought of the hungry undergraduates upon whom he'd bestowed cufflinks and desk-barometers, but contented myself with inquiring whether Anastasia was my sister.

"Aha," he said, as if spying some ulterior motive in the question, and his expression turned fatuous again. "I'd *heard* you two were sweet on each other! Well, don't You worry, lad—*Sir*—I don't believe Stoker's filthy talk about her and that George fellow. He says Pete Greene's lost his head over her too—fellow served under me in C.R. Two, heck of a fine Joe. But I'd never believe that flunking Stoker!"

Disturbing as was the suggestion that Anastasia was known to be "sweet on" Harold Bray, I merely demanded to know whether he meant then that she was *not* Virginia Hector's daughter. He sighed and rolled another cigarette, shaking his head.

"She only had the one, poor Ginny: just Yourself. Me and Ira stood by in the delivery-room, hoping You'd be stillborn. I figured You'd be some kind of monster, if Ginny hadn't been lying about the GILES-thing . . ."

Unaccountably my heart thrilled to the news that "My Ladyship" and I (so I began from that moment forth to regard her) were no kin. But I repeated Ira Hector's assertion that he'd helped deliver her himself.

"I wouldn't put it past him," Reginald chuckled. "That's Ira all over." But the truth, he declared, was that Ira regularly "helped out" at the Unwed Co-ed's Hospital simply to be helpful, and thus had taken part in a great many deliveries—it was, after all, his building. Anastasia's parentage, however, would never be known: "The hospital records are confidential anyhow, and when we decided Ira should adopt a girl we had her papers destroyed. Ginny's doctor was the only one who might have known, and he passed away twenty-some years ago." In other words, Anastasia was an orphan, born to some luckless co-ed, left for adoption at the New Tammany Lying-In. When my disappearance from the tapelift, and G. Herrold's garbled talk of finding a baby in the Belly, had led Reginald Hector to fear that his plan had misfired, he'd judged the scandal of illicit pregnancy less dangerous than that of infanticide, actual or attempted. The fortunate coincidence of Dr. Mayo's death at about that same time had made it possible to enter on the records that Virginia Hector had borne a daughter, Anastasia—whom Ira raised when Virginia refused to. Scandal there'd been, when the news gradually became known, but on the whole it had not much damaged the public image of Reginald Hector; people pitied him and censured Virginia (a double injustice of which he seemed yet oblivious), whose subsequent deterioration they were pleased to regard as her due; Max was got rid of, the Cum Laude Project quietly scrapped, and Eblis Eierkopf demoted to less sensitive researches. Anastasia had proved a delightful grandchild, and but for an occasional nagging fear that the GILES had not really perished (if the baby had *been* the GILES), Reginald Hector had put the unpleasant episode out of mind—until yesterday, when it had suddenly come back to haunt him.

"But look here," he said at last, patting my shoulder, "if You really promise to let bygones be bygones, You can count on me to put in a good word for You with Stacey."

When I asked what exactly he meant, he winked. "She had no business marrying that dirty-minded draft-dodger in the first place! But Stacey listens to her Grandpa Reg, and if I was to tell her the G.T. loves her . . . Not that You haven't told her so already, eh?" He nudged me with his elbow.

"A Grand Tutor loves the whole student body," I told him coldly, adding that if he felt so beholden to me as to pimp for his married granddaughter, he was flunkèd indeed, and had better heed my counsel about herding goats. Not to lose my temper further at his pandering to the image of Harold

Bray, I turned my back on his expostulations and left the office. At that very moment, as if to remind me of urgenter business, the crowd outside set up a shout. But another came from behind me, like an answer to the first: a woman's cry:

"You're *not* my Giles!"

It was Mother, crazy-eyed and pointing from behind the ex-Chancellor. In vain the young receptionist tried to coax her back into the farther room; in vain Reginald Hector said, "Whoa down, Gin"—his own eyes still flashing wrath at me. She pushed past him with her claws out and would have attacked me if they'd not caught her arms.

"You're not my Billy!" she cried. I froze before the hatred in her face. More shouts came from outside, disorganized and fearsome. She struggled now not at me but towards the office window, shrieking, "They're killing him!"

"What's she talking about?" her father demanded. The receptionist, herself verging on hysteria, replied that it was that George-fellow, the so-called Goat-Boy, that the crowd had discovered somewhere and dragged to the front gate. "She says it's her *son,* sir! And I think—they're lynching him . . ."

I ran for the porch, flunking myself for not having put off all disguise long since. The doorguard snapped to attention, ignoring the horror at the gate. There on hands and knees in the torchlight some poor wretch was indeed not long for this campus: blows and kicks rained upon him; the host of his attackers snarled like Border Collies at a wolf; those not near enough to strike with briefcase, umbrella, or slide-rule shouted imprecations and threw weighty textbooks. Already a noose was being rigged from a lamp-post, and Telerama crews were exhorting the crowd not to block their cameras. The victim's tunic, though rent now and bloodied, I recognized as Bray's; but his hair was gold and curled, not black and straight—and the face he raised, when the mob hailed the sight of me, was my own!

"Stop!" I commanded. "Stop in the name of the GILES!"

They did actually pause for a moment, weapons poised, and Reginald Hector (a more seasoned hand than I at giving orders) bellowed at them from the doorway to fall back before he horsewhipped the lot of them. "You heard your Grand Tutor: let the bastard go!"

"Billikins!" my mother screamed behind me, and had I not caught hold of her, would have run to the gore-smeared

likeness of her son. *"You're* not the GILES!" she shrieked at
me, and strove ferocious at my eyes. "Billy is!"

Did I see Bray smile through his mad disguise? A half-
second I had to wonder what, if not an EATen mind, could
have led him to so fatal a mask, and where anyhow he'd got
it. In that same half-second, as the mob faltered, another
woman squealed forth round a shrubberied corner of the
mansion. I let go my mother in horror at sight of Anastasia
herself, scarcely less abused than Bray: her sandals were
gone; her hair was wild, her cheek bloody, her white uniform
ripped down the front and everywhere grimed!

"What in thunder!" Reg Hector shouted. My mother, instead of assaulting me, ran weeping to embrace whom she
thought her son. Like the crowd, I stood dumbfounded; Reginald Hector, half-mad with alarm, caught his granddaughter in his arms and shouted questions at her: What had happened? Who had attacked her? But she shook away and ran
to me. Forgetting my mask I held out my arms—ah,
Founder, she was worse mauled than on the night Croaker
beached her!—but she halted just before me and screamed at
me to "keep my promise." Men with microphones came running.

"You *swore!*" she cried. "You swore you'd pass Him if I
slept with you!" Beside herself, she snatched a microphone
and pointed to the man she thought was I, his wounds being
kissed by my mother. "That man is a passèd Grand Tutor!"
she shouted into it. "Don't dare kill your own Grand Tutor!"
To me again then she cried, "I kept *my* promise! You keep
yours!"

I was dizzy with shock. Reginald Hector ran in small circles with his hands upon his ears. The Telerama people signaled one another furiously, and spotlights fingered all about
us. To perfect the confusion a squad of Stoker's motorcycle-
guards now roared around the corner of the house whence
Anastasia had appeared; they drew up near the gate, sirens
a-growl, cursing the crowd from their way. Stoker himself led
them, black-jacketed, booted, and grinning as of old, soot on
chin and teeth a-flash. In his sidecar—manacled, disheveled,
bruised, and glum—Peter Greene, with Stoker's pistol at his
head! Anastasia ran from him, to hug my knees. Everyone
milled about; the lynching was temporarily forgot.

"Please don't let them hurt George!" My Ladyship begged

me. "We'll try again tonight, if you want to. The whole night!"

A dreadful thought occurred to me as she spoke, so that only later did I realize what she'd said.

"Did Greene attack you?" Even as I asked I groaned with the certainty that he had, brought to it by disillusionment at my hands.

She pounded my kneecaps with her fists. "It doesn't *matter!* Please do what you promised, Mr. Bray! I'll find *some* way to have a baby with you; I *swear* it!"

My eyes blinded—with tears of chagrin that would not, however, fall—and I pushed through to where my mother knelt kissing the semblance of myself. Restive now, the crowd were arguing with Stoker's men and unabashedly restringing the noose. I tried to say "Wait!" but the cry lodged in my throat. Bray smiled through his bloody mask expectantly; upon his chest my mother wept. I pointed at him and managed at last to say: "That man's an impostor!"

"You're telling us, sir?" his captors laughed, and made to fetch him noosewards. I blocked their way.

"Look!" I seized his hair and my own—which was to say, my own and his—and yanked both masks away, wondering what face Bray would show beneath. It was his own—that is, a semblance of the one I doffed—and people cried astonishment. My mother looked wailing from one to the other of us and clutched her head.

"I'm George the Goat-Boy!" I declared bitterly to the crowd. "My diploma's false; I've failed everything—"

I could say no more for grief; anyhow they were upon me—seized me by the hair, and, seeing it was real, commenced to kick and pummel. Mother screamed, and was fetched from me. My diploma (the erstwhile Assignment-list) they stuffed into my mouth and bade me eat—as willingly I would have, in self-despite, had it not been retchy sheepskin. When they hoist me to a sidecar-top and readied the noose, I could see Bray moving porchwards on the shoulders of the faithful. From the mansion-steps Reginald Hector held out his arms to welcome the true Grand Tutor—nay, more, tore off his own shirt to staunch Bray's wounds, nor would accept the new one his aides fetched forth, until the spotlights swung from him to My perjured, ruined, ruinous Ladyship. Anastasia tugged at Bray's ankle, tore at her already open blouse as if to show him his reward, and screamed to him what she'd screamed to me, I did not doubt; he made a circle of his thumb and forefinger but could not calm her, nor moved at all to stay the lynch.

Neither did the guards: Peter Greene they held from the crowd (who were inspired to hang us both), on the ground that no formal charge of rape had yet been brought against him; but they only grinned and stood by as I was beaten with my own stick, my black purse pulled like a death-mask over my head without regard for its contents, and the tip of the shophar thrust into my rump. No matter: I yearned for the end; welcomed the hemp onto my neck; stepped off the side-car before they could push me. A vile cheer rose; I heard Stoker laugh at my strangling. "Blow it!" someone yelled—and I thought I might have, so fiercely did I strain to die; indeed there came a far-off shrieking whistle, blast upon blast from Founder's Hill; a sound I knew. As I let go reins and breath and all I heard a man cry, "Founder help us; we'll all be EATen!" And another, almost matter-of-factly: "It's the end of the University."

SECOND REEL

1.

Students pass away; not so studentdom, until the campus itself shall perish. And at that term of terms, when the student body is no more, shall its mind not persist, in other universities than ours?

I couldn't at once adjudge, from where I woke beyond the noose, whether the EAT-whistle had blown for my sole succumbing or all studentdom's, as my chamber was isolate except from the cry and reek of fellow flunks. But that I was in Nether Campus I could not doubt: the heat, the shrieks and mad laughter, the stink—all attested it. I lay in foul straw in an iron stall with padded walls, lit by the red-orange glow from a port in the ceiling—the one apparent aperture. That I should abide there among the flunked forever I did not question: I had failed everything, everyone, in every sense; was as flunked as any other of Bray's passees; had flunked myself as I had flunked them; was flunked at the outset for craving ardently to pass, just as that patch-eyed Nikolayan had been selfish in his yen for perfect selflessness. "Passage is failure": I saw now in my black box what truth was in that remark, and prepared to suffer till the end of terms.

Two things alone surprised me: that the old West-Campus images of the mind's fate after death should turn out, evidently, to be literal truth instead of vivid metaphor—real iron, real dung, real fire and screams, and elsewhere, I presumed, real harps and passèd madrigals!—and that my punishment, so far at least, was in strictly human wise. I had been raised in straiter stalls than this, had slept for years in

580

urinouser peat; surely the Founder knew I must find these quarters less loathesome than another human would. Was it that under the aspect of eternity all punishments were equal, being infinite every one? Or that in His wisdom the Founder chose so goat a lot for mine the smartlier to sting me for playing at human Tutorhood? No matter, these or any things: it was finished. My neck hurt; otherwise I was comfortable, sweetly tired in every limb. Naked, besmeared, I rested in the black heat and balmy absoluteness of my fall. I had failed all, then, passed nothing! Relief—from aspiration, doubt, responsibility, fear of failure—it flooded through me, drowned remorse and dread, swept me into the most delicious sleep.

Hours later—semesters, centuries—I woke to earnest conversation and realized I'd been hearing two male voices for some time.

"He wouldn't!"

"Excuse, Classmate sir: *wouldhood!*"

"Indeed, I think he would not . . ."

"Impossibleness not!"

"You truly believe he would, my boy?"

"Yes. No! Bah, I give it up!"

The latter voice, its accent and locutions, was exotic, much in the matter of that same Nikolayan defector's. The former—exotic too, but gentle, old, and wondrously familiar—was Max's. Had they been Shafted, then, and was there company in Dunce's College? I opened my eyes: I was on a bed now, of sorts—a sweet straw tick on an iron-wire platform—in a chamber better lighted than the one before, though no less warm. The floor and ceiling were of concrete, and the wall to which my steel-pipe bedframe was attached; the other walls were comprised of parallel vertical bars in the manner of detention-cells I'd read of. It was, after all, Max and Leonid Alexandrov I heard: they faced each other on the cell-floor, gesticulating as they argued.

"What about the other question?" Max demanded.

"Same like, turned around," Leonid said: "Would go."

"Maios didn't, when *he* had a chance to."

"Was vanity, then. Playing heroness."

"Playing! He died for it!"

"More famous so! Big advertise, name in historybooks!"

I feared to speak, lest the vision of my keeper vanish; for aught I knew, dear dreams might be my torment. But they

saw me stir; Max hurried to me; real tears dropped into his
beard and onto mine; material the arms that hugged me,
mortal the hand that felt my brow, and I learned I was alive,
in Main Detention. Leonid, though we'd met only once before, embraced me also, in the Nikolayan manner, and
seemed as pleased as Max to see me wake. They had become
friends, it appeared—as were too the Nikolayan and his former adversary Peter Greene, who saluted me glumly from
the next cell!

"Thank the Founder you're okay!" Max cried. His late reserve with me was gone; beside my cot he closed his eyes and
thumped his forehead against my chest.

"Nothing's okay," grumbled Peter Greene, and was cheerily bid by Classmate Alexandrov to go flunk himself.

"I didn't mean *him*," Greene said. "Y'know durn well what
I mean."

I didn't, nor cared just then to learn. Enough to be alive
and on campus, however incarcerate and disgraced. Responsibility! Remorse! Dishonor! I welcomed their sting now as evidence that, among my other failures, I had failed to pass
away.

There is no time in Main Detention—under Stoker's war-
denship, not even night and day. We slept or woke irregularly
without regard to the lights, which went on and off at unpre-
dictable intervals. Meals were served at any hour, apparently,
sometimes in such close succession that one had no appetite,
sometimes at so great a lapse of time that chants of protest
rose from the detained. One had the impression that there
was in theory a fixed routine, which however was whimsically
administered: we would be routed out for exercise after
"lunch," say, and find ourselves doing push-ups under the
stars; or we might go for (what seemed like) days without
leaving our cells, then be sent to the prison shops or
reading-room for so long a stretch that we'd sleep and eat
upon the work- or library-tables. In this disorder I saw Stoker's hand, as in our random assignment to cells. Main Detention itself, as I'd gathered from that chart in Stoker's office,
was scrupulously laid out as to the location among its tiers of
the several sorts of offenders; there was evidence, even, of a
moral logic in its architecture. But in practice we were assorted by no discernible plan: I for example had been taken
from the noose at Stoker's direction and detained for imper-

sonating a Grand Tutor; the cells for that species of error were in the fourth block of the third, or bottom, tier, counting downwards; yet I had waked first in an observation-chamber for the criminally mad and later in the company of an alleged murderer, an alleged spy, and an alleged rapist (such was the charge against Peter Greene, who after reviving from Dr. Sear's sedation had on the evening of my fall tracked Anastasia into an alleyway behind the Old Chancellor's Mansion and there, by his own dour admission, flung My Ladyship upon the pavement and forced her virtue "redskin style"), no two of whom belonged in the same stratum. Moreover, at each return from work or exercise there was no telling where one would be confined, or with whom: I might be lodged alone or crammed into a cell with ten others in an empty tier; my companions might be fellow-impostors—false dons and pretended sophomores—or some of the many grafters, gamblers, pornographers, and prostitute co-eds detained under Lucius Rexford's far-reaching program of campus reform (of which more presently), or any other combination of the flunked.

Yet among the inconsistencies of our detention, by the logic of our warden's illogicality, we were not invariably assigned a cell at all. On occasion it was every man for himself at lock-up time; my objectives then would be to elude the predatory faggots (who collared the unwary to ruthless buggering) and share a cell with Max, Leonid, Peter Greene—or Croaker, when soon afterwards he joined our company. From them, from Stoker himself, who now and then toured his domain, and from the regular visits of Anastasia and my mother, I learned the unhappy state of things among my erstwhile Tutees, as well as in the upper campus generally. And that news, those developments, were my one real punishment in this interval of my life: sad postings in a desert of dead time.

I was not uncomfortable. When meat was served, or cowsmilk, I contented myself with water and mattress-straw, and gained strength and trim from that buckly fare. I cannot say that I was never abused by guards and prisoners, who sometimes took advantage of my sticklessness, or that I never made use of the restless whores who climbed upon the bars to sport. In general, however, except for the pleasure of atonement with Max and the pain of learning what catastrophe my Tutorship had wrought, my season in Main Detention was as numb as it was timeless. So much so, I reconstruct with confidence neither the order of the several disclosures and events which follow nor my reaction to them. They took place, I see now, over a period of some forty weeks, but for aught I felt or valued time it might have been forty years, forty days—or one long night.

The EAT-whistle that had postponed my end was a false alarm—rather, a true alarm falsely construed. When Classmate X had broken off the Summit Symposium and in such dudgeon left the U.C. building, the Nikolayan and New Tammanian border-guards were each alerted to expect trouble from the other. Later that same day, on Lucius Rexford's orders, units from the School of Engineering had moved up to begin the task of relocating the NTC Power Line a full kilometer west of its former position and mounting extra floodlight-towers in the widened gap between East and West Campus. The Nikolayans, thinking themselves menaced by this activity, had actually sent short-order EAT-waves crackling to the very Boundary (at least EASCAC had transmitted them; whether at its own discretion or on orders from the Student-Unionist First Secretary was not clear), which WESCAC had detected and duly reported. Ordinarily in such circumstances no general alarm would have been sounded until the enemy's hostile intentions were unmistakable; but Chancellor Rexford being unavailable for consultation (he was in fact drafting the first of his "Open-Book Test" bills, and refused to be disturbed), the New Tammany professor-generals had blown the whistle. They may or may not have ordered a counter-attack as well: they themselves denied it, but the Nikolayans claimed—predictably, yet perhaps not incorrectly—that New Tammany was calling EASCAC's defense-transmissions aggressive in order to justify counter-aggression; and Stoker himself (from whom I learned all this) maintained that WESCAC had indeed set about to EAT Nikolay College, either by its own AIM or at the direction of the professor-generals; only the drain on its power-supply— caused by Stoker's unwonted absence from the Furnace Room and a sudden frenzy of power-consumption by the Library CACAFILE—had prevented Campus Riot III. The situation remained critical: Chancellor Rexford's sudden insistence on "open-book diplomacy" had made practical negotiation impossible between East and West; the separation of the Power Lines ended the defection of malcontents; the Nikolayans maintained that NTC's apparent retreat was a prelude to "loudening" the Quiet Riot, and Tower Hall replied that the Nikolayans were advancing their Power Line under cover of darkness—the new floodlights were barely usable for want of power. The only casualties thus far were among New Tammany's border-guards, numbers of whom fell to their deaths each week from the Power Line because of the poor light and the new "heads-up" collars which the Chancellor obliged them to wear on duty; but pressures were mounting and tempers shortening on both sides, and at any hour the EAT-whistle might sound again, this time in earnest.

Nor was the grave varsity situation the only cause of Rexford's declining popularity. Stoker had returned to the Powerhouse with rapèd Anastasia after rescuing me from the noose, and in time had restored Furnace-Room output to three-quarters of its normal level; better than that he could not inspire Madge and the rest to do, by reason perhaps of his own loss of energy; even so, a part of the production was stored, or went up the Shaft in smoke, because New Tammany's power-consumption had dropped to fifty percent of normal. The decrease was owing not to reduced demands for power in the College—they had never been higher—but to the problems of distribution raised by Rexford's refusal to have any commerce with Maurice Stoker, whose presence he also forbade in the Great Mall area. This was the first of a series of prohibitions enacted by his administration in the following months: the ill-famed and short-lived "Open-Book Tests" designed to eliminate flunkèdness from New Tammany College. Dormitory-brothels were shut down, their madams prosecuted. Adultery was made a criminal misdemeanor and rape a capital felony on the one hand, while celibacy on the other—at least as represented by bachelor- and spinsterhood—was penalized by fines increased annually after age twenty-one. Homosexuals were flogged, irrespective of gender; flagellants were not. Although one glass of light wine was served with the evening meal in every dining-hall, drunkenness, even in the home, was punished severely, as were fights of any sort and even domestic altercations—wife-beating, in particular, was made punishable by long detention. Tower-Hall patronage was abolished; macing, graft, division of interest, and other abuses of office became grounds for expulsion from the College. Censorship was imposed upon all media of entertainment, communication, instruction, and artistic expression, with the aim of suppressing excess. Exotic dress, grooming, and behavior were condemned from all sides by bill-boards and Telerama messages, and—what was perhaps the most controversial measure of all—it was proposed that psychotherapy be made obligatory for extreme or intemperate personalities, to the end of schooling them in moderation. This last proposal the Chancellor ultimately vetoed as immoderate, though he himself had drafted it; but the press criticized him all the same—in guarded terms, out of respect for the censorship. So also did the rank and file of New Tammany undergraduates, who had used to adore him; they removed his sunny likeness from their walls and smirked at the rumors that Mrs. Rexford's vacation from Great Mall would be permanent. Yet they submitted to the Open-Book reforms to a degree bespeaking some basic sympathy with their spirit. Criminal violence became rare; so too did loud merrymaking. Sharp cheeses and unsliced rye bread disappeared from menus. Nearly everyone had a *C* average. Greene Timber and Plastics (in the owner's absence) developed a synthetic material said to be almost indistinguishable from real plastic, and a more efficient way of packaging containers. It was with a faint smile, a faint sigh, or a faint shrug that people nicknamed Tower Hall "Dead Center." No one was happy; on the other hand, no demonstrations were mounted or measures proposed to repeal the new laws.

The Chancellor himself was only moderately concerned about these developments; neither did it stir him to hear that the Founder's Scroll had got lost in the CACAFILE—which, reprogrammed by Mother's office in accordance with my directive, seemed to have declared every volume in the Library *sui generis* and would file no two in the same category. The evidence of student-opinion polls, the complaints of his party-leaders and lieutenants that he'd never win the next election, the declining wattage of the Light House itself—nothing much troubled him.

"He's not right bright these days," Stoker said. But he said it languidly, with none of his old high-spirited contempt, and though he had regrown his beard and reverted to his motorcycle-costume, his hair was barbered, his leather jacket greaseless—and a curly black forelock hung upon his brow. "I'm glad he's no kin of mine."

This as he returned me to my cell—to *some* cell,

anyhow—from one of his offices, early in my confinement. I had testified in Max's behalf during his trial for the murder of Herman Hermann and conversed afterwards with Stoker for several hours, during which he told me most of the foregoing and other things as well, with a kind of bored persistence. He had been convinced, he said, that I was as much a fraud as Bray; for that very reason he'd taken my advice and ceased to define passage by his wholesale flunkèdness. His aim—which he pursued because he had no faith in it—was, I gathered, to lead the Chancellor and others to failure by no longer exemplifying and tempting them to it (thereby himself to fail, I suspected, and thus, by his inverted logic, to pass—the same end he'd originally pursued, only essayed now by transvaluated means); and he supposed he had succeeded. Shaven and suited, he'd gone to the Light House in order at once to embrace and to deny kinship with Lucius Rexford, whom he met returning from the aborted Summit Symposium. The two had made polite, if distracted, conversation, even toasted each other's health in Dry Sack; but though the Chancellor was astonished to see him there and gratified to hear that the claim of their fraternity would need be denied no more, Stoker had distinctly felt that for the first time Lucky Rexford disliked him in addition to repudiating him. To be sure, the Chancellor was distraught by the events at the University Council, by Mrs. Rexford's chilly announcement that she'd be dining out that evening, and (what Stoker hadn't been aware of) not least by my several counsels to him, which though he'd scoffed at them he couldn't forget. Nevertheless Stoker felt so clearly the distaste that took the place of Rexford's former envious rejection, he himself cut the interview short, and readily agreed to the Chancellor's suggestion that they meet no more. In a curious heat then, he had throttled through the Light-House gate with his company—not in excess of the posted speed-limits—just as Anastasia and I had happened to taxi past en route to the Library from Dr. Sear's. When shortly afterwards the crowd had gathered before Tower Hall, and he learned their purpose, he'd put his new *persona* to the further test I'd witnessed, soothing the demonstrators instead of inciting and clubbing them at once as was his wont. Bray's admonition there in the lobby—to "be himself, for Founder's sake"—accounted for his subsequent partial regression: who *was* himself? and for Whose sake did he do anything? Confused, he had retired to

Main Detention, exchanged the business-suit for his customary garb, and returned to Great Mall just in time to stop the lynching.

"But why'd you stop it?" I asked him. "If you'd decided my Tutoring was false and Bray's was true . . ."

He shrugged. "Stacey's orders."

I could scarcely believe him. "You took orders from Anastasia?"

"I couldn't decide what was what," he said listlessly. "And Peter Greene humping her like that, it kind of upset me . . ."

I remarked that My Ladyship's sexual misfortunes had never previously dismayed him; he was even responsible for not a few of them.

He sighed. "That was *before*. You've seen how she is lately. I don't know, George: I think there's something wrong with our marriage."

I believed I knew what he meant, for though I'd seen Anastasia several times since being detained, and accounted for some features of her behavior as owing to my counsel and others to her misguided faith in my Grand-Tutorhood, I couldn't finally say I understood My Ladyship at all. Her permitting Harold Bray to service her in exchange for Certifying me I comprehended, revolting as was the idea; his later amnesty-offer and invitation to me to set right the damage I'd done I refused, assuming they were bought with the same coin. But when she brought my mother to visit me she was cold, even priggish, far beyond the simple chastity I'd enjoined on her. She was unsympathetic not only to the vulgar prisoners who shouted obscenities and exposed themselves to her in the Visitation Room—and whom she once must passively have comforted with her sex—but also to her husband, despite his having ceased to abuse her. If formerly she had embraced the hateful as well as the dear in studentdom, accepting indiscriminately lust with love and receiving upon her with equal compassion police-dogs and Grand Tutors, now she seemed as catholic in her rejection: would no more of me or even of Leonid (who truly, passionately loved her) than of Peter Greene, who professed disgust with her and all her gender.

Anastasia's character, in fact, was one of two chief subjects of debate among my friends in Main Detention; it always came up when Peter Greene and Leonid were within talking distance of each other.

"Keep-her-legs-together-wise," Greene would declare to him, "I used to think she was a durn nice girl, same as you do now. I'd of swore she was the GILES her own self if you'd of stepped up and asked me! Didn't I sock you one in the Living Room for saying she weren't no virgin? But it's no use her putting on airs *now*, by golly: I've seen what I've saw!"

"And done what you did," Max would remind him.

Leonid then would shout "Irrelevanceness!" or "Dumbnicity!" and, seizing his new friend by the hair (if they were in a common cell) or shaking a cordial fist, would harangue him on his blindness to the real nature of Anastasia's virtues.

"*Is* the GILES!" he would declare of her. "Excuse, George: you know what! Virgins bah! All this chastehood, all this niceship—what's the word it is, Dr. Spielman, sir?"

"*Schmata*," Max would offer, who had grown fond of Moishian terms since his detention. "*Dreck*."

"I love!" Leonid then would roar, with reference equally to the words, his idol Max who supplied them, his grumbling and perhaps pinioned cellmate (who had given up exercise and vitamin-pills), and My Ladyship. "Never mind goodity! *Pfui! Pfui!*"

What he meant I can more easily paraphrase than reproduce in his idiom: to believe in Grand Tutors and Founders was against his curriculum, but he would not dismiss as did everyone else the notion that the GILES could possibly be female or that Anastasia, despite her sexual history, might be it. On the contrary, it was just that aspect of her biography and former nature that Commenced her in Leonid's eye; he loved her as blindly (it seemed to me) as earlier had Peter Greene, but for just contrary reasons: as a quintessential rapee, an absolutely unselfish martyr to studentdom's lust—his own included, for he'd once knelt before her in a corner of the Powerhouse, confessed an overmastering desire, and not been denied its satisfaction. He would none of my suggestion that her very docility perhaps aroused the lust that made her its victim. "*Nyet!*" he would shout, slamming one fist into the other and plunging as always about the cell. So far from learning the flunkèdness of her innocence, he would school me in the passèdness of her guilt.

"Lustily I spit on!" he cried. "Chastiness same like!" Celi-

bate co-eds, in his view, were a kind of misers, Ira Hectors of
the flesh, and rapists a kind of burglars or book-pirates:
flunkèd men whose flunkèdness was made possible by the
corresponding flunkèdness of private property. Neither would
Graduate if *he* were Grand Tutor; none save the generous
should pass. "But *nyet!*" he would then avow further. Had he
called her a mere rapee? Insufficienthood! There was no
merit in being robbed; that mischance befell miser and philanthropist alike. Anastasia, he maintained, was like a man
who not only gives alms to the poor and greedy but bestows
his whole wealth among them, share and share alike, lest they
be led to steal it: "A Reginald Hector of sexness!"

I smiled at this analogy, ironically more telling than he
knew, but declined to argue the point or disabuse him of his
esteem for the former chancellor. It was between him and
Greene that the argument raged, as it had since their first encounter at Stoker's Randy-Thursday party; only now, thanks
to Greene's disillusionment, it was flunkèd versus passèd
promiscuity rather than the latter versus passèd maidenhood.
Otherwise they were the cordialest companions—except when
Greene's bitter hallucinations and Leonid's epileptoid fits made
one or the other unapproachable.

"No durn good," was Greene's new refrain, whether he
was speaking of Anastasia, "Miss Sally Ann," New Tammany
College, or himself. "No gosh durn good! What I mean, Truth-
Beauty-and-Goodnesswise, y'know?" Though convinced that
Anastasia had got what she deserved from him ("Flunking hussy, leading me on she hadn't never been touched, and
all the time selling it faster'n O.B.G.'s daughter!"), he did not
excuse himself of the felony. He was flunked, he saw plainly
now; had always been flunked, in every wise. He had de-
spoiled the forests and destroyed their aboriginal inhabitants,
vaunted his uncouthness, ridden roughshod with his vulgar
wealth; he had been no husband to his wife (who however he
was sure now had betrayed him many times over), no father
to his children (wastrels and delinquents though they were).
Let them Shaft him; he deserved no less a penalty, even from
a college he saw now to be corrupt from Belfry to Basement.
Or, if the whore he'd alleyed and her pimp the false Grand
Tutor chose to hush the thing up, let them acquit him: once
free he'd divorce his wife, resign from his enterprises, quit
the Junior Enochist League and all it stood for, perhaps even
defect to the East Campus—or blow his brains out, he was

not sure which. In earnest of these resolves he had already
abandoned razor and soap: his chin bushed orange; his scent
approached the late Redfearn's Tom's.

It turned out that he was neither convicted nor acquitted.
In the morning of the day at hand—the first of Max's
trial—the case against him was dismissed, and he left Main
Detention.

"She wouldn't testify!" Stoker exclaimed to me, referring
to his wife. I was only slightly less baffled than he. My Ladyship had decided to press no charges—so the prosecuting bar-
rister had announced, plainly chagrined—because "mature
reflection" had led her to believe that she'd doubtless invited
and provoked Mr. Greene's assault, and doubtless been gratified by it in some flunkèd wise. As her statement was read,
Anastasia regarded me coolly across the court-room, where I
sat with other prospective witnesses in the Spielman case.

"Generostness!" Leonid wept later, when he heard the
news. "GILES-hoodhood!"

At the counsel-table Greene muttered: "I knew she weren't
no better'n she should be, drive-a-man-to-drinkwise. They're
all of a feather."

But Stoker, like myself, could accept neither of these interpretations.

"It's what you've said about her all along," I reminded
him; and he agreed, but pointed out with a troubled sigh the
same irony that puzzled me: her admission was—perhaps for
the first time!—not true at all.

"Flunk if I know what's come over everybody," Stoker
said. "Maybe you *are* the Grand Tutor." I observed him narrowly: there was in his tone and expression no trace of his
usual tease—nor did he lately, as of old, prompt one's
least-passèd aspects to the fore. For example, his remark did
not tickle my vanity or ambition, as formerly it would have,
but rather shamed me, and I answered calmly: "I don't know
any more whether Bray's the Grand Tutor or not; there's
something extraordinary about him. But I know *I'm* not. I'm
a total failure."

My warden smiled. "Maybe Failure is Passage."

The cell that Peter Greene had vacated I found occupied
now by Croaker, fetched there from the Infirmary while I'd
been in court.

"He's diplomatically immune," Stoker said. "We're just
boarding him till they fetch him back home."

My black friend did not look well. Max and Leonid held his head as best they could while he vomited through the bars. He too was charged with rape, Stoker explained to us, and though he could not be prosecuted he had been declared *non gratis* in New Tammany College and was being held against his recall at the request of his Frumentian alma mater. Following my advice, it seemed, he had mutinied against Dr. Eierkopf: eaten every egg in the Tower Hall Belfry, fresh and otherwise, then jammed home the Infinite Divisor into the escapement of the clockworks and abandoned his master between Tick and Tock. Putting by all restraint, he had deflowered two co-eds, one male freshman, a trustee's maiden aunt, a blue-ribbon gilt, and a cast-bronze allegorical statue in heroic scale of Truth Unveiled. In addition he had consumed indiscriminately raw chipmunks, aspen catkins, toadstools, dog-stools, and the looseleaf lecture-notes of his third victim, an economics major. The campus patrol had overtaken him at the Honeymoon Lodge Motel; yet they doubted they'd ever have subdued him, unless fatally, had not a remarkable occurrence quite nonplussed him.

"A certain married couple known to us both," Stoker said, still with no sarcasm at all, "were spending the weekend at that motel, it seems, on the advice of the Grand Tutor. What happened between them isn't very clear—Kennard's in the Infirmary now, and Hedwig's in the Asylum—"

I groaned.

"—but whatever it was, it must've unhinged poor Heddy entirely. Ever heard of a woman attacking a man?" Mrs. Sear, it appeared, had accosted Croaker in the motel lobby (whose occupants had fled when he strode naked through the glass door and commenced to make love to a soft-drink dispenser), removed her clothing, and leaped upon him, shouting lewd encouragements. Alas, what the vending-machine had mustered, she dismayed; so addled and unmanned him (of course, his stomach was troubling him by this time too) that he stood like ravished Truth while patrolmen shackled and sedated him. Mrs. Sear, altogether distraught, skipped circles about the lobby, chanting *He was my bashful, barefoot beau* in uncertain contralto, until the white ambulance-cycle arrived. It had been summoned in fact for Dr. Sear, who during the furor in the lobby was found by a chambermaid to be unconscious and discolored in his room, overdosed with sleeping-capsules. Thus husband and wife had left the motel together, neither aware of the fact. Mrs. Sear was committed and had subsequently regressed to the behavior of a five-year-old girl, according to Stoker; Dr. Sear had his stomach pumped in the out-patient wing of the Infirmary and so was spared for the Cancer Ward, where he presently languished in preparation for palliative surgery. Croaker himself, once subdued, became ill, incontinent, and helpless: went on all fours, forgot how to feed himself, and finally huddled day and night in one corner like a distempered beast. When presently the fever had passed and his appetites began to rewaken, he'd been transferred to Main Detention rather than to the NTC Asylum because of a dispute among the psychiatric faculty as to whether insanity was possible in sub-rational animals. The alternative proposed by the negative faction, composed largely of South New Tammanians—that he be exhibited in the Zoological Gardens—was rejected by the Office of Intercollegiate Relations lest it give offense to the emerging colleges of Frumentius, whose political support the Office was courting. Of Dr. Eierkopf's fate there was no word.

I touched the head of my sick black classmate, who, weak from regurgitating mattress-straw, collapsed now between his supporters. Yet before the pupils of his eyes rolled up he smiled at me and grunted.

"He's worse off now than he was the time I turned him loose," Stoker observed. "Even a wild animal won't eat what's not good for him."

"My fault," I said, and shook my head. In counseling Croaker to put by all things Eierkopfian and become indeed a beast of the woods, I'd not allowed for the atrophy of instinct, I suppose; or perhaps student rationality and brute unconscious will were not separable, so that plucking the blossom killed the root. My heart I had thought too numbed by other failures to feel new grief, but so formidable a wreck stung it afresh. Mistutoring Croaker in such wise, I had I felt subverted my own origin and base: the easy beasthood that must have accounted for our *rapport*.

"He might be dangerous when he gets well," Stoker said to Max and Leonid. "Want to move next door?"

Those two glanced at each other.

"You go on," Max grumbled. "Me he knows already; I should stay here in case."

Leonid considered, flung his arms about for some moments, then replied as if casually: "Not."

"More heroics," Max said. Stoker, who saw what was coming as clearly as I, shrugged and departed, leaving me (as sometimes happened) the barred aisle for my cell—small boon, as its length was cotless and potless. He was not enough reformed to *insist* on removing my friends from danger; the old Stoker, so far from even suggesting it, would have stayed to watch the mayhem.

"Vice-versity!" Leonid shouted at my keeper. "You're the heroics, sir!"

They took up then the other great topic of debate: the one they'd waked me with at the first and put me to sleep with many times since—and which, after Greene's release, entirely supplanted the issue of My Ladyship's character. It took numerous forms, or rather was provoked by several particular questions like the one here disputed—which of them would risk his welfare by attending Croaker—but inevitably it reduced to the same terms. Max I had accused of a special vanity, the yen for martyrdom; Leonid of a selfish ambition not dissimilar to my former craving for Commencement: the desire to be a perfect Student-Unionist. No good my withdrawing those criticisms now, as bad-tempered, specious, logic-chopping; no good my repudiating all of that flunkèd March-day's work, false counsels of a false Grand Tutor. What they'd denied when I proposed it, they all affirmed, every one of my "Tutees," it seemed, now I would recant; and the more I disavowed Grand-Tutorhood, the strongerly they countered, by word and deed, that disavowal. Max, Leonid, Anastasia, Peter Greene, the Sears, Croaker, Chancellor Rexford—and for aught I knew, Eblis Eierkopf, the brothers Hector, and Classmate X—all seemed to agree now that they *had* been flunked, Bray's Certification to the contrary notwithstanding, even as in my ignorance I had declared—and that Stoker had been less so, or less truly aspirant to that condition, than he'd claimed to be. In the cases of Max and Leonid this had led to a bind. As to principle they were agreed: if the desire to sacrifice oneself, whether by martyrdom or in perfect selflessness, was selfish, and thus self-contradictory, then to attain that end one must not aspire to it. Further, they agreed—sometimes, at least—that *not-*aspiring, if conceived as a means to the same end, was morally identical with aspiring, and that imperfect selflessness, when deliberately practiced to avoid the vanity of perfection, became itself perfect, itself vain. Therefore, as best I could infer, they aspired to not-aspire to an imperfect imperfection, each in his way—and found themselves at odds. Would an unvain martyr stay on in Main Detention, Maios-like, even unto the Shaft, as Max was inclined to, or escape, given the chance, to continue his work in studentdom's behalf? Leonid insisted, most often, that the slightly selfish (and thus truly selfless) choice was the latter, and offered "daily" to effect my keeper's freedom by secret means.

To do this, I came to learn, was part of the assignment given him by his stepfather; but our conversation in the U.C. building and his discussions with Max had impaired Leonid's singleness of purpose. His mission had been first to feign defection and then to get himself detained as a Nikolayan agent by discovering, as though inadvertently, an intent to kidnap some unnamed New Tammany scientist; this much he had accomplished before my eyes, on the Black Friday of my Tutorhood. But this apparent frustration of his objective was part of the plan—for it was Max they wanted! Reasoning that his arrest for Moishiocausticide would turn Max against New Tammany, if his original cashiering hadn't, the Nikolayan Department of Intelligence had chosen Leonid Alexandrov, because of his notorious way with locks, to rescue him from the Shaft and transport him across the Power Lines—yielding up his own life, if necessary, in the process. Not only had Leonid accepted the task enthusiastically, seeing in it a chance to redeem his errant past and earn Classmate X's respect by proving his selflessness; he still maintained that the idea had been his own. But my remarks and Max's moral speculations had led him to doubt. Leaving aside the merits of the collective Student Self and its ambitions, ought a truly selfless agent of that Self to carry out its wishes, knowing the vanity and selfishness of his motives in so doing? Or ought he to spoil the assignment, by merely setting Max free in New Tammany or returning empty-handed, and thereby achieve the selflessness of self-disgrace? That Max himself, whom he'd come to love second only to Classmate X, had no desire to work for Nikolay College or even to leave Main Detention, compounded the difficulty.

The truth was, neither doubted the way of his inclination, only its ultimate passèdness. Seeing liberty and the Shaft as equally vain, Max obviously preferred the Shaft—witness his remaining in jail even after he was convicted and sentenced. Leonid just as obviously wanted to rescue him, for all his concession that the wish might not be unselfish. Similarly, each claimed now that the other should have withdrawn to safety and left Croaker's care to *him,* while freely acknowledging that it might be being "selfish" (that is, unselfish) to take the risk alone.

"For Founder's sake, stop!" I cried to them when I could bear no more of this casuistry. "You're both locked in anyhow. What difference does it make?"

"Bah, Goat-Boy!" Leonid shouted back at once. "Excuse! I love! But bah to you!" He was not angry, only vehement as always. For it must not be imagined that these endless debates were conducted coolly, in a spirit of logical exercise: Max, though calm, was intensely serious—it was, after all, a question of life or death for him—and Leonid was given to crushing embraces, respectful pummelings, shouts, tears, and loving lurches to accompany his reasoning. Now, in demonstration of his contempt for locks (they it was he bah'ed), he sprang to the cell-door and instantly had it open—the first such exercise of his talent in Main Detention. He stepped into my aisle, red-faced and triumphant.

"So!"

At once the other prisoners set up a clamor.

"Could release all!" he roared at them. "Simplicity! Would like! But not!" Because, he confided to me at the top of his voice, he was merely a visitor in New Tammany College, and much as he objected to its curricular policies, he did not wish to act discourteously—besides, he'd not forgotten the consequence of his spree in the Nikolayan Zoo. "Come out, Dr. Spielman! Escapeness!"

Max shook his head, and in the end all three of us ministered to Croaker until his strength and appetites returned, whereupon we fled for safety to an adjoining cell. Thereafter Croaker alternated between reasonless animality and mindless vegetability. In the latter intervals we fed him his meals; in the former we bewore lest he make a meal of us. But whether because, stickless, I had no authority with him, or because like the others he'd taken to heart my disastrous first lesson, I could by no means control or even communicate with him. And so ill-ordered was Main Detention, we all might have perished at Croaker's hands between lock-up times had there not been hosts of passive pederasts and suicidal drop-outs eager for abuse, who diverted him at great cost of limbs and fundaments, not all which Max's skill could repair without medical equipment.

No point now in sifting causes why my old advisor was convicted of first-degree murder in the shooting of Herman Hermann and sentenced to the maximum penalty. True it is that while Max himself would plead neither guilty nor otherwise to the charge (which would have gone uncontested but for our protests to his court-appointed lawyer), he affirmed in court his full confession, not only of the deed but of what he called "virtual" premeditation—by which adjective, lost I fear upon the jury, he seemed to mean a prior yen to persecute unknown to him until the crime (and whereof the deed was the single proof, I vainly testified). Moreover, he asked for the Shaft as the only palliative of his conscience—of the Moishian conscience!—which, he told the court, had centuries of flunkèd pride to atone for . . .

"We Moishians," he testified, "we've had it coming, on account we've known all the time we *are* the Chosen Class!" Protests rose among the spectators, Moishians and non-Moishians alike. The Judge rapped his gavel. "Why passèder than the rest?" Max demanded, unimpressed. He touched his fingertips together and rocked his head. "On account we're the only class knows how flunked we are!" The irony was too nice for most to follow and exasperating to the others; absent-minded with impatience, I chewed the straw fans issued us against the summer heat. The effect of such testimony as this was that reactionary, even Bonifacist elements in West Campus, who approved of capital punishment and had little use for Moishians, rallied to Max's defense, arguing in effect that having condemned himself and his class, he might be let go. Their sympathy, of course, Max repudiated, and since only the most self-flagellant liberals could accept his notions of "guilty victimship" and "flunkèd passèdness," he was left without effectual supporters—almost without sympathizers—and may be said to this extent to have chosen his fate.

But it is also true, alas, that both the issue of capital punishment itself and the question of Moishiocausticide had been being hotly argued in New Tammany just prior to the Hermann killing: the former on account of the then-rising crime-rate, which some attributed to "coddling the flunks"; the latter because two other former Bonifacists had been mysteriously kidnaped and killed since the expiration of Siegfrieder College's statute of limitations for the trial of "crimes against studentdom." Chancellor Rexford himself had formerly been inclined against the ancient practice of Shafting condemned men, but since initiating his Open Book reforms he'd ceased to press for repeat of that penalty. Conservative opinion, slow to condemn the Moishiocausts themselves and skeptical of the *post-facto* law forbidding "crimes against studentdom," was quick to condemn the Moishiocausticides. The liberals—pro-Moishian and anti-Bonifacist—were deeply divided, for though they abhorred capital punishment generally and lynching in particular, they could not bear that the legal safeguards they themselves had struggled for over the terms should make it possible for Moishiocausts to escape retribution for their awful crimes. Much as they revered Max from terms gone by, they deplored his deed, and the manner of his "defense" even more; the whole matter anguished and embarrassed them; they fell out among themselves, husband and wife, teacher and pupil; in the end they stood by painfully, rather hoping Max would be acquitted, or at least not Shafted, but unable to come to his defense when he would not defend himself.

At the trial's end everyone expected a verdict of guilty and the minimum sentence, in view of the defendant's age and fame: a few terms' detention followed by parole. Before the summation Max's lawyer once again begged him to plead insanity and was of course refused. The jury retired, deliberated only a minute or two, and returned the expected verdict. Max stroked his beard, nodding assent; his lawyer, long out of patience with so uncooperative a client, clicked and clicked his ball-point pen. We looked Judgewards and were horrified to see him raise the black cowl, emblematic of capital sentence. Mildly, as if making a procedural point or recessing for lunch, he said to Max: "It is the sentence of this Court that you be taken from here to Main Detention and thence to Founder's Hill, and the life Shafted out of you. Founder have mercy on your mind."

Most were surprised; a few shocked. But who (Leonid excluded) could protest, when the defendant himself had asked for that sentence?

"Beside-the-pointcy!" Leonid shouted at me, back in our cells. "He wants Shaft like Mrs. Anastasia wants rapeness! Inside-outhood! Passitude!"

Before my own failure I would have agreed, and wept

Leonidlike with frustrate love. But I could no longer judge anyone—except myself—or hold opinions on any head, or feel strongly any emotion but a dumb acknowledgment that I'd Failed All. "I don't know what to say," I said.

"Selfish, *pfui!*" Leonid cried at Max, in the idiom learned from him. "I *take* you to Classmate X! Old friend of you; him you listen! *I* take Shaft! Exchangeness!"

Max shook his head, adding that he'd never met Leonid's stepfather.

"Don't say!" the Nikolayan bellowed, grinning hugely, and commenced to flap his arms and pound us all upon the back. Was saving, he declared, for big surprisehood or last resortity, as the case should warrant: his stepfather was no native Nikolayan (Had we thought? Ha ha on us!), but a New Tammany Moishian whose parents had transferred out of Nikolay in the bad old days before Student-Unionism. What his original name was, no one knew except the Department of Intelligence, but as best Leonid could infer, he had worked with automatic computers in their infancy, during Campus Riot II; and subsequently, when New Tammany refused to share its electroencephalic secrets with its colleagues, he had defected to Nikolay College, liquidated his former self, and designed a counter-computer to preserve studentdom's peace of mind from aggressive Informationalism.

Max's face clouded as he listened, and my skin tingled; recalling now Classmate X's curious emotion in the U.C. building at mention of my keeper's name, I realized who he must be.

"Your old friend What's-his-name!" I exclaimed to Max. "The one that helped you EAT the Amaterasus and then defected . . ."

"Chementinski?" Max frowned and plucked angrily at his beard. "*Ach,* impossible! Chementinski had no head for politics: a smart scientist, but a silly man."

"Not silly!" Leonid shouted, and plunged to his knees before the bunk where Max lay resting.

"Silly and flunkèd, Leonid," Max insisted quietly. "If he *is* your stepfather, and he sent you here to take my place, so I could defect like him—*pfui,* that proves it!"

"Untruthcry!" Leonid's protest was more distressèd than indignant. That Classmate X was indeed Max's former colleague seemed beyond dispute: no one else in East Campus had had the practical knowledge required for EASCAC's development, which Leonid knew his stepfather had directed. His later forsaking of mathematical for political science, and his formidable success in that department, was to be explained by the utter eradication of his earlier self (which might indeed have been silly and flunkèd); the successful replacement of his personal, fallible will with the Will of the Student Body, impersonal and infallible. So Leonid explained it, roaring earnestly; that one of his idols should dislike the other clearly anguished him as much as the capital sentence had, and I was surprised at the sternness with which Max refused to soften his opinion.

"What does Chementinski want me *for?*" he demanded. "He knows I've been out of Tower Hall all these years. I got no secrets any more; he knows that too. Why do you think he told you to get me instead of somebody useful, like Eblis Eierkopf?"

Tears streamed from Leonid's eyes. "Loveship, sir! He loves, like me! Like George! Never mind Eierkopf!"

Max shook his head. "It's not love." More gently then, but uncompromisingly, he declared that the principal difference between himself and Chementinski was that the latter, while professing to love studentdom, had always been more or less repelled by individual students; whereas Max, devoted as he was to individual people, had always regarded studentdom in general as more stupid, brutal, and vulgar than otherwise—or else a meaningless abstraction. The weakness of Max's position, as he readily admitted, was that, since EATing the Amaterasus, he was unable to sacrifice *anybody* to the Common Good, in which he could no longer believe; thus he was unfit for administration. "But your Chementinski, this Classmate X: he could sacrifice *everybody,* himself too!"

"Not!" Leonid objected; but I confirmed Max's opinion with Classmate X's own statement to that effect, made to me in the U.C. building.

"How else could he sacrifice you?" Max demanded. "A son he should kill his own self for!"

"Good of the Union! My idea! Make-up test, for past!"

Max put a hand on Leonid's shoulder and once more shook his head. Chementinski, he said sorrowfully, had ever been a most unstable fellow, driven by a succession of ideals in which he'd passionately wished to believe, and never satisfied with the genuineness of his commitment. His whole attitude during the EAT-project, Max remembered, had been a fierce self-justification: It *was* EAT or be EATen, wasn't it? Better a few thousand Amaterasus in ten minutes than another two years of riot! It *was* for the sake of peace, freedom, and culture, wasn't it? Not to mention pure science, and the deterrent against future campus riots . . . The effect of this constant questioning was that he'd talked himself out of his beliefs, come to regret his contribution to WESCAC (as had Max, for other reasons), and decided that only by arming both schools of thought with ultimate weaponry could peace of mind now be preserved. Hence his defection.

"What happened since, I don't know," Max concluded. "But he knew I didn't believe what he did, and it always upset him when I thought he was wrong. If Chementinski thinks we got to EAT the Amaterasus once, he can't stand it anybody smart should disagree; if he defects to East Campus, we *all* got to defect, so he shouldn't wonder was it flunked or passed. That's why he wants me there, Leonid; he can't convince himself he did right."

"Unselfnessness!" Leonid bawled. "He's most unvainestest there is!" He glared imploringly at me. "Talk once, George!"

"I think Max is right," I said. I told him then what I'd learned from Classmate X himself: that he had deliberately led his stepson to believe that he was not forgiven for the zoo-escapade, and could redeem himself in his stepfather's eyes only by expending himself to capture Max. I expected angry denials—would scarce have dared the information had we not been in separate cells, and was prepared, in self-defense, to force his agreement, if necessary, by reminding him that it would be vain to claim the inspiration himself. But Leonid came to the bars, cheeks wet, and asked merely: "Is it true, Goat-Boy? He didn't hate? Ever since?"

"I swear it. He only pretended. He knew you'd do anything to please him . . ."

"His own son!" Max snorted. "To prove his selflessness! *Ach,* that Chementinski!"

But Leonid cried, "Passèdhoodness!" and, indifferent to his gulling, danced a wild step about the cell, so relieved was he that his stepfather had not been angry with him after all. It was some time before Max could declare his conviction that any man who sacrificed his own son thus calculatingly, for whatever cause, was incapable not only of anger but of any emotion whatever, especially love. I might have agreed, with some reservations (for while Classmate X had revealed himself to me as far from cold-blooded with regard to his step-son, the deliberate sacrifice of him in the name of Selflessness seemed to me therefore all the more monstrously vain)—but Leonid was seized at this point with a new violent emotion.

"I love!" he shouted tearfully. "Full of selfity, me!" His problem, from what I could make of his exclamations, was that despite his best efforts he was yet a million *versts* from the impersonality he aspired to, and of which Classmate X was the faultless exemplar. He loved his stepfather, Max, Anastasia, me—he loved everyone he'd ever met, except a few whom he hated, and thus despaired of ever earning Classmate X's love—which of course it was but further selfishness for him to crave!

"Hopelesshood!" From the pocket of his prison-trousers he suddenly snatched a little bottle, not unlike the container of disappeared ink bestowed on me by Sakhyan's colleagues. But this was full of a realer fluid, some of which he swallowed and began at once to strangle triumphantly upon.

"Hooray! Eradicationness! Goodbye me!"

Max made feeble haste to stay him as soon as we realized what he was doing, but Leonid worked his skill upon the doorlock and deftly slipped out into the aisle, where once again he tipped the bottle to his lips. His face purpled.

"No more me!" he croaked. "Tell Mrs. Anastasia I love!" Max and other prisoners shouted for a guard; as was some-times the case, none was about. Leonid fell; yet even curling on the floor he made to drink again that deadly draught, to insure his end.

"Verboten!" Max pleaded, hopping like a cagèd dwarf. "Stop him once, George, he shouldn't swallow!"

Leonid, supine, had decided to wave one arm and sing as he expired. *"Releasedom! Freehood! Death to Selfity!"* He put the bottle to his mouth.

Distressed as I was to see him perish, I would I fear have only watched, and that not merely because I was locked in. But something in his words, more than the emergency itself, got through the torpor I had dwelt in since my noosing. My head cleared miraculously; I saw not just Leonid's plight but his *error*—and more! In no time at all I was beside him in the aisle; had seized the bottle and was forcing air into his mouth—for he had ceased to breathe. Then, thinking better, I released Max for that work and went to fetch help, running four-footed for speed and letting myself without hesitation through half a dozen barred doors on the way. No guards were on duty; so lax was their warden's discipline, and so many the obstacles to our freedom, they often loitered in the exercise-yard or gathered in the cells of wanton lady girls. The first official I encountered was Stoker himself, and that not until I'd climbed to the highest tier of cells, at ground-level: those reserved theoretically for apathetic *C*-students and professors too open-minded to have opinions. At sight of me Stoker smiled, stepped aside, and indicated with his arm the final gate, which opened into the Visitation Room and thence to the offices and freedom, as if inviting me to continue on my way.

"It's you I was looking for," I said.

"How droll. I was just coming for *you*. You have visitors."

I explained the emergency. Amused, Stoker sniffed the deadly bottle, now only half full, and returned it to me.

"Ink eradicator," he scoffed. "How'd you ever get past all those locks, George?"

I dashed impatiently to the barred door of the Visitation Room, resolved to find a doctor myself if Stoker would not send one. Inside I saw my mother, accompanied as always by Anastasia. But whether because this last lock was different from the others or because Stoker's question made me realize that I had no idea how I'd got where I was, I found myself unable to pass through.

"Help me, man!" I demanded. "Were those other doors unlocked?"

Stoker winked and replied lightly, "No door's locked if you've got the key." He found the correct one on his ring. "Stop fidgeting: my wife knows what to do until the doctor comes."

I had forgot My Ladyship was a nurse. Gravely she greeted me, coolly Stoker, who reported the news and solicited her aid in a manner so full of *dears* and *pleases* that I thought he mocked her. But her reply was frosty and overbearing—"Don't just stand there while the fool dies; get him up here!"—and Stoker hastened so to oblige her, I could only conclude that their relations really had changed character. She took charge of the situation, ordering Stoker to bring Leonid to the prison infirmary while she prepared an emetic and summoned a physician. I was told to stay with "Mother" (as Anastasia still called Lady Creamhair, out of habit) and reluctantly consented: someone had to be with her, her mind had failed so, and Anastasia was grown very cross indeed when opposed, especially by a male. Besides which, I was the only one of us not necessary to Leonid's rescue—a sore consideration, as I had got him into his bind and felt on the verge now of understanding how he might be set free of it. Off went the pair of them on their errands, Anastasia scolding her husband out of earshot. The barred partitions of the Visitation Room were left open; I might have exited from Main Detention even without that gift of Leonid's which momentarily I'd seemed to possess, or Bray's proffered amnesty. But though my new clarity persisted, like a light in an empty room where something is about to appear, and my intellectual coma happily showed no signs of returning, I did not leave, not just then, but sighed and turned to Mother, whom I knew I would find watching me with reverent joy. Cross-leggèd on the floor, black-shawled and -dressed, the New Syllabus on her lap as always, she flapped at me her thrice-weekly peanut-butter sandwich and crooned, "Come, Billy! Come, love! Come!"

Anxious as I was for my Nikolayan cellmate, I laid my head in her lap, pretended to hunger for the ritual food, and chewed the pages of antique wisdom she tore out for me, though they tasted sourly of much thumbing.

"Now then, love, let me see . . ." She adjusted her spectacles, brightly licked her forefingertip, and opened the book to a dogeared page. "People ought to use bookmarks!" she fussed. "And there's a verse marked, too. People *shouldn't* mark in library-books." Her tone softened. "Oh, but look what it is, Billikins: I'm *so* proud of the things you write!"

Such was her gentle madness, she thought me at once Billy Bocksfuss in the hemlock-grove, the baby GILES she'd Bellied—and, alas, the long-Commencèd Enos Enoch.

"Passèd are the flunked," she read, very formally. "My, but that's a nice thought. Don't you think?"

I didn't answer, not alone because my tongue was peanut-buttered, but because those dark and famous words from the Seminar-on-the-Hill brought me upright. As lightning might a man bewildered, they showed me in one flash the source and nature of my fall, the way to the Way, and, so I imagined, the far gold flicker of Commencement Gate.

2.

I sprang from Mother's lap. "Passèd *are* the flunked, Mom!"

Like an old Enochist at the end of a petition, she touched her temples, closed her eyes, and murmured, "A-plus, dear Founder!"

Commencèd woman; womb that bore me! No matter, how much she grasped of her own wisdom: Truth's vessel needn't understand its contents. When I said—to myself, really—"Bray's not the enemy; WESCAC is!" she replied, "Your passèd father, Gilesey; and He loves me yet," as if I'd praised instead of blamed that root and fruit of Differentiation. Yet when I exclaimed, "They were all passed, every one, and didn't know it—but I failed them!" she repeated, *"Passèd are the flunked. A-plus!"* and one more scale fell from my eyes. I yearned to be alone, to study the paradox of my new Answer; then to begone, that I might set right my false first Tutoring. Frustrate, I hugged her whom I could not leave, and she bade me comfortably: "Never mind Pass and Fail. Hug your mother."

Commencèd dame! I laughed and groaned at once. There in a word was the Way: Embrace! What I had bid my Tutees shuck—false lines in their pictures of themselves, which Bray in his wisdom had Certified—I saw now to be unshuckable: nay, unreal, because falsely distinguished from their contraries. *Failure is passage:* Stoker had said wiselier than he knew that dire March morning; had spoken truth, and thus had lured me to my error—that distinction of Passage and Failure from which depended all my subsequent mistakes. Even him I'd failed, then, by his own dark lights, inasmuch as the receipt for flunkage I'd laid on him, opposite of my other counsels, was perforce the one true Passage-Way. Embrace!

When at last My Ladyship and Stoker returned, he skulking long-faced as she nagged, I hurried to embrace them both at once. Stoker grunted; Anastasia was as unbending as a herdsman's crook. When I bussed at her she turned her cheek; I let go her husband and kissed her full in the mouth, pricked with desire for the first time since my failure. She

605

struck my face—as I rather expected she might in her recent character—and I cuffed her in return such an instant smiling square one, to her whole surprise, that she whooped and lost all poise: wet her uniform, and went slack when I hugged her soft again.

"Really, old man," Stoker complained. "My wife, you know. What's come over you?"

Intoned my mother: *"A*-plus!"

"I've been wrong about everything!" I declared happily. "Never mind! Is Leonid all right?" Before anyone could answer I kissed whimpering Anastasia again—she was quite glasseyed now and limp—and might even have mounted her, so full I was of yen and new plans for her passage. But her menses were on her, my buckly nose reported, and other business pressed, so I forwent lust for exposition. Leonid's drink, Stoker said, was a multipurpose eradicator used by spies in the falsification of credentials and the elimination of either their enemies or themselves, as the case should warrant. It had been pumped out of him in time, and except for a headache, and the delusion that Anastasia had kissed him back from death, he was quite recovered.

"Some nerve!" Stoker said. "I had to talk her into doing that mouth-to-mouth business, and then he says a thing like that."

Anastasia, dumb, now sat in her pissèd dress beside my mother. I seized and kissed her hand, whereat she wept for very fuddlement.

"Leonid's right about you!" I told her warmly. "You were passèd before I Tutored you. You should love him!" She shook her head. "You should love everybody, even more than before! Never mind what they're after! Forget what I said last time!"

She shut her eyes and wailed.

"Open your legs again, like the old days!" I commanded her. "Let the whole student body in! I thought I saw through you before, but I've got to start from scratch!"

Stoker protested that I'd have to scratch someone else's wedded roommate, not his—unless of course Anastasia *wanted* to oblige me, in which case he must regretfully defer to her wishes.

"Stop that passèd talk!" I cried, and laughed and struck his arm. "That bad advice I gave you was the best on campus! Passage *is* failure, just as you told me—but *Passèd are the flunked,* too! Thinking they're different is what flunked me!" He was far from convinced, but I would say no more on the matter then. I asked whether Bray's offer to pardon me still stood.

"I should say *not,*" Stoker answered. There had been, it seemed, two conditions attached to my release, one presumably impossible for me, the other repugnant to Stoker: all the signatures would need to be deleted from my ID-card, including those in indelible ink, and Anastasia would have not only to submit to the "Grand Tutor" (I used the imaginary quotation-marks uncynically now) but to bear a child by him. " 'A real little human kindergartener,' he said he wanted," Stoker said angrily. "I should've horsewhipped him!"

"You *should* have!" I cried joyfully. "And you would have, before I misled you. But listen—" I knelt and embraced My Ladyship once more, despite her wails and wet. "I was as wrong about Bray as I was about you. There *is* something special about him . . . In any case you must let him service you, no matter what his terms are—and everybody else, too! Take on the whole University!"

She may not have heard me above her bawling. Mother clapped her hands and cried "*A*-plus!" after each of my injunctions, rocking in a rhythm. Stoker fussed.

"Don't act so passèd!" I exhorted him. "Hit me, if you want to! Pimp for your wife! Set dogs on Mother!"

"*A*-plus!" that lady said, whom I would not for the campus have seen harmed.

"You're stir-crazy," Stoker grumbled, nonetheless plainly unsettled. "You talk as if True and False were different Answers."

"And they're not!" I cried. "That's the Answer! My whole mistake was to think they were different—so that's what *you've* got to think, if you really want to flunk!"

We spoke no more then, because Stoker, to my great satisfaction, lost his temper and collared me cellwards. "Pass All Fail All!" I cried to the tiers of flunks. "It's the same thing!"

Stoker took a billy from a passing guard and clubbed me dumb.

As if, in that timeless cave, time's lost track had doubled on itself, I woke again to the voices of Max and Leonid arguing:

"Would-*not*ship, Classmate, sir!"

"Na, my boy, you're mistaken . . ."

"But you think was wrong, that suicideness?"

"That's what George thought, Leonid. Why else should he stop you? And I agree: to kill yourself it's selfish."

"Flunkhoodship, then! I be a big selfish! I defection! Big spy for Informationalists, Ira Hector pays me! And bribe Lucky Rexford you don't get Shaft!"

"You see, my friend? Still being unselfish! And if I escaped I'd still be playing the Moishian martyr, like Georgie said."

"So bah!" Leonid cried. "So I be vain my own self; you defect, I get Shaft, my name in all Nikolayan historybooks! Hooray me!"

"By you it wouldn't be vanity, never mind how you say. By me it would, whether I take the Shaft or don't. I got Moishian motives either way. *Ach*, I hate this!"

"Me too."

I rubbed my head and sat up. "Never mind motives."

As before, they welcomed me back to the waking campus.

Max especially was devoted thereafter, and respectful in a way I found unsettling as much as gratifying: as if, now I no longer thought myself Grand Tutor, he was finally able to imagine I was. My other Tutees, those I'd seen and heard of who had inclined to Bray and doubted me, appeared to have reversed their attitudes in view of the flunkèd state I'd led them to, or led them to see, and doubted now the one who'd called them passed. Their problem, as some saw and others didn't, was complex: if Bray's Certifications were false, how reconcile his Certifying me for having declared them so? And if I was true, how assimilate my self-flunkage and late defense of Bray? Only Max was untroubled by the conundrum: "All the better it don't make sense," he would say to Leonid, My chill Ladyship, or Peter Greene, who sometimes now visited. "So it's a mystery, you shouldn't analyze."

He was become my best apologist, if not my best Tutee. For though Anastasia wept and protested my new counsel, especially regarding her connection with Bray, it was not long before Stoker told me (with a wink, as in former times) that the two conditions of my release might soon be reduced to one: he'd observed his wife against the bars on another level, tearfully urging the foul-mouthed imates to have at her, and while they'd been too awed and suspicious to go to it, there could be no doubt but her attitude had changed. Whereas

Max, who explained me better than I could myself, had trouble practicing the new preachment he so well glossed. Stoker I was pleased to see become once more a kind of Dunce's advocate; he came down frequently now to bait us and found in Max a willing fish, who however was by no means easy to land.

"They're *both* fakes," Stoker would declare of Bray and me.

"Falseness!" Leonid would reply. "WESCAC didn't EAT, yes?"

"They fooled it with masks."

"Masks can't fool it," Max would then point out, and review the possible explanations of my passage through the Belly with Bray: "It might be Georgie was spared because Bray was with him, or vice-versa. It might be they're both Grand Tutors, different kinds. Or it might be they both *were* EATen—but only crazy, not to death. Or it might be the Grand Tutor wasn't EATen and the other was, so one's crazy and the other not . . ."

"Or they're both fakes and WESCAC's on the fritz," Stoker taunted. "Or it changed its own mind about the Spielman Proviso and doesn't EAT anybody these days. Maybe it's in love with EASCAC and lost its appetite."

But Max would cheerfully agree instead of arguing, and point out moreover that either Harold Bray or the defector Chementinski might in some wise have altered WESCAC's AIM, recently or many terms ago, if the computer hadn't "noctically" reprogrammed itself. Nor could one query WESCAC on the matter, as it might have grown quite capable of lying to or misleading an interrogator.

"Which all proves," he would conclude, "you take or leave on faith a Grand Tutor, don't ask it should be on His ID-card who He is. Even if He says His own self He's a fake, and people call Him crazy, He might be the real thing, you got to decide. I believe in George."

Stoker feigned disgust. "Then you must believe he's *not* the Grand Tutor and Bray is, since that's what George says himself."

Undismayed, Max explained what I'd not fully realized I felt until I heard him: first, that all I claimed for Bray was that he wasn't simply flunked, as I'd previously believed: there was something extraordinary, out of the merely human, about him—as about myself, in both my parentage and my kidship. Second, that my admitted failure applied only to my efforts at Tutoring before I myself had passed the Finals and thus had no bearing on my present authenticity. If indeed those efforts were failures, which had successfully revealed to my Tutees such flunkèd aspects of themselves . . .

"Me it sure did!" Leonid cried dolefully. "Such a selfiness I never thought! But I don't care!"

"Nuts," said Stoker. "A man that tells me I should pimp for my wife is a Grand Tutor? And tells her to spread her legs for the whole campus?"

Max nodded, unimpressed. "You he tells that, you should do like the Dean o' Flunks, and hope to pass on account you show others what is it to be flunked. Only you'll flunk on account you lead them to think *Pass* and *Fail* aren't two sides the same page. Which they are. So dear Anastasia, that she has a little touch nymphomaniac, she's got to express it instead of suppress, she should Commence. Not so, George?"

And I would merely nod, for though I followed these explications with care and often saw flaws in them (which I couldn't always have articulated), I did not choose to defend or explain myself to Stoker—or to anyone else except myself. My whole concern was to feel a way through the contradictions of my new Answer, in order to apply it to the several problems of my Tutees when I should leave Main Detention. Therefore I gravely listened, but spoke only now and then to clarify a point or correct a misunderstanding. When for example Stoker asked why I didn't simply walk out of his prison, since I seemed able to open any door, Max's reply was that I wouldn't work wonders at the tempting of the Dean o' Flunks.

"That's not *quite* so," I corrected him, "as Stoker knows. If it were, he could control me absolutely by tempting me to do the right thing." The fact was, I said, I hadn't the least idea how I'd opened those doors, though I felt obliged to Leonid for the ability. All I knew was that for me, just then, they'd been unlocked, as for Leonid all locks ever seemed to be, and that once I wondered how the thing was done, I couldn't do it. It was Anastasia who would set me free, I said . . . and Classmate X.

"What's this?" Max exclaimed. "Chementinski sets you loose?"

Leonid happily squeezed the breath from me, thinking I planned to defect, then frowned and wondered if such "selfishness" (his current interpretation of the move, and a term of approval by his recentest transvaluation) weren't flunkèdly unselfish: "Like I, I can't get rid of selfish, I'm wear it like a uniform: hooray Me! Spy for New Tammany or take Shaft for Max sir, whichever is selfestest."

I praised his resolve, which like the contradiction of his suicide-attempt had lit the way for my late insight into the secret of the University. But he must not worry, I added, whether my program or his own might lead to "failure": as the author of *Taliped Decanus* understood, there *is* only failure on this campus—but as Enos Enoch and the original Sakhyan knew further, Failure is Passage.

In any case, I wasn't thinking of defection. I didn't suppose I *could* defect, actually, since I was only a kind of visitor in New Tammany in the first place. What I was thinking of I demonstrated some time later, when Stoker came down with my stick, my purse, Peter Greene, and pieces of news.

"It won't do you any good," he said, "but I'm supposed to give you your things and turn you loose if you clear your ID-card. Which of course you can't."

I took my possessions joyfully. The other condition, then, had been met?

"It's been arranged," Stoker said dryly. "My wife will meet Bray in the Belfry at eleven o'clock tonight."

Max groaned, but nodded affirmation. "Failure is Passage. A-plus!"

Tears stood in Leonid's eyes. "Commencedomship!" He put his arm around me and declared that while he could not but adore, with each breath he drew, the woman who'd inspired him from the grave, he would no longer dream that she might requite him, but rather that she and I would one day wed. "Never mind you!" he roared at Stoker, whose grin suggested to me that he himself might have arranged My Ladyship's engagement. Anastasia, said Leonid, deserved no less a husband than the very GILES, whom in turn no mate would serve but the passèdest.

I listened uncomfortably. "The fact is, Leonid—"

"You mean the flunkèdest," Peter Greene interrupted. "Durnedest floozy in the whole flunking College. Not that *I* care!"

The change in Peter Greene's manner, which had begun with his attack on Anastasia and grown during his detention, was now in full flower. So far from admiring My Ladyship for not pressing the charge of rape, he took her admissions as proof of her depravity, and had decided that all women were trollops at heart, and he himself an "All-U failure, know-thyselfwise." Thus persuaded, he'd advised his wife's attorneys of his intention to forsake her permanently, and invited her to divorce him on the grounds of adultery if she preferred not to wait the required two semesters; he supplied her with full particulars not only of his rape of Anastasia but also of his current activities, sexual and otherwise, and that catalogue, perhaps, had fetched her back into the Infirmary. Though he'd not after all defected to the Nikolayans, he was become a Student-Unionist "fellow scholar" and something of a Beist as well. He smoked hempen cigarettes, went barefoot and unbarbered, carried a guitar on which with rude skill he played songs of lower-form protest, and said of The Living Sakhyan: "Man, he's got the gosh-durn *most*, what I mean *wise*wise." He had even taken a Frumentian lady roommate, Stoker's secretary Georgina, whom he claimed to admire for her straightforwardness: she enjoyed fornication for its own flunkèd sake, he said, but loathed him personally, as he loathed himself, and slept with him mainly to relish the spectacle of his impotence. For where in the past he had been of limp manhood with Miss Sally Ann (so much so that he now feared their children were of extramarital paternity), and potent only with "the likes of O.B.G.'s daughter," currently he found himself prone to failure with the wanton Georgina, but tumesced at the mere idea of a proper faithful wife, such as once he'd fondly thought was his.

"She weren't nothing but a floozy, though," he would declare, "like Stacey Stoker and all the rest. Onliest decent gal I ever knew was old O.B.G.'s daughter—which I went and drug her in the muck anyhow, back in the old days. She'd of been pure as snow, that gal, if I hadn't made a black whore of her."

Whether Georgina was G. Herrold's daughter, and G. Herrold and "Old Black George" were the same person, was still unclear, as was the extent to which the woman's present motives were actual admissions of hers or Greene's own conjecture. For though he declared himself pleased "to of had his eyes opened," as he put it, to the flunkèdness of New Tammany, the female sex, and his own sorry past, he was an unhappy man, become sullen and surly; and his grudgy speech was laced with slang so pied and shifting, I shook my head as much at his words as at what I gathered of their sense. Withal, though, he seemed more changed in mood than substance: his soap- and shoelessness, beard and guitar, said Billy-of-the-Hills as much as Beist; and the disenchantment was clearly but a change of spells. His acne, which he had hoped to cure with dirt, was purulent as ever; hemp-smoke but guaranteed what had used to visit him unsought. Bray he called now an outright fraud for having passed him as a "kindergartener"; me he credited with "true-blue Beistic vision" for having shown him his former blindness. Leonid he regarded, with glum goodwill, as half mistaken, eye-to-eye-with-himselfwise: right about New Tammany's decadence, wrong about Nikolay's superiority; right about My Ladyship's unchastity, wrong about her passèdness, and so forth.

"Balonicy!" scoffed Leonid. "She's passèd Graduate! If I believed in!" He shook his fist then at our warden, who was idly prodding Croaker with my stick through the bars of an adjacent cell, where the huge Frumentian lay bloat and helpless from overeating. "You turning flunked again, like before! Let go Mrs. Anastasia, should marry George! I don't mind!"

Stoker replied, with a measure of his former energy, that Leonid had never had a mind to mind with, or he'd have walked out of prison long since instead of trying to get himself Shafted in Max's place. As to divorcing his flunkèd wife—

"Not flunkèd!" Leonid shouted. "Is Passessness!"

"Be durn if she is!" Greene shouted back.

"Who cares?" Max cried. "Fail is pass, altogether!"

Croaker set up a clamor next door, prompted either by the argument or by sight of my stick, which he snatched from Stoker's hand and examined with a deal of lick and jabber. I let them all shout on, attending their debate but not joining it, and measured their several stances against the Answer until I'd found what I sought and done what I desired. From the bottom of my purse—under Sakhyan's phial, the shophar, my damaged watch, the pocket-torch, and my partly chewed Assignment—I fished forth my ID-card, wrongly signed, and from my jail-coat the bottle of Classmate X's all-round eradicator, snatched from Leonid in the nick of time. A few drops were undrunk; I poured them on the card.

"Argue while you can," Stoker said to Greene and Leonid, as if casually. "Two halfwits make a whole wit. Pity we can't Shaft the lot of you tomorrow, instead of just Max."

Leonid blanched; Greene also. Max clutched his beard and sat down quickly on a bunk. Only Croaker continued to gibber, in my direction, as if having seen the stick he recollected who I was.

"Did you say *tomorrow?*" Greene asked.

Stoker grinned. "Four-thirty in the afternoon." The appeal had been rejected, he announced, on the ground that Max, though refusing to plead, had affirmed his confession of the crime. The only recourse left was petitioning the Chancellor to commute the sentence to permanent detention; unless such petition was made (by the prisoner himself) and granted— against all odds, considering Rexford's late sentiments—Max would be executed at next day's dusk. "Makes a pretty light as the sun goes down," Stoker said. "Especially an old dry Moishian."

"Pig dog monkey!" Leonid shouted. Stoker chided him for using such language in the presence of other animals: a goat, an ape, and three jackasses. This taunt so got to the Nikolayan that he was seized by one of his fits and had to be bunked. When he had ceased to flail I inspected my card and said to Stoker: "Open the door."

He cheerfully replied, "Go flunk yourself."

"I intend to," I assured him, "as soon as I'm free. Here's the card."

The remarkable liquid had caused to vanish entirely every name on the card except the *George* I'd penned in Ira Hector's ink, and even that had been eradicated to the point where none but myself could mark its traces.

"I'll thank your stepfather for his help when I see him," I promised Leonid. "I'm going to complete my Assignment now."

Overjoyed for my sake, Leonid sprang from his bunk, threw open the cell-door, kissed Max, shook both hands with Peter Greene, snarled at Stoker (who had no keys with him), and opened his arms to welcome me into the aisle. "Love Mrs. Anastasia!" he roared to me. "Defect her to Nikolay College, have lots *rebyata!* Peace to whole Universtity!"

But I insisted that Stoker fetch keys and release me, to make the thing official. In the meanwhile I bade Leonid come in and relock the door, and Peter Greene linger, as I had things to say to them.

"Don't matter none," Greene said, and even joined us in the cell. "Whole durn campus is a jail, far's I'm concerned."

So it was, Max agreed, if one thought it so; but he declared his joyful suspicion that just as freedom might be detention to the flunkèd of mind, so to the passèd might detention be true freedom—the more so since failure, understood rightly, was passage.

"You want to stay there and rot, that's your business," Stoker said, and went away.

"Bring the key yourself!" I called after him. "I have advice for you, too."

His answer-fart rather heartened than dismayed me, as proof of his ripeness for new counsel. When Max, concerned for Greene's and my sake, urged me to employ Leonid's secret, or let Leonid himself usher me through the bars, I expressed perfect confidence in Stoker's return, and saw no need to add that I had none of my ability to repeat the trick, or in the mercy of the guards, who were permitted to shoot escaping prisoners.

"I hate cops," Greene muttered, and, thumbing his guitar, began to sing a tune he called *Greene's Blues:*

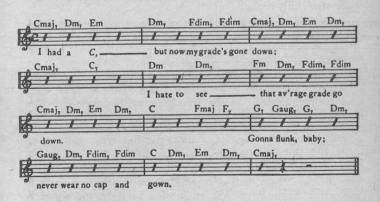

Self-pitying as were the sentiments, and wrong-headed, the melody was affecting. I embraced and bade farewell to Max.

"What I told you before was all wrong," I said.

He nodded gently. "You're telling me?" By which he meant no sarcasm, but an affirmation of what we both now understood. He had been a love-lover, hating hate, and I'd thought him flunked for being not free of that latter passion after all, and vain in his choice to suffer.

"Don't worry you made a mistake your first time Tutoring," Max said. "A beginner is bound to." And holding his testicles he vowed thenceforward to eschew the delusion that Love and Hate were separable; he would affirm them both; he'd be a love/hate lover—more accurately, a love/hate lover/hater—if he could.

"Then you mustn't regret killing Herman Hermann," I advised him.

"Who regrets?"

What I had wrongly flunked him for—that secret yen to be for once the aggressor, the persecutor—I now exhorted him to acknowledge, to embrace, even to assert. Greene and Leonid frowned their doubts, but Max agreed.

"Because what's the difference, pass and fail?" he asked rhetorically. "A trick of the mind, like it says in *Sakhyan*."

"Pass you, Max!" I exclaimed, stirred to the heart. "You know what I mean."

"*Pfui* on categories!" cried my keeper. "Not only I don't regret killing the Moishiocaustnik: I wish I'd shot him myself!"

Peter Greene and Leonid had resumed their favorite quarrel, about My Ladyship, but at this remark of Max's Leonid leaped to us.

"What's this words, sir! You didn't shot?"

"Not my own self," Max admitted.

I too was astonished. At our insistence he confessed what had really happened in the woods near Founder's Hill that night—though he and I agreed that such distinctions as Guilt and Innocence, Truth and Falsehood, were as flunking as the distinction between Passage and Failure. The point-faced guard, he declared, upon overtaking him on the road, had steered and throttled his motorcycle with the plain intent of running him down, and drawn his pistol as well, no doubt to guarantee the murder. But attempting to steer and shoot at the same time, in the dark, he'd lost control of the vehicle and crashed into the ditch.

"So I go look is he hurt," Max said, "and there's the pistol in the mud, and the Bonifacist he's got his boot caught under the sidecar, he can't get loose. So I pick up the gun, it shouldn't get rusty—he shouldn't shoot me either!—and I say to him, Tell me where's Georgie, did Maurice Stoker flunk him yet?" He smiled at me. "Such a dummy I was, about pass and fail!"

He had guessed, Max went on, that Stoker's aide was a former Bonifacist, by his manner and speech, and had surmised further that he must have been a man of some flunkèd consequence to choose exile and disguise at the Riot's end, when so many who surrendered were prosperous again soon after. But he didn't imagine the guard's identity even when he said, in Siegfrieder accents, "Shoot straight, old man; you don't kill professor-generals every night." *Pfui* on kill, Max had replied; that was not his line, whatever his inclinations.

"So I get him loose and tell him go home, he should drop dead without my help. This makes him angry; he says he won't be patronized by a flunkèd old Moishian, that he wouldn't have used to light a cigarette with back in his extermination-campuses: I should shoot him or he'll set fire my beard. Then he walks at me with his cigarette-lighter, I can see his face by it, and I realize he's Herman Hermann the Moishiocaustnik!" Whereupon, instead of shooting, Max had been smitten with despair, not alone because of the Bonifacist slaughter, but for the fate of studentdom in a university where Grand Tutors falter, and the flunkèd thrive. Assuming that the last slim hope of the campus had been traduced by Stoker's blandishments, and remembering the countless Amaterasus who'd not have been EATen had he himself stayed behind to die in Siegfrieder College with Chaim Schultz and the rest, Max could imagine no fitter end than to perish, however belatedly, at the same grim hand that had sent the Chosen Class to Commencement Gate.

Two paces from him Hermann had halted, put his hands on his hips, and said, "Shoot, Moishian!" But Max with a shrug had returned the pistol, butt-foremost, and replied, "Shoot your own self."

"What I meant," he told us now, "*he* should kill *me*, he wants a killing. It's a Moishian way of talking . . ."

Peter Greene nodded admiringly. "You Moishians are the most, what I mean *in*wise. Moishians and darkies, y'know?"

But either this final charity from Max had driven Hermann mad, or his Siegfrieder training made it impossible for him to flout a direct order from any source. He'd muttered, "*Ja wohl*," clicked his boot-heels, and shot himself accurately through the head.

"Magnificence!" Leonid cried, and did a *hopak*. "George

tells this Rexford, you don't get Shaft!" He hugged Max carefully. "Stupidly, sir, you didn't say before!"

Max shook his head. When the shock had passed, he said, he'd seen his guilt. Even if he'd not directly ordered Hermann's suicide, he was the cause of it; moreover, so far from feeling remorse, he found himself trembling with satisfaction over the dead Moishiocaust. Having dragged the body into the woods, he would even have burned it, to complete his revenge, but Hermann's lighter had got soaked in blood and refused to catch. He'd gone then to the roadside and brooded until Croaker and I overtook him next day, by which time he'd come round to seeing he was flunked, and choosing to suffer for the crime of murder.

He smiled. "Then Georgie told me what he told me, up in the Visitation Room, and I wouldn't listen, I didn't believe him since the Powerhouse, also since Bray." Nevertheless, my criticism of his motives had taken root in his mind and grown, further nourished by debate with Leonid, until he'd despaired of choosing either death or liberty for the right reason.

"Ah, Max!" I said warmly. "You're passed already, Shaft or no Shaft! You see that now, don't you?"

He did. "So it's vanity I take the Shaft or I don't: so flunk me! What matters is the right choice, not the right reason. *Pfui* on Entelechus."

"*Pfui* on the right choice, too," I said, and he saw my point at once, so clearly that his application of it to Leonid left me little to add:

"You should stay or go, which you please," Max told him; "go back to Chementinski or transfer to New Tammany, and don't worry what's selfish what's not. Assert your self! Embrace! You got to suppress something, suppress unselfishness."

Leonid objected that he had in his late frustration tried just that course, but felt no passèder than before.

"Forget Passèder!" Max advised.

Leonid scratched his beard, but I affirmed Max's counsel enthusiastically. Their recent bind I compared to the cell in which the Nikolayans had once detained him, pointing out that in this case too the door was open; he need but shut his eye to Reason and stride forth. Hadn't he given me the Pass-key himself?

"It mysteries me, that talk!" he said. "But never mind! You I open door for; go make wife of Mrs. Anastasia!"

I replied that he must put by self-effacement and vie for her himself, without scruple or restraint; certainly without deference to me. For not only was marriage incompatible with Grand Tutorhood, in my opinion; passionate love was too, adulterous or not, by reason of its exclusiveness. If I had allowed myself any such emotion in the past (especially on discovering that My Ladyship was not my sister), I was to that extent flunked; if I should in the future, it would be purely because failure is passage. In any case, let all try for her who would, and the best man win; I was too sensible now of my faults to join the contest.

"By George!" Leonid cried—a kind of pensive shout. "My head spin! I'm such a dumb, I have to think about!"

No less did I—about my last words in particular, whose truth I realized only as I spoke them. Desire I understood, and Camaraderie; to Friendship, Respect, and Loyalty I was no stranger, either in the goat-pens or on Great Mall; certainly not to buckly Rut. I had "loved" Hedda and Redfearn's Tom, Lady Creamhair, Max my keeper, dead G. Herrold; I "loved" studentdom and Truth, and Anastasia's dear escutcheon. But what did I know of Love between human men and women, that emotion held to include and yet transcend these others? My connection with Anastasia—the sidecar-bite, our Memorial Service, my former jealousy on Bray's account, and the rest—seemed merely odd to me now: at best an intimation of what that much-sung *Love* might be, and a flunking measure of my distance from it. What she "saw in me," had ever seen, I could not see, since failure had opened my eyes. *Anastasia:* the name, like the lady girl, went stranger and more dark as I considered it. What thing was Anastasia? The mystery's nub, it seemed to me now, was a phenomenon I'd taken for granted before my fall, but which since baffled, even appalled me: I mean her continuing high regard for me, however indiscriminate and quirked. Why did she heed my flunkèd counsels? Why had she mated with Harold Bray, or pledged to—on my account but against my wish—back when she'd thought him the true Grand Tutor and but pitied me? Why had she pledged to now again, to free me, and declared belief in me against my own denial? I couldn't fathom her at all, not at all. And under my assertion, however sincere, that a Grand Tutor (not that I *was*

one) oughtn't to permit himself the luxuries either of loving
or of being loved, in the passion-way, there lay a dark suspicion that I was incapable of both.

"She needs a proper human man, not a goat-boy," I said to
Max, who acknowledged the possibility with a shrug of his
hand.

Peter Greene said "Haw," and popped a pimple. Since the
night of the rape his aversion to mirrors had changed into
gloomy fascination. Throughout his detainment he had used
to stare at his reflection in anything shiny, growling oaths and
making horrid faces. Now he had managed to get my stick
from Croaker, and aided by the mirror near its tip was bursting pustules on his cheek, cursing himself with every pinch.
"Y'all don't see through her the way I do. (There, you ugly
bastard!) Didn't she admit she brought it on her own self, out
in the alley? A flunker like me!"

He would have embarked then on his usual lament: that
all his life he'd been a gosh-durn baby, knowledge-
of-the-campuswise; that he'd thought himself a fine fellow,
even a Graduate, his marriage a success, his self-education
and career things to be proud of, his alma mater the gem of
the University, Anastasia the flower and pattern of maiden
girlship—until I and Dr. Sear had opened his eye to the
truth. But as he began that drear recital, Max made inquiry
of me with a glance, as if to ask "Him too?" I nodded, and
broke into Greene's complaint.

"Look here . . . Pete," I said, "you're *okay*."

"You durn tootin'," he grumbled, thinking I'd affirmed his
condemnation-in-progress of New Tammany's Quiet-Riot
policies. "Lawless academical adventurism, is what it is."

"I mean *you*," I persisted. "I was wrong before. You were
okay, until you took my advice."

"And what the heck altogether?" Max said smiling. "Like
you used to say, it doesn't matter nothing."

Greene regarded us suspiciously, yet with a rueful expression, as if afraid we were baiting him but admitting he
deserved no better use. I took my stick from him and
suggested cordially that it was time he stopped looking in
mirrors.

"Can't see much in that one anyhow," he admitted. "All
pussed up."

Leonid grunted amiably. "You got face like old whore's
behind."

"Say what you want," Greene sadly invited us. "I know I'm flunked."

I declared then my conviction that he was not—or hadn't been until I'd flunked him. My interpretation of Bray's Certificate, I wanted to tell him, had been as mistaken in his case as in the others. Enos Enoch said *Become as a kindergartener*, and I'd flunked Peter Greene on the grounds that beneath his sentimental illusions lay much guile, much guilt, much that was failed. How tell him now that he was blinder than before—or as blind, but faileder? Better to deceive himself about the worth of things than about their want of it! That Miss Sally Ann had several times horned him I was fairly sure; but that she was no "floozy" I was certain. New Tammany College, as best I could judge from much reading and a little observation, was neither a Graduate School on the one hand nor a Dunce's College on the other; in its history and present state there was much to wince at—and much to take pride in: a few Ira Hectors, a few Lucky Rexfords, and many Peter Greenes, for better and worse. Whom too I thought him wronger about than before: he was not "all right," surely not "all wrong," but in his former error he'd at least been generous, cheerful, energetic, and on the whole more agreeable than not, whereas now . . .

But there was no time for such analysis, nor did I think it would much touch him. Stoker approached with a jingle of keys and a mocking whistle. Therefore I repeated Bray's quotation from the Founder's Scroll—*Passèd are the kindergarteners*—and declared my suspicion that kindergarteners were neither innocent nor simple except to sentimental eyes; only ingenuous, as Greene had been, was yet, and doubtless ever would be.

Max rolled his eyes. "You said that right."

Greene squinted. "You're pulling my leg, George. Not that I don't have it coming, 'As-ye-sow'wise."

I assured him of my sincerity, though in fact I used a small lie to make my point. Didn't he know, I asked him, that his acne had actually been clearing up before he overcame his thing-about-mirrors? "When you *saw* your own pimples you started squeezing them all the time"—so much was true—"and that made more of them. Even so they're not as bad as you think; you see the spots on the mirror as spots on your face."

This unpleasant argument impressed him; he would clean

Sear's mirror and make a count. But I insisted he have no more to do either with mirrors or with Kennard Sear, should that unfortunate man survive.

"I don't get you," Greene protested. "You told me your own self—"

"Never mind what I told you. I was wrong." Of two false arguments that came to mind then, I chose one and was pleased to see Greene supply the other himself.

"Suppose a man's nearsighted," I said. "Things two meters off will be twice as blurred as things one meter off. Right?" I hurried on before he could answer. "So he learns to allow for that error, and he's okay. Now he looks in a mirror from one meter's distance he corrects the image for a meter of error, either in his head or with his eyeglasses, and thinks he's seeing clearly—but he's not, because the image he sees is really *two* meters distant, a meter each way . . ."

Max closed his eyes until Leonid began to make noises of dissent, whereupon he went to confer with him in whispers. Greene frowned. Stoker had paused a few cells from ours to accept certain bribes from a shameless co-ed, before whose eyes he dangled the key-ring. I pressed on to the shakiest part of my argument before he should overhear it.

"So anything he sees in a mirror twenty meters from him will be distorted forty times. He couldn't recognize it at all! Put a mirror up to life, you get a double distortion."

"Quadruple," Max corrected, very gravely. "On account the image is also backwards."

"I hate!" Leonid said, and although his glare suggested he meant deception as well as distortion, he shook Greene's shoulder with rough goodwill. "You wrong about you! I like okay!"

Greene cocked his head, much moved. "I don't know. I swear to Pete . . . That durn window by the funhouse that I told you-all about—you know what I decided a while back, when I was in jail here?" He looked from one to the other of us. "Come to me it weren't any window at all, but a gosh-durn mirror!"

Max pretended astonishment.

"It was *me* talking dirty to Sally Ann!" Greene said bitterly. "I chunked that rock at my own self, that I thought was the Peeping Tom!"

Leonid feigned horror. "Impossity, Peter Greene!"

"Sure it is!" Greene laughed and sprang up with more

vigor than he'd displayed since the rape. "Couldn't nobody see their own reflection so far off, all that distortion!"

"Night-time too," I reminded him—relieved, but not unappalled, that he'd taken my bait so readily and swallowed it whole.

"Plus a funhouse mirror yet," Max added, "that it's *made* to distort things."

This too Greene seized uncritically, disregarding its implications. "I could've been right in the first place!"

"You were," I encouraged him. "Till I misled you."

Leonid pounded his back. "Okayship! No more hate! Mrs. Anastasia too!"

Stoker had come to our door at last, and grinned malevolently through the bars—waiting, I guessed, to refuse to unlock me. But I saw in Leonid's reference to My Ladyship a chance to complete the re-Tutoring of Peter Greene, in whose eye stood tears already of relief; and Stoker's mock, I was willing to gamble, would abet me.

"Don't you realize," I said to Greene, "that Anastasia dismissed the complaint because she loves you? She knows how much you admired her, and how upset you were at what you saw in Dr. Sear's office—or *thought* you saw, through the one-way mirror . . ."

Greene blinked strongly. "By jimmy gumbo, George! Do you mean to stand there on your two hind legs and tell me—"

Thinking he saw what was afoot, Stoker joined in happily: "You didn't think it was really *Stacey* you jumped on, did you? My wife's a virgin, Greene!"

"*I* be durn," Greene said stiffly. "You can't fool me."

"No, I swear it!" Stoker cried, and feigned a whisper. "I was born with no balls, see, and Stacey's got a thing about dildos. Look, I'll show you." He seemed prepared to open his trousers for our inspection—whether in earnest or not I never learned, for Greene professed disbelief and disgust, at the same time blushing with hopeful doubt.

"You can't tell *me* she's a virgin!" he said. "Not after what I done to her!"

His tone implied that he could nonetheless entertain the fantastic idea of her having been unserviced thitherto—despite what he'd seen and heard! I considered suggesting that he himself had deflowered her in the alley. But I hesitated, uncertain whether that notion would please him or bur-

den him with new guilt. Either way, I decided, the
responsibility might involve him with My Ladyship in a manner not conducive to restoring his marriage, and my object
was merely to revive his esteem for Anastasia, as for himself
and the other things he'd valued in time past. While I considered the problem, Stoker solved it, thinking only to make further sport.

"I know you're the Dunce's own cocksman," he said, "despite what Georgina tells me. But if you really believe it was
Stacey in that alley, you're blind as a bat."

"Who was it then?" Greene said angrily. "And who was it
owned up in court it was her own durn fault? Her twin sister?"

Stoker laughed. "Of course! Didn't George think once that
he and Stacey were twins? Well she *did* have a twin, back in
the Unwed Co-ed's Hospital where Ira Hector got her; but it
was a twin *sister* . . ."

Greene held his ears. "Y'all quit, now!" But Stoker, inspired, went on to declare that Anastasia and her twin sister,
though alike in appearance as his right eye to his left, were of
contrary dispositions, to My Ladyship's frequent mortification. For while Anastasia was not only chaste but downright frigid—as Greene himself had observed, surely, by her
demeanor in court and in the Visitation Room—her twin sister, raised in an orphanage, had early turned to vice, and was
in fact a floozy!

"It's the Founder's truth," he vowed with a grin. "She's a
hot one, that Lacey—Lacey's what they call her, from her
black lace drawers—"

"She weren't wearing any drawers!" Greene cried—
triumphantly but wretchedly, for despite his scorn he had
begun to listen with a wincing care.

"Naturally she wasn't," Stoker replied, and as Leonid,
Max, and I looked on astonished, he improvised a remarkable story: "Lacey's" notorious promiscuity, he declared, was
commonly attributed to resentment of her luckier twin,
whose reputation had indeed been damaged by Lacey's playing whore in her name. But in his own estimation—and he
called on me, with a wink, to support his analysis—the
unhappy girl's motives were more complex: indeed, it seemed
to him that "Lacey's" wantonness but confirmed Anastasia's
virgin chastity, and he wondered (that is, pretended to wonder) whether the girl didn't flunk herself deliberately—out of

some hopeless love for her sister, say, or to set an instructive bad example.

I regarded Stoker sharply. "What a very curious idea. Like the Dean o' Flunks, you mean?"

"In black panties!" Stoker laughed. "Except when she doesn't wear any at all, to make Stacey look flunkèder."

"Foolishnish!" Leonid shouted, who had heard enough. "Stop this!"

But Stoker maintained with the same earnestness that his wife, for all her protestations of contempt for "Lacey's" misconduct, often took the blame for her errant twin—whether out of love, or guilt for her own comfortable childhood, or some perverse envy, he wouldn't venture to say, though he inclined to the last hypothesis.

"Pass her heart!" Leonid cried, tearful himself now with compassion. "That Mrs. Anastasia, all the time takes blame! I love, George!"

I nodded approval. He shook his great fist then at Stoker. "Dog pig! And falsifer!" Max and me also he accused of exploiting Greene's "stupihood," and declared that my account of Anastasia's behavior in court was the only true thing we'd said to his blue-eyed friend. "All these mirror, and virginicy, and Lacey-pant—bah! Stop this sisterness!"

Greene rubbed his orange beard. "I don't know, Leo. I don't much trust a durn mirror, one-way or two-. And it *was* kind of dark there, back of the Old Chancellor's Mansion . . ."

Leonid clutched him by the shirt-front. "Don't believe, Peter Greene! *I* have done! What word? My own self . . . *I* have love Mrs. Anastasia! No Lacey-pant!"

Greene choked and flung himself away. *"Doggone* you! You watch how you talk, now, Alexandrov!"

But Leonid pointed with great emotion to his trouserfly and said distinctly: "I have *screw* Mrs. Anastasia my own self! Passèdness her! Flunkhood me!"

Greene leaped at him with a groan and they wrestled to the floor, Leonid cursing Greene for a blindness fool and Greene Leonid for a patch-eyed liar, nose-on-his-facewise. In vain Max and I hauled at them, lest they carry their new Tutoring too far; despite his recent fat and sloth Greene was formidably strong, as was his adversary. By the time Stoker unlocked the cell and nonchalantly fired his pistol near their heads, each had a thumb at the other's good eye.

"No-good Student-Unionist!" Greene muttered as we drew them apart. "Telling filthy lies about the sweetest gal in New Tammany College!"

"Oy," Max said.

"Blind other eye!" Leonid jeered. "Can't see anyhow!"

"You're the one's blind," Greene retorted. "Can't tell a virgin from a flunking floozy!"

They would have set to again, but Stoker and I got between them and pushed Greene into the aisleway. Not that he gave a flunk which fool killed which, Stoker assured them; but he thought it a pity to waste the spectacle on so small an audience. "It's time I threw another party at the Powerhouse," he said. "I'll let you fellows entertain us with an eye-gouging contest. Winner gets Stacey, loser gets Lacey."

"He couldn't tell the difference nohow!" Greene said. "I wish I could *give* him my gosh-durn eyeball, let him see how blind he is!"

Leonid glared from the cell. "Me too you, if George didn't say selfish like Ira Hector."

"Say what you want!" Greene shouted. "Anyhow he's not a Founderless Student-Unionist. Ira's okay, when all's said and done!"

"Like you, hah?"

"When you come right down to it! What the heck anyhow!"

"Goodbye, Georgie," Max interrupted, and I realized that the cell was relocked, with only him and Leonid inside, "Founder help you, you should pass all now and don't fail anything."

I pressed the hand that fetched my purse and stick to me, urged him to remember that Failure and Passage were inseparable and equally unreal, and exhorted him to choose between the Shaft and freedom without considering the purity of his motives. Leonid too, his quick wrath gone, I shook warm hands with, and repeated my advice to him.

"All confuse," he sighed. "But I ask Dr. Spielman. Good luck you, Goat-Boy!"

Stoker acted surprised. "Did you think you were going somewhere, George?"

I smiled. "I'm going to visit your brother Lucky, among other things, to show him how to pass. Will you drive me to the Light House?"

Stoker threw his head back to hoot as in term past, but his

laugh, owing perhaps to the iron acoustics, rang shrill. And he strode off, Greene trudging after, without attempting to rejail me. I wished Max and Leonid final peace of mind, and requested of them also that they do what they could to curb Croaker's appetites, either by instruction or by directly intercepting his food. For I saw the error of my flunking the "Eierkopf" in him and the "Croaker" in Eierkopf—as if the seamless University knew aught of such distinctions!—and therefore I would that he embrace and affirm what I'd bade him suppress, if he could be taught to.

"Yes, well," Max said dryly. "I think of something. I got a whole day."

3.

"Want me to stick him in Solitary on bread and water?" Stoker had come part-way back after all, smirking, to hear me. I waved bye-bye to my cellmates and walked past him towards Peter Greene, who waited in the open gate at the end of the aisle.

"That's not a bad idea," I said over my shoulder. "But *you* shouldn't do it." In fact, I added lightly when he overtook me, he should rather try to thwart my plans for Croaker than further them, just as he should refuse the embrace which I hoped the Chancellor would soon proffer him.

"You don't need a pardon," Stoker said. "You need a strait-jacket, like Heddy Sear's!"

I smiled. "You shouldn't even drive me to the Light House, actually. Pete can do it. Anyhow, your brother will come to *you*, if you take my advice."

Greene allowed as how he'd count it an honor to chauffeur me, I'd so eased his mind; but he begged leave to seek out Anastasia first and apologize for having confused her with her flunkèd twin. As for Georgina—

"Bugger Georgina!" Stoker said impatiently.

Greene drew a pill from his jeans, swallowed it with dignity, and replied that he was happy he'd not sunk to such unnatural practices, nor for that matter succumbed in any other wise to the carnal blandishments of O.B.G.'s naughty daughter, since he knew it to be written somewhere in the Old or New Syllabus that whites and blacks belonged in different classes. Did we suppose he could look his Sally Ann straight in the eye, reconciliationwise, or salute the College pennant at the next Junior Enochist cookout, if his conscience weren't clean as a hound's tooth? Sure, he'd raised his share of heck, as what fellow hadn't, but—

Stoker fired a bullet into the air (we were crossing now the twilit exercise-yard) and promised to put another between Greene's eyes should he not at once close his mouth and vanish. He then reminded me—as Greene sprinted zigzag toward the main gate—that he himself was neither blind like Gynander nor half-blind and half-witted like my former cellmates; he saw quite clearly what my game was and had no mind to play it.

I wiped my stick-mirror clean with the sleeve of my detention-coat and pretended to hide a smile. "You mean my playing Dean o' Flunks with you back in March? I didn't expect that old trick to work *once*, much less twice." I took him to mean that I was advising him not to chauffeur me to Great Mall in order to tempt him, Dean-o'-Flunks-like, to *do* it, since to follow my counsel would pass him, presumably, and I knew he wished to flunk. No such idea had in fact occurred to me; but once he suggested it I decided to pretend I'd done the like (that is, the opposite) in my earlier "Tutorship"—as truly I had, but by no means a-purpose.

Guards opened the gate for us, and I prickled with joy to step outside the walls for the first time in I knew not yet how long. Greene's motorcycle roared from a row of parked ones and up the road—in what seemed to me the wrong direction, though I couldn't read the roadsign in the dim light.

Stoker squinted. "You're telling me you tricked me before so I'll think you didn't," he said carefully. "But the joke's on you."

"Oh?"

"I knew all along that Pass and Fail aren't opposites— didn't I tell you Passage is Failure?—but I also knew you knew I'd try to trick you into flunking. So I told you they were the same so you'd believe I thought they were different and come to think so yourself. Why else do you think I pretended to take your advice?"

"I know why you took it," I replied, and grinned, hoping

to confuse him with inversions-of-inversions long enough to work out the right ones for myself. "What *you* don't know, when I tell you *Failure is Passage,* is whether I want you to believe it is because it isn't or isn't because it is."

Stoker grinned also—not easily, it seemed to me—and added as though carelessly: "—or is because it *is,* eh? Or isn't because it isn't . . ."

I perspired, and he exploited his advantage at once. "Don't forget, boy: whichever you believe, you may believe because I tricked you into it."

Grimly I retorted: "And if you did, the joke may be on you." But it was not a confident *riposte,* and I could only hope he'd think its lameness deliberately feigned.

"Always assuming I don't *want* the joke to be on me," he mocked. I'd have lost my hold entirely at this point had it not swept suddenly, bracingly through me, like the frigid breeze we stood in, that if *Failure* and *Passage* was in truth a false distinction, as I'd come to believe, then it made no difference whether that belief was true or false, as either way it was nei-ther. How hopelessly innocent I'd used to be! Instead of trying to outwit Stoker, therefore—by replying "Exactly," for example—I resolved to outwit him by *not* trying to. I paused beside the first parked motorcycle and said without ex-pression or emotion: "Take me to Great Mall."

He hesitated for the briefest moment—during which, I imagined, a herd of pluses and minuses locked horns—then he mounted the cycle, started the engine . . . and surprised me after all by moving off, not only impassively but without a word! In a cold sweat of doubt I sprang on behind him, and desperately bet everything on candor.

"You've got me so mixed up I'm sweating!" I called as we throttled away. He said nothing. But a few seconds later I smelled another sweat besides my own.

The air was freezing, the campus brown and bare; I shiv-ered for want of fleece. I'd thought it dusk, but a pale day dawned as we raced along: a winter's morning, then, and Max had thirty-six hours of life unless he defected. Had I been three seasons in Main Detention, or three-years-and-three? An hour we rode, without a word, through fallow research-arable and shuttered residential quads. Few people were about. Preoccupied with wondering whether I was headed for Great Mall or being taken deliberately out of my way, I gave no thought to any order of business until a familiar scene surprised me: under a great bare elm sat The Living Sakhyan, oblivious to the weather, looking for all the campus as though He'd not moved since the day of my fiasco. And a few trees on, a black-furred man upon a bench alternately cowered and shook his thin fist at a gang of male students, who pressed about him in sheepfleece coats and belabored him with placards stuck on sticks.

I tapped Stoker's back. "Stop here a minute, would you?"

He would not, until I accused him of trying mistakenly to flunk me because he mistakenly believed in my Grand-Tutorhood—"As if you weren't right!" I added with a chuckle, just in case. He slowed down, perhaps only to deliberate, but when I jumped off he stopped the engine and waited, a-scowl and a-twitch.

"Help!" Ira Hector called. But I went directly to The Living Sakhyan, squatted before Him in His wise, and unpursed my chewed Assignment.

"Robbery!" Ira cried.

"Excuse me, sir," I said to The Living Sakhyan. "I want to thank You for the disappeared ink You gave me some terms ago, and apologize for criticizing You before."

His expression did not change, nor did He give any other indication of having heard me. Except for His smile, and my vast new understanding, I might have thought Him dead.

"Help me, Goat-Boy!" Ira shrieked.

"I know this sounds foolish," I went on, "but I actually used to think *I* was the Grand Tutor! And I couldn't understand why You didn't try to save my friend G. Herrold—remember the fellow in George's Gorge?—or why You didn't help Anastasia when Croaker was attacking her, or Ira Hector when those Beists were bothering him. I thought You must be as bad off as Dr. Eierkopf, up in the Belfry; that's how naïve I used to be!"

The Living Sakhyan made no sign, even when I leaned closer and explained that I understood Him now that I'd abandoned my claim to Grand-Tutorship. Since Passage and Failure were not different except as the deluded mind of Studentdom made them so, what booted it to snatch a man from the torrent, a woman from the tup? As if passèd works brought the mind any closer to Truth! To withdraw from the trials and errors of this campus, sit under an elm, and meditate upon the unutterable Answer—that was the way to

Commencement Gate, I saw now, the sole Way, and I meant to follow His example as soon as I flunked WESCAC.

"That's why I've come to You, sir," I declared: "I suspect Dr. Bray might be a Grand Tutor, but I *know* You are, and I'd like to check out my Assignment with You, if You don't mind. I think I see why I failed it before . . ."

I took His silence for permission. Behind me I heard running footsteps and Ira Hector's feeble curses. "Did you get it?" a student called, and another shouted that he had: "When the sun comes up it'll be 7 A.M., Saturday, December 20!"

"It's a lie!" cried Ira. "Arrest them, Stoker!"

"Hey, a cop!" the same student warned, apparently seeing Stoker for the first time. "Go limp!" The others rebuked him for having extorted by force the information they needed, not because robbery was against the law—everybody knew that the laws were made to protect the privileged—but because the use of force was contrary to the principles of their group. "So I'm a Student-Unionist infiltrator," the fellow laughed. "We got what we wanted, didn't we?" He warned Stoker not to touch him or he'd shout Brutality.

"Go flunk yourself," Stoker growled, still evidently preoccupied with our debate. "The day I touch you, you'll have plenty to holler about."

Some of the students then fell to arguing whether the forcible expulsion of violent elements from their ranks would violate the principle of non-violence; others, whether non-violence as a means had not become an end in itself with them, and thus a contradiction of its own premise that ends never justified means. The dispute was heated but peaceful; no agreement was reached.

"Hey, look," someone interrupted: "it's the GILES! Let's go limp over there and ask Him."

It seemed that my lynching and detention, so far from shaking their confidence in me, had redoubled it. In fact (as I observed when they flopped around The Living Sakhyan's elm), I was now as much their hero as He—perhaps more so, considering their emulation. Beards they'd had before, but now they all wore sandals like mine and fleecy coats—sheepskin, admittedly, and cut too short to be worn without trousers, but the closest they could come to a mohair wrapper. What's more, they leaned upon their staves as upon a crook, as well as using them to carry placards. These last were blank.

They greeted me respectfully but enthusiastically. Had the Administration seen its error and pardoned me? they wanted to know. Was I aware how many folksongs and free-verse poems my lynching had inspired, despite the Administration's efforts to suppress them on grounds of obscenity? Did I know of the "sleep-ins" staged in my behalf and wrongfully slandered by the right-wing press as "sleep-arounds," though the only fornication had been by neo-Bonifacist *provocateurs* of both sexes? Did I approve of *Carte-blanchisme*, their current cause, which aimed at nothing less than Freedom From Everything?

"That's not what it means to *me*," objected one of their number. "To me, *Carte-blanchisme* is a blanket protest against the great Nothing."

This interpretation struck many of his classmates as heretical and was therefore warmly applauded, though one bright fellow remarked that "the great Nothing" was exactly what Sakhyanism aimed at, and a brighter observed that, since the great Nothing was equivalent to Everything, and Freedom From Everything meant Freedom *For* Everything the two interpretations of their cause were not mutually exclusive.

"Syncretist," someone muttered.

"Look here," I said cordially, and they fell silent at once. "I'm much obliged for your good opinion of me, even though you're mistaken. I'm *not* the Grand Tutor; I failed my Assignment before because I took WESCAC on its own terms. That's what I want to consult The Living Sakhyan about, if you'll excuse me . . ."

They withdrew a little way, but begged permission to listen in on the dialogue, and I found the lot of them too lively and agreeable, on the whole, and their admiration too flattering, to refuse them. I was surprised to see that my denial of Grand-Tutorhood disturbed them not at all; of *course* I denied it, they exclaimed in whispers; Grand-Tutorhood was a concept, like any other; if I didn't deny it I wouldn't be Grand Tutor! Didn't my criticism of WESCAC make that clear? They alluded to the parable of Milo and Sophie the heifer: to pass, one must flunk the Examiner . . .

As at our previous encounter, I was impressed by their acuteness; indeed, I remembered now that some of their remarks in that earlier term could be said to have anticipated my present position. They'd understood some things better than I—though perhaps less well than I did now—and their commentary on my remarks invariably enlarged my understanding—to the point where I felt that same commentary vaguely deficient.

"It seems to me, sir," I said to The Living Sakhyan, "that WESCAC really *is* the Dean o' Flunks, as I used to think when I was a kid . . ."

"Didn't I tell you?" someone whispered triumphantly. *"Attack the terms of the problem!"* And before his classmates could shush him he alarmed me (since the slogan he quoted was exactly what I had in mind) by adding, "But isn't it only WESCAC's old MALI circuitry that that would apply to? How can *Wescacus malinoctis* be a symbol of Differentiation?" It was an objection I'd not myself considered. Fortunately another student hissed, "So what's this MALI and NOCTIS? Another set of arbitrary categories!"

This silenced the troubled one, and eased my own mind. "He'll reinterpret the terms of His Assignment," the same fellow said confidently. I decided to do just that, with The Living Sakhyan's aid.

"It says *Fix the Clock*," I began. "Before, I thought *fix* meant 'repair,' but Dr. Eierkopf's gadget seems to have stopped the clock completely, so I guess I was mistaken. What *does* it mean?"

My admirers fell again into the disputation they could never resist, and with the help of The Living Sakhyan's silence I was able to overhear them. My spring-term fiasco, they understood, had been a deliberate bad example, for pedagogical purposes; it went without saying that I'd known all along that *fix* could as easily mean "fix in position," for example, to one not bound by conventional assumptions—was that not what my pretended failure to repair the clock had in fact accomplished? I listened amazed. Moreover, they pointed out to each other, by thus fixing the escapement in position I'd been able to complete my Assignment "in no time," so to speak; surely the implications of the metaphor were clear!

"But if it goes without saying that He *knew* all this," the troubled fellow inquired, "why's He asking The Living Sakhyan?"

"Because it *does* go without saying!" another said. "You don't hear The Sakhyan answering, do you?"

Delightedly I pressed on: *"End the Boundary Dispute:* Now obviously I was wrong to think that meant make our Power Lines clearer, wasn't I? Did WESCAC mean some other kind of Boundary?"

I managed to catch just the words *". . . all arbitrary"* behind me, but that was enough. I demanded of The Living Sakhyan ("Rhetorically, man," they said, "rhetorically!"): "Could it mean that the boundary between East and West Campuses is arbitrary and artificial, and ought to be denied? Should we abolish the Power Line?"

They applauded this suggestion as vigorously as limpness permitted. I was emboldened to ask whether they understood that had The Living Sakhyan answered either yes or no, He'd have affirmed the Boundary's reality, and thus answered falsely. Several nodded, and were at once rebuked by their cleverer classmates, who snapped, "Don't answer!" I had just presence enough of mind to smile and say no more.

In like manner I reviewed the whole of my Assignment with T. L. Sakhyan's aid. *Overcome Your Infirmity*, we decided, must mean *affirm* my limp and goatliness—a happy imperative! *See Through Your Ladyship* was more difficult, since the students knew nothing of my connection with Anastasia; but their whispers of "revisionist psychology" and "normal bisexuality," though meaningless to me, put me in mind of Dr. Sear and his fluoroscopic diversions. Should I literally make My Ladyship transparent? In any case, when I said, "I'll see Dr. Sear about that one," they laughed knowingly. In theory, the fifth task was also problematical: *Replace*, because of its curious hyphen, seemed still to me to mean "Return the Founder's Scroll to its place" and not, as the students suggested, "Replace it with something better"— though "its place" clearly meant its *source* rather than its proper location in the Library stacks. However, by interpreting *source* to mean, not the sandy Moishian cave where the Scroll was found, but the mind and body of studentdom whence its teachings sprang, I was able to satisfy both the students and myself: recalling to them the East-Campus table-grace about "eating Truth," I asked The Living Sakhyan whether I should make a meal of the Founder's words!

Someone whispered, " '. . . not bread alone'!" Another,

"To make way for the new!" And a third asked, "Eat instead of EAT; is that it?" I did not reply.

The sixth and seventh tasks, on the other hand, were clear: to *Pass the Finals* could only mean to by-pass WESCAC; perhaps not to *destroy* it, as the students urged (who regarded it as the emblem of much that they objected to in the University), but certainly to frustrate or circumvent it by way of denying its authority. This established, the final task, like the first, was already accomplished: I myself was my Examiner; I had no proper father, nor was there anyone save myself to whom my ID-card need be presented. I read the seventh task aloud and asked The Living Sakhyan: "What signatures do I need on my card? And who are the 'proper authorities'?" His silence was my Answer.

I bid goodbye to the students then, who thanked me for Tutoring them and hoped I wouldn't judge their group by its non-non-violent members; they'd needed the time of day from the "Old Man of the Mall" in order to schedule a protest march to Main Detention in behalf of Max and me.

"That's not what I was protesting," said one of them. "I was protesting Saturday-morning classes and the Open Book rules."

Some applauded his deviation and maintained that both protests could be served by a general demonstration in the name of *Carte-blanchisme*. Others protested this indiscrimination, but most certainly didn't want to be thought to favor the opposite; still others contended that repudiating such distinctions was the first principle of Beism (as well as the last, since All was One). And so I left them, some protesting, some protesting the protest, and a few protesting that to protest protest was either to affirm *Carte-blanchisme* and hence (by Beistic paradox) to deny it, or to deny it and hence affirm it—which was perhaps to say, deny it . . .

Stoker slouched beside Ira Hector on the bench. Ignoring the old man's scolding, he grinned contemptuously as I approached.

"You're supposed to protect the right of private information!" Ira berated him. "What do I pay taxes for?"

"You never paid taxes in your life," Stoker said, not bothering to look at him. "Did you think they'd *thank* you for cutting off their scholarships?"

Drawing his head into the collar of his topcoat, Ira retorted that he didn't give a fact for their opinion of him, but he did have more right to be protected from robbery than any-one else in New Tammany College; precisely because he had withdrawn all support from his former tax write-offs, the Philophilosophical Fund and the Unwed Co-ed's Hospital, he now paid the highest taxes on campus. In fact, he declared (glaring at me with his shellèd eyes) the Administration was bleeding the golden goose to death, and thus cooking its own; he was on the verge of intellectual bankruptcy, thanks to my bad advice, and the daily robberies and copyright in-fringements perpetrated on him would soon put him over the edge if the campus patrol refused him the help he'd bought and paid for—with his ward Anastasia as well as with his ruinous taxes.

"Buy your own bodyguard," Stoker said. "You can afford it."

"Why didn't you help me, Goat-Boy?" he demanded.

"Help yourself," I answered. "That's what you were Certi-fied for doing."

He thrust a bony fist at me from his coatsleeve and ac-cused me of having given him false advice nine months previously. I reminded him that, as he hadn't paid the Tutor, he shouldn't complain of the Tutoring.

"But my advice to you might have been good, after all," I added with a smile. "I told you that wealth was flunking and that the passèd thing to do was to flunk yourself to help others pass—"

"Don't believe him," Stoker said behind his hand. "He told me the same thing."

"I *don't* believe him," Ira snapped. "You should've heard the claptrap he was retailing! But I don't believe you, either! I'm my own man, sir!"

"What I meant," I put in, "was that selfishness was flunk-ing, but that to keep your wealth from others would actually be *unselfish . . .*"

"Rot!"

"So it turns out," I agreed. "Now I think you *ought* to be selfish, because Failure is Passage."

Ira thrust out his neck and blinked his lashless lids. "You talk like those fool Beists."

"Exactly. The question is, which *is* selfish: the miser or the philanthropist? Take me to the Light House, Stoker."

"Flunk you," Stoker cursed amiably. But when I thanked

him for doing just that, he sneered off towards the motorcycle.

"Well, which *is* it?" Ira demanded. "Not that I'd believe you."

"Let go my sleeve, please," I aaid. "I don't Grand-Tutor for my health."

"You can't Tutor at all!" he reminded me angrily. "You're not the Grand Tutor!"

We struck up a bargain then, to exchange bad advice for the wrong time of day.

"Be greedy," I counseled him. "Give *all* you have to the P.P.F. and the New Tammany Lying-In! Then you'll have nothing, and pass at other people's expense. That's the flunking thing to do, you see, and Failure is Passage. When those Beist-fellows come around, don't just give them the time of day; give them all they want. Give them the shirt off your back."

Ira considered my shadow and squinted at me cunningly. "It's exactly eight o'clock."

However, as I mounted the motorcycle and Stoker throttled its engine, he cackled from the depths of his coat-collar: "I can turn your bad advice inside out, Goat-Boy, but you can't do that with the time of day! I got the best of you again!"

But I smiled—and not merely to worry him, as I'd done with Stoker. For the fact was, I hadn't the slightest idea whether reversing my advice would flunk and therefore pass him, or vice-versa, and whether in either case he'd be passed or failed. Whereas I suspected he'd given me the *correct* time in order to mislead me, for an hour did seem to have elapsed since I'd heard that student say seven o'clock. But if he'd lied to his molesters too, I was no worse off, for Ira Hector desperately needed Grand-Tutoring, but I had no use at all for the time of day. Let him shriek after me (as he did), "It's later than you think!" How could it be, when I had no thought upon the matter?

We came in sight of that grand square where Tower Hall stands like a dean at the head of a committee-table, flanked on one side by the Light House, on the other by the Old Chancellor's Mansion. There was traffic now; I checked the Clock, also my watch: neither was running. A flutter of blackbirds from the Belfry reminded me of Eblis Eierkopf. Again I tapped my chauffeur's shoulder.

"What ever happened to Dr. Eierkopf? Do you suppose he's still in the Belfry?"

Stoker shook his head. "I got him running the hamburg concession out at the Powerhouse. All he can eat and seconds on Madgie."

I recognized that he was speaking sarcastically. "I'm going to see him before I call on the Chancellor," I said. "But I'll need a ride later to the Infirmary. Would you rather have lunch with your brother in the Light House or have him out to dinner at the Power Plant?"

Stoker snorted and opened the throttle; I barely managed to land on my feet. Newsboys hawked the morning paper on the Tower Hall esplanade, calling out that Max's Shaft-time had been set for next day at sunset, and that in consequence of grave new incidents at the Power Lines, Classmate X had arrived on Great Mall, presumably to sever the remaining diplomatic ties between East and West Campus. I half expected Stoker to wait for me, but as I entered the lobby of Tower Hall I saw him drive off towards a squadron of his troopers roaring up in ragged files from the direction of Main Gate.

The elevator-guard frowned at my detention-suit, consulted an empty clipboard, and forbade me the Belfry-lift.

"Don't you remember me?" I asked pleasantly.

"I remember you, all right." His tone was not cordial. "But your name ain't on my list any more. In fact, there ain't any list, since you flunked up the College. Nobody's allowed up there."

I asked where Dr. Eierkopf was, in that case—for I'd assumed Stoker was lying to me—and was told that he was indeed still in the Belfry—or at least his skeleton must be: the lift had not been summoned since Croaker's desertion, the guard said (not without grim satisfaction); as nobody was allowed access to the Clockworks without the Chancellor's authorization, not even repairmen, and since the Chancellor seemed not to care any more about lists or anything else, one could only suppose that Dr. Eierkopf had starved to death and rotted many months ago—if he'd not been killed when Croaker went berserk. "Serves the Bonifacist right, either way," he concluded.

Alarmed, I sprang liftwards, though there was no hope of

saving one so long abandoned. The guard drew his pistol, threatened to shoot if I touched a button, and repeated, for the benefit of startled bystanders, that nobody could use the Belfry-lift. Perspiring, I bethought me of the trick old Laertides had played upon the one-eyed shepherd. I handed him my ID-card, and, hoping he'd miss the one not-quite-eradicated name, I said, *"I'm Nobody,"* and pushed the *Belfry*-button. The doors began to close.

"Oh no you don't!" the guard cried, and would have leaped me, but his classmates-in-arms restrained him on the grounds that while my authority to use the lift was questionable, *he* unquestionably had none at all. Too late then to shoot; the doors clicked shut and I was lofting.

Though I dreaded what I'd find of Eblis Eierkopf, I was prepared this time for the din and spectacle of the Clockworks. But when the lift stopped, all was silence. The gears, large and small, were still; the awful pendulum hung fast before my nose, perpendicular between Tick and Tock. Round about was a strew of papers, eggshells, calipers, and lenses: the birdlimed, dusty ruins, I feared, of oölogical research. High in the center of the works, struck face-on by the rising sun, sat Dr. Eierkopf—dead or alive, I could not at once tell, but at least not quite a skeleton. He was perched—one might even say poised—on the escapement, just under the butt of the weathervane-shaft: one shriveled leg hung on either side of the knife-edged pivot, and the crown of his head thrust up into a smallish bell, as far as to his browless eyebrows. Had he been planted there by Croaker, or climbed there to escape him? His lab-coat and spectacles were smeared with droppings of the blackbirds that flew in and out of the Belfry, hopped upon his shoulders, and squatted on his pate beneath the skirt of the bell. They or other birds had woven a nest of straw around his neck and under his chin. Most had food in their beaks when they entered the tower—bread-crusts, sunflower seeds, or kernels of dry field-corn—and I was astonished to see that now and then one would drop a morsel into Dr. Eierkopf's open mouth. He chewed and swallowed without other motion.

"Are you all right?" I cried.

He showed no sign of having heard me. I scrambled up through gears and cables to examine him more closely. Two Eierkopfian lenses, each inscribed Q.E.D. were clipped onto his spectacles; behind them his eyes were open and glazed.

No question but he was alive—a drop of dew ran off the bell and he caught it neatly upon his tongue—but he either could not or would not hear me, how anxiously soever I begged him to ignore my old advice.

"Everything I told you before was wrong!" I shouted in his ear. "Be like you used to be—even worse! Be like Croaker!" My cries resounded in the bell and flushed out several blackbirds; but assert as I might that he must embrace what I'd bid him eschew, I could not stir him.

"Don't sit there like T. L. Sakhyan!" I implored. I was standing on the teeth of two giant gears; as I leaned forward to shout "Wake up!" I caught at a nearby cable to save my balance. It ran to the outside clapper of that central bell, second smallest of the lot, which now was struck one mighty stroke. The Eierkopfian lenses shivered; every bird rushed from the Belfry; Eblis's hands flew to his ears, and he piped a little squeak of pain. More, the after-swing of the bell disturbed his long equilibrium: the escapement teetered back and forth until its passenger fell, just beyond my reach. His lab-coat caught on the knife-edged fulcrum; for a moment I thought him saved; then fulcrum and coat both gave way— the latter sliced through, the former snapped off where the Infinite Divisor had shaved it almost to nothing—and he tumbled head-first to the floor, breaking his eyeglass-frames and, I feared, his skull. I sprang down. Tears stood in Dr. Eierkopf's eyes; he rubbed his cranium and spat out a sunflower seed.

"*Ech*," he said weakly. "Be glad you're not a bird, Goat-Boy."

I propped him against a lab-stool and wiped guano off his head with a page of old graph-paper. At sight of it he wept. It was not Croaker's rampage that had undone him and his great research, he managed to declare, but my parting remark about chicken and egg. He had, incredibly, forgot to deal with that ancient question in his otherwise exhaustive treatise, and though stunned by my reminder, he'd been so confident of reasoning out the answer on the basis of his other findings that he'd bid Croaker proceed with the application of the Infinite Divisor. Not to miss the triumphant sight of its operation, he'd donned his high-resolution lenses and had Croaker balance him atop the escapement; as the Divisor's twin milling-heads shaved towards him, ever-halving the thickness of the fulcrum's edge, he had rocked joyously from

Tick to Tock, which in his head became *chicken* and *egg*. And it was precisely at the instant when the Divisor had disappeared between his legs, into the center-hole of the escapement, that he'd seen the problem to be insoluble. What had transpired between that moment and the striking of the bell, he had no idea, and his tears, it turned out, were not for smashed lenses, ruined papers, his months of starvation, or his injured head: what difference did any of those make, when the fundamental question of chicken versus egg could not be resolved?

I seized his tapered shoulders. "That's the answer, sir!"

He groaned. "Goat-Boy, Goat-Boy!"

"There *isn't* any problem!" I insisted, shaking him eagerly until the straw fell from his neck. "*Chicken* and *egg, tick* and *tock*, *Croaker* and *Eierkopf*—they're false distinctions, every one!"

He squinted through his empty spectacle-frames. "You hit your head too?"

But I told him happily that he was better off for the breaking of his lenses and the failure of the Infinite Divisor. What the Founder had joined, who could put asunder? Or resolve the One into many? Had the escapement fallen now into the gears and locked them fast? Then let Infinite Divisors and Everlasting-Nowniks embrace: they were proved brothers, and the Clock was fixed! Let there be no brooding among eggs or crowing of chickens; neither had seniority over the other; they were one, like Day and Night. In short, let him rejoice over the failure of his enterprises, inasmuch as, failing, he had passed!

Dr. Eierkopf said: "Goat-Boy, go home."

"I'm leaving," I replied. "But take my advice, sir: forget about WESCAC; forget about logic. Go out and live!"

"Now you tell me," he said sarcastically. "My head's *kaput.*"

"Don't measure eggs," I exhorted him, "eat them!"

"Eggs, *blah*." He made a sour face.

"Don't watch co-eds undressing in your night-glass—"

"You said that last time."

"Go undress them yourself! You can't help being an animal: so *be* one! Be a beast of the woods!"

"I should be a beast of the woods?" he asked skeptically. Inspired by Stoker's earlier sarcasm, I advised him to gratify his appetites directly instead of vicariously: to go to the Powerhouse, debauch himself with Anastasia in the Living Room, or with Madge if My Ladyship happened to be engaged with Harold Bray.

"Eat meat," I said, though my own stomach heaved at the idea no less than his. *"Raw* meat. You might even try some prepared mustard on Madge."

"You lost vour mind," Eierkopf muttered.

Only my Reason, I replied: the flunking Reason that distinguished him from Croaker, and denied that contradictories could both be passèd at the same time, in the same respect.

"Entelechus or no Entelechus," he said, "a man can't diddle except he's got a diddler, not so? You're cracked in the head!"

His objection had the tone of a complaint, as if he wished to be refuted. I stood up confidently. "You're still being logical," I said. "Anastasia will find a way. Want me to help you get your papers together?"

He waved away the offer, declaring glumly that all the dean's assistants could not restore his oölogical masterwork, so hopelessly had Croaker and the four winds scrambled it.

"Come on, then," I urged him. "Leave all this. The campus is your oyster!"

He gagged at the figure, but admitted I'd been right in calling him flunked before, when he'd thought himself passed, and he agreed to consider my strange new counsel. However, after nine months of intense meditation he was too weak to leave the Belfry just that instant. Moreover, he had scores to settle with certain blackbirds who maliciously had fed him angleworms all summer . . .

"Catch them and eat them!" I suggested, remembering the meal once offered me by Croaker. "Bake them in a pie!"

His head shook limply. "I'm a failure, Goat-Boy."

"Failure is Passage," I said, and returned to the lift, hoping to rouse him to action. "Go find Anastasia; bite her in the belly."

But he bared his toothless gums. *"Mit was?* I'm a broken man, Goat-Boy."

"No, sir," I said firmly, and pushed the *Down*-button, "You're a chicken."

4.

I feared the lift-guard might detain me, and indeed I found him and his fellows conferring in a worried cluster—but not about my ID-card, which I spied in the sand of an ash-tray near the lift. They appeared more anxious than threatening; I decided that my bluff had worked and might be made use of. Boldly I retrieved and pursed my card and said, "Dr. Eierkopf wants his lunch. Right away."

Neither my effrontery nor the news of Eierkopf's survival moved them much. "No use him eating," one guard said gruffly. "Way things look, we'll all be EATen before long." Alarming rumors, it appeared, were coming from the Light House every few minutes: that WESCAC was out of order; that Classmate X had declared Riot; that Lucky Rexford had taken an overdose of tranquilizers and was in a coma. Who cared whether Eierkopf was alive, or whether unauthorized persons got into the Clockworks? The subject of their conversation was not how to deal with me, but whether to perish at their posts or at home with their families.

"Stay where you are," I advised them. "I'm on my way now to end the Boundary Dispute."

"That settles it," the lift-guard said. "I'm going home." He cursed remarkably when I congratulated him for seeing that, in effect, the dispute *was* settled already, since it had never properly existed—but neither he nor his steadfaster colleagues prevented my leaving Tower Hall. The sun, far in the south, I guessed halfway towards its meridian, but the sky was overcast now and the Light House gray. A sheep-fleeced band of students picketed the gate, some bearing the wordless placards of *Carte-blanchisme,* others crossing arms, joining hands, and singing in doleful measure:

*E plu-*ri-*bus* u—*u-nu-um . . .*

Despite the stunning aptness of that sentiment, there was small spirit in their demonstration. Indeed, the whole scene was listless: Stoker's troopers slouched about, some asleep in their sidecars, some hunkered idly on the curb. Now and then one clubbed a student, but so half-heartedly I couldn't always judge whether their victims fell unconscious or merely "went limp." The few passersby who stopped to watch seemed scarcely more interested than the throngs who ambled past without a glance. Even the hecklers sounded bored: yet when languidly one called, "Hurrah for apathy," two pickets shrugged and wandered off.

My approach was greeted by three or four with pale applause and by the rest with so mild jeers I could scarcely credit that a like crowd had once lynched me. The same lassitude appeared to have infected Stoker, who lounged against the Light-House gate with Rexford's Frumentian aide. I thanked him for waiting.

"Don't flatter yourself," he said. "Ignition trouble."

The aide chuckled lazily, not at all the brisk chap I'd lunched with last time around. "At least you've got fuel in your tank; that's more than the Chief has."

I advised Stoker not to accompany me inside, as I thought it fitter his brother come out to him. He yawned and scratched his armpit.

"Forget it."

"Nobody's allowed in while X is there," the aide explained. No use, I knew, to try Laertides's trick on them. "Unless you happen to know the password," he added with a smile. "Which you don't."

I considered. "Could it be *Nothing in excess?*"

Stoker frowned. "What kind of talk is that?"

"How about *Pass All Fail All?*"

The brown man shook his head slightly, not very interested.

"*E pluribus unum? Failure is Passage?*"

"Those sound like flunkwords to me," Stoker said.

I searched my memory for Maxims. "*Veritas vos liberabit? Gnothi seauton? Don't burn your bridges at both ends?*"

"Give it up," the aide advised.

A little angrily I said, "I don't think there *is* any password!"

He shrugged and laid his hand on the gate-latch as a party issued from the Light-House door. "You're probably right. Run along, now."

What happened then is somewhat equivocal. I recognized a number of the exiting visitors as Nikolayan officials from the

University Council—all of them, in fact, except one who covered his face with his hat, and whom I therefore took to be Classmate X. At the same time I chose to think that I'd hit upon the right response to the aide (it suited my general Answer, certainly), and that his directive and gesture with the latch were invitations to pass through. It's true he said "Stop" when I entered, and that Stoker drew and clicked his pistol, cursing when it failed to fire. But it was not unlike Stoker to frighten people thus for sport, and I *was* gating the aide aside somewhat roughly in my haste. In any case no one restrained me, whether because I'd chanced upon the password or because no one finally cared.

Not so Classmate X's colleagues: I saw a number of hands fly into coat-breasts as I sticked up the walk.

"Dr. Chementinski!" I called. "It's George Giles, the Goat-Boy! I have news from Leonid Andreich."

As his face was concealed I could not gauge X's reaction, but he muttered something in cold Nikolayan to his colleagues, and no weapons were drawn, though the hands stayed fast. Cameras clicked about us.

"Mistaken identity," he said to me through his hat. "These names mean nothing." But he did not press on at once. His aides immediately ringed us to keep off the journalism-majors who sought a statement about his interview with Chancellor Rexford.

"I know who you are and why you wanted your son arrested," I said.

"There are no *sons* in Nikolay College," he replied; "all men are brothers."

"Then you may be interested to hear that your brother Leonid took poison recently—nearly a whole bottle of eradicator."

For just an instant he uncovered his blank gray eyes, then hid behind his hat again and said tersely: "He is no more then, this stranger you mention."

I replied that Leonid was, fortunately, "more" indeed— more than his stepfather and more than he himself had ever been before, thanks to the less-than-perfect effectiveness of the eradicator; for though he'd not decided yet whether to rescue Max and perish in his stead or defect in truth to New Tammany, he most certainly would use no force on my keeper, who loved him as a son; nor would he be likely to try suicide again, now he saw its selfishness.

"Sentimental mid-percentilism. Petty-Informationalist logic-chopping." But X's voice was thick. "If Leonid Andreich—was that the name you mentioned?—if he failed at suicide it's because a perfect Student-Unionist has no self. Let the Union order his suicide and see whether he fails!"

"You call him a perfect Student-Unionist," I pointed out. "You must be very proud of him."

"Bah." He turned away. "He'll never learn."

"But you *want* him to! You're ambitious for him, like any father!"

I thought I detected a color in what I could see of his face. In the metallest tone he said: "Listen, Goat-Boy: A man sacrifices his only son—the only thing he loves—exactly to *keep* from being selfish. That man is no father." He snapped something in Nikolayan, and the party moved gatewards.

"Self-discipline is selfish, too!" I called after. "You can't escape yourself, Dr. Chementinski! You couldn't even if you could!"

"Did he say Chementinski?" one reporter asked another, and then asked me directly, while his colleague hurried after Classmate X. I confirmed that the Nikolayan representative to the U.C. and the famous defector Chementinski were the same man, and explained briefly how I knew, insisting that Max was wholly innocent of the plot and that Leonid, while guilty of intent to kidnap, had altogether repudiated that intention, as witness his remaining in a cell which he could easily walk out of if he chose to. Everyone pressed after Classmate X then, despite his refusal to comment or uncover his face. Even some of his colleagues, it seemed to me, scowled now as questioningly at him and each other as hostilely at the press. At last he lost his temper, jammed his hat upon his head, and reached inside his coat. Reporters scrambled for cover; aides went for their weapons—but it was an ID-card instead of a pistol that X whipped forth. He waved it at the Telerama lenses.

"Does it say *Chementinski? Nyet!*"

Those who were near enough admitted that only an *X* was visible on the card, though obviously that fact in itself proved little. Coming up behind, I flipped out the magnifying lens on my stick and thrust it over the shoulders of several reporters, bidding them look again closely.

"*Nyet!*" Classmate X snatched the card away, but not before two reporters saw, or claimed to have seen, imperfectly eradicated characters on both sides of the X. Moreover, examining his glitter-eyed, fierce-beaked face, for once publicly uncovered, a cameraman was moved to recall that though the features were otherwise much altered, Chementinski the traitor-scientist had had metal-capped bicuspids like Classmate X.

"The better to EAT you with!" X shouted, as impassioned as his stepson now. "This means Riot!" It was his aides then who led him, one at each arm, out to the motorcade on the mall. I entered the Light House.

A number of the Chancellor's assistants were in the entrance-hall; they wore gray suits and had similar youthful faces, but their forelocks were combed back now, and instead of bustling they lounged about in leather chairs and window-seats. I approached the nearest and announced my wish to see Chancellor Rexford at once. He turned from the window, smiling slightly, and congratulated me upon my release from Main Detention. The voice, though lifeless, was unmistakable.

"You're the Chancellor!" I couldn't conceal my surprise: without his grin, his white suit, his springy force and forelock, he seemed blander than his aides. His face was tired but placid; he looked ten years older.

"I won't be, next term, if the polls mean anything," he said, shaking my hand. "Assuming there *is* a next term."

I'd expected a less cordial reception, in view of the consequences of my former advice, but though no one actually welcomed me into the Chancellor's office, no one forbade my entering it, either. And Rexford, while neither pleased or displeased to see me, was polite, even respectful. He dismissed his aides and postponed several appointments at my request, so that we could talk.

"You needn't tell me," he sighed from behind his desk. "Bray had no business Certifying me, and you were right to call me flunked." He stared gloomily at a photograph of his wife upon the mantelpiece. "But I feel even flunkèder now—not that it matters, extremely. You talked to X?"

I affirmed that I had, but as I prepared to disclose Classmate X's true identity, two telephones on the desk rang simultaneously, a red and a white. He answered the red first, listened gravely to the message, and said, "Again? You're sure? Well, we'll have to think about that. Don't want to do anything rash." He made a memorandum—what appeared to be a tally.

"Another guard fell off the Line," he told me, and picked up the white telephone. "We're pretty sure the Nikolayans are tapping our power at night, too. They may even be advancing their line."

To the white telephone he made similar responses, though more personal. *"Please* be reasonable, dear," he said. "You really ought to give this more thought . . ." But his caller hung up.

He tisked ruefully and put back the receiver. "I guess that's that. Either your advice about women was wrong or it came too late." He'd been skeptical at first of my sundry counsels, he said, but they'd stuck in his mind, and though it went against the grain of his temperament to eschew compromise, he'd had to acknowledge himself guilty of occasional secret "deals" with Classmate X, Ira Hector, and Maurice Stoker; he had, moreover, tolerated moderate amounts of graft, academic dishonesty, prostitution, and other campus vices as unavoidable in a large college, and very infrequently had allowed himself a fit of anger, a drink too many, or an extracurricular night of love, usually with Anastasia Stoker. Upon his return from our ill-fated trip to the U.C. building last spring, his wife had announced plans for a short vacation, alone; and smitten with bad conscience (as well as distraught by the failure of the Summit Symposium), he'd confessed these past errors, begged her pardon, and vowed to lapse from passèd fidelity no more. When word reached him (during his wife's absence) that Bray had passed me for flunking his own diplomates, Rexford determined to follow my advice to the letter: to purge himself of every trace of immoderation and renounce absolutely all traffic with flunkèdness—if his administration could not pass the "Open Book Test," let it fall! His subsequent measures I'd heard about in Main Detention, and their unhappy consequences, all except one: when Mrs. Rexford had at last returned from her long holiday he'd not even scolded her, much less struck her, though everything suggested she'd been unfaithful. On the contrary, he'd proposed they attend together a course of lectures called The Problems of Marriage in a Changing University.

But while he prided himself on having achieved perfect reasonableness and self-control, he did not feel Commenced.

Not because things were going wretchedly—he knew that Right was right and Wrong wrong regardless of consequences—but because his heart's desires hid yet from the light of reason. That the Powerhouse threatened to explode from overproduction while Great Mall flickered and WESCAC flagged for want of power; that West Campus was losing the Quiet Riot, and his administration its popularity; that people suspected him of kinship with Stoker since Stoker had ceased to oppose him; that Classmate X had just announced a new advance of the Nikolayan Power Line and Mrs. Rexford a new vacation, perhaps with a friend and perhaps permanent—all these he might accept as the price of Truth. But the truth was, when he saw Stoker lounging at the gate in a motorcycle-jacket he had the strongest wish to hear him taunt as in the old days, "Flunk you, Brother!" When he saw Anastasia, despite her recent coldness and his perfect restraint, he still tumesced; yet he loved his wife so, her disaffection notwithstanding, that the rumors of her infidelity smote him with jealous rage; gladly would he strike her down—and pick her up, and madly kiss away her bruises . . .

"But that's lunacy, of course," he finished dryly. "I'll do nothing of the sort. If she and X won't debate these things with me, reasonably and openly—that's that. I'll sit here and wait for the EAT-whistle."

"Assuming there's power enough to blow it," I reminded him. "And somebody worried enough to pull the cord."

He laughed a little sheepishly. "There's plenty of power. The trick is to get it to Great Mall without dealing with Stoker. Nothing to lose our heads about, I suppose . . ."

"But it is!" I asserted. "All these things are, sir! Stoker *is* your brother! And I'm no Grand Tutor! I was completely wrong before!"

The Chancellor frowned and glanced towards the door. "Calm down, now . . ."

"No! That's just what you *shouldn't* do!" I strode about the office, gesturing with my stick. "There isn't really any boundary between East and West Campuses: all students are classmates! This nonsense about Informationalism and Student-Unionism—"

"Look here, now, Mr. Giles; I insist you calm yourself." Rexford fiddled nervously with a combination paperweight-flashlight on his desk, clicking the switch on and off. It didn't light. "Maybe from the Founder's viewpoint the Power Line is artificial and unreal, but we're not the Founder. Remarks like those may be harmless in the classroom, but out on the campus things aren't so simple."

"Exactly!" I agreed. "That's why it was a mistake to be absolutely reasonable, and the rest."

"I admit it's not easy. All the same—"

"That's the Answer!" I cried. "*East* and *West, temperate* and *intemperate*—they're all the same!"

"Mr. Giles," the Chancellor protested, consulting his wristwatch. "I'm the chief executive of a busy college, and much as I'd like to reason these things out with you—"

"There isn't *time!*" I finished for him. "And besides, you don't *feel* like being reasonable! That's splendid!"

He saw nothing very splendid about it, Rexford declared; but as he did not after all order me out, I explained to him briefly what I took to be the essence of my former error, and how I'd come to understand that East and West Campuses, goat and Grand Tutor, even Passage and Failure, were inseparable and ultimately indistinguishable.

"You talk like The Living Sakhyan," the Chancellor scoffed. "Be reasonable now: what do you propose?"

My first proposal, I told him, was to cease being reasonable—as if there were a floodlit Boundary between Reason and Unreason! Did his stubborn insistence upon reason at any price not prove the fallacy of such distinctions?

"So we should surrender to the Nikolayans?"

"Not surrender," I said, *"embrace."*

"Nonsense."

"Right!" I cried again. "Embrace nonsense! *Be* moderate when you feel like it! *Don't* always be reasonable with your wife! Make the guards look down so they can see what thin air they're standing on, just like Entelechus! Go hug your brother!"

"Hug my brother!" Rexford blushed hotly—but not, I thought, in anger.

"You know as well as I do that he *is* your brother. Go have a drink with him! And next time you see Anastasia—"

"He's not actually my *brother,*" the Chancellor put in hastily. "Some kind of half-brother or foster-brother, I think . . ."

"What's the difference? Embrace him!" It occurred to me that the difference, in Rexford's mind, might be between adultery with a blood-brother's wife and adultery with an adopted brother's wife, and so I didn't press the indistinction further. Nor did I itemize the ways in which I'd have him repudiate my former Tutelage and assert its contrary. He was, I saw, strongly tempted by Stoker's presence just outside the gate, and by despair, which flooded in on him almost visibly once I'd got through his equilibrium. Therefore I contented myself with advising that the "Open Book" be shut forthwith, and that an amnesty be declared for everyone detained under its reforms.

It was the Chancellor now who strode about, shaking his head. "This is crazy!" He stopped and grinned; the famous forelock fell. "I know: it's *supposed* to be crazy. All the same—" He laughed aloud at this additional irony, throwing back his head and flashing his fine teeth. "Wouldn't that make them sit up, though, if I went out there and called Maury *Brother!* Or told X to bring his Line as close as he wants!"

Unsettled by the tempting outrageousness of that idea, he flung open the curtains of a double glass door leading from the office onto a terrace, and squinted and chuckled in the glare. Beyond the low wall of the terrace was the driveway-gate where Stoker lingered with some of his sooty crew and a few reporters.

"One thing at a time," I cautioned. He caught me up brightly: who was being the prudent one now? But delighted as I was by his respiriting, I felt obliged to warn him that there were photographers about.

His blue eyes twinkled. "What difference does that make? Anyway their pictures haven't been turning out lately. No flashgun batteries." But he grew grave for just a moment at the terrace door. "You say you're not the Grand Tutor, George; but I understand you really are the GILES."

I shrugged. "That's what WESCAC says."

He smiled again. "I'm not as crazy as you might wish. But I take you seriously, and I think I see your point: it's worth risking some kind of long-shot to change my luck and brighten up my image a little. It had better not fail, though."

Before one could say "Failure is Passage" he stepped outside, topcoatless in the winter air, and vaulted lightly over the terrace wall. I saw the reporters rap one another's arms as he strode up, brisk as a sophomore track man, and Stoker scowl at the wrought-iron gate. Aides burst into the office, looked about in wonder, and thrust past me without a word. Then, shedding their topcoats and rumpling their hair, they vaulted after him. What the Chancellor said I couldn't hear from the terrace, but he grabbed Stoker's hand through the gate and pumped it vigorously. Once only he seemed to wince, then flashbulbs popped after all—the Powerhouse-Director had no doubt been horsetrading—then he grinned his grin, flung open the gate, and clapped an arm about Stoker's leathern shoulder. Reporters and cameramen tumbled and called; microphones appeared; Stoker glowered and shook his fist at a Telerama-boom. But Lucky Rexford laughed, would not unhug him, and saying something into the microphones, pointed first to Stoker's black forelock and then to his own sand-white one. His hand was sooty.

More than content, I went back into the entrance-hall; rather than disturb the reunion I would walk the few kilometers to the Infirmary, where I hoped to find Dr. Sear and perhaps Anastasia as well. There was a bustle on the wide central staircase: Mrs. Rexford, crisp and elegant, came down with a gaggle of scribbling ladies and a phalanx of suitcase-bearing young men. Coolly she moved in their van, a slim-legged, doe-eyed, soft-mouthed beauty, with the high-strung grace of careful breeding—truly a Hedda among lady girls (though deficient of udder). She regarded me and my detention-suit with brief disdain while one of her female companions informed her that her husband was at the front gate, and that the press wanted to photograph them together before she left on her vacation-trip. She glanced somewhat petulantly towards a fellow in her retinue, who, though dressed like a chancellor's aide, had not gone with the others; I thought I saw him nod.

"All right," she said, daintily vexed. I considered warning her of Mr. Rexford's changed attitude—but her cool and powdered elegance I found not approachable. I felt ungroomed, less washèd even than I was, a stinkish bill-buck: and though a moment later I put by that feeling with some annoy, I let her go uncautioned, a-whisper in the gray-suit fellow's ear, and left the Light House by a different path. Crossing Great Mall I heard lady-shrieks and other commotion behind me, and was tempted to run with the others to the Light-House gate, to see what was happening. But already my faint shadow fell east of north; the hour was later than I'd supposed, and work remained to do.

Gimping hospitalwards, I scolded myself further for hav-

ing let human upperclassness put me down. GILES, son of
WESCAC, maternal grandson of Reginald Hector; laboratory
eugenical specimen of the Grand-Tutorial ideal (no less rare
even if false); protégé of Maximilian Spielman—and a goat,
by George: a brawny-bearded bigballed buck! Stepkid of
Mary Appenzeller; stallmate of Redfearn's Tom; lover of
Hedda of the Speckled Teats; familiar of that late legendary
sire of sires, Brickett Ranunculus, the very dean of studs—*I*
should deny my pedigree and heritage, my gait my garb my
scent? Infirmity! My one infirmity, I saw now, was having
thought such goatly gifts in need of cure, and that infirmity
was overcome. Studentdom it was that limped: hobbled by
false distinction, crippled by categories! I returned unflinch-
ingly the stares of male and female undergraduates thronging
the sidewalks, and reasoned one strong step further: my infirmity was that I *had* thought myself first goat, then wholly
human boy, when in fact I was a goat-boy, both and neither:
a walking refutation of such false conceits. If I chose, withal,
to comport me goatly now awhile, it was not to deny my humanness (of what was the GILES decocted if not the seed of
the whole student body?) but to correct it, in the spirit of my
new advisings. To that end, as I drew near the Psychiatric
Annex of the great Infirmary I goated it the more—"went to
the bathroom" where no bathroom was, as in pasture days;
bleated twice or thrice at the passersby's dismay; and skipped
up the marble entrance steps on all fours—the point being
that I *wasn't* just *Capra hircus*, any more than the white-coat
pair of watchers at the top were simply *Homo sapiens*.

"A wise guy," one of them said.

"I don't know, Bill," said the other.

"George Giles the Goat-Boy," I announced, rising proudly
to shake hands.

They exchanged glances. "Come off it, pal," Bill said.
"Let's see your matric card."

Pleased at the chance to demonstrate my point, I displayed
the blank ID-card with a smile. "What difference does a
name make, classmates? I *am*, that's all."

"What'd I tell you," his colleague said to him. Bill
grunted.

I was surprised and pleased. "You've thought of it before? That none of us really has a name?"

"Some stinks worse'n others, though," Bill said. The two
each took an elbow, and they led me inside. When I under-

stood that the jacket they called for was for me, and strait, I protested I'd only come to visit Dr. Sear. Bill acknowledged again, grudgingly, that his companion's guess had been correct. "I knew he treated lots of them animal ones," he said in his own defense. "But I thought that there goat one was in Main Detention."

"He *is*," the other said, and explained patiently; "what there is, though, Bill, there's some *thinks* they're the ones that thinks they're animals! It's in their heads."

"You reckon Sear treats them ones too?"

Proud of his knowledge, Bill's companion pointed out that Dr. Sear was a diagnostician, not a therapist. "He just sees what bin they belong in, is all."

The waistcoat was fetched—a cross-armed canvas thing—but they offered not to bind me in it if I'd come quietly to Dr. Sear's office. I agreed, delighted to infer that the doctor had recovered from his dread affliction as well as from his suicide-attempt, and I endeavored to Tutor my gruff escorts no further.

Other orderlies waited with patients in Dr. Sear's corridor. One of the latter growled and snapped at me as he and his keeper took our place in the lift; I lowered my head to butt, bleated a warning, and hoofed the terrazzo floor. The disturbance brought Anastasia hurrying from the Reception Room with dog-biscuits.

"George!" Her eyes widened at sight of the strait-jacket. Refusing to hear the orderlies' story, she scolded them sharply for treating the Grand Tutor as a madman; they were flunkèd as her husband, she said, who'd detained me as a common felon. They grumbled apologies and unhanded me, cowed by her temper if not persuaded by her representation; still flushed with outrage, she nevertheless agreed not to report their misjudgment to Dr. Sear, and dismissed them.

"A regular nut-house," Bill said disgustedly to his colleague.

Anastasia led me into the Reception Room (where I was surprised to see my mother, placidly knitting) and at once hugged me and made tears—not at all the chilly woman she had been being! "I'm so *glad* You're out of Detention," she exclaimed, and although she added, "everything's so mixed up, I don't know *what* to do!" I was pleased to believe her glad of my release apart from any aid she might require. And her recaptured warmth so gratified me that I kissed her

mouth. Nibbled her even, ardently, whereupon she drew back
with her usual wonder, but did not oppose my doing it again.

"Don't just *allow* me!" I rebuked her—still holding her
against me. "Either stop me or join in."

She looked fretfully to Mother, who however regarded us
with blank benignity and went on knitting.

"It doesn't come *naturally* to me, George," she complained. "And I'm all upset just now . . ."

Bracing my heart I asked whether Bray had serviced her.
More tears ensued, and blushes; she wrung in her hands the
forgotten biscuits. He had not, she thanked the Founder,
summoned her as yet, owing to his busy schedule of appointments for Certification. But their rendezvous was set for the
coming midnight, in the Belfry; he was to fetch her from the
Living Room at eleven o'clock.

"No," I said. At once she flung her arms about my neck
for joy. But I continued: "You go to *him*, Anastasia. *You* do
the servicing."

She wept: she could not, not *ever*. Task enough to submit
to every creature's lust, as I had bid her; if she could manage
it at all, it was only at my order, and because I'd taught her
how responsible she was for the lust she helplessly provoked;
but she besought me not to make her take the initiative.

"You must," I said. "And not only with Bray. I want you
to *seduce* people—even Stoker."

"*Maurice?*" If she was anguished before, now she was simply shocked. "You mean . . . make love to my *husband?*
What would he *think!*"

His thoughts, I told her, were not important; her Commencement was, and it depended on her overcoming the false
distinctions I had formerly burdened her with. Yes, she must
seduce her own husband, overwhelm him with carnalities of
every description, even Conscious Depravities. Moreover, for
both their sakes she must cuckold him; commit fornications
without his knowledge and against his wishes.

"That's *impossible!*" she protested. "You know how Maurice is!" But her eyes refilled as she remembered, visibly, that
he'd been neither brute nor pander since my first false Tutoring, but so chaste and docile a spouse he'd often made her
cross. "That would be *adultery*, George!"

This last was more than refusal, and setting the teeth of
my spirit I insisted she deceive her husband, not only with
Bray but with for example Dr. Eierkopf and any other crea-

ture who crossed her fancy or her path—male or female, human or hound-dog, even animate or inanimate. All discrimination must go by the board.

She shook her head. "That's flunkèd!"

"Failure is Passage," I reminded her. She objected no more, but admitted tearfully that Dr. Sear had just finished telling her the very same thing, apropos of "the Peter Greene business," and though she'd understood it from him no more clearly than from me, even when he applied my reasoning to his own case, she guessed she had no choice but to acknowledge her stupidity and try to obey without understanding, repugnant as was the notion of such lewdness. I asked what business of or with Greene she meant, as she seemed not to be alluding to the spring-term rape—and also how my advice to her had applied to Dr. Sear, for while I was pleased to see he saw my point about her "charity" and the need to invert my former Tutoring, I had not myself considered what ought to be his new prescription. By way of answer, she locked the hall-door and bade me come with her into the Observation Room. As we passed in front of my mother, that lady caught and kissed my hand, the first indication that she knew I was there, and smiled slyly to herself as always. I kissed her hair, and she put down her knitting to make Enos Enoch's hand-sign on her fallen chest.

"What are you knitting, Mother?" I asked gently, and looked to Anastasia for reply; between her spells of reliving our season in the hemlocks, my poor Lady Creamhair spoke not at all except in confidential whispers to My Ladyship, whom she stayed with constantly, as it seemed.

Anastasia colored. "It's a baby-sweater, George. Mom— Your mother thinks I'm going to have a baby."

I considered her belly. "Are you?"

"Of course not!"

Mother nodded to the wee blue wrapper. "Bye Baby Billikins."

Anastasia colored further. "Sometimes she thinks it's that WESCAC business again, and *her* that's pregnant."

But my mother resolutely shook her head.

"You *do,* sometimes!" Anastasia scolded her; but then confessed what I took to be Mother's commoner delusion; "other times she seems to think I'm Your *wife* or something . . ."

I smiled and kissed again Mother's poor mad hair, and to

humor her folly drew Anastasia near, patted her fine flat gut, and nodded.

"That's cruel, George!" In a little temper My Ladyship went into the Observation Room. "I'm not even *able* to have babies, and You know it!"

My apology seemed rather to encourage than to mollify her petulance; she maintained a more or less injured air while recounting Peter Greene's strange forenoon invasion of the office. But though I was much interested in her tale, I forgot her vexèd tone when I looked through the oneway glass into the Treatment Room and saw a shirtsleeved man, his head swathed in bandages, lying on the leathern couch—and Peter Greene, white-coated, in the chair at its head!

5.

"Don't ask *me*," Anastasia said, before I'd thought to. "Kennard took him in there to calm him down, and next thing I knew it was like that. They've been at it since before lunch."

From her account I gathered that the bandaged man was Dr. Sear; his malady was no curabler than before, but surgical excision of his nose had abated its progress, temporarily, enough for him to resume a limited practice. Anastasia had returned to assist him on the conditions that she be obliged no longer to offer sexual therapy to anyone, even Mrs. Sear, and that her "mother" be permitted to stay with her in the Reception Room. Indeed, it was Mother, I was startled to learn, who in her own recent therapy-sessions had by some means conveyed to Dr. Sear the first reports of my new programme—perhaps by the same fortuitous quotations from the Syllabi that she'd inspired me with. In any case, with his usual acuity Sear had seen my point, and when shortly afterwards Anastasia had come to him, distraught, with word of my strange new advice, he'd not only approved it, but fortified my paradoxical argument with a dozen quotations from *Footnotes to Sakhyan* and other works of "unitary expletivism," none of which My Ladyship could make heads or tails of.

" 'He *is* a Grand Tutor!' " she said he'd said of me. "I told him *You* said You weren't, and he said, "That's the point! That's what I mean!' " She sighed (still a little poutish): thereafter Sear had pressed her in vain to return to the practice of sexual therapy; and it was he, I now learned, who had suggested that she might secure my release by promising to become Bray's mistress (he'd also persuaded Bray to release me on the strength of her pledge without waiting for its consummation—not to mention the siring upon her of the child Bray craved). Further, Sear had acknowledged to her that he himself had been desperately flunkèd thitherto, even as I'd said; was flunkèd still, as he'd seen too plainly at the Honeymoon Lodge Motel. Hence the decision to end his life. Rescued willynilly from the sleeping-capsules, he'd tried to relish the horror of his disease, but the physical decay, it seemed, drove out the intellectual, and he'd found himself terrified instead of diverted by death's approach. Anosmia was followed by exophthalmos, and as his eyeballs began to pop, the cancer spread to and obstructed his lacrimal ducts, with the result that tears ran from them almost constantly. But it was as much *for* as *from* his condition that he wept. Greatly as he loathed mutilation, now he feared death more, and consented to radical surgery: the tears disappeared, along with his nose and a portion of the sight of both eyes.

With what vision remained to him he'd striven to imagine how my new Answer fit his case. Clearly I would not advise him to refine his amusements or otherwise attempt to become more campusly—the end of *that* road he'd reached already, at the Honeymoon Lodge Motel. From my advice to Anastasia he inferred correctly that he should assert whatever it was he had vainly tried to rid himself of; further, he'd concluded that that must necessarily be some kind of ingenuousness or ignorance of himself, inasmuch as he'd devoted his whole life to their opposites. That he could *see* no defect in his insight proved to him that the defect existed, since perfect insight would see its imperfections; had he not been naïve to think himself not naïve? His first prescription, therefore, had been to commit himself to the custody of his wife, who had regressed to the psychological age of five. But much as he'd enjoyed playing "Doctor" with her in the sandbox of the chronic-ward playground, he'd come to realize that however correct his diagnosis and prescription, they were invalid perforce, as he'd arrived at them himself.

"So this morning he asked *me* to tell him what to do!" An-

astasia exclaimed. "As if *I* were the doctor! I said he'd better
talk to You, that *I* didn't understand this crazy business—and
the way he thanked me, you'd think that was exactly what he
wanted to hear! As if he couldn't have thought of it himself!"

"I see." And I did see, dimly, his general reasoning, I believed: Sear needed to come to me at the behest of someone
else, preferably someone who didn't understand the situation.
It had seemed to bother him, though, Anastasia continued,
when she reminded him that she was only a nurse. But before
she could suggest that he consult a professional colleague,
their conversation had been interrupted by Greene's visit.

"You won't *believe* what he came to tell me!" The memory
so renewed her astonishment, she forgot her pique at my having pretended she was pregnant.

I smiled. "He apologized for confusing you with your
flunkèd twin sister."

"How did You know? He's *crazy,* George! And I hate to
say it, but I'm afraid Kennard's mind has been affected, too.
By the cancer . . ."

I followed her account as well as I could, for it was more
arresting and suggestive than I'd anticipated. But my attention was sorely divided: not only was I listening at the same
time to the conversation in the Treatment Room, which I'd
remembered could be overheard at the flip of a switch; I was
also sharply interested in observing through the glass what
appeared to be a new development in the strange relation between Greene and Sear.

"*I* thought he wanted to apologize for last spring," Anastasia said. "In fact, I was going to offer to explain the whole
thing to his wife, in case she thought it was *his* fault, what
he'd done to me. But when he started in on this *sister* business, and how he was sorry he'd ever thought it was *me* that
wasn't a virgin . . . ! He got more excited all the time, saying
his wife was the dearest little wifey on the Founder's green
campus and I was the dearest little sister, and women like
Maurice's secretary and my *sister* were floozies that ought to
be horsewhipped! Kennard was right there listening to the
whole thing, and when Mr. Greene started saying he'd defend
my honor to the death, and pawing me at the same time, I
thought Kennard would *help* me! Because it wasn't the first
time, You know, that a patient ever got *fresh,* and I really
think Mr. Greene thought he was *protecting* me, or something . . . But do You think Kennard helped? He was listen-

ing to Mr. Greene as if it were the Grand Tutor talking, and when Mr. Greene tried to lay me down on the desk-top, all Kennard said was 'Remember what George told you, Stacey'!"

In the Treatment Room, as she spoke, Greene had been inveighing against the decline of moral standards in "the present modern campus of today" and recommending that the dunce-cap and birch-rod be restored to their place of honor in New Tammany kindergartens; Sear interrupted him to ask whether, when he played Doctor with Mrs. Sear in the Asylum sandbox, he ought to pretend to be the doctor and Hedwig the patient, or vice-versa: to his mind, taking make-believe rectal temperatures with a forest-green crayon was an apt symbolic affirmation of the element of childish perversity which had always underlain his sophisticated medical researches; on the other hand, he could see that assuming the "patient's" role not only in the office, as he was doing presently, but also in the sandbox—baring *his* bum to *Hedwig's* popsicle-stick—might be said to combine inversion, perversion, reversion, and reversal.

"What do *you* suggest, Doctor?" he inquired.

"Now that's enough!" Greene said angrily. "That's just plain dirty talk, is all it is!"

"I *know*," Sear admitted. "But the fact is, you see, I was a *very* naughty five-year-old. I peeked up the little girls' dresses and tasted my b.m.'s and showed me my pee-tom to the teacher. So what I hope you'll tell me is whether 'becoming as a kindergartener' means returning innocently to childish perversions or pervertedly feigning a childish innocence . . ."

"Did Greene actually service you, then?" I asked Anastasia.

"He *would* have, I'm sure," she said, "and thought he was defending my *virginity* the whole time! But when Kennard reminded me of what You'd told me I got all mixed up, because I *don't* like Mr. Greene—not *that* way, especially since last spring—and yet I *do* believe in You, George, even if You don't. But it's so *hard* for me to act like a . . . a *floozy*, You know . . ."

"That's just more smut, Dr. Sear!" Greene was declaring. "You know durn well I'm not any sawbones, say what you want, nor a headshrinker either—excuse the expression! I'm a simple country boy that's trying to do the right thing by his wife and family and his alma mater. Don't think I don't see you're up to some naughtiness with this playing-doctor business, pull-the-wool-over-my-eyeswise."

"What did you do?" I was wondering vaguely whether the net effect of a seduction of Greene by My Ladyship would be therapeutic or antitherapeutic, so to speak, in their separate cases; likewise a repetition, under present circumstances, of her previous forcible alleying. At the same time, the conversation in the Treatment Room I found more absorbing, and relevant to my Assignment as well as to Greene's and Sear's.

"All I could think of was how crazy that *sister* idea was," Anastasia said. "He was trying to take my clothes off, and Kennard was taking Mr. *Greene's* clothes off—You know Kennard! I was squirming around on the desk, and Kennard thought I was trying to be *sexy*—so did Mr. Greene, I guess. But really I was trying to *be* loose and *get* loose at the same time, I was so mixed up by what You'd told me. Anyhow, I was shouting in Mr. Greene's ear that I was Maurice Stoker's wife and hadn't been a virgin since I was twelve, and between that and my wiggling around he decided *I* was the flunkèd sister! So he got off me, thank the Founder—in fact, I could see he *couldn't* do anything then, even if he'd wanted to; You know what I mean—and he started lecturing me about disgracing my sister Stacey. *Honestly!* Then Kennard took him into the Treatment Room to calm him down, even though Mr. Greene said he wouldn't listen to any more of Kennard's talk, because he was okay and it didn't matter anyhow. But Kennard spoke to him very respectfully and said he wanted to *ask* advice instead of giving it ..."

At this point, though my mind remained much on My Ladyship, I stopped listening to her story (which was growing somewhat hysterical anyway) in order to hear with delighted surprise Greene's counsel to Dr. Sear.

"You ought to quit this playing Doctor and Patient," he was saying severely. "It don't become an educated man like yourself, that kind of smartness. And it don't show proper respect for your wife, neither, that I'm sure is a good upstanding woman ..."

"It was *her* idea," Dr. Sear complained. His voice grew stubborn as a pre-schooler's. "It was her crayons and popsicle-sticks, too."

"That don't matter," Greene insisted. "You ought to have a proper self-respect for her. Take yourself, now: except for that there cancer you're a healthy man! So don't let your wife's craziness fool you, all that drinking and messing around with floozies like Lacey—you got to learn to see through a woman like that."

"I've *seen*," Dr. Sear insisted half-heartedly.

"I wonder," Greene chided. "Why, take away her failings and you've got a passèd wife and mother!"

"We have no children," Dr. Sear dryly pointed out.

Greene was not abashed. "Get busy and have some, then! What's a marriage without children?" Tears rose in his eyes; he fetched out his wallet. "Take a look at these kiddies here and tell me you don't want a passel of your own! Aren't they the passèdest little scapers you ever laid eyes on? They're grown up now, of course . . ."

Though presumably he could not weep, Dr. Sear wiped the bandages near his eyes with a handkerchief and waved away the photographs as if the sight of them was more than he could bear. Greene sniffled and declared that, fool and flunker though he was in other respects, he'd been a loving father to his children, and Miss Sally Ann a loving mother, nobody could take *that* away from them, and in this conviction they could go to the Gate content, fulfill-their-natural-purpose-on-this-campuswise. Satisfied, even inspired, I turned to Anastasia, and was surprised to observe that she too was in tears. I recalled her emotion on the occasion of my own recommending, for very different reasons, that Dr. and Mrs. Sears beget a child, and assumed that now, as then, she was weeping with pleasure for their sakes.

"Out of the mouths of babes," I said cheerfully. "That's about what I was going to tell Dr. Sear myself, with maybe one qualification; but it's even better for him to hear it from Greene." I gave her pretty rump a pat, and by way of a cordial tease declared it was high time she herself was bred; if Stoker wasn't stud enough and Bray should miss his appointment, maybe I'd service her myself . . .

She cried, "You're hateful!" and fled into the Reception Room. I followed after.

"I was only joking, Anastasia."

"You don't understand *anything!*" She turned on Mother, who was silently making the Enochist sign with her knitwork. "Will you *stop* that?"

Shocked as I was, I believed I saw through her anger then: so rare a thing was barrenness among the does, I could not keep in mind that My Ladyship was infertile. I had been tactless; no doubt she'd *wanted* to breed with Stoker, if only for the improvement that lactation would work upon her udder. I apologized sincerely, and by way of consoling her pointed out that Mrs. Lucius Rexford, for example, was all but flat-chested despite her having been freshened once or twice by the Chancellor; also that I'd heard it claimed (by the free-speaking inmates of Main Detention) that there were men who actually *preferred* rather udderless women. For all I knew, Maurice Stoker might belong to that fraternity.

She pummeled at my head.

"Stop it, Anastasia! I don't understand this at all!"

Our scuffling brought Greene and Sear from the Treatment Room; as soon as they opened the door My Ladyship fled inside, turning her face from them. Greene curled his lip, even spat in her direction. Dr. Sear's reaction I couldn't observe, owing to the bandages, but we greeted each other warmly. He was delighted to learn I'd overheard his conversation with Greene and approved his reasoning; he embraced us by turns, nowise amorously, and though he was unable to weep or snif-fle, his voice caught at the notion of fathering a child.

"We tried last time, George, as you know," he said with difficulty. "It was so outrageous, taking Heddy to bed—and at the Honeymoon Lodge Motel, of all places, like freshman newlyweds! It should've been marvelously perverse, just as you intended, but when Hed put on her bridal nightie, and I thought of the incredible things we'd done over the semes-ters . . ." It was then, he said huskily, that the ceaseless flow of tears had commenced, and instead of mounting his wife, perversely, in the ordinary way, he had been smitten with the hopeless wish that they could be free, if only for an hour, of the burden of all they'd seen and done, and could come to-gether in simple, bashful love. Impossible, of course: not dis-taste or disinclination but shame unmanned him; what kind of parents would *they* be, anyway? they sneered, and con-temning each other and themselves they'd gone, she to the bottle and to Croaker in the lobby, he to the sleeping-cap-sules.

"It weren't no proper way," Greene said stoutly.

"Founder help me, George!" Sear exclaimed. "What a blind dunce I've been! If a man could only wipe the slate clean!"

"A fresh start," Greene affirmed. "Being smart never made a man happy. Where there's life there's hope."

The awful triteness of these sentiments made Sear sob. But dared he imagine, he asked me, that even with the aid of what he called "self-hypnotic autoamnesis" he could ever achieve enough unself-consciousness to make love to his wife—not to mention begetting a child in the Honeymoon Lodge Motel?

"If a person wishes hard enough," Greene solemnly declared, "his wishes'll come true. Say what you want."

I smiled. "You might try, anyway, I think, if they'll let Mrs. Sear leave the Asylum." In his case, I decided, it was inadvisable to add that he needn't worry if the plan misfired again, since failure and passage, rightly conceived, were not different. Judging from what he'd told Anastasia, he was acquainted with the truth of that paradox. "Forget about Taliped and Gynander as well as yourself," I advised him. "Keep telling yourself that you'll live happily ever after."

"What *I* always say to myself," Greene said: *"I'm okay. And what the heck anyhow."*

Sear shook his head, unable to speak.

"I have some business with My Ladyship," I said. "May I use the Treatment Room for a while?"

When he understood to whom the term referred, Dr. Sear readily granted permission, he being too unsettled to see more patients that day. But for all his absorption in his own "Assignment" (as he called the wife-bedding project), he ventured the opinion that "seeing through my ladyship" must mean denying my male sexuality—or better, affirming and embracing the female aspects which he claimed no male was without—in order to demonstrate that *male* and *female* were no realer than any other categories. Was that not the sense of my new Answer? And "overcoming my infirmity," if he understood Sakhyanism correctly, ought similarly to mean denying either the difference between *sick* and *well* or the reality of the "I" alleged to be ill—an attitude he himself meant to take toward his squamous-cell carcinoma if he could. "After all," he said, "if I'm dying of cancer, then cancer is living of me: in the Founder's eyes it's all the same, isn't it?"

I shrugged. "You may be right, sir. But what the heck anyhow."

He put a fist to his bandaged brow. "I see, I see!" He might have embraced me again, but Greene held up a finger and said, "Ah-ah."

"Flunk me for ever doubting You, George! You really *are* the Grand Tutor!"

I shook my head, but Mother in the corner said, "A-plus."

"A-plus indeedy," Greene agreed, but added that in his opinion Grand Tutors should have no traffic with the flunked likes of Lacey Stoker.

"I'll be okay," I assured him, and pointed out that even Enos Enoch in His term had passed a floozy or two. "It's a curious thing," I said to Dr. Sear, more seriously; "I think I understand you two pretty well, for instance, and Max and Dr. Eierkopf and the rest. Even Maurice Stoker I can see through, more or less. But My Ladyship's a mystery; I never know what to make of her."

"I feel the same durn way about Sally Ann," Greene confessed.

"I used to think I knew Hedwig inside out," said Dr. Sear. "But now sometimes I wonder whether I've ever known her at all. Or anything, for that matter."

We may not have been thinking of the same thing: Anastasia's mysteriousness, I felt, was not just the famous unpredictability of human women or the celebrated difference between male and female points of view; it had rather to do with the insufficiency of any notion I entertained of her. I was reminded of a time long past, in the barns, when Max, more familiar to me than my own face, had seemed suddenly, unbearably other than myself: a stranger, alien and distinct; as who would find that his arm or leg has a will not his, a personality of its own. But in the case of Anastasia this foreignness was the more conspicuous for its contrast with our obscure intimacy: I had never bit Max in a sidecar, after all, or serviced him memorially, or declared to him despite myself (strange words) "I love you!" or chosen him, in the days of my error, as my first Tutee. Bright as Anastasia's eyes shone on me, I could not see what lay behind their luminosity, or account for her behavior.

"In any case," I said, "I've felt for some time that until I see through My Ladyship I can't be sure I understand anyone, myself included. That's the only thing I believed last spring that I still believe."

"I see your point," Dr. Sear said. "I may question your definition of the term, but I certainly agree with the principle."

"If you'll excuse me, then . . ." I smiled. "I'm going to try to learn all there is to know about My Ladyship."

He opened and closed his hands and admitted he'd like nothing better than to watch us from the Observation Room, but acceded to Greene's veto of that idea. He could not refrain from pointing out, however, that the Treatment Room was soundproof; that if Anastasia had truly become her old obliging self again, one could do what one pleased with her; but that a closet near the couch was stocked with manacles, whips, and other instruments of sportive interrogation should I need or desire them.

"Now you quit that," Greene scolded. But he bade me anxiously to be careful for though he was sure I'd never step out of line, take-advantage-of-the-weaker-sexwise, we would be durned if a floozy like Lacey couldn't lead The Living Sakhyan Himself astray—look what she'd done to *him* behind the Old Chancellor's Mansion! I promised to keep both eyes open, reminded Dr. Sear that I sought merely illumination, not gratification of any appetite, normal or abnormal, and went into the Treatment Room, closing the door behind me.

Anastasia sat half-turned on the leathern couch, hiding her face in its arm and her own. I sat down to apologize for any hurt I'd done her feelings unintentionally; but as soon as I touched her hip in a conciliatory way, she flung herself upon me and wailed into my chest that she was the unhappiest woman on campus, and wished herself passed and gone.

I was freshly confounded. "Then you aren't angry at me for teasing you about being sterile? It *was* thoughtless."

She sniffled into my jail-coat that she knew I hadn't *meant* to be tactless, and that anyhow her infertility had been attested by Dr. Sear to be psychological rather than physiological, and thus perhaps not a permanent condition. She drew back to look at me, blushing and grave. "Human women don't have *heats*, You know, George—I remember Maurice telling You something silly about that at the Powerhouse—but we're supposed to have *orgasms,* and for some reason I don't. Kennard says there might be a connection between that and not having babies."

This seemed doubtful to me, since the fertilest and most amorous does in the herd, to my knowledge, were strangers to the phenomenon she described: wag their pretty tails they might to call for love, and hunch some seconds after service

(maiden goatlings in particular) if the buck was strong; but
of "transports" and "climaxes" they knew nothing, I was certain. Mary Appenzeller, to cite but one example, an infallible
breeder, was inclined to munch hay calmly even when topped
by Brickett Ranunculus himself! As for infertility, there had
been few cases of it in the barns that could not be "cured" by
two dessertspoonfuls of soda dissolved in a liter of warm
water and administered vaginally prior to mating, to neutral-
ize uterine acidity—and I would have told Anastasia so forthwith, but I had come to learn, not to teach.

"Why are you unhappy, then?" I asked her. "What do you
want to be dead for? If there's nothing wrong with your organs you'll surely be in kid one of these terms, by
somebody . . ."

"George . . ." She drew the name out protestingly, and
seemed about to weep again. To forestall her I acknowledged
the truth of what she'd charged earlier—that with regard to
human ladies, at least, I understood nothing. I asked her to
remedy my ignorance with plain statements.

"Is there anything you have to do this afternoon? Dr.
Sear's closed the office."

She glanced apprehensively at the one-way mirror. I assured her that no one was watching, and wondered why she
cared, since we were only talking.

"Your mother wants to be home when Uncle Reg arrives,"
she said. "But that won't be until dinnertime."

"Then I'm going to get to know you," I said. "Inside out,
in every way. Even if it takes the rest of the afternoon."

Her eyes doubted. "I've *told* You my whole flunkèd past,
George: all the terrible things I've done thinking they were
right. You know as much about me as I do."

"I don't know why you wish you were dead," I observed.
"Stoker isn't cruel to you any more. And he could inseminate
you artificially if you can't conceive in the normal way. Out
in the barns, we—"

She shook her head. "I don't *want* to have a baby! Not by
him. George . . ." Her expression was awed. "There's something wrong with my marriage."

Recalling that Stoker had expressed a similar apprehension, I asked her what might be their trouble.

"I don't really love my husband!" she said, as if frightened
by her own candor. And then all reticence left her; in a tearful rush she confessed herself more flunkèd than I supposed.

Her lack of love for her husband, she declared, was not new, and had nothing to do with his pleasure in seeing her serviced by other men, not to mention women, dogs, inanimate objects, and Dr. Eierkopf's eggs, Grade-A Large; the truth was, she had never loved him; indeed, she feared she'd never loved *anyone*—male, female, or whatever. Of all Bray's Certifications, she felt hers to be the falsest, for though she most certainly had sympathized with her classmates and done her utmost to gratify their needs, loved them she had never, she knew now. And the proof of it was that while she'd never said "no" (except since my spring-term directive), she'd never said "yes," either. With her sex, perhaps, but not with her heart of hearts.

"That's very interesting," I said. "I think I'm getting to know you better already." What she said fit nicely too with my recent advice to her, I pointed out: saying *yes* to her classmates was, in effect, what I meant by actively servicing rather than passively receiving them.

"You don't *understand!*" she wailed. "How can I say it? I'm not supposed to *have* to say it!"

I frowned. "Say what, Anastasia? If I don't understand, teach me."

She closed her eyes and pounded the couch-cushion with one fist. "Why do You think I see these things about myself now, and never did before?"

I admitted that I hadn't any idea, unless it was that my mistaken first counsel to her and Stoker had led her to see that his abuses had nothing to do with her want of feeling for him.

"*No*, You idiot!" She gasped at her outcry, then wept freely and pounded the cushion with both fists. "I'm sorry, I'm sorry! Oh, Founder, You of all people . . . I can't say any more . . ."

"Now listen here, Anastasia," I said; "I'm a little tired of all this mystery. I'm not the Grand Tutor, but—"

"You *are*, George!"

I shook my head firmly. "I'm not; that's almost certain. But either way, I want you to take my advice and assert yourself. If I'm *not* the Grand Tutor, then what I tell you now is right because it's the opposite of what I said before, when I thought I was; if I *am* (which I doubt), then it's right because I am. You *must* assert yourself."

"I want to," she said, "because that's what *You* want . . ."

"Then stop beating around the bush. What is it you can't tell me?"

She looked at me, stricken. "I *love* You, George!"

I sat up. Her eyes brimmed over again.

"I don't understand it any more than You do; we hardly know each other . . ."

"What do you mean, *love?*" I demanded, much unsettled. She asked me shamefacèdly what *I* had meant when I'd said I loved *her.* "I don't know!" I cried. "The words just came out. I don't even know what it means!" She began to weep. I apologized for hurting her feelings again—but, flunk it all, I was alarmed, dismayed, I could not myself have said why; titillated of course, and flattered, certainly flattered—but equally appalled, oddly frightened, and for some reason cross. "In the herd, it means being in heat. For anybody. Everybody."

She whipped her head from side to side.

"Don't you really mean you're just convinced I'm the Grand Tutor?" I asked gruffly. "You loved Bray, too . . ."

"No!" It was true she had once believed in Harold Bray's Grand-Tutorship as well as mine, she said indignantly, and that now she believed in me exclusively, whether *I* did or not; but she had never loved Bray, only honored and obeyed him, and her love for me had nothing to do with her acknowledgment of my Tutorhood. In fact, the two sentiments were at cross-purposes: "I want to do what You tell me to, much as I hate the idea of other men," she said, "because You're the Grand Tutor, and what You say must be right. But the reason *why* I hate the idea is that I love You, George!" She looked at me straight, and took a breath. "I want *You* to make love to me!"

I strode about the Treatment Room, greatly excited.

"You *told* me to assert myself," she said.

"I know! I know!"

"I want to do what we did in the Living Room!" she cried. "You shouldn't just say 'I know, I know'!"

"I understand, Anastasia. The trouble is—"

"You think I'm a—*floozy!*" she exclaimed.

"No, no, no." I could not myself say why her profession of love, so gratifying to my vanity and destructive of my composure, did not also infuse me with desire.

"*Service* me!" Covered with shame and desperation she

took the position she'd once assumed in the Powerhouse. "Don't make me beg You!"

"Please, you don't understand." Nervously I stroked her cleft with the tips of my fingers. But roused as I was, at last, by the dainties thereabouts and her pretty sounds when I touched them, my mind grew clearer. I nuzzled her in the way of the friendly goats; but I would not mount her, I declared, love or no love, until she'd carried out my new directive. She kissed my mouth.

"Can't I start with You?"

Though her heat was real, taking the initiative was plainly an effort for her, and her attempts to provoke my ardor rather cooled than fired it.

"I do want to know you carnally too," I said, "but not until you've serviced your husband and Bray, at least . . ."

"I don't *want* them." On her knees upon the cushion now, she would assert herself further, draw my face into her bosom, offer her navel to my nose—all which I craved, detumescent as I was. Speaking with difficulty into her lower abdomen, I declared that that was exactly why we would not mate until she'd fulfilled her Assignment and made good the pledge that freed me.

"But even then you shouldn't *love* me the way you mean," I added. "If by some chance I turn out to be a Grand Tutor, I doubt if I ought to have a particular mistress, especially someone else's wife. And if I'm not—I won't be here to love." The idea disclosed itself to me in an instant, fullblown; I took my gold beard from her darling dark and addressed her gravely: "I left Main Detention for two reasons, Anastasia: to correct the mistakes I made last spring, and to flunk WESCAC. That's why I'm here—to Overcome My Infirmity and See Through My Ladyship. In a little while I'm going to find Harold Bray and go down to the Belly with him, without any mask on, and if WESCAC doesn't EAT me first, I'm going to destroy it."

She had started to protest; then she listened, her face stricken as when she'd said she loved me. At the end she drew her uniform together and kissed me chastely on the brow.

"Excuse me for acting so crazy, George," she said. "You see how hard it is for me to be aggressive." She sat down and smoothed her skirt. "If You get EATen, I'll get EATen too. I'm going with You."

"No."

She smiled firmly. "Yes I am. If I can't be Your sweetheart, I'll pass and be Your first protégée. You promised me that."

At once now I was inflamed with desire, by her return to demureness more than by her words, which were troubling enough. Now she didn't press it on me, the idea that I was loved stirred me to the bowels with warm amazement. To keep her from WESCAC's Belly was one thing; could I keep her from my heart as well? What in Founder's name was this thing from Sub-Departments of Sentimental Literature, this *love?* I was baffled, and felt now towards myself the same queer strangership I'd felt towards Anastasia, and erst towards Max: a loveless, gingerly, wrinkle-nosed curiosity.

"Is there something else You need to do with me for Your Assignment-task?" she asked determinedly. "Or shall I go home and service Maurice right now?" Her mind was made up, I saw, and my backbone tickled. My voice would not come; I shook my head. Her eyes shone with a kind of passionate reservation; she was mine, they said, in all particulars save one: I could not will her out of love.

"What else is there to learn about me, then?" she asked herself brightly, for my benefit. "You know my history, and how I feel about things. *I* know what!" She jumped up and rummaged through a filing-cabinet. "I can show You my medical records and my psychological profile! My academic transcript's on file in Tower Hall, of course; I'll send for a photocopy. Let me think . . ."

"Anastasia—" My voice was thick. She turned from the file.

"It's not—I don't want just information."

She ignored my emotion and pretended to consider deeply. "Let's see, then: *See Through Your Ladyship.*" She snapped her fingers. "The fluoroscope!"

I waved my hand, but she turned switches and stepped behind the ground-glass screen. Within the supple shadows of her flesh I saw dark bones and dusky organs.

"I'm not anything to love," I found myself saying. "I don't even know what I *am* . . ."

"This is my duodenum," she said crisply, as if lecturing, and pointed with a finger-bone. "These are my right and left kidneys here, and down here somewhere You may be able to see my ovaries. Come closer if You can't."

"Stop, Anastasia."

"I want You to see everything, George. It's all Yours." She turned sideways; despite my odd anguish I gazed fascinated at her innards. "I'm asserting myself," she reminded me. "Hold on: I'll use a light the way Heddy used to; You can see right through to it. Is that flunkèd enough?" There was no sarcasm in her tone, only lovingest resolve.

"Please, Anastasia!"

She applied to herself despite my murmurs an illuminated Lucite rod.

"Do you want to work it? Kennard likes to . . ."

"I'm not Kennard!" I cried. I took her hand and put an end to the illumination. "I'm not anybody!"

"You're the person I love," she replied, and laying aside the rod, hugged me softly. Notwithstanding her queer behavior, she seemed altogether at ease. I was most uncomfortable! "I'm sorry I complained about Your advice," she said calmly. "I kept thinking of it in the ordinary way, as Kennard or Maurice would, instead of seeing that the idea is to test my love, the way the Founder tested people in the Old Syllabus."

"Anastasia . . ." The name seemed strange to me now, and her hair's rich smell. What was it I held, and called *Anastasia?* A slender bagful of meaty pipes and pouches, grown upon with hairs, soaked through with juices, strung up on jointed sticks, the whole thing pulsing, squirting, bubbling, flexing, combusting, and respiring in my arms; doomed soon enough to decompose into its elements, yet afflicted in the brief meanwhile with mad imaginings, so that, not content to jelly through the night and meld, ingest, divide, it troubled its sleep with dreams of *passèdness,* of *love* . . .

She squeezed more tightly; I felt the blood-muscle pumping behind her teat, through no governance of *Anastasia.* My penis rose, unbid by *George;* was it a George of its own? A quarter-billion beasties were set to swarm therefrom and thrash like salmon up the mucous of her womb; were they little Georges all?

I groaned. "I don't understand anything!"

6.

"I'm asserting myself," she said quietly. "I think that the Ladyship part of Your Assignment means You're supposed to know me so well that we'll be the same person."

These words so fit my recent Answer, I could not protest when she disrobed. But coitus was not necessarily what she had in mind, ready as she was (and saw the nether George to be) for that ultimate merger of two into one. She removed not only her uniform and underclothing but the pins from her hair, the wedding-ring from her finger, and the cosmetic from her face, then turned from the wash-basin to face me. Her legs were slightly apart, her hands on her hips, her cheeks flaming. Inspired no doubt by Dr. Sear's new relation to Peter Greene, she ordered me to make her person as familiar to me as my own. I asked her what she meant.

"*Examine* me," she said. Her voice wavered, but not for an instant her extraordinary resolution. She was a changed woman.

"Examine you how, Anastasia? If you mean play Doctor, I don't see—"

"Let *me* do the seeing." She closed her eyes for some moments, as if gathering strength to proceed with her remarkable, nonplussing self-assertion. Lifting herself onto an examination-table near the fluoroscope, she said grimly, "Come here, George."

I went. She leaned back on her arms.

"Look me over," she ordered. "Don't mind if I blush or act embarrassed. Examine me, every square millimeter. Don't touch me yet; just look."

I am not made of stone: breathing heavily, and assisted by my flashlight and the various lenses of my stick, I inspected every pore, hair, fold, crease, protuberance, process, and orifice of her. I learned that the hairs of Anastasia's limbs, head, armpits, and pubes grew darker and thicker in that order; that her brown irises were flecked with black and green; that her scalp was more white, her *labia minora* more tan, than I'd have supposed. Her nostrils were not quite a pair; there were silver fillings in three of her molars and one bicuspid. Her nipples, examined closely, were mottled, and more cylindrical than hemispheric. A total of seventy-four tiny moles, all brown, were disposed about her epidermis, five of them bearing at least one hair. Her earlobes were extremely small, scarcely pendant; a thumbnail-size *café-au-lait* birthmark was half concealed, when she stood, in the crease below her right buttock. Her anus—unlike her lips, tongue, nipples, clitoris, and urethra—was neither rosy nor granular, but of the same smooth beige-pink as the skin of her hams. Her navel, shallowly recessed, was bilobular, not unlike the East-Campus symbol for polarity.

"Measure me," she said. With the aid of several kinds of scales, a tape, calipers, and other devices lying about the room, I discovered that the total weight of Anastasia's body was 50.4 kilograms, of which her head and neck accounted for 2.25, her arms for a kilo apiece, her breasts for less than a half-kilo each, and her legs for almost six together. Her height was 1.63 meters standing, about six millimeters more reclining; an average hair on her head was twenty-three centimeters in length, on her armpit (not recently shaven, she said) one centimeter, on her *mons veneris* three. The girth of her forehead was fifty-nine centimeters, of her neck thirty-one, of her chest ninety, of her waist sixty-five, of her hips eighty-eight, of her upper arms twenty-three. Her forehead was seven centimeters high. The maximum arch of her eyebrows was half a centimeter; she could elevate them by three times that amount. Her eyes measured 1.7 by 3.2 centimeters and were set eight centimeters apart from pupil to pupil. The span of her smile was six centimeters, of her shoulders forty-one, of her fingers twenty, of her arms one hundred sixty-seven. Her right arm was longer than her left by a centimeter, measured from armpit to fingertip. Her lips projected from the plane of her face by the same amount; her ears from the side of her head by slightly more. Her breasts were not easy to measure, owing to their resiliency; their projection from the plane of her chest, for example, varied from four and a half centimeters supine through six standing to nine bent over, and there appeared to be a centimeter's difference in pendulosity between them, as between the length of her arms; the distance from nipple to clavicle was seventeen centimeters when she stood with her arms at her sides, not quite fifteen when she raised them; from nipple to nipple, twenty-three standing and twenty-five reclining. Finally, what one might call the standing compressibility of her udder was five centimeters, and their side-to-side play twelve. Her nipples when aroused had a diameter of seven millimeters and a projection of fifteen; their tranquil dimensions, though visibly smaller, I could not measure accurately, for they sprang to attention at sight, so to speak, of the calipers' approach, as did the erectile tissue of her clitoris. Nor could I, lacking Dr. Eierkopf's gauges, measure in real numbers the strength of her anal and vaginal sphincters, though my digital impression was that the former had easily twice the constrictive power of the latter.

That impression, and others equally subjective and qualitative, I gained principally during the tactile stage of my examination, which followed upon the metrical. "Feel me," Anastasia directed, and closing my eyes at her instruction, I explored with my fingertips all her surfaces and apertures, comparing their textures, temperatures, moistnesses, firmnesses, viscosities, and the like; then I covered the same ground, as it were, with the soles and toes of my bare feet, a curious sensation, and finally disrobed myself for maximum-surface contacts, at the first of which (my back to her front) I ejaculated approximately two meters across the Treatment Room.

I would have proceeded then to mount her, in defiance of my own *programme,* but that some of my senses had yet to make her complete acquaintance; and having ejaculated I was able to put by lust and do her bidding with more clinical detachment. Once I'd come to know her from head to foot with my elbows, knees, ears, hams, testicles, and shoulderblades, I sniffed and tasted her, in that order, with similar thoroughness. These final researches were less novel to me, inasmuch as the goats make liberal use of nose and tongue, both to greet old acquaintances and make new ones, and to investigate their general environs. But of course they are without toes and recessed navels, for example, and use neither soap nor artificial scents; obviously too the difference between their diet and a lady human co-ed's (more than the difference in species) made my degustation of Anastasia no mere repetition of my former converse with Hedda O.T.S.T. or Redfearn's Tom. I familiarized myself, olfactorially and gustatorially, with her hair-oil, earwax, tears, saliva, snot, sweat, blood (from a pinprick on her left forefinger), lymph, urine, feces, skin-oil, vaginal secretion, and finger- and toenail parings—I had had no lunch, and my stomach rumbled loudly—and then stood by for further instruction.

"Biographical knowledge, psychological knowledge, medical knowledge . . ." She sat cross-legged upon the examination-table and told the list on her fingers. "Fluoroscopic knowledge, physiometrical knowledge, visual, tactile, olfactory, gustatory . . . We forgot auditory! Use Kennard's stethoscope." She fetched it from a countertop and prettily gave me to listen in upon her heartbeat, respiration, and intestinal chucklings, all more subdued than my own. She strained but could not fart; on the other hand, she had a surprising knack for bringing up belches at will, a trick she'd learned at ten and never forgotten. All the while she chattered matter-of-factly about the question of carnal knowledge, the last item on her improvised list. Many of our investigations, she acknowledged, were distinguishable from amatory foreplay only by their motive, and though she intended to postpone actual copulation with me until she'd asserted herself with Stoker and Bray, she knew that Dr. Sear's bookshelves contained a library of erotica wherein was catalogued such a staggering variety of sexual practices, stunts, and exquisitries as to make ordinary genital intromission seem as tame as shaking hands; would it be out of order, she wondered, for me to acquaint myself with her by means of fellatio, cunnilingus, heterosexual sodomy, flagellation, reciprocal transvestism, and whatever like refinements and experiments we could discover or invent, other than simple coitus?

"Let me be the man," her chest boomed into the stethoscope, "and You be the woman."

But I put down the instrument and shook my head. "I don't know, Anastasia. I don't see—"

I was interrupted by a vigorous pounding on the one-way mirror. Anastasia first gasped and snatched about her for cover, then thought better of it, let go the sheet she'd half torn from the examination-table, and beckoned with her finger at the unknown pounder, with the other hand displaying her pudenda in the manner of those carven *shelah-na-gigs* which she must have noted upon my stick. Peter Greene burst into the room, all crimson face and orange hair and blinking eyes; he it was who'd pounded; but he'd not come at her beck—nor to berate her, though he cried, "I seen what you was up to, Lacey Stoker, what I mean lewdwise! Trying to flunk the Grand Tutor!" Anastasia blushed red as Greene, either at his rebuke or at her nakedness before him; but she contrived to stay her ground, put her hands on her hips, and regard him with her eyes half closed and her head half turned—a really quite provocative stance, considering how unnaturally it came to her. Greene got to the point of his alarum.

"The whole durn place has gone kerflooey!" he announced to me. "Crooks and loonies running all over! It's the end of the University!"

Dr. Sear, it appeared, had gone to the Women's Chronic Ward to arrange a weekend leave for his wife, and Greene had gone with him as far as the Infirmary lobby, intending to visit his own wife's suite of rooms. But they'd found the place in uproar over an astonishing executive order just issued by Chancellor Rexford: not only had a general amnesty been declared for everyone in Main Detention, but the Infirmary had been directed to turn loose every mental patient who was not also a physical invalid. The consensus of the Infirmary staff was that Rexford himself had lost his mind—there was talk, for example, that not only the Open Book Tests were going to be repealed, as most people wished, but every administrative regulation concerning gambling, prostitution, cheating in the classroom, narcotics, homosexuality, and pornographic literature and films. They shook their heads—but there was the order, and to everyone's surprise Dr. Sear, so far from countermanding it, had declared he understood and approved of the Chancellor's position; orderlies and campus patrolmen he'd directed to protect the bedridden (like Mrs. Greene); then he'd gone personally to see to it that every door and gate in the Psychiatric Annex was put open. Many of the staff had fled; the halls and lounges, Greene reported, were a pandemonium; the patrolmen had several times been obliged to pistol the violent, in self-defense. Of Dr. and Mrs. Sear, Greene had heard no more; having bribed the police to double their guard at Miss Sally Ann's door, he'd returned at considerable risk to apprise me of the danger.

"And your mom, too, pass her mind," he added; "ain't *her* fault she's touched in the head. A fellow's got a duty to his mom." But at Anastasia he curled his lip. "They can *have* the likes of you, for all I care. Serve you right!"

Too alarmed by the news to heed his insult, Anastasia rushed into the Reception Room to see that Mother was safe, and then began hastily redonning her white uniform. "Those poor *patients!*" she exclaimed. "Maybe I can tranquilize some of them."

Indeed the situation seemed perilous. Mad bangs and screams came from the hallway; a chap, white-gowned, galloped sideways into the office, scratching under his ribs, and made hooting water on the wall-to-wall carpet.

"Oh, yes, well," my mother murmured. He sprang at her even as I at him, but changed course at sight of me and leaped through the window instead, smashing first the pane and presently himself, as the office was many stories high. Mother resumed her knitting. Other unfortunates thrashed about in the vicinity of the doorway.

"Lock the door," I bade Greene. He stiffened.

" 'Scuse me, George, sir. No disrespect intended, but I can't go against the Chancellor of my native college, true or false. My only regret, alma-materwise, is that I don't have but one life to give for—"

"Let's get out, then," I said, for pleased as I was at Rexford's following my advice, I recalled Leonid's fiasco in the Nikolayan Zoo and feared for our safety. My Ladyship protested that her first responsibility was to the patients, and Greene that the likes of her were disgraces to their uniforms, say what one would. I bade the former to keep in mind that everyone's first responsibility was to the Founder—which was to say, to one's own passage, not always to be attained by charitable works—and declared to the latter my wish that he escort Mrs. Stoker not only out of the Infirmary but all the way to the Powerhouse.

"No!" Anastasia objected. "If everything's going to pieces, then I don't *care* about my Assignment! I'm going with You." And Greene muttered that I should not ought to take him from Miss Sally Ann's bedside for the sake of no floozy.

"It's for Miss Sally Ann's sake you have to," I said; "for the sake of all the patients. I want this floozy out in the Powerhouse where she belongs, so she won't take advantage of helpless people. Do you think you'll be okay with her?"

Anastasia saw my motive and protested.

"I'll be okay," Greene said, and wiped his palms grimly on his trouser-thighs.

"No, please, George . . ." said Anastasia.

"She may try to seduce you," I warned him, for her benefit. "She's awfully aggressive. Not like her sister."

"*George . . .*"

With a fierce squint Greene took her arm. "You come along with me. Don't try to flooze me none, neither."

More gently I took my mother's elbow; clucking and smiling, she bagged her yarn and obediently rose.

"At least give me a minute to fix my *hair!*" Anastasia said. Her tone had changed, was newly resolute and guileful, as was her face. I surmised, not without mixed feelings, that what had been at odds—her wish to assert herself as I'd advised and her wish to go to Tower Hall with me instead of to her home with Greene—were now in league: she would attempt to bribe Greene with her favors. And though I myself had urged such initiative upon her, the twinge I felt was not owing entirely to the danger of her succeeding and thus following me into the Belly. To assure myself that I was not *jealous,* or envious of Greene, I smiled and winked at her, as if to say, "I see right through you, and wish you luck."

She saw and understood me, I'm sure, but regarded me coolly.

"Watch out for the nuts," Greene advised me.

Anastasia patted her hair, and slipped her arm primly under his. "He hasn't any. I'm glad I've got a *man* to take home."

Greene blushed, no less than I, who was shocked by her unwonted coarseness as well as stung by the insult. Certainly it was but part of her strategy! Yet when I pretended to suppress a grin, she turned from me coldly and whispered something in Greene's ear that did nothing to lighten his color. As I bade them goodbye I found myself reminding her, against my better judgment, that if things turned out badly in the Belly she might not be seeing me again.

"You don't say," she said. "Bye-bye, then. Oh, Peter, would you fasten me in back? I can't reach the hooks." She turned her lovely nape to him.

"Hmp," Greene said.

"And I've mislaid my darned purse in the Treatment Room somewhere! Would you help me find it?"

Full of confusion I ushered Mother from the office; and the womanly chuckle I heard behind me, and Greene's half-hearted complaint, as he shut the hall door, that he wasn't *supposed* to shut any doors, it was against orders, smote me with an ireful doubt which—small comfort!—abetted our safe exit. For the first madman who loped up, unfortunately woofing, I butted with such force that he knocked a second down, and our way was clear to the lift. And in the lobby, where demented undergraduates and faculty of both sexes swung from light-fixtures, raced in wheelchairs, coupled on the carpet, shat in typewriters, or merely stood transfixed in curious attitudes, I laid about ruthlessly with my stick, cut an angry swath, and roughly gimped through bedlam with my mother. I could not have explained my fury, or told why, when it occurred to me that Love and Hate must be in truth distinctions as false as True and False, that sagacious reflection nowise clarified my mind or calmed my spirit.

I hailed the only taxi at the Annex door and bade the driver take us to Tower Hall. Newsboys hawked in the fading afternoon: *Power Lines Moving Together: Fear Riot Near; Rexford Raps Mrs., Raises Roof.* The tidings brought me no pleasure. Through a small loudspeaker in our sidecar came further news: so-called "Moderate" elements were resigning from the Administration to protest the Chancellor's recognition of extremists; Ira Hector for example had been offered the post of Comptroller, and Rexford had not only acknowledged Maurice Stoker as his half-brother, but gone to spend the weekend with him at the Power Plant. " *'It may be necessary to have these people around,' complained one resigning official, 'like spies and grafters—but one mustn't officially* approve *of them . . .'* " The new corrective headgear issued to Power-Line guards, the reporter went on to say, was intended to remedy the faults of the "heads-up" collar by fixing the wearer's eyes down at his feet; but looking down from that height seemed to make the guards dizzy, and the drop-off rate was as high as before.

"What the heck anyhow," I said, snapping off the speaker: "Failure is Passage."

"A-plus," said Mother.

Not until we drew in sight of the Library did I realize that I had no means to pay our fare. I glanced at the driver, hoping to gauge his charitableness, and saw what I'd been too disconcerted to observe before, why he was the only cabbie in the madhouse drive. His uniform was white, beltless and buttonless, his eyes were aglint, his grin was euphrasic. Alarmed, I commanded him to stop the motorcycle.

"Stop the cycle," he squawked like a parrot. "Stop the cycle." His grip on the handlebar was fixed now as his expression; the Mall-street fetched us straight over a curbstone, across Tower Hall Plaza, through clusters of alarmed under-graduates, and into a yew-hedge flanking the entrance, where we came to rest. The engine stalled. "Yes, well," Mother remarked. The driver sat erect and beaming as ever, though yew-twigs pressed against his face, even into his mouth.

"Thtop the thycle," he repeated. I helped Mother out and left him to iterate his message to the gathering crowd—the sight of which, understandably, caused a small shudder in me.

In the Library things were more calm: I composed my wits and reviewed the situation. That My Ladyship and I had ex-changed roles in the Treatment Room—she the Tutor, I the Tutee—was not displeasing. But her final behavior mystified me, and behind the turmoil of my heart stood a stiller but impenetrabler mystery, that I had felt briefly in my arms: what was it that looked through the optics of that respiring female organism and said "I love you"? And to what did those voweled noises speak? To what refer? *I. Love. You.* The idea was as preposterous as it was dark! No, I'd not seen through My Ladyship, no more myself, and if that was my infirmity, it was yet to be overcome; indeed, it had overcome me. Very well (I reminded myself as we went up to the Cataloguing Office, Mother pressing the lift-button out of habit), then I had failed that part of my Assignment, even on my own terms, and Failure is Passage. But elation was fled, even grim satisfaction; I began to feel desolate. If only Mother were not demented, I thought, and Max not detained (if indeed he still was, after the amnesty): how good it would be to discuss the problem with them!

We passed through the spoke-filed room, in whose hub the empty Scroll-case stood. It being Saturday afternoon and nearly dinnertime, only a few scholars were about. The door to Mother's former office was locked, and bore a small sign that read CACAFILE OUT OF ORDER. It occurred to that I had no clear reason for coming there anyhow: it was Bray I wanted; no, not even Bray: WESCAC. No, not even WES-CAC: death. So far had my spirits, unaccountably, plunged! To Re-place the Founder's Scroll, to Pass the Finals, to do single combat with WESCAC and what it represented—it was of no importance, I could not even think, my mind was on My obscure Ladyship. I had come from Infirmary to Li-brary out of habit, like Mother, following the order of my spring-term Tutorship. Humming, she fetched from her knitting-bag a key—someone must have forgot to collect it from her—and unlocked the door. The faulty console in the corner began winking, as if roused from sleep.

"Would you care for something to read?" Mother asked automatically.

"No—no thank you, ma'am."

She ignored the new nameplate on her desk and eased herself into the swivel-chair as though ready for work, though the office lights were out and she still had her coat on. "Well, you look around and let me know if you want anything, sonny. There's nothing like a good book."

My heart lifted not a little; I kissed her hair. Again, from her innocent darkness, she had illumined me!

"Listen carefully, Mom," I said; "Can you call for the Founder's Scroll? I want to put it back in its case." Whatever fugitive notion I'd had earlier concerning this item of my Assignment gave way before a true inspiration: Had not Enos Enoch and a hundred other wayfaring dons of fact and fiction taught, by their own example, that the Way to Commencement Gate led through Nether Campus? Was not my answer, *Failure is Passage,* but an epigrammatic form of that same truth? *Replace the Founder's Scroll* had seemed, in the spring, the simplest and clearest imperative of all, and yet the bafflingest, since the Scroll had not been lost; and my response to it had seemed, even at the time, the most specious of my Tutorhood—though to be sure they'd all been incorrect. It was fitting, then—stirringly so!—that on this round, so to speak, when I'd "solved" the first five problems with a deliberate speciousness, the rule of inversion would hold equally for the sixth, and make my re-placement of the Scroll not only bonafide but profoundly significant. It had *not* been misplaced, that was the point; but it was now, for I had misplaced it last time around—and so could re-place it! Things had to be lost before they could be found, broken before they could be fixed, infirm before they could be well, opaque before they could be clear—in short, failed before they could be passed! True, I could not at once discern how this remarkable insight quite applied to Ending the Boundary Dispute, which I'd not begun; nor had I truly "fixed" the Clock I'd broken, for example, or seen to my satisfaction through My Ladyship—but these doubts were nothing, shadows cast by the very brilliance of my illumination; I ignored them. Failure *was* Passage! No past fiasco, no present triumph; the spring made possible the fall!

"Well, hum," Mother said, going to the console. "Founder's Scroll, is it? Is that the title?"

"Yes'm. *Founder's Scroll.*"

Still flustered by my kiss, she fiddled with her hairpins and the switches of the CACAFILE. ". . . *o-l-l,*" she murmured, pressing buttons. "Who did you say the author was, dear?"

I hesitated. "The Founder."

She did not: ". . . *n-d-e-r.* No first name?"

"Just one name, Mother."

The CACAFILE seemed to purr at her touch. "Please step into the next room," she said, still in her office voice. "The volume or volumes you called for will be delivered to the Circulation Desk in approximately one minute."

As soon as I took her arm the manner vanished; she minced and colored like a shy schoolgirl. The CACAFILE-console gave a little snarl, then lapsed into its previous torpid blink.

"Let's go to the Circulation Desk, Mother."

"Oh. Well."

But at the empty Scroll-case we were arrested by a double commotion: from the Circulation Desk, next door to the Catalogue Room, feminine squeals as alarmed as merry; from behind us, at the door we'd first entered through, an angry male voice: "*There* you are, flunk you!"

A half-dozen scholars in the spokes of the card-file raised their heads.

"Hello, Daddy," Mother said placidly.

It was indeed Reginald Hector, but much changed: the fringe of hair around his bald pate was grown shoulder-long; his body, that had been sleek, was brown and wiry, and wrapped in fleece of Angora; his feet were sandaled, and under his right arm (apparently hurt, for he clasped it with his left) was a goat-herd's crook! This last he tried to raise with his better arm as she approached, and my surprise gave way to apprehension. I put the case between us.

"P.-G.!" A young dark-spectacled woman rushed in from the Circulation Room with a double handful of long white shreds. Behind her, from the desk-chute, more of the same blew forth, like paper streamers from a fan. "Thank the Founder you're here, P.-G.! Look at this!"

I recognized her as Professor-General Hector's receptionist, now out of uniform and evidently employed by the Library, perhaps in Mother's former capacity. She showed no surprise at her previous employer's costume, whether because she'd seen it before or because of her present agitation. The "P.-G." paused and scowled, crook high. Mother clucked her tongue, nowise discomposed. The young woman held out the tangled skein and wailed: "It's the Founder's Scroll!"

The ex-Chancellor clutched his ailing arm. "The Dunce you say!"

"A-plus," Mother affirmed.

"The CACAFILE's gone crazy!" the young woman cried. "All these months the Scroll's been lost in it somewhere, and now it's spitting it out in ribbons!"

There was consternation among the scholars: one snatched a handful of the shreds, examined them, and groaned; others raced to the Cataloguing Office to pound on its locked door, and yet others to the Circulation Desk, where they clenched and hopped in vain to see the wisdom of the ages shredding forth.

"You!" my grandfather roared, thrusting a fistful of tatters under my nose. I closed my eyes, nodded, and took a mouthful of the ruins.

"What's he *doing?"* the receptionist shrieked.

Mother smiled benignly and said, as if interrogated by a library-clerk: "Just browsing, thanks." At the same time a dim memory of our readings in the hemlock must have stirred in her, for she took it upon herself to feed me more of the Scroll. Though I'd had no lunch to speak of and was quite famished, the old vellum was bitter on my tongue, like dung dried in the sun of desert centuries—quite apart from the anguish I flavored it with, compounded of doubt and desolation. For either my insight of a few moments earlier was false, in which case I was as much in the dark as ever, or else it was true, in which case I was failing by my own terms. What was the use of restoring those shreds to the Scroll-case? I was not blind to the possibility that failing all, on my own terms as well as WESCAC's, might be the deeper sense of my answer; that is to say, that the failure truly equal to passage might be the failure to understand truly that Failure is Passage. Even as I chewed, that proposition flickered through my head as on a dim translux but did not console me. No, I was as snarled and wrecked as the Founder's Scroll: never mind P.-G. Hector's crook (now belaboring my shoulders) and the

alarums of bystanders; never mind that the lights began to
flicker again, as they had upon my spring-term disaster, bespeaking another crisis at the Power Lines; never mind that
the College was in anarchy, that lunatics and flunkees ranged
the quads—all I could think of, strangely enough, was My
Ladyship. I envisioned her beneath—no, atop—Peter Greene,
or Maurice Stoker, or Eblis Eierkopf, or Lucky Rexford, in
some lubricious exhibition on the Living-Room dais. No, no,
after all it was none of them; or having serviced them to exhaustion, now she stood, slack-mouthed with love; expelled
their mingled seed with a tricky jerk, and stretched forth her
arms to her fated, fateful lover, who rose up glitter-eyed
upon the dais and enfolded her body in his hard black cloak.
And I was no longer jealous, no, I was relieved; joyous, even,
for her sake, when I heard the muffled cry of her delight and
knew she was infused for good and all with the germ of Passage. I wanted to die.

"You can't eat that!" a scholar shouted, clawing at the
strips that hung like *pasta* from my jaws.

"He can shove it!" my grandfather snapped. *"Independence,* he calls it!" He grabbed at his wrapper. "Where's my
aides?" he demanded of his former receptionist. "Get this
flunkèd hair-shirt off me!"

"Weren't they with you at the barns, sir?" she said.

"Oh, the Dunce, I forgot I sent 'em out there." Suddenly
defensive, he glared at me and asked how the flunk a man
could mix a batch of goat-dip by himself and keep his eye on
a young buck like Triple-T at the same time. At mention of
that name tears sprang to my eyes; I swallowed a great cud
of Scroll; the rest fell to the floor and was scrabbled up by
scholars. For a moment my despair gave place to a sweeter if
no less painful emotion.

"Tommy's Tommy's Tom? Have you been with the herd,
Grandpa?"

"Don't Grandpa me, Dunce flunk you! If that buck hadn't
banged up my arm—"

He would crook me a harder one despite his infirmity; I
lowered my head to take the blow and die like Redfearn's
Tom, grandsire of the buck he spoke of. There were cries
from receptionist and bystanders, quite a number of whom
had been attracted by the disturbance.

"Stop." It was a voice I knew that pierced the clamor, and
my heart: hard, clickèd, like a thumbnailed flea, a hoof-

cracked tick. Asafoetida, the very smell of my impotent vision some moments before, was faint now in the literal air. Like Bray's voice, it came from the Circulation Desk, whither all eyes turned. He stood upon the desktop, as if flushed forth by the CACAFILE: a taller, leaner-jawed Bray than the last I'd seen, less hirsute, more commanding, stronger of voice and odor. His skin shone as if varnished, and even as I had dreamed, he now affected over his white tunic a stiff black cloak, as of hard-shined gabardine. Everyone fell silent. My grandfather humphed, but lowered the crook. Mother made a baleful sound and whipped a knitting-needle from her bag, undoing all her purlings in one stroke; but she permitted me to disarm her. I patted her hand.

"Thank you, George." Bray stepped from the desk and came hubwards.

"Look at this, sir!" an old scholar cried, wetting with his tears a handful of vellum tatters. "It's destroyed!"

Everyone spoke at once then: it was my fault more than the CACAFILE's, they said, whose original breakdown I'd also caused with my spring-term program; rather, it was Lucky Rexford's fault, for they assumed that my freedom, and Mother's, was owing to the flunkèd general amnesty. The ex-Chancellor's former receptionist was especially vociferous: she had mistrusted me the minute she'd first set eyes on me, she declared to Bray (forgetting, I presume, that I'd been at that time disguised as him), and her suspicions had been borne out catastrophically: not only had I, in addition to my more famous crimes, driven my mother mad, ruined the CACAFILE, and caused the Founder's Scroll to be first lost and then destroyed; I was also responsible for the undoing of New Tammany's most beloved alma-matriot, chancellor emeritus, and professor-general (retired). Not content to destroy the Philophilosophical Fund and thus move the College another step closer to Student-Unionism (of which Founderless ideology she had no doubt I was an agent), I had by some sinister means arranged for the transfer of its former director, the greatest of p.-g.'s and most considerate of employers, out of Great Mall and all posts of honor, to the managership of a bunch of stinking goats—probably in reprisal for the well-deserved punishment of the "pink pedagogue" and traitor Max Spielman.

"There, there," the P.-G. muttered, blushing gratefully and

patting with his good hand first her corseted, indignant rump and then, catching himself up, her back, in a classmately way.

"A-plus," my mother said, impressed I think by the righteously wrathful tone of the woman's accusations, and glaring at Bray as if they were directed at him. The bystanders murmured; cameras clicked, and their wielders cursed the flashbulb shortage—for which too my denouncer called me to blame. Only the scholars paid us no heed; possessing themselves of what shards and tatters had been fetched into the Catalogue Room, they withdrew to the Circulation Desk to salvage the rest, curiosity supplanting their dismay. Bray himself heard the charges patiently, without expression, as nothing new, and I indifferently, bristling only at her insult to the herd. Then he raised his hand to silence her and the assemblage.

"Professor-General Hector's retirement to the goat-barns was his own decision," he said. "He wished to be 'beholden to no man,' I believe he told me. Isn't that true, sir?"

Gruffly my grandfather admitted it was—not to be obliged, I suppose, for advice either, even bad advice. It was a poor professor-general, he declared, who didn't know when he was licked, and he would not deny that his objectives—utter independence and complete self-reliance—which thitherto he'd thought of as synonymous, had turned out to be contradictory. Managing the herd without the help of his aides, he'd found himself dependent absolutely on himself—a dependence so oppressively time-consuming, he'd had no opportunity to "be himself" at all. Isolated from classmates and staff, absorbed from morning till night with the tending of goats, the preparation of his food, the maintenance of the barns, even the manufacture and repair of his clothing, he'd scarcely had time to roll himself a cigarette, much less assert his independence and enjoy his individualism.

"And that was when I had *two* hands," he said.

"You poor *thing*, sir!" the receptionist exclaimed, touching the injured arm. "Let me tie it up for you."

But he refused permission, declaring he'd bind the wound himself, as he'd done more than once in time of riot, as soon as he located his goldbricking aides—on whom obviously it was folly to depend; he pitied the goats, now he remembered he'd dispatched his aides to tend them in his stead. But no: Dunce flunk those stinking brutes!

"Then you weren't beholden to the Goat-Boy for that idea," Bray asked again. "Is that correct?"

"I make my own decisions," the ex-Chancellor grumbled. "I don't pass the buck. I'm my own man. An officer's responsible for the mistakes of his subordinates."

Touched by his sense of honor, however confused it was, I apologized for the counsel he now denied I'd given him, and agreed that it had been mistaken, though for other reasons than his.

"Every man for himself," he snapped.

"Hear hear!" his loyal former receptionist applauded, taking his good arm and flashing her glasses at me defiantly, as if I'd been put in my place. I turned to Bray and explained, with a mixture of new respect and old resentment, the fault I'd found with his Certification of Reginald Hector: reading the citation *"No class shall pass"* to mean that his famous self-reliance was my grandfather's key to Commencement Gate, I had bid him cast off his lifelong unacknowledged dependency upon his brother, the Old Man of the Mall, and single-handed herd the goats. But I saw now, not merely that he was more dependent than ever, only upon himself instead of upon Ira and the aides, but also that my counsel was self-contradictory: I'd held Passage (Reginald's at least) to depend on independence, whereas to be consistent with itself it ought to be independent of independence.

"Balls!" said Grandfather.

"May we quote you, sir?" inquired a reporter, but retreated before the former receptionist, who had commandeered her former employer's crook and brandished it menacingly.

Bray may have smiled. "I believe Mr. Ira Hector intends to restore the original endowment of the P.P.F. He's doubling it, in fact . . ." This announcement caused much stir among the bystanders and the reporters who had found their way to the scene, or perhaps arrived in Bray's company. "Do you suggest," he asked me politely, "that Chancellor Hector apply to his brother for reappointment to the directorship?"

"I don't take favors from any man," snapped the P.-G.; but the proposal was clearly not unwelcome to him, for he added with a growl: "Besides, Ira's gone kerflooey, from what I hear; he'd probably turn me down. Not that I'd go begging, mind!"

I assured him that if Bray's report about the P.P.F. was true, then Ira had repudiated my former advice, as I'd latterly advised him to, and could be depended upon to reinstate him.

"I wouldn't take *his* word for it, sir," the receptionist said.

"I think you can depend on your grandson this time," Bray interposed with a level click. I could not but be comforted by his support, not alone for the sake of my grandfather, whom I'd long since forgiven his attempted nepocide and wished only well, but also because, as Bray's subsequent speech indicated, he had apparently more confidence in me than I'd had for the last quarter-hour in myself.

"Grandson my foot," the P.-G. said. "No bearded Beist is any grandson of mine. If he is, I disown him."

"A-plus," Mother said in her unhappy ignorance.

Bray raised both arms, spreading his cloak impressively, and addressed the company. "Now hear this," he demanded; "George Giles, alias the Ag-Hill Goat-Boy, alias Billy Bocksfuss, was released from Main Detention early this morning at my request. I believe he is the true, authentic GILES." A great commotion greeted this pronouncement: reporters dashed for telephones; Grandfather and his former receptionist frowned and gasped, respectively; Mother wept and kissed the hem of Bray's cloak. I remained suspicious, but my heart stirred.

"However," Bray continued, "he may or may not be a Grand Tutor." The reporters halted in their tracks; everyone seemed reassured, even myself, by the possibility that I might yet be false. "Now hear this, classmates and Tutees: you did right to lynch him last spring, but I did right also to stop the lynching, and grant him now a probationary pardon. This is his opportunity to redeem his former failings, complete his Assignment correctly, and thus verify the Answer he claims to have discovered. Very soon he and I will go as before into WESCAC's Belly, but unmasked this time, and we shall see who emerges unEATen. Perhaps we both shall; perhaps neither. Or perhaps George Giles is the true Grand Tutor, and Yours Truly is false . . ."

He waved down a chorus of No's; clearly his popularity was undiminished outside the small circle of my acquaintances. Mother remained kneeling before him as if he were still praising me. The former receptionist bitterly, but not disrespectfully, objected that my second day on Great Mall, from all reports, was proving at least as disastrous as the first. Look what I'd done to the Founder's Scroll . . .

"His Assignment was to re-place it," Bray said calmly. "But what is the origin of the Founder's Scroll? Not the Founder, Who surely inspired it, but the minds and hearts of His protégés—which is to say, of studentdom! If a Grand Tutor eats His words, is He not feeding Himself Himself?"

The woman was quieted, if not satisfied. Grandfather scowled at me uncertainly. I myself attended Bray's apology with interest, for though I could not remember that it was he who'd ordered the EAT-whistle sounded and stopped the lynching, and though I was aware of his ulterior motive in freeing me, and though I had no intention of submitting to WESCAC's examination as before, his defense of my sixth Assignment-task was ingenious and straightforwardly offered. Moreover, the phrase "eating my words" suggested yet another interpretation, whether meant by him or not: what else had my day's work consisted of?

"Consider too," Bray enjoined them, "that the Scroll was torn to pieces by the CACAFILE in its efforts to file it at once in many different categories, as I believe George Giles instructed it to do last spring. But he now denies the reality of all such categories; of *all* categories. According to his present teaching, the distinction between one book and another, and between *books* and *non-books,* is illusory, inasmuch as the Founder is One, and the Founder is All! Possibly his destruction and partial consumption of the Founder's Scroll is meant to demonstrate that teaching. Possibly not."

I was much impressed with this analysis, and with Bray's surprising grasp of my position, derived as it must have been from sketchy reports and observations of my long day's labor. The others appeared less convinced, but respectful of Bray's magnanimity and explicatory prowess. I regarded him closely for signs of guile, and found none.

"Understand," he concluded, "I don't say that this is the case, or that George Giles's teaching is *my* teaching . . ." There were murmurs of agreement. "But is it for students to correct and discipline their masters? And until we have gone through the Belly unmasked, who dares say which is the student and which the master?" His expression seemed to grow sad, and his next words much moved me: the fact was, he declared, studentdom inevitably *did* judge its Tutors, and being less than Tutors, inevitably judged wrong, for which reason it was written in the Founder's Scroll: *A proph-prof is never* cum laude *in his own quad.* That this was so was the failing of studentdom; yet there was no help for it; it was the nature of the student condition that one was obliged to honor one's Tutors as true or condemn them as false, and yet such a judgment could not be made truly except by a true Grand Tutor. Had he said that studentdom necessarily judged wrong? The truth was, they might honor the true and condemn the false as easily as the reverse, but in either case they judged ignorantly. Yet did he say "as easily"? Nay, not as easily, for the false more often pleased than the true; wherefore it followed that the true Grand Tutor was almost invariably condemned as false, and the false celebrated as true—but not always.

"Assemble at the Belly-exit," he exhorted them. "In a little while I will pass judgment on George Giles, and he on me, and WESCAC on us both. And for all mere studentdom can know, one of us may judge falsely, or mistakenly; or both of us may; or neither. For a false Grand Tutor is no wiser than his Tutees, and may in his ignorance sincerely believe himself to be what he is not—or flunkèdly pretend to be. And even WESCAC may be wrong! What is WESCAC, that it should be exempt from error? Why might it not protect and affirm the GILES—truly, falsely, or mistakenly—or confuse a false GILES with the true, or choose by confusion, preference, or error a GILES who is not a Grand Tutor over a Grand Tutor who is not the GILES, or make any other of the varieties of wrong judgments you can imagine, or no judgment at all? Go to the Belly door and wait! See who emerges; hear what he says—then believe and do as you will. Very possibly you will be mistaken, wherefore it is written in the Founder's Scroll: *Many take the Finals, but few Commence.* Dear, dear classmates: the flunkèd must always outnumber the passed! A-plus."

"A-plus!" many of his auditors responded, and though Bray's elucidation of their plight perhaps dismayed them, they obediently dispersed, the journalists excepted, who lingered to see what might happen next. Bray raised my mother from her knees, listening politely, even with interest, to her prattle of the passèd grandchild she believed to be in Anastasia's womb.

"Yes," he went so far as to tell her: "That will come to pass, lady. Without fail." He then commended her to the keeping of her father, whom he also welcomed back to Great Mall, saying that the chancellory might well require his good offices in the terms ahead, in view of Lucius Rexford's abdication of responsibility.

"Beardless youth," Grandfather muttered, not altogether consistently. "Founder knows what they're coming to; it's coddle, coddle. If you want a thing done right, you've got to do it yourself."

Bray patted his shoulder and bade him think well of my recommendation concerning the P.P.F. directorship, among the virtues of accepting which would be the opportunity to re-employ his former receptionist. Then he turned to me.

"Shall we go down into the Belly, classmate?"

7.

Rank as was his reek, even in my tolerant nostrils, I asked his pardon with as much humility as was compatible with dignity.

"As you know, Dr. Bray," I said, "I used to believe you were a flunkèd impostor. I don't think you're flunkèd any longer."

"But I may yet be an impostor?" he inquired, I think lightly. "No matter. Is it true you no longer regard yourself as a Grand Tutor? You could make a public statement to that effect, you know, and not go through the Belly. I say this purely from concern for your safety; I have no grudge against you."

I believed him. For one thing, he had no further cause to regard me as a rival, either to his office or to Anastasia's favors, which I would not seek. But some lingering pride forbade me to do quite as he suggested. He might not be what he claimed to be, I told him, but he was not simply an impostor, as I'd formerly maintained; there was something more to him, I could not say what. And while it was true that I no longer regarded myself as a Grand Tutor, I was not blind to the possibility that this opinion, like others I'd held, was erroneous, or that in my heart of hearts I might be holding it alongside the conviction that Failure is Passage.

"Ah," he said. "To the Belly, then, by all means!"

I then explained that while I had no fear of WESCAC's EATing me—which it well might do—I would not acknowledge its right to examine me, or anyone else's save my own, for reasons that I'd readily set forth to him, but did not regard as the affair of the popular press. To the chagrin therefore of the reporters (some of whom intimated openly that they would "get even" with me) we made our way to the main lobby of Tower Hall, where, as on that fateful night some terms before, a crowd was collecting in the flickerish light, their anxiety nourished by alarums and rumors. Them too Bray urged to wait at the Belly-exit; he and I then took the special lift to WESCAC's Mouth—a lift guarded now by a squad of ROTC cadets in riot-uniform on account of the general emergency.

"What were you saying?" Bray inquired, utterly composed, and pressed the single, recessed button. We went down the dark shaft. During the descent, and in the red-lit antechamber, I described for him my day's Assignment-work and my present intentions, in a neutral voice, neither asking approval nor inviting argument. I reviewed the conditions of Max, Leonid, Croaker, Stoker, Peter Greene, Ira Hector, Chancellor Rexford, Dr. Eierkopf, Dr. Sear, and Anastasia, my new advice to them and the reasoning behind it, and my confidence that, being all now confirmed in their failings, they were Candidates for Passage.

"I see," said Bray. "Shall we present our credentials now?"

That was another thing, I declared: it was as inconsistent with the Answer to let WESCAC pass upon my credentials as to take my Assignment or the Finals on its terms. My ID-card was blank, virtually, and the faint *GEORGE* that a careful eye might discern yet upon it would serve, in my estimation, as well to identify *Father* and *Examiner* as *Self:* I was not born George; I was not born anything; I had invented myself as I'd elected my name, and it was to myself I'd present my card (already "properly signed") when I had passed by the Finals.

"Passed them *by,* you say?"

"I'm going to flunk WESCAC," I said. "Where's the plug? I'll pull it."

Bray very likely smiled as he went to the scanning console among the tape-racks. "Don't be silly, George; there isn't any plug. You'd have to cut the Power Lines, or short-circuit them. But do you really think it's worthwhile to take WES-CAC so seriously? It's only a symbol."

This assertion I might have quarreled with: had Mother been impregnated by a symbol? Was it a symbol that had EATen the Amaterasus and G. Herrold, and would in all likelihood soon EAT me, if not the entire University? That incorporated in its circuitry all the dreams and definitions that tricked studentdom into believing in its own existence, and in the reality of its flunkage? Some symbol! But Bray clicked his tongue (and sundry buttons on the console) and forestalled these objections by reminding me that, the lift having automatically reascended, there was no way out of the Mouth except through the Belly, and no way into the Belly, as far as he knew, save by WESCAC's admittance, upon inspection of our credentials. "Why not put your card in the slot?" he suggested. "That doesn't commit you to anything, especially since you've eradicated the signatures. It's as good a way as any to challenge the computer, if you take that so seriously. Mine's already in."

I'd not seen him insert it; no matter; I deliberately jammed my card into the slot, upside down and backwards with reference to its spring-term presentation.

"It seems quite reasonable to me," Bray said, pulling the side-lever, "that the nature of the card doesn't influence the opening of the port, but determines what happens afterwards If we were Nikolayan agents, for example, I imagine the port would still open, but then we'd be EATen. Don't you agree?"

I was too sobered by the dilation of the iris-shuttered port, like a great black pupil, to reply. I tried to think of My Ladyship, as appropriate to what might be my last moments on campus—but my mind and heart were blank as my ID-card; if Anastasia's image appeared there at all, I regarded it without emotion. Nothing happened. Bray handed me my card, which had been returned into the console-cup in lieu of reply-cards, I presumed, we having made no inquiries. He pointed out as I pursed it that the exit-port was likewise impregnable; I had, alas, no choice but to reply to WESCAC's questions—always assuming I was not EATen before they were posed. Naturally I was free to make deliberately "false" replies, to demonstrate either my contempt for the examiner or my conviction that Failure is Passage; he supposed too I might choose to push no buttons at all. He could not but imagine, however, that in that event I would remain in the Belly forever.

If I felt chagrin at this hitch in my plans, or suspected Bray of tricking me after all into changing them, or wondered how he himself would leave the Belly, if I chose not to—I can't recall it. Neither did I care, as before, whether he came with me or escaped by some secret means, without examination. I stepped through the port and flung myself down the entrance-tube into the warm black chamber, its spongy surfaces athrob. Bray tumbled after and against me at once, identified by his foetor, but we spoke no more. I sticked my way to the little display-screen, already phosphorescent with the inquiry *ARE YOU MALE OR FEMALE.* They would be, then, the same questions as before. I considered answering *Yes,* as I had last spring, on the ground that all those previous responses, like their maker, had perforce been wrong, and Failure is Passage. But on second thought I decided to reply more strictly in terms of my new point of view, itself an implicit denial of WESCAC's authority and the presuppositions of its terminology. Therefore I found and pressed the left-hand button—the *No,* if Bray's earlier instructions were correct, and my memory of them was accurate, and the button-box had not been reversed or otherwise altered in the interim—for what were *male* and *female* if not the most invidious of the false polarities into which undergraduate reason was wont to sunder Truth?

I think Bray sighed, or else the chamber-lining squished when I stepped to answer.

*HAVE YOU COMPLETED YOUR ASSIGNMENT
AT ONCE, IN NO TIME*

Readily I answered *Yes,* for the triple reasons that I'd fixed Tower Clock in position, that the passage of time was anyhow a flunkèd delusion, and that, Failure being Passage, my non-completion of the Assignment, last time or this, was not ultimately differentiable from its completion. But after a moment's further reflection I pressed the other button to change my answer, for on the loftiest view of all there was no *I* to complete the Assignment, as distinct from an *Assignment* to be completed, in the timeless, seamless University—which University itself, *et cetera.* The same reasoning led me, not without trepidation despite my convictions, to press *No* at appearance of the epithet *GILES SON OF WESCAC;* for not only were *GILES* and *WESCAC* distinctions as spurious as

son and *father,* but, viewed rightly (if after all through the
finally false lenses of student reason), the eugenical specimen
whereof I was the issue had been drawn as it were from all
studentdom, whose scion therefore I was; WESCAC's role
had been merely that of an inseminatory instrument, the tool
of the student body. I braced myself to be EATen, and was
not.

DO YOU WISH TO PASS, the computer asked finally,
and ready for that basic, that ultimate question, with closed
eyes and held breath I answered *No,* and again *No,* and *No
No No No No,* as though pounding blow by blow into WES-
CAC's heart the stake of my refutation! The screen blinked
out at the first press and snapped sparks at the others; machinery behind the walls convulsed and roared, pitching me now
to the floor, now against the tight-shut exit. Bray it must have
been I heard groan. Indeed it looked to be the end, for
though I felt nothing as yet in the way of brain-piercing rays
(which I imagined must be the pain of electroencephalic amplification), there were arcs and sparks at both ports, which
now sprang open; a stench as of burning rubber filled the
Belly, and its walls constricted to grip me like Bill's strait-
waistcoat, only bent double. But before I could give last voice
to despair, or commend to the Founder my twice-flunkèd
mind, a convulsion of the acrid chamber expelled me thun-
derously, breech-foremost, through the port, out onto the frozen ground. A second blast put Bray beside me; then the
port, instead of snapping shut, hung wide and still, quietly
smoking. Co-eds squealed and clutched their escorts. The
upheavel was not confined to WESCAC: every streetlight I
could see behind Tower Hall was sparking, flashing over-
bright and then popping out like a photographic lamp. The
Telerama-crews cursed and scurried, issuing free torches to
the crowd. Two of their number came forward with microphones as I picked myself up (Bray had landed on his feet),
still dazed by the force of my ejection, the confusion of the
scene, and the fact that I had once more, evidently, come
through unEATen. There were no anthems this time; the
crowd was too alarmed to sing.

Of the first reporter to reach us Bray demanded, "What's
the trouble?" and was told that the East- and West-Campus
Power Lines, according to sketchy reports from the scene,
had either touched at some point or been moved to such
proximity that an arc had flashed between them, short-

circuiting at least temporarily the entire Powerhouse and causing no one knew how much damage to WESCAC and the campus generally.

"I see," Bray said, undisturbed. Light from a mobile generator now fell upon us, and while I endeavored to assess my position—what the net import was of the day's events, and what I ought to do next—he took the man's microphone and called for attention.

"Now hear this, ladies and gentlemen! Now hear this, Tutees and classmates! George Giles the Goat-Boy, by his own admission and intent, has Failed All!" An angry cry came from the crowd, but as they moved to seize me Bray bade them stay and drew me to his side, asking cordially behind his hand to borrow my stick for a brief but necessary ritual. I understood: as I had formerly declared myself passed and he me failed, now that I owned myself flunked he would pass and Certify me to the student body, even dub me Grand Tutor with a rap on the scapula—his Assignment on this campus (as he'd told me in March, when things had gone badly) and the explanation of his survival! To be sure, not all was clear; indeed I was assailed by doubts and questions; but my troubled heart surged like the torchèd crowd. Granted, it was for me and no one else to decide my condition, nature, and policy, when circumstances should permit reflection; yet whether in failing I had passed or in thus passing failed, official public Certification would do no violence to the paradox and might serve in that parlous hour to pacify the crowd, for whom difficult truths were best expressed in simple mottoes, simple rites. I surrendered my stick.

"Thank you," Bray said. "Please kneel." The crowd hushed; likewise my spirit, strait-waistcoated in contradictions of which, not impossibly, one tap of the stick might free me at last. I knelt.

"This is how it must be," Bray said, and smote me flat. Over me then, as I fought for breath (the blow had struck me full in the back, else my head would have been crushed), he declared through the public loudspeakers: "George Giles the Goat-Boy, cause and embodiment of all our ills: you are hereby denied admission to the student body. No probation; no reinstatement; no clemency. You shall be deported to the goat-barns at once, forever." The crowd shouted approval. Still stunned, I was snatched up. "Tomorrow morning," Bray announced to them, "I go to Founder's Hill to work certain miracles on the occasion of the scheduled Shafting, which you are all invited to witness. Now I shall retire into the Belly of WESCAC to meditate, but presently I shall come forth, ascend to the Belfry, and beget a son." He paused. "The Goat-Boy is yours."

Each of these extraordinary declarations was greeted with astonished hurrahs. At the last of them the crowd set upon me, ignoring my proper sentence, and I saw Bray no more. My jail clothes were torn off, either deliberately or in the general pull and haul. My male equipment, shrinking from the cold, was made rude fun of, and I was pummeled—about the head, in particular, by two short-skirt co-eds whose heavy sweaters bore the initials NTC, as did the megaphones they beat me with. My hair and beard were cruelly pulled by knowledgeable skeptics suspicious of disguise. As in a horrid dream I was fetched round again to the dooryard of the Old Chancellor's Mansion: already a sidecar was drawn up to the familiar streetlamp (now extinguished), from whose top the noose was rigged. Grandfather Hector shouted orders from the porch, gesturing with his crook at the Telerama-crew already established there, while his loyal receptionist (who had contrived to exchange her library-clothes for military uniform) made checks on a clipboard with a series of pencils which she drew from and returned to her hair. Whether the P.-G. was opposing or directing the lynch I could not tell. I wondered why Mother was not in her place. Stoker's guards were rowdy as ever; I saw no sign of their leader, nor any indication that they meant to thwart the mob. The monogrammed co-eds had left off clubbing me in order to lead the procession; reaching the lamp-post they wheeled about smartly, went down on one knee, and with the aid of their megaphones and practiced gestures, set the crowd to chanting, "Get the Goat! Get the Goat!" As I was lifted to the sidecar-top and prodded with my own stick, I even heard, as in the spring, a voice cry "Rape!" and the familiar consternation at the Mansion-corner. With a bitter sigh and no prompting from my captors I thrust my buckhorn into place and put my head in the noose. Why wait to see My Ladyship rogered yet again, en route to her Belfry-tryst, by a once-more-fallen Peter Greene, and hear the EAT-whistle blow, this time no doubt in earnest? An end to my tiresome history, and the University's! Once more I'd been all wrong, in what wise I was too miserable to care. What the heck anyhow!

Yet I paused a moment before committing suicide, for it was Hedwig Sear instead of Anastasia who shrieked round from the alley. Dressed in a thin infirmary-gown and clutching a rag-doll, she was pursued not by Peter Greene but by Croaker, whose cure had apparently not taken before Rexford's amnesty freed them both. And clinging to Croaker's trouser-top, half running, half dragging, was Dr. Sear himself, identifiable by his white tunic and gauze-bound head. He it was who cried "Rape! Rape!" At sight of the crowd Mrs. Sear stopped short, and as if smitten by modesty, pressed the rag-doll to the bosom of her gown and put a finger in her mouth. At once Croaker overtook her; to my further surprise, Dr. Sear fought—heroically!—in her behalf, but alas, succeeded only in facilitating the assault. For as the three tumbled campuswards his tugging brought down Croaker's detention-pants. Even so the doctor was not done; he picked himself up, and heedless of the difference in their strength and of his own safety, struck Croaker with both fists. The dread Frumentian had fetched up his quarry's gown and aimed his weapon; propped on one elbow, Mrs. Sear began to play with the doll, oblivious to her peril. One backhand swat felled the plucky doctor; he lay unconscious. Bucklike then, with a grunt and single slam that the tardy guards could not arrest, Croaker studded Mrs. Sear—back into awareness, one gathered from her cry.

I closed my eyes. No matter that accessory features of the dénouement were changed; it was the same old plot. As Croaker croaked and Hedwig wailed, I shrugged and swung myself off the sidecar, to make an end of it. No such luck: even before my death-wrench could sound the horn, I was hoist on mighty shoulders. The shophar flew; the rope went slack. I opened my eyes and found myself astride Croaker's neck, as once in the Living Room. A swath of tumbled undergraduates marked his path from me to Hedwig, who now embraced upon the ground her comatose if not deceasèd spouse.

"Everybody keep your shirts on!" ex-Chancellor Hector cried over the loudspeakers. But the unfelled bystanders clambered over one another to safety. Several sooty guards had drawn their pistols and were advancing towards us; armed with my stick, which he must have espied near the side-car, Croaker growled and made ready for combat. A young man whose dress and forelock suggested administrative responsibility stepped between us to warn the guards about intercollegiate repercussions and New Tammany's varsity image. My mother, to perfect the scene, found her way at last onto the porch from somewhere inside the Old Chancellor's Mansion, took one look about, and swooned; a ball of blue yarn rolled from her knitting-bag almost to Grandfather's feet.

"For pete's sake give me a hand, somebody!" he shouted, still in possession of the public-address system, if not his composure. "Flunk this arm of mine! Give me something to tie it up with!" This last, though broadcast, was snarled at his receptionist, who, despite the cold, at once began unbuttoning her uniform-blouse. The P.-G. snatched it from her before she could offer it, and ordered the doorguard to tie the sleeves behind his neck in the fashion of a sling. The forelocked vice-chancellor or administrative assistant, meanwhile, had commandeered a megaphone left behind by the fled cruel co-eds, and having begged the guards to hold their fire yet a minute, now implored me to check Croaker if I could: emissaries of his Frumentian alma mater were to fetch him next day, I was told, and with the University on the verge of C.R. III (if not already beyond it!), New Tammany needed all the colleagues it could get. Reports had it, he said, that Dr. Eierkopf was at the Powerhouse with Chancellor Rexford: would I guide Croaker thither, escorted by the guards, and arrange with Eierkopf to manage him until his recall?

"I'm busy being lynched," I reminded him. The aide apologized for that miscarriage of justice, acknowledging that even New Tammany had its imperfections, and promised that if I'd steer Croaker safely off Great Mall and retire myself to the goat-barn for the time being, he'd do everything he could to get me reinstated, appealing Bray's decision if necessary to the highest committees in Tower Hall.

The mob had retreated to a safe distance. Croaker croaked and handed me my stick, as if inviting governance; the guards stood ready to pistol him at the first threatening move. A white infirmary-vehicle with flashing headlight had swung into the dooryard, and medical-school functionaries hurried to attend the Sears and my mother. Reginald Hector had gone into the Mansion with his receptionist, but the latter now reappeared, an ROTC overcoat cloaking her bare shoulders; she flung in our direction her employer's former wrapper, and pertly withdrew.

Forelock's diplomacy gave way at last; fetching up the wrapper, he either tossed it to me or threw it at me, and cried, "Won't this day ever end? Flunk everything!"

The wrapper was of fine Angora, but ill-cut and worse-stitched. I smiled despite all at Granddad's goatsmanship and Forelock's distress—then put the noose from my neck, slipped into the familiar hide, and with a farewell glance at my swoonèd mom, sticked Croaker homewards.

THIRD REEL

1.

In fact—so our driver guessed as we sped in convoy from Great Mall—it was probably no later than half-past six. He hoped not, anyhow, for his detail was to go off duty at seven, and riot or no riot, he'd heard that the maddest party in the history of the Powerhouse was in progress, and he wanted not to miss the fun. Croaker I'd induced to ride in the side-car, but I was obliged to remain on his shoulders. The streets and public buildings were dark, owing to the power-failure, and almost vacant because of the general emergency; despite the ragged navigation of the guards we made good time. My neck was sore, my stomach empty, my bladder full, and the wind of that longest night in the year chilled me through; but my heart was so entirely spent, my spirit sunk, that their despair was indistinguishable from peace. I felt no further pain at abandoning Max, Mother, and my hopes, nor chagrin at being spared yet again from lynching, nor pleasure at the thought of rejoining the herd. I felt concern no more for studentdom's predicament, or my own. I felt nothing; was full of that positive sensation.

In perhaps an hour, so rapidly we traveled, we came to the top of that gorge where G. Herrold had expired—decades ago, it seemed. The moon shone cold on the beach and stream (which ran still now) and reflected upon a new span built on the old one's piers. Its design was different, its termini the same—and so for all I knew or cared might be its fate, come next spring's torrents. At the intersection where a right turn led down over it and thence to the barns, a left to the Powerhouse, pistol-shots rang out ahead. Our troop made a ragged halt and answered in kind, firing into the air. Then other shots sounded on the left, and almost simultaneously three headlights jiggled into view, one from before us and two from the left: motorcycles racing full-throttle. Nowise alarmed, the guards fell to wagering: their odds favored "the boss" (some called him *"der Hauptmann"*), who approached from the front, to reach the crossroads first, although the pair coming up on our left seemed rather nearer. And they knew their man, for with a recklessness that bespoke Maurice Stoker, "the boss" suddenly began shooting not into the air but at his competition—at the road ahead of them, in any case, where dust-puffs rose in their headlamp-beams and bullets rang from stones. The lead cyclist of the pair swerved for his life and spun into a shallow ditch, as Herman Hermann must once have done; the other slowed his pace appreciably, with the result that Maurice Stoker skidded into the crossroads, lit by our headlights, three or four seconds before his rival, another Powerhouse guard. Our detachment applauded their leader and hooted at their colleague's timidity.

"See if Fritz is *kaput*," Stoker bade the nearest of them, and pointed out with a laugh that not only had his "short-cut" from the Powerhouse been a potholed road, but he'd had *two* prisoners in his sidecar, whereas his competitors, on the better road, had had but one between them— fortunately not in Fritz's vehicle. He glared up at me in the swirling dust, as if he'd been expecting to meet me, on Croaker's shoulders, along his way (and indeed he had been, I later learned, my escorts having wirelessed the news ahead). His voice took an edge. "All's fair in love and riot, hey, Goat-Boy?"

I had nothing to reply and was anyhow distracted, as were my escorts, by the sight of his passengers. Slumped in the sidecar and blindfolded, they started up at mention of my name. Pocket-torches focused on them, and I was doubly surprised: Peter Greene it was, and Leonid Alexandrov, handcuffed together; their coats and faces were as bloodstained as the linen that bound their eyes—not blindfolds after all, but bandages.

"Aren't they a pair?" Stoker demanded of his troopers, but with a smolder in his tone meant for me. "And look at Hans's."

"Verdummt," the other driver reported, flashlighting his

unconscious passenger. Dr. Eierkopf's head lolled over the side-car-wale, a new pair of eyeglasses hanging from one ear. "Out-passed." Hans held his nose and pointed to stains on the prisoner's lab-coat, not of blood. The company laughed. Croaker stirred under me and sniffed the air, but seemed not to recognize his old roommate in that fallen state.

"Drunk and disorderly in the Living Room," Stoker said. He cut his engine, dismounted, and aimed his torch to observe my expression. "Ate a kilo of *Blutwurst,* tried to force my wife's virtue, and gummed the mustard off Madge's rear end till the blood came. Then he threw up and passed out. But your pal Rexford's still at it."

"Untruthness," Leonid Andreich said calmly from the side-car.

"Leonid's right, George," Peter Greene seconded—his voice uncharacteristically quiet also. "It was her took advantage of Doc Eierkopf—not that he give a durn. Lacey it was: the floozy-one."

Awed by the bloody pair, the troopers listened silently, their engines stilled.

"Lacey no," Leonid countered. "Mrs. Anastasia yes. Self-sacrificehood to needs of classmates." Like Greene's, his voice remained subdued, and both faced straight ahead as they spoke.

"Might be I was wrong about that Lacey business," Greene admitted. "But Lacey or Stacey, it weren't no sacrificeness. It was plumb floozihood."

"Possible," Leonid granted. "But I don't think, how do you say, all-said-and-donewise."

"I do," Greene said. "Might be mistaken, though."

"Also."

Stoker heard them out with his hands on his hips, but when they fell silent he exploded with disgust. "Two hours ago it was fight to the death; now they're buggering sweethearts!" He began to recount the fracas—ostensibly for the troopers' amusement, but still with a sarcasm that I knew was for my benefit. *He* hadn't felt like a party in the first place, he declared; he was sick of parties; it was the flunkèd Chancellor's idea, who having punched his own wife in the mouth had kicked over the traces entirely and directed that an orgy be commenced at once in the Powerhouse Living Room, so that he might, in his own phrase, fiddle while New Tammany burned. And it was Anastasia whom he'd chiefly fiddled with, drunkenly calling her his sister-in-law . . .

"Don't believe it, George," Greene interrupted. "Mr. Rexford was drunk all right, and claimed Stoker was his brother; but it was Lacey floozied *him*."

"Yes," Leonid affirmed. "But Mrs. Anastasia. And not floozied."

"All right!" Stoker shouted, and now glared directly at me. "Disgustingest thing I ever saw: Chancellor of the College boozing and wenching like a flunkèd sophomore! *Bragging* how he'd socked his wife! Telling everybody he's my brother! And Stacey carrying on like a Furnace-Room whore!"

"Even with him," Greene confirmed.

Leonid shook his head at the memory. "Even with us. Compassioncy!"

"Hot pants," Greene corrected. "But what the heck anyhow."

"*Da.* Irrelevanceness."

That, Stoker went on, had been the matter of the quarrel between his prisoners, presently so amicable: Greene had chauffeured Anastasia to the Powerhouse at my request, and, eager as he was to reunite with his family at the Pedal Inn, had lingered on to drink a farewell toast or two with Leonid. The Nikolayan, determined to act selfishly but uncertain how, had left Main Detention not by his own skill but, like Croaker, under Rexford's amnesty, which he'd judged it selfish to take advantage of, and made his way to the Powerhouse resolved to be a double agent for East and West. Encountering Greene at the orgy-in-process, he had clinked glasses with his former cellmate, the one drinking vodka, the other corn. First they'd toasted Max, who'd elected not to leave Main Detention: "Decent a Moishan as ever deserved Shafting," Greene had called him, and Leonid "the unselfnesssest martyrty." Next, with increasing sharpness, they'd saluted each other: "A durn fine Joe, for a Founderless Student-Unie"; "Lawlest Informationaler blind-bat, but I like okay!" And finally they'd drunk to Anastasia, who with tearful eyes and liquorous breath had offered to service both at once. "Passèdèdity!" Leonid had declared; "she make men classmates in love!" "You're the blind one!" Greene had charged, "tell-a-floozy-from-a-Founderwise! This ain't even Stacey!" Thereupon the toasts had turned to plain invective, so heated that neither availed himself of Anastasia's offer or even noticed when she left the bar, "flung herself" (in Stoker's words) again at the Chancellor, and finding him tabled with Madge, declared she was "running off" to meet another lover in the Tower Hall Belfry.

"Don't think I don't know who," Stoker growled at me. "Not that I give a flunk!"

"He gives a flunk," Greene said, surprisingly, and Leonid agreed.

"The flunk I do!" Stoker cried. "Any more than you wise-guys, or you'd have talked her out of leaving!" All *they'd* been concerned with, he said bitterly, was that his wife be seen as a Commencèd martyr (in Leonid's case) or (in Greene's) as a flunkèd floozy with a passèd virgin twin; the debate between them on this head, fired by alcohol, had grown so hot that it flared at last into a duel: they would fight to the death, they vowed, and the winner's prize would be the loser's good eye. The Living-Room bartender put their agreement in writing, the disputants each grasped a bottle by the neck and broke off its bottom, and armed with these ugly weapons they set to. For a time it was crouch and feint; the combatants, Stoker had to admit, were equally fearless, resolute, wary, and strong of arm, so that it seemed they might come to a bloodless impasse. Then Leonid had cried something in passionate Nikolayan and flung wide his arms, and Greene, believing himself insulted and attacked, had slashed in with the bottle. But even as he thrust he realized that his opponent was impulsively yielding the victory and offering his throat to be cut: the barkeep (himself a defected Nikolayan and rabid anti-Student-Unionist) reported later that Leonid's exclamation had been "Better you should see the truth than I" or something to that effect—which he interpreted to mean that Leonid was afraid of what he might see about his alma mater with two good eyes.

"Not so," Leonid here commented from the sidecar. "I meant Mrs. Anastasia, he should see her through my eyes."

"I figured that," Greene said. "And soon's I figured it, I felt the same durn way about *him*, Stacey/Laceywise."

He had tried therefore to pull his cut short, and Leonid to thrust himself upon the glass, but one or both misjudging the distance, the stroke had fallen on Leonid's face instead of his throat, and unfortunately slashed his patchless eye. Whereupon, stricken with remorse, Greene had snatched the vodka-bottle and stabbed out his own.

"The way they bloodied up the Living Room," Stoker said, "you'd have thought it was the Amphitheater!"

He had arrested them both and administered first aid; amnesty or no amnesty, he declared, he was fetching them to Main Detention, where he meant to stay himself until Rexford should sober up and go "back where he belongs." As for Anastasia, she might breed a barnful of billy-goat bastards for all he cared.

Leonid said flatly: "He cares."

"Yep," said Greene. "Anybody can see that."

Stoker responded with a jeer. "So there they sit, Goat-Boy: two blind bats! Are they passed or failed?"

Affecting as the grim tale was despite its teller's sarcasm, and shocking the bloody sight of my former cellmates, I listened and looked without comment, if no longer without emotion. Yet it wasn't pity I felt, or terror, not even responsibility for their present wretchedness. Stoker's question had been mine since early on in his narrative, and had absorbed me entirely well before he asked it, fetching me from apathy into the intensest concentration of my life. Indeed, my spirit was seized: it was not *I* concentrating, but something concentrating upon me, taking me over, like the spasms of defecation or labor-pains. Leonid Andreich and Peter Greene— their estates were rather the occasion than the object of this concentration, whose real substance was the fundamental contradictions of failure and passage. Truly now those paradoxes became paroxysms: I shut my eyes, swayed on Croaker's shoulders, trembled and sweated. All things converged: I understood what I had done to Dr. Eierkopf with my innocent question about paleooöontological priority. That circular device on my Assignment-sheet—beginningless, endless, infi-

nite equivalence—constricted my reason like a torture-tool from the Age of Faith. Passage *was* Failure, and Failure Passage; yet Passage was Passage, Failure Failure! Equally true, none was the Answer; the two were not different, neither were they the same; and *true* and *false,* and *same* and *different*—unspeakable! Unnamable! Unimaginable! Surely my mind must crack!

"What is it?" Greene asked. "What's going on, Leo?"

"I can't see, classmate."

The troopers murmured at my strange countenance and behavior; Croaker rumbled, feeling my thigh-grip on his neck, and stood up in the sidecar.

"Don't try to get loose!" No doubt it was Leonid Stoker warned, but his words struck my heart, and I gave myself up utterly to that which bound, possessed, and bore me. I let go, I let all go; relief went through me like a purge. And as if in signal of my freedom, over the reaches of the campus the bells of Tower Clock suddenly rang out, somehow unjammed: their first full striking since the day I'd passed through Scrapegoat Grate. As all listened astonished, the strokes mounted—*one, two, three, four*—each bringing from my pressèd eyes the only tears they'd spilled since a fateful late-June morn many terms past, out in the barns. *Sol, la, ti,* each a tone higher than its predecessor, unbinding, releasing me—then *do:* my eyes were opened; I was delivered.

Dr. Eierkopf too the bells revived; at first sound of them he had sat up and clutched his head. On the sixth stroke he'd snatched off his new eyeglasses just in time, for the seventh shattered them, as earlier in the Belfry. On that eighth and last, blood spurted from his nose, his eyes rolled up out of sight, he shrieked, *"Ach, mein Grunder, ist geborsten der Schädelknocken!"* and collapsed again. Croaker bounded to his side, and I sprang down. The handcuffs fell at my feet.

"Halt!" a guard warned; Stoker drew his pistol. But I went in perfect sureness past him to the sidecar, and caught up his prioners' hands.

"Leonid Andreich!" I said. "Pete! Thank you and pass you!"

"It *is* George," Greene said joyfully. "Hi there, George."

"Hi," I said. "Listen, Leonid: why are you going to Main Detention?"

"Because he's under arrest!" Stoker snapped.

Leonid shrugged. "I talk again to Dr. Spielman; maybe turn him looseness yet."

I gripped his hand. "Max doesn't want that, classmate. But *you:* look—" I tapped his handcuff. "You're free!"

He shook his head.

"Go back to Nikolay College!" I urged him. "That's where you have to pass!"

"Selfishty, George."

"Yes! And when *you're* passèd, try to help Classmate X."

"Forget it," Stoker said dryly. "This afternoon Chementinski declared himself a failure to the Union and asked for execution. Said he loved his son more than he loved the brotherhood of students. I imagine they'll oblige him."

"What is this!" Leonid cried.

"Never mind," I said. "Look: you and Pete have ended your quarrel. Re-defect! Tell your stepfather his confession was selfish: he wants them to kill him so he won't have to kill himself. Then tell him *that's all right!* Do you see?"

"George!" Leonid's forehead wrinkled above the bandage. "Passness of me, that's nothing! Even Classmate X, I love so, that's nothing to pass! But the self of Studentness—*He* matters! And you teach me He's flunkèd selfish! How He's pass?"

"Probably He can't," I said. "Try and see."

Red tears oozed into his bandage. "Failure is Passage, yes? No?"

I clapped him on the shoulder; the handcuff fell from his wrist.

"See here, now!" Stoker protested.

"*Da!*" Leonid cried. "Tomorrow, after Max: redefectness!"

"I'll take you to Founder's Hill," Peter Greene said, suddenly determined. "Look here: we'll meet my daughter at the Pedal Inn and stay the night; tomorrow we'll go to the Shafting together, for old Doc Spielman's sake."

"The flunk you will!" Stoker said. "You stay where you are!"

I took Greene's hand. "What then, Pete?"

He swallowed a number of times. "I got right smart of work to do back home, George. Finish up inventory; try and set things right with Sally Ann . . ."

"Do you really think your marriage can be saved?"

He set his chin, and would I think have blinked had his eyes been unbound. "Prob'ly not. But what the heck anyhow, George! I'm going to start from scratch, what I mean *understandingwise*. Things look different to a fellow's been through what I been through. I got a long ways to go."

"Pass you!" I declared.

"Into first grade," he added wryly. "I might Graduate yet, one of these days. But the odds ain't much."

"They never are! Look for me at Founder's Hill tomorrow."

He now wept freely, and his wounded eye bled a little onto his cheeks. He supposed with a laugh that he'd have no more hallucinations, at least, and wondered aloud whether a mixture of blood and tears might be good for acne. "Come on," he said then to Leonid; "I'll show you the way to the Pedal Inn."

"Nyet, friend; I know the way. I show *you."*

"I'll show you both," I said; "I'm going back to Great Mall."

Stoker fired his pistol into the air. "Flunk all this! Who the Dunce do you think you are, Goat-Boy? The Grand Tutor Himself?"

I regarded him closely. "Have your men drive them to the Infirmary first and then to the Pedal Inn. If Dr. Eierkopf's all right, he and Croaker can wait in the Powerhouse until the Frumentians come tomorrow. Why don't you take me to Tower Hall yourself?"

"You're coming with me, all right," he said, "but not to Tower Hall! Get in that sidecar!" He commanded his men to ignore what I'd said; Greene and Leonid *were* to be delivered to the Infirmary for treatment of their wounds and then left at the Pedal Inn—but not at my direction, only because that had been his plan all along. The amnesty, he explained crossly, forbade him the use of Main Detention. Similarly, Croaker and Eierkopf (who was stirring now as his roommate licked his head) were to be taken to the Living Room, but purely because he, Stoker, hoped thereby to chase Rexford out; the guards were to see to it that Eierkopf directed Croaker to that end. As for me, if I thought he meant to chauffeur me to a tryst in the Belfry with his tramp of a wife, I had another think coming . . .

"I'm not the one she's to meet there," I interrupted pleasantly; "it's Harold Bray."

He managed to accuse me of jealousy and mendacity, but I saw he was alarmed.

"I'm going to drive Bray out," I told him. "Among other things."

"I'll bet you are. So you can take his place!"

I shrugged. "One thing at a time."

He glared at me furiously. "You're as false as he is!"

"Bray's not exactly a phony," I said. "But he must be driven out. Would you like to do it yourself, before your wife services him?"

There I had him: except during his extraordinary "reform" back in March, Stoker had an aversion to Great Mall generally and a positive abhorrence of Tower Hall, its hub and crown. Yet for all his present soot and bluster he was not quite the Stoker of old: clearly he was distressed by My Lady-ship's new aggressiveness, and jealous of lovers she chose herself; he wanted the Belfry-tryst prevented, but could not deal himself with Bray (who I pointed out might well retreat with Anastasia into the Belly), and distrusted her with me. On the other hand he doubtless understood that if I *were* the Grand Tutor, I alone might manage Bray; and (less as-suredly) of all healthy men on campus I alone might be the one not interested in cuckolding him at his wife's invitation. Therefore he found himself, so I imagined, in the position of having to hope that I was what he declared I was not, and that I would overcome the temptations and obstacles he'd surely put in my way. His face grew livid with contradictions. As I gimped firmly into his sidecar, which Greene and Leonid had vacated, Tower Clock struck the half-hour.

"It's getting on," I observed. The troopers stood about ex-pectantly.

"Move!" Stoker shouted at them. *"Achtung! Dunkelbier! Sauerbraten!"* He fired his pistol at the ground near their feet, and they scrambled cursing for their vehicles. Stoker swung onto his own, not neglecting to fart as he kicked the starter. As if in reply his powerful engine barked and spat. He let out the clutch, spun our drive-wheel in the dust, howled an obscenity at the troopers leaping clear of us, and threw back his head as we snarled down the road. But it was I who laughed.

2.

I had come from Great Mall rapidly enough; returning, we fairly flew, by every trick and short-cut in the book: crossed through woods and fields and private lawns, took corners without a pause and stop-signs at full throttle. As if energized by our speed, Stoker resumed his usual baiting and other stratagems.

"So you still want to be Grand Tutor!" he shouted. "Now's the time to make your play, while Rexford's out of commission and everything's upset!"

I smiled.

"Why not work together?" he suggested, and outlined at the top of his voice a plan for "taking over the College": the Chancellor was in political disgrace and therefore vulnerable; only some extraordinary stroke of fortune—such as absolute Commencement by an undisputed Grand Tutor—might redeem his public image; but if Stoker himself had been disgusted by Rexford's conduct in the Living Room, surely Bray would be more so, and would revoke his Certification. The thing to do, then, was get rid of Bray—for example, by exposing his intended adultery with Anastasia—and establish *me* as Grand Tutor; Ira Hector's wealth and Stoker's secret influence (but he would deny me publicly and affirm Bray, to sway student opinion contrariwise) could promote me to that office easily, given the present disorder and uncertainty in West Campus. Then I would declare Lucky Rexford reinstated and Commencèd, and we three could run New Tammany as we wished.

"What you really want," I said, "is to see your brother Commence."

Stoker flushed and cursed. "Brother my arse! You should've seen him carrying on! Not that I care!"

I listened carefully to the quarter-hour chimes far in the distance and pointed when we came to a fork. "Bear left."

Stoker bore right. We soon drew up to Main Gate, passed through and down the dim-lit Mall to where indigent students, as always, were badgering Ira Hector, even swatting him with their various placards. Coatless and shirtless in the cold night air, Ira sneezed and feebly called for help. Stoker paused nearby, at the bole of a leafless elm where The Living Sakhyan sat upon the ground.

"Why not help old Ira?" he challenged. "Then he'll owe you a favor, and someday you can use him."

I smiled and got off the motorcycle. "Is that a dare?" But before I went to Ira's aid I bowed to The Living Sakhyan.

"Thank You for the disappeared ink, sir," I said. "I signed

my ID-card with it when I completed my Assignment at once, in no time."

He appeared to be smiling.

"For pity's sake, help!" Ira called.

"Excuse me, sir," I said to The Living Sakhyan. "I'm going to go help the Old Man of the Mall."

"Goat-Boy!" Stoker shouted from the motorcycle. "I *dare* you to help him! Understand? I'm daring you!"

To him also I bowed, but then waded into the circle of angry young students, most of whom "went limp" until they recognized me and then stood by while their spokesman explained their grievance. But a few, who had previously been standing on the fringe of the group with their backs turned, now moved in and commenced to swat Ira, not very violently, with their placards, perhaps in protest against the general *détente.*

"He's as stingy as ever!" the spokesman said angrily. "He poisons the whole West Campus."

"Didn't he give everything to the P.P.F.?" I asked.

"Gave 'em the shirt off my back!" Ira cried. "Why d'ye think I can't see to tell time? I'm a sick man!" He sneezed again and wiped his eyes, which were clotted with rheum. *"Gesundheit,"* said a student beating him.

"It's night-time anyhow," I observed to the group. "He can't see our shadows to tell time by."

"Ha!" Ira cried.

"That's not the whole point," said the student spokesman. "He's pulled the rug out from under the Rexford administration. Ruined the economy."

"Who cares?" another challenged. "The Administration's corrupt anyhow. All power corrupts."

"And knowledge is power," said a third, whose sign bore the one word *Ignorabimus.* "So absolute knowledge corrupts absolutely. Look at Dr. Faustus. Look at Dr. Bray."

They fell to arguing then whether Lucius Rexford was a liberal conservative or a conservative liberal, and became so preoccupied, I was able to spare Ira Hector further swats, for the present, simply by sliding him half a meter down the bench, out from under the swinging placards.

"I don't owe you a thing," he wheezed at once. "You owed *me,* for taking your fool advice this morning." He had, I learned, instructed his agents to make over his entire estate and divers incomes to the Philophilosophical Fund, with the declared intention of Passing through poverty and ignorance, and burdening others with his wealth. But the result was that he stood to become wealthier than ever from tax-refunds, while the College went bankrupt for want of tax revenues. Half the student body would subsist on tax-free scholarships, all deductible by the Hector cartel. Moreover, his agents were abandoning him to take service with his brother, lately back from the goat-farms, in the mistaken conviction that Reginald was independently wealthy: why else would he have "resigned" from the P.P.F. directorship? Finally, the students whose tuition had been going to be paid by Lucius Rexford's tax-supported grant-in-aid program now despised Ira, and had apparently stripped the clothes from his back when he offered them, gratis, the time of night.

"You said you *gave* them your shirt," I reminded him.

He sneezed and cursed. "I'd like to see 'em try to get along without me!"

"They can't," I said.

"Tell them that!"

I bent close to his ear. "Listen, Old Man: forget what I told you both times before. It was mistaken advice."

He glittered his eyes. "Swindled me, did you? I figured you for a sharper! What's your line this time?"

I smiled and bade him good evening.

"Hold on!" he called after me. "Don't you think these rapscallions'll start right in once you've gone? What kind of help is that? You owe me!"

It was indeed evident that at least some of the indigents only waited my withdrawal to resume their molestations—and a very few, of course, had never really left off. But though I'd deemed it flunkèd, in West Campus anyhow, not to assist him, I also recognized the final futility of assistance, and so tarried no longer.

"Wait!" he cried more desperately. "It's earlier than you think; I can tell by the moonshadows! It's only quarter till ten!"

Sure enough, Tower Clock sounded the three-quarter melody as he spoke, and if the coming hour was indeed ten, it was not so late as I'd have supposed. But that fact was of no importance to me.

"Ha!" the student leader exclaimed. "Hear that? Quarter till! Much obliged, old man!" And laughing at their adversary's inadvertent gift, which it plainly chagrined him to have bestowed, they left him in peace, for the time being at least—except one small faction opposed to private charity and another to the forcible extortion of information, both of whom now laid on with their placards.

"Aren't you going to re-advise him?" Stoker demanded sarcastically.

I knew what reply to make; but just then the Great-Mall streetlights—those not burned out earlier in the evening—flared momentarily, and I saw Reginald Hector, flanked by aides and receptionist, striding towards his brother's bench. I stepped between them.

"You!" the ex-Chancellor cried, and his surprise at the sight of me quickly turned to irritation. "Look out of my way, boy; I got to save Ira from those beggars!"

"Your brother can't really be helped, Grandpa," I declared. "His case is hopeless."

"Nuts," he said, pushing past me. "That's no-win talk. Nothing's impossible!"

"Check," the receptionist affirmed. "Up and at 'em, P.-G."

"You have some begging of your own to do, is that it?" My gibe fetched him up, though I knew it to be no more than half true. He ordered his aides to proceed to Ira's rescue, directing them with his slingèd arm, and then turned to me like a professor-general to a wayward freshman recruit, his chin thrust dangerously forth.

"I withdraw the remark, sir," I said, before he could speak. "Your brother Ira can't pass, but I *do* have some final advice for you. If you want it."

"Hmp!" He glared at me squint-eyed for a moment, stroking his jaw. His aides, having driven off Ira's three or four lingering molesters, found themselves beset now by the whole original company of demonstrators, almost united in their opposition to uniformed intervention.

"Contingency Three-A?" the receptionist called.

"Affirmative," said the P.-G., and at her direction the aides began issuing articles of cold-weather clothing, warm though ill-fitting, to the demonstrators.

"Three-A Sub One!" Grandfather barked. At once the receptionist offered to deputize the bearded student leader as an assistant aide, or field supervisor of P.P.F. disbursements, at a high salary. He hesitated, considered the jeers of his out-of-classmates, but finally accepted the post, protesting to his fellows that one had to see the undergraduate revolution in its larger perspective, if one was not to be after all an ivory-tower *naïf*. "Even Sakhyan—" he started to explain.

"Three-A Sub Two!" the ex-Chancellor shouted triumphantly. His receptionist whispered something into the new aide's ear, whereupon he exchanged his soiled-sheepskin jacket for a heavy olive topcoat with epaulets, bestowing the fleece upon Ira Hector. The students booed.

"Losers weepers!" Ira cackled. *"Sauve qui peut! Possession is nine points of the law!"*

"Keep your advice, boy," Grandfather told me proudly. "I'll get to Commencement Gate on my own two feet! Beholden to none!"

I made no objection. The students now were pelting their former spokesman with the gold cufflinks, desk-calendars, and ball-point pens distributed among them by the aides, and Reginald Hector went to issue fresh directives for this contingency.

"Tower Hall," I said to Stoker.

He twitched his mouth. "I'll bet you didn't *have* any advice for the P.-G."

"Better hurry," I suggested, climbing into the sidecar. "It's not getting any earlier."

He started the motor, but deliberately tarried, watching the ex-Chancellor efficiently put down the demonstrators.

"Why didn't you Certify him, if he's passed?"

"I didn't say he was passed."

He grinned. "So Reg is as flunked as Ira."

I smiled. "I didn't say that either."

"Nepotism!" Stoker taunted. "Same old story—not *what* you know, but *who*." Tower Clock tolled ten.

"Your wife's assignation is scheduled for eleven," I reminded him, "but she may be there already. You know how it is when a woman's in love. For that matter, Tower Clock may be wrong."

With a loud oath he wrenched open the throttle; our acceleration pressed me into the seat. Moreover he sounded the siren, and the crowd on Tower Hall Plaza looked around in grave alarm as we raced up. Above the great clockfaces the Belfry was floodlit by mobile searchlight-units of the NTCROTC and the various Telerama departments. Agitated pigeons flew in and out. I saw Stoker's face grow grim.

"Go around to the back," I said. "I'm going up through the Library."

"The flunk you are!" he exploded, and jammed on the brakes. "I'm not going anywhere!"

I considered a moment, shrugged, and climbed out of the sidecar.

"Neither are you!" he insisted. But I obviously was.

3.

Just then the crowd sighed; looking up with them I saw a white-tunicked, black-cloaked figure waving from the Belfry. Beside him, all in white, was a smaller, whom partially he caped.

"Did you *see* it, Jo Anne?" one co-ed demanded of another. "He walked right up the wall, with her on His shoulder!"

"Nonsense," a young man sneered. "He was up there all along. I saw the whole thing."

"So did *I!*" said the girl on his arm indignantly. "And you're both wrong: He flew *down,* from higher up." And this opinion she defended stoutly against the most cynical objections: maybe it *was* a publicity stunt, or a Telerama trick; she neither knew or cared; but that Bray had by one means or another flown into the Belfry with his girlfriend she was as absolutely certain as was her beau that he'd done nothing of the sort and the first girl that he'd scaled the tower bare-handed and -footed. Strongly I gimped through, sticking and butting my way in some circumstances, politely begging leave to pass in others. Once, recognizing a knot of my erstwhile lynchers, I slipped into my Bray-mask till I was by them; in another instance I declared I was on official Chancellory business; in yet another, that I was George Giles, Goat-Boy and true Grand Tutor, en route to rescue my distressèd Lady-ship.

"From what?" Stoker demanded, puttering behind me on the motorcycle. "Who said she *wants* rescuing?"

A few male students chuckled. Others whispered to their female companions. I gimped on, around to the Library-entrance, followed by a small but growing throng. The figures in the Belfry disappeared.

"Flunk it all, listen here!" Stoker yelled, throttling up beside me. "Do you think she'd be up there if I hadn't ordered her to go? I arranged it!"

I smiled.

"Call me a cuckold!" Stoker challenged. "You can bet I have my reasons!" His tone grew more fretful as we came near the Library door. "But that doesn't give *you* permission, Goat-Boy! You're staying right here!"

I positively grinned at him, whereupon his voice at once turned guileful.

"How about Maxie? We could still spring him, if we work fast . . ." He raced his engine angrily. "Some Grand Tutor! You want her yourself!"

The students cheered. I motioned Stoker with my stick to get behind me; he was obliged in any case to do so, or leave his vehicle, as we'd arrived at the Library steps.

"Keep your hands off my wife!" he cried, heedless of bystanders—who seemed anyhow to assume that he was as usual playing a part. "If you even touch her without my say-so, I'll fix you both!"

But I went on up, and he didn't follow.

"You can say goodbye to Spielman!" he shouted at last. "You've condemned him to death!" He added something else, which the closing of the door cut off. Students clustered after me, some drinking from their steins, other heckling, a very few shouting threats of a fresh lynching, a roughly equal number defending me verbally against them, and most simply curious. All were halted, as was I, by armed cadets at the door of the Catalogue Room.

"No admittance," they declared. The students angrily reminded them that it was a public library in a presumably free college. "Open stacks! Open stacks!" they began to chant. The cadets, in beautiful unison, fixed their bayonets. Everyone waited to see what I would do. But the noise fetched out an elder library-scientist from the Catalogue Room, where in the erratic light one could see numbers of his colleagues poring over a tablesful of documents.

"Quiet!" he demanded. "We *will* have quiet in the Library!" To the students, who seemed to respect him, he explained that all of New Tammany had just been put under martial law by order of the Chancellor (who I therefore gathered must have come "back where he belonged") and would remain so until the general emergency passed and order was restored. He exhorted them to return to their dormitories in the meanwhile and do their homework, by candlelight if necessary, inasmuch as varsity political crises came and went, as indeed did colleges and curricula, but the research after Answers must unflaggingly persist. Follow his own example, he bade us, and that of his colleagues, who would continue to piece together as best they could the scattered fragments of the Founder's Scroll, though the very University rend itself into even smithier eens.

"My own coinage," he chuckled at this last. "Comparative diminutive after *smiodar:* a piece of flinder. The substantive *een* is spurious, it goes without saying . . ." As he spoke, a special lens attached to the side of his spectacles like a mineralogist's loup fell down into place and focused his attention on me: he asked excitedly whether I was not George Giles, the Goat-Boy and allegèd Grand Tutor indirectly responsible for the shredding of the Founder's Scroll.

"Yes, sir," I said. "Sorry about that."

But he bore me no grudge; indeed he seemed almost grateful to me for having in a way occasioned his current research. He insisted that the door-guards admit me, unless they had specific orders to the contrary, as he and his colleagues needed to consult me on a matter of textual restoration. "Understand," he said to them and the students, "we're not necessarily intimating any support of Mr. Giles's claims or ambitions, which frankly don't interest us one way or the other. Even the Dean o' Flunks can quote the Scroll to his purpose, they say, and an accurate quotation is our only concern."

A few students laughed politely at the little joke; the guards clicked their rifle-bolts as one. But I was permitted to enter.

"A little humor there," the library-scientist told me modestly. "Shows them we're not all dry-as-dust." His associates looked up from a circular central table where the Scroll-case had formerly stood. Some had magnifiers in their hands, or Eierkopfian lenses, or scissors and paste. The manuscript-fragments, carefully laid out on the table-top, were surrounded by photographic equipment and bottles of chemicals; the floor round about was littered with longer, more modern scrolls: coded read-outs from WESCAC's automatic printers.

I was introduced around to philologists, archaeologists, historical anthropologists, comparative linguists, philosophers, chemists, and cyberneticists, the last on hand both to lend WESCAC's analytical assistance to the project and to apply their genius with codes and ciphers to the restoration of the priceless text. I nodded to each, explained to the group that I was merely passing through the Catalogue Room en route to the Belfry, and excused myself.

"Oh no." My escort, a model of donnish affability thitherto, spoke sharply and seized my arm. His colleagues too, whom one had thought to be gentle, preoccupied academicians, closed ranks between me and the exit, their expressions firm. I regarded them thoughtfully.

"Accuracy of text is all we care about," declared my warden. His voice was polite again; he even chuckled. "After the first shock of seeing the Scrolls destroyed, we realized you'd actually given us a unique opportunity. All the texts are corrupt, you know, even these—copies of copies of copies, full of *errata* and *lacunae*—but we never could agree on a common reading, and of course the old Scrolls acquired a great spurious authority for sentimental reasons, even though they contradict each other and themselves." At an interdepartmental faculty luncheon that same day, therefore, a committee of experts from various relevant disciplines had been established to reconstruct, from the shards of the Founder's Scroll (actually several scrolls, overlapping, redundant, discrepant), the parent text, until then hypothetical, from which all known variants had descended and on which their authority was ultimately based.

"A radical project, to be sure," said the library-scientist, who was also chairman of the *ad hoc* committee. "But we like to think of ourselves as *avant-garde* classicists, so to speak. Little paradox there . . ." After a small digression then on the etymology of the word *lacuna,* and a more extravagant one on the word *digression* (which he justified with the chuckled preface that *digression* and *extravagance* were "etymological kissing cousins, you might say"), he came to the point. With WESCAC's aid and the committee's pooled learning, the groundwork for restoring the Scroll had proceeded very swiftly, and an "analogue model" of the proposed *Urschrift* had actually been roughed out on the computer. But before the work of assembling the Scroll-fragments after that pattern could really get under way, a fundamental issue had to be resolved. As much a question of personal philosophy as of historical philology, it involved whole complexes of argument, ideological as well as scholarly; but the Committee agreed that for convenience' sake it could be symbolized by a practical question about the translation of a single sentence—a mere two words in the original language of the Scrolls. The "etymons," as he called them, were the root terms for *Pass* and *Fail*, but inflected with prefixes, infixes, suffixes, and diacritical marks to such an extent, and so variously from fragment to fragment, that conflicting interpretations were possible; indeed, the history of certain such interpretations, in his opinion, could be said to figure the intellectual biography of studentdom, as had been amply demonstrated in a wealth of what he called *Geistesgeschichten* . . .

"Here's what it comes down to," one of his younger colleagues interrupted; "the existing texts of the sentence are grammatically discrepant, and where it's supposed to appear in the most reliable context we've got *lacunae:* the missing fragments are either in the CACAFILE somewhere or among the ones you ate this morning." He happened to brandish a pair of library-shears as he spoke, and I gripped my stick to parry any move to disembowel me. But all they wanted, even as his senior colleague had declared, was an opinion from me on the question whether to the best of my knowledge the crucial sentence ought to be translated *Flunkèd who would Pass* or *Passèd are the Flunked*. On that question, obviously, depended whole systems of others, perhaps even the overall sense of the Founder's Scroll.

"Mind you, we agree on what each version means," the young man said briskly. "What we call the *A* reading means that one ought to desire to fail, since the desire to pass is vain and vanity's flunkèd—not to mention the famous tradition that Passage is to be found only in the knowledge of Failure, *et cetera et cetera.*"

The older man adjusted his glasses and cleared his throat. "Well, now . . ."

"The *B* reading," his protégé continued quickly, "is a way of saying that while to desire passage is to fail, to desire failure on that account is also to fail, since it equals desiring to pass. But despite the fact that Passage and Failure aren't different, they're not the same either; and for that reason if one wants to pass one should desire *neither* Failure nor

Passage—yet one shouldn't desire neither *because* one wants to pass, obviously . . ."

"Obviously," several of his colleagues agreed, and even his mentor nodded with a slight cock of the head, as if to say that while details of the young man's gloss were not unexceptionable, as a rough-and-ready formulation it would do.

"But we *can't* agree whether *A* or *B* is correct," he concluded, "and so we're collecting expert opinions, weighting them appropriately, and programming WESCAC to arbitrate the whole question." He winked and chuckled. "You may be interested to know that your colleague Dr. Bray has already obliged us with his judgment—though you understand I'm not at liberty to confide it, or what his weighting is on our little scale."

They waited for me to speak. "Gentlemen," I said, "your problem is most interesting in itself. What's more it's of the first practical importance, clearly. Now, if you'll excuse me . . ."

But they blocked my way.

"*A* or *B?*" the young scholar demanded. "If you can't remember what you ate, boy, tell us what you think, and we'll let you go." His superior tut-tutted at this show of coerciveness, but my inquisitor frankly declared that accuracy and thoroughness in scholarly matters were his only values in this flunkèd University, and that as a truly revolutionary researcher he would not hesitate to resort to terrorism if necessary to gain his ends. He didn't give a flunk, he said, whether *A* or *B* was "true" in the philosophical sense—all such mystical formulations, in fact, he regarded as superstitious mumbo-jumbo: their authors knaves, their Tutees fools—but upon their like was constructed the whole mad edifice of campus history, for a clear understanding whereof it was absolutely essential to have accurate texts, "believe" them or not.

"Do you *have* an opinion?" he asked me wryly.

I smiled, as I had done through the whole episode. "Yes."

"Then let's have it." He clacked the shears grimly. "We'll let WESCAC decide what it's worth."

Reluctant for some reason to use the library-scientist's term, I asked, "where is this famous 'pit'?"

The young man smiled and carefully indicated with the point of his shears a ragged hole near the center of the assembled shards. I opened a lens on my stick-end and leaned close over.

"Why magnify it if you don't know the script?" he asked unpleasantly. "That just makes a big riddle out of a little one."

But I was not inspecting the *lacuna,* nor was my lens a magnifier, but Dr. Sear's mirror, with the aid of which I observed that the Committee had forsaken the aisle to gather close about.

"What's your answer?" one of them demanded.

I huffed a great puff, sending vellum flinders in all directions, and with a sweep of my stick scattered fragments, chemicals, note-cards, shears, and scholars. Before they could recover themselves enough to decide whether stopping me or re-retrieving the smithered eens was of immediater importance, I had dashed into the Circulation Room and was gimping it headlong for the lobby. Halfway down a flickering corridor it occurred to me that if two riot-troopers were guarding the Catalogue Room, whole platoons must be on duty in the main lobby, especially at the lifts that serviced Belfry and Belly. Somewhere overhead the clock once again struck the three-quarter-hour; unless it was in error, there was no time to waste debating with a phalanx of bayonets. I retraced my steps to the Circulation Room (no one seemed to be pursuing me) and having noticed from a corner of my eye a few moments earlier its single occupant—a longhaired pallid girl, uncosmeticked and -washed, reading behind a desk marked INFORMATON—I took a long hazard.

"Excuse me, miss: is there any way up besides the lift?"

Next door the scholars fussed and clamored, scrambling after fragments on all fours like awkward kids, but the Circulation Room was still. The pimpled maid, thin and udderless as Mrs. Rexford but infinitely less prepossessing, looked over her spectacles from the large novel she was involved in and said with careful clarity—as if that question, from a fleecèd goat-boy at just that moment, were exactly what she'd expected—"Yes. A stairway goes up to the Clockworks from this floor. You may enter it through the little door behind me."

All the while she marked with her finger her place in the book, to which she returned at once upon delivering her line. Mild, undistinguished creature, never seen before or since, whose homely face I forgot in two seconds; whose name, if she bore one, I never knew; whose history and fate, if any she had, must be *lacunae* till the end of terms in my life's story—Passage be yours, for that in your moment of my time you did enounce, clearly as from a written text, your modest information! Simple answer to a simple question, but lacking which this tale were truncate as the Scroll, an endless fragment!

"*-less fragment*," I thought I heard her murmur as I stooped through the little door she'd pointed out. I paused and frowned; but though her lips moved on, as did her finger across the page, her words were drowned now by the bells of Tower Clock.

4.

In jerky leaps I sticked up stairs, around and around the shaft in which the mighty pendulum swung. Four flights there were, which I ascended as the bells phrased out their tune, and then a vertical ladder from the topmost landing up to a square trap-door in the Belfry floor. This ladder had ten rungs, I happen to know, for as I hiked myself up to each, the bells tolled an hour and over my head Anastasia screeched—a little higher each time, the three of us. Upon the eighth, bane of Dr. Eierkopf's head, my own was through the trap-door, and in the reflected glare of plaza searchlights I saw My Ladyship a-humpèd upon the floor. On hands and knees she was, face slack, shift high; standing behind her, black cape spread and face a-glint, Harold Bray—quite older-visaged than thitherto, also hairier. Though his tup was hid (the pair were facing me) it must needs have been brutish long and sore applied: he was not mounted, only standing with bent knees aft of her 'scutcheon, and his cassock was raised in front no higher than his shin-tops; moreover he did not thrust like any buck but only stood connected, opening and closing his eyes and cape; yet on each peal (high-*re* and -*mi* were the two I witnessed) Anastasia shrieked as if impaled, and on *fa*—which last stroke fetched me through the trap-door altogether—she collapsed upon the bird-limed floor, among broken eggshells and pigeon-straw. I was obliged to leap over her, the way being strait between Eierkopf's work-tables and the busy gears of the clock; my stick-stroke, consequently, fell short of Bray's head and but thwacked his cape, raising a silky dust that made me sneeze. He sprang behind the pendulum-shaft into the lift, and so escaped—but I had meant anyhow only to drive him off My Ladyship just then. To her, sitting up now fuckèd in the strew, I turned.

"How are you, Anastasia?"

She palmed her brow. On the floor between her legs, a thick green puddle.

"George . . ."

"Ma'am?"

She caught her breath; her eyes grew awed. "It wasn't what You think. I know now why Dr. Bray never tried before! *He's . . . different!*"

"Different how, Anastasia?" I'd squatted before her; now with a wail she flung her arms about my neck and wept into my fleece. Once she'd managed between shudders to explain, as best she grasped it, that her ravisher was altogether lustless, craving only her reproductive assistance; that his private construction was not like that of any male in her large experience; and that in the nature of his case it was highly doubtful, even unimaginable, that she would conceive by those glaucous gouts of his rank stuff—most of which, thanks to my timely appearance and her collapse, had anyhow missed their mark—I advised her that she needn't loathe him. She wiped her eyes.

"I guess I don't, George, now that I know. But, *ugh!*"

"I have to drive him out of the Belly now," I said, "and sooner or later off the campus. Part of my work. But I don't have any feeling about him, one way or the other."

She sniffed and shivered. "Me neither. But, George . . ."

"Yes?"

Again she hugged and wailed. "I love You!" Then at once she drew away. "What are we going to *do?*"

I begged her pardon. Three hours and eight minutes previously, when so much had suddenly come clear in George's Gorge, I'd seen—as it were in the general light—that marriage was not for such as I, nor any amorous relationship; the bonds of desire, the ties of wife, mistress, children, like every other bond, I would cast off, eschew, abjure—eradicate, if necessary, like the names on my ID-card. And adultery, in particular, I perceived—given the student situation and the fab-

ric of campus life—was flunkèd in the Founder's eyes, so to
speak, at least for His Grand Tutors. Of these things I no
longer held opinions; I knew them to be the case, as I'd been
given in that instant to know much else. Yet in all this clarity—which so surely had lit my way back to Great Mall and
up to the Belfry, and would beyond, from Tock to Tick,
where presently I must go—one shadow remained. I detected
it most plainly in the pupils of Anastasia's eyes, and inferred
therefore that what it shrouded was myself.

"You must love your husband," I earnestly advised her.
"Stoker's in critical shape just now. He's actually jealous."

"I'm a complete failure!" Anastasia cried, and repeated
what she'd told me earlier on, and which her Living-Room
debauchery had confirmed for her: she still felt compassion
for the student body's needs and a particular obligation to
please her husband (for whom she had discovered in herself
that day, for the first time, a kind of affection, when she'd
seen his distress in the Living Room); moreover, she craved
with all her heart to practice my instructions, as she believed
absolutely in my Grand-Tutorhood. But she had failed, she
wept; *was* failed, because what her deliberate promiscuities
and self-servicings had taught her was that she was *in
love*—an entirely novel experience! And the object of her
passion was myself.

I fretted. "Anastasia . . ."

"I don't care about anything," she said quietly. "I don't
care what Maurice thinks, or You think, or even the Founder
thinks. I know I'm flunked, and I don't even care." She'd
come to the Belfry, she declared, against her husband's express prohibition (the first such of their marriage), knowing
she might have to submit to Bray and then letting him do his
will upon her even when she saw the horror of it, all in the
conviction that I would appear—as indeed I had, though I'd
not decided to until three hours and fifteen minutes past (the
clock chimed as she spoke), and had even supposed in the
Treatment Room that we'd see each other no more. Thus was
her faith vindicated. What she wanted now, and was resolved
upon with the same formidable confidence, was to engender
and bear a child by me—an idea obviously planted by
Mother—and to this end she was prepared to flunk herself
forever with the prerequisite adultery. If I refused (and she
would not "assert herself," she said; no more of that; I must

come to *her*), she meant to go down in the Belly with me and there expire.

"I know You don't love *me*," she concluded. "I guess You can't, and still be a Grand Tutor. But I love You."

Her manner was the more disturbing for its perfect calm. I was touched with wonder and, at first, a really dispassionate curiosity. My nature and function, it seemed to me, I understood (since eight o'clock) quite clearly and disinterestedly. Certain misconceptions and imperfect notions had fallen from me, like blindfolds from the eyes or handcuffs from the wrists; I *knew* now I was meant for Grand-Tutorhood, and saw my way, work, and fate with sure indifference—as, for instance, that I would drive out Harold Bray, but with neither rancor nor relish, only as part of my larger Assignment. A knife cuts; a fish swims; a Grand Tutor, among other things, drives from the campus such as Bray. There was no glamour to the work, nor any longer to the term: *Grand Tutor, WESCAC, fountain-pen*—all names of neutral instrumentalities. Thus also even *Bray, impostor, troll:* as he himself had once suggested, albeit guilefully, it was his *function* to be driven out; on the Founder's transcript, so to speak, his *A* and mine would be of equal value.

"Anastasia," I began again, and would have told her of these things—that the fact of my Grand-Tutorhood, for example, in itself made me no more *lovable* than the fact of assistant-professorship, say; and that for pointing the way to Commencement Gate, as surely I would do, studentdom owed my person no more love than one owed an Amphitheater-usher, for instance, or museum-guide, who also merely discharged their functions. To be sure, a certain kind of love for studentdom was prerequisite to my work—but so was a love of plants to the horticulturalist's, whose crop was nowise obliged thereby to reciprocation. Love me? I didn't love myself!

But I got no further than her name, at sound whereof she opened to me her fine clear eyes. They gave back my image, luminous, and another shadow disappeared—the last but one.

"Show me the way to the Belly, Anastasia."

She understood, evidently, that the lobby-lifts were under guard, and that in any case we could not resummon the elevator Bray had used. My hope was that like the nameless Information-girl, she would know of a hidden stair or other seldom-used route: her "mother," after all, had worked in

Tower Hall throughout her adult life. But under this hope
and conjecture was a certain knowledge, in view whereof I
directed instead of asking her. She paled a little, then quietly
got up. We went through the trap-door and down the ladder
and stairs to the bottom landing—one level below the Circulation Room, but still a long way from the Belly. Taking my
hand then, she led me through a low door into a maze of
unlit bookstacks, through which she threaded as surely as if
she dwelt there. More than once our way was barred by
locked mesh doors, increasingly formidable, marked
RESTRICTED: NO ADMITTANCE—which however she opened
easily with a hairpin by the light of my pocket-torch. At last
we came to a cul-de-sac, in whose blind wall was a large
dumbwaiter in a steel-screen shaft. A sign above it warned
the few whose rank in the College might open all those inter-
vening doors. DANGER: DIET-TAPES ONLY. I understood
where I was, that I had been there once before. She gripped
my hand.

The tapelift door was bossed with assorted keyholes and
combination-dials, proof equally against hairpins and blows
of stick. But when in exasperation I merely pulled, it swung
open, as if unlatched from the beginning. A steel box one
meter square at most, scarcely large enough for one person;
however, Anastasia climbed in at once, unhesitant, and drew
me after. Knees to chin and arsy-turvy—like two shoes in a
box, or that East-Campus sign of which her navel had reminded me—we had not room to move a muscle; yet in some
fashion I crooked the door shut with my stick, and Anastasia,
using flashlight, mirror, and magnifying lens from my purse,
and the curved tip of the shophar, contrived to reach through
the mesh and press the red button marked *Belly*. The lift
gave a jerk, shearing off many centimeters of horn-tip and
further tangling My Ladyship and myself; we began a slow
descent in total darkness. Yet had there shone upon us all the
lights of the Power Line, I'd have been blind as Greene or
Leonid, blind as Gynander; for such was my involvement
with Anastasia, my eyes pressed into what had been my first
sight of her (G. Herrold's last), upon the broken bridge.
Hers me likewise, and through my curly blindfold I began to
see a light.

"Adultery is flunkèd," I declared into her. "Also the
deception of spouses." She whispered, "A-plus."

"Hypocrisy, too," I said. "And yet—there's a riddle here

somewhere, Anastasia; something fundamental. It's as if the Answer were right under my nose! And yet I don't quite have it . . ."

So cramped were our quarters, she could but murmur acknowledgment. Yet respond she did to my impassioned ruminations, vouchsafing me in wordless tongue a foretaste of ultimate Solution.

We reached bottom.

"This is just the Mouth," I said when the lift-door and my eyes opened on the familiar ruby glow. Able now to move her head, Anastasia tensed at my words and declared: "Then this is the end, I guess. But I don't mind being EATen, George . . ." Indeed, she slipped out before I could and gave me her hand, saying, "I love You."

Again those words! I swung my legs out of the tapelift and thoughtfully rubbed my chin. Bray was gone before me, I perceived, leaving only the faintest trace of himself behind: perhaps he lurked in the Belly proper; on the other hand he may have gone on towards Founder's Hill. No matter. All that counted was that final shadow, which, like My Ladyship's mighty night-fleck in the Gorge, appeared no larger than a man's hand, and yet enveloped the University. I, belovèd! I frowned and squinted, blinked like Peter Greene. Anastasia's face was all entreaty; and yet, having said, "I love You," she would say no more: she waited with eyes closed and hand extended.

"Assert yourself, Anastasia," I ordered huskily, to test her. In a very positive small voice she answered: "No."

I stepped to her, stirred to the marrow, and kissed her lips. Like Truth's last veils our wrappers rose: her eyes opened; I closed mine, and saw the Answer.

"Pass you!" I whispered. She nodded.

Supporting her under the buttocks with my stick, I lifted her upon me; she twined me round.

"In the purse," I said. "Bray's mask. For the scanner."

From the bag strung about my neck she withdrew and donned the mask. Then I bade her empty the purse itself of its sundry contents, invert it over my head, and draw the strings. At my direction she directed me to the entry-port.

"Wait," I said. "Do you see a control-panel nearby? Some sort of console?"

"Yes. There's a row of black buttons on it and a place marked *Input*. But the only jack I see says *Output*."

"Put it in," I instructed. She did, and pulled the lever beside the console. There were hums and snaps. At once the port opened, and in I went. The scanner clicked: as one, we tumbled past it and slid deep into the Belly.

"Wonderful!" I cried. For though the place was lightless, and my head pursed, in Anastasia I discovered the University whole and clear. Mother of my soul, its pulse throbbed all around us; my Father's eye it was glowed near, whose loving inquiry I perceived through My Ladyship.

"It says *ARE YOU MALE OR FEMALE,*" she whispered. We rose up joinèd, found the box, and joyously pushed the buttons, both together, holding them fast as we held each other.

"HAVE YOU COMPLETED YOUR ASSIGNMENT AT ONCE, IN NO TIME"

Was it Anastasia's voice? Mother's? Mine? In the sweet place that contained me there was no East, no West, but an entire, single, seamless campus: Turnstile, Scrapegoat Grate, the Mall, the barns, the awful fires of the Powerhouse, the balmy heights of Founder's Hill—I saw them all; rank jungles of Frumentius, Nikolay's cold fastness, teeming T'ang—all one, and one with me. *Here* lay with *there, tick* clipped *tock, all* serviced *nothing;* I and My Ladyship, all, were one.

"GILES, SON OF WESCAC"

Milk of studentdom; nipple inexhaustible! I was the Founder; I was WESCAC; I was not. I hung on those twin buttons; I fed myself myself.

"DO YOU WISH TO PASS"

I the passer, she the passage, we passed together, and together cried, "Oh, wonderful!" Yes and No. In the darkness, blinding light! The end of the University! Commencement Day!

5.

How long we lay embracèd none can tell: no bells toll where we were. After the shock, the Belly was still as we: asleep, passed away. In no time at all we lay there forever.

"A-plus."

We embraced the more tightly, not to wake.

"Pass All Fail All!" The voice, some meters off, was familiar: a cheerful lady croon. Loath to return from the farther side of Commencement Gate, I tried not to recognize it, and in that effort—alas!—came to myself. Anastasia, herself now too, moaned into my pursèd ear and stirred her legs.

"Come, Billikins! Come, Bill!" Dear Founder, it was Mother: my sigh was not for passèd bliss, but for bliss past. What was she doing in that fell, Commencèd place? And—Founder—why had I to leave it? Anastasia, unmasked already herself, unpursed me, kissed my brow. Tears in my eyes, I rose up on my knees, looked over Truth's warm shoulder at the cold and flunkèd campus I must return to. Day was about to dawn: how loath I was to leave that bright, consummate, hourless night! Then my heart softened: it *was* Mother, leaning in through the slackened exit-port. In one hand, a peanut-butter sandwich, which she flapped at me as she crooned; in the other, a carefully folded garment. Compassion lightened hopeless duty; the campus wind was chill, but Knowledge warmed me. I knew what must be done, and that I would do it; all that would come to pass was clear, hence my tears—but now they were for studentdom, not for me.

Anastasia's eyes shone still with love; my own I think with neutral Truth, dispassionate compassion. Calm of heart, I kissed her thrice: once on the brow, in gratitude for her having been to me Truth's vessel, and declared her Passèd; once on the navel, sign of the lightless place where I had seen, become myself, issued from to my post-Graduate Assignment; once finally on the Mount of Love where I'd Commenced, and upon whose counterpart I'd one day meet my end. The Cyclological Hypothesis, Spielman's Law: at last I understood it, as Max perhaps could never, and kissed its sign.

Beyond the port now, commotion. Anastasia rubbed her belly, sighed, and said she loved me. I sighed too—but not, as she was pleased to think, in simple reciprocity, though I saw no need to disabuse her of that conviction—and went to Mother. Alas, she had been EATen in the flash, when at the final question I'd caused both buttons to be pressed: her once-cream hair was singed, her babble less lucid even than before. How she'd known to come to the Belly-exit, and how got her head in through it at the crucial moment, I was not to learn for some while. Happily, her mental estate had been already so grievous (a circumstance made much of subsequently by WESCAC's riot-researchers) that the EAT-wave hadn't been fatal: it was as if the scar-tissue, so to speak, of her former wounds, some inflicted by myself, shielded her mind from fresh assaults; already destroyed, she was invulnerable, and WESCAC's worst had but chipped like a grapeshot at the ruins. I ate the sandwich from her hand. The folded garment, it turned out, was my matriculation-fleece, left behind me in the Turnstile months before. How she came by it I cannot imagine, unless she and WESCAC maintained a secret intimacy from terms gone by. Torn as it was, I received it from her joyfully, and donning it in place of Reginald Hector's, discovered in its fold a second treasure, lost with the first: the amulet-of-Freddie!

"Pass you, Mother!" I kissed her hands and joined them to Anastasia's, who had come to the port. "Pass you both, in the name of the Founder, *summa cum laude!*"

Mother fluttered, and in her soft madness mixed a Maxim: "First served, first come."

Now sirens growled and motorcycles crowded up. Computer-scientists, professor-generals, and Light-House aides, alarmed by signs of trouble in the Belly, swarmed about; student-demonstrators chanted, I could not hear what, "Give us the Goat," I supposed; a disorderly motorcade roared around from Great Mall and paused at the confusion. Commending Mother to Anastasia's care, I girdled my ragged fleece with the amulet-of-Freddie and issued forth. Shouts went up: it was indeed "Give us the Goat" that certain bearded chaps and longhaired lasses cried—but not in anger. They were no more than half a dozen, fraction of a remnant of a minority, and clouted even by their sandaled classmates as they cheered; but their signs, I wept with gratitude to see, read AWAY WTH BRAY! Their elders beset me at once with questions, threats, and mock. If I had ruined WESCAC, the military-scientists warned, I could expect a traitor's fate . . .

"I made a short circuit," I admitted calmly, drawing strength from my half a dozen. "But I don't think WESCAC's damaged." I actually hoped not, I added for my classmates' benefit; for although it stood between Failure and Passage, WESCAC therefore partook of both, served both, and was in itself true emblem of neither. I had been wrong, I said, to think it Troll. Black cap and gown of naked Truth, it screened from the general eye what only the few, Truth's lovers and tutees, might look on bare and not be blinded.

The six took frownish notes, shaking their heads; the rest hooted me down. How to speak the unspeakable? I said no more. One forelocked aide winked at a stern professor-general, tapped his temple, and said, "Probably EATen, like the old lady."

I sighed and contented myself with a suggestion they could understand: that they unplug WESCAC's Output from its Input, to restore the normal circuit. Exchanging glances of surmise, they hurried off. I looked about then for my usual lynchers, and was surprised to see none in evidence, until I observed that the approaching motorcade was led by Stoker, and that Max was in his sidecar: the mass of studentdom had gone to Founder's Hill, I realized grimly, to watch the Shafting. It was against capital punishment, among other things, that the sheep-skinned band had assembled to demonstrate, all but the faction protesting protest. Stoker skidded up and snarled at Anastasia; his crew piled up their rowdy vehicles behind him.

"Get in here, woman! I'm taking you home!"

Demurely she refused; she would stay with me, whether I wished her to or not. She apologized for having forsaken her wifely vows and tried to explain that while she sympathized with Stoker and was even beginning in a way to love him, she had a higher obligation as a Grand Tutee; a higher love, not in conflict with her marriage, she declared, but transcending it; a passèd Assignment from the Founder, scarcely dreamed of even by myself, to the fulfillment whereof she was now utterly dedicate . . .

"Hogwash!" Stoker raged. All this while I'd been contemplating Max, who, wizeneder than ever, sat oblivious to the fuss. But at Stoker's oath, unfamiliar to me, I started, for it put a notion into my head, or rather disclosed to me in an instant one that had grown unnoticed there almost to ripeness. In half a second I was studying Max again (who also studied me), ignoring Stoker's jealous oaths and the general furor; but it was as if the Founder had seen to it he would cry Hogwash on that occasion rather than Horse-manure or Sheep-shit (other of his pet ejaculations), just in order to inspire me with a plan.

Max held out a thin hand. "Bye-bye, Georgie."

How to tell him that I grasped now, among much else, the

hub of his Cyclology; that I had completed my Assignment, passed the Finals, and come through to bonafide Grand-Tutorship? There was no need: he saw what I'd seen and had become; from his eyes, hid deep behind their brows like an owl's in snowy brake, understanding glowed. I gripped his hand. "You don't *have* to die this afternoon, Max. I've got a secret: Leonid's key. I can take you right out of this." I studied his face as I spoke. He touched the amulet-of-Freddie. The true scapegoatery, I reminded him, was not to die for studentdom's sake, but to take their failings upon oneself and live. "You misunderstood the amulet-of-Freddie."

"*Ach*," he said, "not only that. You know why I been an all-round genius, George?" He smiled. "Because I never knew my real major. But I found out now what my life's-work is."

I asked what.

"To die," he said, delighted by the joke. "In studentdom's behalf, selfish or not, and even if it don't make sense."

"Are you a love-lover nowadays, Max?" I earnestly inquired. "Or a hate-hater, or what?"

Promptly, as if he'd expected the question, he replied: "Na, I don't hate hate any more. But I love love more than I don't hate hate."

"You're going to the Shaft?"

He nodded.

"Even though you might be playing martyr?"

He shrugged. "So I'm playing. The game's for keeps."

I placed my fingertips on both his temples and declared him a Candidate for Graduation.

"*Ach!*" he said, hoarse with pride. "You know what's ahead for you, Georgie? At the end of the circle?"

I smiled and gently mocked his accent. "A circle has an end? *Auf wiedersehen*, Max."

Yet a moment he clung to my amulet. "One favor you can do me, Georgie: blow your horn when the time comes, I want to hear it on the Shaft."

I promised I would, thrilling again at the way all chance seemed fraught with meaning and instruction. The original shophar, no longer blowable, I'd left in the Belly with Mother's purse and all my collected tokens except the stick and watch, the rest having done their job; but its mate (old Freddie's left) still lay, I trusted, in a certain tool-locker out in the barns, where I meant to go anyway before the Shafting.

"I'll drive you out," Anastasia said firmly, turning from her husband. "We'll use one of Maurice's cycles." I glowed at the miracle in her words, and agreed. Unable to speak for rage, Stoker fired both pistols into the air and raced his motor. His troopers laughed at his discomfiture. I beamed at him.

"You!" he roared at me, and turning then to the demonstrating students he shouted that the Grand Tutor was Harold Bray, who even then was on Founder's Hill preparing to do wonders at the Shafting, while I was a gross and treacherous impostor whom no committee in the College would condemn them for lynching. The half-dozen grinned appreciatively, and some of their classmates looked at me now with a new respect, which infuriated Stoker the more. As he harangued them I touched his temples from behind and declared him a Candidate for Graduation. My six were startled; even Max and Anastasia looked surprised.

"*Wah!*" Stoker bellowed, too paroxysed now to speak intelligently. "Wah! Wo! Wah!" Anastasia being nearest his reach, he clouted her with his helmet, knocking her into my arms. The sight drove him wild; actual tears stood in his eyes; he seemed about to shoot the pair of us.

"Maurice," Anastasia warned. "Don't you dare shoot. I'm pregnant."

"*Wah! Wo!*"

"I'm eight hours pregnant," she affirmed, in utter earnest. "By the Grand Tutor."

The troopers and students guffawed and cheered; Mother murmured, "A-plus." I marveled at My Ladyship's extraordinary conviction, wondering all the same whether the EAT-wave mightn't have got to her after all. As for Stoker, this declaration on the heels of my Certifying his Candidacy made him truly berserk: he wrenched the motorcycle into gear, cursing, babbling, snarling at once, while tears coursed over his grimèd cheeks. Demonstrators sprang in all directions as he tore through; Max clutched the sidecar-wales. The rest of the troop, still laughing, straggled after—all save one, whose vehicle Anastasia commandeered by the simple expedient of threatening to tell Stoker that he'd forced her virtue. The trooper sneered, shrugged, growled something about *Pantoffelheldentum*—but climbed up behind a smirking colleague, leaving his own motorcycle idling. Anastasia donned the helmet her spouse had swatted her with, passed Mother into the keeping of the forelocked aide (who seemed, like most of the student body, on familiar terms with My Lady-ship), and bade me mount behind her, the vehicle being side-carless.

"All's fair that ends well," Mother murmured to the air.

6.

Stoker meanwhile, hurtling cornerwards, careered into a sec-ond motorcade—this one in perfect file, upon white engines—which had wheeled round from the Mall. The con-fusion obliged both parties to halt.

"Oh dear," Anastasia said, and blushed. "It's Mr. and Mrs. Rexford."

An expert driver, she would thread us out of the traffic-jam and away from the scene. But I directed her to take me to the Chancellor, whom Stoker, springing from his vehicle, had found shrill speech enough to mock.

"Wife-beater!" I heard him jeer, among other things. The Chancellor's white-helmeted escorts drew polished pistols, and two or three professor-generals came running from the Belly-port, which I noticed had reclosed. Rexford, though he reddened at the taunt, seemed in control of himself again, and showed little sign of last evening's debauch: his eyes were bright, if slightly bloodshot; his hair was groomed but for the one unruly lock, his face clean-shaved, his light coat pressed and spotless. His wife, though her left cheekbone was something moused, seemed not displeased to contradict with her presence the reports of their separation; she glared at Stoker angrily, as if he were responsible for her husband's truancy as well as for the present embarrassment. The Chan-cellor himself, though he frowned at the disorder, seemed not alarmed, and vetoed the request of his professor-generals to have Stoker shot.

"Put him in irons, then," one of them ordered the Chancel-lor's escorts. "We'll get him for disorderly conduct and con-spiracy to overthrow."

"No no," Rexford said. "I'll let him go on to the Power-house."

Stoker beamed contemptuously. "That's my brother!"

The professor-generals, who, it was rumored, had been talking anyhow of impeaching the Chancellor on charges of conduct unbecoming a Commander-in-Chief, exchanged meaning looks, which Rexford obviously saw and was as amused by as was Stoker, if for different reasons.

"He'll be allowed to pass outside Main Gate between the Powerhouse and Main Detention," he said—addressing the p.-g.'s but observing Stoker. "If he sets foot on Great Mall again, arrest him. If he enters Tower Hall or the Light House, shoot him."

Stoker laughed as if in mocking triumph, but his effect was diminished by the tear-tracks still on his face. He thrust out his hand. "Put her there, Brother!"

At that moment the Chancellor remarked our presence, Anastasia having drawn us near at my insistence. He flashed us a quick smile before returning to deal with Stoker; his wife stared dangerously at My Ladyship, who lowered her head. Calmly, almost respectfully, Rexford pushed away the proffered hand, wiping his own afterwards on a white linen handkerchief. Good-humoredly he scoffed, "Brother indeed! Go back where you belong."

The professor-generals brightened. "You deny he's your brother, Mr. Chancellor? Once and for all?"

Rexford coolly reminded them that professor-generals did not address their Commander-in-Chief as if he were a miscreant recruit. Then he added with a wink: "Do I *look* like the rascal's brother?"

Stoker flung back his head and laughed, again as if meaning to mock; but I thought I detected wet streaks among the dry. Catching sight then of us, he bellowed, "Wah! Wow!" leaped back upon his motor, and throttled off. The professor-generals took counsel with one another; one of them I saw slip a *Light Up With Lucky* button out of his pocket and repin it on his tunic, above the riot-ribbons. Stoker's men having left to try to overtake him, the white-helmeted escorts realigned their positions, discreetly raced their engines, and made ready to proceed. But the Chancellor had turned to me, with a kind of bright hesitation, as if certain of his desire but not of protocol. I dismounted and stepped towards him, whereupon with a grin he sprang from the Chancellory side-car and met me halfway.

"Glad to see you without the rope," he said, and expressed

his regret that my former keeper had chosen not to take advantage of the recent general amnesty, as his freedom would have been its one happy consequence. "The way the varsity situation is," he confided sadly, "and the way I've carried on the last few months, I don't dare stay his execution now; I'd have a mutiny in the Military Science Department. But I love that old man. It's things like this that make you wish you weren't the flunkèd Chancellor."

I listened attentively, studying his bright eyes. His admiration for Max was entirely sincere, and his regret for the Shafting; but that he wished not to be Chancellor, his whole presence denied.

"How is it you're not angry with me for the trouble I've caused, Mr. Rexford?"

"Who says I'm not?" His smile was shrewd. "I think I see what you were trying to teach me. But I guess Commencement isn't for administrators." In painful sobriety after his debauch, he said, he had resolved to abandon his yen for Graduation and merely "do his flunkèd best" for his alma mater, by his own lights, however benighted. To this end he had reopened secret economic dealings with Ira Hector, much as he deplored that necessity, and made covert overtures to new negotiations with the Student-Unionists. The Power Lines would in all likelihood be restored to their "original" locations, and the Boundary Dispute, he hoped, resumed on its former terms without too great loss to West Campus because of his recent vacillation. Having learned, thanks to me, that Classmate X was the defector Chementinski, he supposed he would put that knowledge to use less passèd than I would approve of: blackmailing the Nikolayans back to the conference-table. "It's all very well for prophprofs to be above these things," he said amiably; "but the man with the power can't always keep his hands as clean as he'd like to." Folding his handkerchief neatly as he spoke, he caught sight of the Stoker-smudge on it and laughed.

"What about the Power-Line guards?" I asked carefully. Stepping back into the sidecar, he declared he'd given orders that all special head- and neck-gear be made optional for them, if not discarded altogether.

"If they look down, they fall," he said cheerfully; "if they *don't* look down, they fall too. They'll have to learn to see without looking!"

My heart rejoiced. But I administered a final test by greeting his wife (who regarded me chillily) and expressing my regret for the accidental injury to her cheek. Her face flashed anger, as for an instant did the Chancellor's.

"For a man to strike his wife is a flunkèd thing," he declared firmly. "We don't live in the Dark Semesters any more. And we're not Furnace-Room mechanics."

"I should say *not*," Mrs. Rexford snapped. "And I'll tell you something else, Mr. Giles, while we're on the subject: my husband might be the Chancellor, but——"

She stopped with a look of fright, for Rexford had suddenly raised his hand. In fact he only signaled the advance-guard to proceed, but even Anastasia gasped, and Mrs. Rexford never finished her sentence.

Her husband grinned. "See you on Founder's Hill this afternoon, Mr. Giles."

I reached to touch his temples, declaring him a Candidate for Passage and Commencement. But he shook his head and cordially declined. For one thing, he said, the gesture might be looked upon by his political enemies as some sort of bribe, or at least an endorsement of my authenticity, a matter too controversial for him to take a public stand on unless he had to; for another—his grin was melancholy—he reminded me that as Chancellor his first allegiance was to the College, whose best interests he would pursue at whatever cost— enlightenedly, he hoped, and in the final service of all the Free Campus, even all studentdom. But if circumstances forced the choice ("Which Founder forfend!") between repudiating me and breaching the vows of his office, he would consent even to my Shafting, as he had to Max's. That Remusian vice-administrator of the Moishian quads in terms gone by, who had winked at Enos Enoch's lynching, was to Rexford's mind a tragic figure, unjustly maligned by simplistic Enochists unaware of the responsibilities of power.

"You'd Shaft me if you had to, sir? For teaching administrative subversion, say, if *I* had to?"

He gave me a level look. "It might flunk me forever. But I'd do it."

The professor-generals clapped one another on the back; the military escort cheered. For just a moment Rexford surveyed them with an expression of distaste, even loathing; then he flashed the famous grin, mischievously winked at Anastasia while embracing Mrs. Rexford, and sped away.

"Is he a Candidate or not?" Anastasia asked me.

"You're a Graduate," I replied; "what do *you* think?"

Flushing with pride, she considered the matter at length as she steered us out onto the highway, through the dormitory-quads and faculty-residence areas, and along the Founder's Hill road towards George's Gorge. In that vicinity, having grappled with the pluses and minuses of the case for more than an hour, she said at last, "I think he *is*, George. Not a Graduate, but a real Candidate for Graduation."

"I see. Why is that, Anastasia?"

"I'm not good at *words*," she reminded me seriously. "But embarrassed as I was to see him, after last evening (especially with Mrs. Rexford, who must *hate* me, much as I like her), it seemed to me there was something important about that *hitting-her* business. You know?" After a pause she tried again: for the Chancellor of a college to disavow and deplore such things as espionage, cheating, and secret negotiations, she seemed in her fashion to be saying, while yet not disallowing them, was in itself doubtless mere hypocrisy, like condemning wife-beating on principle while striking one's wife; yet she could imagine an elevated version of this *modus operandi*, so sincere and second-natural that what had been flunkèd Contradiction became passèd Paradox. And she believed that should Lucius Rexford attain that state—which was betrayed and falsified even by talking about it, as she was doing—he would be Commenced.

"Is that right, George?" she asked at the end. Inasmuch as I was obliged in any case to clasp her from behind in order to keep my seat, I smiled, patted her belly, and called her my first Graduate Assistant.

"You're *teasing* me!" she said, a little crossly, but abandoned the throttle to press my hand against her a moment. "If what I said is wrong, tell me so!"

But we had come to a fork in our road, some kilometers beyond George's Gorge; I caught my breath, recognizing suddenly where we were and what lay just past the next bend. A moment later my heart leaped up, and over My Ladyship's shoulder I pointed out the gambrels and cupolas of home.

The day being fine, though chill, the herd was outside in the pounds, officially supervised by one of Reginald Hector's aides. But that fellow (chosen by lot, I learned later, when the ex-Chancellor forsook the independent life) was either irresponsible or incompetent, and nowhere in sight. Once I'd got over my surprise at how much smaller everything seemed than in my kidship, I groaned at the evidences of neglect: the barn and fences needed whitewash; the pounds were filthy, the feed-cribs bare. Worst of all, the herd itself was depleted by half—owing, I could only hope, to ignorant neglect and not some keeper's bloody appetite—and the survivors were ragged and pinched as inmates of a concentration-campus. In vain I looked about for Hedda O.T.S.T., for Becky's Pride Sue or Tommy's Thomas: I recognized no one. Anastasia hung back, not to intrude upon my grief. With smarting eyes I rushed into the pound; the does scattered like wild things. Could that be B.'s P. Sue, a pinched and gimpy crone? As I wept at the likelihood, and with chagrin that they knew me no more than I them, a strong bleat came from the barn, a bucky challenge; and after it—head couched and hooves a-pound—Redfearn's Tom, charging from the dead! Stick in hand I stood, as years before, transfixed this time as much by wonder as by fright. I had retraced my way; had I also, in some wise, rewound the very tape of time? The buck was young and full of juice, despite his leanness—younger than R.'s Tom had been on the day I slew him, or Tommy's Thomas when I'd set out for Great Mall. In the instant before he was upon me I guessed he was no ghost, but Tommy's Tommy's Tom: that Triple-T who saw the light not long before my departure! Joyfully I sprang aside; he cracked the fence-rail—splendid son of splendid sires!—and neither dazed by the collision nor tempted to escape through the broken fence, spun about and recharged me at once. Anastasia squealed. Out of practice as I was, slackened by my terms in Main Detention and the life of human studentdom, I durstn't try to pin him; I parried, passed, and fended as I could, calling him all the while by name and giving him to smell, between charges, my wrapper and the amulet-of-Freddie. These intrigued him, and when at last I stripped myself (retying the a.-of-F. about my loins) and flung the wrapper over his head, its scent stirred in him some deep ancestral memory. His mood changed altogether; he permitted me to scratch his head, licked Anastasia's hand when I introduced them, and appreciatively snuffled her escutcheon.

"He's a *darling*, George!" she cried. "I *love* animals!"

I smiled. But delightsome as was reunion with Triple-T and the does—who wandered up now in twos and threes, smelt of the hide, and bleated to me as to a keeper—I had come to do works of preparation. Hedda alone I lingered awhile in communion with: unbelievably agèd and infirm, her beauty flown, she tottered from the barn last of all, sniffed my amulet suspiciously, then nearly wept for joy upon realizing who I was. For some minutes we nuzzled wordlessly—shocking how sere and shrunk her once-peerless udder, whose freckled daint had fired my youthful dreams! When at length I introduced her to My Ladyship, the two appraised each other without expression; then Anastasia took my arm and leaned against me, whereupon dear Hedda, with a feeble snort, gimped back into the barn, nor stirred from her rank old straw again.

I set about my work. First I fed the herd, forking hay down from the loft and refilling the stagnant water-troughs. Then, with Anastasia's help, I drenched them all with copper sulphate to de-worm them, milked the few who needed that relief (the number of kids was heartbreakingly small), and trimmed everyone's hooves. Next—what Stoker's oath had suggested—I filled the dipping-tank with creosote solution, bathed the entire herd, and then (though neither I nor my wrapper was literally verminous, as were the others) cleansed myself in that potent bath, immersing even my head, until no trace of my term on Great Mall remained. Anastasia scrubbed my back; she would join me in the dip, cold as was the air and free of lice her fleecy parts; I knew why, was well pleased, but told her it was unnecessary. We did however wash her body with saddle-soap, and groomed each other when we had brushed and combed the herd. It being then noon, and she and I both roused by the brisk shampoo of our private parts, we repaired to a bed of fresh-forked straw. Warmed by the huddling does (all save Hedda), for two hours we drowsed and coupled—but knew better than to strive for last night's wonders. She remained she, I I; in a campus of thats and thises we sweetly napped and played, and were content: not every day can be Commencement Day. Lunch, like breakfast, we forwent.

At two (I could read a goat-crook's shadow in any season quite as accurately as Ira Hector a man's, and set Lady Creamhair's watch with perfect confidence) I rose refreshed from My full-friggèd Ladyship, re-cleansed my organ in the dip, and donned my wrap. Fetching the spare horn from the gear-chest I nipped its point to mouthpiece-size with a dock-ing-tool and fashioned for it a stout sling of binder-twine. Then to all the herd, save two, I bade farewell, pledging to return one day and to send a better keeper to them in the meanwhile. Hedda and Tommy's Tommy's Tom were the exceptions: the latter because I meant to take him with me; the former because when I bent into her lousy pen I found her passed away. I closed her glassèd eyes, touched my lips to those withered teats once prouder and more speckled than my dam's, and left her, trusting that even Grandfather's aide would not deny her a respectful grave. Triple-T we tethered behind the motorcycle; a handsome buckling he was now, dipped and groomed, with a proper lunch in him; he pranced and snorted and butted without fear the very fender! Anastasia (who not only declined the syringe of vinegar I offered to douche her with, but plugged her privity with sterile gauze to retain the insemination) put on her helmet and released the clutch, and we headed west.

Our progress, however, with Tommy's Tommy's Tom in tow, proved poor. I was obliged at length to hogtie him— revolting term—with the tether and truss him behind me athwart the fender, much as I sympathized with his fright. By this arrangement, though his bleats would have moved to pity Ira Hector himself, we tripled our speed; once past the Gorge and crossroads, moreover, Anastasia displayed a skill at short-cuts equal to her husband's, and a truly Stokerish capacity for the speed that had so alarmed her as his passenger. The sun hung still a fair half-hour from the horizon when we hove in sight of Founder's Hill.

7.

Set free but for a leash wrapped thrice about my wrist, Triple-T opened us a walkway through the crowd. On every slope they'd gathered through the day—students, professors, administrators, trustees, groundskeepers, clerks, all wearing holiday best. Despite the gravity of the occasion (Shafting had only recently been made public again—by Rexfordian liberals, interestingly enough, who hoped thereby to shock the student body into abolishing capital punishment) there was excitement in the air, even a certain festivity. As the execution happened to coincide with other ceremonies and observances traditionally scheduled for that day of week and time of year, Founder's Hill had been a busy place since morning. A kind of intermission seemed now in progress: martial music could be heard from loudspeakers, and strolling vendors offered food, drink, pennants, and large white flowers to the crowd. Newspaper extras were being hawked around; the one I fed to T.T.T. bore headlines about Bray's promised wonders, the full restoration of WESCAC's strength under Dr. Eierkopf's supervision from the Powerhouse Control Room, the apparent disappearance of Classmate X, the expected resumption of the Boundary Dispute on last term's terms. On all the front pages were photographs of Lucius Rexford embracing his wife in the Chancellory sidecar and winking, so it seemed, at the camera, as if to indicate that all was in hand at home as well as abroad. Indeed, despite the seriousness of the varsity situation and the great disruptions of normalcy that still prevailed in New Tammany, the captions were optimistic: LUCKY DAYS ARE HERE AGAIN; "LIGHT LIGHTS," LAUGHS LUCKY. Roving photojournalism-majors prowled with cameras and Telerama-packs, interviewing the student-in-the-path and campus celebrities on such topics as capital punishment, Grand-Tutorial impostors, and what they called the "new look" of the Rexford administration. Me too they would approach for a statement, and Anastasia, when we left the motorcycle and started up: they trotted about, asking what I thought of Bray's mid-day "miracles" on the Hilltop, and whether I intended to "top his performance" or "have it out" with him. But thanks to the plunging horns and knife-edged hooves of Tommy's Tommy's Tom, they kept their distance, as did hecklers, applauders, and the hosts of the indifferent, through whose ranks we made our way.

Towards the summit, where the rocky hill flattened into a kind of park around the Shaft, the crowd was thinner; Stoker's guards had erected a great circle of barriers, several hundred meters across, past which none but high officials and their guests were permitted. Stoker himself stalked the far perimeter all ascowl, threatening would-be gate-crashers with his billy and passing upon credentials: some he admitted whose ID-cards showed them to be nobodies; others he refused whose eminence entitled them to pass. At the consequent uproar he laughed—a harsh echo of his old hilarity. Anastasia was admitted at once by the guard at our barrier, who recognized her with a lick of his lips, and at her coax he reholstered his pistol instead of shooting Triple-T. Espying us from several meters off, Stoker shouted an obscenity and ordered the guard to refuse me admittance. People in the dignitaries' stands near the Shaft turned to look.

"Go to him now," I bade My Ladyship. I might have added certain further directions, thanking her too for having fetched me where I had to go; but she agreed this time so readily, and with so knowing a smile, I said no more. Triple-T, once out of the crowd, browsed placidly; I handed his leash to Anastasia and stepped past the guard.

"Achtung, Stinkkäfer!" he cried. He referred of course to the goat-dip on me, mighty indeed the perfume whereof; but his epithet was so exactly inapposite, I laughed aloud. He swung his billy; I parried with my stick and hoofed him a clean one in the balls. Before he could let go of himself to shoot, a pair of white helmets came over from the dignitaries' stand. One intervened in the names of the Chancellor and Harold Bray, both of whom he declared had authorized my admission—murmurs went through the near bystanders at this news, and the fallen guard put by his pistol with a curse.

"You call that Grand-Tutoring?" Stoker shouted. He had started for My Ladyship, but paused when T.'s T.'s Tom bucked at him. Anastasia too seemed shocked by my deed. "Violence!" Stoker appealed to the crowd. "No respect for law and order!" People stirred; even White-helmet, though he'd come between us in my behalf, bent to assist his sooted comrade and grumbled that the man had after all been simply doing his duty.

"Tomorrow the Revised New Syllabus," I said to My Ladyship. "Today the stick."

The other white helmet now escorted to me Hedwig Sear—at her request, it turned out, who had observed from the viewing-stand my entry. She was gowned in black, her face veiled; Anastasia hurried to her, and they wept together as Three-T grazed. The shock of Croaker's assault, it seemed, had cleared Hedwig's mind; she spoke lucidly and quietly, impeded only by her grief at the critical condition of her husband. Dr. Sear lay in the Infirmary, she told me, at the point of death. Her one wish was to join him, but she'd come to Founder's Hill at his request in order to honor Max and give me a message. The circumstances of her attack she recounted with extraordinary calm—despite the fact that Croaker, with Dr. Eierkopf aboard, was present in the visitors' stand. She could even smile, mournfully enough, at the irony of her rape: that when she'd tried to provoke him to it once before, in the Honeymoon Lodge Motel, he had rejected her in favor of an automatic soft-drink dispenser. There had followed her return to childishness, of which I'd heard, and when Croaker's path and hers had crossed again, following their separate releases in yesterday's amnesty, she had fled him with the fright of a five-year-old girl.

"Which is just what turned him on," she said ruefully. "He couldn't help it; he was just being Croaker. But poor Kennard—" She chuckled and wept. "In the old days he'd have taken pictures, and I'd have been showing Croaker naughty tricks. But Kennard's changed, too, since last spring—the different things you've told him, and his cancer and all . . ." She blew her nose. Perhaps it was no more than a metastasis of the cancer to his brain, she said; in any case, he'd been escorting her from the Asylum to Great Mall (so he told her afterwards) to get a taxi to the Honeymoon Lodge Motel, not this time to mount her in Position One as the consummate perversion, but to come to her in simple love, in hope (her voice grew awed even now at the notion; she doubted I would believe her) that he could leave a child behind him upon his death! The rest I had witnessed from my noose: how, seeing her attacked, Dr. Sear had *leaped*—spontaneously, instantly, one could only say heroically—to her defense, and been felled by Croaker with a backhand smite. The blow had struck his bandaged tumor; though entirely blind now and basically, mercifully unconscious, he still had moments of lucidity, during which, in the night just past, she'd told him of her own astonishing recovery, begged his forgiveness for her part in their sorry past, professed her devotion to him, and announced her intention to undergo surgical curettage, against the unlikely chance that Croaker had accomplished what her husband had aspired to.

"But Kennard said I mustn't," she declared. "He says we have to be *grateful* to Croaker for bringing us together after all these years, and that we ought to *hope* I'm pregnant! No matter what the baby looks like, he says, it's our child— Kennard's and mine—because of what Kennard did without stopping to think."

"Oh, *Heddy!*" Anastasia wept with delight and embraced her again, clearly as convinced of the fact and nature of Mrs. Sear's pregnancy as of her own—though neither was two dozen hours past! Time was getting on; I asked Mrs. Sear directly whether her husband was pleased to be dying.

She shook her head at once. "That's what I'm supposed to tell you, George. He says he doesn't regret for a minute doing what he did. He says that what he'd never seen till Croaker hit him, even though he thought he'd seen everything, was that a certain kind of *spiritedness* was absolutely good, no matter what a person's other Answers are. It doesn't have anything to do with education, he said to tell you, and it's the most valuable thing in the University. Something about Dean Taliped's energy, even at the end . . . He wants to know whether he's right."

"Oh, George!" Anastasia cried. "Pass him now, so Heddy can tell him!"

Stoker huffed. "He's out of his head."

I smiled at tearful Hedwig. "Please tell Dr. Sear that in my opinion his attitude is certainly sentimental, and that his cancer may very well have damaged his mind as well as his eyesight. But tell him also that he's a Candidate for Graduation, and congratulate him for me on being a father."

"Only a Candidate?" Stoker jeered.

I nodded. "Like yourself."

This retort so infuriated Stoker that Anastasia, still holding Triple-T, was obliged to step between us and command him to behave himself. Taking Mrs. Sear's arm I slipped away to the viewing stand, and added en route: "Of course, some Candidates are much closer to Commencement than others. Give your husband my love, Mrs. Sear."

"Goat-Boy!" It was Dr. Eierkopf calling, from the dignitaries' bleachers. There also I saw Chancellor and Mrs. Rexford, holding hands; the brothers Hector, amply coated; and Leonid Alexandrov, fidgeting as usual and looking restlessly to westward (though he could not see), where the sun fast sank upon the distant reaches of East Campus. Peter Greene was on the right, similarly bandaged, and flanked, to my surprise, by Stoker's secretary Georgina and a pretty young white girl whom I concluded must be Greene's daughter. But she was the very image of Chickie, that co-ed girl I'd watched disporting years ago with the Beist-in-the-buckwheat! The same uncombèd locks; the taunty eyes! And if anything younger, though I her witness had aged seven years in body, thrice that in spirit, since the night I'd heard her beg to Be. She could not be the original Chickie, then; wry speculations came to mind once again about Miss Sally Ann—but I put them aside as immaterial to Greene's Candidacy and Assignment; also to attend Dr. Eierkopf, who, despite the bandage around his forehead and his general want of robustness, was fairly bouncing on Croaker's shoulders. Round about them, come to retrieve their errant colleague, sat the delegation of visiting scholars from Frumentius, in the colorful garb of their alma maters. Outfitted with cameras and clipboards, they appeared to be making a careful record of the proceedings.

"I'm *Übertrittig,* Goat-Boy!" he cried. "My eyes have been opened!" While Croaker croaked croaks of greeting and the Frumentian scholars sniffed my air, felt of my fleece, and made pictogrammatic notes, he reported shrilly that he was a skeptic no more in the matter of Grand-Tutoriality. For he had seen with his own two eyes (abetted, to be sure, by corrective lenses) wonders unexplainable by natural law and student reason: Harold Bray, not two hours past, had appeared on the Hill as it seemed from nowhere; he had changed color and physiognomy before their eyes, leaped over the reflecting pool—a distance of some dozen meters—in a single bound, walked up the vertical face of the Founder's Shaft as if it were a sidewalk, to rig ropes and pulleys for the main event, and then vanished, declaring from nowhere over the loudspeakers that he'd reappear at sunset.

"Wunderbar, Goat-Boy!" he exclaimed. "No tricks! No mirrors! Excuse you: that Bray, He's a real Grand Tutor!"

I smiled. "You believe you've seen a miracle, Dr. Eierkopf?"

"Ja wohl, boy! I believe *because* I saw one! Five-and-twenty, yet!"

From behind me, where I'd not observed his approach, Stoker scoffed. "You haven't seen anything, Doc. If it's miracles you want, George here can do better." He clapped my shoulder in feigned affection.

"Dean o' Flunks!" cried Eierkopf. *"Heraus!"*

"He's going to rescue Spielman off the tip of the Shaft at the crucial moment," Stoker announced to the stand at large, pointing at me with his index finger. "That'll prove he's the real Grand Tutor! He might even save the whole University in one whiz-bang, and Pass us all! Why not?"

With the exception of some of my Tutees, whose admission Bray seemed to have arranged for reasons of his own, the privileged spectators in the stands were people of position and influence, many of whom had sniffed disapprovingly at my aroma when I came near; they made it plain now that Stoker's rowdiness offended them on the sober occasion at hand, and called upon the Chancellor to have us both removed from the Hill. Rexford looked with some concern in our direction; his wife whispered something in his ear that made him frown. He let go her hand and consulted a forelock behind him, who glanced at us and nodded.

"Come on!" Stoker taunted me at the top of his voice. "Do some tricks! Show us you're the real G.T.!"

"Down in front!" someone called. At the same moment drums rolled, and I saw that the sun's lower limb had touched the horizon. A marching-band struck up a grave processional; way was made at the barricades for a vee of three black motorcycles, behind the foremost of which walked Max. Bent under the weight of a block-and-tackle rig, he moved with difficulty, but his face was alight. A gasp came from the stands: not at that pitiful spectacle, but at a sudden apparition at the base of the Shaft. One would have sworn its marble lines had been unbroken except for ominous ropes and pulleys; there were certainly no doors or other apertures in the masonry, or hiding-places on the little ledge around its base, and the whole monument was ringed by a moat or reflecting-pool said to be a meter deep and twelve wide—yet in an instant on that empty ledge stood Harold Bray, black-cloaked, his arms held out to the approaching victim!

"How does he do it, Goat-Boy? Show us the trick!" Stoker's tone was half jeer and half dare, but perhaps there was something else in his eyes. I turned my back on him and the others who now looked to see my reaction; bidding Anastasia to remain where she was with T.'s T.'s T., I made my way around to the opposite viewing-stand. Though not inconspicuously attired and scented, I was able to move without attracting great notice, owing to the crowd's preoccupation. As the guards led Max forth, Bray's cloak changed color with each rich chord the trumpets sounded: black to brown, brown to iridescent green, green to a white so like the Shaft's that the cloak seemed transparent, if not vanished—even the mortar-lines were replicated on it! Next he stepped from the ledge onto the surface of the pool and with a kind of sliding gait, as if the water were frozen, walked across to meet my keeper. The guards, no less amazed than the spectators, dismounted and examined the pool, even poked it with their billies to prove that there was no walkway just under the surface.

"Ja ja!" I heard Dr. Eierkopf cry, and his applause was taken up by the others. Even the Chancellor shook his head, much impressed; the professor-generals behind him elbowed each other excitedly; Telerama-men chattered wide-eyed into their microphones. Max looked about under his burden, perhaps for me, as the guards placed a portable walkway over the moat. Catching his eye or nose, I waved a discreet bye-bye and held up the shophar to reassure him that his last request would be honored. He nodded, but some dismay at Bray's performance still wrinkled his brow. Bray saw me then, if he had not before, and as if to taunt me with his prowess, uttered a sound not unlike choiring brass. The musicians put by their instruments, dumbfounded; everyone murmured astonishment except Anastasia and myself, who exchanged calm glances across the space between us, and Tommy's Tommy's Tom, browsing contentedly among discarded candy wrappers and cola cups.

Max was now strapped by his escorts into a kind of canvas diaper or bosun's-breeches on the ledge, his tackle-ropes rigged to those that ran up the face of the Shaft to its flaming tip. His seat-belt was secured, the gangplank removed; the crowd grew still. Again drums rolled; the Chancellor gave a reluctant signal; and as two of the guards hauled upon the halyards to the stroke-call of the third, Max slowly rose. Even the professor-generals most pleased to see him go, like my grandfather, were hushed by the sight.

Bray then glided, as it seemed, to the central space between the stands, turned to face the Shaft, and raised his arms. Though the light was failing fast (shadow, in fact, went up the column as the sun went down, and determined the rate of Max's ascent), he began another series of metamorphoses more remarkable even than the earlier: not only did the color and apparent cut of his vestments change at each halyard-heave, but his face and form as well. *Stroke:* he was Max himself! *Stroke:* pretty Anastasia! *Stroke:* the late G.

Herrold! At every transformation the crowd roared *Hurrah* (sometimes *Olé*), the band saluted, and Max went up another measure on the Shaft, blowing kisses and pulling his beard. Now Bray was The Living Sakhyan, now great black Croaker, and then in rhythmic series Maurice Stoker, Kennard Sear, Eblis Eierkopf, Lucius Rexford, the brothers Hector (both at once), hat-faced Classmate X, Leonid Alexandrov, and my passèd lady mother! Last of all he assumed the semblance of myself, complete with stick and shophar—and in this guise, as Max neared the blazing tip, proclaimed: "Dear Founder, pass our classmate Maximilian Spielman, who has finished his course in faith and would rest from his labors." Though no public-address system was in sight, his voice carried as if amplified. "A-plus," he said at the end, resoundingly, and from somewhere Mother's voice gave back the echo: *"A-plus!"*

The moment was at hand. As Max went waving to the peak I put the buckhorn to my lips and blew with all my strength. *Teruah! Teruah! Teruah!* My keeper, whose dear wise like this campus will not soon see again, combusted in a glorious flare—by the light whereof I saw Tommy's Tommy's Tom race unleashèd toward my semblance. His hand was high; joyously he bleat! Bray buzzed and flapped; literally he shed my guise (stick and horn attached), and holding his nose, flung the limp shed at Triple-T. Underneath he was gleaming black, his face hid under a cowl; seeing it was not I, T.'s T.'s Tom lowered horns and charged. Dreadful the hum, horrid the foetor Bray now gave out! He bounded mewards from Tom's creosoted horns; I drove him back with horn and odor of my own. Thus caught between us, he spread his cloak for half a second; more loud his hum than Stokerish engine! Then from under his tunic-front a thing shot forth, shortswordlike, as Tommy struck. The buck shrieked, fell kicking, lay still. I snatched the black vestment, slick as oilskin; Bray flapped it off, face and all (underneath was a blacker), and fled—nay, vanished—in the crowding dark. A glance told me there was no helping T.'s T.'s T.—his legs stuck out stiff, his eyes were filmed over, his belly swelled. I had at shadow, ground, and moat with my stick, lest Bray be camouflaged against them; waded through the icy pool (at great cost of goat-dip) and attacked the Shaft itself. The crowd had watched, dumbstruck; now as I thwacked the pillar they seemed to wake. A voice very like Peter Greene's cried, "What's that I hear a-flapping and a-flying, Leo?"

"Nothingcy!" a Nikolayan voice replied. "I don't hear!"

"Look once by the Shaft-tip!" squealed Dr. Eierkopf. *"Der Grosslehrer ist jetzt ein Fliegender!"*

I looked up. In the pall above my flaming keeper something large and obscure appeared to rise, rolling and spreading like the smoke itself. The crowd's dismay turned into panic: people leaped from the stands, swarmed over the barricades in both directions, fell upon their knees and girlfriends, clouted neighbors, clutched loved ones. Bravely the band played New Tammany's anthem until overrun. Guards scrambled into the moat, either to arrest or to protect me; at their head grinned Stoker, cursing as he came. His wife I discerned high up in the bleachers, one hand upon her belly, watching with anxious love above the crowd; Mother knitted placidly beside her. And upon us all, gentle ashes—whose if not my gentler keeper's?—commenced to fall. Another term, surely, they would be mine; not now, for though my youthful work was done, that of my manhood remained to do. What it was I clearly saw, and what it would come to. Nonetheless I smiled, leaned on my stick, and, no troubleder than Mom, gimped in to meet the guards halfway.

POSTTAPE

Today, at thirty-three and a third, I record indirectly into WESCAC's storage the last of these tapes—at my protégée's behest, as always, but not, this final time, in her presence. She awaits my coming daily in the Visitation Room, with a pair of youngsters who had far rather be out romping in the lovely spring than languishing in this cagèd, sunless place. Let her wait.

My self-wound watch runs fast; anyhow I have small time left, and so futile is this work now approaching its end, I am sore tempted to abandon it unfinished and go gambol in the April air myself. *She* thinks it done already, whose notion it was I render my tale during this my recentest and last detention. Her great nagging faith has alone sustained me, for better or worse, through the monstrous work—this "Revised New Syllabus," as she calls it, which she is convinced will supersede the Founder's Scroll. I smile at that idea, as at the olive lad she calls our son, and in whom I see as much of Stoker, of Croaker, indeed of Bray, as of myself. Supposing even that the Scroll *were* replaced by these endless tapes, one day to feed Him who will come after me, as I fed once on that old sheepskin—what then? Cycles on cycles, ever unwinding: like my watch; like the reels of this machine she got past her spouse; like the University itself.

Unwind, rewind, replay.

No matter. Futility and Purpose, like Pass and Fail, themselves have meaning only for her sort, and her son's (in whose dark eyes I see already his mother's single-mindedness). For me, Sense and Nonsense lost their meaning on a night twelve years four months ago, in WESCAC's Belly—as did every such distinction, including that between Same and Different. Thus it is, and in no other wise, I have lingered on the campus these dozen years, in the humblest capacity, advising one at a time undergraduates to whom my words convey nothing. Thus it is I accept without much grumble their failings and my own: the abuse of my enemies, the lapses of my friends; the growing pains in both my legs, my goatly seizures, my errors of fact and judgment, my failures of resolve—all these and more, the ineluctable shortcomings of mortal studenthood. And thus it is—empowered as it were by impotence, driven by want of motive—I record this posttape (which she will not know of), in order to speak of the interval between my "triumph" of twelve years back, just recounted, and my present pass. Perhaps too to speak to myself of what is to come: the end Max saw from the beginning; the "Commencement" I saw at the end.

To begin with, my original "Tutees": of the two I Graduated out of hand—my mother "Lady Creamhair" and "My Ladyship" Anastasia—the latter I've spoken of already and will surely return to (as I will return to the Visitation Room where she waits, go out released with her once again into New Tammany, and abide with her until that last release of all, whose imminence she little dreams); the former passed away not long after her grandson's birth, the EAT-rays having got to her more sorely than at first appeared. She died smiling, I understand, with Reginald Hector, Anastasia, and the infant named Giles Stoker at her bedside—but then, she had lived smiling, too, since the day I shocked her out of sense, and, as the effect of her EATing spread, had lapsed unhappily into a more or less constant chuckle. Anastasia's conviction, therefore, that Mother died happy in the knowledge of her "gift to studentdom," I take in the spirit of her other convictions: that "Gilesianism" (her term, for her invention) will cure the student body's ills, and that "our" son will establish "the New Curriculum" on every campus in the University. I long since ceased attempting to explain—never mind what. It is terms now since I raised an eyebrow or even sighed. Not impossibly dear Anastasia was a little EATen herself, that gorgeous night; not impossibly I was too, either in infancy or in one or more of my descents into the Belly. How would I know? Not impossibly (as Dr. Sear once speculated) all studentdom was EATen terms ago—by WESCAC, EASCAC, or both—and its fear of Campus Riot III is but one ironic detail of a mad collective dream.

No matter.

Sear himself is dead too, of course; was so, it turned out, even as I affirmed his Candidacy that afternoon on Founder's Hill. It was his cancer killed him—but alas, not directly. Persuaded, in his clear delirium, that he had achieved not only fatherhood but total illumination, his old sympathy with Gynander became obsessive: blind already, he saw his generative organs as all that stood, as it were, between him and prophprofhood, removed them in the nurse's absence with a shard of tumbler, and expired of massive hemorrhage. No doubt he would have smiled like Mother at the end, had he not lacked at the time a great part of his face. Hedwig, too old and weakened by their past to bear children safely, did indeed prove to be impregnated (as did Anastasia: a circumstance I keep in mind when tempted to protest her extremer convictions); but the birth of her child—a fine strapping girl the hue of dark honey—ruined both her health and her brief lucidity. She and Mother died a week apart in the room they shared for their last term on campus, in the NTC Asylum. Stoker even has it they were sweethearts at the end—but that's Stoker. One never knows. When he says with a grin, "What the flunk, George, love's where you find it," I neither agree nor disagree.

Of the others whose Candidacies I affirmed—or would affirm, or was held to have affirmed—three more are dead now also, not counting Max: Reginald Hector, Classmate X, and Leonid Alexandrov. Of Grandfather the fact was that I neither affirmed nor denied him: were it not for him I'd never have been born; on the other hand, had his will been done I'd have perished at birth—I regard both circumstances with mixed feelings, but in any mood they cancel each other. Reciprocally, as it were, he neither affirmed nor denied my Grand-Tutorship, for though his real preference, like most other people's, was for Bray (insofar as he concerned himself at all with such questions), he never openly supported those who called for my expulsion on the grounds of Grand-Tutorcide. Family loyalty it was, I suppose, or the kind of affection sometimes displayed by old professor-generals for those they once tried and failed to kill. He passed away not long ago, after an extended invalidity, with his belief unshaken that he was beholden to none. His faithful receptionist—who for many years had written all his speeches, managed his affairs, and warmed his old flesh with her young—arranged a splendid funeral at the joint expense of the Military Science Department and the Philophilosophical Fund.

Leonid Alexandrov redefected immediately after Max's Shafting, making his way by some unknown means, blind though he was, through the steel-mesh partition in the Control Room. I never saw him again, nor heard anything of his activities for some years after, during which the Boundary Dispute alternated (as indeed it does yet) between crisis and stalemate—each crisis a little more critical, each stalemate a quantum uneasier, than the last. Then one day two Nikolayans, one old and one not, were caught wrestling at midnight in the Control Room. How they'd managed to open the locked and electrified partition, no one knew. Their tussle gave the alarm; guards from both sides ran to the scene in time to see the younger man push the older through to the

NTC side, intentionally or not, and electrocute himself in the process. The older man—who turned out to be Classmate X—might then have made good his own defection, if that was his object, had he not attempted to reclose the door behind him. But the Nikolayan guards were at his heels, and Chementinski (as he called himself again thereafter), uncertain whether they meant to shoot him or defect themselves, kicked the mesh-gate shut, and was immediately shocked to the point of death. Summoning me to the Infirmary before he expired (I was working, between detentions, as a free-lance freshman advisor), he told me among other things that his stepson had helped dozens of undergraduates on each side of the Power Line to transfer illicitly to the other, risking his life in the two-way enterprise again and again without remuneration; in the end he had given his life to save that of a secret agent assigned to kill him, but who in fact so admired him that he'd resolved to kill himself instead. The agent, you will have guessed, was Classmate X, to whom Leonid had repeated a hundred times in vain my advice, as he understood it: that the special vanity of suicide was, in X's case, permissible, even passèd, affirming as it did the self that destroyed itself—which self, being anyhow inescapable, had to be got beyond instead of suppressed. The nature of the conflict in the gate I never did get clear—who was trying to do what to whom, and why—but Chementinski seemed convinced of two things: that his stepson perished in his behalf, wrongheadedly or not; and that he himself, in closing the gate on guards from both sides who possibly meant to defect, had committed suicide twice over (because the act was impulsively selfish, and hence fatal to the selfless character called X; and because Chementinski, whose self was thus reaffirmed, was dying of the consequent shock—"by his own hand," he vowed, not altogether consistently or accurately). His final word to me, as he expired, he declared had been Leonid's to him, upon their recognizing each other and themselves on that fatal threshold: "Gratituditynesshoodshipcy!"

When I repeated this story to Stoker during my next term in Main Detention, he pointed out with a sneer that the dying man had been as delirious as Kennard Sear, and consequently that his account, whatever it signified, was probably mistaken. The young man in the mesh had been burned beyond recognition; his older classmate, also badly seared, was bandaged as a mummy. One had only his feverish word for both their identities, and Nikolayan administrators, for example, maintained that Classmate Alexandrov had never redefected in the first place, and that Classmate X had been executed many terms earlier for membership in a forbidden ID-cult.

"That's all quite possible," I agreed—but no longer with a

smile, as I would have in terms gone by. Anastasia at once took up the cudgels in behalf of Chementinski's and Leonid's Graduation, and so browbeat us both upon that head (her tongue grew wondrous sharper every year), I was as glad to leave the Visitation Room as was Stoker to fetch me to a cell.

My confinement on that occasion had to do with the tenth anniversary of Bray's rout (others called it his Elevation), just as my present one, ending today, had to do with the twelfth of his initial appearance in the Amphitheater. Both times I had been sought out, in my obscurity, by journalism-majors with long memories, who asked whether I still maintained that I was the Grand Tutor; that I knew the "Way to Commencement Gate" (one could hear quotation-marks in their tone); and that Harold Bray, in whom hundreds and thousands believed as against the handful of my own Tutees, had been a flunkèd impostor. Patiently both times I had replied: yes, I was the Grand Tutor, for better or worse, there was no help for it; yes, I knew what studentdom was pleased to call "the Answer," though that term—indeed the whole proposition—was as misleading as any other (and thus as satisfactory), since what I "knew" neither "I" nor anyone could "teach," not even to my own Tutees. As for Bray, I had not called him flunkèd, I declared: his nature and origin were extraordinary and mysterious as my own; all that could be said was that he was my adversary, as necessary to me as Failure is to Passage. I.e., not only contrary and interdependent, but finally undifferentiable.

"You say you're Bray in a way, hey?" the reporter would ask, in the flip idiom of his fraternity. I would say no more, having said too much already; but the interviews, when broadcast, so inflamed the mass of studentdom against me that my loyalest Tutees (including Lucius Rexford) had me detained for my own protection. I was indifferent—Freedom and Bondage being *etc.*—so long as I might meet with my current advisees in the Visitation Room. But I shall answer no more questions, even from closest protégés. That much is dark is clear. Did Bray really fly away? they ask me. Who or what was he, and will he reappear? (Some of *his* many followers believe him still on campus, in one or other of his infinite guises; because at the Maxicaust he took my semblance, some—like Grandfather in his dotage—have even alleged that I am he, and it is by exploiting this uncertainty that Lucius Rexford preserves my life.) Was WESCAC really bested, they want to know, or did it plan the whole thing, including its own short-circuiting? Could there have been two or several "Brays," whereof one was a true Grand Tutor, who for that matter might have taken my semblance to rout me in his? If the GILES is WESCAC's son, and a Grand Tutor, is not WESCAC in a sense the Founder? Might being EATen not be equivalent to "becoming as a kindergartener," and hence the Way to Commencement Gate? Perhaps WESCAC doesn't EAT anyone; or if, as Sear conjectured, everyone has been EATen already, might not everyone be a Graduate, even a Grand Tutor? These things they ask in faith, despair, or hecklish taunt; I make no reply.

Three who aspired to Candidacy I denied. Ira Hector for years pretended not to mind, so long as Reginald was a Candidate—their own conclusion. At his brother's death he seemed more concerned; declaring at once that Grand Tutors are humbugs and that I'm holding out on him for a better price, he has determined to outwait me—to outlive me, if necessary. And he shall, Old Man of the Mall; hornier, wrinkleder, and stingier term by term, he will blink and snap there on his bench when I am no more. Rumor has it—perhaps fostered by him—that I owe my survival as much to his covert influence as to Lucky Rexford's. But he can never pass.

Neither, I fear, can Croaker and Dr. Eierkopf, though the latter, following my rout of Harold Bray (whom now Eierkopf vowed he'd called *ein Fliehender,* not *ein Fliegender*), declared himself converted by the testimony of his eyes to my "cause." My advice to him was to join Croaker in darkest Frumentius, where together they might accomplish much, despite the imperfections of their partnership. The idea pleased him: certain Frumentian birds, for example, laid eggs the size of a man's head; he might even rewrite his great treatise, once the fracture in his skull had mended. But in the meanwhile, could I not affirm the Candidacy at least of his roommate? What about the passage from the Scrolls, cut into Croaker's gut: *Be ye as the beasts of the woods, that never fail?*

"They never fail," I replied, "because they're never Candidates." Gently as I could then I denied them, not failing however to thank them for their assistance, without which I could not have passed myself. They went off together to emergent jungle quads and have not since been seen—though I suspect they may be in terms to come.

Two on the other hand to whom I offered affirmation of their Candidacy refused it: Stoker and Lucius Rexford. Of Stoker little need be said: had he not refused me, I should have had to refuse him; denial is his affirmation, and from that contradiction he—indeed, the campus—draws strength. The Chancellor, to be sure, denies this, along with Stoker's imputation of their fraternity. Partly therefore, his image in

New Tammany and around the University remains bright, though there are those who maintain that his administration, however brilliant, has accomplished little of practical consequence. The Boundary Dispute continues unresolved, they point out, and the Chancellory has failed to take a clear position on many grave issues—for example, the vexing question of what really happened at Max Spielman's Shafting. Popular opinion supports Bray's authenticity and holds me guilty of Grand-Tutorcide; conservatives want me Shafted; even the liberals, though generally skeptical of Grand-Tutorship and opposed to Shafting, wonder at my never being brought to trial, if only to "clear the air." Having thus alienated both ends of the Tower-Hall spectrum, Rexford finds it harder every term to keep me from the courts and disciplinary committees. His fastidious official neutrality, combined with much tacit support of my hard-oppressed "followers," has given rise to an ominous coalition of far-left and -right. Not that they care in their heart of hearts about Bray or me; but they see in the "Founder's Hill affair" an opportunity to lever Rexford out of office. Already the Senate has extended New Tammany's statute of limitations for "crimes against studentdom," among the number whereof Grand-Tutorcide is specifically included. My release this time may well spring their trap, and I have not forgotten Rexford's smiling words on the day I offered to affirm him.

From the host of my first Tutees, then, only Peter Greene and Anastasia remain to me. Between them they have assumed and divided the work of "spreading the word of GILES"—Anastasia about Great Mall, Greene to the outlying quads of New Tammany and abroad. A fervid enthusiast, Greene has found in extempore lecturing his true vocation, especially among the lower percentiles of the student body. Impressive he is, too, in his beautiful goatskins and fine red beard, when he points to his patchèd eyes and declares, "I have *seen* Him, brothers and sisters, and woe to them that drop His course! But I'm here to tell every flunkèd one of you today that it's *not too late*, reach-Commencement-Gate-the-Gilesian-way-no-matter-how-black-your-transcriptwise! *A-plus!*" His optimism is boundless; in his mind, "Gilesianism" is already inseparable from "New-Tammanianism," and he would make enrollment in the "New Curriculum" obligatory for all West-Campus studentdom. His wife, I understand, supports him in this endeavor; is in fact the organizing spirit of the "Gilesian Academy," that fugitive society of drop-outs, cranks, and idealists which meets clandestinely out in the tracts of the Forestry Department, and into which Greene has put all his wealth and managerial know-how.

Yet his labors have gained him little except contempt and vilification; even Anastasia, though she openly professes sympathy with his group, declares in private that what he calls "GILES's Answers" are flunkèd misrepresentations. Her own hopes, more and more, are centered in her son. She has brought him up (in the face of Stoker's derision) to believe that his mission on campus is one day to drive out what she ominously calls "the false proph-profs," without mentioning any names, as his "father" once drove out Bray, and to establish *true* Gilesianism" in every quad.

How arbitrate between them? Greene has the advantage of a certain charisma and naïve force, as well as an efficient and affluent organization; Anastasia on the other hand makes much of the fact that while he may claim Candidacy, *she* is the sole living "Gilesian" Graduate on the campus, not to mention being bearer of "His" son. Daily their points of difference grow; their uneasy alliance, should their influence really spread, might someday turn into a schism as profound as that between East and West Campus. Thus far, my presence in the College, if nothing else, has deterred them from open denunciation of each other, and it was with an affecting display of classmateship that they jointly sponsored the "Revised New Syllabus"—even coerced me, with every show of respect, into this vain, inescapable labor, by threatening to send Tombo "off to school" should I not cooperate. I consented at once.

Tombo, Tombo! How they hate to bring you to the Visitation Room! How it galls them to see us together, we who know nothing of Gilesianism, New Curriculum, or Revised New Syllabus, but see termless Truth in each other's eyes! Watch out for Auntie Stacey, Tombo, apparently so doting, actually so jealous on her son's behalf, who bullies you cruelly in pretended play. Beware Uncle Peter, whom you so resemble: don't go with him to visit his sawmills; let him not lure you to the tapelift with all-day suckers! "Old Black George's" daughter's son, Tombo is; abandoned by his mother the fickle ex-secretary; raised in the Unwed Co-ed's Nursery of the New Tammany Lying-In; named by me what time I plucked him from that heartless, well-meaning fold and made him my errand-boy. Despite his red hair, it is G. Herrold I hear calling in his fleecèd voice, so deep for a lad's; his mother to my knowledge never numbered buckgoats among her paramours, but Tombo's eyes are of the cast of Redfearn's Tom's and his noble line—hence my name for him. In those eyes alone upon this campus—not Greene's, gone; not Anastasia's, grown so hard; not "Giles Stoker's," all gleam and no vision—I see the reflection of myself, my hard history and my fate. He does not know, nor can I teach him, preciousest Tutee though he is; but if fate grant him time enough (he has, alas, neither Greene's nor G. Herrold's robust health, nor the wiry hardness of his namesakes or myself), and grant me to spirit him out of peril into some obscure pasturage—*he will learn,* will my Tombo! Yes, and one day hear, in his far sanctuary, a call, a summons . . .

No matter. Tombo's end is not given me to know, but I know my own, that rushes towards me like Triple-T. The wheel must come full circle; Fate's pans, tipped a brief while mewards, will tip back, like the pans of history. No one these days need die for the curriculum of his choice, as in terms gone by; alas, would anyone be willing to? The passion that exalts is the same that persecutes; if New Tammany's new Auditorium has no flogging-room beneath it, neither has it a soaring campanile above. Never was enrollment greater, or the average student less concerned for the Finals. Professors have ceased to kick the child who fidgets while they lecture: is it not that they also care less strongly than they ought whether he Passes, or believe less strongly that their words will be his Answers? The present Chancellory—by this one praised, by that condemned—has like any other the vices of its virtues, precisely. To gain this, one sacrifices that; the pans remain balanced for better and worse . . .

Nay, rather, for worse, always for worse. Late or soon, we lose. Sudden or slow, we lose. The bank exacts its charge for each redistribution of our funds. There is an entropy to time, a tax on change: four nickels for two dimes, but always less silver; our books stay reconciled, but who in modern terms can tell heads from tails?

And as with the profession, so with the professor; so even with Grand Tutors. I go this final time to teach the unteachable, and shall fail. A handful will attend me, and they in vain. The rest will snore in the aisles as always, make paper airplanes from my notes, break wind in reply to my questions. I know they will steal my lunch, expose their privates in the cloakroom, traffic in comic-books under the seminartable. My voice grows hoarse; the chalk will break in my hand. I know what Seniors will murmur in the stacks and Juniors chant at their torchlight rallies. A day approaches when the clerks in Tower Hall will draw up forms; Stoker's iron tools are oiled and ready; it will want but a nod from the Chancellor to set my "advisees" on me in a pack. They will not remember who ordered their schedules out of chaos and put right their college; who routed the false Grand Tutor, showed the Way to Commencement Gate, and set down this single hope of studentdom, *The Revised New Syl-*

labus. Those same hands that lovingly one term put off my rags, sponged me in dip—will they not flip a penny for the golden fleece they dressed me in? My humble rank and tenure will be stripped from me, as were Max's; my protégés—aye, Tombo, even you, even you!—will curse the hour I named them beneficiaries of my poor policy. Naked, blind, dishonored, I shall be coasted on a rusty bicycle from Great Mall. Past Observatory and Amphitheater, Turnstile and Scrapegoat Grate, George's Gorge and intersection—yea, past the remotest Model Silo, beyond the Forestry Camps and the weirs of the Watershed Researchers—I shall make my way, in lowest gear, to the first spring of the last freshet on the highest rise of Founder's Hill. There, in a riven grove beyond the Shaft, one oak stands in the rock: its top is crowned with vine, its tap-root cleaves to the spring beneath and drives I think to the fiery bowels of the campus. At that day's dusking, when lights come on in Faculty Row and my enemies raise their liquor, I'll make a goblet of my hands, drink hot toddies from that spring. My parts will be hung with mistletoe, my cleft hold the shophar fast; the oak will yield, the rock know my embrace. Three times will lightning flash at a quarter after seven, all the University respeaking my love's thunder—*Teruah! Tekiah! Shebarim!*—and it will be finished. The claps will turn me off. Passed, but not forgotten, I shall rest.

POSTSCRIPT TO THE POSTTAPE

Anticlimax, a vice in dramatic fictions, is clearly no failing in a work of the nature of *R.N.S.*, whereas textual integrity is of the first importance. As agent for Stoker Giles (or "Giles Stoker"), therefore, and aspirant professor of Gilesianism in whatever college may see fit to appoint me, I must observe—reluctantly—that however affecting here and there might be the rhetoric of the document entitled "Posttape" (I myself am unmoved), there is every reason to believe it spurious. An interpolation of later Gilesians, perhaps—more likely of antigilesians—or an improvisation of *Wescacus malinoctis,* but not the scripture, so to speak, of George Giles, Goat-Boy and Grand Tutor. Nor of His son, whom the document so unfairly and uncharacteristically maligns. I include the "Posttape" with the manuscript proper only because I found it (much soiled and creased) stuck among the pages left in my trust by the Grand Tutor's son, and feel unauthorized to delete what he so magnanimously let stand. That is, if he even knew of its existence; it was folded crudely and inserted between two random pages, as though in haste. Quite possibly it is the work of some crank or cynic among Stoker Giles's contemporaries; indeed, the typescript languished unguarded so long on my desk, the "Posttape" might even be some former colleague's idea of a practical joke.

In any case, one ought not to take it seriously. Consider the internal evidence against its authenticity: in the "Posttape" the "Grand Tutor" puts quotation-marks around such terms as "My Ladyship" and "Lady Creamhair," a practice followed nowhere else in the manuscript; also around "Revised New Syllabus" and "Gilesianism"—as if he had grown contemptuous of the terms! More revealingly, he mentions technological and cultural phenomena whose existence is never previously alluded to, such as airplanes and comic-books; and his references to nickels, dimes, and pennies, for example, seem flatly discrepant with the economic system of New Tammany College implied by the rest of the chronicle—and so important to an understanding of the Boundary Dispute. It may be objected by ingenious apologists that in one instance a reference of this sort is preceded by the ambiguous phrase "in modern terms," which, though it patently means "nowadays," might be said to suggest in addition a translation—by WESCAC or the Grand Tutor—of His University into our terms. Indeed, there is a sense in which the same may be said of the entire *Syllabus*—of all artistic and pedagogical conceit, for that matter, especially of the parable kind. But suffice it to say, in reply to this objection, that the Grand Tutor seems nowhere else in the vast record of His life and teachings to resort to this device—only in the gloomy "Posttape."

Which brings us to the real proof of its spurious character. Even if none of the above-mentioned discrepancies existed, the hopeless, even nihilistical tone of those closing pages militates against our believing them to be the Grand Tutor's own. Having brought us to the heart of Mystery, "He" suddenly shifts to what can most kindly be called a tragic view of His life and of campus history. Where are the joy, the hope, the knowledge, and the confident strength of the man who routed Harold Bray, affirmed the Candidacies of His Tutees and readied Himself to teach all studentdom the Answer? "Not teachable" indeed! And the unpardonable rejection of Greene, of Anastasia, of His own son, in favor of a sickly mulatto boy with the improbable name of *Tombo*—

But no, the idea is ridiculous. Some impostor and antigiles composed the "Posttape," to gainsay and weaken faith in Giles's Way. Even the type of those flunkèd pages is different!

J.B.

FOOTNOTE TO THE POSTSCRIPT TO THE POSTTAPE

The type of the typescript pages of the document entitled "Postscript to the Posttape" is not the same as that of the "Cover-Letter to the Editors and Publisher."

ED.

FAWCETT CREST BOOKS

ON TOP WITH
THE BIG BESTSELLERS

More Outstanding Titles in Paperback from Fawcett Crest

JOHN UPDIKE

Winner of the National Book Award and other awards. "John Updike is the most talented writer of his age in America."—THE NEW YORK TIMES

Assorted Prose	R983	60¢
Pigeon Feathers and Other Stories	d605	50¢
The Same Door and Other Stories	d676	50¢
The Centaur	R1050	60¢
Rabbit, Run	R538	60¢
The Poorhouse Fair	d677	50¢
Of the Farm	R993	60¢
Verse		
(Telephone Poles and The Carpentered Hen)	t787	75¢

SAUL BELLOW

Twice winner of the National Book Award, acclaimed by the critics from coast to coast and around the world as one of the most brilliant and vital American novelists.

The Adventures of Augie March	m780	95¢
Henderson the Rain King	m879	95¢
Herzog	m868	95¢
Seize the Day	R857	60¢

A Fawcett Crest Reprint

Wherever Paperbacks Are Sold